ANGRY HEAVENS

ANGRY HEAVENS
STRUGGLES OF A CONFEDERATE SURGEON

DAVID MICHAEL DUNAWAY

Certain characters in this work are historical figures, and certain events portrayed did take place. However, this is a work of fiction. All of the other characters, names, and events as well as all places, incidents, organizations, and dialogue in this novel are either the products of the author's imagination or are used fictitiously.

Archway Publishing books may be ordered through booksellers or by contacting:

Archway Publishing
1663 Liberty Drive
Bloomington, IN 47403
www.archwaypublishing.com
1 (888) 242-5904

Scripture taken from the King James Version of the Bible.

ISBN: 978-1-4808-8089-4 (sc)
ISBN: 978-1-4808-8090-0 (e)

Library of Congress Control Number: 2019909940

Print information available on the last page.

Archway Publishing rev. date: 7/30/2019

This novel is dedicated to my wife, Sandy Dunaway, who shares my love of the South. You are the best of me, my inspiration. Your goodness is reflected in every noble deed done by every character in this work.

Thank you for listening to every new page over morning coffee and for never getting weary of hearing each revision no matter how many times you had heard it before. Your enthusiasm for my work made it possible for me to enter a wonderful world of words and tell this story.

O war, thou son of hell,
Whom angry heavens do make their minister.

Henry IV, pt. 2, 5.2

PREFACE

The Nature of Historical Fiction

The story told in *Angry Heavens* seeks to be truthful as its characters would have it told. But also the truth is as personal as it is powerful. A balance between these two things is what I continuously sought as the author and narrator.

As any work of historical fiction, this work is a blend of my imagination and history's people, places, and events. I leave the determination of which is history and which is imagination to the reader. If at some point you ask yourself, "Did that really happen?" then I have accomplished my goal.

As a reader, you can read from start to finish without the need to check the veracity of my words. This *is* a work of fiction, and as such you can certainly enjoy it (I hope!) without ever using Google to check my facts. However, I do hope that you will, on occasion, google dates, events, characters, or places named in relation to specific events.

Of course my major characters frequently interact with their historical counterparts. That is the fun of writing a novel with history as a backdrop, and it is the best way to see this story. The Civil War is the backdrop against which my major characters live, work, fight, and question their beliefs about everything they hold sacred.

Finally, I must point out that the names of my characters are names typically used during the period in which they live. Yes, even going back to the 1600s. Beyond that, they are my creation.

Author's Perspective that Inspired This Work

The states that make up the southern geography of the union more than 150 years after our story are still known collectively as *the South*. This is an expression mostly pejorative in nature to those who were born, who lived, or who were raised outside these regional borders. To those who were, by the grace of God, born and raised in the South, the very same two words hold a mostly unexplained, and perhaps unexplainable, reverence bordering on religious fervor.

However, unlike the religious zealots who ignore the multitudinous horrific transgressions carried out in the name of whatever almighty being they worship, true southerners readily admit their collective past sins. They distance themselves from the atrocities carried out against an entire innocent race of persons who lived in and produced, but never benefited from, the economy that fashioned the almost mythical antebellum South.

The mythology that the South was white-columned neoclassical mansions overlooking hundreds of acres of cotton tended by hundreds of slaves is a purposeful misrepresentation grown into a mythos. According to the US Census of 1860, 75 percent of Southern families did not own a slave. But the 25 percent who did own other persons have created a great open wound that has yet to heal for more than fifteen decades afterward, as our protagonist fears in his diaries.

The story in this recounting of the antebellum lives, the lives during war years, and the postbellum lives of our characters does not seek to explain away the horror of the ownership of one person by another. Such is beyond explanation by rational people. Rather, our characters demonstrate a conundrum of southern life that remains today. How could they who did not embrace slavery fight and die for a homeland that seceded to maintain the damnable institution?

As the descendants of the characters in our story might say today:

> We, of the South, are not who others think we are, but we still carry the great open wound that was the Civil War.
>
> We recognize that we, unaided by the conscience we professed to own, inflicted the first wounds at Fort Sumter and kept them open to the life-draining infections of war.

The wounds of slavery were intentionally inflicted by a people who were from the South but not Southern. They were selfish, belligerent, loud, angry, and worst of all, inhuman.

These people are important to this story only in their roles in perpetrating and executing a war that would leave the South's image in flux 150 years after Appomattox. As the writer of the stories of the Bailey and the Merriweather families, I have worked to studiously assure that the mythology of the antebellum South plays no role in this telling other than as history.

The antagonist of this story is the war but not the Union soldiers across the battlefield. The soul of the story resides in the war's effects, primarily on the two families, the Baileys and Merriweathers. They dearly love their South and fight for it despite the unseemly workings of the national and regional politics that brought the war to fruition. The effects of war on the entire union have been told of many times since the cannons last roared as the armies fought around Appomattox. But seldom has the story been written of the terrors inflicted by war on the people who played no role in the events that led to secession or the first shots fired in Charleston Harbor.

The heart of the South is not embodied in the economics of slavery, not in the Confederate Battle Flag, and not in the statues of the officers and sacrificial young men that adorn courthouse greens. Nor is it the refrain of "Dixie," written by an Ohioan for Northern minstrel shows. It was and is found in its people, who are kind and gentle, distinct and diverse, proud but not vain, God-fearing and honest, and good and generous to a fault, people from a place where "Yes, ma'am" and "Yes, sir" are taught from when a child first starts to speak.

The heroes of our story, aside from the Baileys and the Merriweathers, are the honorable people of the South. The South was and remains, despite all of its flaws, *the* unique regional culture within the Union. The people within its undefined borders do not ignore its history. However, that history does not taint in any way southerners' love for their homeland. That is the conundrum of the South, isn't it? Others (especially Yankees), then and now, cannot understand our love for this land and the appreciation given to the Almighty every day for being born southern.

ACKNOWLEDGMENTS

When I conceived the telling of this story three years ago, I told myself that I was going to learn to write by writing. The reader will be the judge of whether or not I succeeded.

For me, writing *Angry Heavens* has been a journey of love, passion, discovery, and frequent aggravations. I encountered late nights when the search for a phrase would not let me sleep or when a paragraph defied all attempts at revision until I took it utterly out of its context and parsed it as if it were a separate work unto itself not connected at all to the words and ideas that gave birth to it. I made revisions upon revisions upon revisions until it seemed that every word was different from what I had first intended.

I quickly learned that stories don't follow a linear logical pattern. They tend to burst forth like fireworks, and sometimes they begin with an ending. Sometimes they have a purpose. Sometimes they are just for the telling. Such writing is hard on the intellect and the soul.

I never believed in the idea of the muse that artists speak of. Hell, I never thought of myself as an artist. I still don't. My former students describe me as a storyteller. I am proud to own that label.

The master of the written word and the most exceptional southern writer of any generation inspired the telling of my story. Pat Conroy's beautiful words set the standard for every other storyteller—especially those who call themselves southern.

Conroy, in an essay for *The Writer*, describes writing like this: "Good writing is the hardest form of thinking. It involves the agony of turning profoundly difficult thoughts into lucid form, then forcing them into the tight-fitting uniform of language, making them visible and clear."[1]

All I can add to that is amen.

I offer my heartfelt thanks to my dear friends and my best critics: Sharen Buyher, who lives in Oakland City, Indiana; Laura Lee Pike, who resides in LaGrange, Georgia; and Dee Archer Fanning of Charleston, South Carolina, all of whom tediously read the "final" manuscript and who made profoundly important suggestions. There was never a doubt from the first word on the first page to whom I would send the final manuscript for review. This work would not have been possible without their selfless contributions.

Thanks to Civil War enthusiast Tim Armstrong from Fort Branch, Indiana, for helping whenever I got lost in the details of battles, commanders, and locations of command posts. He helped me with my portrayal of history, ensuring that if it was not entirely accurate, at least it was reasonable in its intent and essence.

Thanks to every student who has ever sat in one of my classrooms in Alabama, Kentucky, Indiana, or North Carolina for letting me know that stories bring meaning to learning.

To the great writing teachers at every stage of my life, *God*

[1] Pat Conroy, "Pat Conroy: Interpreting the World through Story," *The Writer* (June 12, 2012).

bless you. You are and shall be long remembered and much appreciated.

Thanks to every person who is helping preserve the battlefields of the Civil War. The research necessary for this work was made ever so much easier by the work of the American Battlefield Trust, which visually brings back to life the battles and battlefields.

Finally, thanks to everyone who venerates being southern and celebrates the sacrifices left on the battlefields that dot our landscape even though the South's cause was wrong. You are the impetus for this story of two families who loved their land beyond measure and gave everything for it. As they loved the South in 1861, we, in kind, love it equally today.

PROLOGUE

Some call it fate. Some call it predestination. Some call it the will of God. In Norse mythology, three female divine beings called Spinners dwell within the roots of the great ash tree at the center of the universe and weave the events of our lives into a tapestry, one thread at a time.

Whatever we call it, without dispute, events are unknowingly intertwined in such ways that when viewed separately from each other, they cannot logically have any connection at all. Yet when these events are seen with the advantage of time, we denote their relationships as clearly as a spider's web hung across a wide path on a dewy morning. And as mystical as how the spider spanned such a distance are the forces that transform improbabilities into reality.

Such are the connections between the Baileys of Charleston, South Carolina—descendants of County Galway Irish farm folk—and the Merriweathers of Richmond, Virginia, who sprang from the loins of a prosperous London merchant family.

For the Baileys and the Merriweathers during the dark weeks and months of the Civil War, time became an enemy. The result was that the ill-timed delivery—or worse, the frequent loss—of precisely crafted letters meant to share news of home and front turned these letters into a missile as deadly to the psyche as the Minié ball or to the body as grapeshot.

During the Civil War, letters, unlike the carefully preserved diaries, suffered the quirk of being lost in transit or arriving irregularly, already in tatters from the rough handling, causing rampant homesickness at the front and trepidation at home for a loved one's safety. Because letters came so sporadically, they were read over and over in the long interludes between correspondences and kept near to hand. Dates became smudged, pages misplaced, and entire letters simply lost, with only the memories of what was written lingering until they, too, were lost to time and circumstance.

The disquiet caused by the vagaries of letter writing was at least as disconcerting as the solace contained in the written words of a beloved. It was very hard for the soldiers at the fronts and for families back home to get information about their loved ones. The families, especially, were left to rationalize that the only hope they could derive day by day was from getting no bad news. Therefore, they chose to find solace in not knowing. What a small bit of faith that must have been.

PART I
THE BAILEYS

CHAPTER 1

Ties Old and New

An unwavering family memory of the old country was passed down through the DNA of stories told in front of glowing hearths on cold winter nights. The Jacobites' vision of a Catholic Ireland independent from English rule was inherited through the generations from father to son and from mother to daughter. The Baileys of Charleston considered themselves not so far removed from their homeland as to have forgotten the tyranny their family had suffered at the hands of the English, and therefore they had no interest in the slave trade. But it would have been a grave mistake to think that they were anything but Southerners.

James Patrick Bailey, the future patriarch of the Charleston clan, and his wife of three months, Siobhan Brennan Bailey, set sail from Norfolk, Virginia, to Charleston aboard the coastal trader the *Chesapeake Queen*, which arrived in Charleston on May 13, 1794. They arrived with few possessions except each other but had a great ambition and a cache of herbal remedies that were passed down to James from a small tenant farm on the River Clare in County Galway, Ireland.

By the birth of their only child, Matthew Conroy, James had begun to grow as a merchant in a growing Charleston. He was a keen observer and a quick learner. Growing up on the banks of the Chesapeake Bay, James had lingered at the water's edge on the warm summer days long after his mother called him in for supper. The blue crabs were his fascination, and they were easily caught with a scrap of chicken left over from the slaughter, which was a weekly event. Putting the chicken into a tin or jar and burying it for a few days made it even better. Crabs would fight each other to grab onto a putrid chicken neck, and if James pulled gently on a piece of twine tied to the bait, the crab would hang on until James could reach down in the silty gray water and pluck him up. More than a few times, the crabs had let go of the chicken to latch onto a finger with their powerful claws. Their grip was not injurious, but it was painful for a while.

That many of the crabs had only one big claw and a much smaller second claw caused James to imagine a great crab war where the claws were used like swords and lost like arms. But remarkably, they seemed to regenerate, and James wondered why a human finger would not grow back. "If a lowly crab can do it, why not us?" he asked his father.

"There is more that we don't know about nature than we do know," his father responded—which was a totally unacceptable answer for James.

His father continued, this time with a lesson on preserving the bounty of nature that the Almighty had provided for them in the great estuary of the Chesapeake. "It is true that the crab meat inside his shell is quite tasty, but if we open that shell, the crab will die. So, if you want crab for supper, you should just snap off one claw, leaving the other so the crab can fend for himself. Only a few of those claws makes for a tasty pot of your mother's crab chowder. Then we can leave the crabs to be caught again and again."

Thus began James Bailey's fascination with nature and its cures. As a young businessman in Charleston, he sought out reading materials about nature's cures, but such were scarce, so he asked questions—lots and lots of questions to anyone he thought might add to his knowledge—and he added new cures and remedies to his stockpile, often obtained in trade with local Native American tribes. He was affectionately known, usually, as Doc James, and there were few people in Charleston proper—merchants, seamen, or slaves—who had not heard of the Irishman looking for home remedies.

Although his business began with medicines sold from a pushcart, some of them admittedly "snake oil," James soon recognized that if he could open a general store, he could expand his offerings beyond just remedies and have the customers come to him. Over the years, most customers, even if they were coming in for potatoes or rice, almost always sought his advice for their ailments, inevitably leaving with a potion or a poultice.

Mother Unknown

Matthew Conroy Bailey barely knew his mother, Siobhan. She had died of pneumonia in the winter of his fifth year, unable to regain her strength after giving birth to a stillborn daughter, Mary Catherine. She was devastated at the loss but not really surprised, as she had not felt the baby's kick in many weeks. Still, she had hoped.

The burial day was damp and cold and gray, as only a southern winter day can be. It was an appropriate day to bury a promise unfulfilled. Very ill herself, Siobhan wrapped the tiny pine coffin containing the remains of Mary Catherine in wool blankets and cradled it to her breast. As she bent to lower the coffin into the small grave that would hold for eternity the daughter she had so desired, James stepped forward.

"Here, let me help you," he said. "The fresh dirt is slippery with rain."

"Get away from me! This is *my* daughter. I will bury her," Siobhan snapped as anger escaped from the deep recesses of her soul. She laid the small coffin on the soft dirt in the grave, burying the last bit of her will to live alongside it.

As James helped Siobhan step into the carriage, she looked back one last time and let out an inhuman wail as the first bit of gray loamy dirt pounded on the pine coffin holding her baby. In a fortnight, Siobhan would be buried next to her.

A Father's Influence

As a child, Matthew, on rare occasions, had memory flashes of his mother's skirts with their crinoline petticoats layered under checked gingham. He also remembered that she would sometimes sing as she scurried about the house preparing supper.

He never could pinpoint the events that caused these flashes, but he welcomed them nonetheless. As time passed, the flashes faded to sparks, growing farther and farther apart until eventually he could remember only that, at one time, he had had memories of his mother, but no longer.

Matthew loved his father, but he missed his mother. As an independent little boy who wasn't prone to getting into trouble, Matthew was left by himself (looked in on by a neighbor) as his father made his rounds with his pushcart of vegetables and home remedies. At night, James would teach Matthew to read using his tattered old Bible from the old country as his textbook. Matthew took to reading with a natural gift, and soon his father was asking his customers if they had any books they might sell him or exchange for a purple eggplant or a head of cabbage. Often, his customers simply gave him the books. Matthew read his small library so many times that he memorized most of the passages. On a rare occasion, James would purchase a copy of the *Charleston Courier* newspaper, which Matthew would read until the paper fell apart in his hands.

At eight, Matthew began going with his father on his daily rounds. By this time, James had purchased an old mule and a secondhand or thirdhand wagon. It had no springs to soften the cobblestone streets, but it beat walking and pushing a heavy cart. James began by having Matthew take customers' purchases to their houses and return with money. Not long after, Matthew became responsible for accounting their earnings. As good as he was at reading, he was even better at arithmetic, and the daily earnings were his father's perfect teaching tools.

When Matthew was twelve, his father rented a storefront as a general store that carried both remedies and sundries. But James did not abandon the wagon. When he left to make deliveries, he allowed Matthew to tend the store. Three years later, James purchased the storefront, and Bailey's Remedies & Sundries was born.

By the time Matthew Conroy Bailey took the business reins from his father, Bailey's Remedies & Sundries was a well-established and respected Charleston business.

CHAPTER 2

A New Patriarch

Matthew Bailey had learned well from his father, James, and he took the sale of remedies a step beyond any other in Charleston. As his father had peddled his pushcart filled with some curatives and also "snake oil" antidotes, Matthew had a new idea to add to the business. He reasoned that if he began regularly calling on the growing number of physicians graduating from the Medical College of the State of South Carolina in Charleston, he could make connections that would be profitable for both parties. The physicians would have no need to keep drugs on hand because they knew their patients had easy access to them through Matthew Bailey. Further, this meant for Matthew a source of customers they could count on and, for the doctors, a small kickback for what Matthew Bailey dubbed "scripts" with symbols.

A New Matriarch

The success of the business on occasion allowed the Baileys to mingle with Charleston society. Making inroads into Charleston society was not a goal of Matthew Bailey, but it most decidedly was for his new wife, Lauraleigh.

Lauraleigh O'Brien Bailey had met her future husband, Matthew, rather predictably at Saint Mary's Catholic Church. Matthew Conroy Bailey, the bachelor son of Charleston merchant James Bailey, was not a regular attendee at Mass, but the spirit moved him to attend on a mild summer Sunday in 1819. He was taken immediately with the crystal blue eyes speckled with gold and the sunset-tinted tresses of Lauraleigh as she sat her pot of seafood chowder and a large bowl of buttered grits on the table with the other food that would feed the congregation at its annual church dinner-on-the-grounds feast.

Having learned the art of conversation at the feet of his merchant father, Matthew was never at a loss for starting a conversation with a total stranger, especially one as beautiful as the creature before him on this Sunday afternoon. Well and truly smitten, and with the confidence of youth, he introduced himself. "Miss O'Brien? I am Matthew Bailey, and I believe we share a common heritage. Do you fancy exploring that possibility over a bowl of your seafood chowder?"

"Well, Mr. Matthew Bailey, while you may be correct about our connections to the old country, you are mistaken that I would fancy a sit-down with you, a man I do not know in the slightest. However, I might abide a bit of conversation if you are willing to help me serve this stew and these grits and attend to the cleanup afterward."

"It would be my honor, Miss O'Brien."

Matthew's church attendance was about to increase significantly.

From that day and every day since, he never failed to refer to his love as Miss O'Brien, although when she became his wife, he relented slightly, calling her "Miss O'Bailey," but never Lauraleigh. He reserved her Christian name for the intimate moments they were able to carve out of a busy life. In fact, his children could never recall a time when their father referred to their mother in any way other than "Miss O'Bailey."

In quick succession, Lauraleigh Bailey gave birth to four children: John Calvin, Andrew Ryan, Mary Assumpta, and Joseph Paul. Joseph's life in the Bailey family lasted but a few days. He was born premature after a particularly difficult pregnancy, disrupted by almost constant nausea and severe anemia brought on by Lauraleigh's aversion to eating any red meat. Her stomach, it seemed, was in a constant state of unrest. While she had had typical bouts of nausea early in each of her previous pregnancies, nausea was her constant companion throughout her pregnancy with Joseph, and she simply had no desire to eat. When compelled to eat out of concern for her unborn child, she seldom kept any food down more than a few minutes. So instead of gaining weight during her pregnancy, she was an emaciated shadow of herself, spending most of her pregnancy in bed too tired to rise from it and dress.

Joseph died less than a week after his birth. A family tragedy, it was not unexpected. Premature and weighing only two pounds, he had little chance at life. His lungs were underdeveloped and his heart enlarged from trying to overcome an inadequate number of red blood cells brought on by Lauraleigh's anemia. Lauraleigh was unable to nurse him, and although a wet nurse was found, Joseph never took to the nipple and simply starved to death.

Lauraleigh Bailey, the staunch emotional bulwark of her growing family, would not rouse from her bed following

Joseph's burial in the family plot, where two small headstones marked the graves of Joseph and Mary Catherine, daughter of Siobhan, who was wife of James and mother of Matthew. Lauraleigh was critically depressed.

As she grew thinner and more frail, where she had been voluptuously developed with an attitude to match, Matthew approached his father about what he could recommend. His father told him of a remedy that some said had magical properties—Saint-John's-wort. The next morning James Bailey traveled to the farms and woods north of Charleston, where he picked a dozen stems of the brightly colored flowers, took them back to Matthew, and showed him how to make a tea from the flower petals.

Matthew sweetened the slightly bitter tea with honey, added a dash of whiskey for good measure, and stayed with Lauraleigh until she had drunk it all. He followed his father the next day, and for the next two weeks each morning he left at the day's first light to pick the Saint-John's-wort flowers and prepare Lauraleigh's morning potion.

The Physician

The direct connection between the Bailey family business and the medical community had an unexpected influence on Mathew Bailey's children. He was not surprised when his eldest son, John Colin, enrolled in the Medical College of Charleston. As a child John had taken in every stray, injured, or emaciated cat, dog, rabbit, raccoon, or fox that he could ensnare or entice, and he soon released them—at least the wild ones—back into nature. The house always had a feel of a menagerie about it, much to the dismay of his mother and the delight of his sister.

John Colin was a natural healer. As a medical student, he thrived looking for ways to advance beyond the knowledge of his professors. A questioner, he daily danced close to the line of insubordination with his questions that often began with, "But, Professor, why ...?" John was graduated by the Medical College of Charleston with much more than the rather rudimentary knowledge that was typical of his classmates.

The medical arts as learned and practiced in the early 1800s, like most professions, were learned through an apprenticeship. John Bailey was no different, except his father, Matthew, had a firsthand knowledge of the good, the not so good, and the downright dangerous doctors practicing in Charleston. So when John Bailey began talking about his upcoming apprenticeship, his father introduced him to Dr. Aaron Salvador.

Dr. Aaron Solomon Salvador was the nephew of a distinguished Charleston Jewish family. His uncle was the first Jewish colonist elected to public office and the first Jewish American killed in the Revolutionary War. Like his uncle, Dr. Aaron Salvador had built an exceptional reputation in both the Jewish and Christian communities of Charleston. When John Bailey completed his apprenticeship with Dr. Salvador, he left with not only a significantly increased knowledge of medical practices but also an unrepentant belief that a true healer did not pick and choose his patients. Illness was the physician's enemy, not the color of a man's skin or the religion he practiced.

When John looked for a place to open his practice, his father quickly suggested the two-story apartment a few blocks from the family business. It had been vacant for some time and seemed a perfect fit. John could live on the second floor and practice on the bottom floor—a fine arrangement for any newly minted physician setting up practice in the spring of 1845.

His practice began slowly, but with a natural connection to the family pharmacy next door, he soon built a reputation as a physician of exceptional diagnostic skills. As he settled into his practice, it was not without controversy. He drew criticism from other physicians for opening his doors to any person who required his skills. Being shunned by Charleston society suited John just fine as it allowed him more time to read and contemplate remedies frequently outside the practice of most other Charleston physicians.

John Bailey's personal medical studies steered him as though by compass to the embryonic field of surgery. As he grew in his knowledge and skills, his patients were the testaments to his persistence and his techniques. Farmers with broken legs and infected bites or cuts found in John Bailey a physician who turned away from traditional salves and balms and turned often to the scalpel (somewhat to his father's regret as an apothecary). He was unafraid to lance and surgically remove infected tissue around a pustule or to open a leg punctured by a compound fracture in order to set the bone. But even the simplest surgery was a harrowing experience for patient and physician alike. And this weighed heavily and constantly on his mind.

Dr. John Bailey routinely treated the seamen of Charleston's docks for a variety of ailments. One such person was Bartholomew Jennings, a seaman aboard the coastal schooner the *DeMille*. In early November of 1847, Jennings had picked up a bag of oysters for supper for the crew. But while shucking the Low Country delicacy, his oyster knife bounced off the oyster shell and embedded itself in the palm of his left hand. Because he had not stopped to treat his wound, the hand soon became infected to the point he could hardly pull up his pants after his morning constitutional. The *DeMille* was headed north to Norfolk in three days, and he dreaded the prospect of Captain Jeremiah Gaffney's wrath if, once they were out to sea, he saw that Jennings was useless to him. Jennings knew he had to go see Dr. Bailey.

The men of the *DeMille* and Dr. John Bailey were well acquainted as the captain, gruffer than a hard-shell Baptist preacher on Pentecost Sunday and just about as devout, knew he could not keep his men away from the delights to be found at the Three Sisters brothel in "French Town," so called because each house was painted the color of each madam's hair. However, he could make sure they did not carry any unexpected passengers home to their wives back in Norfolk. And so, routinely, his men paid a visit to Dr. John Bailey the morning they were to depart Charleston.

As Bartholomew Jennings made his way to Dr. Bailey's office, he already felt weak in the pit of his stomach at the thought of the scalpel slicing open the infected hand. Even the two slugs of whiskey that he had downed aboard the ship did little to calm him.

As he stepped a foot across the threshold of the office, he almost turned around, but he had come this far, and how could the reality be worse than his dread? It was worse. It was always worse.

After two slugs of better whiskey provided by Dr. Bailey, Jennings bit hard on the leather-covered hilt of the dagger he carried in his belt. Dr. Bailey opened the wound quickly and expertly, excised pregangrenous flesh, dosed the hand with alcohol, closed the wound with catgut, and covered it with a pine tar infused–bandage. Jennings would heal quickly if Captain Gaffney did not throw him overboard first.

Jennings pulled on his shirt and turned to Dr. Bailey. "Doc, I been seein' you a coupla times a year now, and I think you done so much cutting on me that I cain't tell your scars from them I got in my bar fight fracases."

"Bartholomew, what's your point?"

"Well, I think you will agree that I don't shy away from the hurtin' once I make it in the door and have a couple of shots of your good whiskey."

"I cannot disagree with that, other than you conveniently left out the shots you downed to get your courage up to come see me in the first place." Bailey smiled.

"Yes, sir, there is that," Jennings admitted. "But I got to tell you, Doc, that my whiskey courage just ain't workin' like it used to."

Bailey paused a moment, as he truly never forgot about the pain that he often inflicted at the point of a scalpel. "Bartholomew, I wish I could offer you something better than whiskey and the leather hilt of your dagger."

Jennings, getting up a different kind of courage minus the whiskey, spoke respectfully, "Doc, you always treated me right 'n' kindly. Cain't complain about that. Will that bag of oysters I left out by the back door cover what's I owe you?"

"More than, Bartholomew. More than. Safe voyage, and stay away from Captain Gaffney for a day or two if you can."

Entrepreneur

Andrew Ryan Bailey suffered from middle child syndrome. Four years younger than John and seven years older than Mary Assumpta, his knowledge and opinions were discounted on the one hand for the elder John's years of education and on the other by Mary Assumpta's temperament and her cuteness, neither of which could be ignored. Mary Assumpta demanded attention whenever she was present. Most humiliating of all, Andrew Ryan was often asked to look after three-year-old Mary Assumpta, especially during his mother's prolonged recovery following the death of Joseph Paul.

Andrew Ryan, as the family called him, developed into a replica of his father—quiet, observant, steady, and humble in a family where boisterousness was de rigueur for his other two siblings. As a student, Andrew Ryan was proficient if not remarkable for his achievements. Finishing the eighth grade at fourteen, Andrew Ryan was expected, and happy, to embrace the anticipated apprenticeship at the feet of his father in the family business, where his personality fit perfectly in dealing with a variety of customers seeking foodstuffs or remedies.

Six months in, he was manning the store as his father made his routine rounds of Charleston's physicians. By eighteen, he was married and had bought one-quarter interest in the family business from his father.

Andrew Ryan proposed to his father that they take a step backward to expand the business.

It was a cold, damp January day in Charleston. It was the kind of cold that seems to chill you to the core with wind blowing off the Charleston Harbor and whipping down the alleyways and narrow streets, totally unlike the dry cold of a Maine or Vermont winter day. It was a southern cold: humid, biting, relentless.

Andrew Ryan had gotten to the store early that morning and started a fire in the wood-burning stove. As the fire started to heat the public portion of the business, he gathered the battered old coffeepot from the back room and filled it with water from a cistern just outside the back door. He added a cup of coffee grounds roasted on the same stove along with a teaspoon of chicory to the water and put it on the stove to boil.

It was not yet daylight when his father, Matthew, arrived just as the coffee had started to boil, filling the room with an aroma of Jamaica. At least that is what the trader who sold them the green coffee beans had told them it would smell like. Jamaica or not, the aroma was comforting on a cold Charleston January morning.

Matthew Bailey poured his first cup of coffee of the day. His son was waiting for his father to pass judgment as he saucered the boiling coffee, unwilling to wait until the dark liquid cooled in his cup.

"Ah. Well done, my son," his father said as he noisily slurped the coffee from the saucer. "Andrew Ryan, you have learned many important things about buying and selling over the years. Perhaps none of these things has been as important as how to make a good cup of coffee on a cold morning."

His father presented him an opening to talk buying and selling, and Andrew Ryan now seemed divinely propelled as he had been considering a plan for increasing their sales. This was clearly the time, so he grabbed the opportunity. "Father, now that I have a stake in the family business, I have a proposal to increase customers by 10 percent. Would you like to hear my idea?"

"Son," his father responded, "I would listen to a plan that would increase our sales by 1 percent. Tell me what you have in mind, and let us talk about it over another cup of this coffee."

Andrew Ryan began his pitch: "I have been thinking that we should go back to Grandfather's pushcart philosophy. We take our business to where our customers are—especially those customers who are uneasy or unwelcomed in the store by other customers.

"We can load a mule-drawn wagon with vegetables, fruits, meats, and fish, if the weather is cool enough—whatever is in season—and miscellaneous sundries and remedies. And just one day a week, I will take it into Clifford's Alley."

His father knew that Clifford's Alley was the section of Charleston where free blacks and slaves had isolated themselves from the larger white community, and it caused him some concern about how such a move would be viewed by other customers. He also worried that their views might put Andrew Ryan at some personal risk. The Baileys had built a reputation that their business was open to anyone who needed their services. It was not unusual to see a black man or woman in the store picking up goods for his or her master. And more frequently of late, some small number of free blacks had come into the store—almost always with another black person, so other customers would assume they were together: two black slaves.

"Andrew Ryan, your mother and I have clearly raised you right, and Father Quigley will be proud of you as well, but this is not as easy as it sounds. I do not worry about you in Clifford's Alley or amid any other poor residents of Charleston. God's people are good people. However, there are some of our customers who are not God's people, and I fear they may cause you harm."

"I have considered that, Father, and I have already spoken to Reverend Simon Abraham Tyler Jacob Billington, pastor of the Emanuel African Methodist Episcopal Church, and he has assured me that on the day I am in his parish, he will have members of his church posted throughout Clifford's Alley to alert me if trouble approaches."

Matthew Bailey was pleased with his son's planning before he had even broached the subject that morning. He was also satisfied with the chances of the plan's success. "I have just one suggestion, and it is to appease your mother's inevitable fears for you. I want you to pay a visit to Father Quigley and ask him if he, too, will keep an eye and ear out for potential trouble. And just to be sure he listens, take him a pound of that coffee you brewed up this morning. It will go down well with his daily dose of scotch.

The Feminist

Mary Assumpta Bailey was the youngest child and the only daughter in a Charleston family with two older brothers who alternately spoiled her and harassed her as the little girl in the family. Mary Assumpta joyed equally in both. She could be a little lady in lace, frills, and curls on Sunday morning for Mass and a tomboy in pigtails and long pants for an afternoon of fishing with her father on Wappo Creek just across the Ashley River.

Mary Assumpta was ever the precocious child, ungainly and awkward, known as much for her temper as her curls that gleamed of rust and gold in the midday sun on a summer day. Mary Assumpta established her independence early as a force of uncommon intelligence and common sense within her family. As a youngster barely in her teens, she was in regular attendance at her brother's medical office as an organized record keeper, with organization being a skill her brother lacked. And in her fourteenth year, after countless requests, her brother finally allowed her to observe in a minor surgery—the removal of a carbuncle from the backside of a merchant seaman.

Having grown up around brothers who regularly skinny-dipped in the creeks flowing into the Ashley River, Mary Assumpta at fourteen was neither surprised nor intrigued by the male anatomy. But the nature of the carbuncle on Bartholomew Jennings's backside and why it needed surgery did surprise and intrigue her.

"Okay, John," she began as surgery was about to commence, "I understand that when Mr. Bartholomew sits down, his ass hurts ..."

"Mary Assumpta, how many times have I warned you about your language in this office?" John reprimanded her and hoped she did not see the smile on his face as he turned his back to pick up the scalpel. Mary Assumpta was 100 percent Irish Catholic and had the language that went with the designation—most of it learned from her brothers.

"Okay. Okay. Sorry, Mr. Bartholomew," Mary Assumpta said with feigned humility.

"Not to worry, lass. If that's the worst I hear today, I will be looking for the second coming anytime now!" Bartholomew was a hesitant believer, but he did like to hedge his bets.

As he cleaned the site of the infection before using the scalpel, John gave Mary Assumpta an anatomy lesson and Bartholomew Jennings a reprimand.

"The anatomy of the carbuncle starts with a hair that, rather than growing outward and penetrating the skin, turns and grows inward, causing an infection and pus to gather around the site of the hair. And Mr. Jennings here, rather than coming to me as soon as he arrived in port, paid a visit to the Two Brothers' Tavern, sat on his buttocks for much of the night, further irritating the boils beneath the skin that form the carbuncle, and was knocked on his backside at least once by a fellow patron when the two could not agree who crewed the fastest coastal trader. Luckily he had enough to drink that nothing was broken, like his coccyx, which would not have been so easily repaired or quickly healed."

"So why not just apply one of Father's poultices rather than the scalpel?" Mary Assumpta asked.

Jennings agreed: "Yeah, Doc. Why not?"

Turning back to pick up the scalpel, Dr. Bailey explained, "Well, that poultice would probably work, but Captain Gaffney might wonder why you have to stand to eat for the next week. And you know he barely abides your trips to the Two Brothers' and the Three Sisters." Bailey was giving Jennings a veiled reproach about his visits to the local brothel, hoping Mary Assumpta assumed it was another tavern.

Mary Assumpta smiled at Bartholomew, who knew that she knew well the commerce plied by the Three Sisters. She knew whiskey was sold, sure enough, but that was not why he patronized the business.

"Okay, Mr. Jennings, time to bite down on the hilt of that

dirk in your belt. I am going to make my cut." And he did, excising the carbuncle swiftly and with little damage to the skin and muscle.

"That warn't so bad. You through now, ain't ya, Doc?" Jennings asked hopefully.

"I wish it were so, Mr. Jennings, but I have exposed four boils, and I must now lance the head of each and expel the pus contained in them. Unfortunately, there is no delicate method for this procedure."

"Mary Assumpta, pour Mr. Jennings another dose of that whiskey there on the counter," Bailey directed his sister, who by now was fully into the role of nurse.

"Is it that serious, Doc?" Jennings asked haltingly.

"Not serious, Mr. Jennings, just likely painful as there is no other way to clean those pustules than by applying pressure with my thumbs against either side of the infected area.

"It will rather be like the pain you felt when you were knocked down last night in the Two Brothers', but without all that whiskey. And it will last longer because I must press every drop of pus from the site or it will just get infected again, and neither Mary Assumpta nor I want to see your ugly hairy arse [here he reverted to the Irish pronunciation] in here again before you sail." Everyone smiled, perhaps Bartholomew less that the others, but he did appreciate the humor.

Mary Assumpta cleaned up the site with alcohol, getting a final yelp from Bartholomew. She then applied pine tar to the site and covered it with a clean scrap of cloth folded four times to keep the pine tar from seeping through to Bartholomew's pants and causing even more embarrassment than he had experienced already.

"Mr. Jennings," Bailey said as Jennings pulled up his pants, "while I clean up back here, you can settle up your bill with Mary Assumpta out front."

Mary Assumpta surprised no one in the family when two years later, a year away from finishing her schooling in the eighth grade with Sisters of Our Lady of Mercy, she announced that she, too, was pursuing a career in medicine. At the dinner table on a lazy May Sunday afternoon, Mary Assumpta, in her sixteenth year, made her announcement: "Mother and Father, I have decided that I am going to be a doctor like John."

Her mother, Lauraleigh, reacted first, saying, "But, Mary Assumpta, your father and I had so hoped that we could present you to Charleston society this summer. Now you have just cast our plans on the rocks."

"But, Mother, those were never my plans. Those were your plans. I have no interest in Charleston society or in marrying some spoiled gentleman farmer who is more boy than man and has never worked a day in his life."

"Now, Mary Assumpta," her father interjected, "let's not rush into a decision that you may very well regret. Darling, there are just no women doctors. No man is going to let you examine him, and most women are of the same opinion."

"Well, I will just be the first in Charleston."

At seventeen, Mary Assumpta Bailey applied for admission to the Medical College of South Carolina at Charleston.

July 15, 1851

Admissions Committee
Medical College of South Carolina at Charleston
Dear Sirs,

I wish to apply for admission to the fall class of the Medical College of South Carolina at Charleston.

I have graduated with honors from the Sisters of Our Lady of Mercy Grammar School and have been continuing my science and mathematics schooling through the tutoring of Dr. John Bailey, a graduate of your institution.

Additionally, I have worked as a nurse in Dr. Bailey's medical office, assisting him with routine medical and surgical procedures. He can attest to my knowledge in those areas.

My father is able and willing to pay for my tuition a year in advance to demonstrate the genuineness of my application.

I look forward to your response.

Sincerely,

Mary Assumpta Bailey

Despite her family's dismal predictions for her admission, Mary Assumpta was sure that she would be admitted given that she met the one primary requirement—she had the ability to pay tuition.

Mary Assumpta was never a child who doubted her own abilities. At ten years old, she and her brothers had hauled their skiff to the eastern shore of the Ashley River to launch it and paddle upriver about a mile until they reached a bank where the marsh grasses had receded and left a small sandbar. They called it "the Bailey Beach." The bar tapered off gently into deeper water and made for the perfect place to swim on a hot Charleston July day.

On this particular day, the spirit of sibling competition was strong. As they took turns paddling upriver, Mary Assumpta's two brothers dared her to swim across the Ashley River and back. John and Andrew Ryan, of course, never considered the river current or the potential of alligators bedded up in the reeds that grew profusely on the far side of the river. They never considered it because they had never thought that ten-year-old Mary Assumpta would take them up on the dare. She did.

No sooner had they beached the skiff than Mary Assumpta dove into the cool water and started across the river. When she was about fifty yards from shore, it occurred to John that Mary Assumpta might get into real trouble. He hurriedly pushed the skiff into the water, and he and Andrew Ryan began paddling furiously toward Mary Assumpta.

As they neared the swimming Mary Assumpta, they begged her to return to the boat. "Mary Assumpta, that is enough. We were only kidding. Swim over to the boat and we will haul you in. You win the dare."

Mary Assumpta ignored their pleas, rolled over on her back, and casually began a lazy backstroke toward the far side. "I am not getting in that boat with you two sissy boys."

Another twenty-five yards and she rolled back over and swam strongly toward the shore about fifty yards away. "Dammit to hell, Mary Assumpta. Get in the damn boat right now." John was getting really worried, and Mary Assumpta simply ignored him. She reached the far bank and turned around without her feet ever touching the muddy bottom.

As Mary Assumpta swam steadily, albeit slowly, on her way back to the beach, she began to tire, her arms feeling like limp rope. As her arms tired, she simply floated with an occasional kick to keep herself moving in the general direction of Bailey Beach, allowing her arms to recover. Thirty minutes after she had entered the water, she crawled onto the beach and promptly retched up her breakfast. Then she smiled triumphantly.

On August 5, 1851, Mary Assumpta received a response from the admissions committee of the Medical College of South Carolina at Charleston:

August 1, 1851

Jackson C. Hawthorne, MD
Provost and Professor of Diagnostic Medicine
Medical College of South Carolina at Charleston
Charleston, South Carolina

Dear Miss Bailey,

We regret to inform you that your application has been rejected, as the Medical College of South Carolina at Charleston is not currently admitting females to the study of medicine, nor do we foresee a change in this policy in the near future.

However, we congratulate you on a fine record of achievement in your education and your work in the medical office of Dr. John Bailey.

Perhaps you may want to consider a career in nursing, which does not currently require any credentials beyond a grammar school education.

Very cordially yours,

Jackson C. Hawthorne, MD
Provost and Professor of Diagnostic Medicine

Mary Assumpta had had her heart set on following John's path into medicine, all the while being smart enough to know that she would not likely be admitted to MCSC. Still, the letter tilted her young world to the brink of destruction.

There had been few times in her brief seventeen years when she had been genuinely heartbroken. On this day she was devastated. Emotionally, for the first time in her life, she doubted her abilities, even though she knew logically that she was smart enough to master the study of medicine.

After picking at her food during supper, Mary Assumpta asked to be excused and retreated to the familiar comfort of her upstairs bedroom. Forgoing dessert meant to Lauraleigh Bailey that something was really bothering her youngest and most resilient child.

When Lauraleigh knocked on Mary Assumpta's closed door, she heard what she thought were sobs. The last time she could remember Mary Assumpta being overwhelmed with emotion that brought her to uncontrollable tears was five years earlier when her father had had to shoot her dog Amos, who had shown definite signs of distemper. That day and the next Mary Assumpta refused to come out of her room until her brother John intervened with a new puppy procured from one of his patients.

When her mother entered the room on this day, the shutters had been closed, and Mary Assumpta was drawn up into the fetal position, her body racked with her sobbing. The feather pillow that covered her face was now soaked with tears. A new puppy clearly would not change the emotional state of Lauraleigh's daughter on this day.

Lauraleigh sat down beside her and said not a word, just caressed her tangled and cerise curls. Soon, Mary Assumpta let her mother take her into her arms, and she sobbed even more violently on her mother's shoulder. Lauraleigh, the mother of two unemotional boys, had never experienced the depth of despair that her daughter showed this day. She could only hold her, somehow knowing that anything else would be useless.

Finally, after many minutes, Mary Assumpta found her voice. But "Oh, Mother" was all she could say before retreating once again into body-shaking sobs.

PART II
THE MERRIWEATHERS

CHAPTER 3

On a wet and windy late summer morning in 1760, Timothy Meriwether, a religious studies graduate of Oxford's Merton College, sat for the first time at his faculty desk in the College of William and Mary library in Williamsburg, Virginia. He smiled, knowing that his father would have been proud that he carried on the scholarly family traditions. He stifled a laugh knowing that his grandfather David would have been equally proud of the adventurous spirit that brought him from the comforts of Oxford, England, to the turmoil that was beginning to simmer in the colonies.

The patriarch of the Virginia Merriweathers had arrived in the United States, and when he signed his first employment contract with the College of William and Mary, he noted that the bursar had spelled his name as Timothy *Merriweather* instead of Meriwether. *Fitting,* he thought. *A new name for a new home.*

On fall days of 1760, when he felt as if he had finally settled in to the small apartment steps away from the campus, a hand-warmed snifter of brandy in hand, Timothy Merriweather—sometimes wistful, sometimes maudlin—remembered the history of the English Meriwethers from whom he had sprung. His life in the world of academia was a gift heritage from Oxford and Cambridge passed down from his father. But the Meriwether clan had begun as much simpler folk. Timothy knew well the stories of the *first* Meriwether, Wyllm (the) Merchant from Meranwyrthe in County Kent. He cherished the story of how Wyllm became *William* and Meranwyrthe became *Meriwether* when he moved his family to London. He proudly and often thought of the stories of the first coffeehouses in London and Oxford built by his grandfather David Meriwether and how he—an uncommon commoner—was appointed by King Charles II as an envoy to Spain. But Timothy's most-cherished memory was of his father, Charles, who broke with family tradition and chose to study medicine and religion instead of business. Above the door of Timothy's small study in the William and Mary College library was a plaque of Cambridge walnut upon which was engraved the epitaph from his father's tombstone in the Cambridge University cemetery: "In the beginning was the Word, and the Word was with God, and the Word was God" (John 1:1 KJV).

The Eccentric

Timothy Merriweather prospered, as had his father, Charles, in his scholarly pursuits. At Oxford as a student, and now as a professor at the College of William and Mary, Timothy continued the path of scholarship begun by his father. He considered their studies no less than a critical mile marker in the progression of the human species toward godly perfection. Their writing and lectures centered on one little-explored theme of Christendom: *Does the Bible endorse slavery as an acceptable practice?*

Their conclusions and their lectures, typically fiery, were often unpopular in the halls of academia and in the aisles of the cathedrals in England and Virginia. It was a fact of life that slavery and empire building thrived together in a symbiotic relationship of evil.

Timothy Merriweather was known as "the Eccentric" among his students because he often came to class unshaven and with his hair uncombed because he had spent all night reading and writing in his library office. While walking across the tree-lined campus, a fellow professor, Franklin Randolph, had overheard students laughing about his colleague. Having been granted tenure just the year before, he recognized the symptoms of unproductive and potentially dangerous overzealousness in Merriweather. Randolph had dubbed the symptoms as "the ivory tower effect," which frequently robbed an academic of the broader perspective necessary to judge whether his scholarly work possessed any practical purpose at all.

Franklin Randolph conspired that day to bring balance to the life of Timothy Merriweather, whether he desired it or not. It began with a lunch at Christiana Campbell's tavern, a short, pleasant walk from campus. As they walked together, Randolph broached the subject of the students' laughter the day before. "Timothy, did you know our students have a pseudonym for you?" Randolph began.

"Well, Franklin, I am far from surprised. I thought we all were victims of our students' creative imaginations," Timothy replied with no surprise at all in his voice.

"That is certainly true, my friend, and we should be concerned that we are not pushing them hard enough had they not anointed us thusly," Franklin agreed. "However, the source of your moniker worries me a bit."

"Worries you? Why in God's name does it worry you?" A little harshness had entered Timothy's voice. Randolph ignored it.

"It is a playful name, 'the Eccentric.' It seems you earned it by the number of times you have come to class looking rather tattered from an all-night session of reading and writing."

"I cannot deny that it has occurred a time or two," Timothy responded, a wry smile on his face.

"Timothy, I am not worried about the name, and neither should you be. I am, however, worried that you may be losing perspective—that intellectual commodity that keeps us eccentrics reasonably sane. I fear that you are working too hard toward earning tenure and that, in so doing, you may hinder its attainment."

"Franklin, I appreciate your concern," Timothy responded. "But I cannot let down my family, who have financially and spiritually supported me in making this, as they see it, drastic move."

"Timothy, I think you overexaggerate their expectations. Your father, especially, knows the rigors of academic work and its effects on the mind and body.

"We're here," Randolph said, opening the door to the tavern and ushering in Merriweather. "I believe that table in the far back left corner has been reserved for us."

"Are you sure? It seems someone has already been seated there."

"Indeed. That is my sister, MaryAnne, who is visiting me this week from Boston. I think you will enjoy her unique perspective on most matters of conversation, but especially on the politics of the day."

Timothy was momentarily transported to Pireas, Greece, and back to an excursion he had once taken with his father to explore the world of the ancient Christian church. He remembered being served coffee in a small outdoor coffee shop overlooking the translucent cerulean Mediterranean Sea. The server was the daughter of the owner, and he had never been so overpowered by a first impression as he was on that mild day in Pireas.

Until today.

With black lustrous hair, no makeup, and kissable lips that stirred Timothy to his male core, MaryAnne Randolph was striking. All thoughts of scholarly activities evaporated from Timothy's mind like the sun burning away the fog on a spring morning.

A year to the day he had met MaryAnne Randolph in Christiana Campbell's tavern, they married in Boston's Old North Church. Later that same year, tenure as a professor of religion was granted to Dr. Timothy Merriweather.

The youngest child of Timothy and MaryAnne Merriweather, Nicholas Randolph, was born in 1780. Nicholas Randolph Merriweather was baptized into faith by his uncle Franklin Randolph in the Wren Chapel on the campus of the College of William and Mary. He would later be grandfather to James Edward Merriweather.

Black Dog of Melancholia

Nicholas Randolph Merriweather grew into manhood as the United States began to grow into its promise. To both, it seemed that there were only endless possibilities. At twenty-seven, he graduated from the College of William and Mary School of Law founded less than twenty years earlier by then Virginia governor Thomas Jefferson.

Nicholas chose to begin his law practice in the capital, Richmond. Simply, Richmond held too many possibilities to ignore. There he apprenticed for two years under the tutelage of Edmund Randolph, his mother's uncle and former Virginia attorney general.

Two years into his practice, Nicholas met and married Ramona Gail Lee, whose distant relatives would include a rather famous Civil War general. Ramona gave birth but lost her first child to a hateful strain of ague soon after birth, and the second died when he ran in front of a carriage as his mother watched helplessly from her porch.

Ramona retreated into darkness. Her existence was reduced to eating, performing daily ablutions, and sleeping for twenty hours a day. Nothing could bring her peace, for nothing could bring her answers. Her pastor, well-meaning but shallow as he was, told her that God had a plan for her life that included the deaths of her two precious children. She rejected a God who would include such a plan for her life, one that included such painful deaths to her innocents. Her physician initially prescribed laudanum to help diminish her emotional anguish. She put it away because she wanted to grieve. She wanted the pain her babies had experienced. She did not need the laudanum to descend into the darkness of her soul. A helpless Nicholas immersed himself in his work. And she was left not only alone but also to her dark inclinations, which she translated into sexual liaisons with dozens of strangers and an equal number of acquaintances. Some continued for months. No relationship was involved—only sex and anguish. How she managed not to be impregnated was a mystery, and her dalliances were known to anyone who desired to know them.

Nicholas sought the advice of his father, who advised him to love and forgive and at some future point try to forget. "But I am not in love with her, Father," Nicholas implored on a visit to Williamsburg.

"Just love her," his father retorted.

"Are they not one and the same?" Nicholas argued.

"The emotion of being in love is a noun that follows the act of loving, a verb. Love her. Let her and God see your love; she will return to you one day."

"How? How can I?"

"It will not be easy, but can it be any harder than what she endured at the deaths of her children?"

"But, Father. Her meandering. How do I ever forgive that?" Nicholas almost wailed.

Timothy Merriweather took his son's hands in his hand—the hands of a father, a pastor, a scholar. "Nicholas, she did not do those things to hurt you but to hurt herself. That is the beginning of your forgiveness and her own."

The journey back began with flowers—every morning put on her nightstand before she awoke. It continued with meals that Nicholas prepared himself. No more tavern meals for either: an excuse eliminated, a tenderness begun.

For three months he slept on the floor by her side of the bed, before he eased one night to rest on top of the duvet. A week later he slipped under the bedcovers. Another two weeks and they touched feet accidentally during the night without a gasp or groan from Ramona Gail. In six months they held hands for the first time in five years. In three years, Winston Arthur Merriweather was born—the father of James Edward Merriweather.

The Merriweathers were firmly planted in the rich soil of Virginia, not as businessmen, as had been their forefathers in London, but as professionals—scholars, attorneys, and physicians. The trait that all the Virginia Merriweather progeny shared with their English progenitors was an unwavering sense of right and wrong. As early businessmen and in service to the king, their integrity reigned over reward; truth over convenience; wisdom over opinion.

When Timothy Meriwether, the religious studies graduate of Oxford's Merton College and the first Merriweather in the United States, continued his scholarly pursuits at the College of William and Mary in Virginia Colony, he did not start his studies afresh; rather, he continued a path begun by his father, Charles, as a student at Oxford and as a don at Cambridge. It was built around a central theme: *Does Christianity endorse slavery?*

Their conclusions and their sermons, often fiery, were often unpopular in halls of academia and in the aisles of the cathedrals in England and Virginia, where slavery was a fact of life of empire building. As the family continued into law and medicine, the aversion to slavery was a common thread in their professional work.

Many discussions over Sunday dinners of fried chicken, corn bread, butter beans, and peach cobbler were held about the conundrum of being Southern in a South that included slavery. The Merriweathers were not a family of exceptional means financially or politically, so most of their discussions ended where they began—as enigmas debated during Sunday dinner. As the South moved toward separation from the Union, one thing was clear: if called, they would serve.

Wedding Bells

Beatrice Elizabeth Williams Merriweather was the daughter of Raymond Williams, the law partner and longtime friend of Winston's father. The two attorneys had struggled in their early years in Richmond, finally seeing the reasonableness of joining forces in a single law practice. When Nicholas and Raymond signed the contract setting up the joint practice in a small storefront office on the corner of Thirteenth Street and Main, it was also as if a silent contract bound the families together.

A year later Winston and Beatrice were born a month apart. The two children grew up on the same street, attended the same Sunday school, and were friends long before they became lovers. Their courtship had been not so much a courtship as an inevitable evolution. The length of the relationship had only increased the desire in each to get on with the day.

On her wedding day, in the anteroom of Saint John's Episcopal Church in Richmond, Beatrice Elizabeth Williams fretted to herself that she was the plain sister to the elegance of her older sister, Martha. Whether it was wedding day jitters, or the rivalry of a younger sibling, or being consigned inevitably to wearing Martha's hand-me-downs, though they were practically remade to fit Beatrice's made-for-childbearing hips by her mother, Beatrice was antsy and ready to be done with the ceremony so that the fun could begin.

Truth be told, Martha *was* elegant, and she was also a Southern bitch. Beatrice, on the other hand, was not plain in any sense of the word. Where Martha was thin and stately, Beatrice was statuesque—the epitome of the promise of delights saved for her husband-to-be. Beatrice, despite her shapeliness, tended toward tomboy, compared to Martha's innate prissiness.

At 5:30 p.m. on June 22, 1820, with candles burning softly in every window, Beatrice held tight to the arm of her father, Raymond, and walked expectantly to meet Winston, who waited for her at the altar. As she seemed to float down the aisle, the crowded sanctuary expelled a simultaneously whispered "My goodness" as the wedding dress sewn by her mother emphasized each curve, dip, and hillock of her youthful body. On this day, Beatrice Williams, to Winston's delight, was definitely not a tomboy.

Winston Arthur Merriweather had waited to marry until he had, at least semisuccessfully, begun his medical practice. At just under six feet in height, Winston was darkly tanned as a result of his passion to be outdoors at every opportunity. His hair was light brown with lighter highlights from the bleaching of the sun. He could not be described as muscular, but neither was he gangly. He possessed a quiet strength from long strides up and down the hills that rose from the James River and were his second home.

Today he wore his father's dark gray wedding suit—a little out of style, but so filled with nostalgia and tradition that there had never been a question of his acceptance when his father offered it to him. As with the wedding of his mother and father, his grandfather the Reverend Timothy Merriweather, professor emeritus of the College of William and Mary, presided at the wedding—perhaps the end of a long tradition of religious scholarship expressed in the Merriweather family's marriages, births, and burials.

Grandfather's Counsel

On a mild spring day in April before their wedding, Winston and Beatrice traveled with Beatrice's mother the fifty miles by carriage to Williamsburg, where they were to receive the blessings and counsel of the Merriweather family patriarch. As they entered the office of Winston's grandfather behind and above the chancel—a bit larger than his first cubbyhole in the library had been—they did so with not a little trepidation. "The Eccentric," as his students called his grandfather, had well earned that reputation in his classroom, but he never carried it beyond the classroom walls. This day he was dressed in neither professorial nor ecclesiastical garb. Instead, he looked the role of a kindly grandfather. Before he served the tea and biscuits, they all held each other's hands as he prayed for the couple.

"As the essence of all love, heavenly Father, bind these two souls to your bosom this day in holy togetherness, and place the words in our mouths and ears that you desire for us to speak and hear this day and every day. In Jesus's holy name, amen." It was a sincere and elegant prayer that Winston and Beatrice, and later their children, would repeat each day of their lives.

Tea, just now cooled enough to drink, was poured and homemade shortbread cookies were served—a fitting way to begin a conversation rather than the lecture the young couple might have anticipated. After a half hour or so of scriptural advice for husband and wife, Father Timothy looked to the couple with a wry smile. "Well, surely you have something to ask of me, for as you know, clergy and professors never experience marital discord, Winston. Just ask your grandmother!"

"Grandfather," Winston haltingly began, "Father said that you gave him a sage admonition that he says was the best of any kind that he's ever received."

"Yes," Grandfather replied. "There was a particularly rough patch that your parents were going through, and he came to me for advice. Has he not told you of it?"

"Only that God spoke through you as clear as a church bell on a December Sunday morning, but he did not tell us what you said. Father told us that Beatrice and I must hear it from you, not from him, because pastors are much closer to God than mere attorneys who, he said, are a bit closer to hell's fires than to heavenly advice."

His grandfather laughed out loud at Winston's aphorism—a perfect reward since Winston had practiced it in his head hundreds of times on the carriage ride from Richmond.

"Winston, your mother entered a state of mind following the death of your younger brother and sister that is simply unknowable by physician or clergyman, much less a husband trying to get by and care for his wife. Troubles happen in life—to all of us. Some people blame them on fate, some on the Almighty's testing of us, some on the sins of our forefathers. I blame them on life.

"I know that my God does not harm innocents just to demonstrate his omnipotence. My God has no plan that includes deaths of children.

"Winston, I know your mother tried to find her own way out of the depths of the hell in which she was trapped. To her everlasting credit, she clawed her way back toward some sense of reality as only she could understand it. It was beyond the comprehension of any of the rest of us. Our only recourse was to pray and love and be patient, and to trust that she and God, in his time, would bring her back. And he did.

"My advice to your father, and now to you, Winston, and you, Beatrice, is to love each other in the hard times as you easily love today. Love is an emotion unafraid of the tempering fires of life."

Circumscribed by Secession

In rapid succession, three children were born to Winston and Beatrice—all boys. James Edward was born in January 1821, barely nine and half months after the wedding, long before Winston and Beatrice learned to be a proper husband and wife, but early enough to have a few tongues wagging about Richmond. John Raymond was born eleven months after James, and Timothy David waited awhile and was born an entire year after his older brother Raymond.

Two things that came happily easy to Winston and Beatrice were lovemaking and, thankfully, childbirth. Beatrice was naturally blessed with wide hips and had developed exceptionally excellent muscle control from her days of climbing hills and valleys with Winston as a teenager. After Timothy David was born, the third child before the couple turned twenty-five, they were sure that they were to have a large and boisterous family, something each desired as they grew up mostly with each other and not siblings.

But as the sisters of fate would spin their web, there were no children for another five years. As a physician, Winston could not explain it other than to say, "It was just not meant to be," which was as good a medical explanation as any of the day. And then it happened. Rachel Lee, Patrice Jemima, and Daniel Jefferson were born—all within another five-year period.

After the birth of Jemima, it was apparent to parents and offspring alike that it was time to build a bigger house.

The Physician

The children born to Winston and Beatrice Merriweather were to come of age defined almost wholly by the prelude to the inevitable War between the States. James Edward, John Raymond, and Timothy David were old enough to have started careers and families when the untimely shots were fired by an unprepared Confederate artillery battery on a poorly supplied Union brigade at Fort Sumter in the middle of the Charleston Harbor.

James Edward grew up in a home consumed with five essentials common to all Southern families: religion, heritage, meaningful work, food, and community—pretty much in that order. He never looked farther than his father's medical practice for guidance to fulfill each of these essentials in his life.

When he was five years of age, his sister Rachel Lee was born. His father, believing that good hard facts were better than easy fabrications, invited James into the bedroom to observe the birth of his baby sister.

After Rachel Lee was cleaned up and delivered back to her mother, Beatrice, and James Edward's father was washing up, James ventured an observation: "Father, I was frightened by Mother's yells, and then the baby came out all covered in blood."

"James, the miracle of childbirth is not without its pain,

but as your mother will tell you in few days, it is worth it," his father replied.

"Do all women go through this same thing?" James asked, one of a hundred questions on his mind.

"Most do. Some have it easier, and sometimes the mother or the child, or both, does not survive, especially if they do not have a doctor to help them."

"Then I want to be a doctor so that I can help."

"My son, I expect you will do exactly that." His father, Winston, smiled inwardly at just how clinically James had approached the entire process. If he was squeamish, it never showed on his face.

James would be there for the births of his second sister, Patrice Jemima, and his brother Timothy David. His path in life was settled.

The Theologian

If James was the scientist, ever curious about the natural world, then John was equally inquisitive about the world of the metaphysical. From his first experience as an altar boy at Saint John's Episcopal Church, John was enthralled with mystery, majesty, and the magic (as he called it) of the church. John questioned Father William Bishop incessantly about the children's Bible stories in ways that surprised even the seasoned old priest.

"Father William, did a fish really swallow Jonah? Was it a whale? Could he live inside the fish for three days? Did Noah *really* get all the animals of the world on that one boat? Did Peter actually walk on water?"

One at a time, Father William explained the theology behind the stories to his young acolyte, not dismissing the Almighty's power, but not settling for the unquestioned literal interpretations either.

By age twelve, John was heard on many Sundays reading the Bible verses to the congregation that would make up the text of Father Williams's sermon. By fifteen he was assisting with the serving of the Holy Eucharist.

"I do believe that we may have another pastor in the Merriweather family," Father William was heard to say to Winston Merriweather as they enjoyed a brandy following a Sunday lunch.

"You certainly may be right, but he has a lot of growing to do yet in the ways of the world, which are apt to challenge his beliefs. We will rejoice if the Almighty calls him to his church, but we will let nature take its course for the time being. He has university and the opposite sex to contend with first."

John never wavered and followed a long-standing family tradition of academic work in the area of religious studies at the College of William and Mary. There he earned an AB, an AM, and a DD, and also served as an assistant professor of Latin and Greek. But his greatest joys were in his marriage to Katherine Willamine Jackson of Williamsburg the week after he graduated with his AB degree, and in serving as pastor of the small Episcopal church dedicated to the seamen of Newport News. Willamine kept his ambition grounded in family as his seamen parishioners kept his faith rooted in the real world.

The Officer

Timothy David, the third son in three years and six months of marriage, was born to Winston and Beatrice Merriweather on November 23, 1824. The baby in the family for almost six years, Timothy, by age five, was fighting for his place among his older brothers. By age sixteen he was a plebe at West Point. Timothy Merriweather wrote to his father a short note at the end of his second week:

August 15, 1839

Dearest Father,

My deepest apology for not writing sooner, but honestly, there has not been a moment to write, and every minute is reserved for the upperclassmen to whip us plebes into fighters or to harass us into leaving. Of the class of fifty who entered two weeks ago, forty-five remain.

I am pleased to say that I am one of the forty-five and plan to continue to be so until I am commissioned as a second lieutenant. The mental stress is as relentless as the physical exertion, but I see its purpose if I am to be an officer in the army of the United States. Battles provide no time given to relaxing or, it seems, to thinking either.

I begin my studies on Monday with classes six days a week in analytical geometry, elementary surveying fieldwork, French, English grammar, rhetoric, and military history.

I must close. I hear my cadet colonel making his rounds to give us hell (sorry, but my language is already getting a bit salty) one more time before lights out.

Your exhausted son,
Timothy, Cadet Fourth Class

Timothy David Merriweather graduated West Point Military Academy and was commissioned a second lieutenant with his father, his mother, and his older brothers in attendance on May

27, 1844. Upon his graduation, Second Lieutenant Merriweather was transported by the War Department to Fort Leavenworth, Kansas, in anticipation of the conflict brewing between Mexico and the United States. By the end of the engagement, Timothy David Merriweather had risen to the rank of captain. His rise in rank would continue, as would his duties in the newly acquired Southwest territories, with little rest between fighting Mexico and turning then to the Indian tribes indigenous to the area. By the beginning of the Civil War, Merriweather, hardened and fully committed to a career in the US Army, had risen to the rank of lieutenant colonel.

A looming personal decision would be harder than any foe he had yet faced.

The Southern Belle

Rachel Lee Merriweather, had she resided in England, would have been categorized as the prototypical English beauty: dark blond hair, flawless skin unblemished by the sun's rays, and cerulean eyes with flecks of gold. She was stunning and knew it.

Rachel Lee enjoyed the company of young men and to this point had seen no practical reason to marry in her early twenties. She would leave that to her friends. Rachel Lee was simply having too much fun. All that changed when, at twenty-six, while attending a party at the home of US senator James Murray Mason, she caught the eye of a distinguished, somewhat older gentleman, the prominent Richmond attorney and Virginia assemblyman Richland James. Richland James's opinions were well respected in Virginia politics and beyond. He was known to frequently bend the ear of Senator Mason and was an instrumental advisor to Mason when he drafted the Fugitive Slave Law of 1850. Richland James was an up-and-comer.

Rachel Lee, trying to look coy but not pulling it off, sat on the brocade love seat drinking white wine and talking with her longtime socialite friend, Mason's middle daughter Virginia. "Why, Rachel Lee, I do believe that gentleman across the room talking to Father is spending more time looking at you than listening to my daddy drone on about Washington politics," Virginia Mason whispered in Rachel Lee's ear, trying to elicit a blush.

"He is handsome in an older sort of way," Rachel Lee responded. A late evening tryst was never out of the question for the free spirit of the Merriweather clan. As that thought moved from her subconscious to her conscious mind, Richland James extricated himself from James Mason and eased over toward Rachel Lee and Virginia, who seemed to be sharing a private bit of humor at his expense.

"Rachel Lee," Virginia whispered, "I do believe that he is coming our way, and he looks like a strutting banty rooster in those fancy pants."

"He does fill them out rather well." Rachel Lee giggled in return just as Richland James stopped, executed a perfect bow, and introduced himself. "Miss Virginia, you get prettier every time I see you. Isn't it about time you found yourself a husband?"

"About time if you listen to Daddy. But I never listen to Daddy," Virginia responded with a giggle.

"Mr. James, let me introduce you to my dear and very single friend Rachel Lee Merriweather. Her daddy is Dr. Winston Merriweather."

"Yes." James drew out the word. "I believe I had the pleasure of meeting him at a Richmond Hospital fund-raiser, but that was not nearly as pleasurable as making the acquaintance of Miss Rachel Lee."

He again bowed, extending his hand. "Miss Rachel, it is my pleasure to meet you. Might I ask if you would be so kind as to walk with me to the wine table, allow me to refill your glass, and perhaps have you tell me how I have gone so long without our paths crossing?"

Intrigued and never one for shyness, Rachel Lee rose, took his hand, and walked with him through the crowded room to the buffet that held at least twenty bottles of fine French wine. As they walked from the parlor to the dining room, not a few heads turned as a couple not seen before in Richmond seemed to float rather than walk across the waxed and polished oak floors.

Richland and Rachel Lee were practically inseparable from that moment on and were married six months later in Saint Paul's Episcopal Church. At age twenty-seven, Rachel Lee delivered twins, Jemima Beatrice James and Richland Morehouse James Jr., with her father and her brother James as attending physicians.

The house of Richland and Rachel Lee James, which had often been the scene of raucous socialite parties, was now a dignified, if slightly over the top, Victorian home in the heart of Richmond only five blocks removed from the statehouse, the center of politics in Richmond and, soon to be, the entire South. Richland James relished its proximity to power. Initially, Rachel Lee flourished in the glow of the powerful and notables whom she entertained weekly for her husband. However, her pregnancy so soon after marriage changed her mood to one of enduring the inevitable, and once the twins arrived, she had no interest in socializing, a change not unnoticed by her husband, who often was left to entertain as the sole host. There was a rift, but James was also devoted to his children, so the fissure never grew beyond bothersome.

The Contrarian

Patrice Jemima, like her sister Rachel Lee, had not married early, but for entirely different reasons. She had never shown an interest in boys at any age. But was intensely interested in history and politics, both so very common in Richmond. By fourteen, she had read every political treatise on both sides of the Revolutionary War. By sixteen, she had tracked down and devoured every manuscript written by her scholarly relatives at Oxford, Cambridge, and William and Mary. She was not interested in medicine or religion—the scholarly pursuits of her relatives—but she was fascinated with the idea of knowing more about a topic than anyone else on either side of the Atlantic.

"PJ," said Rachel Lee, calling her sister by the name she had used for her almost since birth, a name that stuck with the rest of the family, "why are you not going to the spring cotillion? All the handsomest boys in Richmond will be there lining up to dance with us. You don't have to bring one home, but wouldn't it be fun just to tease them to the point that they are lathered up like a racehorse but with no way to let off all that pent-up passion?"

"Rachel Lee, one of these days that pastime of yours is going to get you into big trouble that you are not going to be able to talk your way out of. Besides, I prefer to think that Southern ladies should have a bit more substance to them than frilly knickers that Southern boys want to get into," PJ countered sarcastically.

"Oh, for heaven's sake, it is just for laughs. The boys at the cotillion know that I am just having fun. Hell's bells, PJ, we go to church with most of them."

"Rachel Lee, has it never occurred to that pea-size brain of yours that young women promenading around at the cotillion look remarkably like a bunch of heifers at an auction? No thank you, ma'am. I will keep my fifteen-year-old behind firmly planted right here in Daddy's study reading Machiavelli. He is ever so much more attractive than your silly Richmond boys."

Patrice Merriweather never wavered in her ambitions, even as the lone female student pursuing multiple degrees in history and political science at the University of Virginia. As she worked on her master of arts, she taught undergraduate history and worked on her thesis: *Social and Political Dialectics in a Changing South.* So well received was her research that she was invited and joined the prestigious faculty of the History Department, where her debating skills earned her the name "the she-devil's advocate." Her most memorable debates often centered on the political and social consequences of the impending war. Interestingly, few people truly knew on which side of the war her sentiments lay as she could argue both sides equally well.

Soon she would be forced to choose.

The Free Spirit

Daniel Jefferson was the youngest of the siblings. He worked for a while as a law clerk for his grandfather Nicholas and in his father's medical practice once his brother James moved to Charleston to apprentice. In fact, Daniel Merriweather had no idea of what would make him happier than a drunken night at the local tavern and awaking the next morning with a hangover and smelling of the two-bit whore in whose bed he found himself. Daniel was possessed of an unsatisfied spirit.

At twenty-one, Daniel Merriweather, on a lovely late spring day, left home after telling his mother that he was headed to the James River for a day of fishing. Daniel did not return home that night, or the next, or the next. However, given Daniel's propensity for not spending nights in his own bed, it was five days before the family became worried enough to contact the Richmond police. Based on superficial evidence gathered by the mostly uninterested officers, the police reported to the family that Daniel did indeed spend some time fishing, according to regulars who fished along the same area of the James River that Daniel had been known to frequent previously.

This starkly simple police report was the last his family

would hear of their youngest son. Ten years to the day he had disappeared, the family erected a headstone in the cemetery of Saint John's Episcopal Church.

Daniel was a sweet child, smart as any of his siblings but quieter and more introspective. There was never a doubt that Daniel loved his family, but he attended more than participated in family gatherings, and his absence was only noticed after several minutes. His mother, Beatrice, would sadly confide to her husband, Winston, "Just when does one miss silence?"

Daniel was as much of a mystery to his family in life as he was in death. Still, every week his mother placed flowers on his tombstone and prayed that he was not dead, all the while knowing she prayed in vain.

A Shadow from the Past

James Edward would not know until he was eighteen that his father harbored a dark family secret.

On his first day back home after his second year at UVA, expecting a joyous homecoming, James instead found a noted darkness in his father, Winston. He had not seen this side of his father before, or perhaps he had simply been oblivious to it as a self-absorbed teenager and a physician's son. But he was distant. Not unloving, just withdrawn. The handshake at his entrance was perfunctory, and dinner was uncommonly quiet in a house that was never quiet with his younger siblings about.

The next morning as he began to make rounds of houses with his father before returning to his surgery office, James ventured a question. "Father, are you ill? You hardly spoke to me yesterday."

"James, when you were born, your mother and I made a decision: that we would not talk about our family secret until you were mature enough and ready to hear it. It was the right thing to do because it let us move forward without continually looking backwards. By focusing on keeping the secret, we did not have to think about the secret itself. But eighteen years ago, I had a nervous breakdown and was unaware of anything around me for almost four months. The darkness, as it was whispered of in my family growing up, had afflicted my mother, brought on by the tragic deaths of her two young children in the period of a month. I think we have spoken of this on occasion, but what we have never spoken of was her retreat into madness for almost a year."

"Did you figure out what brought it on?" James asked, still not quite believing what he had just heard.

"Perhaps it was your birth so soon after your mother and I were married. Perhaps it was the wagging tongues who spread rumors that you were born a little too soon. Most likely it was simply the stress of trying to get a practice going with a newborn and the sleepless nights that go with any new baby—and your mother was pregnant again within a month of your birth. Likely it was a combination of all these things and a bit of inheritance thrown in too. I have concluded that there is little doubt at this stage of studying dementia that aspects of it are likely inherited."

"Have I inherited the propensity for it, do you think?" James asked, clearly worried.

"No way to know right now. Your mother and I watched you very closely for signs of unusual moodiness or general unhappiness, but you never exhibited any of those traits. It will be wise for you to monitor your own moods, eat well, get adequate sleep, and find ways to relieve the anxiety and stress that will come with your chosen profession. There have been debates within the medical profession about whether it is better to be somewhat removed from the patients or to be personally involved. It will not be an easy choice for you to make. My suggestion is that you find a middle ground."

"Father," James, now intrigued, asked, "how did you live during those months when the world was dark to you?"

"Your mother knew that my secret could never emerge, for if it did, my career would be over. Your great-uncle the Reverend Timothy traveled from Williamsburg to Richmond to pray with and advise your mother. It was he who first told us of the story of your grandmother and grandfather and his advice to my grandfather during his deepest moments of despair and his young wife's retreat from reality. What we had going for us most was our age and our love. Your mother never gave up on me. She talked to me and read my favorite novels to me, and she talked about our future and our family. I remember hearing her words as if they had come from a very long distance, and there were times when I would almost break through the smothering darkness with her assurances of our future, but my self-doubt would pull me back down into the depths of despair. But then I heard your laughter as you responded to your mother's teasing, and the present very gradually began to emerge almost as a physical presence—at first like a faint candle and gradually like a bright sun that warmed my soul as it would warm my skin on a summer day.

"Your mother says she knew on that June day eighteen years ago that I was going to be okay when I sat up, put my clothes on, and asked for eggs and bacon for breakfast. That day was eighteen years ago yesterday. I get a bit melancholy sometimes on the anniversary, and yesterday was one of those times. But it always passes, and I move on, thankful for the love of a remarkable woman.

"I know you wonder if it will hit you like it affected your grandmother and me. No way to know, but it is not uncommon to skip generations. Should it happen, we will deal with it with love and compassion. Right now, you need to focus on always having balance in your life in all things. That is my advice.

Trust in God, but know that he does not reside in churches alone. Believe in yourself, but when the time is right, totally give your trust to a good woman. Find a hobby totally unrelated to medicine, but treat it in moderation too. Eat well, but do fear the occasional indulgence. Stay attached to your family first, then to your ambitions. Nothing is more capable of bringing balance than family. And remember, if you are a physician without balance in your life, you are a doctor, but you are not a healer.

"Now, let's see how Mrs. Bohannon is feeling this morning," his father said as he knocked on the door of her quaint cottage.

PART III
A NEW TAPESTRY

CHAPTER 4

Meeting of the Minds

Dr. John Bailey's skills as a surgeon lifted him above the typical Charleston physician, and he was often asked by his alma mater to teach others his methods. As his students graduated and spread beyond the borders of South Carolina, so did Bailey's reputation as an innovative practitioner. In early May of 1851, with its mild days good for traveling, John Bailey made a pleasant trip to Charlottesville, Virginia. As the invited speaker of the University of Virginia Medical School, he lectured its students on the topic of "The Use of Hygienic Surgical Techniques as a Curative in the Hospital and the Physician's Office."

As alumni of the very same medical school, Drs. Winston A. Merriweather and James E. Merriweather—father and son—decided to attend the lecture. The idea of using surgery as a restorative rather than as a radical procedure appealed to both father and son, and perhaps a destination closer to the Blue Ridge Mountains might provide a bit of cool in an otherwise oppressive heat wave.

As they made their way to Charlottesville, the road once outside the city of Richmond was still muddy from a recent thundershower, but it was more than passable for their two-horse carriage. However, as they bounced along, they still groaned about the recent lack of foresight by the Virginia legislature in thwarting the approval of a turnpike linking Richmond to

Charlottesville. It seemed that weather and the roads were always good for starting a conversation.

They hoped to make it to Columbia before nightfall, some forty miles from Richmond and two-thirds of the way to Charlottesville. They would stay the night at the Wild Turkey Inn. The proprietress at the inn knew James Merriweather well as he had stayed a number of nights in her care on his thrice-yearly trips between Richmond and Charlottesville as he pursued his medical education. James hoped that she would not tell his father that some of those visits had included a late night visit to his room by a comely local Columbia lass he had met over dinner in the spring of his first year.

Once they entered a smoother section of road, Winston Merriweather decided to raise a subject with his son that he had been putting off for some time.

"James, you have been practicing with me now for almost a year, but I sense an uneasiness in you just of late. Anything we need to talk about?"

James *had been* edgy, and he was not surprised his father had picked up on it. His father was particularly perceptive of feelings, one of his most valuable assets as a physician. That his father had opened the door pleased James, and he stepped through it.

"Father, of course you are right. I trust it has not affected my work with patients."

"No, not at all, James. But it has affected your mother. She is worried about you too. She told me last week that you left her talking in the middle of a conversation."

James spoke over the sound and rhythm of the horses' hooves. "I *am* sorry for that. I owe everything to you and Mother and would never purposefully cause you disquiet."

A bit unsure, he continued, "My time as your apprentice has been rewarding beyond measure. What I have learned far exceeds, by any reasonable measure, that which I brought with me when you accepted me as your understudy."

Sweat stung his father's eyes, or perhaps it was tears mixed with sweat.

"Father, I think it is time I move beyond Richmond, at least for a while, and study with another about his care for his patients who can teach me new techniques."

His father, wiping his eyes on his sleeve, coughed and regained his ability to speak. "James, as I believe it should always be the case, the master often learns much from the apprentice. Such has been the case this year. So, of course I support you. Now let's nudge these nags toward the Wild Turkey and supper, and then we will talk some more of it."

The Encounter

In the surgical teaching theater on their third day out of Richmond, Drs. Merriweather and Merriweather joined a sizable number of other colleagues and a goodly number of medical students, obviously required to attend, who were seated on the floor around the walls.

It was crowded, thankfully. Dr. John Bailey was not sure how he was to be received. It was hot, unfortunately, but that would present him with some practical opportunities to talk about sanitation during surgery. After an hour of lecture and another of questions, the temperature in the surgical teaching theater had become beyond tolerable as the day wore on toward noon.

As the assembled passed out of the teaching theater and walked beneath the hovering oaks' branches over the brick-lined walkways, Winston Merriweather, a step or two behind John Bailey, caught up and introduced himself and his son.

The elder Merriweather had been surprised and impressed by John Bailey's presentation. On his return to Richmond,

Merriweather wrote to Bailey, and their correspondence commenced a series of events that would eventually join the Merriweather and Bailey families.

Dr. Winston Merriweather
324 Franklin Street
Richmond, Virginia

May 20, 1851

Dear Dr. John Bailey,

It was my great pleasure to be in your audience for your lecture on "The Use of Hygienic Surgical Techniques as a Curative in the Hospital and the Physician's Office" recently at the University of Virginia. I know little of the techniques of surgery beyond the removal of limbs, which in the past I have deemed beyond salvage, and amputation has been the limit of my surgical expertise.

I have seen firsthand the impact of the loss of a limb, not only on the patient but also on his family. Therefore, using surgery as a targeted curative rather than as a blanket solution was of particular interest to me and to my son James Edward, a newly graduated physician apprenticing with me this year.

Additionally, your willingness to treat the disease or disorder regardless of the status of the person in society is an issue that I have also faced here in Richmond. We are of like minds that every person, citizen or slave, white or colored, Christian or Jew, deserves our best effort as we are asked to give it. As you so eloquently said, “It is the disease that is our enemy, not our patients.”

James is ready to move on and to learn from another younger than I. If I may be so bold, I wonder if you would consider being his tutor in his second year of apprenticeship.

I welcome your return correspondence.

Yours sincerely,
Winston Merriweather, MD

CHAPTER 5

Enthusiasm or Arrogance

Correspondence between Dr. John Bailey and Dr. Winston Merriweather had produced the desired results for James, but only after Bailey wrote and received a return letter from Dr. James Merriweather's professor of diagnostics, Dr. Thomas Adams. A very busy man, Dr. Adams was straightforward:

> Thomas Adams, MD
> School of Medicine
> University of Virginia
>
> June 25, 1851
>
> Dear Dr. Bailey:
>
> James Merriweather was younger than most of my students when he matriculated with me, and he suffered from a bit of expected youthful exuberance. He was at times just shy of being defiant with his questions. However, to his credit he also came to me having grown up in a medical family and having assisted his father no few times in his practice. Therefore, his accumulated knowledge was often greater than his classmates'.

It has been my experience that my students grow up during their studies. A bit of age and a great deal of knowledge are prodigious teachers of the adage that "the more we learn, the more we learn just how much we do not know." I find that this maxim remains true for me today.

I believe that you will be very pleased to have Dr. Merriweather's assistance in your practice and that he will be fortunate, indeed, to have you as a tutor.

Yours in medicine,
Thomas Adams, MD

Well, thought John Bailey, *I do believe I recognize a bit of myself in James Edward Merriweather. Perhaps a little insubordination to challenge me where I have grown stale in my thinking is just what I need.*

Bailey wrote to James E. Merriweather on the same day he received his response from Dr. Adams.

The Offer

Dr. John Bailey
319 Meeting Street
Charleston, South Carolina

July 15, 1851

Dr. James Merriweather:

It is my intention to let you know in this letter of my decision regarding your request for apprenticeship.

I have inquired with patients whose names and addresses you shared with me, and I have corresponded with Dr. Thomas Adams of the University of Virginia Medical School.

Patients describe you "as caring as he is professional," saying, "He stayed with my husband and read to him throughout the day of his death. Dr. Merriweather's presence brought peace and acceptance to our family in this difficult time."

Dr. Thomas Adams wrote that you brought significant knowledge with you when you joined his program and that you matured as you grew in knowledge and experience.

Dr. Adams also wrote that you had a tendency to ask some very probing questions that, in his words, were "just shy of being defiant."

Worry not, Dr. Merriweather. I spent significant time myself in the office of my professor based on my "questioning techniques." These days I find that I ask the same kind of questions of myself less and less, and it will be refreshing to have a like-minded colleague to push me as you pushed Dr. Adams.

I am pleased to offer you an apprenticeship in general practice and surgery beginning no later than September 1, 1851. As part of your apprenticeship, you will be provided with all necessary medical supplies beyond your personal medical kit and a stipend of not less than 15 percent of the net monthly profits. And if you desire, you may lodge at no cost in a vacant bedroom in my apartment above the practice. You will provide for your own board, but I expect that there will be ample opportunity to dine at the Bailey dinner table.

If these conditions meet with your approval, I will look forward to your correspondence accepting this apprenticeship.

Yours sincerely,
John C. Bailey, MD

CHAPTER 6

Sailing to Charleston

The Blue Seas, out of New Bedford, Connecticut, rode high and traveled fast with fair seas and favorable winds typical of the middle of August. Even so, James Merriweather was totally out of his element. His sole ventures on the water had been in rowboats and sailing skiffs on the James River in Richmond. Even had he been asked, he was of no use to the crew and didn't want to be. Instead, he turned to his avocation—writing. A diary writer, he used his time to record life on board *The Blue Seas* and, occasionally, his plans for his future.

August 18, 1851
Off the Outer Banks of North Carolina

I have remarkably been free of any mal de mer as The Blue Seas has stayed rather close to land. We often see glimpses of tall pine trees off to the starboard. At night we anchor in peaceful harbors where we often see dolphins swimming around our ship, trying, it seems, to decipher the nature of this big fish that has entered their world.

Given that this is a coastal trader, our stores are fresh, and Cookie is a wonder, often serving up fried fish caught that day, interestingly with grits.

Grits were a staple of my mother's kitchen but never served with fish. I have found that I rather like the combination. I sleep in a hammock on deck, with the gentle rocking of The Blue Seas and the cool sea breezes making for pleasant sleep.

August 19, 1851
Wilmington, North Carolina

Soon we will be docking in Wilmington with an opportunity to get my land legs back under me. Even with North Carolina's long coastline, Wilmington is only its second commercial port. The Blue Seas will take on stores of tobacco that has been curing in tobacco barns since last fall and may be sold in Savannah or transported back to New Bedford. The decision rests with the market and our captain, a shrewd merchant indeed.

After a bit of exploring Wilmington, I have to wonder what Charleston will be like. I wrote to Dr. John Bailey several weeks before my departure to express my gratitude for accepting me as a surgery apprentice in an area for which he is a recognized expert in Charleston. I am not sure how I will practice following my apprenticeship, but I am confident in my skills as a general practitioner, having learned at the side of my father while caring for his patients.

August 22, 1851

We should be in Charleston in another day. This landlubber will be grateful to plant himself solidly on terra firma again. Our last two days have been the worst of the trip as an early season cold front stirred the seas into formidable (at least to me) six-foot waves. Unlike the predictable swells of calm seas, the stormy weather whipped our sails, seemingly from many directions at the same time, causing The Blue Seas to pitch and yaw in unpredictable ways. The seas came straight at us and often over us. Crew and passengers alike chummed over the side repeatedly.

Knowing that I was a physician, they turned to me for help. Fortuitously, I had packed a rather large store of peppermint that my father often prescribed for nausea. My observation is that perhaps it helped, but nothing as much as a return to calmer waters.

August 26, 1851
Charleston, South Carolina

As we made our way into the Charleston Harbor at the confluence of the Ashley and Cooper Rivers, Fort Sumter sat on our starboard side, guarding the entrance to the harbor. We docked in the late afternoon, and my first impression was of the many church steeples. No wonder Charleston is called the Holy City.

I will sleep one more night on The Blue Seas, and tomorrow I will find a place to lodge and explore Charleston. I meet with Dr. Bailey on September 1. I am both excited and anxious to begin this new phase of my life.

CHAPTER 7

Discovering Charleston

James Merriweather was glad to be ashore as he stepped foot on the Charleston docks, however, his head continued to tell him he was still on board the ship as the world seemed to rock to and fro whenever he stopped to get his bearings.

As he made his way to 319 Meeting Street, he carried only two items—his medical kit and his two changes of clothes in the leather suitcase his parents had presented to him as a going-away gift. Merriweather was again struck by the beauty of the church steeples of Charleston. Over the last year his parents had insisted that he attend church with them at Saint John's Episcopal, the church where Patrick Henry had declared, "Give me liberty or give me death." His parents' insistence was as much about marriage making as it was about religion, and their scheme was not unknown to their son, so James was a rather reluctant participant at best on Sunday mornings.

Merriweather, a thoughtful if not passionate religious person for his twenty-three years, told himself as he walked that it was time to return to the Episcopal church of his upbringing and see what it had to offer in this time of growing unrest in the South over the issue of slavery. But that could wait. Right now he wanted to impress his new tutor, Dr. John Bailey.

Unsure of which direction to take to Bailey's office,

Merriweather approached a man in clean seaman's garb who seemed sure of his direction of travel.

"Sir, if I may bother you for directions, I am looking for 319 Meeting Street and the medical office of Dr. John Bailey. Could you point out the proper course I should be taking?"

"Dr. John Bailey, you say?" The seaman seemed a bit overly interested, and Merriweather began to wonder if he might be accosted for his suitcase.

"Yes, Dr. John Colin Bailey. I am his new apprentice as of this morning."

Obviously impressed by James Merriweather's revelation, the seaman responded, "I tell you what, young feller, I will just take you thar. Doc Bailey and I are right well acquainted. My name is Bartholomew Jennings."

"That would be just perfect. How is it that you know Dr. Bailey?" Merriweather asked.

"Oh, I see the doc ever' time I am in port. You know, cain't carry no social disease back to my ladies in Norfolk."

Given that this was a bit more information than he was expecting, Merriweather experienced a slight case of trepidation, wondering what he had gotten himself into after working with his father's rather genteel clientele for the last year. But the feeling eased, and in minutes they were at the office of Dr. Bailey.

Bartholomew opened the door and, without even looking around, loudly declared his presence: "Doc Bailey, I got a young feller here who says he is comin' to work for you. You might need to come on out here."

"Bartholomew Jennings, pipe down right now." A very feminine voice, but on the sultry end of the alto scale, chastised the seaman to little effect, as he had a big smile on his face as a result.

James Edward Merriweather had just seen his future bride, Mary Assumpta Bailey.

First Impressions

To James Merriweather, surgery was more art than science. Surgery as a therapeutic in sanitary surroundings was largely a foreign concept. Operations on internal organs were unknown to him and most other physicians. Patients during his apprenticeship often died from the shock of the pain from a routine procedure, or more likely from rampant infections following surgery.

In 1851, surgery was nothing if not crude—except in the office and in the operating room where Dr. John Bailey was practicing.

James Merriweather was to learn new purposes and ways of surgery during this next year, but on the morning of September 1, 1851, he just wanted to officially let his tutor for the next year know that he had arrived and was ready to begin his advanced studies as soon as he could put down his suitcase and have a conversation with him.

Dr. Merriweather, with the unrequested assistance of Bartholomew Jennings, was introduced to the young woman assisting patients and Dr. Bailey.

"Dr. Merriweather," Jennings began before Merriweather had a chance to speak, "I want you to meet the prettiest little colleen in South Carolina. This here is Miss Mary Assumpta Bailey."

"Miss Bailey, it is my pleasure to make your acquaintance. I am Dr. Merriweather, Dr. Bailey's new apprentice."

Merriweather paused a moment, considering whether to ask the obvious question. "May I ask if you are related to Dr. John Bailey?"

Mary Assumpta, always ready to play the coquette, blinked her blue eyes several times and responded, "You may ask, and I might respond."

"Now, Miss Mary Assumpta," Bartholomew chided her,

"you're just bein' ornery. Answer the man and quit wasting his time and mine. I need to see the doc too."

"Yes, I am John's sister. And you'd best not forget it." She hoped she had not taken her little game too far, as James Merriweather's good looks had not escaped her inspection.

"John told me to be looking for you any day now. Welcome to Charleston, Dr. James Merriweather." She drew out his first name to let him know that she had done a bit of research on the new apprentice.

"Bartholomew, would you help Dr. Merriweather take his bag upstairs to his bedroom?" The exaggerated next few words were not lost on Merriweather, nor was the playfulness beneath them. "Y'all know that Mother would not think it proper for a young lady such as myself to be alone upstairs with a stranger."

Mary Assumpta opened the door to the stairs, and Bartholomew grabbed up Merriweather's suitcase before he could object. "It is the second door on the left. I believe John left the key in the lock. Feel free to take it with you when you lock the door. We have another, I am sure."

New Home

Merriweather deposited his suitcase on the four-poster bed that was positioned opposite the fireplace. Large windows on either side faced toward the harbor to catch the evening breezes. Above the mantel was a large painting of what he took to be an Irish landscape with sheep on rolling hillsides and the outline of a cathedral just beyond the lowest hill, giving the distinct impression of a community that lay in the valley just below the grassy hill. He would try to remember to ask Miss Bailey about it. Perhaps that might warm up the otherwise chilly reception he had received from her.

He made sure as he placed the suitcase on the bed that he did not dirty the immaculate white duvet that covered it or wrinkle the multicolored quilt folded across the foot. The bed was clearly worn from use, and he surmised that it must be a family treasure.

He surveyed the remainder of the room, finding a three-drawered side table on the door side of the bed for his personal items, a wardrobe to the left of the door where he could hang his two shirts and two suits, and a washstand on the wall opposite the wardrobe. These three pieces of furniture were clearly new and beautifully built, as he learned later from John, by Ray Hendersen. Hendersen was a first-generation Swede who learned to work in wood by building sailing skiffs with his father in Malmö on the shores of the Öresund, the sea between Sweden and Denmark. The carefully made skiffs were highly prized by the sailors of Malmö, for whom sailing seemed to be genetic. Ray Hendersen had sailed into Charleston as a seaman aboard an English two-masted schooner that had ported in Charleston to add tobacco to its larder of sugar and rum procured on the Caribbean island of Saint Croix and had stayed. Charleston provided the ocean he craved and maybe a market for well-built Swedish sailing skiffs.

After a year of scraping by and finding out that Charlestonians were not keen on recreational sailing, Hendersen turned his woodcrafting hands to building furniture, having correctly assessed a market for custom furniture built for the growing middle class who found Hendersen's furniture equal to the best imports from Europe at a significantly reduced cost.

The table, the wardrobe, and the washstand were crafted from aged local walnut trees and finished with a rubbed tung oil finish that produced a sense of depth in the golden-brown walnut. The doors of the bureau and the washstand and the top of the bedside table were inlaid with the pattern of a magnolia blossom made from lighter ash wood. The harp arms of the washstand were carved with magnolia leaves.

On the washstand, Merriweather found a white basin with matching ewer and soap dish, and a washcloth and hand towel folded and draped precisely on the wooden shaft joining the two filigreed side pieces that together made a perfect harp.

The washstand's drawer contained several more bars of soap wrapped in tissue and sealed with a dab of wax stamped with a seal that indicated their origin was Paris. *Hmm,* he mused, *I wonder who was so thoughtful?*

Back on the first floor, he discovered it was to be much easier to arrange his belongings in the upstairs bedroom than it was to arrange a conversation with Dr. Bailey. He found that he was alone as he stood at the foot of the stairs. Neither Miss Bailey nor the seemingly ever-present Mr. Jennings was anywhere to be seen on a perusal of the room and what he could see of the hallway that led to the back of the first floor.

As Merriweather turned to walk back outside and survey the surrounding neighborhood, Mary Assumpta Bailey floated (at least it seemed to Merriweather) from the back hallway, and she spoke as a person clearly in charge: "Well, I see you are still here, Dr. Merriweather. Are you just going to stand there, or are you going to assist my brother with his morning patients?"

House Call

James Merriweather found John Bailey both more and less what he had expected. The surgeon was more knowledgeable, more willing to test out theories in his practice, and intolerant of thoughtless mistakes—even less so of casual omissions. John Bailey was not a tyrant, far from it. But he was demandingly scientific in everything. He left little room for the art of medicine.

To James Edward Merriweather, it seemed his year as an apprentice both flew by and dragged on, occurring, as he remembers it, often in the same day. Yet here he stood, alone in the early evening, looking back at the new sign that hung above the door:

SURGERY AND GENERAL MEDICINE
319 MEETING STREET
DR. JOHN C. BAILEY
DR. JAMES E. MERRIWEATHER

As James made his way to a celebratory dinner at the Bailey home, he was transported back to his first week, in fact his first day, as an apprentice under the tutelage of Dr. John Bailey.

Harry Coulter owned a small tailoring business some five blocks west and north of 319 Meeting Street—not uptown yet, but moving in that direction as his reputation continued to grow.

Fifty-five years old and married with three adult children, Harry's wife, Clara, was an extraordinary cook, and it showed in Harry's fifty-two-inch girth. For the last three days, Harry had been unable to walk more than a few feet without collapsing in pain, and therefore he was unable to walk the two blocks to his business. And as harvest was approaching when farmers would have funds to purchase new pants and shirts to replace last year's, he was worried, with reason, that he would see his income suffer significantly if his shop did not reopen soon. So as soon as he finished his breakfast of country ham and biscuits slathered in butter and topped with sorghum molasses, Harry had sent Clara to fetch Doc Bailey.

Drs. Bailey and Merriweather arrived by carriage at the home of Harry and Clara Coulter in the early afternoon of the same day. James remembered well the next event. Before they exited the carriage, John Bailey gave James Merriweather the instructions for his first lesson.

"As I question Harry about his symptoms and palpate the foot, I want you to take Clara aside and talk with her about Harry's habits—what he eats, how well he sleeps, how often he urinates, and anything she might want to offer."

"The wife? Really? You want me to talk with the wife instead of the patient?" James replied, a bit perturbed.

"James, we are looking for cause and effect. The symptoms will be obvious; the causes, less so. But if we only treat the symptoms, we may obscure the cause and do more harm than good. Trust me."

As soon as James Merriweather rapped the brass doorknocker against the oak-paneled door announcing their presence, but not a second before, they heard a wail that seemed to rattle the shingles on the side of the small cottage. The doctors, not waiting to be invited in, rushed through the door to find Harry lying on Clara's prized horsehair sofa—the only thing of worth she inherited from her mother—with one leg on the floor and the other, his big toe clearly red and swollen, resting on two feather pillows.

Once they realized that Harry Coulter was not in danger of dying, John Bailey pulled up a stool to take a look at the big toe, now the size of a large lemon. In the meantime, James and Clara Coulter sat at the table over a cup of coffee to talk about her husband's lifestyle.

When James Merriweather discussed Harry's habits with Clara, she explained all, and in great detail. Harry, according to his wife, loved his red meat, usually with several pints of ale each evening. And he insisted that Clara, an excellent cook, always serve her husband bread—usually biscuits—and potatoes. And always there was a cobbler or pie for dessert. On the other side of the equation, Harry was not fond of green vegetables or exercise. Harry's only exercise most days was walking the one block back and forth between his business and home. Even a noontime walk home resulted in Harry devouring leftovers from the night before. Most days at work, Harry sat at his sewing counter, only moving off his stool to turn to the ironing board behind him.

Merriweather thanked Clara for her information, and when she turned back to the stove, he detected a smile. She had enjoyed talking about her husband's bad habits to this young doctor.

As John Bailey finished his examination, he asked James to join him outside, much to the distress of Harry Coulter. "Doc, am I going to lose my foot? Is that what y'all are going to talk about that you don't want me to hear?"

"No, Harry, I don't think you will lose your foot or even your toe. I just want to confer with Dr. Merriweather about what we want to do to get you back to work."

The Lesson

Outside the door, Bailey and Merriweather shared their information. The diagnosis was relatively easy once Bailey determined that Harry had not fallen or stubbed his toe, but he wanted to see if his pupil had made any connections between the diagnosis and what he learned from Clara that might help in treatment.

Merriweather said that he had seen gout in his father's practice, and usually his father prescribed bed rest and the symptoms became tolerable within a week or two. Not good enough for his tutor. John Bailey led Merriweather to consider Harry's diet in light of his disease.

"Did you know any of the patients you observed in your father's practice well enough to know their lifestyles? Were any obese? Were their diets similar to what you learned today? Can you draw any conclusions? Don't worry about causes right now. Can you make some connections that might inform us of how to treat Harry Coulter?"

Methodically, the process went on for several minutes, long enough for Harry to issue another wail. "Doc, give it to me straight. I am dying. Oh God, Clara. I *am* dying."

"Harry, shut your moaning until the docs get back in here." Clara had heard Harry's dire predictions before.

John Bailey explained to his pupil that he did not yet know why a diet high in red meat often caused gout. However, he knew from practice and accumulated documentation that when he placed a gout patient on a diet rich in vegetables, rich in fruits, and limited in red meat, those patients improved, and the condition did not return as long as they maintained the diet, increased exercise, and lost weight. That was enough. He would eventually find the scientific reason.

That day outside the door of Harry and Clara Coulter's cottage, James Merriweather started his journey toward becoming an uncommon physician.

Once Bailey and Merriweather came back inside, it was James Merriweather who talked with Harry about the next steps as John Bailey spent time with Clara. James Merriweather's explanation to Harry about the connection between diet and his sore toe was not perfect, but it was an excellent learning opportunity provided by his tutor. It was also a good lesson in bedside manners as Harry Coulter was distraught at the remedy for his swollen big toe.

"Doc Bailey, get over here. This wet-behind-the-ears insignificant person thinks he can tell me to stop eating my steak and potatoes. Hell, Doc, part of the reason I work so hard is to be able to eat well. Now he tells me I have to eat chicken and vegetables, have dessert only once a week, and eat an apple and walk at lunch instead of coming home." Harry was almost foaming at the mouth as his words of anguish were coming out so rapidly. Clara, on the other hand, had to sit down, she was laughing so hard at her husband's dilemma.

When John Bailey told Harry to drop his pants and pee in the mason jar Bailey had brought for the purpose, this was almost the final straw.

"Damn you, Doc. You might as well shoot me right now if this gets out that I had to pee in a jar in front of God and the missus."

Clara, tears of laughter streaming down her face, escorted Drs. Bailey and Merriweather to their carriage.

Opposites Attract

In the year of James Merriweather's apprenticeship, nothing about Mary Assumpta Bailey had escaped his notice. He knew every freckle on her face. He could describe in millimeters the left dimple on her face and knew by how much it was asymmetrical to the right. He could describe the color of her hair with more than ten adjectives. He could tell the position of each gold fleck in her eyes. But he could not say whether she fancied him in the least.

Perhaps tonight's dinner celebrating the end of his apprenticeship and the beginning of his partnership would provide him an answer. He did not foresee it happening, but nonetheless, one must have hope.

Fittingly, as he knocked on the Baileys' front door, it was Mary Assumpta who opened it and invited him into the parlor for drinks before dinner.

"Welcome. It has been so long since this afternoon, Dr. Merriweather," said Mary Assumpta as she gave him a perfunctory hug and kiss on his cheek.

"So we are to use formal addresses tonight, are we, Miss

Mary Assumpta?" He returned the shuttlecock to her court with a smile.

"It probably *would* please Mother. I trust you know she still does not trust any Protestant male—and especially one whose ancestor had worked for King George—in the same room with her sainted daughter." She used her grandfather's west Ireland accent on the last two words for added emphasis.

Well, well, well, thought James to himself. *Is this a sign, or is Mary Assumpta just toying with me in her own home?*

Probably the latter, he told himself as he entered the parlor to applause by the entire family gathered there. *Well, you little minx. You set me up,* he thought. Even so, he was genuinely touched by this welcome from the family of his new partner. Hopefully, they incorrectly assumed the blush on his pale English face was a result of their surprise and not of Mary Assumpta's uncharacteristically playful welcome.

More Than a Partner

"Thank you all for that, but I trust you know it was unnecessary. Now, would you do it again if I left and came back in? When John has welcomed me every morning over the last year, it has usually been, 'Good to see you. Now get to work.'"

"Damn right!" John Bailey agreed. "Now come over here and get yourself a glass of this wine so we can have our first proper toast of the evening.

"To a doctor who keeps *me* on *my* toes, to a damn fine apprentice, and to an even better partner. Let's raise our glasses to Dr. James Edward Merriweather."

As James was about to speak in response, Matthew Bailey stopped him. "Hold on a minute, James, before you dazzle us poor Low Country folks with your fine Richmond eloquence. I have a gift to you from all of us. After all, you are mighty close to being family." James thought that just maybe Lauraleigh Bailey was frowning a bit as her husband said those last words.

Matthew Bailey presented James with what was clearly a framed picture of some sort. As he tore off the wrapping paper, Merriweather discovered a framed oil painting of the front of the surgery with the new sign he had just been admiring a few minutes before, clearly visible with his name below that of John Bailey. The import of the painting, done by well-known Charleston-born artist Charles Fraser, was not lost on James Merriweather, who knew of Fraser's portrait of the Marquis de Lafayette of Revolutionary War fame. He was aware that the family had paid no small price for this gift, and he was genuinely speechless, so he took another large sip of his wine.

"My dear, dear friends and colleagues. What an unexpected pleasure. It will hang in my office at the surgery, which I never go into because John keeps me so busy. So perhaps Mary Assumpta can admire it for me and remind me of its beauty and significance every so often."

Another frown from Lauraleigh Bailey at the smile this elicited from Mary Assumpta.

James Merriweather now refilled his wineglass and offered a toast of his own. "To the finest teacher and mentor a doctor could ever hope to have. To my friend, landlord, and partner, and to this truly remarkable family. Thank you all. Now can we please eat before I embarrass myself further?"

He presented his arm to Lauraleigh Bailey and escorted her to the dining room, where he found that he was seated squarely between Andrew Ryan and Matthew Bailey and as far away from Mary Assumpta as Lauraleigh Bailey could arrange at a table for seven.

After an exceptional dinner of Low Country seafood that concluded with bourbon bread pudding and conversations over coffee back in the parlor, James Merriweather bid goodbye and thanked everyone again for the painting, which he would hang tonight before he retired to his bedroom above the surgery.

As he walked in the cooling evening, breezes blowing in off Charleston Harbor, he determined that if he were to court Mary Assumpta Bailey, he would have to engage in an uphill battle. For where her daughter was concerned, Lauraleigh surely held and controlled the high ground in this family.

No problem there; he liked a challenge. Good thing. He was in for one.

CHAPTER 8

Courtship in Secret

The early evening of October 15, 1852, was unusually brisk for Charleston, where October weather was more damp and warm than bracing. Mary Assumpta Bailey was shivering as she stepped from her hansom cab, into the surgery and general medicine office at 319 Meeting Street, and into the arms of Dr. James Merriweather.

Perhaps, she thought, *I am shivering because I am again deceiving my mother about my destination.* Mary Assumpta had told her mother she was meeting her closest friends, Cleo Lambert and Megan O'Hare, for an evening of card games and girl talk. She knew she could trust Cleo and Megan to keep her secret, but she also knew her mother had a keen sense of changes in her daughter. And Mary Assumpta knew that she often returned with a "particular blush" to her after an evening with James. The friends did actually get together for tête-à-têtes from time to time so that they could at least tell partially truthful lies if quizzed by a parent.

But tonight was not one of those nights when such a thing was possible. Tonight belonged to Dr. James Merriweather. Tonight she would give her whole self to him. Tonight she would become his lover. James had not pressed her toward lovemaking; their heated kissing and fondling had given him the signals that he only needed to wait and not push the issue. Mary

Assumpta was love's passion abroil in a religiously repressed Roman Catholic's nineteen-year-old body. She would not remain repressed much longer; of that, James Merriweather was confident. Even so, it was important that he remain a gentleman.

Mary Assumpta Bailey had been all business with her brother's new apprentice for most of his first year. Even so, she told her girlfriends that she would have to be blind not to notice those dark eyes of his and his boyish smile.

James Merriweather stood six feet tall and weighed a muscular 190 pounds. His brown eyes were the color of brewed coffee, and his Virginia accent was as smooth and slow as titi tree honey poured on a steaming buttered biscuit. Mary Assumpta Bailey thought that James's personality was like her mother's, red-pepper-jelly sweet with just a hint of heat on the back of the tongue when you least expected it.

If James Merriweather knew his effect on the opposite sex, he hid it well with his social graces. He had worked with Mary Assumpta every day for more than a year before he broached the subject of courting her, and then he'd done so only after he had accepted her brother John's invitation to become a partner in the practice.

Perhaps it was the repressed feelings for the other that each had kept at bay. Perhaps it was fate working again. But whatever it was, at her family's dinner celebrating his joining the practice, the two of them barely kept their emotions in check—mainly with the help of Lauraleigh Bailey, who recognized the signs and purposefully kept them as far apart that night as social customs would reasonably allow. Still, Mary Assumpta and James Merriweather recognized the mutual desire to explore the fires they had kept banked for a year and that now threatened to burst into flame right before her mother's eyes.

Mary Assumpta knew that her mother did not approve of James Merriweather. Not because he was unkind or not of the proper social class, but merely because he was Protestant and English, and the Baileys were well and truly Irish and Catholic. And Lauraleigh Bailey intended that her grandchildren be so as well.

Of course her mother's views meant not a jot to Mary Assumpta. In fact, they had the opposite effect of tempering her actions. For James and Mary Assumpta, the fall of 1852 was filled with the kind of excitement that only love on the sly can produce: lunches filled with furtive looks and hands held and feet crossed beneath long tablecloths, stolen kisses at work, and surreptitious late afternoon meetings after John had left to join the family for dinner. Even though she was late for dinner, Mary Assumpta would just say she had been shopping at Annah Catherine's Dress Shop, which she did often, especially since she had co-opted Annah into verifying her "visits" should her mother drop by the dress shop herself.

And joyfully, Dr. James Merriweather and Mary Assumpta Bailey courted in secret until just before Christmas 1852, when at yet another clandestine rendezvous, Mary Assumpta whispered to James the most profound and explosive revelation of their brief love affair: "I am two months pregnant."

Uncertainty

A cold and damp draft permeated the small apartment above the surgery. Under the white duvet, the lovers, entwined in each other's bodies and emotions, were oblivious to the temperature. They talked sotto voce for no apparent reason other than Mary Assumpta had revealed her secret to James in a whisper.

"Mary Assumpta, I don't know whether to laugh, cry, or shout to the heavens, because I now know for certain that you will marry me."

"And just how in God's name are you so sure that I want to marry you?" Mary Assumpta parried his assumption.

"Interesting that you should bring God into this conversation," James returned, "for that is precisely how I know."

"What? The Almighty spoke to you personally, did he?"

"Not in so many words, but yes," James said with a laugh in his voice as Mary Assumpta sat atop his loins, her pink erect nipples peeking through her fiery curls that cascaded down her shoulders almost to her waist.

How is it, James wondered, *that the glimpse of hidden treasures can be so erotic?*

Mary Assumpta was clearly enjoying her temporary dominant position and could feel that James was enjoying it equally. "I did not know you were on such intimate terms with the Deity. Please, tell me more about this marriage since I have yet to hear an invitation from your lips." She emphasized her feistiness with a rolling of her young muscular hips, which practically sent James into a state of delighted apoplexy.

Almost breathless, he explained, "First and second, you *are* Catholic, and childbirth out of wedlock is a mortal sin. Third, given that Lauraleigh Bailey is God's Catholic voice to Charleston, she is not about to let her 'Miss Magnolia' lapse into social disgrace. And I almost forgot, fourth, you *do* love me madly. Therefore, there is only one logical conclusion."

"Only *one*? I thought my brother taught you to consider all possible solutions. Perhaps there might be at least one more you have not considered," Mary Assumpta said as she relieved his apparently stressful condition.

Almost breathless now, he answered, "Nope, I have studied them all, and you *will* marry me, but not until I ask. So I am asking."

"What if I would rather we run off and board the first rum trader headed to Jamaica, junk everything we know about Charleston, and just live the rest of our lives as lovers?" Mary Assumpta's breaths were now shallow and came more rapidly.

Panting, James replied, "I don't think I heard a yes in that idea."

"Of course, you heard a yes! Yes! Yes! Yes! God in heaven, yes!"

Little did the lovers realize how prophetic Mary Assumpta's words in jest about running away from Charleston were to be.

Spent in blessed exhaustion, the lovers lay a bit longer, and then Mary Assumpta rose, dressed, and made her way home, late to family dinner yet again.

Unexpected Announcement

"Stop by Annah Catherine's again, did you?" her mother quizzed.

"Not today, Mother. I stayed over today to help James finish up sterilizing the scalpels. We have a surgery in the morning." Mary Assumpta was surprised at her boldness. This was the first time she had used staying late to help James as an excuse.

John Bailey knew the scalpels were not in need of sterilizing because he had disinfected them himself before he left for the afternoon, but he said nothing. He understood his baby sister's close-to-the-truth subterfuge. She had confided in him early on in their courtship that she and James were meeting from time to time. He just did not know how often "from time to time" was or what she meant by "meeting."

Her mother's annoyance with her passed, or so it seemed, and Mary Assumpta served coffee and cobbler. "Everyone," she said excitedly, "I have an exciting announcement that I have wanted to share, and I think this is the perfect time."

Oh God, no, John Bailey thought to himself. *She is not about to tell us that she and James are getting married.* He braced himself for his mother's impending emotional explosion. However, he would find himself totally surprised, and pleased, by his sister's announcement, which was to have nothing to do with marriage. Still he sensed that another announcement, one he dreaded, would come sooner rather than later.

"Y'all know how much I wanted to attend the Charleston Medical College. Of course you do. I pouted for a month until John 'gave' me a job at his surgery.

"It has been four years now, and I have helped John, and now James, with every procedure from the ordinary to suturing up after surgery unassisted. I am not a physician, and it appears I will not be one no matter how much I desire it." Mary Assumpta paused before continuing.

Lauraleigh Bailey picked up on her pause. She was sure where her daughter's announcement was heading. "We know, dear," she said in her practiced and patronizing manner. "Now that you have gotten that nonsense out of your system, you can just settle down and become a wife and mother."

When her mother uttered the words *wife and mother*, Mary Assumpta choked on her bite of cobbler, convulsively coughing until she spit it out on her plate—to her mother's consternation. *Does Mother know? Does John suspect? He would be the one to notice the very slight bulge in my waistline*, Mary Assumpta wondered as she took a sip of coffee to help clear her throat and gave herself a moment more to recover her composure. *No, my big brother would not tell Mother even if he does know. I am just imagining things, if for good reason.*

"So sorry. A piece of crust went down the wrong way. And yes, Mother, I know it is totally impolite to spit food back out on my plate. I apologize for that."

Fully recovered, she went on. "Now where was I when that cobbler attacked me? Oh yes, my pouting about medical school and my announcement. James and I had lunch this week with Dr. Hawthorne, the provost and a professor at MCSC. James arranged the meeting and went with me to discuss the idea of starting a program of nursing for women who are barred from medical school but would like a career working in medicine. And Dr. Hawthorne said my proposal had merit.

"That's my news. That and the fact that Dr. Hawthorne asked that we develop a one-year curriculum for nursing and a plan for how to enroll the first students a year from next fall. Obviously, James and I have a lot of work to do. And, John, we want your help too. We will meet with Dr. Hawthorne again in two months."

In two months Mary Assumpta would be worrying about other, more pressing issues, and the appointment would be forgotten but not missed by either party. Mary Assumpta would be busy in ways she could not imagine at dinner tonight, and Dr. Hawthorne had never been serious to begin with in his invitation for more information.

John was proud of his baby sister, and he, too, thought the program a good idea. She was already the equal to a majority of the physicians practicing in Charleston. He knew that her plan was risky. A nurse with a sound knowledge of medical practices working closely beside physicians was not an idea acceptable to every doctor. However, he also knew what an asset Mary Assumpta's knowledge and skills were to his surgery. Right now she could handle the routine bouts of ague, scrapes and cuts, and the aches and pains of his older patients, freeing him and James to focus their time on practicing new techniques and attending to the more critical needs of their patients.

Lauraleigh Bailey, with apparent disdain for her daughter's announcement, snapped, "Well I, for one, see no purpose in it.

All I seem to hear is 'James this' and 'James that.' Sounds to me like you are getting a bit too cozy with Mr. James Edward Merriweather."

Silence enveloped the dining room like a thick fog rolling in off Charleston Harbor. With her pronouncement, Lauraleigh Bailey sighed deeply and loudly. "I think I am feeling ill. I am going up to bed. John, will you come up in a few minutes and check on me? Mary Assumpta, dear, you can clear the dishes and wash them before you retire."

"Of course, Mother," Mary Assumpta replied with obvious disappointment that her rather revolutionary news had been received with such contempt.

"Well," said her father, "I think it is just the kind of thinking that this family has been known for. Your mother will come around. You let me know if I can help. I think my contacts with the physicians who use our business will be right pleased. Now I guess I'd better go see if I can mend some fences. Seems like that's all I do lately."

Alone as she cleared the table, Mary Assumpta said out loud to no one, "I wonder if Father will be quite so confident about Mother when he hears my next announcement."

First Letter to Her Beloved

With the dishes washed, dried, and put away, and with her mother's words still running around in her head like an ear-worm's melody, Mary Assumpta retired to her bedroom to write a love letter to James that she would slip under his door in the morning before he came down for the day.

My Beloved Physician,

I love you more than I can put into words. And because I now carry a part of you inside me, I miss you more than ever when we are apart. That precious person inside me is a new life—a pure and profound truth. Unformed right now, but yet still our baby, our holy creation, he (or she) will know God through us as we will understand our Maker's love for us in ways heretofore secret to us through our baby.

Before we make love again, we must plan for when and how we will approach Father, although I do not think him too difficult to convince. However, after tonight (more about this when we can talk), I can predict how Mother will react after she hears our news. She will explode. I am sure of that. Will her eruption produce steam and then she will simmer down as she usually does, or will she spew hot red molten lava that consumes us all? Either is possible. We must pray for the former, but we must prepare for the latter.

Remarkably, however Mother reacts matters little as long as I have my beloved physician at my side.

Well and truly yours,

Red

Christmas Plans

James Merriweather had been at the Bailey family home far too many times to remember, usually for dinner at John's invitation, when he had noticed James had not eaten well in many days. But James had not seen the Bailey home in its Christmas finery. It was a thing to behold, particularly as he would not make it back to Richmond this year to his mother's Christmas artistry.

It was early evening, just after dusk on a cloudless Christmas day. As he stepped from his carriage, Merriweather saw that candles burned in every window. A large pine bough wreath with a dark maroon velvet bow hung on the front door. Winter-red holly berries were interlaced in the pine branches forming the wreath. The four columns framing the porch were encircled with more of the pine boughs, but these were interwoven with large magnolia leaves painted gold with a silver starburst decorating the middle of the wreath.

The magnolia leaf theme continued inside the home. In the center of the parlor was a seven-foot fresh-cut red cedar tree decorated simply with arrangements of five gold magnolia leaves strung together and stems of bright green holly leaves and red berries attached to the cedar limbs. A large silver and maroon plaid bow topped the tree with four ribbons coming from it and extending all the way to the bottom layer of branches. Many decorative boxes opened earlier in the day surrounded the base of the tree.

A bone china Nativity of obvious costliness adorned the mantle, and on the wall above the crèche, a wrought iron star of Bethlehem with a burning candle at each of its points provided all the light the room required.

The effect was stunning.

Mary Assumpta greeted James at the door with a stem of mistletoe, a perfunctory kiss, and a giggle that went with it. Nothing more. She took his coat, put it away, and led him to her father's study, where Lauraleigh Bailey was serving cheese straws and eggnog laced generously with Irish whiskey and a bit of cognac.

At the beginning of the evening, James and Mary Assumpta sat on opposite sides of the room, part of the plan that they had made just days before. Conversation drifted back to the recent addition of James as a partner in John's medical practice, to the weather that had been particularly enjoyable throughout December, and to politics that had not.

James, with Mary Assumpta—at her insistence—had met with Matthew Bailey earlier Christmas Week and explained to him of their plans and his daughter's condition. And James asked for Mary Assumpta's hand. Matthew was not surprised.

He had been a young man once, and he knew the strength of will and the passion for life that resided in his daughter. Matthew told the couple that he would have wished circumstances had been more traditional, but he would try to prepare Lauraleigh as best he could for the Christmas Day announcement and the emotions that surely would follow.

Mary Assumpta told James that she knew the family would return to the parlor after dinner for coffee or drinks before dessert. They would announce their engagement and Mary Assumpta's pregnancy at that time, hoping that Christmas goodwill and good wishes would soften the potential for a major explosion from Lauraleigh Bailey. There would be a display of emotions. They were sure of that.

They only hoped it would be short-lived and that Lauraleigh Bailey would embrace the love they shared for each other. They were wrong.

The Announcement

Christmas supper was the final celebration of Christmas in the Bailey home. It was a family tradition that had begun the evening before with midnight mass at Saint Mary's Catholic Church. The first meal of the day took place after Mass and long before dawn just as it was celebrated at the Bailey farm in County Clare the night Ulrich Bailey wed Bridget O'Flaherty during the midnight mass of 1690.

Cooking in the Bailey house was not relegated to a hired cook, although finally the Baileys could have afforded one. Lauraleigh and Mary Assumpta had worked since morning getting everything ready. Cooking was not drudgery in the Irish home; it was a sacred sacrament that historically held many marriages together in the toughest of times.

Tonight's meal began with she-crab soup made with fresh heavy cream and more butter than eaten by the family in a week. It was thick with pieces of crabmeat, and a curlicue of golden sherry was suspended on top of the thick soup.

Carolina ham, as it was each Christmas, was the main feature of Christmas supper. The meat had been cured with salt and sugar for forty days the previous winter and then smoked with hickory wood for twenty-four hours in a small shedlike smokehouse that would hold a half dozen hams. The smoked ham was then wrapped in muslin and hung in the root cellar to be unveiled in all its finery at Christmas supper. On Christmas Eve Lauraleigh Bailey scrubbed the mold that naturally formed on the outside of the ham and placed it in a tub of water to reduce its saltiness. She changed the water often, though she would not tell anyone except Mary Assumpta *how often*, until the saltiness was just perfect, not overwhelming.

On Christmas morning, Matthew's job was to stoke the woodstove in preparation for the roasting of the ham. The roasting usually took three to four hours depending on the size of the ham and the oven's temperature, which varied every day based on the day's temperature, the humidity, and the moisture of the wood used to build and sustain the oven's heat. The roasting process required close monitoring and was always more art than science.

When Matthew Bailey brought the Christmas ham of 1852 to the table, it was steaming, covered in a brown sugar, honey, and mustard glaze with cloves prickling its surface. John quickly followed him with a large bowl of collards, Andrew Ryan with a platter piled high with baked sweet potatoes, and James with a plate of two-inch-high biscuits. Lauraleigh and Mary Assumpta were the royalty at this supper served by the menfolk. They looked it and enjoyed the attention.

Christmas supper was not a time for heavy subjects, so conversations were limited to praise for the cooks, discussions of the weather, and hopes for the New Year.

The meal completed, Andrew Ryan asked to be excused to visit his love interest, the comely colleen Sarah Murphy whose family lived on the outskirts of Charleston, some five miles from the Bailey home.

"Home soon after midnight, Son?" his father asked with a smile on his face.

"Maybe. God willing and the creeks don't rise," Andrew Ryan retorted with the standard southern aphorism worthy of most any question.

Taking their cue from Andrew Ryan, the women rose to move to the parlor as the men cleared the table and reset it with dessert plates, coffee accouterments, and two pecan pies ready to be cut and served with coffee once supper had settled a bit.

As he entered the parlor several minutes later, John praised his mother's cooking one more time. "Mother, you will have James thinking we eat like this at every meal, and he will soon be expecting a bigger portion of the profits."

James added his praise as well. "Mrs. Bailey, that was truly memorable. Thank you and Mary Assumpta for all the work you put into supper and for inviting me, an outsider, to dine with you on this evening. My mother will be very jealous when I tell her about this in my next letter to her. I know she will be asking me to get that she-crab soup recipe from you." James spoke in as normal a voice as he could muster. However, he was unsure if sounded too enthusiastic and perhaps had given her reason to wonder about his motives.

"Why, Mr. Merriweather, you can get that recipe in any restaurant in Charleston." James noted that, clearly, Lauraleigh Bailey did not intend to give him even the smallest acknowledgment of attachment to the family. He was an outsider. Not Doctor, not James, only Mister—the Protestant interloper.

"Well, I sure understand why you would want to hold on to

the recipe. It was that good," James replied, hoping to mend any unintended gaffes on his part.

James made his way to the tufted gold brocade love seat where Mary Assumpta was already sitting. She had, unobserved she hoped, saved room for him by placing her shawl not on her lap but on the space next to her. As he started to sit, he confidently took Mary Assumpta's extended hand and interlaced his fingers in hers. Act I had begun.

Matthew Bailey sat down next to Lauraleigh, who, he noted, was visibly perturbed. John sat in a leather wingback chair that was catty-cornered halfway between the love seat and the sofa but not in the direct line of the verbal lava flow that he knew was coming. He had noticed the handholding and bodies touching from shoulders to thighs and to ankles. Not a good sign.

Mary Assumpta started to speak, but a half cough was caught in the back of her throat. Nerves. *You can do this,* she told herself.

"Everyone. James and I have two announcements. James, perhaps you should go first?" Mary Assumpta finally said, her voice just above a whisper and filled with tremolo.

"Mrs. Bailey, Mr. Bailey, John. I have asked Mary Assumpta to marry me, and she has accepted." With this, he pulled a small package from his coat and presented it to Mary Assumpta: a ring set with a single lustrous black pearl complemented by garnets on each side on a band of gold. "Mary Assumpta, this pearl represents the uniqueness of our love; the garnets, your fiery personality; and the gold band, the precious unbroken bond that we shall share in our marriage."

Tears streamed down Mary Assumpta's face, streaking her makeup and revealing her freckles. She had not expected an engagement gift as she knew James struggled with his money because he did not yet see many profits of his partnership with

John. James handed his fiancée his handkerchief, but as soon as she dried her eyes, the tears started again. James moved closer, putting his arm around her shoulders.

Thus far, John and Matthew were silent though tears welled in their eyes at James's gesture. No tears in Lauraleigh's eyes. Rather, her face was dark red from her neck to her forehead and up into her hairline. She was not embarrassed or excited. She was about to erupt. Before she could speak, James continued.

"Mary Assumpta and I want you all to be the first to know of our happy news. We plan to marry in a simple ceremony soon after the first of the year."

Shattered Dreams

Lauraleigh could contain her anger no longer. "Matthew, what in the hell is going on? Did you know about this? Did he not ask you for my daughter's hand?"

"Yes, Mother, he did," Matthew responded calmly. "James and Mary Assumpta came to me on Monday of this week with a humble and proper request, which I granted. They are undoubtedly in love."

"You granted?" Lauraleigh responded angrily, spittle emphasizing her vehement challenge to her husband's words. "She is my daughter, and I will determine whom and when she will marry."

Lauraleigh asserted a side of herself that was heretofore suspected but unseen by her husband, and he responded more demonstrably than he would have wished.

"As long as I put my pants on every morning and keep this family afloat, then yes, I will make the decision because it is my place to give my permission, and I joyously gave it."

Lauraleigh had never seen her husband so assertive, and it caused a tectonic plate shift in her emotions. Molten lava began to spew uncontrollably, aimed directly at James and Mary Assumpta.

"How dare you, James Merriweather? The goddamned English Protestants drove my people off our land. You usurped our rights as Irish citizens. You refused to allow us to speak our own language. You gave my people the untenable choice of converting to your unholy Protestant religion or losing their land.

"No! You damn well cannot marry my daughter. Not in my lifetime."

She seemed to be finally spent. Mary Assumpta chose this moment to break the deathly silence that had, at Lauraleigh's pause, invaded the parlor like the fog of death on a battlefield with the awful stench of pathetic violence.

"Mother, Father, John. I have one more piece of news. I am pregnant. I have missed two periods. And, John, with your keen eye, I expect you have noticed a bulge in my waistline."

If total silence can intensify, it did at that moment.

"I know this is hard news to hear, but I want you to know that we created this baby in love. I will carry the baby in love, and we will raise him or her in a loving home. James and I want you to celebrate this event as well as our marriage. It is the reason we will marry soon after the New Year."

Lauraleigh Bailey expelled a funereal-like wail as if she had just heard the news of a tragic loss of a loved one. This was how she accepted the announcement of her first grandchild.

"Oh God! Matthew, we are ruined. We will be the laughingstock of Charleston. All that I have done to make this family respectable is gone. We are ruined by you, James, and you, Mary Assumpta.

"Now, both of you go to wherever you have been whoring and do not ever come back to this house again. As of this night, I no longer have a daughter."

Mary Assumpta rose and went to her mother to try to console her. "Mother, you must know I love James genuinely and totally. We have a future as doctor and nurse working together. We will have a family that you would be proud of."

"I gave birth to you, but I do not know you. You betrayed this family and me. You have committed a mortal sin, and you will be excommunicated from the church as well.

"I don't know what will happen to you, and I do not care. You are gutter trash, and you belong in a brothel. I will pray that God punishes you in childbirth so I can be rid of you and the bastard offspring of your unholy union. Damn you, James. You are a gobshite shat from the arse of a Richmond whore.

"Mary Assumpta, you will hear from my attorney that you have been removed entirely from my will. Now get the hell out of my house, the both of you."

James Merriweather put his coat and his arm around Mary Assumpta's shoulders as they made their way to the front door. "Mother, will you at least come to the wedding?" Mary Assumpta pleaded.

"I would rather be eaten by rats and covered with snakes than step foot in your wedding. You are dead to me. How can I attend the wedding of a corpse?" Lauraleigh laughed hysterically at her metaphor.

"I wish you both a life of poverty. I will pray that God punishes you every day of your sorry marriage. Now get the hell out of my house, you two goddamn whores."

Gentle Love

James picked up Mary Assumpta and carried her to his carriage, not out of chivalry but because she was so overcome with grief that she could not put one foot in front of the other. The carriage delivered them to 319 Meeting Street, where James carried Mary Assumpta to the upstairs apartment above the surgery.

He laid her gently on the bed and covered her with the duvet that still had the scent of recent lovemaking. He filled the bathtub nearly full of pleasantly warm water, went back to the bed, gently undressed his wife-to-be, carried her to the bath, and gently lowered her into the large white porcelain tub.

He had not used the French milled soap that he found on his washstand his first night in the apartment, a special Mary Assumpta touch. He unwrapped the soap and inhaled the fragrance of patchouli. He gently ran the soap over every inch of Mary Assumpta's body. In any other circumstance, this would have aroused him. Tonight he was Aphrodite's apostle washing his beloved goddess in an act of guileless worship and adoration. He finished by gently washing her hair. He dipped the ewer he had brought from his nightstand into the warm water and poured the water lovingly over her ginger curls as she tilted her head back in total trust. As he washed her hair with his patchouli-scented soap, he massaged her scalp and the back of her neck until she almost slipped beneath the water asleep. Dipping the ewer once more into the water, he rinsed the soap from her lovely body and hair. As she stood in the tub to let the water drip from her body, James dried her hair.

With her hair damp and starting to curl uncontrollably, he picked up another towel that had been draped on a chair near the fire to warm. He would not let her dry herself. Not tonight. Tonight, he was the servant to the bravest woman he had ever known. She stepped, dripping, from the tub on the towel used to dry her hair. James started with her back, using the warm towel to dry the crease of her backside and down her legs. He had her bend each foot back like a smithy would hold the leg of a thoroughbred as he dried her feet. She was almost asleep as he dried the droplets on her face and in the creases beneath each breast. As he toweled her stomach, he saw for the first time, with a lover's eye, the bulge in her abdomen.

The altogether lovely task completed, he once again picked Mary Assumpta up in his arms and placed her under the covers, where she was asleep before he could pull the duvet up to her chin.

Soon the molten lava would all come rushing back down the mountain, but this night, in this ridiculously small apartment, was theirs.

They would face the eruption soon enough.

CHAPTER 9

The First Day of a New Life

Christmas Day 1852 would forever stain their feelings of Christmas for James and Mary Assumpta. The approaching days' decisions would remove the gentleness and kindness of Christmases past and replace them with momentous choices that would change the course of their lives in ways they could not have imagined.

On Sunday morning, which seemed a lifetime away from the events of last night, James rose early, having slept little the night before. In an interesting way, thanks to Lauraleigh Bailey, the stress of clandestine meetings was over. He and his fiancée would sleep here together until they could decide on their next steps. They needed to talk to John and Matthew, but they could not do that today, so today they would plan for the meeting and a wedding.

James had built a fire in the small fireplace, brewed a pot of coffee by the fire, and warmed two leftover pastries out of the dozen he had purchased at Amélie's Breads and Pastries on Christmas Eve.

Amélie's was typically the first face he saw every morning. Amélie had come up from New Orleans and quickly developed a loyal group of customers, mainly because she opened early. Even before she opened the doors for business, the smell of fresh baking announced her day's offerings to every open window within blocks. Every morning James began with strong French roast coffee with a touch of chicory and warm pastries. He knew he should be eating better, but it was too convenient and too good.

Rousing and tossing her covers off her still naked body because the fireplace had quickly warmed the single room, Mary Assumpta spoke in a still sleepy rasp. "Am I imagining things, or did I actually sleep in your bed last night? And, as it seems, unmolested. Doctor James Merriweather, you *are* a gentleman. And now you bring me breakfast pastries and coffee? Father has never done that for Mother."

She slipped into her camisole, her knickers, and her dress from the evening before, leaving off the heavy petticoats. It was at this point, with this inane set of everyday actions, that Mary Assumpta realized the life-altering enormity of last night's events.

"James, I have only this one set of clothes, and they are dirty. We can't buy clothes today—and maybe not tomorrow either."

James thought for a moment. It was a real problem that faced them, one to which they had not given a single thought. "Well, while you stay here and tidy up the apartment"—at that point Mary Assumpta hurled a shoe at him, but he continued—"I will go to John's home straightaway. If I leave right now, I will catch him before he leaves for Mass, and I can ask him if he will arrange with your father to gather up some of your things this afternoon while your mother takes her Sunday nap. John can put enough in his carriage to get you by for several days until we can arrange a meeting with your father and John to plan our next steps."

"Okay. But hurry! This crinoline slip is terribly itchy. But before you go, we need to settle on a day and time to meet with Father and John, so you can tell John."

James thought for a moment—this was earlier than he intended to reflect on this. In fact, he had not thought about it at all. *Freedom through procrastination,* he said silently to himself.

"Perhaps we can meet first thing tomorrow morning, here in the surgery, before your father walks down to open his business? John and I have no surgeries until Wednesday, and we can just fashion a sign for the door to turn away any walk-ins. Sound all right to you?"

"Yes, it is all right, but when you return, I want us to sit down and talk about that meeting with Father and John. We need to spend the rest of the day doing only that."

"*Only* that?" James asked playfully, which merited the other shoe as he closed the door to make his way to John's home.

Pain of Metamorphosis

When James returned, Mary Assumpta was busy writing at his desk and did not hear the door open or his footfalls on the pine floor. So when his shadow walked across her writing tablet, she screamed.

"Whoa. Whoa. It is just me!" He laughed as she pounded her fists on his chest.

"That was not funny at all, James Merriweather. We will just see if you get any afternoon dessert!" she retorted with a big smile. He responded with crocodile tears.

"John was about to leave when I caught him. He said he would talk to your father and bring some of your things around by evening. He said he was having Sunday dinner at your house, so it should work out well. John also said if he did not tell us something different this afternoon, we should just plan to meet with him and your father here at six o'clock in the morning."

"Well, that leaves us the rest of the morning and the afternoon to outline what we can see that stands directly in front of us over the next few days, and we can think in broader terms about what lies beyond that. Okay with you?"

Mary Assumpta had already been thinking about how to get started on the things to talk about when they met with her father and John. For the next hour, they created a list as they bantered, usually with good humor, about the most important things to get clear tomorrow morning, assuming there would be more morning meetings to come.

Once the preliminary things for Monday morning were laid out and arranged by category, James suggested they talk through each one so that the two of them could be in agreement before the meeting. *Important to be united,* thought James to himself.

"Do you want to go down the list, or would you rather start with something easier than our relationship with your mother?" James asked before beginning.

"No, we might as well tackle that one first. I expect the others will be easy by comparison," Mary Assumpta said, her tears over the Christmas night eruption expended for the moment at least.

"Maybe I can start our discussion of it?" James asked as he took up a pencil and paper.

"You have lived with your mother for eighteen years. How would you describe her? Perhaps that might help us understand her outburst last evening."

With obvious difficulty, Mary Assumpta began. "When John and Andrew Ryan and I would traipse in the woods after a hurricane, we would find huge water oaks with massive trunks—limbs and roots as big as trees themselves. They had been blown over, roots and all, by the winds. When we would start exploring more around the tree, we would often see that those huge trees were green and evidently healthy on the outside, but when we would dig around down at the base of the trunk, we usually found out that the magnificent tree was actually black and hollow and rotting on the inside—literally a shell of what it appeared outwardly."

After a pause to gather her emotions, she finished her thought. "Mother is like one of those old water oaks, and our announcements showed her as she actually is, not as she appears to others. In its way, that is as sad to me as the excommunication from her life." The tears and sobs came with this disclosure to James of what she had known but could not admit to herself before now.

James knocked his chair to the floor in his rush to comfort Mary Assumpta. He eased her to the side of the bed, and there he just held her for many minutes until her heaving sobs and wailing requiems for the mother she no longer had, or had known for some time, finally subsided.

She drifted to sleep, spent. James lay beside her and held her, although she was aware of nothing but her inner demons during her nap on this Sunday afternoon after Christmas in 1852.

A knock on the door startled Mary Assumpta awake. She felt beside her. James was gone. For a moment, she was disoriented when she heard the knock again, along with James's voice. "Mary Assumpta! For God's sake, will you open this door? I am about to drop your unmentionables on this dirty hall floor." James had returned from a trip downstairs holding an armful of Mary Assumpta's underclothes and nightclothes in folded stacks. He would make at least one more trip for a sizable number of dresses and coats that John had also delivered.

"Bless you, my hero. No more laundry duty for you." Mary Assumpta giggled as she took the clothes from his arms and placed them on the bed for now.

Mary Assumpta's cathartic revelation of her mother's inner thoughts was a metamorphosis. The struggle to emerge on the other side of such a life-altering admission produced a freedom of full personhood she had not experienced before. She was not happy, but she was free of the shadows that had clouded her life since the death of her brother Joseph Paul.

She would not forgive her mother. Not anytime soon. There were plenty of the old country's stories in her blood too. But she could move forward.

So she and James, over several glasses of smooth golden peach brandy, compiled the list as best they were able, knowing their conclusions would likely change in the morning. It was shorter than either had imagined:

1. Future relationships with both families
2. Date, place, and size of the wedding
3. Living arrangements until the wedding
4. Living arrangements after the wedding
5. James's business arrangements with John

Father's Perspective

The next morning, Mary Assumpta gave her father the biggest embrace she could muster and held onto him until her heart and her breathing finally slowed. "How is Mother?" she asked.

"She is as she was when you left last evening," her father responded. "Her proclamations have been replaced by stony silence, and I believe I like the commandments better than I do the godlike transcendence with which she has enveloped the house."

"Will she reconsider her decision about the wedding?" Mary Assumpta asked, hoping for the answer she knew would not be forthcoming.

"Oh God, no. Of that position, I am sure. Perhaps when her

first grandchild is born, she will soften her stance toward the entire matter. Before then? You and James need to build your life together. Space is what she needs. In fact, she has moved her things to the guest room. I saw her today in the evening and then only for a short time, as she retired early to read and, I hope, to pray, but I do not know since she locked her door."

"Oh, Father. I am so sorry that I have caused the rift between you and Mother."

"As you probably have figured out already, the lessening of your mother's affection for every member of the family began with the death of Joseph Paul, and it has declined steadily ever since with each setback, no matter how minor or temporary. Over the years she has spent less time with us and more time at Saint Mary's Church. One would hope that the latter would have positively affected the former, but it has not. Mary Assumpta, had it not been your announcement, it would have been something else. Of that I am convinced.

"Darlin', you must not stop loving your mother. This conflagration is two days long. She has loved and cared for you your entire life. Let that count for something. Will you promise me that?"

"I will try, Father, but try is all I can promise," Mary Assumpta responded, fighting to keep her anger at her mother at bay, especially now in the presence of her father, who she could see was hurting too.

"I can ask no more at this time," her father responded.

"Now can we get on with this meeting? I think I heard John and James making coffee back in the kitchen." He put his arm around his fiery-haired daughter. With her head on his shoulder, she walked to the table in the small kitchen area of the surgery devoted to a little cooking and much disinfecting of instruments.

The Wedding Chapel

Before James was to begin as they had decided yesterday, Mary Assumpta had whispered to him, "Start with number two. I will tell you why later." So James went down the list of their concerns.

They set the wedding for Sunday, January 9, 1853, at 3:00 in the afternoon. Sunday afternoon seemed to everyone to be the natural choice with Saturday night hangovers reducing at least some of the wagging of tongues, as would a week between the ceremony and the next church services.

Choosing a site was harder than setting the date, but only a little. Matthew had talked to Andrew Ryan, who also knew the streets of Charleston from his rounds with his apothecary cart. They both agreed that a small, recently built Methodist church just off Meeting Street close to the harbor was an excellent location. The church was Charleston to its core, simple, elegant, and smelling of sea salt. Its pastor, Reverend Wesley Green, tended his flock of mostly seamen during their stay in Charleston before they harkened back to sea.

It seated no more than fifty people in simple handcrafted pews. They sat on heart-of-pine floorboards salvaged from barns destroyed or abandoned in hurricanes up and down the coast. The interior and exterior walls of the church were rough cypress boards; the windows and the door were framed with the rough-hewn cypress lumber. The front door to the chapel was brass and had led to the captain's quarters on the merchantman *The Wellington*, which had run aground south of Charleston in a winter storm a year before. The altar rail was salvaged from a long-forgotten vessel when the piece of deck to which it was attached washed ashore during a hurricane. The fifteen-foot piece of brass had been found peeking out from the sand, but it was easily recognizable by seaman Bartholomew Jennings, who was walking the shore on that August afternoon looking for just such "treasures" as might be found following a hurricane. Now it had been given new life. Its brass shined bright once again.

The pulpit was made from an old cypress tree pulled from the Shem Creek swamp. Charleston furniture maker and ex-seaman Ray Hendersen oversaw its conversion into a pulpit like no other. Instead of the table his imagination had seen in the wood when he first found it, he would fashion a glorious pulpit and donate it to the church.

Hendersen sawed off the stump horizontally about five feet above the bottom of the roots. Then he cut a six-inch-thick slice of the stump vertically from the middle of the widest portion of the stump at the bottom. This would be the front of the pulpit—narrow at the top and broad at the bottom. Several tree-sized roots still spanned out from the trunk where it touched the floor. He cut horizontally across these roots so that they would sit flat, appearing to be growing out from the floor.

The effect was spellbinding.

The twin of the first slice, but only three inches thick, was cut and then cut in half so the halves produced the two pieces to form the sides of the pulpit. Roots were retained on both side-pieces. The top on which a preacher might sit his sermon notes was two 6" × 3" boards side-glued with dowels and clamped. Eventually, they would be sanded smooth, rubbed with tung oil, and attached to the top of the front section with more dowels and glue.

Once the pulpit was finished with the tung oil on the front, there could be counted 210 yearly rings. How long the tree had lain in the swamp—probably blown over by a hurricane—before it was pulled out was anyone's guess. This lectern could easily be five hundred years old, felled two hundred years before Martin Luther.

The windows were made of melted wine and liquor bottles and other colored glass and poured into a mold that would fit into the two square windows on either side of the church and the two at the rear. A small cypress cross was placed in each molded window while the glass was still soft. When the rays of the sun shone on a window, blending the myriad glass, the rays produced the colors of the sea on the floor and the pews, and an image of a cross stood out in bas-relief.

The parishioners who built the church kept it immaculate between the visits of the circuit-riding Reverend Green, who preached every other week. On off weeks, a functioning Sunday school managed to survive.

The church was formally called the Seaman's Methodist Chapel of Charleston. But every seaman who had ever received its ministrations knew it simply as the Stump. Only Ray Hendersen knew that the word *stump* was actually a synonym for the word *pulpit*, but to those who had labored, and to those who served and were served by the small church, *stump* was the most beautiful word in God's English.

After Matthew and John had described the Stump, there was no doubt left about the where of the wedding. Of course, they would refer to it to others as the Seaman's Methodist Chapel of Charleston. But to James and Mary Assumpta, it was always the Stump.

God continued to smile on the couple that day. The Reverend Wesley Allen Green was going to be preaching in Charleston on January 9. John told the pastor the situation that required a speedy wedding, asking if they could use the church and if he would be willing to officiate. Wesley Green laughed at the request. "Brother Bailey," he said, "if I limited my congregation to the holy, I would not have the church you see before you or anyone to fill its pews. I would be honored to offer my blessing and God's to your sister and her fiancé." John was to find out much later that Pastor Green was the son of a prostitute and a sailor. He only knew of his parents' "vocations" because he had pried the information from his adoptive parents before he preached his first sermon at the Stump.

The size of the chapel took care of the size of the wedding party. There would be no reception for the couple. They only needed each other, and to retreat to a place to live so they could begin to look ahead instead of behind.

Wedding Gift beyond Measure

These were the easy things, relatively. But now John and Mary Assumpta needed to make decisions with moral implications that could ruin reputations and livelihoods of the people who depended on them. There was no room for niceties at this point in the morning.

"Father and John?" It was now Mary Assumpta's turn to speak for the two of them. "Before we go any farther, James and I cannot adequately express our gratitude to you both for your help and understanding."

"Mary Assumpta," her father spoke in measured tones, "I was your age once, as was your mother, and we faced decisions no different from you and James. That you took love's most immediate course does not make you all wrong and your mother and me right. However, your decision will appear wrong in the eyes of an intolerant Charleston society if we are not careful. So we must plan for how we will deal with it, and dealing with it begins tomorrow morning."

Mary Assumpta put forward her idea of staying with friends Betsy Jennings and Fiona Carroll for the next two weeks. Her father disagreed, but with a gentle touch.

"Mary Assumpta, I know that you think your friends will

not become party to the rumor mill, but you cannot be so sure about their parents. Gossip is a mighty force of evil and all but impossible to resist. Until the wedding, you need to stay out of sight except for work. For the next two weeks, you plan to stay at the Indigo Inn. It is not far from John's office and it will be a nice treat. I suggest that you and James only see each other at work and only for work. It will do you both good."

Mary Assumpta began to disagree, but she caught herself as she realized her father was plainly trying to protect her from the ugliness of ignorant people, and she was beginning to see some daylight through the clouds of her despair. Besides, his risqué pun made her smile.

"Why don't you invite them to the wedding instead?" her father suggested. "I will deliver your message to them next Sunday morning at Mass."

Mary Assumpta accepted the changes graciously. "Father, that is obviously a good idea. I sure hope some of your wisdom rubbed off on me. I have a feeling I will be needing it in bucketsful."

James would stay in the surgery apartment for the next two weeks while Mary Assumpta stayed at the Indigo Inn. James could not disagree, knowing that he would see Mary Assumpta every day, and they could easily sneak some time together.

It was now time for those hard decisions, and James and Mary Assumpta faced them with a frontal approach.

"John," James began as he poured himself and Matthew a new cup of coffee, "Mary Assumpta and I both agree that I must dissolve my interest in our partnership."

"Now wait just a minute. That is the dumbest thing that has been said at this table this morning," John Bailey insisted. "We can work this out. You will see. You two go away for a couple of weeks to New Orleans or Baltimore, and when you return, this will have blown over. Such things are like hurricanes. They blow and bluster and sometimes cause damage, but soon they are forgotten."

"I would agree," James returned, "except for one thing—your mother. Her reaction to our announcement on Christmas was anticipated—not to the degree, but we all knew she would react loudly and emotionally. But she has resented my presence in the life of your family since the day I arrived to begin my apprenticeship. We are, it seems, total opposites. She is Catholic. I am Anglican. She is Irish and attached to the land. I am English born from scholars and professionals.

"The roots of your mother's contempt for us will run long and be profound in this small town that is not as big as it thinks it is. It means nothing to me. But it has been, at best, a smoldering fire. Her manners were all that kept Mrs. Bailey from barring me from the house before now. And I cannot endure the knowledge that my actions would unfavorably affect your reputation.

"Finally, I will not intentionally or unintentionally cause damage to your relationship with your mother, but the only way to do that is to separate myself from our partnership. This decision is not for negotiation. Mary Assumpta and I are settled that we must move on."

Matthew Bailey, quiet for the last few minutes, spoke up at the idea of moving. "What do you mean, 'move on'?"

James continued, "We have talked about three possibilities and would like your advice. There is a possibility of moving to the outskirts of Charleston, but again, Charleston is exceedingly small when the gossipmongers are about doing their dirty deeds. So we don't see staying here as a good solution.

"We also talked about moving to Richmond near my parents, but the risk, even a small one, of affecting my father's reputation is not one I am willing to take. So that, though better than Charleston, we also eliminated."

Mary Assumpta spoke up. "We discussed most seriously about moving to Wilmington. It is not Charleston, but I think it might feel like home. However, it is a significant trip back to Charleston to visit with you all, and maybe one day with mother, so, though we did not eliminate it, it doesn't seem to be a good choice. But it appears to be our only option."

Mary Assumpta's father spoke again, and again insistently. "I cannot disagree with your analysis of these options, but I have one more that I would like you to consider."

A smile now creeping on his face, Matthew continued. "A few years ago, I bought two hundred fifty acres and a farmhouse in decent shape on Horlbeck Creek just west of the Boone plantation. I have had a tenant family farming the property for me and keeping up the house, but they received a better offer, as fate would have it, from the Boone family. If you all are willing, I would like to deed that property to the two of you with the sole right to buy it back from you, at your best-offered price, should you decide at some later time to sell it."

Mary Assumpta responded emotionally. "Father, you cannot do that. That is *your* investment. We cannot take it, though we are overwhelmed by the offer."

"And just how would you interpret my deeding it to you as anything but a sound investment? I cannot think of a better way to keep the property in the family." Matthew argued his point with his hardheaded daughter, knowing that she would see sense in it even if she at first rejected it for other reasons.

"Look," Matthew continued, "it is about fifteen miles as the crow flies from where we are sitting right now, but it might as well be fifteen hundred. It is not easy to get to. The only way is by boat, and that takes two hours. And then there is a nice long walk from the dock at the mouth of Horlbeck Creek at the Wando River to the house.

"My point," Matthew concluded, "is that we are both near to

and far from each other, far from your mother and the wagging tongues of Meeting Street but near enough should you need John or me, and perhaps your mother, as time passes. We can see you often enough, and you can make a trip to Charleston without too much trouble. I wish the trip to see your parents, James, were easier. However, it is just a boat ride to Charleston to catch a coastal trader to Norfolk and then on to Richmond by rail. A four-day journey in most likelihood, and as rail lines will soon join us to Wilmington and on to Richmond, the journey will be half that.

"So do we have a deal?" Matthew asked.

James nodded to Mary Assumpta and she to him. "We have a deal," they both said together, but James added one caveat to the deal: "We will begin paying you in yearly installments as we are able to see a profit."

"Let's ford that creek when we come to it," Matthew interjected. "First you have to learn the *science* of farming—an honorable and rewarding profession. To turn a profit, you must plant the crops in demand in Charleston and harvest at just the right time when prices are good. And finally, you must factor in the Almighty's plaything—the weather. You will learn the business, and I have some good friends about a mile from you up the creek who will be most glad to help. The Billingtons, Nathaniel and Audrey Lee, are childless and would love nothing more than to adopt the both of you and the little one on the way. Once we get you married, we will sail over, and I will show you the place and introduce you to the Billingtons. I expect you will have ample opportunities to keep up your doctoring once folks on that side of the harbor hear that there is a doctor in their midst."

James, tears welling up in his eyes, accepted the journey that was ahead that would lead him and Mary Assumpta to a new and singularly different life. "We gratefully accept the generosity of your offer, and we promise to learn to be gentleman and lady farmers. And I confess that with the growing turmoil on the national political scene, raising a child on the farm away from the quarrelsomeness that shall be soon enveloping Charleston really appeals to me."

"We have plenty to do," Mary Assumpta inserted, bringing the morning to a close. "Can we meet again on Wednesday? And, John, can you do without James today? We have even more to talk about than when we started the morning." Everyone agreed with hugs and handshakes.

Matthew left to walk the six blocks to his pharmacy. James left to walk the two blocks to Amélie's. John eased back to his office, and Mary Assumpta bounded up the stairs to wait for James to return with pastries. *How did James know that I am craving sweets?* she thought to herself.

She lay on the unmade bed and wondered out loud to the heavens, "And how can I feel so good but so scared at the same time?"

No one answered. They never do.

PART IV
THE FARM

CHAPTER 10

Memories in the Mirror

The wedding seemed an eon ago to Mary Assumpta, yet it had only been four weeks. For two weeks after the wedding, the Merriweathers stayed in the small apartment above the surgery and continued to work with John. They needed every penny they could earn to purchase the essentials for life on the farm. They ventured out only to have an early meal each evening and returned home to plan for the farm. As odd as this whole arrangement seemed, and was, they were newlyweds, and they enjoyed every minute they could steal from working on the farm.

The wedding was a simple and classy affair: candles on the altar rail and in each window; ribbons salvaged from Christmas wreaths on each pew; an immense white and silver bow decorating the cypress pulpit; a white cotton runner from the front door to the altar; James in a dark blue suit; Mary Assumpta in a floor-length off-white off-the-shoulder satin ball gown purchased for coming out but never worn; Matthew Bailey in a dark brown—almost black—suit; the Reverend Green in his clerical robe; Father Joseph, persuaded by Wesley Green to participate, in his finest priestly attire. James, Anglican. Mary Assumpta,

Catholic. The service in the simple Seaman's Methodist Chapel. It seemed right, neither Catholic nor Protestant, yet both.

It is a shame, Matthew Bailey thought during the vows, *that Lauraleigh is not here.* Matthew did not see Mary Assumpta's mother on that Sunday though he had knocked on her locked door. He begged her to come, but she reasserted her hard stance: "I do not have a daughter getting married today."

"Come on, Lauraleigh. If not for you, do it for Mary Assumpta."

"Dammit, Matthew. I told you I do not have a daughter. Now leave me the hell alone."

And he did.

A Gentleman Farmer

After two weeks of clearing out, cleaning up, patching up, and replacing where necessary, Horlbeck Creek Farm—it had to have a name—was beginning to feel the tiniest bit like home to James and Mary Assumpta Merriweather. The couple still smiled each time they thought of themselves as James and Mary Assumpta Merriweather.

Farming methodically, the same way he had learned to approach medicine, had an appeal to James Merriweather. He was not entirely foreign to preparing, planting, and harvesting a garden. Few Southerners were.

His father had turned to vegetable gardening as his form of relaxation after taxing days of caring for his patients. James had helped his father, Winston, in the family's larger than typical Richmond garden.

Each year the Merriweathers planted a quarter acre of tomatoes, corn, butter beans, okra, purple hull peas, and at least three varieties of squash. Along the borders of the plot Winston Merriweather grew peaches, eating and canning pears, and his personal favorite, quince.

James had never given much thought to the garden. Mainly he was his father's helper, even when he was apprenticing with him during his first year out of medical school. He was the muscle behind the high-wheel hand plow cultivator, and he and his brothers and sisters helped his mother, Beatrice, pick and preserve the vegetables for winter. But, of course, that was after they had eaten more than half the garden.

James tried to build a library of books about farming to no avail. He wrote to John, asking if he would pay a visit to S. G. Courtenay & Co. Booksellers on Broad Street to inquire if they published books on farming. They didn't, but they did sell the indispensable *Farmers' Almanac* for 1853, which he purchased and mailed to James and Mary Assumpta.

James was pleased to get a copy of the *Farmers' Almanac* but was a bit disappointed that John's letter that came with the package indicated there was nothing else on the Courtenay & Co. Booksellers shelves to aid a novice farmer. So James did what he always did when he needed unvarnished advice; he wrote his father.

February 8, 1853
Horlbeck Creek Farm

Dear Father,

It was so good to see you and mother at the wedding. I had hoped to see the whole family, but I understand the difficulty of their travel on such short notice. I trust you and mother are doing well and adjusting to the idea that you will soon be grandparents! I am both *ready and totally unprepared to be a father. I expect those emotions are universal for all new fathers.*

Mary Assumpta sends her love to you all. She is obviously pregnant now but continues to be in good health and maintains a busy schedule of trying to get this place in order for us to begin planting at the end of March. It will be a late start as I understand most farmers here try to get seeds in the ground in early March. It can't be helped as we just cannot be ready before then.

I have tried to find books on the subject of farming, but it seems it is handed down more by word of mouth than word of books. So with that in mind, I am writing this letter to pick your brain about planting a garden for the family that can produce enough vegetables for eating this summer and preserving for the winter.

Sincerely,
James

Visiting the Neighbors

While James awaited the reply from his father that would take at least a fortnight, he paid Nate Billington a visit. The mile's walk up the Old Shell Road gave James an opportunity to be with himself for a while. It seemed, and in actuality was, that neither he nor Mary Assumpta had done anything but work full steam since the Christmas Day announcement that set off Volcano Lauraleigh. For the two weeks leading up to and following the wedding, the stress had been, more often than not, emotional, the kind that one feels when life's control is just beyond one's fingertips. The stress wasn't so much as a result of not knowing where their lives were headed; it was the destruction that seemed to follow in the wake of their decisions even when they knew the decisions to be right and proper.

We, and no one else, put the events into motion in the heat of love's passion, James reckoned to himself. *But the real question is, would I make the same decision again?*

As he was in sight of the old gate that opened to the oystershell path in the swept dirt yard to Nate and Audrey Lee Billington's weather-beaten farmhouse, he put aside that question for the moment. Each corner of the house sat on two sandstones that had been hewn to a roughly rectangular shape. The house was wider than it was long. Two more sets of foundation stones, equally spaced apart, supported the width, and there was one set on each side of the length. With only one set of foundation stones on the short side, settling had occurred over the years and the length had a noticeable sway, but overall it was decidedly stout enough to survive its share of hurricanes over the years.

As James stepped up on the porch that spanned the front of the house, a feist dog greeted him. He was small but bigger than a Jack Russell, but still with a Jack-like temperament when strangers invaded *his* territory. His feet and belly were muddy from a recent trip to the nearby swamp in search of squirrels. A man who possessed a good feist squirrel dog could eat fried squirrel all winter long. The mud faded into the dog's brindle coloration—another trait of the feist dog and one that made him almost invisible to squirrels in the trees when they looked for predators on the ground. He barked with a high-pitched squeal, letting his master know that someone who did not belong was on the property.

"Rufus!" The shout came from the darkness behind the screen door. "Stop that barking. I said stop it."

When Rufus continued, Nate Billington came out of the door in a rush with a sagebrush broom that the dog obviously recognized as an instrument to be feared, since he ran off the porch and under it, still whining at a pitch that opera singers would envy. "Rufus. Don't make me come under there," Nate said with a laugh. James was observing a game they had obviously played many times before. Rufus stuck his head out from under the porch, but the squeaking had stopped.

"Dr. Merriweather, how are you settling in?"

"Now, Nate, I have already explained that if we are to be neighbors, I am just plain James."

"Okay, James, but it still feels funny, and the missus fusses at me about it."

"Perhaps I can explain to Mrs. Billington," James responded.

"Well, that remains to be seen. Come on in and let's talk about what's on your mind over a cup of coffee and Mrs. Billington's peach cobbler. The cobbler is from last year's preserves, but it is still mighty good."

The inside of the farmhouse was as neat as the outside was battered. Nate had built the cabinets in the kitchen and most of the furniture over the years, including a beautiful old pie safe, from which he took an uncut lattice-top peach cobbler.

As Nate was about to cut into the cobbler for the first time, Audrey Lee walked in from the back porch. She was not what James expected, dressed in an obviously homemade dress. Although it was homemade, it was anything but homely. The complementary colors she had dyed into the cotton cloth blended seamlessly into each other, rather like the colorful Charleston houses on Revolutionary Row. Her hair, long and drawn into a ponytail, was still mostly blonde, the color of wheat ready for harvest, and streaked with gray that did nothing but enhance her natural beauty. Her arms and legs showed the musculature of farmwork. One best not ignore Audrey Lee Billington at a first meeting.

"Nathaniel Billington! Put down that knife right now. That

cobbler is for supper tonight with Reverend Baker." Audrey Lee spoke with a molasses-slow and sugar-sweet Low Country accent.

Just as she had chastised her husband, she saw James and quickly backtracked. "Okay, go ahead and cut it since we have company. Dr. Merriweather, how are you this morning?"

"Fine, Audrey Lee, but I would feel better if you would just call me James."

"My mother would rise up from her grave and tan me good even at my age if she heard me call a doctor by his first name. You're just gonna have to get used to me calling you Doctor.

"Nate, you might as well cut me a piece too while I fix a new pot of coffee. You cannot serve company that black sludge you call coffee that's been in the pot since five o'clock this morning."

James had liked Audrey Lee immediately, and he was anxious for Mary Assumpta to spend time with her too.

"Well," James started as they waited a moment for their coffee to cool, "I am here for some advice. As I was growing up, I watched my father and helped him plant and tend his quarter-acre garden behind our home in Richmond. But that was nothing like farming. Nate, how do I get started this spring, since I am starting late, without making a complete fool of myself?"

"James." Nate laughed. "If every farmer worried himself silly whenever he did something stupid, we wouldn't have any farmers. Learning from our mistakes is how farmers learn."

"Well, that makes me feel better, but how do you make a living if you make mistakes often?" James asked.

"Well, I did not say I made mistakes often," Nate corrected James. "I said I just learned from them when I did make them and didn't make the same ones again. Every farm is different. Even though you and I are just a mile apart, our soil will be different, and believe it or not, the climate will be slightly different too. You will make mistakes learning about your farm."

"Nate, I guess my number one questions is, how do you suggest I begin this first year, especially since I am starting in late March at the earliest?" James was relieved that he was asking his most pressing questions so early in the conversation.

"Well, first I would not worry about starting late. Late is a relative term given the length of our growing season. We start earlier, but it will still be hot here in July, although not nearly as hot as a hundred miles north of us. Plus, the showers off the water means we don't have to worry much about drought even if it is hot. We can grow things a little longer and sometimes even get in two plantings.

"It is true that some things do better at the beginning of the season, but I would not even worry about those. Vegetables like English peas or cabbage are good to grow for your family, but you will probably not make a profit from them because you cannot transport them beyond a day or two after harvest. You can go ahead and plant some cabbage even now; it might make it or might not. Just don't worry about it."

James felt better hearing Nate's advice, but his biggest concern was still the number of acres that he would need to cultivate to produce any profit. "Nate, how many of my two hundred fifty acres will I have to plant to reasonably expect to make a profit?" James asked.

Nate laughed again. "James, my boy, if you plant what it takes to feed your family this summer and through next winter and keep an animal or two fed, you will be a huge success. I would say you are maybe three years away from making consistent profits, and there are a heap of maybes in that proposition.

"Start with an acre," Nate advised. "Bigger than the size your father planted, but easily manageable. The smaller-sized garden means mistakes have less impact. Start with some proven crops like peas and butter beans.

"Plant some summer squash, but not too many. They can produce so much that you can't eat them all, and squash are just not good for canning. Plant a few rows of corn because corn is susceptible to all manner of pests depending on the year, but it is worth a try.

"Be sure to plant some crops that you harvest in the fall like pumpkins and winter squash, and particularly potatoes. Sweet potatoes especially take very little work. Pests (except for rabbits) don't bother them, and when they are harvested, they keep all winter long.

"That is the kind of garden I plant these days. My days of working from dawn to dusk are gone. My arthritis just won't let me."

James perked up at the medical topic of Nate's arthritis. "You come see me sometime. I think I have something that will help with your achy joints. Maybe we can trade some medical advice for farming advice. Deal?"

"Deal. And I know I have some proven seed that I will throw in to sweeten the transaction." Nate was excited to be talking farming with someone who knew the medical profession inside and out, and also excited to maybe get some help with his achy joints.

As he rose from the table, James suggested, "What about you and Audrey Lee coming by our place in a few days, and we will continue this conversation? I think we will have the house reasonably cleaned up by that time."

"I will do it," Nate said. "And I will bring a friend you need to meet."

"Audrey Lee," James called out, "thank you for that cobbler. I trust Reverend Baker won't be disappointed that we got into it."

"He will get over it," Audrey Lee said.

Yep, thought James. *I do like Audrey Lee.*

As James closed the gate, Rufus ran from under the front porch, this time wagging his tail while giving out a happy yelp. *Got to get me a dog,* James reminded himself as he was enjoying the company of Rufus.

As he started for home, for some reason James could not recall the conversation he had been having with himself about the stresses he had been feeling before he arrived at Nate Billington's farm.

Must not have been important, he reflected to himself. Walking with a confident step, he began to whistle the old church song "Bringing in the Sheaves."

Gentleman Farming

February 20, 1853

324 Franklin Street
Richmond, Virginia

Dear James,

Your mother and I were pleased as always to receive your recent correspondence. I hate that my response will likely be too late to do you any good at all this planting season. Nonetheless, here are my thoughts on planting that I have learned over the years the hard way—trying things and finding those that worked and those that failed miserably or simply were not worth the effort required to make them succeed.

My first piece of advice is simply to start small. You cannot expect to turn a profit as late as you are starting. However, you can grow enough to provide for the family, and that should be your first goal. I know that you have likely put some money aside, and between that savings and what you can grow, you will be able to provide for the family. You know that Mother and I are ready to help if you need us. But knowing you, I don't expect that to happen. Still, keep the idea in the back of your mind.

My second piece of advice is to prepare your soil. There is nothing more important than this. You cannot expect to grow quality vegetables from poor soil. You will get some, but they will be few, and the plants will die back at the first sign of difficulty because they will have no roots. (Seems to me some people are about the same way.)

Third, find out what is easy to grow, not just in Charleston but also in that creek and river basin area, and focus on that. You will be planting the same thing as everyone else, but you are not trying to make a profit; you are learning the prerequisites for being a farmer.

Fourth, don't plant something just because you like it or fail to plant it because you don't like it. Use your training to look for nutrition. You will be surprised at how easy you can learn to like the taste of most anything when you are hungry—and when you have grown it yourself.

Fifth, assess the amount of sun where you are considering putting the garden. Sunshine is even more essential than the soil preparation. Even a little reduced sun can ruin crops like squash as shade increases the humidity around the plants, and fungi will attack the plant, the blossoms, and the fruit. Potatoes do okay in partial shade, but little else will.

Plant things that are easy to preserve or that last through the winter. Tomatoes out of a jar are mighty good in the middle of April. Okra is one of the plants that may repulse you, but it will grow in the hottest days of the summer and produce until the first freeze. Too, okra can be canned with tomatoes or peas or pickled like cucumbers. Very versatile plant. Peas and beans provide fruit most of the summer and can be canned and dried.

Sixth, learn from failure as much as from success—and don't blame the weather. Everyone has the same weather. Some years you will ask yourself why you ever thought you could make a go of a garden. The next year your larder of canned vegetables will last far after the next year's harvest, and you will be ready to write a book about how to garden.

Finally, get yourself a mule. Take it from someone who knows: you will kill yourself trying to turn the soil with a push plow. You will question yourself a hundred times about how you could have been so stupid as to have paid good money for such a hardheaded creature. Then you will swear that that mule is eating up all your profit. Truth is, until somebody invents a steam-powered mechanical version, the flesh-and-blood variety will become your best friend.

I wish I could have given you more practical advice. I bet you can get some reliable guidance from that friendly farmer and his wife I met at the wedding. Seems like a real nice old couple.

I am always here to help.

Father

P.S. Get yourself a dog for the times when Mary Assumpta won't let you near her during the last weeks of pregnancy. Trust me, you will need somebody who *always* loves you!

James was just finishing up reading his father's letter out loud to Mary Assumpta when Nate and Audrey Lee arrived in a beat-up old carriage pulled by a swayback roan. Rufus was dancing ahead of the aged swayback horse, and, of all things, a mule was tethered to the back of the carriage.

CHAPTER 11

Neighbors and an Old House

James and Mary Assumpta ran to greet their first visitors to Horlbeck Creek Farm.

Their time together since they'd arrived toward the end of January had been a blessing filled with long days of hard work that left little time in the day to worry about the trivialities of what might have been. Hence, their supper conversations were focused because of their immediate needs and their weariness. They were asleep as soon as their bodies hit feather pillows and the mattress they had brought with them along with all the furniture from James's apartment above the surgery. John had given them the table and four chairs from the surgery kitchen. They had had no need of a sofa until now. They soon found that Nate and Audrey Lee were much more kitchen people than sofa people anyway.

Nate and James shook hands vigorously and began immediately making small talk. Audrey Lee was hardly out of the carriage when she was giving Mary Assumpta a big hug—manifestly enjoyed by both. As they finally let go of each other with whispered smiles only understood by women and never shared with men, Audrey Lee turned her maternal attentions to James. "James Merriweather, if you won't let me call you 'Doctor,' then you must learn that those hugs are a mandatory form of greeting in these parts. Get yourself over here and give me a proper welcome."

Nate, ever the gentleman, gave Mary Assumpta a genteel hand, but Mary Assumpta surprised him by pulling him into a full-body pregnant-woman hug. "Welcome to Horlbeck Creek Farm, such as it is. Okay if we move inside?" Mary Assumpta said. The February wind, always laden with moisture from the Atlantic, chilled Mary Assumpta in ways that she had never experienced before. *Pregnancy*, she thought as she chugged up the three steps into the house.

The house was thirty feet on a side. A small porch, only enough for two rocking chairs, kept the weather from the front door and was placed squarely in the middle of the front side. The kitchen, the dining room, and a future parlor made up the front half of the house. The right back half of the house was a bedroom with the opening covered only with a faded curtain. A door would come later. The left back half behind the kitchen would eventually become another bedroom—this one for the children, in the plural.

The pine floors had cracks between the boards and open knotholes that James had patched with pine tar and sawdust from the limbs he had cut when cleaning up. It was not a permanent solution, but it would do for the winter. Even so, the floors were spotless and smelled of the turpentine that had been used to clean and disinfect them.

The house was faded lapstrake that had weathered to a gray patina and covered the outside, and the old folks said it would provide a natural protection better than whitewash. At any rate, James would not have time to whitewash it anyway. The house was surrounded by a picket fence to keep wandering livestock from the yard. The yard was swept except for the path from the front gate to the front steps. The walk was made from small pea gravel from the creek restrained by logs that made up either side of the pathway. The previous residents had planted a few canna lilies as foundation plants and had transplanted several wild rhododendrons and azaleas that were doing well on the shady side of the house but not so well on the sunny side.

James stoked the still hot coals in the stove with a couple of pieces of wood as Mary Assumpta put on a pot of coffee. With coffee poured and sugar cookies passed around, the menfolk began a walking survey of the property while the womenfolk retired to the rocking chairs on the porch and talked about whatever womenfolk talk about when menfolk are not around.

The Mule

"Well, Nate, can you tell me what you see at a first look?" James asked to start the conversation about the property.

"James, you are in pretty good shape to start the family garden right here on the left side of the house." Nate bent down and picked up a handful of soil.

"See this sandy-brown texture and color of the dirt? That is what we call 'loamy,' and you should count your blessings because, with the right amount of natural fertilizer such as manure and compost, you can grow most anything in it. It drains well; it is naturally soft; and it does not require a lot of breaking up to prepare it for planting. In fact, there are some farmers around who plant without tilling the soil every other year to conserve the land from wind and water erosion.

"Begin by top-dressing the garden plot with manure and compost if the last tenant left you any. I can supply you with plenty of manure, and if there is no compost left, just go into the creek swamp, where you will find plenty. You'll also want to add ashes from the limbs that you have been cleaning up and burning. That adds potash to the garden.

"Once you have staked out the size and location of your garden plot, lay out the rows of the garden on paper. You will find it is much easier to harvest by keeping some plants away from others. Put your squash and potatoes on the outside rows so their vines can run and not interfere with other plants. Plant more tomatoes than you think you will ever need because they are finicky. Some years they will be coming out of your ears, and other years you will barely produce enough to eat. Use okra to shade peppers that don't like hot days. Peas can grow up the cornstalks. See what I mean?

"For all your plants, pay attention to those that grow the biggest, yield the most fruit, and resist pests. Keep back seeds from those plants for next year. As I told you at my place, I have more than enough seeds to get you started this year."

James just shook his head. So much to learn. "Nate, that seems like a lot to take in. You going to be around if I need help?"

"Does it look like I am going anywhere?" Nate laughed.

"Oh, by the way, how much stock do you put into the *Farmers' Almanac*?" James asked.

Nate laughed again. "It's good reading, but it is not based much on facts, more like on intuition. Some of their predictions seem to work, but just as many fall flat on their asses. Your own trial and error will still be the best way to learn.

"James, there is one thing we have not talked about, and that is how the heck you are going to till up that garden plot once you have the top-dressing in place."

"I have not gotten that far," James admitted.

"Well, I have." Nate laughed again. "See that old flop-eared piece of stubbornness tied yonder to the carriage?" James nodded that he did. "That is Jake, and he is now *your* piece of stubbornness if you will have him."

"I can't do that, Nate. Besides, how will I feed him?"

"Well, Jake will do just fine on the grass that grows most of the year. And when that runs out, I have some hay that will just be sitting in my barn. Way too much for my milk cow."

"How are you going to plow your garden if you don't have Jake?" James asked.

"I will come borrow him from you, of course."

Nate was on a roll now. "My coffee cup is empty. What do you say we see if we can refill it before we finish our tour?"

The Barn

With refilled blue and white enameled metal coffee cups, James escorted Nate to the barn. The barn was as James found it, full of spiderwebs and dirt dauber and wasp nests and in general disrepair. However, there were some tools, large and small, lying around, all with rust, but to Nate's eye, a pretty nice selection.

"James, looks to me that you are in pretty good shape. Everything needs a good cleaning and oiling, of course, but I don't see that you are lacking anything major that you need to get started working behind ol' Jake. The harness needs a good oiling, as do the plow handles, but I think you will be ready shortly with a little work."

"Really? Ready? I don't even know how to hook up the plow harness to Jake, much less how to give Jake the commands to get him to work."

"My advice is to take a little time to get to know him. Just walk him on a lead around the farm so he can learn the land, and when you complete the prep work, come and get me. Then Jake and I will show you how a plow mule is a farmer's best friend."

Rufus came zooming around a stack of hay bales with a barn rat half as big as he was in his mouth, his teeth firmly attached behind the rat's neck. He was shaking the life out of that rat, and when it was dead, he laid it at Nate's feet. Rufus was not only a squirrel dog but was also a ratter, a necessity around the barn.

"Okay, Nate, where do I find a dog like Rufus?"

"They are pretty hard to find. I'll check with the owner

of the bitch that birthed Rufus and see if she is going to have another litter anytime soon. Then I'll let you know. But you'd better clear it with Mary Assumpta. A dog, and especially a puppy, is a lot of work."

Having established that all the implements necessary to till and plant a garden were on hand, although they needed cleaning and oiling, Nate and James walked the 250 acres that made up the farm.

Hidden Treasures

The lane that led from the road to the house evenly split the farm into two halves. As one walked toward the house, one noted that the left half was an orchard of peach, pear, and apple trees ready, it appeared, to bear a first substantial crop of fruit in the upcoming year. Additionally, there were a half dozen blueberry bushes, two turkey fig trees, and three arbors. One arbor was for the small red muscadines and two for the larger golden scuppernongs.

"James, do you know what you have here?"

"Well, it appears I have some fruit trees and grapevines."

"What you have here, my boy, is a gold mine. That last tenant did you a big favor by planting this orchard, I'd say probably four or five years ago, and now the trees and vines are ready to bear substantial fruit."

"What do I need to do?" James asked for what seemed the hundredth time.

"It is a bit late to apply fertilizer; instead, I would put a ring of compost around each tree out to the outer braches. The compost will keep down weeds and will more gently feed the roots than manure. You can add manure around the trees next fall. The most worrisome thing," Nate continued, "will be the bugs on fruit trees and birds on the blueberries, figs, muscadines, and scuppernongs."

"So what do I do about them?"

"I mix a gallon of soapy water to a cup of oil, like bacon grease. Then I take a mop, dip it in the bucket, and splash the mixture on the trees once the fruit has started to show up. The idea is that the oil and soap will smother any insects. Just repeat it after each rain or if you see insects building up on the fruit. It is not perfect, but it is better than letting the bugs eat your harvest.

"For the birds, an ol' scarecrow or good dog will do the trick. Of course, picking the fruit often is the best way. The birds want ripe fruit, so pick it right as it is getting mature."

James felt some relief finally. "Okay, I see I have some work to do, but it doesn't seem too hard. I would guess all of this fruit can make for good canning too."

"The fruit preserves, especially the turkey figs, are outstanding and will keep for more than a year if you seal them well in the canning jars. Audrey Lee can show you how to do that. It is not hard, but you do have to pay close attention to doing it right."

As they took a look at the two fig trees near the house, Nate suggested that James cut them back. "The hardest thing about picking figs is when the tree gets so big that you can't reach the figs, but the birds can reach them for sure! So keep them trimmed back and let them grow out instead of up."

Beyond the Fruit Trees

Nate could see that James was pondering the next step, the big one: making a living from the land beyond what was needed to feed his family.

"James, you are going to reserve these hundred acres or so not planted in fruit for growing vegetables that you can sell in Charleston to restaurants, grocers, and believe it or not, ship quartermasters. But remember, this is not the year to do that. This year you are going to work only on the one-acre family garden. You will make a little money or maybe a goodly amount from the sale of the fruit to the same people. You will need to make a trip to Charleston early in the growing season to meet up with these people and let them know your plans for this year and beyond. Ask them what they would like to have, then start planning for planting those things next year. The easiest way to *grow broke* farming is to plant vegetables that no one wants." Nate laughed at his pun.

"What about hay for Jake? And don't I need a milk cow and some hogs at some point?" James asked, finally having broken through into thinking like a farmer.

"Yes, you do need some hay for Jake. I think planting an acre of hay will be more than enough for this year. As to the cow and the hogs, you are going to want to have them, but maybe not this year. Perhaps after the fruit harvest you can begin thinking about that."

"I see," James said, laughing, "that we are back where we started."

"Yep, that happens a lot in farming." Nate laughed. "Why don't we go see what the womenfolk have been doing and maybe rustle up something a little stronger than coffee?"

"Well, it does appear that the sun is beyond the yardarm, and I do believe I have a bottle of ten-year-old whiskey put away for special occasions. I think this surely qualifies."

James eased into the bedroom and brought out a barely touched bottle of scotch whiskey and two shot glasses. Sitting in the two rocking chairs on the front porch, he and Nate celebrated the official christening of Horlbeck Creek Farm.

"To Horlbeck Creek Farm. Long may she prosper," Nate toasted.

"Hear, hear," James agreed, feeling at least a little confident in his future for the first time since he'd arrived on this piece of God's earth on Horlbeck Creek.

Adopted

As James and Nate had surveyed the prospects for farming, Audrey Lee and Mary Assumpta were busy gauging the prospects of family life on the farm. Farming was entirely foreign to Mary Assumpta—as much as child-rearing was to Audrey Lee.

"Audrey Lee," Mary Assumpta gently inquired, "did you miss not having kids running around the house?"

"There were certainly times like the holidays when something just seemed to be missing, or harvesttime when we surely could have used the extra hands, but Nate and I have had a full life together. We have always been closer, I think, because we both tried to fill the gap by loving each other even more. I can sure tell you one thing: we are excited to have you and James expecting and so close that we can help anytime we are needed. I expect you will just have to run me off sometimes once your baby comes!"

"Audrey Lee, I will need all the help I can get. James thinks that because he is a physician, he is also ready to be a father. I know him better than that. He is great at anything technical—like the farming advice he is getting from Nate. I have no doubt he will make a go of this farm in short order, but fatherhood? I expect he will be over his head within minutes after he delivers the baby."

And so the conversation continued to baby clothes, bassinettes, breastfeeding, and midwifery.

"Mary Assumpta, I know that James is more than qualified to deliver your baby, but should you desire a woman's touch, I want you to know that I have delivered dozens of healthy babies in these parts over the years. I guess it started as a way to be involved in something I would never experience. As I became more experienced, women with no doctor close, or those just desiring a woman's presence, kept calling on me. I read everything I could find, which was not much. And on a trip over to Charleston one fall, I made it my goal to meet with Jane Clayton, the most well-known midwife in Charleston. We correspond to this day. I am not trying to be pushy; I just want you to know that if you need or want my services, all you need to do is send James to get me."

Mary Assumpta saw that Audrey Lee could fill an empty space in her life—the role she had no doubt that her mother would one day regret that she had missed. And with Audrey Lee's interest and experience in medicine, not unlike her own training with her brother John, the two women had much more in common than Mary Assumpta could have imagined.

And to think that it was here on the banks of Horlbeck Creek that she'd met a fellow female traveler in the ways of medicine.

God, she thought to herself, *you sure work in some very mysterious ways.* And at that, she turned away from Audrey Lee and genuflected. She felt closer to the Almighty than at any time in many weeks.

CHAPTER 12

New Baby—New Parents

Mary Assumpta had been in labor for most of the day when she grabbed James by the testicles as he sat by her bedside. "You take Jake and go get Audrey Lee right now, or you are sleeping with Jake the rest of our marriage. I mean it, James. Get your ass out of that chair and go. I will be just fine for thirty minutes."

Four hours later, on July 30, 1853, Colin Edward Merriweather was born. He was seven pounds (weighed on the produce scale brought in from the barn) and twenty-one inches—measured on a yardstick Audrey Lee used to measure the cloth for her dresses. Bald as his godfather Nate, with a wisp of red-tinted down, Colin had the temper of his grandmother. He was beautiful to everyone who saw him on the day he entered the already-turbulent world that was to become his South.

Colin was born at a fortuitous time of the year for his father and mother. The figs, now left for the birds and yellow jackets to consume, and the apples, which would bear fruit in the early fall, were the only fruit trees still producing anything. The garden had slowed down except for the okra, which had to be cut every other day; a few squash and bell peppers that needed picking once or twice a week; and the sweet potatoes and Irish potatoes that would be ready in another couple of months. Ol' Jake took care of himself with minimal attention. Glad to be out from under the plow and harness and the clumsy directions of his new master, he was totally content to wander the unplanted fields that led down to the banks of Horlbeck Creek.

Mary Assumpta was a natural mother. James was better at fatherhood than Mary Assumpta had expected. Still, she could see that he was nervous when he took Colin up to change his diaper.

On a trip back to Charleston to sell his fruit at the city market, James purchased the newfangled invention guaranteed to make baby changing easy and quick—the safety pin. However, for James, the process was neither easy nor quick. Mary Assumpta often found him talking to himself as he tried to fold the cotton square exactly as Audrey Lee had instructed him. So afraid was he that he would stick Colin with a safety pin that he often took him back to Mary Assumpta to finish the job, which always drew a smart remark from his wife.

Settling In

James's favorite time of the day on the farm had been the cool of the evening when all the chores that could be done in a day were done. He would sit on the front porch with a glass of whiskey diluted generously with branch water from the clear cold spring that bubbled up through the limestone behind the house. But these days his favorite time was the early morning, at what the country folks called "wolf light"—not dark and not yet dawn.

He would make himself a pot of strong coffee, pick Colin up from his bed, change him, and walk with him to the front porch, where he would sit in the old rocker and talk to him about what lay ahead of them and about his grandparents back in Richmond. Whenever the baby began to fret, James would dip his index finger into the jar of titi flower honey that he used to sweeten his coffee and place it to Colin's lips. Sometimes Colin would ease back to sleep as his daddy rocked him, but seldom would the baby sleep for more than a few minutes at these times.

It seemed James might just be getting the hang of this fatherhood thing. Regardless, it surely felt good.

Too soon, the dawn would slip out through the loblolly pines and sweet gum trees at the edge of the creek as a yearling buck, just losing his spots, would ease out of the trees to test the air for predators before beginning to graze. And James would take his lovely progeny back to his mother for his morning feeding and take himself to the barn to start another day of farming.

If he were lucky, Nate and Audrey Lee would break up his day with one of their many visits to look in on their godson and their adopted family. Now that ol' Jake was a semipermanent fixture at Horlbeck Creek Farm, Nate had taught an old cow to pull the carriage. They were surely a sight coming down the lane in that old carriage with Bessie pulling on the reins and Audrey Lee fussing with her hair and fussing at Nate to go faster because Colin was getting older every minute.

The first cool breezes of a fall that was yet a month away teased Horlbeck Creek on October 30. On the trip home, Audrey Lee would snuggle up and ask Nate if he would start a fire in the fireplace when they got home (and he would comply as he always did), even though both knew they would end up opening the windows once the fire was roaring. The reminder of good things sure to come seemed always to be on the first cool evening in October. Colin Edward Merriweather turned three months old on this kind of day.

The goodbye wave to Nate and Audrey Lee at the end of their visit was a signal moment in James and Mary Assumpta's life at Horlbeck Creek Farm, although they did not notice it at the time. They had become emotionally if not financially safe with their new lives as farmers. In truth, they were not really satisfied but willingly accepting of their current state.

CHAPTER 13

Drumbeats

A light sleeper, James Merriweather roused and turned over in bed toward the window of his farmhouse near Horlbeck Creek at what sounded to him like thunder. Thunder was not uncommon in April in coastal South Carolina; however, when James had retired not long after dark the evening before, the almost full moon was clearly visible. The deep, resonant sound of thunder across the flats of the Low Country surprised him enough that he rose from his bed and went to the back door, which faced in the general direction of the ocean from which most thunderstorms had their origins. He walked out a few yards from the door, and as he looked above the tree line, he saw flashes of light that seemed to indicate lightning strikes, followed shortly by the bass rumble of thunder. As he turned to return to his bed, and perhaps a predawn tryst with Mary Assumpta before eight-year-old Colin awakened, James noticed just above the roofline of the farmhouse the same waxing moon he had seen the evening before. But this time he saw it as it was making its way to the horizon, accompanied by an asterism of stars, but strangely no clouds.

Anyone who made a living from farming, as James now did, developed a sense of the weather, and his weather sense told him that all was not typical for an April morning south of Horlbeck Creek in Charleston Harbor. He wakened Mary

Assumpta with a kiss on her brow, a soft shake of her shoulder, and a "Red, are you awake?" whispered in her ear. Red was his pet name for her when no one else was around.

"I am awake now. In the name of the God of all things great and glorious, what time of the night is it?" Mary Assumpta asked pertly and more than a little annoyed.

James replied, "I think it is just near dawn. But that is not what is important. Listen and tell me what you hear to the south of us."

Mary Assumpta heard the same sounds. "Thunder, you think, so early in the spring?"

"No. I fear the booms are not thunderclaps but the thunder of cannons. My guess is the fools in Charleston or those in Fort Sumter have started a storm that shall not pass quickly," James responded despondently.

Mary Assumpta put on her plaid housecoat and made her way to the kitchen to ready coffee as James stoked the stove with firewood and kindling. Soon the house was filled with the smell of coffee as the reverberations of cannons and the flashes of shells bursting above Fort Sumter continued.

An Irish Temperament

Over many cups of coffee that April morning in the farmhouse kitchen, James Edward and Mary Assumpta Merriweather had the first significant argument of their eight-year marriage as their son Colin slept on his feather mattress in his bedroom on the north side of the house and away from the sound and lights.

"So," Mary Assumpta challenged James, "what are you going to do now that war is surely soon upon us?"

"I don't think that I will have much of a choice," James replied in a calm voice. "We could leave now before the fighting begins and go to Kentucky or Maryland."

"We could do that," Mary Assumpta said, taking up his

logic. "But that would mean uprooting our family, abandoning our home, and starting again in the middle of a war in an area likely to be contested by both sides. Not a reasonable prospect at all."

James responded unexpectedly, "In the final analysis, I don't think this is directly about you or Colin. It is about me. I see no way, at my age, to escape enlisting. If I don't volunteer, I will eventually be 'volunteered,' and I much prefer the former to the latter."

"But, James, we are just starting to make a go of this farm. We should be able to pay Father at least a little in repayment this fall.

"But if you enlist, what is to happen to our son and me? Can you really expect us to work this farm?" Mary Assumpta asked rhetorically.

James thought, for what seemed a long time to Mary Assumpta, before he spoke again. "Could you perhaps ask your mother to accept you back in the fold given these circumstances?" James had broached *the* most taboo subject of their marriage—Lauraleigh Bailey's formal estrangement from her daughter. Therefore, when James broached the subject, he added a heart pine knot to an already blazing family bonfire.

"Goddamn you, James Merriweather! Are you really serious?" Mary Assumpta's language was frequently salty as a result of growing up with boys, but this epithet was never uttered toward others and especially not under their roof with a child nearby.

"On my damn wedding day, my goddamn mother made it perfectly clear that she no longer had a daughter. Dammit, James, she disowned me. If I never see her again, it will be too soon." Mary Assumpta spit out these words with as much hurt as anger. Hurt and anger at her mother, but equally with her husband for not understanding the depth of her wounds. Tears streamed down her cheeks, and she let them fall to the floor. She had not experienced a catharsis of this intensity since she left her home on Meeting Street in 1853.

"Red," James said as he reached to touch her face. "Let's put this aside for a while and just bide our time until we must make a decision."

"Bide your own time, you damn gobshite!" Mary Assumpta pulled an epithet from her Irish upbringing, one she had heard her grandfather use when a customer failed to pay him after he had allowed the customer to purchase on credit. It was *the* worst profanity she knew.

"As far as I am concerned, you are already dead, as you are to surely be in God's good time if you enlist.

"If I can practically raise myself, I sure as hell can survive without a husband. Now get out of my sight and go make your goddamn plans—and leave me be."

Uncertain Future

With those stinging words resounding over and over and over in his head, James walked out the back door as dawn was breaking. He eased slowly down the lane recently planted with cypress trees on either side and to the road that led west and to the landing on Horlbeck Creek.

James had never seen such forlorn emotions from Mary Assumpta. She had maintained a sense of composure even when her mother had not attended the wedding and, instead, sent her attorney to deliver the document removing Mary Assumpta from her will and her life.

Mary Assumpta was Irish, and so she was, it seemed, naturally strong in her opinions, but up to this point she had been equally strong-willed. Never had James seen her resigned to fate's spiderweb of entrapment.

As he walked, he pondered two simultaneously contradictory

ideas. First, he was Southern to the marrow of his bones, and that meant that he would serve the South in the coming conflict. However, his spiritual upbringing was in the Episcopal Church, where his forefathers developed a long tradition of religious scholarship around the evils of slavery. And finally, politically, he saw no future for a South where slavery remained.

When he arrived at the dock, he sat and dangled his feet into the water where Horlbeck Creek joined the Wando River. The thundering sounds were unmuffled now as they made their way across the Charleston Harbor up the Wando and to his ears. He knew the sounds of cannons, and he knew that he must return to Mary Assumpta and an uncertain future.

His socks and feet had dried in the morning's first sun, and as he laced his boots, rose worriedly, and started back toward home, he realized with an epiphany of sorts there on the banks of the creek that uncertainty would be *his* certain future. The acceptance of that sure fact was his starting place on the morning of April 21, 1861. He prayed that he could explain it to Mary Assumpta. The uncertainty of Mary Assumpta's reaction was his first confident step. He realized he could not foresee her reaction, but he had to take the step nonetheless, and so he left the dock and walked the familiar oyster-shell-covered Old Shell Road back to the farm.

Too Close for Comfort

On the morning of April 11, 1861, at 4:30, the Charleston Battery under the command of Brigadier General P. G. T. Beauregard opened fire on Fort Sumter, and the Civil War began.

By good daylight, a carnival-like excitement had engulfed Charleston. People hurried in carriages and on foot down to the battery in hopes of seeing Fort Sumter's quick surrender. They were to be disappointed as the cannon battle lasted for two days.

By 9:00 a.m. it was evident that there would be no patients

today in the medical office of Dr. John Bailey. However, soon the familiar face of Bartholomew Jennings protruded through the doorway, the rest of him still on the wooden sidewalk. He yelled, "Doc Bailey, it's a-happenin'!"

"For God's sake, Bartholomew, what is happening?" John Bailey asked with frustration in his voice that he regretted as soon as he noticed it, for he was never short with Bartholomew.

He was a character, that was for certain, but he was always faithful and usually funny, and seldom, if ever, hyperexcited about anything. On the contrary, he was generally so laid back—often with the help of a shot of rum—that one had to tug it out of him to get him even to admit he was hurting, much less describe where it hurt and how much. Not today.

"Doc," he said almost out of breath, "the garrison down at the Cummings Point Battery has been firing on Fort Sumter since dawn. That is what all the commotion is about. Folks are yipping and yelling about how we gonna whip them Yankees' asses all the way back to Boston and how we gonna be our own country in a few months. I'm enlisting as soon as I can. I don't want to miss the fun."

"Hush up, Bartholomew. You are too old to do any such thing. Your scraggly old ass would be the first one killed. Probably by another Rebel just to pretty up his platoon."

"The Yankees are firing back, but there was jest a little bit of damage down at the battery. If you ask me, they couldn't hit a bull in the butt with a bass fiddle," Bartholomew said proudly.

"Let's hope so, Bartholomew, let's hope so," John Bailey said with distinct skepticism in his voice as he returned to his office.

The cannons at Fort Sumter were not so much poorly aimed as they were at a disadvantage as there were few munitions, and what were on hand had no timed fuses, so the Union commanders were reduced to firing solid cannonballs, and that sporadically to conserve their supply.

On Saturday, April 13, Major Robert Anderson surrendered the fort and his eighty-five men. Remarkably, only one person was killed, and that was by an accidental explosion while loading a cannon for a ceremonial hundred-cannon salute agreed on by Confederate general P. G. T. Beauregard. After the accident, the salute was reduced to fifty cannon shots.

The Confederate Battery suffered no casualties in the exchange of cannon rounds.

Son of the South

For Dr. John Bailey, this signal of the beginning of the conflict meant that critical decisions had to be made that would affect him and those he loved in profound and unexpected ways. He retreated to his office and his thoughts.

He loved the South and its rural-based traditions that dominated life even here in the city of Charleston. The land. Gentility. Politeness. Manners. "Yes, ma'am" and "No, sir." Independent thought and action. Contracts sealed with a handshake. Slow-paced days. Honor. Family. But John Bailey was not naive to the cancer of slavery that diminished the South.

Bailey's surgical practice was known, not always popularly, to treat anyone who came through its door—planter, foreman, free black, slave, rich, or dirt-poor. When people were sick, there was no distinction between them.

Bailey stayed away from the political discussions of secession and the economic necessity of slavery and focused on his medicine. He did not support secession, which had begun on December 20, 1860, and included the states of Alabama, Florida, Georgia, Louisiana, Mississippi, South Carolina, and Texas. Today, his remaining hopes for a compromise were dashed as surely as the cannons' rounds that exploded over Fort Sumter, the Union stronghold in the middle of the Confederate Charleston Harbor.

John Bailey would not sleep this night. He would think deeply about the South and its rich rural culture and the stories he had heard often growing up about the oppression of the Irish at the hands of the English and their surrogates. He knew the Bailey clan in the United States began when Catholics Ulrich Bailey and his wife had refused to convert to the Church of Ireland at the demand of the English and instead sailed for a new land and a new start.

He could not unthink the connections he had made in his mind that the industrial North was trying to impose its will and way of life on the South. *I am not so different from Ulrich,* he thought, *except I do not have another country where I can start again. I am honor bound to fight for my culture, for my way of life, and for my independent thought and action.*"

John Bailey knew at that moment that when the time came, as it soon would, he would enlist as a medical officer in the Confederate army.

Inevitable Decision

James Merriweather arrived back at the farm at midmorning and found no lack of things to do around the barn in preparation for spring planting, which was upon the farm. He turned to his chores before he returned to take up the conversation with Mary Assumpta that had ended abruptly a few hours before.

He honed the turning plow until the edge of the blade gleamed and rubbed the leather harness with tung oil until it was supple and soft, and then he did the same for the wood to which the metal plow blade was attached. Next, he found Jake's harness and the reins and finished them with the last of the tung oil.

Jake was a fine creature. Though of humankind's creation and not of the Almighty's, Jake was an excellent specimen of mule. Jake was as smart as his horse mother and as hardworking as his donkey father. No question that he could be hardheaded at times, but James and Mary Assumpta had learned that it was almost always for a pretty good reason. More than a few times when pulling the plow, Jake had stopped dead still and refused to move forward an inch. On investigation, it was found that a snake was just ahead in the unplowed field. Neither Jake nor his masters distinguished between black snakes and rattlers. James usually dispatched both with the blade of a sharp hoe.

James fed Jake his ration of oats, brushed him down like a racehorse, then made his way back to the farmhouse after cleaning his boots of manure and mud.

As he looked through the kitchen window, he saw that Colin was now up and finishing his breakfast of bacon, eggs, biscuits, and honey. As James entered, he did so with an exclamation: "Well, I sure hope your mama left some breakfast for dear ol' dad."

"We did," Mary Assumpta said. "The eggs are in the basket. The bacon is on the slab hanging above the window, the lard and flour are in the pantry, and the buttermilk is on the counter if you fancy biscuits."

"Colin," Mary Assumpta told her son, "why don't you go feed the chickens and let the cows out into the pasture while your father and I talk some adult talk."

"Aw. I never get in on the good stuff," Colin said with a smile as he made his way out the back door, headed to the chicken coop.

As Colin left, James put his arms around Mary Assumpta, who did not resist. "Well, I see you are still a bit picayunish."

"A little," said Mary Assumpta. "By the way, your breakfast is warming in the oven. Honey and butter are on the table, and I have fresh coffee ready.

"Now, let's start again," Mary Assumpta said as she kissed him and handed him his breakfast.

She continued, "I know that you are right in your thinking

that you will end up in the war or be thought a traitor for sure. And Lord knows, this family doesn't need any added burdens. I just ask one thing of you—that you return to medicine as your service. You will not be totally protected, certainly not from the aftermath of the battles, but you will not be directly in the path of Mr. Lincoln's cannons. Will you do that for us?"

"You continually amaze me, my love. Exactly the argument I was going to make to you. Like your family, you know that I will never condone slavery. My forefathers would doom me to a certain hell were that true. But at the same time, I could not foresee abandoning the South in her time of greatest need.

"And I promise that I will not enlist until the last possible reasonable date. I will be here preparing this farm as best I can for the dire days that surely lay ahead if this conflict turns the way I see it inevitably turning."

Mary Assumpta wrapped her husband in her arms, her ruby tresses falling over his face as she kissed him, before she led him to their bedchamber. "Where is Colin? He does have a propensity for opening the bedroom door at the most inopportune moments!"

She undid the buttons of the plain dress of a farmer's wife and smiled as it slid to the floor, brushing her breasts and arousing her nipples as it slid over them. "Oh, Nate Billington asked Colin to go fishing with him. He will not be back until sundown."

James, clearly aroused by the proposition of an entire afternoon in the arms of Mary Assumpta, responded to her good news. "Well, I guess that preparation for war can wait one more day."

Antebellum No Longer

There were those on both sides who, like Bartholomew Jennings, thought fighting soft-bellied Yankees or the redneck

Rebels would simply be a short-lived lark, and there were rather educated citizens who believed the fight would be short-lived as well. However, all had failed to judge newly elected President Lincoln's resolve accurately. Lincoln was of one mind on the issue of ending slavery and slave trading within the borders of the United States. However, he was not sure what came next. But he was resolved that the best way to deal with the matter of slavery, its end, and the introduction of millions of new Americans into society could only be accomplished with the union intact.

So even more important to Lincoln was the matter of whether or not a group of like-minded states could, on the basis of political disagreements, of which there was never a lack in Washington, decide to withdraw from the union.

To the Northern sentiments, the cannon fire on Fort Sumter was not an exercise between a former artillery instructor and his pupil; it was an attack on the territory of the United States by an armed militia intent on doing it harm.

Interestingly to the Confederate politicians gathered in the temporary capital of Montgomery, the transfer of Union troops from Fort Moultrie to Fort Sumter, a Union command post squarely in the middle of Confederate Charleston Harbor, was likewise an illegal intrusion by the Union into the sovereign nation of the Confederacy.

Thus, the War between the States, the Civil War, the War of Northern Aggression, the War of the Southern Rebellion, the War for Southern Independence, began.

CHAPTER 14

Lessons of War Told to a Young Boy

On his ninth birthday, Colin Edward Merriweather walked the mile to the mouth of Horlbeck Creek where it entered the Wando River to go catfishing from the dock with his uncle Nate.

For nine-year-old Colin, life had been good. He was loved. But he did not live protected from life. He had survived both chickenpox and measles. He could walk behind ol' Jake and plow a reasonably straight row. He had killed rabbits, squirrels, and a deer with the double-barrel muzzleloader shotgun his father had received as a gift from a wealthy Low Country farmer whose leg he had saved after the farmer had gotten caught in a wild hog trap while he was hunting with the shotgun.

Colin learned to pole Nate's pirogue on the creek and around the marshes of the Wando River as long as he stayed in view of the landing. His uncle Nate showed him how to make a crab trap from limber willow branches, and he and his father often spent spring and fall nights until early in the morning crabbing off the dock at low tide. He could gig frogs from the pirogue with the long pole he had fashioned from an oak limb.

Colin's personal knowledge of geography was restricted to up and down Horlbeck Creek, the occasional trip up the Wando River in Uncle Nate's pirogue to run limb lines set out the day before, and every inch of the 250 acres of Horlbeck Creek Farm.

Colin knew his grandparents in Richmond and his grandfather and his uncles in Charleston, although he never visited either. His mother told him stories of how the Baileys came to America to escape the tyranny of the English and thus began his earliest lessons in the immorality of enslaving other people. His father relayed stories of how the Merriweathers' personal journey traveled from commerce to scholarship and service through the spiritual and medical arts. When Coin asked his father why he was not a doctor anymore, his father said, "Colin, you will understand why when you are old enough." He was not yet old enough. But soon that would change.

Colin's mother taught him to read at age four when she noticed his interest in the books on farming his father had bought in Charleston. His study of practical farm mathematics began soon after, and biology lessons came as an essential part of farm life. His understanding of animal anatomy grew each time he trapped or shot a rabbit or a squirrel and cleaned it for supper.

He ate figs and peaches fresh from the tree, tomatoes from the vine, and watermelon fresh from the garden and cooled in the creek. He rose early to slop their two hogs, and he grew lean and strong pitching hay for ol' Jake and Beulah, the milk cow, and shoveling their manure for the garden and the fields and fruit trees. His back grew tired from picking beans and peas with his mother and father just after daylight on June mornings. Okra and squash stung his arms when he cut them, and the corn leaves left minute cuts on his face nettled by his sweat when he walked the corn rows to pick corn for supper.

Colin's freedom had been almost without boundaries until that June night in 1862 when his father sat down with him after their evening meal to tell him he was going to war.

Facts of Life Learned Too Soon

"Uncle Nate, can I ask you a question?" Colin inquired as they sat on the dock, keeping an eye on their lines and a hand on their poles, waiting for the tug of a channel cat.

"Yes, child. What is it?"

"Why did my daddy decide to go to the war? I asked Mama, but she starts crying every time I bring it up. Doesn't he love us anymore?"

"Yes, son. He loves you right now, even though he is away from you, as he did the day you were born."

"I believe you. But that just doesn't make good sense to me. If Daddy loves us, why wouldn't he just stay?"

"Colin, let's pull these lines in for a bit because we need to concentrate on what I am about to tell you. We'll throw 'em back in when we're done."

They pulled the lines in, took the small bream used as bait from the hooks, and put them back in the bait bucket. The bucket was made of sweetgrass woven by Audrey Lee. The grass let enough water flow through to keep the bait alive. They tied it off the dock with a string and put it back in the river.

Colin found a spot in the shade of a sweet gum, and they ate the sausage and the honey-filled biscuits Audrey Lee had prepared for them.

"Colin, what I am about to tell you is how *I* see things. Why is that important?"

Nate often treated his godson like he was a small adult in a little boy's body. The next few minutes were not going to be easy as Colin's unique gifts of understanding were going to be tested.

"Because I still need to ask Mama too?"

"Yes. You know that me and your aunt Audrey Lee love you and your mama and your daddy like you are our own family, right?"

"Yes, sir."

"And that I would never tell you anything or do anything that would hurt you?"

"Yes, sir. Are you about to tell me something bad has happened to my daddy?" Colin asked, perceiving the tenor of the conversation far beyond his years.

"No, child. Nothing like that. I am just going to try to tell you why your daddy may not be home for a while."

"Okay. I guess," Colin almost whispered as he moved closer to his best friend.

Going to War

"Do you remember me telling you that my father, Tyler, fought in the Revolutionary War here in South Carolina?"

"Yes, sir. You said he left his father's farm to go and fight the Redcoats."

"Do you remember what I said about why?" Nate asked.

"Yes, sir. South Carolina and the other colonies wanted to be free from King George because they thought they were not being treated right. And you said that since he lived in South Carolina, he had an obligation to fight." Colin struggled a bit pronouncing *obligation* before he got it right.

"I'd better be careful what I tell you. You don't forget nothing. Do you know what that word *obligation* means?" Nate probed, ever his godson's teacher.

"Well ... I think it means that you owe money to somebody else," Colin ventured.

"It can mean that, but it can also mean that your feelings tell you that you oughta do something just 'cause it is the right thing to do. Does that make sense?"

"Yes, sir. I think so. Is it like I ought to obey Mama just because she is my mama?"

"That's exactly right, but here is the interesting thing about your obligation to your mama. No matter how old you are, you *always* will owe that obligation to your mama. One day, if you are lucky, she will be very old, and you will be obliged to take care of her like she took care of you when you were tiny."

"Okay, but what does that have to do with my daddy going to war?" Colin was clearly puzzled now.

"Well, my father went to fight the Redcoats because he felt he needed to pay back something for what South Carolina had done for his family. Do you remember what I told you about the skirmish at Gibbs Plantation?"

"Lord Cornwallis was marching toward Charleston, and the Patriots stopped him at Gibbs Plantation right before he got into town. And your daddy was part of the soldiers who beat those Redcoats."

"That's what I told you, but there was something I didn't say to you because you were too young when I told you that story. My daddy was one of eight soldiers wounded that day, and he lost his right arm just below the elbow."

"I think I am lost again, Uncle Nate."

"I bet you still want to know what that has to do with your daddy, right?"

"Yes, sir. Then can we go back to fishing?"

"Yes, we can. Just a little longer. I talked to your daddy before he left to join the Confederate army, and he told me he joined up for two reasons. Can you figure out what they might be?" Nate probed his pupil.

"Well, I figure one had to do with an obligation, but I don't know what it was. We're not fighting the British anymore."

"Your father's obligation was to where we have all been raised and where we live. All of your daddy's relatives and your mama's too have lived in the South since they arrived in America. He knows that y'all could not have the kind of life that you have if he were not a Southerner. Like all of us, he loves the South."

"Yes, but if we don't own slaves, and if you don't own slaves, how can we be Southerners?" Colin asked his uncle Nate in the complete innocence of his nine years.

Slaves Come to Horlbeck Creek

"What a question for such a small boy. Now let me see if I can answer that question for you. Simply, we are Southerners in spite of slavery. Not because of it."

Before he answered Colin, Nate thought back to the story his father had told him about the day that slavery came to Horlbeck Creek.

It was July 4, 1776. The delegates to the Continental Congress met to approve the final wording of the greatest document in the history of the freedom of humankind—Thomas Jefferson's Declaration of Independence—which brought freedom from English rule to the people of the colonies. Most of the people, that is.

For two people—husband and wife holding each other, standing on the small and elevated stage on Market Street in Charleston—July 4, 1776, was another day of ignominy and hopelessness. Moses and Sarah—it does not matter about their surnames, for those were about to change again to that of their soon-to-be new master—stood as a group to be auctioned off like so many farm implements. Actually, that is what they were, human machines used to increase the profit margin of farming or make life easier inside the house for the family. Nothing more.

The auctioneer began with a description of the two slaves standing on the platform. "Two fine specimens here. A buck and a fertile bitch." The auctioneer drawled out the words. "The owner, John Van Landingham, guarantees they are well trained, docile, and willing to work. They will sell as a pair of fine African flesh. Who will start the bidding at three hundred dollars for the lot."

Jacob Billington did not bid immediately. He wanted to see if the price stayed reasonably within his budget. He had talked to Van Landingham before the auction started to find out why he was selling. "Well, sir," Van Landingham had said in response to his question, "I am just too old to work my land anymore, and I can work my kitchen garden by myself. And to tell you the truth, it costs me more to feed them than I was getting from them in work."

"They ever give you any trouble, sir?" Billington inquired.

"No more than usual. This family is a very religious group, and sometimes Moses has overstepped his training and tried to convince me that the Bible condemns slavery. But I don't pay him no mind. That's about all.

"I have owned these coloreds for sixteen or seventeen years. Hell, I can't remember anymore. I do remember that I even brought in a preacher to marry Moses and Sarah. Sarah's been working since she was old enough to hold a hoe or pick cotton. I think you are gonna find they are worth your money if you decide to buy them."

"Come on, gentlemen," the auctioneer chastised the crowd. "Will nobody give me three hundred dollars for this pair? They are in prime working condition, and they got a lot of years left. They can be trained to do most anything."

Finally, an old farmer in dirty overalls bid $200 for the two adults. A voice in the back of the small crowd bid $250. No one else made an offer until Jacob Billington spoke up: "I'll give you three hundred dollars for the lot."

"We got three hundred dollars. Three hundred twenty-five, anyone? Anyone?" the auctioneer urged. "Three hundred dollars once. Three hundred dollars twice. Sold to Jacob Billington for three hundred dollars."

Moses and his wife left the auction block with Jacob Billington pulling them toward his wagon by a rope around their waists that tied them together. Once they were in the wagon, Jacob fastened them again with a second rope to keep them from jumping out.

The trip back to the Billington farmstead on Horlbeck Creek took the rest of the day as Jacob traveled north until he could board the ferry that crossed Wando River and tied up at the crude loading dock at the mouth of Horlbeck Creek.

Jacob had never owned slaves before, and he pondered on the way home about what he would tell them when they arrived at the farm. He knew they would have to sleep in the corncrib with the mice and the weevils until he could use their labor to build a log cabin where they could live permanently. Plenty of time for that before winter. Until then, they could sleep on corn shucks and make a fire to cook on in the yard between the crib and hogpen.

The log cabin that was to be living quarters to the Billington slaves was completed just before the fall rains set in. Cedar logs were notched and set on each other until the wall reached a height of six feet. They used clay and straw to caulk the cracks between the logs. The slave quarters had a single door that faced Jacob Billington's back door about forty yards away. The floor was dirt—loam that was not easily compacted and was always dusty. But Moses and Sarah had been here before. Moses took the same kind of clay from the creek bank that later would be mixed with straw and allowed to dry in the sun into bricks to make Sarah's chimney. Instead, for the floor, Moses just allowed the clay to dry, and then he pounded it into a fine powder using the wide, flat sandstone that would mark the entrance to the front door.

Once he had gathered a bucket of clay powder, he took a

second bucket of oyster shells picked up from the banks of the Wando and repeated the process until he had a fine powder the color of scudding clouds on a winter day. The contents of these two buckets, one fine clay powder, the other powdered oyster shells, were mixed together in the mule's watering trough until they were a dusty pinkish-white mixture. Moses took this mixture, a bucket at a time, to Sarah inside the cabin.

The cabin on this Saturday was the temperature of mid-July noontime instead of late September. Inside the hot and humid cabin, Sarah took the powdered clay and oystershell mixture and spread it on the loamy floor that Moses had earlier dampened and tamped down to as hard a surface as it would make. The sand of the loamy dirt would never compress and harden like clay, as the sand would allow little spaces in between grains. If all worked out according to plan, the fine clay and oystershell mix would get right in those spaces, harden up when it was wet, and make a smooth floor.

Sarah spread the mixture until it was roughly an inch thick. The process was repeated until the entire floor of the 12' × 12' floor was evenly covered. Moses and Sarah then took a straight board and used it to screed the floor until it was level to Moses's practiced eye.

Sarah then sprinkled water on the floor to knock down the dust. Moses followed behind her, tamping the mixture to a consistent density. Once the entire floor had been sprinkled and tamped, Moses, working from the back of the room to the door, liberally sprinkled water on the floor until it was saturated.

Moses and Sarah would sleep at least one more night in the corncrib, listening to the scurrying of the mice in the corn and the whispering of the wings of the barn owl that made her home in the barn as she swooped to capture her supper of corn-fed mice.

Sunday broke mild and sunny again, just what was needed

to heat the interior of the cabin so that the floor would set evenly. By evening the floor was less dirt and more like a primitive but workable concrete. It was a surface that Sarah could keep clean as long as she could get her boys to leave their shoes outside the door.

In the advancing dark of evening, Jacob Billington and his youngest son, Mason, helped his slave family move their two rough beds, an eating table, three chairs, and a food preparation table into the small, dark cabin. Moses had built the furniture from scrap lumber from around the farm and a number of thick planks he'd found washed up on the banks of the creek.

Once the potato harvest was completed in a few weeks, Moses would begin the process of constructing a fireplace and cooking area on the outside back wall opposite the front door. Sarah would hurry him along as she did not relish the cold and damp nights in the cabin they had built for their owner Jacob Billington. However, she knew she could not rush her husband, for when it came to making anything, he was a perfectionist.

It was October. The morning was cloudy and cool, a good day for digging potatoes before more clouds came with rain. Jacob and his youngest son, Mason, were in the field with Moses and Sarah lending hand this day. Leaving potatoes in the ground to the whims of Low Country weather was a sin as Jacob and Moses saw it. So the work was fierce and merited a longer than usual dinner break under a nearby black walnut tree.

As dinner break was winding down, and before resuming digging potatoes, Moses eased over to where Jacob Billington was sitting. "Mr. Billington, suh, I sho would be proud if you and

Mason might stop by on the way in from the field to see what we done with the cabin."

"Moses is proud of his work," Jacob said to Mason as they walked toward the cabin when the potato harvesting was done for the day. "Son, don't forget to compliment Moses and Sarah on their work on the cabin."

The cabin and the handmade furniture was remarkable. The latter was not just simple sticks held together with twine or rope but was furniture built by a craftsman, and Jacob told Moses so.

As Jacob and Mason started out the cabin door that evening, Moses, who had observed his master to be a practicing and sincere Presbyterian, asked if Jacob would say a prayer to bless their new home.

Jacob was surprised by the unexpected request, but he was pleased. "Dear God of all mankind, bless this home and this family who dwells within it. Amen."

Jacob did not indicate that he knew the irony of his words, but they were not lost on the other Billington family that now resided on the homestead on Horlbeck Creek.

It was April 2, 1780. This day for Sarah and Moses as slaves on the Billington farm was like any other they had experienced the last three springs. Just before first light when shadows play tricks on the eyes and the night animals are still moving toward their daytime beds, Sarah left the slave cabin and walked the forty yards to the big house, though it was not really very big, and opened the back door quietly. If she was the first one up, she made a fire in the stove, put water on to boil for coffee, and began preparing breakfast for the family. She and her man would eat the same meal but on the back steps, where they would have to shoo away the dog and the chickens.

Before Tyler Billington left to fight the Redcoats back in January, he did like a cup of buttermilk if any was left over from his mama's biscuit making. However, since Tyler had left for the war, the biscuit making was left to Sarah, who almost always fixed drop biscuits, eggs and bacon, and coffee. There would be at least two kinds of preserves, but one of them would always be figs from the tree in the backyard. Some days there was bacon, and some days there was cured ham. Both were fried. Some days the eggs were fried and some days they were scrambled, but every day they appeared in the savory remains of the bacon or ham.

Moses knocked on the screen door and asked if breakfast was ready yet. "Shush you, Moses Billington. You gonna wake up the missus, and she been feelin' poorly lately. I think it's 'cause she ain't heard nothing from Tyler in two weeks. She 'bout ready to send Mr. Jacob to go find him on the other side of the Wando."

"Okay, Mama. I waitin' out here on the steps, but that ham sho' does smell good. You hurry now, you hear?!"

Bringing out the biscuits and figs, Sarah asked, "What we doin' today, Moses?"

"I reckon we goin' to plant that back forty with corn. The ground is warmed up enough to plant them corn kernels." Moses was a master of reading nature's signs and the moon phases and knowing when the ground was right for germination and the last frost was past. Today it was right, and he hoped that down the way one day he would have a chance to demonstrate what he knew.

One day. Maybe one day, Moses thought to himself, daring never to say anything to Sarah, *we gonna plant our own corn.*

Moses and Sarah cleared away the sticks and limbs blown on the fields by winter winds before Moses tilled the forty acres to be planted with field corn for milling. Jacob was busy working the ground of the acre-sized kitchen garden, planting sweet corn. Once the sweet corn was in the ground, they would all turn to transplanting the tomato plants that had been growing on a table next to a window in the big house exposed to the southern sun. Mrs. Billington was not too pleased with tomato plants growing inside her house, but she did love a tomato fresh from the garden, and so she said little when Moses and Jacob placed the box by the window some weeks earlier.

Moses took great pride in his work as a farmer, and he almost always had a system for doing something simpler or quicker. This year's tomatoes were an example. In mid-February, Moses built a long rectangular box about three inches high and divided into twenty-five 2' × 2' squares. Each square was lined with an almost-rotted piece of burlap and then filled with a compost and soil mixture into which two tomato seeds would be placed and watered. The warmth of the southern sun in the window and Sarah's attention had produced a box full of healthy tomato plants ready to transplant when Moses decided the last frost was past. This was the week that Jacob and his slaves, Moses and Sarah, would gently remove the plants from the box and transplant them in the kitchen garden.

"Moses," Jacob declared, "we are getting ten-inch tomato plants in the ground when before we were just planting the seeds at this time of the year. It would be a good six weeks until they were this tall. If this newfangled system of yours works, we may just beat everyone else to market." It never occurred to Jacob that he might share the proceeds with Moses.

On the day the corn went into the ground, Jacob Billington's oldest son, Tyler Billington, lost his right arm to the musket fire of General Cornwallis's Redcoats, and the lives of Jacob Billington, his wife, and his sons changed in a way that was beyond their comprehension up to this point in their lives.

The Ultimatum

"Uncle Nate. Uncle Nate!" Colin called out as he shook Nate's shoulder, waking him from his apparent daydream. Colin was used to Uncle Nate's daydreaming. But today's dream frightened him with its length and the mumbling that went with it.

"Sorry, Colin," Nate said. "For a minute there I was back remembering the stories that my father told me about the first slaves brought to Horlbeck Creek. Let me see if I can tell you a little bit about what I was dreamin' while I try to answer your question.

"In early May 1780, when *my* father, Tyler, returned from fighting the Redcoats after he had lost his arm, he talked to *his* father, my granddaddy Jacob, about freeing Moses and Sarah. My daddy said he had been fighting for freedom and believed that it just wasn't right to own another person. He told his father that he could not live on the farm anymore if his father continued to own slaves. My granddaddy Jacob sure didn't want to give up his slaves, and he thought on it for almost a week. He knew the right thing to do. He just didn't want to do it. But finally, seeing how much my daddy had given for the family's freedom in losing his arm, he freed his slaves, and then he hired them back and paid them for doing the same jobs they had been doing. Then he rented them a place to live and paid them to paint it and fix up like a proper house. He wrote off the first six months' rent 'til they could get up and going."

"Why did he own slaves in the first place, Uncle Nate, if he did right by them when his son asked him to?"

A hard question but a reasonable one from a boy who has never encountered a slave or an owner, thought Nate Billington.

"Colin, that is a question my grandfather asked himself in his prayers every night after that. My father helped him see the evil things that he had hid away from himself."

"What does 'hid away from himself' mean, Uncle Nate?"

"Let's think on it this way. You believe in God, right?"

"Yes, sir. My mama and daddy taught me about him, but I still don't understand much about what they told me."

"That's okay," Nate said as he tousled his godson's hair. "God is like that sometimes—hard to understand, I mean. But you do understand that God is all around us all the time?"

"Yes, sir. Mama said he sees everything we do, so we should try to do right all the time."

"And do we do that? Do right all the time?" Nate asked gently with not a hint of accusation in his voice.

"No, sir. Sometimes I don't do my chores until Mama fusses at me. Is that what you mean?"

"Well, kinda," Nate said, and Colin knew he was about to be asked for more. "Have you ever hurt an animal just because you were mad at it?"

"One time I hit Beulah with a board because she kicked over the milk pail. Is that what you want me to say?"

"I want you to tell me about it, but only if it is the truth, and if you have never talked about it before, not even in your prayers. I won't be angry with you. We have all done things like that."

"Okay. I never told anyone about hitting Beulah. Not even God."

"Did it bother you—what you did to Beulah?"

"Yes, sir. For a while. Then I forgot about it until right now. I am really sorry about it," Colin answered with a sincerity that was easy to overlook in one so young as he.

"Do you think God knows what you did to your milk cow?"

"Yes, sir, I guess, if what Mama says is true. Do you think God is mad at me for hitting Beulah?" Tears welled in Colin's Irish-blue eyes.

"Disappointed maybe, but not angry. God has been waiting for you to understand what you did, and he heard you just now. God is very patient, and now he has forgotten that he ever saw what you did to Beulah." Nate shared a bit of his Presbyterian upbringing with his godson.

Colin rose and gave his friend a mighty hug at Nate's assurance that all was well with God. "Was it like that with your granddaddy and God?" Colin asked, wiping the tears away with the back of his hand, not seeing the tears in Nate's eyes too.

"Yes, Colin. It was exactly like that. My granddaddy bought those slaves because he thought it would help him make more money on his farm, and he told himself it was okay because he knew a few folks who had made a lot of money doing the same thing.

"My granddaddy even used the Bible to fool himself into thinking it was all right to own another person. He knew he was raised better than that, but that money and believing what other folks thought was more important to him than doing what was right. Pride is like that. It can cause us to hide away things and to convince ourselves that what we did was not evil in the first place. When my daddy came home from the war with his right arm shot off and he told his father what he thought about owning slaves, all the lies my granddaddy had told himself over the years, he saw in his son's words that day."

"Is that why you never owned slaves, Uncle Nate?" Colin asked, now reversing the role of teacher and pupil.

"Every time my daddy would take me with him to Charleston to sell our produce, I saw people who were slaves, and on the way home, Daddy would tell me the story about the day he came home from the war. He taught me that being a Southern gentleman and loving the South had nothing to do with owning slaves. Your mama and daddy are like that."

Daddy's Duty

"Then why is my daddy fighting?" Colin asked, getting back to the crux of their conversation.

"Because your daddy loves this land. He loves the good people of the South. He didn't enlist for the few people who own slaves and who have most of the money. He did it for the people who work hard for their families and their churches and their communities and who help others when they need it. That was his duty. He wants you and your mama to live in that South, and he is willing to fight so that you can.

"You gotta few more minutes left in you for me to talk about the other reason your daddy enlisted? It won't take long, I promise."

"Only if you promise that we can go back to fishing again when you're done." Nate knew he didn't have long, as Colin was now sprawled out on the cool grass and looking up at the clouds, his eyes drooping.

"Okay. Here goes. When my daddy came home without his arm, he knew he was lucky. A Redcoat musketball had hit him just below the elbow, and it broke both bones in his arm and caused lots of bleeding."

"What was lucky about that?" Colin asked. He was clearly ready to be finished and get back to fishing.

"He was lucky because his commander, Lieutenant Colonel Laurens, got him to a doctor in Charleston. Otherwise he would have died. That is the other reason your daddy enlisted—so he could save the lives of soldiers like my father who will die unless he is there to save them."

"I think I've got it now, Uncle Nate. Even though he didn't want to, Daddy went off to war for Mama and me and to help those boys like your daddy by goin' back to bein' a doctor?"

"Yes, little man, you got it."

"When will he come home, Uncle Nate?"

"Colin, that will depend on God, the generals, and the politicians, but mostly on the politicians."

A Prayer for Uncle Nate

Mary Assumpta Merriweather began Colin's birthday still angry with her husband for not being here on his son's birthday. But she realized about midday that she had almost missed her son's birthday too. She baked up some shortcake, picked some late strawberries, and mashed them up with a bit of her precious supply of sugar. She would cover the biscuit-like shortcake with the berries and a little heavy cream for dessert that evening.

Colin came bouncing in toward dark with a half dozen eating-size squealers already skinned and ready for the skillet, a smile on his face, and an Uncle Nate story. Mary Assumpta occasionally worried about some of Uncle Nate's stories. He sometimes forgot that Colin was not yet ten. But when Colin told his mother the story of Nate's father's sacrifice at the hands of the Redcoats and his grandfather's decision, she knew that now she could have that conversation with her son she had been putting off for so long.

"God bless you, Nate Billington," she said in her prayers that night. It was the first time she had prayed in a very long time.

PART V
THE BEGINNING OF THE BEGINNING

CHAPTER 15

Richmond Letters

July 4, 1862
Horlbeck Creek Farm

Dearest Mother and Father,

I write to tell you that I will soon, in the next few days, be joining the Army of Northern Virginia. I have searched myself for reasons to avoid this inevitability, but finally I could find none that would satisfy my sense of obligation to my home state and to the new Confederacy of States. It is of no little consideration that I write this letter on July 4. However rashly our Southern leaders may have acted in separating us from the union, the act is done, and young men are dying in numbers that the physician at the core of my being cannot ignore as long as I know that I can save the precious lives of the men of our Southern wives and mothers.

I have prayed hard on the issue of slavery and have asked the Almighty to relieve me of the contradictions of going into a war whose purpose is to the evil status of slavery. He has not provided me with another path. I can only pray that he will guide my beloved South to seek a new level of humanity at this war's end.

I have never been tested as I have in the weeks since I first talked to Mary Assumpta about the direction of my inclinations. She has flailed against me in her spirit and with a corporeal anger that is wholly Irish in its source. Worst of all, she has given up her fighting and accepted the inevitable. I have never before seen Mary Assumpta when she did not believe that she was more powerful than any element of the environment that surrounds her. For all of our marriage, she has been a force of nature, at times a hurricane and at other times a gentle whisper of the wind through pines in early morning. But at every turn, she has been guided by the purpose she sees before her. My decision has left her directionless, it seems.

God assails me with reasons to stay here on this farm with my wife and son, and I argue with him, as did Jacob at Peniel. I am confident that God takes no side in war except to abhor the concept of it. I know the family is his natural expression of the relationships he desires to see between members of his creation. What I know to be true still falls short of what I believe I must do. I believe that God has been pushing me my entire life to help save his creation, and I feel that most acutely as battle reports reach us in our isolation here on the creek. I have argued with him: "Do you expect me to save the lives of soldiers at the expense of my family?"

Mary Assumpta assures me with resoluteness that she and Colin will survive if they cannot prosper. She is strong, but is she really that strong? In the final analysis, I have chosen to believe her. I pray that I am right.

I will be making my way toward Richmond and the War Office and my enlistment. I shall ask to be assigned to General Lee's army, as he is the point of the spear in our fight against the Yankees. I shall try to see you both after I enlist, but I fear the forces of this storm shall push me steadily and forcefully in other directions.

As I will be on the road for many days, I suggest that you forward any correspondence to me in care of the War Office. I will endeavor to respond, as I am able.

Your faithful son,
James

July 15, 1862
324 Franklin Street
Richmond, Virginia

Dearest James,

Father and I were delighted to receive your letter of July 4. The conundrum of the date was not lost on us either. It is a sad time here in Richmond. The war seems to have consumed every aspect of our lives as citizens. Yet we journey on as best we can and as far as we can see the road in front of us. Our family, going back to England, has always been a family of forward thinkers and movers, but these days we move as if we are walking at twilight, seeing only a few feet ahead and stumbling and groping our way.

As your mother, I cannot say that I am delighted with your enlistment, although I knew in my heart that it was inevitable. I cannot fathom the depth of your pain in leaving Mary Assumpta and Colin. I pray for them morning and night.

You have made the right choice in not postponing the unavoidable, as Robert E. Lee is now in command of the Army of Northern Virginia. In the early days of the war, Father and I met General Lee and his wife, Mary, at a fund-raising dinner for the Richmond Hospital at the home of a mutual church friend, Randolph Jackson. Mary had recently taken up residence on East Franklin Street here in Richmond, and we still see her frequently at Saint Paul's.

I was most impressed with General Lee's humility and his concern for the boys under his authority. Of course, at that time he was not yet in command, but you could see in his quiet confidence that he would quickly rise to higher levels of responsibility in the war effort.

Please be as careful as you are able, James. What you are doing is a noble undertaking, and no doubt your medical skills will allow many boys to return to their wives and families. I just pray that you will as well return in good health to Mary Assumpta and Colin.

If you find that you have the time, please come home, if only for a few minutes, after your paperwork is complete at the War Office. If not, I understand. Write as you are able.

Love and blessings,
Mother

First Letter Home

July 30, 1862
War Office
Richmond

My Dearest Mary Assumpta,

I arrived in Richmond today after a rather interesting journey. I departed Charleston on July 20, as fate would have it, upon the coastal trader the Demille, where I was reacquainted with our friend Bartholomew Jennings, who constantly bombarded me with questions about you. Thankfully, he made the journey seem short, even though we did detour to Wilmington, where I stayed at the Star Hotel for one pleasant night. Wilmington is a very cosmopolitan city, even now with the war. I expect it may be my last pleasant night until I return to your arms. We then traveled to Norfolk and on to Richmond by rail.

Darling, I am officially Captain James E. Merriweather and a member of the medical corps assigned to the Army of Northern Virginia and General Robert E. Lee. You can guess my pleasure when I walked up the steps to the War Office, asked how I might enlist in the medical corps, and was shown into the office of Lieutenant Colonel John Colin Bailey.

I fear I spent far too much time reminiscing with John about our time together. He asked of you, and I told him that I hesitantly left you and Colin in the capable hands of Nate and Audrey Lee. He quizzed me incessantly about my desire to serve as a combat surgeon. He assured me that he could find a place for me in the War Office teaching other physicians. I am sorry, as I know it will not please you, but I insisted that my place was with the wounded, not the healthy.

John understood and then he told me the story of his journey to the War Office, as follows:

Having entered the war as a surgeon with the rank of captain, John's advanced surgical techniques became known for the first time at the early-in-the-war Battle of Manassas—the battle that convinced politicians on both sides of the profane silliness of the idea of a "Ninety-Day War."

According to John, casualties at Manassas simply overwhelmed the rudimentary medical facilities, yet John was still able to save lives. Once the Yankees had retreated to Washington, the commanding officers, seeing a notable difference in wounded treated at the hands of John compared to those treated by the other physicians, called him to the tent of Brigadier General P. G. T. Beauregard, the commander of the army.

Speaking softly and with the lexicon of the author and inventor he had been in a former life, Beauregard said, "Captain Bailey, I have seen your handiwork with our wounded boys, and I think you are simply too valuable to be this close to the battlefield. I need you training our other battlefield physicians in the surgical techniques I saw today. Can you do that?"

"General," John said, "I am honored that you think

that I can be of service of any kind to the army of the Confederacy, but, sir, I am a surgeon."

"Captain." Beauregard's voice became even softer. "I understand. But today's battle will not be the last of its kind. I surely expect that battles that are to come will banish today's encounter into the realm of a skirmish.

"Son," Beauregard continued in his thick-as-gumbo Louisiana drawl, "when I see something as unique and unprecedented as I observed in your surgical skills, the inventor in me acts on it immediately. Yes, you can save many lives working alone, but we need more just like you if our boys are to survive the days ahead to return to their homes. There will be opportunities for you in the surgical tents, but right now I need you overseeing and training others."

John said he took a deep breath and responded. "Yes, sir, General," he said, "I will serve in whatever capacity you think best serves our boys."

Beauregard promoted him on the spot with, "Thank you, Captain Bailey. As of this moment, you are now Lieutenant Colonel Bailey. Congratulations, although I suspect you get no delight from a battlefield promotion. However, you have earned it, and it will serve you well as you work with some pretty big egos."

"Thank you sincerely, General. I will labor to earn your confidence in me."

"Lieutenant Colonel Bailey," Beauregard said, as he pushed his chair back from his battlefield desk, stood, and executed a crisp salute, "see my adjutant in the morning. He will make it official and will make sure that you have the proper accouterments for your uniform."

As soon as John had finished his story, he

pointed me toward his adjutant and ordered him to complete my enlistment as a captain assigned to General Lee. I stumbled about a bit and told him that the rank was unnecessary, fearing nepotism, but he assured me that it had nothing to do with you and everything to do with the year I had spent by his side learning his techniques. I trust him that that is so.

I picked up my uniform, and with two days before I reported to General Lee, I made my way home to see Mother and Father. I enjoyed a supper of fried chicken; a discussion with Father about his impressions of General Lee, having read Mother's letter delivered to the War Office; and a pleasant night's sleep in my own bed. Mother even did a bit of tailoring of my uniform.

I shall be off tomorrow early as soon as I get acquainted with the horse I have also been assigned. Once I have settled into some kind of routine, I shall write again.

Yours most faithfully,
JEM

Surgeon's Diary

Perhaps as a premonition of personal dark days ahead, but most likely simply as a means of putting to words feelings that he would not share with Mary Assumpta, James Merriweather began a diary.

Innocuous and mostly official sounding at the beginning of his service, as the war progressed, the diaries would reveal dark thoughts that, on August 8, 1862, Dr. James Merriweather would never have thought he possessed.

August 8, 1862
Richmond, Virginia

My first feeling upon being given the rank of captain in the Confederate army medical corps was that I was totally undeserving of it. Was I the beneficiary of my brother-in-law's nepotistic generosity? John assured me that the rank is deserved and not unusual for exceptionally well-trained physicians who enter the service. Still, I feel overwhelmed and wonder how I shall be received when I meet up with General Lee's forces in a matter of days.

I carry my orders assigning me to the medical corps of the Army of Northern Virginia that I am to present to General Lee's adjutant. Still, I am uneasy about how I shall be received by the commanding officer of the medical corps. I know that I am likely to be a bit rusty, having practiced my surgical skill only intermittently on the inhabitants of the farms around Horlbeck Creek. I know that once I am engaged in an operating theater, it will all come rushing back.

In some strange way I feel like the child I was when I left home to move to the University of Virginia. I know there is no turning back, yet still I am apprehensive. Neither was I then, nor am I now, the neophyte enthusiastically about to enter the fray. I have stilled my anxieties by reading my Bible, especially Corinthians 13. It brings me peace to go into this conflict with love rather than aggression.

I was astounded at the War Office to see the numbers of enlistees, so many of them boys with peach fuzz still on their faces, practicing their Rebel yells and anxious to kill their first Yankees. I shall be traveling with many of them tomorrow to meet up with General Lee's forces. I know with sure dread that I shall meet many of them again on my operating tables.

I meet with the other enlistees tomorrow morning at 6:00 at the War Office, where we will all be notified of our final destination to which we will march.

I stop now to pray for Mary Assumpta, Colin, Nate, and Audrey Lee. I am keenly and remorsefully aware that I can do no more. Such is the path I am traveling with a heavy heart.

JEM

Surgeon's Diary

August 10, 1862
Outside Richmond, Virginia

I got my orders, and I have not had to travel far to join up with General Lee's forces, which were bivouacked only a day's travel from Richmond following his successful Peninsula Campaign. He drove Yankee general George McClellan from the outskirts of Richmond, and for the time being Richmond is again safe.

The word here is that we will travel to

Manassas to battle the combined forces of John Pope and George McClellan. I have yet to treat a wounded Confederate soldier as the army gathered here is healthy. Its casualties were left in Richmond, and I expect John will be called on to treat them.

Nonetheless, the consequences of war are all around me. Only those of us who are newly enlisted talk to any measure. The battle-hardened men who defeated McClellan do not take joy in their victory or in the rumors of another go at the Yankees at Manassas. Mostly they stare. "The thousand-yard stare," my colleagues call it. We assume they are reliving the all-consuming fear of being torn apart by grapeshot from cannons across the battlefield and the closer buzzing of musket balls as they tear the air around them like angry hornets.

In my three days here I have made my rounds of as many tents as I have been able to see if there is any assistance I can render. By my second or third visit I had begun to see a revival of the spirit. Some talk of their wives or sweethearts back home, real or imagined, and two soldiers asked me to write letters for them. Neither talked of the war, only of their memories of home and their expectations of a return in a few weeks.

I wonder how long it will take these boys to recover the next time. Even now the next battle looms over us like a silent malevolent predator.

It is time for me to retire, to pray for these

boys and their leaders. Right now, it is all I can do.

JEM

Surprise from Home

Mary Assumpta had thought about writing her husband hundreds of times, eventually making a pact with her soul that she would not write until she first heard from James. It was important, she told herself, that she needed to learn to endure the wordlessly long, longing days before James's first letter if she was to ever fight off the insanity once his fighting officially started. Emotionally suffocating, the night's quiet was worse than her days. No matter how hard she had physically worked at her daily chores, it was hours upon hours before she would silently cry herself to sleep.

Mary Assumpta did not know the day the war would start for her, but she knew it would begin with James's first letter home.

The war on Horlbeck Creek began on August 8, 1862.

It was evening, Colin already tucked in. Mary Assumpta sat at her kitchen table in the small farmhouse to write the first letter to her husband, who had now been gone from her embraces for a month that seemed like an eternity.

August 8, 1862
Horlbeck Creek Farm

My Dearest Physician,

I am so very pleased with your appointment as captain in the medical corps of the Army of Northern Virginia. However, I would be less than honest if I did not tell you that I am torn between the solace I feel that you are again in the Father's plan as a physician and the concern for your well-being that abides deep within my soul.

We are doing well here at Horlbeck Creek. Nate took Colin fishing for catfish on his birthday, and they had a long talk (as only Nate can talk) about why it was important for you as a Southerner to go to war for your land as his father had fought for South Carolina in the Revolutionary War. I gained a greater measure of understanding myself of your motives when Colin told me the story of Nate's father.

I had a letter from Father recently, and he is doing reasonably well with the business, but it is slowing down as people are beginning to see difficulties ahead and are not purchasing as many goods as before the war began. In some sad news, Father said Mother is not doing well. Her hysteria and retreat from reality has worsened Father's ability to care for her, even with a full-time nurse.

I worry about Mother and that I may have brought on this dementia, although Father assures me that he saw it coming before her blowup on that Christmas night many years ago. I pray for her daily, but I am ready neither to forgive nor to think about a visit to see her. Perhaps one day that will change.

My darling, I have saved the good news for last. You are to be a father again! As of this writing, I think that I am about three months along. I am feeling well—much better than with Colin. You must not worry about me, but rejoice that the Almighty has blessed us with another child. I recently told Audrey Lee, and she is already acting the mother hen, making sure I eat correctly and do not overexert myself. Toward that end, Colin is a blessing. I cannot say that he joyously does his chores and many of mine, but he can do them and does them reasonably well without me fussing at him. He wonders if you will be home for the baby's *birth, as do I. I pray this conflict can end swiftly and you will return to me soon.*

Ever your loving wife, with greetings from your son,
Red

Letter to Charleston

Since moving to the farm on Horlbeck Creek, to Mary Assumpta Charleston seemed an ocean away, though it sat only a morning's sail across the harbor.

Equally at first, Matthew Bailey had been an infrequent visitor to the farm he had deeded to James and Mary Assumpta, giving the new family a chance to settle into a life very different from the one the couple had hoped for. Lauraleigh Bailey's explosion created an unanticipated new life away from the surgeon's office and the family home.

As she had with everything before the move across the harbor, Mary Assumpta attacked farmlife, and as a consequence, her well-intended correspondence with her father was a casualty of her vigor.

With James at war and Horlbeck Creek Farm about to enter its own war, Mary Assumpta realized that she must renew the relationship with her father that she had known as his only and very spoiled daughter.

August 15, 1862
Horlbeck Creek Farm

Dearest Father,

Please forgive my failure in not writing more often. Whenever you have visited Horlbeck Creek over the years, I have promised myself that I would always write you in a few days. Then a few days have led on to several and several to many, and you know me; I have never been good at apologizing. It rather feels like missing church for a few Sundays, and then the Sundays multiply for fear of all the embarrassing where-have-you-been, I-hope-everything-is-okay, and we-missed-you-so-much expressions. Silly of me, I know. Then and now.

The days here at the farm are long and hard without James's help to bring in the last pickings. Thanks to Nate and Audrey Lee, we are now finished except for the potatoes, an occasional squash, and the okra in the small garden. Unlike past years, Colin was actually more help than hindrance. He handled ol Jake and the wagon, and that kept him out of the way of the adults. Of course, he loved sitting up above it all and shouting commands to Jake—commands that Jake mostly ignored, knowing himself when to move the wagon forward and when to stop. I have found this mule to be stubborn but far from stupid.

I miss James so very much. I have not heard from him in three weeks, and I guess from this point forward letters are likely to be irregular. He has enlisted with General Lee's Army of Northern Virginia (ANV), and once they learned he was a surgeon (and a graduate of the University of Virginia), they made him a captain and placed him under John's command. John assigned him to the medical company of the ANV. Remarkably, John and James are still connected.

James seems happy to be back with a scalpel in his hands. However, I do fear for his safety as the medical tents are always only slightly removed from the fighting. Pray for him and for us, and don't forget Nate and Audrey Lee. I can see already that if we make it through this, they will be the reason.

I have one other piece of news. James seems to have given you the gift of another grandchild before he left. No nausea with this one—thank God in heaven. I am feeling fine, but my belly is *beginning to grow. No one else knows, not even James yet (hopefully my letter will get to him soon), so please keep it to yourself too. And no, I am not returning to Charleston.*

I must admit that Charleston has been on my mind lately. It is amazing where the mind goes when the body is left with only routine tasks like shelling beans. That is, more than anything else, the reason for this letter. Is everything okay at home? I am still not ready to forgive Mother, but I do worry about her and about you and Andrew Ryan.

Please forgive me for being so lax in my correspondence. I promise to improve.

Your loving Horlbeck Creek family,

Mary Assumpta and Colin

Conflict Looms

Outside Richmond
August 12, 1862

My Dearest Mary Assumpta,

Since my last letter to you, I have been bivouacked outside Richmond with troops returning from the successful Peninsula Campaign. General Joe Johnston was injured by a Union artillery shell fragment and was replaced by General Lee, much to the jubilation of the brave fighters. From what I hear from the soldiers who are making their way to our encampment from the campaign, I believe we shall see a different war now that General Lee is in command of the Army of Northern Virginia. In fact, the success of the defense of Richmond and the defeat of Yankee general George

B. McClellan is in large part due to General Lee's arrival on the scene.

General Lee will not accept, it seems, a defensive war. If his success in the Peninsula Campaign is any indication, he will take the fight to the Yankees and drive them from my precious Virginia. Only time will tell.

Those who are bivouacked here are assuming that we are assembling to march toward Manassas, where the Yankees gathered after they retreated, tails between their legs, after departing the east bank of the James River. As I shall be moving with General Lee's column, I am not certain of when I will write again, but I am intent to record my travails and travels in my diary so I can relay them to you in all good time, my darling. Please pray for me as the conflict looms before me.

Now to more joyous expectations. I have been counting off the days in expectation of your first letter to me. I do miss you and Colin so and, I must admit, even Nate and Audrey Lee. I know that they have helped you in every way that they can, and I pray that the harvest was both bountiful and reasonably easy on your back and shoulders. I wish that I could have been with you, but I do sincerely believe that my duty to our future togetherness is best served here.

When I close my eyes each night, as I am about to do now, my last conscious thought is always of my lovely colleen and the family who waits for me on the banks of Horlbeck Creek.

Yours faithfully and fully,
JEM

Distressing News from Home

Charleston, South Carolina
August 19, 1862

Dearest Mary Assumpta,

I am jubilant to know that I will again be a grandfather! You must let James know as soon as possible. He will need every incentive to keep his spirits up as he tends to the wounded and dying—the primary commodities of war. He is not unfamiliar with either, but he is also not immune to being overwhelmed by the immensity of destruction when armies collide on the field of battle. In today's war, a rifle's accuracy is measured in hundreds of yards, not in dozens of feet. As you asked, I pray for him daily as he is surely doing the work of the Almighty.

I am doing passably well since last I saw you. Andrew Ryan has recently enlisted in the Confederate navy and is posted here in Charleston, so we see him often, though he is very closed-mouthed about his duties at the naval yard. I miss his work with me at the store, but I am managing okay as people have reduced their purchases because they can see a scarcity of money coming shortly. But we will always have customers, even if many are on credit. Worry not. I have enough funds put away (and not in the bank) to keep us afloat for several years if need be. Our family attorney, Ralph Jordan, is the only person who knows the location of my funds. Should something happen to your mother and me, you should contact him immediately.

Now, I am afraid that I must write you of distressing news. I hesitate, but I think it best to tell you now. Your mother has progressed from occasional mild bouts of hysteria and depression to total madness, and she is now a patient at the recently completed South Carolina State Hospital for the Insane here in Charleston. I know this will trouble you, but your mother's doctor of many years, Dr. Frazier, and I agree that this is the only reasonable course for the time being.

Since we first saw her mental state on that Christmas night in 1952, she steadily, if slowly, descended from anger to bouts of depression to hysteria that has no sense of reality to it at all. She often asked me to bring Joseph Paul to her room, and when I could not, she descended into days and days of grieving as she had at his death.

I hired a nurse to stay with her, and up until the last few weeks, she was docile during her depressed days and happily hysterical on other days. At very rare times, she emerged as Mother again and asked after each of you children. Yes, even you. I treasured the suppers we spent together on these days, but typically, as the day seemed to vault into darkness, so did her depression.

Of late, in the last two weeks really, her hysteria progressed from destructive to violent. It was no longer safe for the nurse to care for her, and I made the hardest decision of my life to seek a court order requiring her admittance to the state asylum.

I implore you that there is nothing you can do. I see Mother during weekends, and she no longer recognizes me. I have written John and have given him this same advice. She is well cared for. Restraints are removed whenever she is docile. Unfortunately, that is for only a few minutes each day. Dr. Frazier sees her as part of his regular weekly rounds, and he and I talk afterward. At this point, he advises me that he is giving her mild doses of laudanum to help her rest from fighting against the restraints. He tells me that he has seen cases where removing the patient from familiar places gives the brain the time to reset itself toward normality. Pray that she moves in that direction. I have expressed my concerns about the side effects of the laudanum, and he assures me that he will work to keep her from becoming addicted to it. However, he cautions me that right now, addiction is less to be feared than the physical harm she may cause to herself by fighting the restraints.

Mary Assumpta, there is no blame to be apportioned here in your mother's condition. I saw it progressing long before it manifested itself at the announcement of your marriage. I should have told you, but I just rationalized it away by saying it was Mother being Mother.

The best thing that you can do for yourself, your mother, and me is to bring another grandchild to Horlbeck Creek Farm. The Almighty continually renews his creation, and I can think of no more godly thing you could do at this ungodly time than to do exactly what you are now doing. It will be hard. But doing it will be right.

I close with all my love and prayers for you all, knowing that they are returned in kind. Trust Nate and Audrey Lee. One of the reasons I bought the farm in the first place was that they were such good people that I wanted them nearby.

Hug and love on Colin for me, and stay strong for James.

Love and blessings to you all,
Father

The War Begins

August 20, 1862
With the Army of Northern Virginia

My Dearest Mary Assumpta,

Your lovely letter of August 8 finally reached me today with the news that I will again be a father. Such joyousness I have seldom ever experienced, and I have such sadness that I cannot be with you in coming weeks.

I have told the news to anyone who would listen, so much that they have begun to call me Papa, which I rather fancy when compared to some less flattering names I was called when I lanced a boil on the backside of a crusty first sergeant.

We have been moving for the last week in preparation for the battle that looms ahead on the plains of Manassas where the Yankees have grouped and where it is rumored they have a rather large store of food and supplies.

General Lee marches with General Longstreet to bolster General Stonewall Jackson's forces that have been in the area for several days looking for the supply depot.

Even though we have not engaged the enemy, I have nonetheless been busy honing my skills as a surgeon. Wagons turn over. Men are thrown from their mounts. Rattlesnake strikes are not uncommon in the August heat. Treating deer fly and yellow fly bites are a daily occurrence. One fellow who must be allergic to the yellow flies had both hands so swollen that I hardly could find his fingers.

We eat reasonably well with salt pork, beans, and hardtack, the staple of lunch and dinner. Occasionally we are treated to fresh roasted chicken, but we inquire not at all about how the hens were acquired.

Our mail call came earlier today, and so it is time for me to make my routine walking rounds of the camp to check for ailments and to write the occasional letter home.

I shall write as circumstances allow, but I fear that with fighting swiftly approaching, it may be many days before I am able to write again. So, my dearest, my beloved companion, I close with a prayer for you on my lips as I know you pray for me.

Yours in my thoughts and prayers, and with every hope for a swift return,

JEM

Honesty from Home

August 20, 1862
Horlbeck Creek Farm

My Dearest Physician,

I only recently received your letter from your encampment outside Richmond awaiting orders to march to Manassas and to battle. James, my heart is heavy with the realization that you are, in fact, inexorably heading to war. I am so worried for you that my days are constantly filled with dread.

My mind is constantly occupied with disquiet that, in his omnipotence, God shall exact his full measure of retribution for my sins upon you, my beloved. As unreasonable as you will no doubt tell me that these fears are, they remain nonetheless my constant companions, and I am afraid they shall dog my every step until you return to Horlbeck Creek.

I am consoled by the knowledge that at Horlbeck Creek you dwelled here not of your choosing but to satisfy me. In the last almost nine years on the farm, surely you did creditable penitence for my sins of arrogance and the overbearing pride that has not yet let me forgive my own mother. My darling, come home to me. I am in need of rescue from myself. I am simply awash in self-recrimination.

I am so sorry for the tenor of this correspondence, but until your letter, I held out some prospect, small as it surely was, that you would not be accepted as a son of Virginia into the Army of Northern Virginia. Now I know differently, and I am without hope, only despair.

As time passes and puts all things into perspective as only it can, I promise that I shall be the positive war wife that you need. For now, honesty must suffice.

With love and prayers,

Red

Surgeon's Diary

August 31, 1862
General Lee's Encampment
Outside Manassas, Virginia

Before I record my reactions to my first battle as a field surgeon, I think it necessary that I record for my own future reflection the events that produced this noteworthy victory, though it appears most costly to my virginal soldier eyes. The words that follow are my own only as I have tried to recollect what I heard around evening campfires from officers preparing for and fresh from battle.

Lee's victory in the Peninsula Campaign that saved Richmond and the South from a quick end to the war at the hands of the Yankees produced two changes for which the Union army and General George B. McClellan were ill prepared: the dynamism that is Robert E. Lee as commander of the Confederate army, and his propensity for aggressive military tactics. This combination turned an apparent Union victory into a humiliating defeat as General Pope and his forces were in sight of Richmond and was to be repeated at the Second Battle of Manassas.

General Lee surmised that Yankee major general John Pope intended to attack the Confederate railroad, so on August 25 General Lee sent Stonewall Jackson to defend the lines. Jackson, even more aggressive than his commander, marched quickly toward the Yankees, who in rather typical Yankee form chose caution over forthrightness. Thus, Jackson's forces quickly captured the lightly defended railroad stop at Bristoe Station and speedily pushed on to Manassas Junction where, on August 27, he took the Yankee depot unopposed. There, Jackson's men found newly constructed warehouses and railroad cars on half-mile spurs filled with stores almost beyond the imagination of the soldiers who had been living on hardtack and salt pork. They found a square mile of military goods awaiting the day that Pope's and McClellan's forces would combine for another advance on Richmond.

General Jackson's men indulged on the likes of molasses and an unusual delicacy—light bread. To these fighters it was like cake compared to the hardtack found in their knapsacks. Some even feasted, I am told, although I cannot confirm it, on pickled oysters, canned lobster, and German wine. Damn Yankees feast while we fight for our land on the most meager of rations. Surely the goodness of our men shall see us through to ultimate victory over such rapacious indulges found in the North.

I have let my anger subside with a cup of coffee, and I will seek to continue in a more objective rendition of the second Manassas campaign.

General Jackson, in his typical fashion, did not occupy Manassas but moved on until he found in nearby Groveton the perfect ambush point, a partially finished raised railroad bed. On August 28, the Yankees encountered fire from General Jackson's forces as they moved their force toward Centerville, Virginia. It appears from what I can glean from jubilant officers that Yankee general Pope, having found General Jackson, was preparing a direct frontal attack the next day directly at his impeccably defended position. What Pope did not know was that as General Jackson's men were eating their way through Manassas Junction, General Longstreet was quickly moving toward Manassas as well.

On August 29, Pope, believing that General Longstreet was more than a day away, ordered assaults on General Jackson's position. The attack came the next day about 3:00 p.m. What he did not know was that General Longstreet was in perfect position to unleash his artillery on Pope's forces as they moved toward General Jackson. Totally hemmed in and caught in the withering crossfire, the Army of the Potomac, as the Federals are known, was slaughtered. The Second Battle of Manassas was over.

To this point in my life as a physician and surgeon, I have seen every feature of the human body. I have seen its beauty in birth and health and its baseness in depravity and death. An essential requirement of my calling is to develop callousness to the smells and sights of the human condition at its worst, and I was confident until the last four days that my immunity to such sordidness was beyond attack. I was wrong.

Since the twenty-eighth, when General Jackson engaged the Yankees in earnest at Brawner's farm, I have thought over and over of a verse from a poem by Robert Burns I learned in grammar school. I cannot get it out of my head. It goes round and round like some crazed creature that will not be quieted. Neither whiskey nor sleep calms it. I awake to its incessant rhythm and its verses. My only respite is when I am too intensely engaged in surgery and up to my elbows in muscles and viscera to think at all. But as soon as I retreat from the surgery tent and clean myself of excrement and tissue, it returns again in greater force.

And man, whose heav'n-erected face
The smiles of love adorn,—
Man's inhumanity to man
Makes countless thousands mourn!

For the last two days we have been encamped southwest of General Jackson's forces along the unfinished railroad bed and northwest of General Longstreet's artillery. Although General Jackson's fortified railroad bed provided his men with ready-built trenches, still his casualties have streamed, endlessly it seems, back to our medical tents as the Yankees kept coming without regard to the bodies of their mates piling on top of each other, killed at point-blank range by our muskets. With such disregard, it was inevitable that they would inflict horrible wounds on General Jackson's foot soldiers. And they did—unrelentingly—until General Longstreet unleashed his artillery on the unsuspecting Yankees, who did not know that he had outflanked their forces to the southwest.

I can only imagine, and that is more than enough, the damage done to the mothers' sons in blue. I pray that God gives them a swift journey to a final peace.

JEM

Soon We March

September 8, 1862
Manassas, Virginia

My Most Precious Love,

I am just today in receipt of your letter of August 20 and know that I must respond and set your mind at ease about my current condition. My heart hurts for you and Colin as days pass into weeks with your not knowing whether I am well or ill. While I feel the selfsame emotions, I know that you have Nate and

Audrey Lee to look after you; therefore, I acknowledge that I do not worry as much as you.

No doubt by the time this missive reaches you, you will have heard the news of our boys' valiant defeat of the Yankees at Manassas. General Lee was remarkable in his planning, only surpassed by the execution by the infantry of General Stonewall Jackson and General James Longstreet's artillery.

Since the Peninsula Campaign and General Lee's defeat of the Union forces as they sought to surround and choke the life from Richmond, our men have come to firmly believe, as do I, that victory is not just possible but also imminent. I must not say more.

I am well, if tired from the stress of wagon after wagon of wounded who were brought to our surgical tent at General Lee's headquarters for two days of the actual fighting and for two days after the battle as men were found barely alive in the woods around Groveton. Some we save if only by the crudest of surgeries, but others die from the pain and shock of our efforts.

Now, days removed from the battle, we continue to fight off disease and infection from wounds and dysentery from the unclean conditions in which our men must constantly live.

I continue to grow in the surgical skills that I learned as John's partner—usually in surgeries performed after the heat of battle has passed when I have time to repair rather than remove.

We march north in the morning, away from Virginia, but I am unable to tell you more. Please keep heart, my darling, and pray for me that my hands may do God's work. If I know that, all else I can keep in perspective.

My deepest love for Colin. I pray daily that you are taking care of yourself and the new addition soon to arrive at Horlbeck Creek Farm. Give my grateful best to Nate and Audrey Lee.

Forever yours,

JEM

CHAPTER 16

Marching to Slaughter

September 14, 1862
Antietam
Near Sharpsburg, Maryland

My Dearest Mary Assumpta,

We are marching with General Lee into Maryland. I can send this to you now, knowing that by the time it arrives the battle will be over and, God willing, we will be well on our way to Washington and an end to this struggle.

I fear that General Lee's outwitting of the Yankees at Manassas and the capture of the Federal supply depot with its hordes of food have given our men a false feeling of an easy war and an irrational sense of blind forgetfulness when it comes to the dead and wounded. At some fundamental level, I accept that putting the horrors of battle behind us and moving forward is an evil necessity of the battlefield and the surgeons' tent. But we do so, I fear, at our own peril.

While the majority of the wounded have been transported back to hospitals in Richmond, many remain for our continued treatment with the merciless hope that they can be returned to their units to face death yet again on another near battlefield. The dead we bury near where they fell. The August heat prevents all else. And so we march on to the next engagement, trusting in others to remember them as they surely deserve.

Although we have yet days to travel, we know that we are really but hours away from another bloody confrontation. The men all hope we again meet McClellan's army as his indecisiveness and inferiority against General Lee will pave a quick road to Washington. I pray they are correct.

While there seems almost no control once the fighting begins, we have days when the generals are readying for battle, preparing to fling young men to their deaths. Recently, as we have traveled from Manassas, two other young physicians and I have met as we find spare moments to develop our own strategy for our side of the surgery tent—as if such is even possible given the insanity of battle.

I learned from John that even if the surgery is an emergency, the moments taken in planning before making the scalpel's first cut are moments of life given back to the patient in scores. We have resolved that before we hear the first cannon's roar, we will set out trays of bandages, buckets of water, folding tables for the surgical saws and knives, and what little antiseptics are available as this is a commodity unknown to the quartermaster corps. We will bring to the tent a cast-iron washpot filled with white-hot coals and cauterizing irons. Finally, we will set about a supply of whiskey-soaked, tightly wrapped gauze as this is the only dulling of the senses we can offer.

The pain of surgery often produces its own unconsciousness. At Manassas, I observed young and old alike just give in to the pain and lapse into insentience. However, tragically, many never saw the light of day again. I am unable to explain this occurrence, and it troubles me greatly. I shall write to John and seek his knowledge and advice.

My darling, enough about medicine. My life is not entirely consumed with battle. There are many times where the monotony of "soldiering on," step after weary step, is an assault on the mind from the sheer boredom of it. I know that I am fortunate to ride a faithful mount that was battle-seasoned in the Richmond campaign before I received him. He is a solid black gelding without a single white hair. I call him Coal because his coat is that black and shiny. A big horse, he is three years old and stands seventeen hands tall. He is gentle but does not know how big he is! So, I have taken to working with him to respond to the touch of my knees on his shoulders and a gentle touch of the bridle on his neck. Colin would be thrilled to ride Coal. He is a gentle giant unless he is given the rein, and then he can fly across the ground.

Our evenings are oftentimes given to card playing as one of our few diversions. As I am Richmond's worst poker player, I stay away except to listen to others' stories of home and engage in their laughter that seeps to the surface, from where I do not know. A few men are musicians. Billy O'Keefe is the best among them, playing Irish ballads on his uilleann. The *wail of his pipes surely reminds us all of the reality of where we are. So we have told him he must play soon after supper. His playing is remarkable, but we much prefer the after-supper serenade conclude with Norman Yeats's banjo or, even better, the strum of Jimmy Turnipseed's guitar. Nothing like the guitar on a still night to calm the wandering and restless thoughts of an injured mind.*

Mostly I just read. I always start with the Bible. Seems that I have worn paths to the book of Job and to Genesis and the story of Abraham and Isaac. I confess that I do not attempt to understand either, yet they seem so very comparable to sacrifices being asked of the young men on both sides who equally believe that their mission is God-blessed. Perhaps Grandfather wrote about such mysteries in his scholarly pursuits. I must find out when I return.

My darling, when you read this, I know with assuredness that I will have taken your mind off the war as I will surely have put you sound asleep. But such is my life—fits of mania interspersed with tedium, both beyond description.

As we are traveling soon, I will write again after we have settled following the Maryland Campaign and send both letters together.

Yours in love and faithfulness,
JEM

Surgeon's Diary

September 19, 1862
In retreat from Antietam Creek

I began my last diary entry after Manassas with a brief and, I thought, cogent recounting of the battle strategies as I heard them. I wrote those words with every intention of continuing them after each battle. After experiencing the horrors of Antietam Creek, I realize that I am not equipped intellectually or spiritually to talk of the sons of the South as but so many chess pieces moving against the unseen enemy. I shall limit my diary to my own thoughts and experiences as a surgeon.

What I encountered in the surgery tent on September 17 can only be described as hell on earth. Whatever conception I had developed of the depravity, the bloodletting, and the evil that is the pain of hell, it bore little resemblance to the images on my surgical table this day.

My colleagues and I had carefully laid out supplies as we had them, but ten times as many would not have been sufficient for this day. Men and boys were delivered to us with wounds suffered at point-blank range by muskets and bayonets. Others had been torn apart by cannon. One soldier was mistakenly brought to my table, his head cleanly removed by a chain shot, which whirled into the troops as if they were wheat ready for the scything.

I prayed for him. Yet he was lucky. A quick death from an unknown hand is much preferred to a lingering death from infection and filth, knowing that if you survive, you will never walk behind another mule to till your fields of corn.

The last two nights I have seen the images of carnage in my sleep. I do not see the bodies as they arrived at my table but rather as my mind conjures up how their injuries occurred. My mind seems able to deal with the actual bodies before me as I work. The work is its own solace. But when my mind should be at peace, it is in its most vigorous state. I have supposed that since I have never fought in battle, I have no frame of reference from which my mind can draw, and therefore, literally it seems, it draws its own images, however horrific or unrealistic those explanations may be. I have no other insights.

I pray that as I become more accustomed to the sounds and smells of battle and the stories I hear from the men who return to our encampment, my mind will adjust back to the physician's detachment with which I am familiar. But I am unsure if this is mental progress or retreat.

One final thought so that I do not forget it. Every soldier comes to our surgical table without regard to the severity of his injury. So I may stitch a bullet wound for one patient and for the next amputate a leg. It seems to me that there must be a more logical means of working with the multitudes of wounded who seem to appear at our surgical tent as if out of the miasma of battle all at one time.

There are three groupings of the wounded, I think: those whose injuries are minor and will recover regardless of the speed of treatment, those with injuries so severe that they will receive no benefit no matter what we do, and finally those who will recover if treated but who will die promptly if untreated.

In what order should we treat? I must write John Bailey and ask his opinion on this topic and on the topic of men who die from the severity of pain associated with the wound or surgery.

JEM

Aftermath

September 20, 1862
Northern Virginia in Retreat

Mary Assumpta,

Of only one thing this day I am sure—that you are the reason I arise each morning.

I understand now why the young men around our fires at night talk about their loves in the present as if they saw them but yesterday. Thoughts of you are the only things that guide me through the ungodliness of my existence each day. When the cannons have stopped rumbling and the last of the boys have been brought to my table, I turn my thoughts to you. You are all that saves me. Without you, I am left with only my own feeble explanations of how two peoples of a common land could come to such a place of ritual killing as this. There is no idea, however seemingly noble, that is worth the life of a single boy, much less the hundreds to whom I have tended at Antietam. Such is beyond my human mind to grasp.

During these days, my faith in a benevolent, caring Almighty has been totally ripped from me just as I have seen arms and legs and faces ripped from the bodies of young men not yet husbands and from husbands who will never see fatherhood.

Darling Mary Assumpta, I cannot continue this plaintive lament any longer, for I cannot bear to relive the images that are becoming my companions. Nothing at Manassas prepared me for the sheer carnage I have been asked to repair or to remove from the young bodies brought to me here at Sharpsburg. I believed that my colleagues and I had planned so that such a catastrophe could never overwhelm us as physicians. I was wrong. We were at the mercy of Beelzebub, for surely my God could not ordain such butchery. That he must have permitted it has shaken the foundation of everything that I have ever believed was good and righteous in this world. My deepest apologies for those thoughts.

I go now and retire to my bed with the only peace on which I know I can rely—the tender mercies of your love and prayers.

Yours,
JEM

Pandora's Hope

October 1, 1862
Horlbeck Creek Farm

My Darling Companion,

I have not heard from you in such a long time that my heart aches at not knowing and throbs with worry for you so that I am fretful the baby shall be affected by my heart's incessant pounding, which must sound like cannon fire inside my belly.

We get news so seldom here on the creek. Only just in the last week have we read of the tragic defeat of our brave boys at Antietam. Such carnage at the hands of the Yankees. I know you battled for the bodies and souls of our boys as surely as if you, yourself, were fighting in the farms and fields around Antietam Creek.

My soul hungers for you, conscious all the while that my longing must go unsatisfied. I am daily resigned to accept a Pandora-like hope, infrequently satisfied. It is hope not that you are moving surely to safe harbor, for that I am denied, but that no reports of your death must somehow make content my unsettled heart.

Be strong, my love, and be assured that I pray for you day and night without ceasing.

I am sorry, but I must put this letter aside for a time as even the thought of you in such danger as was all around you at Antietam, with my not knowing of your sure safety, is more than I am able to ponder. I shall write again when the baby and I have returned to a state of passable, if not persistent, peace.

Now I must rest, praying for the day when you return to me in all hope, grace, and loveliness.

Red

October 2, 1863
Horlbeck Creek Farm

My Darling,

I hope that when you read this letter, you are able to forgive the weaknesses of yesterday's missive. While they are my true feelings, and therefore you should know them, they reside in my heart only temporarily, and then they are gone—to where I do not understand. They return only in hours of lonely desperation when I cannot conjure up your face or remember the tender feel of your hands on my body.

Here we are getting by better than many, I suspect, who must bear the destruction of their fields by battle and pillage even as the harvest is nigh upon them. We have more than sufficient stores until we can plant again in early spring. Audrey Lee and I put up twenty-five jars of beans, twenty jars of corn, and thirty jars of tomatoes. We also put up ten jars of succotash, good by itself or as a starter for soup for the wet, cold days of January. Even now we have just planted collards and turnips in a small patch just beyond the back porch. If we are able to keep the deer and rabbits at bay, they will be an excellent addition to our pumpkins, winter squash, and Irish and sweet potatoes.

Colin misses you so much and has finally learned to restrain the impulse of asking every day if I have heard from you. He studies hard, and Nate takes him hunting and fishing around the creek whenever he is able. Yesterday, I called Colin to me after supper, and he felt the baby move for the first time. I am not sure if he slept at all last night thinking of all the things he will teach his new baby brother. He has no doubts that it will be a boy.

I have been without any nausea for a month now, and Audrey

Lee, who checks on me (more often than needed!), says I have a glow about me. I am not sure about that, but I feel really good. I am able to do whatever I want, and I thank our everlasting Father for the blessings of health and contentment he bestows upon me as the new soul grows within.

I regret that our mutual correspondence is irregular—days and perhaps weeks after events have occurred. But rest assured that I read every letter until it is tattered, and I keep them all in the seaman's chest that Bartholomew gave us for our wedding. Worry not that your news is late, and worry not about us here on the creek. Mercifully the war has not affected us much except for the distance it has brought between Charleston and us and the delay of news and correspondence that would bring us a measure of peace.

I am yours in everlasting love,
Red

Wisdom from the Creek

October 5, 1863
Horlbeck Creek Farm

My Dearest Surgeon,

I praise the Almighty that you are alive and physically unscathed by the fighting at Antietam Creek. I received both your letters yesterday and spent most of the day reading and rereading until the imprints of the oil from my fingers became permanently embedded in them with your thoughts.

I wish that I could, for an instant, travel to you, hold you close, and reassure you that what you feel is as natural as the horror you face is unnatural. I do not confess to know from experience or from study the ways of the human mind, but since Father *told me that Mother had lapsed into a more or less permanent state of insanity or dementia, as the preferred term seems to be known these days, it is as if the eight different letters of this newly minted term make it more palatable and therefore more treatable than insanity. Regardless, it has caused me to reflect on Mother's break with reality and if it was gradual or immediately caused by my actions.*

I write you about my thoughts in the hopes that they may help you understand the path your own mind is traveling as it seeks to fathom what heretofore it could not even imagine, much less accept as reality. Here is what I think is happening to you and to all who experience war's revulsions for the first time.

Because your background as a surgeon and a gentleman will not allow you even to contemplate physical retreat from what you see during the battle, and given the fact that you see it over and over for hours without respite, your mind during the hours of surgery retreats into another room of your brain where it does not have to experience what your eyes clearly see. The training you received as a surgeon from John has conditioned your conscious mind that you and every surgeon must retreat from the wounds to the muscles and viscera in front of you and just allow the training to take over.

The following is a crude example. I see it rather like plowing that half-mile-long bean row with Jake. Both Jake and I retreat into a kind of unconscious level of competence where we need not think but only perform as we have learned to perform by plowing countless rows before the one in front of us. Often, I find that when Jake and I reach the end of that long, long row, I will not even remember how we traversed the distance except for beginning and end. Now here is the interesting part: that level of unconscious consciousness frees my mind (I don't know about Jake's) to wander into heretofore unexplored rooms of my thought. Exploration, if I try to do it purposefully (and I have), falls flat in frustration.

Two things seem to be necessary for this to happen: (1) the ability to do the job, whatever that job might be, at a high level as if it were by reflex, and (2) a willingness to let the unconscious mind travel where it will.

I believe that this is what is happening to you during the heat of battle. Then when rest comes, your unconscious mind, freed from the conscious mind's attention to tasks at hand, seeks to make sense of what it has observed from the distance of the upper reaches of your beautiful mind.

I suggest that you begin to embrace the nightly visitations of your unconscious mind. Should you awake, perhaps recording the images as you remember them will help you put them into the past to be considered at a future time. And if you cannot remember them when you awake, embrace them nonetheless as your mind "emptying the refuse" of yesterday so that you may begin the next day anew. I sincerely believe that how you perceive them will ultimately produce good or ill.

Please begin and end each day knowing that as you arise and retire, prayers are making their way from Horlbeck Creek to the ears of the Father, beseeching him to keep you safe in body and spirit. Worry not that your faith has been challenged; I would worry more if it had not been. I spoke to Father Joseph one time about why God caused evil to affect good people. I shall never forget his words. "Child," he said, "God gives us all free will to choose good or ill. Never mistake the evil that men do to each other as having any connection to the Father.

"God's nature," he said, "is pure love, and giving mankind the freedom to act for good or evil is the ultimate act of that love."

I think that your questioning of the Almighty's purposes is an example of that love at work in you. Accept it. Affirm it, but also pray on it.

I love you. I embrace your soul and hold it close to my heart *continuously. I know, my beloved physician, exactly who you are and who you could never be. Question everything else except for two things: who you are and who we are.*

Love, prayers, and blessings,

Red

CHAPTER 17

Fredericksburg Prologue

After the defeat at Antietam, the Army of Northern Virginia withdrew in haste to the friendly confines of Virginia. Yet the Rebels won a victory of sorts, even in defeat. Union president Lincoln was confronted with the fact that the Union army had not pursued the Confederates across Antietam Creek and dealt them a blow that could have ended the war. His wrath, for it could hardly be characterized as anything less, was exacted on the Union commander Major General George McClellan.

On November 5, 1863, Lincoln signed the order removing Major General George McClellan and replacing him with McClellan's good friend General Ambrose Burnside.

As Lincoln was playing swap-the-commander, Jefferson Davis was embarking on a campaign to offer words of encouragement to the Confederate armies in the lower and western portions of the South. He was hoping that his words of encouragement would bring new recruits to his decimated and dwindling army of the Confederacy.

However, General Lee's spies had informed him and President Davis that Union major general Ambrose Burnside was massing a force along the Rappahannock across the river from Fredericksburg, hoping to inflict a knockout blow with the capture of Richmond. This development weighed heavily on Davis even as his commanders in the south and west reminded him that there were Confederate armies other than the Army of Northern Virginia.

After Antietam, Lee was moving toward wintering his army when the 150,000 Union soldiers along the Rappahannock convinced him that Burnside likely had every intention of swiftly crossing at Fredericksburg, bullying aside the much smaller Army of Northern Virginia, and quickly pushing the 60 miles to Richmond.

There was only one question about Fredericksburg that caused Lee nightmares. It was whether or not his army could arrive in time to oppose Burnside. His worries were genuine, and only an intercession by the hands of the Fates who chose to weave a different tapestry saved, if only for a time, Richmond and the Confederacy.

Worry and Hope

October 10, 1862
Horlbeck Creek Farm

My Dearest JEM,

It has been nearly a month since I have had a letter from your hand to my heart. I fear that I pester you with such thoughts, knowing the life-and-death engagements in which you find yourself almost daily. Every day that I do not receive a letter, I pray an unusual prayer—that your message has become lost, for I can find hope in believing that the vagaries of this war have consumed your precious letter. Otherwise I cannot bear to consider that you have not written to your family here at the farm in almost a month.

Enough of my mealy-mouthing. Evening currents, precursors to the sure-enough fall breezes in November, are finally relieving us of the endless summer that began early last spring and increased in hellishness upon your leaving in July. Even now, Colin and I work from before dawn until the sun is well risen and racing toward its zenith. I work inside, and Colin feeds the livestock, checks the garden, and brings in water from the artesian spring. The sun has finished the squash, cucumbers, and beans, but the okra thrives. We do love it in every way we can cook it, but that love comes with a price. Colin threatens those okra plants every day with an early death as his arms sting from their nettles.

Once the sun comes up hard and hot, we retreat to the porch and shade of the water oaks that make his studying and my stitchwork tolerable. We eat our lunch on the porch—usually tomatoes with a bit of Audrey Lee's fresh cottage cheese when we can get it. We still have a few tomatoes coming, although not enough to can, so we will enjoy eating them to the first frost.

I had a letter from Father last week. He says that Charleston is still in the hands of the South but the Yankees harass shipping around the mouth of the harbor just enough to raise prices on the goods that do get through, although he says most ships do get through and the shipowners are just gouging the merchants with prices that border on the unreasonable. Mother remains in the care of South Carolina State Hospital for the Insane. Father says that she is no worse than when he last wrote, but she only infrequently recognizes him. I would like to see her one day, but I am not yet ready. Irish hardheadedness runs deep in these veins as you well know. Father says that Andrew Ryan is working with navy engineers on something called a submarine. But beyond that, Father says he is totally secretive.

Nate and Audrey Lee always ask about you whenever we see them. We swap visits every week, and Audrey Lee and I have a small hen party while Nate and Colin do a little cleaning up around the garden and the barn and find an hour or so to walk down to the creek. Nate has a special fishing spot he calls the "blue hole" because it is deeper than the surrounding water. In the summer, catfish gather in its cool depths, and usually they are hungry for the gob of wigglers that Colin has dug up from the compost pile. Most times he and Nate bring back supper of catfish and the occasional green trout. Nate has sworn Colin to secrecy about the location, and he will not even tell me. But they have to walk a mile or so to get to it and then crawl their way under heavy underbrush. Maybe he will show it to you when you return. So come home soon before they fish it out.

My belly grows almost daily, it seems, but I still feel remarkably well. Audrey Lee says the second baby is always easier. Or have I already told you that? After evening prayers, when I have retired each night and the baby stirs before settling down, it reminds me just how much I actually miss you. Take care, my love. I need you more than you will know (until I see you again!).

As I have put off my sewing this morning, I must go now and fix our lunch. Colin wants to send you a letter with some questions about what you are doing, and I think I can put him off no longer. So be looking for his letter soon. Until then, he sends you his best, and we pray for you morning and night.

With deepest and most sincere desire for your return,

Red

Faith Renewed

October 15, 1862
Northern Virginia

My Dearest and Precious Mary Assumpta,

God has intervened, and my faith has returned, battered but leaning forward. Since Antietam I have found some solace as we have begun preliminary preparations for our wintering grounds north of Richmond and south of Maryland. I am unable to tell you more.

In the days since we retreated from Antietam, my medical undertakings are more closely aligned with my knowledge and skills than to the madness that seems to be de rigueur for the battlefield surgical tent. I have tended to men who have a realistic chance of recovery even staying here with the rest of the army. I am not amputating but using surgery actually to repair wounds. I do confess that I remain uncertain about aiding these boys, mainly so that they can one day return to the battlefield. However, I rationalize, I suppose, that the more I can see them restored to health, the better they will be to withstand the rigors of battle. It has not been unusual in a three-day battle to patch up boys more than once and to have them return to fighting less than their full selves.

Our army is at such a disadvantage just in numbers of troops, compared to the multitudes of Union boys thrown upon us. Only the knowledge of General Lee has prevented this war from reaching a quick and unfavorable end. We came within a whisker of total defeat at Antietam, which was really a draw, yet the Yankee newspapers laud it as a Union victory. Had McClellan possessed a whit of Lee's aggressiveness, I expect I would be languishing today in a Yankee prison camp in the heart of Richmond.

In the last few days, I have had time to actually think about a better way to treat our boys in the surgical tent in the midst of battle than the milieu of mayhem that I have experienced thus far. I have contemplated a technique that John and I talked about from time to time should we have to tend to possibly hundreds of severely wounded as a result of a hurricane that could visit its destruction on Charleston any year.

I think I wrote you about it earlier, but I confess that it may simply be a figment of the nightly visitations of the war upon my mind.

The process seeks to divide the wounded by likelihood (or lack thereof) of my care on the surgical table to save the injured. I will not bore you with the details again, but let me just say that with the lull we have experienced and the opportunity to work with the less than severely wounded, I have been able to conduct experiments of a sort without endangering any of the men beyond the inconvenience of being treated by me later rather than sooner in the same day.

A colleague of mine, Lieutenant William Joe McCarty, who also graduated from the UVA Medical School, and I have bonded as partners based on our common experiences of being routinely dressed down by Professor Wisdom Strikeleather. After anatomy lab, we would return to the lecture theater the next day to be summarily informed of the hundreds of future patients we were sure to kill based on his observation of our pitiful dissection techniques. In fact, he called the entire class "a bunch of weak-minded miscreants" most every day as he greeted us.

It was restorative to have that bit of fond memory to remind me there was—and shall be again—another more civilized time. But back to my experiment. Willie and I select twenty-five wounded at random, and each of us, without consulting the other, groups those wounded into categories based on the severity of their wounds. We then talk over coffee in the evening about men in our three categories and compare our groupings. Over three days of grouping twenty-five different soldiers each day, Willie and I have agreed on the grouping 75 percent of the time. This is much higher than we had thought and offers promise for the process.

If circumstances allow, next week we will do it again, but between now and then, Willie and I will develop a rating system that we both agree on, discuss the intricacies of its application, and then we each apply it independently of the other. It is nice to see a bit of optimism in the midst of such desperation. Surely your prayers for me have been answered as God has provided me this diversion that shall improve the survival rate of our patients in the surgical tent during battle. Much yet to be done. Keep those prayers coming.

Your devoted husband,
JEM

Surgeon's Diary

October 29, 1862
Northern Virginia

I never knew a lengthy cessation in the fighting could be so busy. Our camps can be found from all along the fifteen-mile road from Winchester north to Bunker Hill.

I am officially encamped with General Lee at his headquarters at Stephenson's Depot.

However, I spend most of my days, and often nights, in the home of Jesse and Iris Conklin, who have turned their home outside Winchester, as have many others in and around Winchester, into a hospital. I estimate that between the homes and the public buildings also serving as care units, we have as many as six thousand men wounded at Antietam quartered around this small community.

The Conklins have given up their own bedroom, the largest in the house, so that ten cots can be placed in the same space. They sleep on pallets on the floor on the back porch so they can be near the kitchen if they need to help with boiling water for an emergency operation. Every reasonable space of their modest farmhouse is taken up with cots or medical supplies. The blood of the young men who lay there in their last moments will forever stain the dining room table used for surgery. Sometimes the table has three boys on it at the same time. The Conklins' dining table is likely the last piece of furniture these men will rest upon on this earth. They are here because they have not responded to our best battlefield ministrations, or else they suffered additional, if unintended, injuries in our retreat from Antietam.

Those who have a chance of recovery are treated in their cots—although *treated* is not the proper term. There really is no treatment beyond what they have already received except for changing bandages and cleaning wounds with warm salty water. Their treatment is in the hands of the Almighty, although the Conklins, devout Presbyterians, have taken this on as their Christian duty. Having raised three rowdy boys who now ride with Jeb Stuart's cavalry, they treated lots of cuts and scrapes through the years, making bandages from scraps of cloth and ointments from pine tar and turpentine. I do find it most sad that we seldom even have the rudiments of antiseptics, and once again scraps of fabric donated by the citizens of Winchester must suffice for bandages.

JEM

Fears Relieved

November 1, 1862
Horlbeck Creek Farm

Dearest Husband,

Dear God in heaven, I finally received your letter. Thank God. Fears relieved.

I had not given up hope, but I was praying my rosary at every spare moment in our somewhat uneventful days here on the creek. Interesting that you were asking for prayers even as I was delivering them to the Almighty. He does work in mysterious ways.

I rejoice that your doubts of faith in him and yourself have been assuaged.

November, as you well know, finally brings a relief from the summer heat that seemed to last through the end of October. A few winter squash are holding on, and we have not harvested our late sweet potatoes—waiting on the first frost to dig them all. Colin has laid out some boards on sawhorses so that we can properly age the potatoes before we transfer them to the root cellar with our winter squash and a good supply of apples that are already there.

Colin surely has your intellect. He just amazes me with his questions about mathematics and engineering. I, of course, cannot answer most of them and tell him he will just have to wait for your return. Nate helps him a lot. Nate may not arrive at the answer in the way Colin's textbook proposes, but his practical knowledge from so many years on the farm is amazing in its own way. He has solved so many problems through the years that I do not think there is anything that he couldn't build if given time to work on the problem at hand. He is best at adapting materials for uses that you and I would never have considered. So Colin may be taxing my brain, but I think Nate is still staying up with him. Whenever Colin is stumped, he trundles over to Nate's on the back of ol Jake. Nate will tell him how a farmer would have solved the problem the book proposes, and with the book and Nate's experiences, everything seems to come together for Colin. I think he is getting so much more than the book learning that made up your education and mine—until I started working for John as his nurse.

The last time Colin visited Nate, he came home with a surprise for me, one I was not really keen on at the time. A small dog was trailing behind Colin and ol Jake, just prancing like he owned most of Charleston and half of Savannah! He is an interesting dog and of a breed I have not seen before. He stands about sixteen inches tall, and I figure he weighs about thirty pounds right now and could stand to add some more weight as his ribs protrude. Nate said he showed up one day at his farm and would not leave, so obviously Audrey Lee just had to feed him. Nate says he really is keen around quail and doves on the ground. And when he gets close enough to the birds that he can smell them, the dog will lift his left leg, stick out his nose, straighten his back, and stick out his *little stumpy tail just like he is pointing to where those birds are in the underbrush.*

Nate figured the dog must have come from one of the plantations up the river, so he took half a day and walked over to the Boone plantation to see if they had heard about a missing dog. When no one claimed him, Nate did! For Colin. I am not sure who was the happiest, Nate, the dog, or your son!

On the way back from the Boone plantation, Nate heard cannon fire and figured Boomer would be a good name for him. That's how Boomer became our new family member. He was so dirty when Colin came striding up with him that I could not really determine his color. Of course Colin wanted to bring him inside right then, but I put a quick end to that! So down to the creek they went with a bar of soap and some towels.

When Boomer and Colin returned, I hardly recognized either one, they were so cleaned up and presentable. Boomer, it turns out, is copper and white with the copper tending just a tad toward orange. He has splotches of copper hair on his left side that look like a checkerboard and a big area on his right side coming over his back like a saddle. His chest, his belly, and his feet are white with little speckles of copper hair. His face is copper with a white blaze going around his freckled copper nose right up between his golden eyes and forming a heart on the top of his head. Imagine that. On the backs of his legs, he has long hairs growing that look like feathers more than hair. His copper ears are about as long as a beagle's but with shaggy hair on them. When he gets excited (which is most of the time), he perks those ears up and his golden eyes shine like a late evening sunset on Charleston Harbor.

Nate vows to help Colin make Boomer a hunting dog, but I am not sure of that as I have let Boomer sleep with Colin every night. During the day, they are inseparable. Colin misses you so much, and given that there are no friends near, Boomer seems to be God-sent. Whenever Colin heads over to Nate and Audrey Lee's,

Boomer prances right behind. I think he knows Audrey Lee has saved him some fatback from her beans as a treat.

Boomer is quite a handful and just what Colin needs to occupy his time and his mind.

I am doing well. As I calculate it, I am now in my sixth month and beginning to show rather dramatically. Good thing we live on the farm where pregnant women are a fact of life and not put under wraps. I do get tired a little easier, but life right now is slowing down as winter approaches, so all things considered, the timing is good. I am just praying that I will give birth in time to recover and help Colin with spring planting. The baby has really begun to kick—not quite like Colin—more like a lady, I hope. I have been thinking about names, and I don't believe that it is too early for you to share your thoughts on the matter. I am thinking that boy or girl, this baby must have a name from her (or his) English heritage. Let me know your thoughts about that. Maybe it can help take your mind from more dire matters at hand.

I told Colin last time that he could include a few lines in my next letter, so his correspondence is on the next page. I should not want him to see in my words that I miss his father—body and soul in equal amounts.

Until I hear from you again, I am yours in all respects,
Red

Son's Letter to His Soldier Father

October 31, 1862
Horlbeck Creek Farm

Dearest Father,

I know that you are very occupied with treating all our brave Confederate lads, so I will not add a lot to Mother's letter to you. I wish that I could be by your side or, even better, fighting the Yankees with General Lee. Have you met him? Is he as great as what we hear at whipping the Yankees and making them run with their tails between their legs? I bet he is. I hope he is.

I know Mother has told you about our new addition. No! Not the new baby—Boomer. He is brilliant and quick and smart and just the best friend I have ever had—not counting you, of course. I have taught him to sit, and fetch, and speak for his treats. He is right beside me wherever I go. Boomer is so quiet that sometimes I think he is sneaking up on me like he does the birds he smells when we are out rambling in the woods. Nate sure picked a good name for him. He said that when they were walking home, and when Boomer heard that cannon's fire, he threw back his head and howled at those Yankees! We don't know if it was the Yankees, but for sure Boomer howled and barked at those cannons!

Do not worry about Mother. I am taking good care of her just like you told me to do on the morning you left when you took me aside where she could not hear what you were saying. I think she knows, by the way, because sometimes she calls me her "little man." Sometimes she even forgets and calls me James Edward Merriweather when she is really mad at me. It is kind of like I used to hear her call you when we stayed too long at Nate's and supper was cold by the time we walked in the door.

Right now everything is fine with us on the

farm. We have plenty to eat, and we haven't seen any Yankees, although we do hear cannon fire from the harbor pretty often. I am keeping up with my studies just as you told me. We don't see much of Grandfather, but I understand that it is hard to cross the harbor. Nate seems to like taking his place anyway, and I like it too, but still, I miss Grandfather almost as much as Mother does.

I hear Mother calling me for supper, so if I don't want her to confuse the two of us again, I better hurry in and give her this letter.

Your devoted son,

Colin Edward Merriweather

Surgeon's Diary

November 5, 1862
Richmond, Virginia

Granted furlough from the commander of the medical brigade, I traveled to Richmond to meet with my brother-in-law Lieutenant Colonel John Bailey to discuss my ideas and preliminary research on the feasibility of employing a triage methodology in treating battlefield injuries as they are brought to our surgical tents.

John, like me, had heard of such a technique used by French doctor Dominique Jean Larrey late in the Napoleonic Wars, but it was never applied routinely in our current conflict. John was most interested in the rudimentary research conducted in Winchester following Antietam. At the conclusion of our discussion, we decided that our next step would be to train two nurses to employ the system at the next opportunity.

John and I further discussed the strange phenomenon of what I have begun to think of as the "shock into unconsciousness" often followed by ultimate death occurring during surgery even though the injured limb may have been successfully removed and the wound cauterized appropriately. John had seen the evidence of this condition—the rapid shallow breathing, the cold clammy skin, and the rapid and weak pulse. The cause seems at first obvious—the pain of the wounding, transportation, then surgery and cauterization. Yet there are some with comparatively minor injuries who also suffer and die with the same symptoms.

John has agreed to study the condition further and advise field surgeons of any potential treatments. We are not very hopeful at this point.

Before departing to go back to General Lee's encampment at Stephenson's Depot and to hospital work at Winchester, I was able to have a pleasing supper of late summer vegetables and corn bread and a hot bath in a tub. My bath was followed by a restful night's sleep in a bed, and in the morning I had a breakfast of eggs and leftover corn bread lathered in butter topped with peach preserves. God knows how John procured them, and I did not ask.

I stopped off in Winchester to check on my patients at the Conklin home and was saddened to find that Lieutenant James Conklin, the youngest of the Conklin boys, had been killed in a harassing cavalry raid behind Union lines. Thankfully, General Stuart was able to recover his body, and he escorted it personally to the home of Jesse and Iris Conklin. There he saw him buried with full military honors, a tattered CSA battle flag draping his simple coffin. As I watched the ceremony and the tears that unexpectedly formed in General Stuart's war-aged eyes, I knew why his men held him in such reverence. More than all the words said that day, Jeb Stuart's tears consoled the Conklins in ways beyond measure or simple explanation.

After checking in with Dr. McCarty and telling him the news of John's support for our triage efforts, my mount Coal and I made our way to General Lee's encampment, to a meager evening meal and a chance to rest for us both. Tomorrow I hope to meet with General Lee's adjutant to discuss the plans for the triage process and the enlistment of five nurses to be trained.

Surgeon's Diary Addendum

November 15, 1862
Northern Virginia

After returning to camp on November 6, I finally got an opportunity to meet with Lieutenant

Colonel Walter H. Taylor, General Lee's aide-de-camp, on November 10 and make my proposal to him about allocating and training five nurses to conduct triage duty during the next battle. Colonel Taylor received my verbal report well and asked several piercing questions of the kind I had come to expect based on his reputation as a deep and logical thinker and a brilliant organizer and tactician. I left him my written analysis of the preliminary research that Willie McCarty and I had completed and a letter of correspondence from John Bailey in Richmond.

I pray for his recommendation, but I am steeled for a less than enthusiastic reception.

JEM

Bits and Pieces of News

November 20, 1862
Horlbeck Creek Farm

My Dearest JEM,

What follows does not substitute for a letter, and my composition teachers at Sisters of Our Lady of Mercy Grammar School would be most upset with me that it does not. But I have been feeling a bit poorly lately as the baby has become rather restless, and so a tad here and tad there as I feel like writing will have to do for now.

All the crops are in except for turnips and collards. The turnips do us no good, but the deer sure love them. For some reason, they have no taste for collards. We completed a good harvest that will see ol Jake and us eating sufficiently until we can do it all over again next spring.

November 23

First frost of the season. It had been getting cooler all of last week, and Nate promised Colin that he would take him deer hunting the first day it was cold—unless it was on Sunday, of course. It turned cold yesterday morning, unusually so for Charleston, and Nate and Colin headed to the woods about midafternoon. Nate had planted a patch of turnips just for the deer down by the creek bank, and he and Colin sat down with their backs to a big swamp oak several yards away from the turnips and waited.

Nate told me before they left that it could be dark before they returned. Still, as it was beyond dusk and moving quickly toward dark, I was getting a bit perturbed at Nate and worried about Colin. So I found myself looking every minute or so out the kitchen window that faces the lane. It was just about good dark, when colors turn to gray, and white and black begin to blend together, and images have no substance, when I thought I saw movement down the lane. "No," I told myself. "Just my mind playing ghost games with my eyes again." Still, I saw movement, I was pretty sure, but I could not make out the shape. It was strange as it looked like two men walking and holding the hands of a child in between them. Well, that sure did not make sense. Finally, about fifty yards from the house, I could tell it was Colin and Nate, and the child they were dragging was a deer that they each had by the horns, leaving a trail of blood up the lane.

As they got closer to the light from the window, I thought Colin had been hurt. His face was covered with blood, as was the front of his shirt. I screamed and rushed out to them. I yelled at

Nate, "What have you done to my son, damn you!?" Nate and Colin just broke out laughing, which made me scream louder, salty tears streaming down my face.

I was not raised on a farm. I didn't know that a boy got bloodied when he killed his first buck. Nate almost got bloodied too as I beat on his chest with my fists amid my tears and then hysterical screams of laughter!

November 24

Yesterday after we all had the big laugh at my expense over Colin's bloody face, and before they came in the house, Nate and Colin hung the deer from the rafters in the barn up high enough that no other animals could get at the carcass. They had gutted him down by the creek bank so skinning and butchering could wait a day in the cool weather.

Nate and Audrey Lee made their way over after morning service, and after lunch Nate and Colin made quick work of the deer and salted away the meat in the barrels that already had been emptied of salted pork we had eaten since this time last year—keeping out a nice leg roast for each family.

As the "men" went about their tasks, I began feeling particularly weak. Audrey Lee helped me to bed and gave me some midwifery advice about taking it easy. She is right, as she usually is. Giving birth to this baby is still a long way away, but I must admit I am a bit anxious from time to time. Something is just not the same as with Colin. But aren't all babies different? Probably nothing a dram of Audrey Lee's homemade sherry cannot cure.

November 26

As it turned out, Audrey Lee was worried enough that she stayed the night while Nate went on home to feed the stock and put his leg of venison roast in the springhouse until Audrey Lee could cook it.

I needed the rest, I guess. When I finally got up at mid-morning today, I was feeling much better. Yesterday after I lay down to rest my head, Audrey Lee swept the floors, straightened up, fixed supper for Colin, and put the leg of venison in a pan of salt water with a brick on top of it to soak out the gamey taste before roasting. Not sure what that brick does, but she swears by it. I cooked it for supper tonight for Colin and me. It was sure good with the sweet potatoes and onions we roasted with it, so I guess that brick worked.

November 28

It has been a month since I have heard from you. I miss you so desperately.

Yours always,

Red

Surgeon's Diary

December 2, 1862
Northern Virginia

With reports of Union forces gathering on the shores of the Rappahannock, we have begun preparing to march toward Fredericksburg. Three days ago, Colonel Taylor called me to his tent, where he spent an hour questioning me about the triage process I proposed. I was astounded at his knowledge of my research and the proposal, but I could not determine if his being so well versed in my own words was good or bad for the proposal.

In the end, Colonel Taylor said it was his communication with John Bailey in Richmond, along with John's positive endorsement, that swayed him to give triage a trial run at the next battle, which seems shortly upon us. He reduced the nurses from five to two and assigned me two of the youngest nurses. No matter. We shall succeed.

I met with the two nurses. Bobbie Jean McCarty had followed her new husband, Willie, from Columbia, South Carolina, to the fighting. Maggie Adams is the thirty-year-old widow of Private Ranson Adams of Atlanta, who was killed at the July 1 Battle of Malvern Hill. Maggie, after a month's mourning, decided that she would take up the fight for her husband in the only way she knew how. She believed that had she been present when her husband was returned from battle to the surgery tent, she could have saved him. I pray that Maggie will never know the true story of his wounds and that he was killed instantly and did not suffer. Even so, her belief is a good thing for her and especially for the boys she nurses.

Neither Bobbie Jean nor Maggie has had any experience with medicine, but both were farm girls, long desensitized to the sight and smell of blood and entrails.

As we move on toward the next battle, the four of us travel together so that we may teach and learn along the way. At pauses Bobbie Jean and Willie steal time to be together, and Maggie and I talk about our lives back home. Once General Lee has stopped for the day, the intensity of the learning increases as Willie and I quiz our pupils and each other on the types of battle injuries that we all have witnessed and how we would handle them in the triage process in the upcoming campaign.

The ladies have developed a desire to see the process in action. Like some others, they have doubts that removing two nurses from treating injuries to put the wounded into categories will save more men.

I cannot see how we can possibly cause more deaths. And on that thought, I retire for this day.

JEM

Rejoicing

December 14, 1862
General Lee's Encampment
Fredericksburg, Virginia

My Most Lovely Mary Assumpta,

General Lee showed his superiority again yesterday as the Army of Northern Virginia inflicted significant damage to the Army of the Potomac. The battle had been brewing since Thursday, when the Yanks crossed the Rappahannock on a pontoon bridge and laid waste to the town of Fredericksburg with little resistance from General Lee, who was, we were to learn, massing his army on the hill known as Marye's Heights that sits above the demolished city. Yesterday, the Yankees attacked the hill and suffered the consequences of such a tactic that is foolish even to my nonsoldierly eyes.

With our victory here, there is once more hope for a rapid and propitious end to this War of Northern Aggression. Surely Mr. Lincoln can assess the divine rightness of our struggle for a nation for our Southern people, as our far-outnumbered army, again and again, is superior to his Union forces.

As you can tell, I am pleased that we prevailed, but I am overjoyed to inform you that our trial run of the triage process was most successful. While we did not have the kind of rush of wounded that we experienced at Antietam, we still were able to assemble the wounded into groups for, I am convinced, more effective treatment. I know that there will be more Antietam-like battles ahead, but I am rather confident that triage will prove its worth. Over the next few days, I look forward to many meetings with our team to hear their reports. There are many other things that I should tell you about life here, but I fear that I would only inevitably return to the success of triage.

So I shall turn to images more pleasant. As Christmas quickly approaches, you and Colin are never far from my thoughts whenever I have a moment to rest from my duties. Each evening I read of the events leading to the birth of our Lord as my devotion before retiring. Interestingly, in my mind, as I read the Yule story, Mother Mary is a redheaded colleen, and the Blessed Baby resembles our Colin at his birth.

I am not sure of the next steps for this army and for me, but in the surgery during this battle I observed many, many men without shoes, their feet wrapped in rags. Yet they fought when called upon at Fredericksburg. We must acquire shoes, clothing, and food over the oncoming winter months or our war shall end ignominiously here in Fredericksburg.

My hope is that I will find more time to write to you and Colin as an inevitable lull, I think, must be at hand for both armies. Should this not reach you before Christmas Day, when you do read it, remember that nothing in this world can surpass my love for you and Colin.

Overwhelmingly and desperately in love with you,
JEM

Christmastime on the Farm

December 28, 1862
Horlbeck Creek

My Dearest and Most Precious JEM,

The best thing I can say about Christmas of 1862 is that peace on earth actually seemed a possibility. Father visited us unexpectedly on Sunday of Christmas Week. There was an unofficial Christmas truce, so he was able to find a boat to transport him to Horlbeck Creek. At breakfast on Monday morning, Father insisted that we travel back with him to Charleston first thing on Tuesday morning.

At first I resisted, but Colin, of course, would have nothing except to sail to Charleston. Since he would have little else special with which to celebrate the season, and given that I was feeling well—the baby has been calm for several days now—we decided that we would just do it.

Colin rode ol Jake up to see Nate to ask if he would look after the animals until we returned on December 27, and of course Nate agreed. The small single-sail flat-bottom oyster boat arrived just after dawn on Tuesday, December 23, to pick up Father, and we sailed straightaway to Charleston without incident other than, unusual for me, I suffered from mal de mer.

To be on the safe side, we sailed up the Cooper River and disembarked north of Drum Island, where Father had left his carriage in the care of a local blacksmith whom he regularly supplied with ointments for burns from his furnace. Once we were in Charleston proper, there was no worry. Father says it appears that for now the Yankees have given up attempts to invade the city and are focusing on trying to blockade the harbor instead.

As we rode up to the homeplace, Mother's absence was painfully evident as there were no Christmas decorations to be seen at all. I did not expect much, not in time of war, but most other homes at least have wreaths on the front door. Our house was unique in the absence of anything reminding us of Christmas. Colin constructed a primitive wreath of cedar and holly, and I found an old red hair ribbon of Mother's to form a bow. It was painful to see the tears in Father's eyes.

Darling, Charleston proper has not yet experienced wartime destruction, but it has certainly suffered. A little more than a year after the great fire that laid waste to so much of the city, little rebuilding has taken place. Father says that many people have just moved to the country, taking with them what cash they saved from the fire or withdrew from banks that were most reluctant to allow more than minimum withdrawals.

Father's store and John's practice were unaffected by the fire, although Father's business is far from where it was before the war, and the windows in John's practice are boarded up with a sign on the door: Closed Due to War. See Dr. Raymond Ebenezer for Assistance. You will surely remember old Dr. Ebenezer. He once came to John suffering from jellyfish stings, and when John told him the best thing to do was to just piss on the welts, Ebenezer huffed out of the office, only later that day to be arrested for indecent exposure! I remember that the judge set ol Ebenezer free because the entire court (including the judge) was laughing so hard that the judge could not restore order.

Father says Dr. Ebenezer is one of only two or three "physicians" continuing to practice in Charleston.

Father took me to visit Mother on Christmas Day, but she did not know me. She seemed to recognize Father, but he says that is more because of his visits and because she remembers his face, but Mother doesn't recall any of their marriage. At some point, Father had brought her one of my old dolls, and she was holding it to her breast, rocking to and fro and singing to it, calling him Joseph.

Pray for Mother, but pray more for Father. He must continue to care for her as his wife although she does not know him except as a kindly gentleman who visits her each week. Mother lives in a totality of her own creation.

Mother seemed happy the day I observed her—I cannot call it a visit—but Father says that her bouts of angry hysteria are becoming more frequent. At these times she must be restrained to her bed, and Father cannot bring himself to see her in such pain, so he stays away.

Perhaps I might have at least attempted to reconcile with her, but Father says that was never my choice but instead was Mother's. Still, to see her in this place among so many who are afflicted like she has softened my resolve to never reconcile. Father says that is most likely never to be a choice I shall face.

Before I forget, Father arranged with Bartholomew Jennings to drive us in the carriage to the Christmas Eve service at "the Stump." The Reverend Green continues his ministries, but these days much of his work is with parents of boys killed in the Virginia campaigns. Parents who live without bodies to bury turn to the reverend because he understands their grief from time spent with families of seamen lost at sea.

Seeing Bartholomew again was worth the trip to Charleston. He stayed with Colin during our visit to Mother and joined us for the evening Christmas meal afterward. I have promised Colin I will tell him the full story when he is older.

Yesterday when we arrived back home at the dock at the mouth of Horlbeck Creek, there was Nate fishing and ol' Jake grazing with the wagon nearby. When we pulled back up to the house, the smells shouted that Audrey Lee had prepared a sure-enough Christmas meal for us. She had cooked a venison roast and a ham, roasted sweet potatoes, green beans, corn bread, and corn bread dressing with bits of fat from the ham throughout. Apple pie from her preserves was dessert. Father sent us back with a bit of his precious coffee (thankfully without chicory), and we finished the whole lot of it that afternoon just talking and eating Audrey Lee's pie.

While we were gone to Charleston, Nate took the antlers from Colin's deer, cleaned them up, and wrapped them at the base with leather he had tanned from a hog he slaughtered last year. He attached the antlers with two hidden screws to a piece of weathered barn board that he had cut into the shape of an oval. Just below where the antlers were attached to the board, he had carved the following:

C. E. M.
FIrSt BuCK
11-22-62

Colin didn't see the mounted antlers until he went into his room to put down his rucksack from the trip. In a minute or two, the yelling commenced because when he turned toward the dining room, there they were, hung right above the door where he could not miss them. God bless Nate and Audrey Lee.

And God bless you, James Edward Merriweather, and keep you safe until you return to my arms. That thought is the only gift I desire this Christmas.

Yours in everlasting love,

Red

Surgeon's Diary

December 30, 1862
Fredericksburg, Virginia

I have been lost in hell. It has taken me fifteen days to regain any measure of composure so that I can record my impressions of Fredericksburg and its aftermath. Thanks to unconscionable blunders by General Burnside and our own luck in arriving at just the right time, the slaughter was one-sided and as brutal for the Union army as it was fortuitous for the Army of Northern Virginia.

Compared to Antietam, our casualties were few. It provided an exceptional opportunity to employ the triage process as a trial, as the small number of wounded gave us time to assess the process and make adjustments as we worked. It was, by my calculations, reasonably successful. However, I think that I cannot use it again. The tragedy that occurred the day after the battle ceased has so negatively colored all considerations of triage that I want no association with it.

In the false dark of early evening on December 16 as men were celebrating the success of another Confederate victory with shouts of "Bring on DC" and "Abe, here we come," tragedy pierced our hearts and darkened our souls—mine beyond repair, I think.

Willie McCarty and his young bride eased away from the camp in hopes, I assume, of finding a soft bed of pine needles where for a few moments their lovemaking could wash away the blood of the last three days. It was a chilly evening, and Willie had given his topcoat with officer epaulets to Bobbie Jean. He had put on a clean blouse under his captain's jacket. Bobbie Jean still had her hair in a bun and had not changed from the dress she had worn during the day.

It was not until the evening bugle call that the absence of the McCartys was noticed. Nurse Maggie Adams first missed Bobbie Jean. She waited fifteen minutes after the bugle call, figuring Bobbie and Willie were exchanging last embraces and kisses before retiring to separate quarters. But as fifteen minutes drew out to half an hour, Maggie became worried and sought me out. She relayed to me that Bobbie

Jean had told her that she and Willie were going to sneak away from camp after supper for a woodland tryst before bedtime. Maggie and I agreed that we would go out and try to find the lovers and get them back to their proper tents without drawing the notice of the sentries.

Geographically, the only suitable area was the level pine forest to the south of the camp near a creek that would have muffled sounds of lovemaking. While it was not yet good dark, Maggie and I approached the copse in opposite directions.

Less than five minutes into our search, Maggie yelled out my name in horror. I made my way to her by following the sound of her sobbing and praying. As I drew near enough, in the gathering dark I saw an almost headless form. I ran to Bobbie Jean but knew without palpating her wounds that any medical assistance would be useless. I asked Maggie if she had seen or heard anything of Willie, but she said she had not. As I left to find Willie, Maggie stayed with Bobbie Jean, cradling her limp body to her breast. I began to circle our position in widening circles, and on my second circuit I almost tripped and fell over the body of Willie.

To the killer who would have crept unseen and unheard toward our camp, Willie and Bobbie Jean McCarty, in the dusk of evening, must have appeared by their clothing to be CSA officers and easy prey. It seemed that as Willie had bent to pick up an armload of pine needles, the commando, his face likely covered in dirt and charcoal, sliced Willie's throat with a practiced stroke. I found Willie resting facedown in the dirt, a pine bough clutched tightly in his right hand. How did the killer find Bobbie Jean? Perhaps he had heard Bobbie Jean moving about the creek while washing up a bit. Whatever it was that attracted him, the silent predator left Bobbie Jean on the creek bank where eddies inches from her head swirled with the stain of her blood. Clearly the assassin had no idea that his second "officer kill" was the wife of the Confederate he had executed moments before.

As the bodies of the husband and wife were collected on a mule-drawn cart, there was found underneath each an ace of hearts with these words penned in black ink within the heart: Greetings from Abe.

The story of the twin murders, for this was not killing in war but in pleasure, spread through the Army of Northern Virginia like cloud-to-cloud lightning across a June sky. The story spread to the Union brigades across the Rappahannock almost as quickly. Only a communiqué from General Burnside to General Lee quelled the emotions on both sides of the river. Burnside wrote to Lee that he had ordered that any sign of joy among Union troops would be met with swift and harsh discipline. From reports from the western front, he identified the assassin as a former Union soldier, Abraham Whetstone, who had been court-martialed and sentenced to death by firing squad by General Ulysses S. Grant for brutality to civilians at the battle of Fort Donelson on the Cumberland River, but Whetstone had escaped in the middle of a storm before he was to be executed the next morning.

Enclosed with the communiqué was a personal letter from General Burnside to the families of Willie and Bobbie Jean McCarty expressing his condolences. His letter was accompanied by a telegram from President and Mrs. Lincoln declaring that the assassin would be caught and justice would, as the president wrote, "propel him swiftly to the everlasting fires of perdition."

Maggie accompanied the coffins back to the families in Macon, Georgia. She never returned to our ranks.

After the initial uproar, and according to scuttlebutt passed among the Union and Confederate armies, Whetstone, to be executed the next day, escaped by cutting the rope binding his wrists with the razor blade he kept hidden in the heel of his left boot. Once free of his bindings, Whetstone killed the Union sentry guarding the horses with the same razor blade. In the middle of an unexpected thunderstorm, unnoticed by almost everyone, Whetstone stole a saddle, a rifle, and a bowie knife. As he eased the horse almost silently away—the sounds of hoofbeat softened by the wet ground—a second sentry at the outskirts of the encampment called out to him to stop and identify himself. According to the story, this was the assassin's first kill with the bowie knife that he used to kill Willie and Bobbie Jean.

With the loss of the three people most knowledgeable of the triage process and most dear to me, I am not of the mind to see it resurrected. Perhaps at some future date, should I become immune to the horror so often laid before me in this conflict, I will teach others of its benefits.

JEM

CHAPTER 18

French Leave

Following defeat at Fredericksburg, Union general Ambrose Burnside was so devastated by his repeated failures that he wrote to President Lincoln and offered his resignation. The president refused even though Burnside's critics had labeled him the "Butcher of Fredericksburg." Burnside, hoping to redeem his name after Lincoln refused his offer of resignation, launched a second offensive against the Army of Northern Virginia in January 1863, but winter weather was an enemy greater than Robert E. Lee. Burnside's Army of the Potomac became bogged down in the Maryland mud, with the campaign eventually being derisively known as the "Mud March."

The Army of the Potomac was in disarray and dismay. Burnside again offered to resign, and this time Lincoln accepted.

In late January, Lincoln named Major General Joseph Hooker to lead the Army of the Potomac. Lincoln sincerely hoped that he had finished the deplorable game of swap-the-commander, as it was dubbed by his critics.

He would be wrong. In reality, Lincoln's changes in command were of little consequence to either of the two armies facing each other across the Rappahannock River.

The winter was not a time of fighting in the east. As Burnside found out, no matter how well he could predict the actions of his enemy across the river, the unpredictable winter weather undid the best schemes. So winter was a time for resupplying the armies with essential goods. Many of Lee's fighters had answered his call at Fredericksburg with little but rags for shoes, and now as winter worsened, increasing numbers took French leave and just walked away. No one blamed them or challenged them as the condition of the Army of Northern Virginia had deteriorated to the point that surrender on humanitarian grounds was discussed at the lowest and highest levels of General Lee's army.

The inability to reliably resupply the Confederate army would inevitably be more disastrous than the Union's battle plans. Without the industrial capacity to support its own war, the South relied on its European allies—principally England and France—to supply arms, food, and other essentials necessary to prosecute a war. Of course, this being no secret to the Union, capturing or at least blockading the East Coast ports became a primary strategic objective of the Union war plans. New Orleans was the first major Southern port to fall during the spring of 1862. For the Union, this provided a mile-wide highway from New Orleans to Vicksburg. For the South, the Mississippi was no longer the vital pipeline through which goods could travel to the railhead in Vicksburg and from there east to Tennessee, Georgia, and the Carolinas on to the Army of Northern Virginia, whose goal was nothing less than to capture Washington, DC.

Foraging nearby farms and cities for cured meat and winter vegetables was a detested but necessary evil if the Army of

Northern Virginia was to survive the winter. Southern civilians gave and then gave some more, retaining barely enough food to see themselves through to springtime. The dire need of the army for the most essential items created within the average Southerner and the combatants a view that this was a war of desperation and survival—not just temporary, but a glimpse of the future.

Fortuitously, supply trains from the port of Wilmington, North Carolina, and to a lesser degree, from Mobile, Alabama, brought food, clothes, shoes, and weapons supplied by the factories in Europe to the Army of Northern Virginia. With the supplies came a renewed anticipation for the spring and summer battles that loomed just beyond the winter's horizon.

Letters in Time of War

The letters to and from the front were a constant consternation to James and especially Mary Assumpta.

James's day moved swiftly from dawn to dark. Frantically during battle and methodically afterward, it always moved. There was a little time for reflection, so diary entries became more predictable than did the letter writing. Letters required a significant tact to give Mary Assumpta a feel for her husband's circumstances, but not so much a feel as to generate alarm. Therefore, letters needed time and creativity. Diary entries were cold hard truth written at the end of a long day.

Mary Assumpta's time flowed more slowly. A thousand times between letters she worried for her husband's safety. Newspapers from Charleston reported casualties, but she read a newspaper no more often than she received a letter from James at the front. Her worries were her constant companion, and the accompanying anxiety affected the growing life in her womb with a fetal disquiet and a pregnancy noticeably different from her first with Colin. Letters relieved her for a few days, but they were far apart. When she felt most alone, the doubts returned. In the back of her mind where her deepest fears dwelled, she believed something was amiss with her unborn child.

James's war diary was printed and kept in several small bound notebooks he had picked up in Richmond before he reported for duty. He added to his supply on his visit with John Bailey after Antietam. It was not that his letters from Mary Assumpta were less precious than his diaries. Things that he would not say to his wife, he wrote to himself. The journals, empty or completed, were kept dry and dark and covered in his trunk. So dates and names of places, people, and battles were well-preserved.

James's psyche, fragile at best, had been dealt an immense blow. The murder of Willie and Bobbie Jean McCarty and the decision of Maggie Adams not to return to nursing caused him to withdraw into himself as a daily occurrence. This occupied his time and energy, even as the war ceased for a time.

Mary Assumpta and Captain James Merriweather were as loving and loved as any two war-tossed lovers in any conflict. They wrote regularly, yet in the time frame after Fredericksburg and before Gettysburg, there were huge gaps in their correspondence. Unreasonably so. Mary Assumpta was in the last stages of her second pregnancy, and little could be done outside the warm farmhouse. James was in the midst of the major winter lull in the fighting after Fredericksburg. Both were series of events that should have produced more letter writing, not less.

War, all war, is a series of mishaps and misadventures defying every plan and plot. Human beings—foes, friends, acquaintances, and lovers—within this maelstrom are thrown together. And with them, their personal letters and official dispatches are sent into the ether. In the end, there are some preserved, most with gaps in telling the stories, and there are those just as important that are lost to all time. These communiqués—lost, found, and in tatters—illuminate the war with their personal stories and struggles. They inform us at least as much about events as the historians do.

One is remiss in consideration of the matters of war without considering the purely metaphysical. James and Mary Assumpta wrote of events that existed yet did not coexist. Instead, their written words resided in two worlds separated by time, distance, design, and purpose. Each wrote to the other knowing before placing pen to paper that when their letter arrived, if it arrived, their worlds were likely to have changed paths in their orbits of fate. They knew that which they wrote had already been eclipsed by new events whose stories had not yet been told. Such uncertainty.

For James and Mary Assumpta, the uncertain knowledge of events at home and at the front were their constant companions, bringing both hope and despair in equal measure.

Surgeon's Diary

January 8, 1863
Fredericksburg, Virginia

"Long is the way, and hard, that out of hell leads up to light," wrote John Milton.

And I understand.

Willie and Bobbie Jean were such excellent people. With their murders, I descended into hell and dwelled there for some time, unable and unwilling to see beyond my own pain. For days my tent and my cot burned with hell's fury.

My only contact with this earth was the ground beneath my feet when I left the tent to relieve myself. For days, when I pissed it smelled of sulfur to my nostrils, and I could not get far enough away from my tent to keep the odor from following me to my bed.

Finally, I ran out of whiskey. There was none to be had by anyone in our encampment, and there was enough food to barely stay alive. My rescuer, Chaplain Father Michael O'Malley, tells me that I roamed about the camp crying out for whiskey. Why he decided I was worth rescuing, I am not sure. Surely I am not the only person among us afflicted by the evils of liquor.

Regardless, he was a God-sent healer. No prayers over me that I observed (although I am sure there were many). No preaching of the evils of excessive drink. He knew that I already had experienced that lesson firsthand. He stayed with me, and as I became able, we talked.

We knew each other professionally, having seen each other in the postsurgery tents as we looked in on the boys, but we'd never taken the time to talk until now. As I became more lucid, I was surprised to find that he was a parish priest from Richmond and that he knows of my father's medical office and his practice of buying slaves, freeing them, and then turning around and employing them as he is able. We talked eventually of how we found ourselves engaged in this war though we are both personally opposed to slavery. Father O'Malley said that had the Vatican required that he serve the Army of the Potomac, he would have been on the other side of the Rappahannock tending to the needs of those boys. I understood entirely.

We talked first of how I became *his* patient—of what brought on this role reversal. As we became more comfortable with each other's company, we talked of political and philosophical views. We talked of the war and our roles in it—of how those roles were changing us in unexpected ways.

We shared family stories and laughed uncontrollably as I told the story of how my grandfather and religion professor Timothy was known to the students at William and Mary as "the Eccentric" because he often came to class unshaven and with hair uncombed, having spent all night reading and writing in his library office.

We talked of family and friends destroyed by this war. Father O'Malley urged me to speak about the murders of Bobbie Jean and Willie McCarty, and for the first time I released that horror from inside me. I cried. I raged. I drew into a ball of emotion, and still he waited on me patiently until I came back to him again. In the act of finality, of expressing it to another person, I told him about my vision for triage and why I could not regain that dream. And still, he listened. When I had talked out my horrors, my fears, and my decision to abandon my plans, we talked of other things, more mundane but not unimportant.

We talked of land and heritage. He is familiar with the area of Ireland from which Mary Assumpta's father's people came. Father O'Malley grew up poor and Catholic, which, as he explained, was the status quo, as was joining the priesthood to escape poverty and bring honor to his family in Galway. As a young priest in 1858, and just graduated from All Hallows College in Dublin, he was assigned to Saint Peter Catholic Church in Richmond. He spoke of his congregation's just-formed acceptance of him as a pastor when he was assigned to the Army of Northern Virginia. It seemed, he said, that the Vatican assumed, as most people did, that the war would be short and that Father O'Malley could resume his duties at Saint Peter in a short time.

We talked of God and less of religion. I told him of the ups and downs this war had caused in my beliefs in the Almighty. Of times when I felt sure I had been cursed, punished, and abandoned. I was surprised to find that Michael O'Malley was not unfamiliar with these feelings and questions of the reality of the Divine in the actions of man. Assuming God existed, we talked about his expectations of us as people, our expectations of him as a deity, and how these two ideas determined the basic relationship of God and man. Our conversation of the Almighty ended with two unfinished discussions: the nature of God at his most elemental, and whether God uses evil for his purposes. Our religious upbringings took us down predictable paths, so we reached no conclusions but agreed to continue the conversation.

Finally, we talked of slavery. Father O'Malley told me of the abhorrent conditions in the slums of Galway and his view of the English government that had reduced Irish people to peasant slaves through the control of land-ownership by the nobility, and he forgave my English Protestant heritage. Michael talked of his struggle spiritually when he was assigned as a chaplain to the Army of Northern Virginia and did not know whether or not he could minister to the members of an army to a significant part fighting to maintain slavery as an economic engine. In the end, he said it came down to his duty to the church, which he said must succeed among so much that is evil. I found his struggle, not unlike my own and my duty to my land, of equal measure to his duty, and like his, my struggle is unsatisfying.

Throughout the day of talking, I found a depth to this young priest that was not unlike that of Grandfather Timothy—a connection spanning time, nationality, and religious tradition.

With a promise of return the next day, he made his way to minister to his flock as best as he was able, no doubt doing it with sincere compassion for their wounds of body and psyche.

Before I retired, with his wisdom ringing in my ears, I wrote this mantra to guide me in the upcoming days:

I am resolved to do my duty,
To do what I can do,
To stay within that framework as I am able,
Knowing that God will be satisfied with my efforts.

JEM

Casualty on the Creek

January 8, 1863
Billington Farm
Horlbeck Creek, South Carolina

Dear Dr. Merriweather,

I know of no way to tell you this that will not hurt. Mary Assumpta lost the baby in the early hours of Wednesday a week ago. Audrey Lee and I were by her side when the baby boy was stillborn. According to Audrey Lee, it was clear that the baby had been deceased for some time as he was only big enough to fit into my two hands.

I have hesitated in writing this letter in the hopes that Mary Assumpta would rouse from the overwhelming sorrow that has consumed her this last week. However, except for the burial of Baby M, she has not risen, taking what little soup Audrey Lee can coax her to eat and taking care of nature's call without leaving the bed.

So it has fallen to me to tell you of the events that preceded this sad event and of the days that have followed up to this letter.

It was evident when we visited on New Year's Day for a supper of black-eyed peas and collard greens that Mary Assumpta felt mighty poorly. She did not just have "the pregnant regrets" as Audrey Lee calls that time when the lady is very much with child but still has a month or more before delivery. She was really hurting in her belly. Audrey Lee and Mary Assumpta had calculated way back that the baby should be born early to mid-February, so both womenfolk were mightily concerned with the pains Mary Assumpta was experiencing so much before that time. Audrey Lee is really good at calculating these things, so I expect she was right this time too.

After supper, Audrey Lee sent me and Colin to ride back to the house to get her kit bag of medicines and such. When we arrived back, Mary Assumpta was in such pain that she was crying out for you and for her mama, Lauraleigh. I sat by her as Audrey Lee went to the kitchen to brew up some herbal tea of red raspberries, Saint-John's-wort, spearmint, primrose, and wild yam. I stayed by Mary Assumpta's side while Audrey Lee worked in the kitchen, and judging by the way she would grab my arm when one of those pangs would grip her, I knew she was hurting bad.

Mary Assumpta got a cup of the tea down. As the rest of the tea boiled down to be used as a poultice, she rested some. But it did not last long, and she was crying for Jesus to save her baby. Audrey Lee gave her another few sips of tea—this time laced with a big dram of whiskey—and applied the warm poultice to her belly to bring some small relief. This went on until near midnight. Colin tried to stay up to help his mama, but he finally gave it up, went to his room, and dropped off to sleep in the early morning.

Just before dawn, Audrey Lee called out for me to hurry in from the kitchen and help her—the baby was coming. With a final but not so painful push, Mary Assumpta gave birth to your son. As I looked down at the tiny little boy, Audrey Lee gave me a very small shake of her head to tell me the baby was stillborn. Mary Assumpta asked if it was a boy or girl, and Audrey Lee told her it was a little boy and that I would take him into the kitchen and clean him up.

As I washed his little features with a gentleness I did not know these old and calloused hands could muster, I heard Mary Assumpta ask Audrey Lee why she had not heard the baby cry. Audrey Lee did not answer her directly but told her I would bring her son to her presently. As I finished drying off the baby's head, I heard Mary Assumpta cry out in what can only be described as the pain that souls in hell must utter, and I knew that Audrey Lee had broken the news to her that her pregnancy had been unfulfilled with life at its end.

As I laid the little boy into Mary Assumpta's arms, tears were streaming down her face and onto the face of the little boy whom you will never hold as she held him now. How I wish you had been there. I was a terrible substitute for the strong man she needed.

As Audrey Lee helped Mary Assumpta clean up, I knew that it was my job to go and break the news to Colin. James, a farm produces its share of nature's tragedies, but a lifetime of farming had not prepared me for what I had to do that early morning.

As I went into Colin's room with the antlers above the door declaring his journey into manhood, he was sleeping with his back to the door. I eased down beside him and touched him on the shoulder with the hands that had just washed his brother-never-to-be. As he turned over, he was wiping his eyes, and I knew he had not been asleep at all, knowing that tragedy had struck his house early that morning. Before I could speak, he asked if his mama was all right. I told him she was but said the baby was stillborn. We talked a bit about what that meant until he was ready to walk with me to see his mama. I asked him if he wanted to see his brother, and he told me he did.

As we eased through the door, it was apparent that Audrey Lee had taken the baby in anticipation of Colin's arrival and was wrapping him in one of his mother's bright scarves worthy of a little boy. When Mary Assumpta saw us, she reached out her arms, and Colin ran to her. As his mother cried, he soothed her as best he could, and when she would not be soothed, they cried together for ages in each other's arms. All cried out, Colin asked if he could see his brother, and Audrey Lee brought the baby to him and Mary Assumpta. As we all gathered there in the false dawn with our heads bowed, I prayed for Mary

Assumpta, for your boys and you, and for myself and Audrey Lee.

We buried Baby Merriweather as soon as Mary Assumpta was able to rise from her bed, dress, and with Audrey Lee's help make her way outside. Just there inside the fence of the kitchen garden, in a tiny wooden box made of barn wood, the baby still wrapped in Mary Assumpta's bright scarf, we lay Baby Merriweather in his final resting place adorned with a cross fashioned by his brother on which he carved "Baby M. 1-2-1863."

Mary Assumpta will recover. Colin, Audrey Lee, and I will see to it.

Yours in sorrow,
Nathan Billington

For Good and Ill

January 14, 1863
Army of Northern Virginia
Winter Encampment

My Dearest Mary Assumpta,

I trust that you have received my letters of Christmas Day and again on New Year's Day. I celebrated the day of our Lord's birth and the New Year with a heavy heart for the families of Bobbie Jean and Willie McCarty, who were so brutally murdered the day after the fighting at Fredericksburg ceased. I will not burden you with a retelling of the events or my reaction to them, but a month removed, I remain unsteady of mind and body. For a while, I took medicinal shots of whiskey to aid me through the day, knowing that I was substituting one evil for another. And evil it was that was dragging me into a hell from which I wondered if I should ever emerge. However, with the help of our chaplain, Father Michael O'Malley, I have given up the drink. We talk instead—at least once a day. Don't worry for me; I am in good hands.

The weather here has been remarkably awful. Last week we had thirty straight hours of windblown rain. The mud became so thick that we lost horses and mules whose hearts gave out as they tried to pull wagons through the mire.

The word here among the officers is that there will be no further campaigns until spring. Many of our boys have no shoes, have limited ammunition, and must ration food supplies. Pray that our European allies are, even as this letter is being written, loading supplies on railcars bound to us from the docks at Wilmington. Without their help, this war is headed toward an unfortunate end even though we have driven the Yankees from our soil.

I pray for you and Colin and the baby you are carrying morning and night, and soon I look forward to receiving a letter announcing the birth.

Although I would not have you believe that I do not struggle with this hellish conflict, I do come and go with good days and bad. I rejoice in the good and contemplate the ill, trusting that such is all that I can reasonably do in the service of the Almighty. No matter the day,

I am most assuredly and devotedly yours,
JEM

Fanciful Thinking of a Bored Mind

January 16, 1863
Army of Northern Virginia
Winter Encampment

My Precious Mary Assumpta,

What a glorious day was today. I have read your Christmas letter over and over, savoring every word and turn of phrase. The last letter I received was from late November when Colin had killed his deer and nothing since. I was crazy with all manner of silly and outrageous worry. Now all of that is gone as the sun burns away the winter fog.

I am so pleased that you were able to travel to Charleston with your father and Colin, but saddened at your description of the city. The fire could not have come at a worse time for rebuilding with both men and supplies in short supply.

When I read that you had stepped forward toward reconciliation with your mother, I said a prayer of thanksgiving. Perhaps your mother does hear you but cannot respond. It is so important that your healing has begun. I will pray for your mother's recovery and study on it too.

I traveled to Richmond recently to talk with John again about the surgical condition we call "shock," but he was unable to suggest to me a remedy for the unwellness that takes so many men who survive battle only to die of this puzzling malady. I returned to camp with three textbooks written about the connections between mind and body. Many physicians consider any suggestion of a reaction between a person's mental state and their physical wellness, or lack thereof, to be poppycock.

I have seen far too many cases to consider it anything other than worthy of study. We have many who return to physical health but who live in another day and time, far away from the terrors of the battlefield. Perhaps there is a connection between their afflictions and your mother's. I will do my best to find an answer. In the meantime, I will pray earnestly for your father and mother. Both are fighting battles without bullets but with wounds deep and painful nonetheless.

Personally, I have not yet retreated beyond this world in the daytime, but my night terrors, especially since the murders of Bobbie Jean and Willie McCarty, visit me almost nightly. Perhaps I shall find some answers to my own demons too.

Enough of these dark words on this cold and clear day. Sounds like Bartholomew was just the same as last I saw his ugly face. I am not surprised. He is a kind soul and a friend to be trusted. So glad to hear the Stump remains a refuge. It surely provided us with a place of solace and joy on our wedding day. I hope to see it again soon.

Nate and Audrey Lee are surely blessings to you and Colin. Though this conflict has caused me to doubt any working of the hand of a divine providence, it is hard to deny that the Almighty satisfied two needs when he plopped us square in the laps of those two would-be parents.

General Lee continues to resupply our forces, as does the Army of the Potomac, and it is only a matter of time until we clash again. Pray that somehow this *war will end before another young husband is lost to the cold hand of death.*

I sometimes think we should put politicians on the battlefield instead of boys. But lately, I don't believe that we even need to put the politicians on the battlefield, just bring them into my surgical tent. I am confident they would see the reason to halt the killing in the tide of blood and bile lapping at their feet.

I know that is only fanciful thinking of a bored mind, and I will do my duty as I have promised. And no doubt that need will arise as certain as springtime. Until then, I will try day by day to move away from the insanity that took the lives of my dearest friends, not in battle but by wanton murderous killing, so that I can fully return (without the need for libation) to caring for the men with whom I am entrusted.

Give my love to Colin and to Nate and Audrey Lee. I pray for you all and especially the little one you carry. Remember, you and Horlbeck Creek are my refuge. I will return to you.

Mary Assumpta, dear and darling Mary Assumpta, I am forever yours,

JEM

Surgeon's Diary

January 20, 1863
Fredericksburg, Virginia

Forsaken. Punished. Worthless. Wandering. Alone. In hell. Broken.

Dear God, why have you shattered me again with such pain? Have I not suffered enough in this heaven-forsaken war? For whatever sins I have committed or shall commit, have I not been punished enough? Have you not allowed Satan to have his way with me in my dreams and my drunken stupors? Why would you rain such hurt upon me by killing my precious son? What in your name have I done? What must I do to rid myself of your wrath?

January 22, 1863

Father O'Malley procured a scarce dram of morphine, and I have slept for two full days. I think he was with me much of the time, but I may have wishfully dreamt it.

I am still unable to deal with the enormity of my distress at the letter from Nate informing me of the stillborn boy child on January 8. I shall never be able to repay the debt I owe to Nate and Audrey Lee for caring for my precious Mary Assumpta. Of all the injuries of this war, none shall be greater than the open wound that I shall personally carry with me for the remainder of my days because I was not by Mary Assumpta's side or there to comfort Colin and help him understand the uncertainty of birth. I can only pray that they will find a way to forgive me.

I need to write to Mary Assumpta. I cannot find the words.

January 23, 1863

Michael O'Malley has helped me to accept my pain as real and connected, albeit unlike the pain that Mary Assumpta felt on that day and since. He has shown me that the intensity of my feeling of guilt is amplified by distance, circumstance, and lack of knowledge and has persuaded me that I should accept the pain but not the guilt. According to him, pain at its most primitive tells us we are alive. Guilt convinces us that we do not deserve to live.

Still, I am hurting in ways I cannot understand. My training has not prepared me for this eventuality. I cannot intellectually objectify it the way I can with a death in the surgical tent, and I am not sure where I will go from here.

January 24, 1863

Tomorrow I travel with Michael O'Malley to Richmond to take an extended leave to be with my parents until I am ready to return to my duties.

I don't know whom he convinced or how, or by what logic he made the case, but my orders read as follows:

By orders of General Robert E. Lee, Captain James Edward Merriweather, MD, is hereby granted leave until April 1, 1863, or such time that he is ready to return to his duty station with the Army of Northern Virginia. Said leave is to be spent in Richmond, Virginia, in whatever accommodations he is able to procure. He is to consult weekly with Lieutenant Colonel John Bailey, his temporary commanding officer, to wit to develop techniques for treating the condition of surgery commonly referred to as "shock."

Upon his return, he is to report directly to me.

Lt. Col. Walter H. Taylor
Adjutant General
Army of Northern Virginia

January 25, 1863

We left at dawn this morning and arrived in Richmond at noon. The day was cold, but thankfully there was no rain, of which we have been afflicted for much of January. After reporting to duty at Richmond headquarters without seeing John, I was mounting Coal to make my way home when Michael O'Malley, about to mount his own horse and return to his duties probably after dark, took me aside to give me his orders to be completed during my leave. He said, "James, I have two situations for you to consider, and they are intertwined with each other. I have one question about them for you to answer.

"In the murder of your friends and the stillbirth of your son, what role would a loving God have played in those two tragedies? Write to me when you are sure of your answer, and I will make a trip to Richmond, and we will talk."

With that, he shook my hand, mounted his horse, and rode north. I draped Coal's reins over the hitching post again and went back inside headquarters to write this diary entry so that I would not forget Father O'Malley's question, for I knew that he would not forget.

My entry completed, I rode west toward my parents' house at 324 Franklin Street, and to peace.

JEM

The Priestly Missive

January 26, 1863
Winter Encampment of the Army of Northern Virginia

Dear Mrs. Merriweather,

Let me begin by introducing myself. I am Father Michael O'Malley, and I am a chaplain assigned to the medical corps of the Army of Northern Virginia. My home is Richmond, where I minister to parishioners at Saint Peter Catholic Church.

Before I go any further, I must express my profound sorrow at the stillbirth of your son. I do not know why such things happen, but my faith in the goodness of the Almighty will not allow me to believe that he causes such deaths and pain such as you have endured. One day we shall know. Right now, know that I pray for you and your son, Colin, daily. I know Captain Merriweather will correspond with you as soon as he is fit to do so.

In fact, I am writing this letter at the request of your husband. He is not hurt and unable to write but rather is in a transitional period between assignments and is unable to correspond for a few days. You will surely hear from him soon after this correspondence as he becomes settled in his new duties.

Captain Merriweather and I have been acquaintances since he joined the surgical unit under General Lee's command. However, until recently we only knew each other's name and little else. But in the past few days, we have become friends and confidants. I write to you on his behalf regarding the nature of our conversations over those days.

I am unsure if you are aware of the tragedy that befell your husband's good friends the McCartys. Therefore, I will try to concisely retell the story because it is critical to the purpose of this letter.

On Tuesday, December 16, a day after the Battle of Fredericksburg had ceased and the men of the Army of Northern Virginia were celebrating a victory, Lieutenant and Mrs. McCarty slipped away from the camp to find some quiet personal time in the midst of the raucous celebrating. When they were missed as dark drew near, Captain Merriweather and Nurse Maggie Adams went to look for them and found them murdered less than a hundred yards from the camp in a copse of pines where a fast-running stream would have muffled the sounds of a struggle. The perpetrator left a calling card by which he is well-known to the general staffs of both the Confederate and Union armies. He has murdered civilians and Confederate and Union sentries from Mississippi to Virginia. He never knows his victims but merely looks for the unsuspecting.

The duty fell to your husband to prepare the remains and arrange for transport back to their home in South Carolina. Nurse Maggie Adams agreed to accompany the bodies, and before she departed, she confided to Captain Merriweather that she would travel on to her family's farm in Dahlonega, Georgia, and would not return to the Army of Northern Virginia.

We have all learned to cope with death in battle, to put it in a dark and bottomless cave in our minds, and we do not allow ourselves to spelunk these dark recesses where the nameless corpses are entombed. The deaths of Willie and Bobbie Jean McCarty were a horror that Captain Merriweather could not restrain within his mind, and he turned to whiskey. He resided in a state of drunkenness where he could not remember the past and could see nothing of merit in the future. Fortunately, the whiskey, like everything else in our miserable existence here, was in very short supply. When there was no more liquor to be had from the stores, he roamed the camp begging anyone to give him even a thimbleful to assuage his pain.

He came to me pleading for Communion wine, not knowing that I had been substituting water in Communion for weeks. When I told him the news, he fell at my feet sobbing. Not wanting anyone to see him in such misery, I grabbed a redheaded private who was walking nearby, guessing he might just be Irish, and we carried Captain Merriweather back to his tent. After I'd promised Private Patrick Flynn a special dispensation from the Vatican at the war's end, we cleaned the vomit from the wooden floor of the tent and washed it down with lye soap until it smelled reasonably clean. Next, we took to the task of cleaning up Captain Merriweather himself. I had worked in the slums of Glasgow as a neophyte priest, and Captain Merriweather's condition reminded me in a strange way of home. I believe that the clothes Captain Merriweather was wearing were the same clothes he had on the day that Maggie Adams started south with the bodies of Willie Joe and Bobbie Jean McCarty. At any rate, we found a clean set of gray woolen trousers, a white blouse, a tunic jacket, and remarkably a pair of clean socks in his trunk.

He never awakened as we washed and dressed him, and I held him erect as Private Flynn made his bed with a set of sheets and a wool blanket that Flynn had procured from where I did not know. Nor did I ever ask. God provides.

Finally, James roused and began to talk to me once he saw my clerical garb. I listened to his pain for the rest of that day and most of the next, but less and less every day after that as he reemerged as himself. As he and I talked, we found common ground even in our uncommon religious upbringings. The war has taken a toll on every man in the Army of Northern Virginia. In that regard, James and I are brothers-in-arms in combat's aftermath.

Madam, your husband is a good man, and his goodness and his ability to see beyond the "what is" to the "what might be" has served him for good and ill in this war. In our conversations, it was evident to me that he feels deeply about you and your son and his obligation to you. I know that James sometimes feels he is shirking that duty. And when he questions his steadfastness to his promise to you and at the same time sees that his best work yields few gains, he is open to suggestions from evil forces that would easily be repelled were he his true self.

Mrs. Merriweather, your husband is a medical wizard. He knows that what resides in his head as an idea can improve the odds of the wounded returning intact to their homes. His work with triage at Fredericksburg is an example. He saw an idea come to fruition even though it was yet neonatal at best. But he could see beyond the small success of triage in that battle to the fullness of its possibilities. A man who lives balancing on the edge of today and tomorrow is ripe for disappointment at every turn. Therefore the decision came to abandon triage altogether after the deaths of Willie Joe and Bobbie Jean McCarty. James could not see himself carrying the vision to its full reality, and I expect he was right, if for the wrong reasons. I also expect that if this war continues, he will return to triage as a way to honor his friends. Death, especially unexpected and tragic death, closes our eyes to future possibilities, yet I believe that God, in one of his greatest acts, reaches down and transforms our painful recollections that bog us down in grief into fond memories that once again propel us forward. James, as will we all, will one day celebrate the lives of Willie Joe and Bobbie Jean McCarty, who made the ultimate sacrifice in service to the men and boys of the Army of Northern Virginia.

Because your husband will be needed so desperately as winter turns to spring and this unholy war once again rages, I approached General Lee's adjutant, Lieutenant Colonel Walter H. Taylor, with a plan to bring James back to his complete self. I requested that Captain Merriweather, because he was not critically needed in camp during this lull, be transferred temporarily to Richmond to serve directly under your brother Lieutenant Colonel John Bailey. Further, I suggested that Captain Merriweather's assignment should be to work with Colonel Bailey in seeking an understanding and remedy for the condition known as "shock of war," which takes the lives of so many men during and immediately after surgery. I further suggested that he be allowed to seek accommodations outside those provided by the army. Toward that end, he will, I am sure, return to reasonable normality at his boyhood home. I can think of nothing more rehabilitative than delving into the problem of shock with his mentor, working regularly with his father in the daily routine of a physician's office, and then coming home to a supper prepared by his mother.

As I daily pray for James, I pray also for you, Colin, and your heavenly departed infant son. Should you need my services, I welcome your correspondence directed to me as your parish priest or a friend of your family.

Sincerely,
Father Michael O'Malley

CHAPTER 19

The Petri Dish

In the winter of 1863, in the middle of the War between the States, Washington, DC, was wild and wide open for business of most any kind. There were 212 eating establishments, 88 whorehouses, 5 theaters, 29 hotels of varying repute, 16 saloons serving whiskey, another 15 specializing in oysters, 22 rum mills, and 85 grocery and liquor stores. This was the perfect petri dish for the outlaw Abraham Whetstone in February 1863.

His bloody desires temporarily satiated with the murders of Willie Joe and Bobbie Jean McCarty, Whetstone easily made his way through the farmland of Maryland and on to Washington, DC. He was low on cash, but for Whetstone having cash was not a concern—he just took what he needed and left behind no witnesses, at least none who could or would identify him.

In the early afternoon of Tuesday, February 3, Whetstone stopped at the Wounded Duck Tavern just outside the city limits of DC. Shabby and little more than a shack, it suited him perfectly. He purchased a pint of ale since he never drank whiskey—he said it dulled his appreciation of the art of bloodletting—and got recommendations for a local boardinghouse that was cheap and that asked no questions.

Whetstone didn't come to DC to satisfy lust for blood kills. He could do that anywhere. He often thought to himself that killing was so easy—people were so gullible—that he must be a superior member of the human species. Whetstone decided as he made his way to DC (in fact, it was the sole reason to come to DC) that it was time to expand his reputation, and to do that he needed to expand his operation. He would find others who lusted for the sight of blood spattered on the walls of an otherwise pristine home. He couldn't find them in countryside—just too much room. The armies of the North and South certainly had their share of soldiers like him and were adding to the numbers of bloodlust psychopaths with each battle, but he was too well-known in those circles. He reasoned that DC was the perfect place—not quite the North and not quite the South. *Hell,* he thought, *there must be a few like me in Congress*—a thought that made him smile to himself.

Adding Evil to Evil

Shivering in the cold dusk, Whetstone made his way to Hell's Bottom and the boardinghouse of Mary Skirett in the northern section of DC, which charged two bits a day for a room and supper and provided a stall and hay for his horse in the back for another two bits. Hell's Bottom was not a neighborhood frequented by strangers or police. Problems were solved with a gun or a knife, and no one asked questions. Whetstone had found a home.

Whetstone put his horse away and climbed the back stairs to his 8' × 8' room. It smelled of sex and piss, but he had slept in worse. The room came with two buckets, one for nightly eliminations and one for washing up. He took the latter and filled it at the pump on the side of the house opposite the outhouse and the horse pen. As he was making his last stroke of the pump handle, he caught a movement in the peripheral vision of his left eye. He stopped pumping, threw the bucket of water in the direction of the movement he had seen, in one continuous motion ripped his pistol from its holster before the water arrived to drench whoever was watching him, and fired a shot that purposefully missed by a hair's breadth.

"What the shit are you doing?" A distinctively Georgia-accented voice showed the man's disdain at suddenly being soaked on a cold February afternoon.

"You are damn lucky that a bullet did not arrive before that water. Now get your sorry Rebel ass out here where I can see you before I lose my patience and give you a third eye."

David Little—and he was small, almost petite—walked out of the bushes behind the pump with his hands up. In his left hand he had a small Allen and Wheelock .28-caliber five-shot revolver, and in his right hand, he held an Arkansas toothpick more rusty than honed.

"Boy, you ever killed anybody with either of those pathetic excuses for weapons?" Little shook his head. "I thought not. Now lay them down and back away." Little complied. As Whetstone bent down to pick up Little's weapons, Little hit him behind the ear with sap filled with bird shot.

Whetstone, stunned but not incapacitated, whipped his Union-issued revolver across David Little's face, breaking his nose, which bled like he had been shot instead of pistol-whipped. Before Little could get back on his feet, Whetstone grabbed him by the collar, holstered his revolver, and exchanged it for his bowie knife. Before Little comprehended what was happening, Whetstone flicked his bowie knife to the side of Little's head in one fluid motion. The pain came immediately. For a few seconds Little thought Whetstone had just slapped his head with the blade of his knife, but when he touched his hand to the side of his head, his hand came away bloody.

"Goddamn! What have you done, you damn maniac?"

Whetstone bent down, picked up Little's right ear with the tip of the bowie knife, and presented it to him. "Here, pissant, put it in your pocket. After I fill my bucket again, go wash your face off under the pump and then follow me to my room. I just might have a use for an asshole like you."

CHAPTER 20

Resurrection

Mary Assumpta had returned to her motherly duties with Colin some days ago after Nate risked a late night boat trip across the Wando to Charleston to summon her father because there was little more that he and Audrey Lee could do. Mary Assumpta needed family to jar her from her melancholia. Audrey Lee and Nate were partners in her tragedy of stillbirth, and neither was willing to try hard love on their "adopted" daughter.

It was now February 18, 1863, on Horlbeck Creek Farm, and Mary Assumpta finally sat to write a letter to her husband for the first time in a month and a half. When she looked back, there was only one way she would ever see this past January. Bleak. Tragic events. Emotions raw and frayed into depression. Miserable weather that, day after day, mirrored her soul.

"Dearest JEM," she began, and did not write again for three days. Knowing that her failure to write had caused consternation and unworldly worry for her husband, who was fighting his own demons, she rationalized to herself that, as irrational as it really was, writing now would only make things worse. The feeling from the deep recesses of her teenage memory was like that which she felt upon returning to church after an absence of a couple of weeks. She knew she ought to be there, but she just did not want to face all the false well-wishers who would make a scene of welcoming her back. She knew she ought to return, and she did not need anyone to remind her, most of all the parish hens who fed on gossip feigned as nicety. So two weeks drew out to three and four. Logic played no part in her reasoning.

She knew that James needed her to write, but her irrational childish logic let her put it off even after her father returned to Charleston, although she had promised she would do it the next day. The next day was just not good. She felt poorly. Three dragged into a week and then two weeks, with her having written nothing more than "Dearest JEM."

Audrey Lee and Nate came midmorning, and while Nate and Colin cleaned out the barn, Audrey Lee decided she had to have a Sunday "Come to Jesus" meeting with Mary Assumpta. She quietly knocked on the weathered doorframe. There was no answer. She found the pencil and paper with its two words on the table, and she saw Mary Assumpta staring out the window toward the barn as she washed the same pot over and over.

"Mary Assumpta," Audrey Lee called to her forcefully, hoping to jog her from the self-imposed misery that was clearly written on her glazed-over eyes. It worked.

"Audrey Lee. What a nice surprise. I didn't know you and Nate were coming this morning. What brings you out our way?"

"You, Mary Assumpta. You are why we came. And when I saw you staring again into the fog of February, I knew we had made the right choice." Audrey Lee added a smile to lighten what she had said and was about to say.

"Mary Assumpta, you and James have suffered your separate hurts in silence. You must today, once and for all, accept that he has suffered no less than you. He was not here when his son was stillborn, but it affected him no less. You and he both retreated into the darkness and remained there, in part because you wanted to be there. Were you hoping to cause the other to feel the pain you felt? I don't believe that. You both are too good to be so vengeful, but whether you are doing this purposefully or not, that is what staring out that window borders on. Life is full of tragedies, and then we die. But in between each misfortune, we must return quickly to lives full of love, forbearance, and joy whenever it can be found. But mostly joy is manufactured. You have had no joy in your life because you chose to have no joy.

"I am sorry to be so blunt, but love must sometimes be hard-edged if we are to see its purpose. I hope you can understand that this is my purpose this morning."

Knowing that she had written two words of a letter and put it away, Mary Assumpta knew Audrey Lee was perfect in her purpose and her methods. "Audrey Lee, I know you are correct. It is just that ..."

Audrey Lee broke in immediately. "No, Mary Assumpta. No more excuses. You do not have reasons. You only have excuses. Your husband is at war, but Colin is right here. James may not ever know your excuses—that will be up to you—but Colin sees them every time you stare out that window, every day that you do not talk about a letter you just wrote to his father. If you will not do this for yourself or for James, do it for Colin—and do it today." Audrey Lee was clearly spent. Tears poured from her eyes.

As Nate and Audrey Lee stepped up into the old wagon, Audrey Lee spoke to her husband, saying, "Nate, I don't know if my words reached Mary Assumpta, but I think maybe my tears did. It was as if they washed over her, taking the pain with them, and before I could wipe my eyes, there was the old Mary Assumpta comforting me and drying my tears."

The old wagon bounced and rattled on the rutted clay road

to home, and Audrey Lee snuggled close against her husband in the dying sun and the damp cold of the late mid-February afternoon.

Breakthrough

Mary Assumpta and Colin ate a supper of corn bread and dried beans soaked overnight and cooked in fatback—the perfect meal for a winter day, especially one so cathartic as this one. With supper finished, Colin helped with the dishes and hung the covered iron pot high on the porch away from the coons. They would enjoy the beans again tomorrow. Then he retired to his bed to read Melville by the oil lamp.

Finally, his mother sat down again to write to her husband. Although paper was precious, she wadded up her first attempt and threw it on the dying coals of the fireplace, where it burst into flame and turned to ashes. *Perfect,* she thought. A fitting metaphor for what should happen to the darkness that invaded her soul. Flame. Ash. Potash for the garden.

In a few minutes, Mary Assumpta called Colin from his reading. He walked into the room to see his mother standing in front of the fireplace with a paper in her hand. She took her son to her breast and spoke softly to him, "My darling son, since your baby brother died, I have chosen to live in a very dark place. I chose it. It was my choice, and I regret what I have done to you with my selfishness. I called you out here to tell you and show you my resolve that from this point forward whatever may happen, I will be your mother, and we will prosper with God's providence."

She showed Colin the second sheet on which she had written "January 1 to February 22"—the dates into and out of her depression. She explained the symbolism she had discovered earlier of the flame, the ash, and the transformation. They tossed this sheet on the embers, and arm in arm they watched it flame up and turn to ashes almost instantaneously. They embraced for a very long time, for it had been a very long time for such an embrace, and they both reveled in it. Then she kissed his head and sent him back to *Moby-Dick*.

And she wrote to JEM:

February 22, 1863
Horlbeck Creek Farm

My Dearest, Dearest Love,

There are no words to express my love for you, yet I have come to see on this day as I pen this poor expression of that love that the absence of our words to each other has only convinced me more of our love, and in ways that fill the ether beyond speech and writing.

I have just this day emerged from the hellish dwelling place of my own making after the stillbirth of our son. I have accepted that fact and its companion—that my choices have affected you as well. We are remarkably blessed to have such friends as Nate and Audrey Lee and Michael O'Malley who could write in our stead and transcribe the thoughts that we, ourselves, could not bring from brain to pen.

I just want you to know that when we next meet I will lead you to the tiny grave covered with smooth rocks from the creek, with the cross at its head, and we shall say a prayer not of sorrow but of thanks.

My sorrow is now blown away on the winter wind, replaced with gratitude for being chosen to carry that precious angel whose feet never touched the loamy soil of this earth but who, like Elijah, was taken directly to meet the heavenly Father.

We have something that we still need to do for our son, but it is not onerous. Our angel requires a name for his headstone. To carve it on the cross will surely bring needed closure for Colin.

I suggested the name Colin Edward ten years ago. I think you should choose the name of our second son—with fitting Protestant and Catholic names, of course. And next you see Father O'Malley, ask him to bless it with a prayer.

My darling JEM, how I wish that I could have been with you in the battles of this past fall and with you now in Richmond. I will leave it at that. Just know that you are in my prayers as I know that I am in yours.

I promise that from now on my letters will bombard you—at least until spring planting. It will seem that you are back on the farm. And before I seal each message and send it on its way, I will speak it to you so that when you read it, you will hear my voice, my love.

Colin has been reading that volume of Moby-Dick that you purchased for him before you left. I am not sure how many times this makes, but he never tires of reading the tales of the sea until his eyes close in sleep each night and he drifts away to fight that great white whale. I don't hear any pages turning in his room, so I'd best go and tuck him in with a kiss from you.

Please write me soon, but more than that, get well. Trust John and your mother and father to give you the proper treatment. Put yourself in their hands and in the hands and prayers of Father O'Malley.

Yours returned,

Red

Restoration

By the time Captain James Merriweather had traveled the three miles to his parents' house on Franklin Street, the morning's freezing chill had diminished, but the temperature still remained in the low forties. He made no effort to hurry, reasoning that a cold breeze off his gelding's neck reddening his face would just give his mother more reason, as if she needed it, to fret over him. With Coal setting his own pace, they would be there soon enough.

As the Kentucky coal-black gelding slowly walked the three miles, his rocking gait put Merriweather into a state of conscious unconsciousness, and his unconscious mind wandered where it chose without direction. As it did so, the story of the prodigal son flooded and ebbed in Merriweather's thoughts. He pondered what the prodigal must have thought as he was greeted by his father. And what of the older brother? Did he just stand near? Stare into nothingness? Was he joyous like his father or hostile at the lavish reunion? Merriweather would have to ask Michael O'Malley about that. *I am not the prodigal,* James thought to himself, *but there will inevitably be lingering stares and covered whispers on my arrival. "What is he doing back home?" "Why has* my *boy not returned?" "Why is Merriweather so special?"*

With the joy of the homecoming, Merriweather thought, *there are always the "What took you so long?" and "How long will you be staying?" and "What are the expectations while you are here?" questions that dawdle after the unrestrained hugs and kisses of the long-awaited reunion have passed.*

As he walked the last hundred yards with the horse trailing him, his reins dragging the ground, James realized that he was about to begin his journey of restoration that had started when Michael O'Malley first approached General Lee. Merriweather moved almost cautiously toward his childhood home with the trepidation not uncommon to most reunions.

As he turned and walked down the carriage lane on the right side of the house that led to the carriage house and stable in the back, his mother, Beatrice, caught just the slightest glimpse of his neck, but it was enough to send her into an emotional state that she had had every intention of avoiding.

She ran to the back door, yanked it open, screamed, "Jimmy's home!" and threw herself into his arms. God, how he hated that nickname Jimmy, but Lord how he loved the hugs and kisses that came with it. Unexpectedly, his father soon joined in. Winston Merriweather had closed his office at lunch and come home on a hint supplied by John Bailey. James had expected his father to be at his doctorly duties until past dark as he was every day and especially this time of year.

James's father backed away to get a fuller look at his elder son. He thought that he was not frail, not in a traditional sense as a result of measles or chickenpox, but he was not the young man sure of foot and idea whom they had last seen just a few months ago when he had spent time with them before he reported to his duty station. His mother sensed it too, and she hugged him even tighter.

"James," his father spoke first, "let me put your horse up while you head inside and begin answering all the questions your mother has for you."

"No need for you to do that, Father. He is my responsibility according to the army, and he can be a handful."

"He is certainly a beautiful animal," his father responded. "What do you call him?"

"He responds to 'Coal,' as in 'black as.' He came to the army out of eastern Kentucky, and he can take a notion and act his own mind. Why don't you let me have him?"

"James, I have worked with a hardheaded horse or two. I expect we will get along just fine. Does he respond to his name?"

"He does if you begin every command with 'Coal.' He really is a good guy. Unlike so many horses that I see beaten into submission, Coal responds to firm positive commands and treats when he complies."

"Get along, Son, and go see your mother. I'll be in presently."

Mother and son walked arm in arm up the back steps and

into the kitchen with its familiar smells of simmering winter squash, a pot of coffee on the Oberlin wood-burning cast-iron stove, and a pork roast surrounded by sweet potatoes in the oven. As the family grew, the house that had once been a country house with few neighbors was now surrounded by Richmond. A house that had seemed so large so many years ago today seemed so small to have raised all five children.

The stove and washstand took up the entire outside wall with knotty pine cabinets above, and on the opposite wall were counters with cabinets above—all built by James's father. His father had overbuilt just a bit, and there was barely room enough to walk between the stove and the cabinets. *I think every one of us has a scar from where we brushed against that hot stove without thinking. Rites of passage*, he thought and smiled.

"James, come on in to the parlor. I have some shortbread cookies I made this morning, and there's a pot of coffee. Your father and I were going to have coffee and cookies to hold us over until supper. He'll be in, in a minute, but we might as well go ahead, just in case he is reliving his childhood with that horse."

The opening graces of a wartime conversation were completed with cookies and coffee. James said nothing of significance, and his parents asked nothing in return. Afterward, he made his way to the upstairs room he had last slept in the previous July. *Hard to conceive*, he thought, *of all that I have seen, heard, smelled, and experienced in hardly more than six months*. He placed his kit bag on the dresser and sprawled out on the quilted bed, preparing himself for the harder questions that were sure to come at the supper table.

James and his parents navigated the early part of supper

without hitting any mines. As he settled into the comfort of a meal at home, the conversation changed. Merriweather visually described battles and his surgery tent. *Interesting,* he thought, *that often in the South the most severe conversations must occur with food included as if it is a lubricant without which hard discussions cannot be had.*

James's parents seemed to absorb the horror of Antietam—as much as a description can convey. However, the murder of the McCartys so near the camp and for no reason whatsoever was beyond their ability to rationally accept as they had escaped the ugliness of the war thus far.

However, the status of Mary Assumpta was like a dark and deep gulf enveloping them all throughout dinner. No one risked the estrangement that bringing up the subject might bring to this first precious meal back together.

Finally, James recognized that only he could legitimately steer the wallowing conversation in the direction of Mary Assumpta. But before he could talk about his wife, he had to address his own problems.

He told his parents of his descent into an alcohol-induced stupor after the murders of his friends, his temporary emergence at the hands of Father O'Malley, and then the most unwelcome correspondence he was likely ever to receive—Nate's news that his son had been stillborn on January 1, 1863. Once that had been said, it was easy for him to speak of his second journey into the depths of melancholia and his ascent back to reality with the help of Michael O'Malley.

James took a deep breath and talked of Mary Assumpta, of her own inability to cope with the death of their son, of the impact that he believed his own absence had had on her despondence. He confessed that he had not written home since Christmas.

Only halting breaths penetrated the silence at that dining

table until finally Winston Merriweather, rising and wiping tears from his face with the bright white and precisely starched and ironed napkin, suggested that they all get coffee and apple pie from the kitchen and then return.

They gathered in the kitchen on either side of the stove. Pie was cut and coffee was poured, but words were still not spoken. Finally, they returned to the dining room to talk long into that dark February night.

The next day, breakfast was eaten with subdued conversations not far removed from silence. No one wanted to return to last evening's revelations. After the dishes were cleared, Winston Merriweather suggested, "James, why don't you come with me to the office for at least the morning? Do you good to see what proper medicine looks like, and I could use your help. Richmond is in the middle of a particularly nasty strain of the ague. Sound like a plan?"

Hesitating only for a moment, sensing that his father was offering him first steps on the road to his full restoration, James willingly accepted. "I think that is a grand idea. However, what if I come in after lunch? I need to make personal contact with John Bailey before he writes me up for being on French leave."

It was the first bit of humor Winston Merriweather had seen from his son since he arrived yesterday. It was a good sign.

Vow to Mary Assumpta

February 8, 1863
324 Franklin Street
Richmond, Virginia

My Dearest and Lovely Red,

There is no reason for my failure to write before now. I have started dozens of letters, ultimately putting them down in hopes I would hear from you the next day or the day after, thinking that then I would respond. I should understand most of all the power of words to heal. Please find the place in your heart to forgive me, for although I have not written, I have prayed morning and night that the Almighty would bring you blessed relief. Since I heard from Nate, I have questioned a thousand times my decision to enlist. I needed to be there with you. Yet I fear, having seen what I have seen, that had I not volunteered, I would have been conscripted to most likely a much worse assignment.

All I can do is promise to do better. And I shall.

I do trust that by now, Father Michael O'Malley has written to you with details of my present "reassignment of duties" and what brought me back to Richmond. No need for me to retell the events of which Michael has written. Ah, Michael. Some skeptics do not believe in angels among us. As for me, I know differently. If Michael O'Malley is not a heavenly being come to earth, he is likely as close as I shall ever see to one. And him a papist! All I can say is that you told me so. Perhaps I should reassess my denominational leanings on my return, although Father O'Malley would never suggest it. He is a man of God, not necessarily of religion.

I arrived here in Richmond a fortnight ago with Michael as my traveling companion. I presented my orders to headquarters expecting to see John, but he was outside Richmond tending to our wounded, quartering in civilian homes turned into makeshift hospitals.

I surprised Mother for sure, but I am not sure about Father. I think perhaps your brother slipped him a bit of information about my new assignment. I have had a pleasant two weeks of meeting with John in the mornings and working in Father's office in the afternoons.

John was aware of my drinking and bouts of deep melancholia, and I assume that Michael informed him of the exact reasons for my reassignment of duties, or more likely Lieutenant Colonel Walter H. Taylor, General Lee's aide-de-camp. Regardless, I have Michael O'Malley to thank for my temporary reassignment of duties. I have come to think of it as a time of restoration.

John and I have been exploring the condition of shock that I have written you about before. I think that we are making progress in identifying the symptoms exhibited by patients before they lapse into this almost always irreversible condition. We have a strategy that I plan to employ at my next opportunity—which I hope is yet a good ways away.

I have taken the opportunity to talk with John and with Father about my personal battle with melancholia. John, always the scholar and reader, had acquired before the war for his library a book by the English *scholar Robert Burton. I am now reading it at every opportunity, and what I have uncovered thus far makes perfect sense to me. Burton, in addition to being a scholar, also suffered from melancholia or what he labeled as "depression"—or a decline in one's positive attitude toward the world. And, darling, here is the part that is most interesting: he suggests, based on his trials on himself, that it can be reduced or even prevented with a healthy diet, sufficient sleep, music, and "meaningful work," and by talking about the problem with a friend.*

Those are all the things that war removes from us all. And I must confess that I have seen an increase in my own energy and mental attitude just from working with John again.

Enough about my medical research.

The lateness of the hour has crept up on me as it used to do when we were working together, and I have promised Father that tomorrow I will make his house rounds with him. It promises to be a full day.

I look forward to "talking" to you again tomorrow, and may our prayers to the Almighty on each other's behalf join together in the ether and rise to him as one.

With boundless love and affection,
JEM

Love in Kind

On March 3, James picked up Mary Assumpta's first letter since Christmas from his mailbox at Richmond headquarters. And until he departed in mid-April, she was faithful to her word. One week it was seven letters with several arriving on the same day. The next it might only be three or four. The mail service was better during the lull, but it was far from guaranteed.

Mary Assumpta's faithfulness to her promise required similar behavior from her husband. However, the mail delivery to Horlbeck Creek, never a thing of efficiency in peacetime, coughed and sputtered, and some weeks it died completely. But eventually, most of James's correspondence reached the hands of its intended recipients. Whenever a letter arrived addressed to Master Colin Merriweather, anyone walking down the road to the Wando River would have thought the war had ended. Colin jumped up and down and ran around the house, inside and out, when he received the envelope and again when his father wrote him a sentence or two and directed his son to keep it *top secret*, just between the two of them.

Before, when the Merriweathers were at low points and no letters came, time seemed to drag on like an endless row of butter beans begging to be picked on a hot and muggy July morning. For good or ill, now with the anticipation of letters every day, it seemed their days passed in unnatural and hastened time.

It was the end of March—too soon for Mary Assumpta. She had delayed thinking about planting for almost a month. Her letter to James on March 28, a beautiful and balmy Saturday, was stained with tears whose source she did not quite understand as she told him that she would not to be able to "talk" to him every day, as planting had to begin on Monday. Planting took two weeks of struggling from just after dawn to just before dusk, and what energy she had at the end of the day had to be reserved for Colin and supper.

She knew that James would understand; he knew the strains

of this time of year. He knew that things would return to a kind of patterned normality once the seeds were in the ground. But he knew that by that time, he would likely be back in General Lee's army. There his days would be long, hot, and generally unpleasant as the army prepared for the battles that were as surely ahead of them as were the blossoms on the tulip poplars around the creek's swamps.

In the evenings after supper and with a letter written to Mary Assumpta, James would read his Bible and reflect on God and the stillbirth of their son and the murders of his friends. James, a lapsed Episcopalian, had attended church regularly with his parents in his youth, and the lessons had stuck to him like beggar's-lice during a fall walk in the woods. He did not recognize until his first battle that deep in his soul he was yet a spiritual person. He took out his diary and read again the question Michael O'Malley had left with him: "In the murder of your friends and the stillbirth of your son, what role would a loving God have played in those two tragedies?" The phrase *loving God* were underlined, so at the time Michael must have put particular emphasis on those two words.

He had procrastinated for a month, and now the time was upon him to write to Michael that he was ready for their discussion, or else Michael was likely just to show up at Richmond headquarters, look James in the eye, and ask, "Well?"

James was reasonably sure that he must address Michael's interrogatory not with scripture but with the experiences that had shaped his soul since his birth. He began with the assumption that God had not fully formed his soul at birth and, therefore, life's experiences mattered in understanding the Almighty. At least that was his rationalization for putting the King James Bible aside.

He set his thinking in two cojoined courses. First, he had to conclude for himself the nature of God. When everything about the Almighty was boiled down to its most elemental form, what was his nature? Once that was done, if James could do it, he could enter the more difficult second path. He must answer for himself, and Father Michael of course, what God's most basic nature said about how he treated his creation.

Nice going, James, he thought to himself. *Why not work on topics that theologians have debated for the millennia?* With that thought, he lay down and slept. When he awoke at daylight, he was surprised. He was always a restless sleeper, insomnia his frequent companion. He had no nightmares, and he didn't think that he'd dreamt at all. Best he could determine, he never even rolled over. *How did that happen?* he thought to himself.

Priestly Assessment

On the tenth day of his journey into the spiritual unknown, James Merriweather wrote Father Michael O'Malley that it was time for his return visit to Richmond and that he would have a companion on his journey to rejoin the Army of Northern Virginia at its winter encampment.

James told his brother-in-law to expect a cleric with flaming-red hair and beard and a pronounced Irish brogue to pay him a visit sometime in mid-April.

Midafternoon on April 10, 1863, Father Michael O'Malley tied his mount to the hitching post and walked up the twenty granite front steps of the CSA headquarters building in Richmond to inquire about Captain James Merriweather. Lieutenant Colonel John Bailey, hearing his brother-in-law's name, came out and introduced himself to Father Michael O'Malley. He ushered him to a sofa in his office and served him a rare cup of real coffee.

"Father, I have been expecting you. Welcome. I know you want to meet with James, and I'll get you directions to his parents' home in a few minutes. First, I want us to talk a bit. That okay with you?"

"Colonel, I expect you know from General Lee's office exactly the reason for your brother-in-law's change of orders to Richmond. So I am comfortable with any discussion related to that."

Lieutenant Colonel Bailey and Father Michael O'Malley informally discussed brother-in-law and pseudoparishioner Captain James Merriweather's progress and his expressed eagerness to return to duty. It was an enlightening conversation for them both. Bailey explained that he based his opinion of Merriweather's fitness on a comparison of his history with Merriweather as an intern and medical partner and the unique skills that he brought to the battlefield surgery tent.

John Bailey used a term O'Malley had not heard before. He explained that he had observed that when James arrived, he was in "medical retreat"—unwilling, or perhaps unable, to use his exceptional skills as a physician and surgeon. He would only discuss using the barest acceptable medical practices. John Bailey expressed concern for his brother-in-law as this was opposite of the Dr. James Merriweather as he knew him.

John Bailey described for O'Malley his work with Merriweather to this point. He noted that after giving James a few days to reclaim his family connections under the care of his mother and physician father, he and Merriweather explored for several days the phenomenon of shock and mapped a plan to gather data about it and correspond with each other about their findings. This was Bailey's first goal for Merriweather.

Once he saw that Merriweather showed enthusiasm for battlefield research into shock, Bailey smoothly introduced the subject of triage. As their discussions progressed, they moved from "Colonel" and "Captain" to John and James, partners in medicine, a relationship of special and enduring respect and substance.

As they talked about the value of triage, Bailey could see the heart of the medical entrepreneur return to his brother-in-law. He encouraged Merriweather to put together another team and give triage another try, but only when he was ready.

"Colonel Bailey," O'Malley inserted, "have you had a chance to explore if he discussed with his parents the deep melancholia that he experienced?"

"Father," Bailey began, only to be interrupted by a loud harrumph coming from his visitor. "Yes, Father? Did I say something inappropriate?"

"Looks like you and I are in this relationship for the foreseeable future. How about I promise to address you as John and not as Colonel and you address me just as Michael without the Father moniker?"

"Deal." Bailey had never gotten comfortable with his army title. He returned to the question about melancholia. "James confided in me that there is a history of this depressed state of mind occurring in his family. It is manifested in a retreat from reality, which you saw dramatically and whose remnants I saw. You should bring up to James the work of Robert Burton. I gave him a book by Burton to read. Burton studied the condition and concluded that everyday things like healthy food, enough sleep, work that makes a difference, and talking about the problem with a friend eliminated or reduced the state of depression. Sound familiar?"

"Indeed it does. In fact, that very book was required reading in my preparation for the priesthood at All Hallows College in Dublin. I am glad to see that some of that classwork will come in handy after all. I look forward to getting reacquainted with Mr. Burton," Michael replied with a big smile on his red-bearded face.

Bailey continued, "James and I discussed this, and he knows that I was going to have the same discussion with you. So you need only keep up your excellent work.

"You are most likely to find Captain Merriweather at his father's medical practice this time of day. If, after listening to him, you also think that James is fit for duty, come by here on your way back to the winter encampment. I will have James's orders ready to present to General Lee."

Meeting the Episcopalians

Father O'Malley presented himself at the Merriweathers' front door just as shadows from the water oaks along the streets were lengthening and the temperature was cooling. Spring was in the air, but winter's last gasps could be felt in the breezes of late afternoon and early morning.

James had mentioned to his parents that Michael O'Malley's visit was forthcoming, but he did not tell them that the visit might be at their home. However, he knew that Michael would likely appear where he was most unexpected just to add a bit of levity to the deep discussions that lay ahead.

Beatrice Merriweather answered the knock at the front door sort of expecting it to be Father O'Malley. But she was unprepared for the man who stood under the portico. He was dressed in rather ragged Confederate gray accented by his untidy shock of red hair and full red beard. "May I help you, sir?" Beatrice asked, totally unaware that James's expected visitor stood before her. "If you will come around to the back door, I have leftovers from dinner that I am more than glad to give you so that you can be on your way." Beatrice, not unreasonably, had mistaken Father O'Malley for one of the French-leave soldiers who rather routinely begged for food from homes in the area.

"I do beg your pardon, ma'am. I must look a total mess after traveling from our encampment in Winchester without cleaning up at all. I am Father Michael O'Malley here to visit James. I apologize for not looking at all like a priest."

"For sure, you don't look like any priest I've ever met." Beatrice was still a wee bit wary.

He chuckled to himself at her last observation.

"Perhaps if you will call me Michael instead of Father, it will be better suited to my current state of dress."

"Of course. Forgive me, Father, for mistaking you for a ruffian. Oh, for heaven's sake. I am so sorry." Beatrice was getting flustered.

She tried getting control of her words. "Father, I want to thank you for tending to James. Well, hell, I did it again."

The words spilled out of Beatrice Merriweather's mouth like feet slipping on an icy walk. Once started, there was no controlling it. Her face was now the color of Michael O'Malley's beard.

Michael O'Malley started laughing at the use of profanity by an obvious Southern lady, and the chance for a conversation rapidly declined because he could not stop himself from loudly guffawing. Finally, Beatrice came out on the porch. All pretenses were erased as O'Malley reached out his arms and she willingly accepted his embrace. As the hug smothered her face in his flaming beard, the beard tickled her neck, and she started laughing again. Michael O'Malley had not stopped laughing since the unconventional greeting began. It finally ended when Beatrice pushed herself away so that she could wipe her eyes.

"If you will move your mount around back, you will find a stall next to James's horse and plenty of hay. While you are taking care of that, I will make us a pot of coffee. Just come in the back door and make your way to the parlor."

Finally somewhat in control of his emotions, Michael proposed to Beatrice, "If you promise not to tell James, I will not either." She quickly agreed. Both knew their promises were sure to be short-lived. It was just too hilarious to ignore in such a humorless time.

After their first sips of coffee, they heard James and his father making their way to the carriage house. After putting up the carriage, they entered from the back door to find Beatrice still giggling. "Well, Father O'Malley, I see you saved your finest vestments for this visit. I must congratulate you on your impeccable decorum," said James Merriweather with obvious delight at finally getting the best of his friend.

"Dr. Winston Merriweather, may I introduce Father Michael O'Malley. And I have no idea who this lady is sitting next to him so consumed with laughter." James enjoyed the chance to see his mother not only smile but also outright laugh.

"Father O'Malley," Winston Merriweather interjected. "I have been looking forward to meeting the man who has been able to reacquaint my son with the spiritual dimension of our world. Welcome to our home. Consider it yours for as long as you are in Richmond and as often as you come this way."

"Thank you, Dr. Merriweather, but as I have explained to every ultrapolite person acquainted with your family, *please* call me Michael."

"Done, if you do the same for me. We keep an informal home and will trust you to take every advantage of our lack of social graces."

Beatrice poured James and Winston coffee and returned to the parlor to sit again next to Michael O'Malley on the settee. They looked at each other and nodded, knowing that they might as well tell the story of the Southern belle and the Irish French leave deserter. It took awhile for the story to be told as the storytellers could not contain their laughter.

"Finally," Michael related, "your lovely mother became so flustered at just calling me Michael and not Father that she exploded with, 'Well, hell! I did it again,' which threw us both into a conniption fit worse than before."

"Beatrice Merriweather, I never in my life heard such language in our home." James's false condemnation drew more laughs.

Finally getting control of her emotions, Beatrice rose and left the men to talk about whatever men talked about these days, which was always the war. She needed to prepare supper. She turned and spoke to their guest. "Michael, you are staying for supper, and you can sleep in James's brother's room down the hall from James. I will hear no objections."

"Yes, ma'am," Father Michael O'Malley replied with false subservience to the woman of the house.

Long into the Night

James and Michael talked late into that first night and most of the next day—mostly about James's battle with nightmares, insomnia, and melancholia. James brought up Burton's work on depression and was surprised that Michael was more familiar with it than he. They agreed that James's focus would be on discussing his experiences and feelings with Michael. They might not be able to control the diet portion of Burton's recommendations, but they would make every effort to find and forage, especially for vegetables. James spoke to Michael about the positive effect that having a purpose, whether doing research on shock or thinking about triage again, had already had on his attitude toward his work.

"Michael, it has given me direction. I am amazed at the negative effects the drudgery of wartime medicine has had on my feelings about life in general. I don't think it can be proved, but I have surmised that how I approach my patients likely has an impact on how they approach their own health."

"James, it seems to me that this one conclusion about purposefulness is reason enough for you to follow Burton's regimen as it already seems to have brought meaning to your work. And I promise to nudge you when you need it and to be a ready ear. I know that I am not immune to the evils of melancholia myself, so I expect mutual benefit from our arrangement as we dig more deeply into Burton's work."

Michael was satisfied that James was ready to return to his assignment as a field surgeon, but Michael also was not naive. He knew there would more than likely be a return from time to time to the depression of the spirit as the worst of the war was likely ahead and not behind.

At the end of his second day in Richmond, Michael told James his decision on James's fitness to return to surgery, and he suggested that early the next day they visit the rabbi of the Kahal Kadosh Beth Shalome Synagogue. He explained, "I wrote to him some time back and told him a bit about your journey, saying that one day soon we would show up and ask to use his sanctuary and perhaps call on him from time to time during our discussion. The synagogue's sanctuary will suit our needs perfectly. It is small enough to facilitate our conversation and large enough for pacing should bewilderment require it.

"Benjamin Cowan is *my* counselor. He and his wife, Abigayil, have guided the congregants of Kahal Kadosh Beth Shalome for the last thirty-seven years, but his family goes much farther back than that."

Michael told James the story of Benjamin Cowan's parents, Jacob and Rachel. Perhaps it was the emigration story of Benjamin's parents that first drew Father O'Malley to Rabbi Cowan.

They emigrated from Poland and settled in the harsh immigrant ghettos of Baltimore. Jacob spent his first weeks in Baltimore in taverns on the edge of polite society but near enough to the ghetto that he was not considered an outsider. Jacob's ambition was to pick up in Baltimore the jewelry trade he had apprenticed in during his Warsaw years. As he nursed ales in tavern after tavern, the name of one jeweler was repeated more than any other—Joseph Bruff, a fellow Jew.

After visiting and browsing the merchandise at Bruff's shop, Jacob and Rachel presented themselves to him, not as customers but as unpaid apprentices looking only for a safer place to sleep at day's end than the streets of the ghetto. Jacob made such a proper presentation of his skills in silverwork, which he had learned in Warsaw, that Mr. Bruff offered them exactly what they asked, a room behind the storefront about the size of a large closet but clean and free of rats.

Within a week Bruff offered them a raise: leftovers from his kitchen and a pallet of quilts on which to sleep. For a month, Jacob and Rachel worked with this arrangement and were glad to have it. Then leftovers became full meals, and on Fridays

Rachel was asked to help Joseph's wife, Ester, prepare for the Shabbat meals to which Jacob and Rachel were soon invited.

Jacob very quickly picked up the silversmithing art from Joseph Bruff, allowing Bruff to focus on designing jewelry. As Jacob worked behind the scenes, Rachel became the friendly face first seen by customers. In the process she got to know the customers as she served them tea and the traditional Jewish candy halvah, which she made weekly in Ester Bruff's kitchen. It was not long before the master jeweler offered Jacob the opportunity to apprentice with gems and jewelry.

This arrangement lasted until Rachel gave birth to her first child in the back room of the jewelry store, a healthy baby girl they named Ester for their benefactor. After her first visit to see her namesake, Ester Bruff found that she could no longer abide Jacob, Rachel, and Ester living in the back room of the storefront. So Joseph and Ester opened their home to their new family of "granddaughter" Ester, and of course Jacob and Rachel—the children they had never had.

This arrangement lasted a year until Jacob became restless—not because he was tired of his adopted family, but because he wanted to start his own jewelry business. There were no secrets in the Bruff home or business; therefore, once Jacob had a plan in his mind, he presented the idea to Joseph. Joseph would not hear of Jacob going to moneylenders and backed Jacob himself. In 1765, Jacob opened his own jewelry store specializing in pearl jewelry on Lovely Street adjacent to the newly erected Methodist meetinghouse. Jacob easily acquired his pearls from the oystermen of Chesapeake Bay and combined them with small precious stones that he acquired from Joseph Bruff. Initially he sold his creations in Joseph's store. He did this until his own work produced customers. Joseph lost money on the transaction, but he smiled each time a customer chose a Jacob Cowan pearl necklace or brooch.

By 1770, Jacob and Rachel Cowan were well-known as merchants and as thorns in the sides of the Redcoats. Their home was a sanctuary for insurgents who carried the message of revolution within the colonies. In March of 1778, when Count Kazimierz Pulaski, the Polish mercenary recruited by Benjamin Franklin, recruited his first cavalry unit in Baltimore, Jacob Cowan quickly enlisted. Speaking fluent Polish with a flair for horsemanship, he steadily rose in the ranks. Six months after enlisting, he was General Pulaski's adjutant until Pulaski was killed at the Battle of Savannah.

After the war, Jacob never returned to Baltimore. On his way home, he stopped for the night in Richmond, where he saw the potential of the rapidly growing merchant class in the capital city. So instead of returning to Baltimore, he put down roots in Richmond, buying a storefront on Main Street with his army wages. A month later, he brought his wife and daughter to join him. The Cowan family soon established themselves in the small Jewish community, and Benjamin was born in 1786. At his bar mitzvah, Benjamin declared his intentions of becoming a rabbi. With no rabbinic seminary in the new United States, Benjamin began his studies at the age of eighteen, at the direction of Rabbi Moische Sokol, and served as an assistant rabbi, although without pay, for the next five years.

Moische Sokol was a healthy man, and Benjamin could not foresee a reasonable opportunity to lead the congregation. Wanting to start his own family, he accepted his father's offer and became a partner in Cowan & Son Jewelers.

Yet Benjamin Cowan did not relinquish his desire to become a rabbi. However, at forty years of age and married, he found his rabbinical dream surely slipping away as he became entirely engaged with the jewelry business. But the unexpected happened. Rabbi Sokol fell dead during the Passover Seder of

1821, and Benjamin Cowan became a rabbi at forty—a position he still held thirty-seven years later.

"James, my Protestant friend," Michael continued, "Benjamin and Abigayil are the closest things to family I have in America. And Benjamin is easily the wisest and most independent man of God I have ever encountered. He knows no boundaries. He tried to enlist as a chaplain, but at seventy-seven he was far too old for the war, although it did take Abigayil putting her foot down before he agreed to stay put. So before I left for the army, I spent days with him seeking and probing his mind for guidance in serving a cause of which I was most unsure.

"That is why we have come here today to the Kahal Kadosh Beth Shalome Synagogue, to chase his wisdom again. Are you ready?"

"I am," James replied almost in a whisper, awed by the potential of the unlikely theological convergence that awaited.

Rabbi Benjamin Cowan

The priest and the Protestant stood at the front door of the rabbi's home, a two-story brick structure as modest as the synagogue two streets away. Michael knocked.

"James, as it is yet early, I expect that Benjamin is still reciting his morning prayers, so Abigayil will likely greet us."

In a moment, the front door, red and trimmed in gold, opened. A stunningly beautiful woman greeted them. Tall with lustrous dark brown hair to her shoulders, she had eyes that were almost black, mysterious in their depth.

James was even more astounded when Abigayil Cowan threw herself into the arms of Michael O'Malley, who undoubtedly knew what was about to happen when he knocked on the door.

Not so with James Merriweather. Abigayil pushed Michael inside and welcomed James with only slightly less vigor than given to Michael. James, not one to turn away an embrace by a beautiful woman, was clearly stunned.

"I ... am ... James Merriweather," he stammered in introduction, still flustered.

At this point, still standing in the small foyer, Michael O'Malley and the woman still yet not introduced to James exploded into laughter. These introductions had been planned for whatever day Michael and James appeared on the Cowans' front stoop.

Having now moved to the small parlor, the woman before him introduced herself with the accent of a person raised in a traditional Hebrew family whose first language was Yiddish. "I am Abigayil Cowan."

"Did I not tell you that Benjamin married a child bride?" Michael added to the introduction.

"Michael O'Malley, he did no such thing!" Abigayil responded in false indignation. "I was a young woman—a very young woman!" She followed her declaration with a deep and wonderfully raucous laugh.

"Perhaps I should explain," said a voice at the top of the stairs—obviously Benjamin Cowan. As he made his way down the stairs, more easily than might be expected for a man of his age, he continued, "I had prepared as a rabbi until I was twenty-one, and then I worked with my father as a partner in our jewelry business. I was too busy for a family. But at forty, a miracle happened—well, not for Rabbi Sokol." He chuckled. "But for me. I was a rabbi and unmarried."

"I was seventeen," Abigayil said, picking up the story. "Our families had been intertwined back in Poland. So when my father received a letter from Jacob Cowan proposing marriage to his rabbi son, he agreed immediately. I took a little more persuading, but only a little." She held her thumb and index finger close together.

"A year later we were married. So, you see, she was not as young as Michael likes to say," Benjamin added with a smile. "God has blessed us both with good health and, to my old eyes, Abigayil with beauty that does not age."

"Benjamin. That is enough. My hair may still be brown and my skin smooth, but my bones tell me my true age whenever I climb those stairs. You, my love, have a white beard and a wrinkled forehead, but you climb those stairs without a thought."

James finally felt comfortable enough to speak. "It sounds like you have made a fine marriage," he said with thoughts of his own wife and child on the farm in South Carolina.

Benjamin walked with James and Michael the two blocks to his synagogue, opened the door, and ushered them inside to fabric-covered brick walls and simple pews. There were two windows on each side wall. At the eastern end of the space was a simple table on which was a lighted menorah. Behind and to the right of center was the ark that housed the sacred scrolls. It was a simple cupboard but no less precious for it. To the left of the ark was a raised platform, the bimah, where the Torah scrolls were opened and read.

"My friends, this house is your house except for the ark, of course. I shall sit on the back pew and pray that your labors produce much fruit. Should you need me, you need but interrupt my prayers or my sleep and ask." Benjamin chuckled at that last thought.

"Bless you, my friend and counselor." And with that, Father O'Malley made the sign of the cross, and he and Rabbi Cowan bowed with folded hands to one another. Michael O'Malley prayed for wisdom and courage.

And They Began

"James—and Benjamin, because I know you are listening—I want to repeat the question I posed to James back in January just before I left to return to the army's winter headquarters: What role would a loving God have played in the murder of your friends and the stillbirth of your son?"

Benjamin, unable to restrain himself, lightened the heavy mood with, "My God, Father, why didn't you give the boy a difficult question with which to wrestle?"

Rather than diving immediately into the question of Jehovah's role in the tragedies of the human condition, Michael asked James about the process of reflection that he used to get at the question.

The first hour was a give-and-take on self-reflection as a means of understanding the Almighty. Michael hoped that he might personally gain some insights from James's medical/scientific approach, but his main purpose was to help his friend build a framework from which he might attack his personal demons when discussion with Michael was out of the question.

Michael was mightily impressed as James discussed his initial assumptions about the importance of life's experiences in understanding the unseen spiritual world. In doing so, James had attacked two almost unquestioned creeds of the Judeo-Christian faiths: a predestined future set at birth and the infallibility of the Almighty in the daily affairs of humankind.

"No small starting place," Michael told James. "You have leapt wide chasms of orthodoxy and centuries of theology!"

"For me it was simple," James responded. "Either God was responsible for the murders of my friends and the death of my son or he wasn't."

Michael nodded, not so much in agreement as in fascination at James's logical approach. James continued. "I began by giving him the benefit of the doubt. To do that, fate, or predestination, or God's will, or whatever one calls it had to be put aside. So I considered the alternative, which is that man is born with a soul but that it is not fully formed."

"Benjamin," Michael called, "I know you are listening. You might as well join us."

"I thought you would never ask." Benjamin laughed as he walked up to the front pew where Michael and James were seated. He sat down on the edge of the bimah.

"*Your* thoughts, Rabbi?" Michael prompted him with a smile.

"James has stumbled on one of religion's great conundrums. If we give God the credit for the good in our lives, must we also allot him the blame for the bad?"

Although James likely did not pick up on Benjamin's casual use of the name God, Michael realized again that his friend was a very independent-thinking rabbi indeed. It was very likely that the name God was seldom used in this synagogue. Even in writing, *God* would be written as *G-d* because it is irreverent to use the Almighty's name.

James, now comfortable with Benjamin in the mix, decided it was time that he shared his personal experiences with the juxtaposition of God and war. "As the war began, I had no doubts of God's fidelity to the Southern cause. Even in my first experience with so much death, still I believed. But after Antietam, I distrusted any God whose plans resulted in the slaughter of so many on both sides of the conflict. Then when my friends were murdered, my distrust grew into full-blown disbelief, and I retreated into melancholia and then the bottle. After I dried out and returned to the world with Michael's help, with the news of my son's stillbirth, my disbelief and depression returned."

With tears in his eyes at James's painful retelling of his

story, Benjamin thoughtfully and softly spoke. "We Jews sometimes believe that we have a corner on pain and suffering. We have turned away from God. We have wandered in the wilderness. And what have we learned? The Almighty, Yahweh, God, Allah—whatever name you give—always returns to his children. Even when his children engage in unholy wars in his name."

Michael nudged James. "Have you considered *why* God never gives up on us?"

Just as James was about to answer, there was a quiet rap on the door. Abigayil poked her head in to ask, "Isn't it time for a break? I have a picnic lunch if you are interested."

Dinner on the Grounds

Abigayil had already spread a blanket on the new spring grass under the edge of a live oak tree that shaded the left side of the synagogue. After everyone was seated, Abigayil revealed her picnic lunch of fried chicken, fried sweet potato slices sprinkled with sugar and cinnamon, fresh-baked bagels from a traditional Polish recipe she brought with her to the United States, and a bottle of red wine. All had been blessed by her husband early in the morning before their guests arrived and was therefore kosher.

Rabbi Benjamin, ever the considerate theologian, asked Father Michael to bless their meal. "Benjamin, I know that you blessed this food this morning before it was ever prepared by Abigayil. So instead, may I have a prayer of thanksgiving for Abigayil's work?" Benjamin nodded and Abigayil blushed.

With not a hint of religiosity in his voice, Michael prayed, "Holy One who cares for us all and guides us toward the light of all goodness, we ask that you so guide our minds and voices this afternoon as we consider you. We offer thanks for these friends and for this food lovingly prepared by your beloved Abigayil."

And after a long pause, he said, "Amen."

Before returning to their discussions, James would have nothing less than to carry the remains of their lunch and accompany Abigayil back home. His absence gave Michael and Benjamin an opportunity to discuss what had transpired in the morning.

"Your thoughts on the morning, Benjamin?"

"Michael, I can sense James's spirit, and it is as good as it is troubled. But certainly you are traveling with him in a direction that, based on what I've seen this morning, has already produced remarkable insights for a man not of the cloth, shall we say."

"Anything that you suggest that we touch on this afternoon, assuming that there is some afternoon left after we ponder the nature of Yahweh?"

To a casual observer it might have appeared that Benjamin Cowan closed his eyes and nodded off for a moment. Michael O'Malley knew better and waited patiently on his mentor. After a minute, Benjamin offered his thoughts. "I believe that it would benefit James to receive the same advice that I gave to you: 'See the man in front of you. Focusing on those who control the forces that placed him there is just wasting your energy on things and people beyond your control.'"

Michael paused for a moment. "Benjamin, would you offer that advice to James? I believe it will mean a great deal to him knowing that you gave him the same advice as you gave to me. I think it will also make things easier in future difficulties that are sure to come if we refer back to your advice, rather than it coming from me."

Benjamin patted his Roman Catholic pupil on his head. "Of course, my friend. It would be my honor."

And the Afternoon Was Deeper

Returning from his chivalrous duties, James opened the front door of the synagogue to see the late April afternoon sunrays through the windows shining on radiant dust specks stirred up with the breeze that accompanied his opening of the door. *Hmm,* he thought, *this could easily be interpreted as blessings from the Almighty.*

"Well, gentlemen, what is on the agenda for the rest of the afternoon?"

"Just the opening I needed," Michael said. "Seems to me that perhaps we have kept the weightiest question until our bellies are full and our eyes heavy, hoping for a nap. You must excuse Benjamin if Morpheus overtakes him and he just naps right here on a pew." Michael was prodding Benjamin who, he knew, never napped.

Once James was seated, Michael posed the question for the afternoon. "We talked this morning about how the Almighty does not interfere willy-nilly in the affairs of mankind. Rather, he chooses to let man go his own way within the world, interacting with natural forces God put into motion at the moment of creation. Now let us hear your thoughts on the nature of a Creator who would give such free will to his creation."

James broke his thoughts down into another logical/scientific sequence. "I first asked myself how I could align my concept of the God of the Old Testament with the God of the New Testament, assuming any alignment was even possible.

"Benjamin, if this is touching on a sensitive topic, please speak up."

"Not at all, James. Michael and I have been down this road before. But I am very interested in your views of my God of the Old Testament."

James was somewhat surprised, yet he realized that he

should not be so given Benjamin's openness in the morning's discussion, so he moved the discussion forward.

"From my earliest teaching about God, I learned that God is unchanging. With that premise, I concluded that the God of the Old Testament equals—in all things—the God of the New Testament. That was my first epiphany into the nature of the Almighty. But that was just the start, and more ideas seemed to rush in and swirl around me with that conclusion."

"James," Michael said, in awe of the amateur theologian before them, "I understand totally. When I have experienced this kind of rush and looked at the moment later, I have concluded that it was as close to hearing the voice of God as I was likely ever to experience."

"I think I understand, but I saw it a bit more scientifically—as ideas playing out logically as I considered them. It was more of 'if this idea is true, then this other idea must always be true or cannot ever be true—or the entire logical sequence falls apart.' Does that make sense?"

"Perfectly," Benjamin added. "From my perspective, it is meaningful that you have referred to the flow of ideas as rushing about you. In both the Jewish and Christian scriptures, Yahweh's spirit is referred to as a rushing wind. Could this be what you experienced?" Clearly Benjamin had finished the thought with a rhetorical question.

Michael, having experienced Benjamin's rhetoric and penchant for expanding on a rhetorical question, intervened quickly. "James, tell us a bit about what came next."

"Well, once I had concluded that God's nature was the same regardless of the text I read, I had to ask myself, which image of God is true? The angry and vengeful God of the Old Testament willing to destroy all of mankind except for Noah's family, or the loving God willing to sacrifice everything precious for the humans he allowed to have free will in the first place?"

"And?" Michael asked, metaphorically on the edge of his seat.

"I concluded that God created man to begin with out of love, and that has not changed since the Almighty himself cannot change. Therefore, God's inherent nature and steadfast inclination always had been and still is to love his people. And the different images of that nature were man's interpretation and not God's intention."

"Well." Benjamin stood and stretched his seventy-seven-year-old frame. "What did you conclude about the infallibility of the scriptures?"

"Rabbi," James said, purposefully using the title of respect, "actually I had not parsed that logic out yet, but my from-the-seat-of-my-pants view is that the scriptures were written by man, and anything that man touches will never be infallible no matter how many other men say that it is so."

"Oy vey! I have a heretic in my synagogue!" said Benjamin, expressing his false dismay. "Careful, the walls may tumble in on us."

"Binyamin," Michael said, emphasizing the Hebrew form of the rabbi's name, "you will give our pupil nightmares just when we are about to rid him of them."

"I think I am safe." James laughed. "If the walls have not fallen before now with the likes of you two questioning Jehovah, I expect I am safe enough. But let me finish the answer to the question you asked of me this morning.

"If the Almighty's most basic nature is love, then he could not, by that assumption—which I believe to be true—have even been associated tangentially with either the murder of my two friends or the death of my unborn son. I *have* concluded that he grieved over both of those events, as it seems to me that he must always whenever man chooses evil over good or when the natural laws he put in motion result in unintended harm such as the stillbirth of a child."

Advice on Returning to War

"Well spoken, James, as was your reasoning about the nature of Yahweh, the Almighty," Benjamin said as he rose to face James and Michael. "Michael asked me if I would pass on to you the advice I gave to him before he assumed the duties of chaplain in General Lee's army. Does that sound like a good way to end today's discussions?"

"Indeed it does. I would be most grateful, Rabbi."

"James, as a physician, as much as a rabbi or a priest, you are heaven's emissary to those whom you treat. And as such you must resist the easy temptation to look beyond those whom you seek to heal for the reasons—beyond the obvious ones—for their wounds. When you start down that path, you end up again asking *why* God would permit such grievous deeds to be inflicted upon the man in front of you and by extension upon you. And I think we have covered that sufficiently, at least for today. Here then is the advice I give to you, my new friend.

"See only the man in front of you. Look neither left nor right nor behind. Waste not a single thought on those whose ideas and actions placed him there. God is embodied in the man you see on the table in front of you. Serve that man, and you serve God.'"

Two days later after goodbyes at 324 Franklin Street, Michael O'Malley and James Merriweather stopped by to see Colonel John Bailey and pick up Merriweather's reassignment papers. Manners were observed. Salutes were given. Hands were shaken, and well-wishes were exchanged.

And like with the rehabilitation of a priceless old masterpiece, the restorers in Richmond had done their work. Captain James Merriweather returned with Father Michael O'Malley to the war.

PART VI
THE END OF THE BEGINNING

CHAPTER 21

Chancellorsville: The Agony of Victory

Restored, Captain James Merriweather returned to the Army of Northern Virginia encamped just outside of Fredericksburg, the site of General Lee's last triumph and Merriweather's retreat from reality.

What Merriweather found was entirely different from his last few months in Richmond. Richmond had experienced an unusually severe winter too, accompanied by an incredibly high number of deaths due to the ague. But his parents' home was warm, and there was adequate food still available in Richmond if one knew whom to approach or was a proficient gardener and canner. His parents' garden was substantial, and the previous spring they had overplanted Irish and sweet potatoes and winter squash, not in anticipation of a severe winter but anticipating that the fighting so near to them was soon to affect them directly.

Merriweather reckoned that the men looked more like zombies than soldiers readying for battle. The soldiers of the Army of Northern Virginia, even here on the last days of April, were surviving on a quarter pound of meat and sixteen ounces of flour daily, while ten men shared a pound of rice for up to three weeks. Merriweather wondered how in the name of God these men were to fight the battle that was sure to come when the Federals had dry roads on which to march. Yet a springtime battle was as predictable as the daffodils that had sprung up in the woodlands around the camp with the first warm days. That it would be fought somewhere in Spotsylvania County, Virginia, within easy marching distance of the Rappahannock was also predictable.

To Chaplain Michael O'Malley, the smell of testosterone exuded from young men in need of proving their manhood, as if it needed proving again, was mixed with the nervous sour sweat of the fear of death. And there was little he could do. The war was coming again, and coming soon.

The Battle of Chancellorsville came, and Lee was again master of his counterpart in blue, General "Fighting Joe" Hooker, even though the cost in Southern lives was enormous: 1,665 were killed, 9,081 wounded, and 2,018 captured or missing. In victory, Lee lost 22 percent of his Army of Northern Virginia.

One could argue that the most decisive Southern victory of the war and Lee's greatest triumph to date was also the first step toward Appomattox Court House.

Renewal

With the typical mild winters that morphed from fall to spring with only a little discomfort along the way, the winter of 1863 was hard on South Carolinians, but not at Horlbeck Creek Farm. Mary Assumpta's hard winter of despair was short-lived, ending in February when she received the first letter from James since Christmas. True to his promise in his letter, he sent letters weekly from then on, although they came in bunches or not at all. The Confederate States' mail service seemed without concern for senders or recipients, time, or schedules.

Nonetheless, Mary Assumpta knew that James was safe in Richmond with his parents. Her brother sent word to Mary Assumpta through their father in Charleston, figuring it was more reliable and quicker than trying to send her a letter addressed to Horlbeck Creek Farm. In the letter delivered to her by her father in early March, John described James's recovery from all signs of depression and his renewed enthusiasm for "medical science," as James now called his bent to discover, even in the middle of war, new methods of healing. John wrote,

> I am convinced that James has placed the evils of war in perspective by fixing on the opportunities for learning new avenues of healing and teaching them, as he is able, to his fellow physicians. His spiritual healing is in the skillful hands of Father O'Malley, who will also administer to his depression as Michael and I are now referring to his melancholia.
>
> In preparation for James's return to you, perhaps you can ask Father to see if he can ask among his older physician friends in Charleston and find a copy of the book *The Anatomy of Melancholy* by the English scholar Robert Burton. It is an old book but well worth the reading. Might just do us all a bit of good to read about melancholia as this war seems now to have a life of its own and is in no hurry to expire. James has my copy, and Father O'Malley is familiar with the book.

With assurances from John and James, Mary Assumpta attacked life as though she were fighting a one-woman war in the Battle of Horlbeck Creek Farm.

Rabbi's Advice Passed On to Mary Assumpta

April 21, 1863

Rabbi Benjamin Cowan
Richmond, Virginia

Mrs. James E. Merriweather
Horlbeck Creek Farm
Charleston County, South Carolina

Dear Mrs. Merriweather,

A week ago I had the pleasure of spending the day with your husband and my dear friend Father Michael O'Malley as we queried the traditions of each other's faiths in pursuit of understanding the nature of the most elusive of beings, Jehovah, the Almighty, the Father, Yahweh, God.

James told me the story of his fall from grace in the face of the unrelenting evil of killing and murder, and sought my advice.

Our day had ended as we said our final prayers for each other. As the late afternoon shadows crept through the windows of the small synagogue and Father Michael walked next door to say his goodbyes to my wife, Abigayil, James and I walked toward Michael and Abigayil. He asked me to write this letter to you and pass along the advice that I gave to him, and to Michael some months before, on how to love and trust in the face of unrelenting tragedy.

Before I put pen to page, I sought out my wife,

Abigayil, about James's entreaty and asked for her wisdom as a wife of a rabbi. James and I—we are not so different. We heal the broken of mind, of body. Often we fail. And we question Jehovah. Yes, even a rabbi. Especially a rabbi! As the wife of a rabbi, Abigayil has a special kind of insight. But first, so that I can be true to James's request, here is the advice (or thereabouts) that I gave that day:

> Look at the soldier in front of you. Do not fret about those for whom you have already done all that you can do. Do not concern yourself with how many are yet to lie upon your table. Do not let your mind contemplate the minds of those whose ideas and actions placed wounded men on your table. God is found in the man you see on the table in front of you. Serve that man, and you serve God.

Benjamin Cowan

A Wife's Advice to Mary Assumpta

Let me begin my portion of this letter by addressing you as Mary Assumpta and not as Mrs. Merriweather, as I try to leave the formal forms of address to the men. James spoke lovingly of you in our brief time of conversation during the lunch we all shared. I feel almost as if I have met you already. James spoke of you almost as though you were sitting there in the circle on the blanket with us.

I will do my best to do justice to James's request and to Benjamin's advice. My stubborn old Jew is as wise as he is old. Just do not tell him I said that about him.

The advice he gave is also how he tries to live. Because he was appointed as rabbi at forty, Benjamin was often so consumed with how little time he had left in his life to serve Yahweh, he became consumed with the thought that he was not accomplishing as much as *he* believed the Almighty required of him. Seven years into his ministry, he almost lost the congregation because he was so obsessed with doing everything for everyone that he failed far too many who needed him—oftentimes just to talk and to listen attentively. Benjamin did not know how to care for his congregation one person at a time, and I almost lost him. He contracted tuberculosis and did not leave our home for nine months. During his forced reflection, he developed the philosophy embodied in the advice he gave to you and James and Michael.

I sense a common stubbornness in James. I pray that in his brief time with his parents and your brother, and also Michael and Benjamin, he can now apply Benjamin's advice. It seems that driven men such as ours must depart the community of this life into the depths of aloneness and meet death face-to-face before they are able to employ the "Benjamin rule," as I call it.

Michael seems to be an exception. Pray for him. It is easy to see that he and James have found ways to support each other.

Enough about our men. I believe that you and I share a common "affliction"—we married older men! "We all are given gifts," Benjamin reminds me, "in order to become who Jehovah imagines us to be." Sometimes I want to give my gift back to the Almighty.

To Benjamin I am his wife, and heaven save me, sometimes I am his mother. I am his friend and even his rabbi. When I see that Benjamin is at odds with himself morally or spiritually, I intrude on his thoughts. I make coffee, and we sit and talk about where we have been in this life. My heart remembers. I remind him where we have been together. We drink together, and Yahweh moves us gently forward into our future.

My "rabbinical" advice to you? Although you cannot at this moment sit with your husband and serve him coffee, you can set aside some time every afternoon or early morning and let your heart remember for you both. In your letters, write to him of your life on the farm and how his son is growing into a man too soon. Be honest about your hardships. He knows you have them. Not to mention them is to make them worse than they really are in his imagination. But take a few lines to remember for him, to *talk* to him with your written words. Our menfolk are forgetful beings. From time to time, they need reminding about what is really important and that "she" resides in the bedroom under the covers in frilly nightdresses waiting for him and him alone. Don't remind him too often. You don't want him going on French leave. Remember for you both, until

Providence returns him to you again. Don't leave his returning to the Spinners dwelling within the roots of the great ash tree at the center of the universe. Sometimes the Almighty needs a bit of reminding too.

I pray that soon we shall bring you and Colin (and, yes, James and Father O'Malley) into our home so that we may remember together.

Warmly yours,
Abigayil

A New Plan for Planting

April 20, 1863
Horlbeck Creek Farm

My Very Dearest and Most Desired James,

Thank you, dearest, for the letters and letters you have written. Sometimes they arrive in trickles and sometimes in floods. No worries. My life is renewed as I read each one and can see the restoration of your life. I trust that when this conflict is done, I will be able to meet Father Michael and tell him thank-you for bringing my JEM back to me.

I pray that my letters to you are actually getting through. I have written almost every day, but the mail service to and from the farm is most erratic. You will likely remember that before the war, it was hit-and-miss at best. Nowadays, it is mostly miss.

My spirits are good. Getting a garden in the ground on the back six acres will do that to you. I expect you are saying, "Six acres?" We agreed that planting more than three acres would be beyond my ability to manage—and with my kitchen garden added to it.

Blame it on Nate. He and Audrey Lee (and I think your son!) conspired to present me a proposal one afternoon when I was tired and weak from working outside turning over the kitchen plot. Nate said that it really did not make good sense for the two families to plant three acres each when we lived just a mile apart. He proposed that since perhaps our farm had the better soil, being closer to the creek, we plant six acres to be worked by both families.

So Colin, Nate, Audrey Lee, and I work the eight plots that we have dubbed Angel Acres in honor of Baby Merriweather.

We laid out a wagon path that starts about fifteen feet from the fence surrounding the kitchen garden and runs straight almost to the creek. Then we laid out six one-acre plots roughly parallel to the creek, three on one side of the perpendicular wagon path and three on the other. Then we laid out a second wagon path below the six acres. Below this we laid out two more acres, and the kitchen garden is the last plot and sits closest to the house.

The pathways and the plots that we laid out form two crosses, and anytime we walk to Angel Acres we must pass by Baby M's grave and marker. We touch it and say a silent prayer for a good harvest and for your quick return.

Back in late March a platoon from General Longstreet's army approached every family on Horlbeck Creek requesting that we donate (demanding that we hand over is more like it) two-thirds of our corn and half of any cured meat that we had on hand. We had little, but we gave what they asked. Now we are not far from the same fate as the army met this winter, barely having enough to eat. The lieutenant in charge said that it looked like times are only going to get harder, especially if the Yankees capture Wilmington.

Ten days ago we heard the sounds of cannons off to the south for what seemed like dawn to dusk. Three days ago, Nate flagged down a wagon from Boone plantation coming back from the Wando dock, and the driver told him it was the Confederate cannons at Fort Sumter pounding away at nine Yankee ironclads. He said that they had damaged and beaten back the fleet and had sunk one of them. I guess Charleston remains free of Yankees for a while longer, although Father says in his infrequent letters that goods are very hard to come by as the harbor is barricaded except for the occasional blockade-runner.

I write all of this to tell you that as we have laid out the Angel Acres and the kitchen garden, we have done so with a sodden view of our future. We are planting three acres of corn and an acre each of beans, peas, sweet potatoes, and Irish potatoes. We will plant tomatoes, okra, and peppers in the kitchen plot.

It will be hard to keep any livestock—given how little corn we will be growing—except ol Jake. So we hope the corn will be enough to sustain him and us. We are really counting on the potatoes to get us through next winter if the tide turns against the Confederacy and we must live only on what we grow. As you can see, we are not planting with any expectation except that we stay alive. That is not as dire as it sounds. We still can get fish from the creek and the Wando, and I held back from the soldiers enough fatback to season whatever we eat.

Between our two families we will be just fine, and you should not worry. Farming and hard times are like summer and sweat: where you find one, you usually find the other.

Our supper has been devoured by your son, and dishes await my attention. Then thankfully to bed. I shall sleep with your name upon my lips.

Lovingly yours,
Red

"What Things, Mama?"

May 5, 1863
Horlbeck Creek Farm

Dearest and Precious Husband,

I received the missive from your rabbi Cowan. Instead, I really should say that I got a missive from Abigayil Cowan. Benjamin wrote a few lines and included the advice he gave to you as he best remembered it from that day. However, based on the remainder of the letter from Abigayil, I expect Benjamin remembered it correctly in my letter.

Growing up Catholic, married to an Anglican, and having had awhile now to blend those two not so different religious orders together, I thought my ideas about the Almighty were pretty well set in stone. Abigayils words and Benjamin's (and yours about Benjamin) have set me to some hard thinking since I received the messages from them.

Just today as I was washing the final two sweet potatoes from last year's harvest in preparation for roasting them for supper, I was deep in thought about things not of this earth, and Colin walked up on the porch and stood in the doorway looking at me. He stood for a good few minutes, and I never saw him. Finally, unable to tolerate my pensive silence any longer, or just because he was hungry, he spoke to me gently for fear he would frighten me, "Mama, is something wrong?"

"No, Colin. I was just thinking about being between a rock and a hard place."

"Okay, Mama, you have to tell me what that means."

The boy will leave nothing unexplained, so I told him about having two opposing ideas, saying that having to choose one or the other might be equally unpleasant.

Colin responded, "Kind of like having to slaughter our last hog, or else feed him and have us go hungry."

"Yes, Colin, that is it exactly." Damn, but that boy is scary smart sometimes. I went ahead and shared Benjamin's advice with him and told him about Benjamin being a rabbi and your friend—and Father O'Malley's friend too.

We talked a bit about the Catholic Church and the Anglican Church being two orders in the single Jesus-based religion of Christianity. Of course he wanted to know why Benjamin's beliefs were different. So I did my best to explain what I was taught about Judaism and why my views were now changing based on letters from you and your friend the rabbi.

"You see," I told him, "that is why I seemed so far away when you came in. I was in a faraway place thinking about God in ways that I never had before."

"Kind of like how I think about Daddy and wonder what he is doing right at that time while I am plowing with ol Jake, knowing there is no way to really know?" Colin asked in childhood honesty, which revealed so much of how the war is affecting him, not having his father at home.

"Darling Colin, I think your idea is really close. Of course, we do find out about Daddy when I get a letter from him." I didn't think I needed to say anything more for fear he would worry himself into a sleepless night. Of course he thought of it himself and asked me precisely for the information I was holding back.

"Mama," he said completely guilelessly, "do you think Daddy doesn't tell us everything because he worries that it might disturb us too much?"

Damn son of yours, James Merriweather! Now I had to tell him that there were some things about the war we were just better off not knowing. Then, of course, he asked, "What things, Mama?"

The best I could do at that point was to tell him to go feed

Boomer, ol Jake, and the chickens, and then come back and get to work on his studies before supper.

James, if you gave your parents this kind of grief when you were his age, no wonder they were glad to be rid of you when you moved to Charleston. Of course, I am pretty sure they had no inkling that you would become intertwined in a hotheaded Irish family only three generations removed from the home country, still bearing an animosity for all things English—especially English Protestants.

I wonder, did the Almighty bring us together or just look the other way when we made love for the first time in the apartment above John's office? Now that notion is undoubtedly an example of a rock and a hard place. As were you, as I recall.

Whew! I'd better stop right there.

Let me close with this thought: I continuously pray with your name on my lips that your prayers are answered swiftly, that blessings come to you daily, and that the Almighty grants you grace in everything you do.

Only you, my love,
Red

A Good and Godly Man

May 12, 1863
Command Headquarters, Virginia

Dearest and Precious Red,

I trust that you will accept my apologies for no letters since April 26. As I wrote at that time, the Yankee newspapers from Washington indicated that a Union army led by General Hooker somewhere in the

Fredericksburg–Chancellorsville area was imminent. It began on April 29.

I shall not go into any detail of tactics except to say that General Robert E. Lee can do more and get more from fewer men than any other commander on either side of this conflict. Our poorly fed and poorly provisioned Army of Northern Virginia whipped the Yankees—there is no better phrase—and sent them back across the Rappahannock and into Maryland.

As this was my first conflict since I returned from Richmond, I know that you are worried about my well-being. Well, I am just fine. Not great. Anyone who tells you they are doing great in this conflict is either lying outright or self-delusional. There were times in the field hospital when I had to pause and remind myself of Rabbi Benjamin's admonition to me, and each time it worked to the benefit of this surgeon and the soldier on his table. I wrote to you soon after returning to duty with my version of his wise advice, and I hope that you have received a letter with those same kind words directly from the source by the time you receive this message.

Not everything was satisfactory in the Chancellorsville victory. By the time this letter reaches you, you will likely have heard of the untimely death of General Stonewall Jackson, a good man, a godly man, and the best of General Lee's lieutenants.

On May 2, when news reached our field hospital that General Jackson had been gravely wounded, Dr. Hunter McGuire pulled me aside and said that he had observed my surgical techniques and asked that I travel with him to attend to General Jackson, who had been taken to Dowdall's Tavern. I could not refuse. Once Dr. McGuire observed General Jackson's wounds, he directed the ambulance to take the general to Second Corps' field hospital at Wilderness Tavern. There, assisted by Dr. Claude Paisley, who was assigned permanently to the Second Corps field hospital, Dr. McGuire and I did everything we could, including amputating Jackson's severely damaged left arm, knowing all the while that our best efforts were likely in the end to be futile.

General Jackson lived another seven days, but he contracted pneumonia, and as he knew that he was undoubtedly approaching his death, the general prayed that he would die on the Sabbath. The Almighty granted his prayer, and one of the great sons of the South died on May 10. I was not there at his passing, but others reported that his final words were "Let us cross over the river and rest under the shade of the trees." I firmly believe that God granted him that final peace. As he was carried by wagon to his home in Lexington, soldiers lined the road with hands held in statue-like salutes, and the hardest men I have ever seen cried that day for their "soldiers' soldier" and for their South. For they knew there would not be another. The word that is passing among the men is that General Lee said that losing Stonewall Jackson was like losing his own right hand. Such was the bond between the two stalwarts of our army. For everyone, the excitement of the improbable victory has been more than tempered by the loss of General Jackson.

Red, I think that if I could return to camp and to tending to my wounded after the experience with General Jackson, I am on the path as Benjamin set it out for me.

During the experience at Wilderness Tavern, I found another valued colleague in Dr. McGuire. He seems to be a physician to whom I may be able to present my ideas about shock and triage. And Dr. Claude Paisley, the physician from Selma, Alabama, who assisted with the care of General Jackson, may be another. I did not have an opportunity to talk with him about my ideas for triage. However, he seems to be of a mind that is not set that we are currently doing the best we are able in the care of the battlefield wounded. His questions about the initial care General Jackson received before he reached the field hospital seem to attest to his interest that we do better. I really look forward to making additional contact with Dr. Paisley.

Darling, my most profound apology for the tenor of this correspondence. I shall do much better tomorrow. Rest easy, my love. I pray that every day brings me closer to you.

Yours eternally,
JEM

Surgeon's Diary

May 12, 1863
Northern Virginia

I followed the rabbi's advice. I survived my most recent encounter with my enemy—myself. I confess that it was not easy. Not from the first soldier on my table to the last. But I survived, and I do also confess that I was a superior physician for the men whom I served.

I was well and truly startled when Major McGuire asked that I travel with him and assist with General Stonewall Jackson. I have thought a bit about why the major chose me given my recent past. Perhaps he does not know of my "troubles," but I doubt that, given the grapevine that flourishes in any army. Or maybe he knew about it, but he read John Bailey's written assessment of my fitness to return to duty, and that was sufficient when added to his observation of my past performance. Or possibly he has experienced, to a lesser degree, the same malady as I.

It seems logically that my depression, as a condition, is not unusual in any time of war, for we see it frequently among both soldiers and officers. With most, it eases with time. With others it is manifested in desertion or, worse, suicide.

As I think on it now, I can only conclude that his decision to choose me to assist him with General Jackson was likely a combination of all of these factors. Regardless, I am grateful.

Major McGuire spoke to me of his observations of my surgical techniques and asked if I might meet with him and discuss my background before joining the Army of Northern Virginia. I look forward to it and the possibility that the discourse may lead to a discussion of the promising process of triage and the issue of shock among the wounded.

Lieutenant Paisley seems to be cut of the

same cloth as the late Willie McCarty and would be a valued colleague in the investigation of triage, but I am thinking probably too far ahead, until I meet with Major McGuire.

The men, and I include myself, have an almost otherworldly allegiance to General Lee, which he has rightfully earned. However, I must not close this entry without mentioning the effect the death of General Stonewall Jackson has had on this army. I did not know that General Jackson's troops held him in such high esteem and affection—nearly equal to that of Robert E. Lee—until I personally witnessed their sorrow as the caisson-like wagon transporting his remains back to his home in Lexington, Virginia, passed near them. Tears flowed and rigid salutes were held long after General Jackson's transport was out of view. That is an image of this war that I will always carry with me.

JEM

Surgeon's Diary

May 14, 1863
Fredericksburg, Virginia

This will likely be a short entry but one I expect to return to many times until this war's end.

Victory has been easy for this army. Many attribute it to God's blessing for the South's cause. I am not in that lot, for I cannot conceive that God blesses a cause that is, at least in part, fought to sustain the practice of slavery. Even those who have no tolerance for slavery, and there are many in this army and beyond, nonetheless seem to see the Almighty's provident hand in the ease of the victories since General Lee assumed command during the Peninsula Campaign.

When I returned to Fredericksburg, I found an army that was only a little flesh and bone. Shoeless. Feet cracked open from the constant walking on frozen ground. Butternut uniforms more in tatters than whole. I have no idea how Chancellorsville was won with such as these except for the power of Robert E. Lee to conjure up in terms understood by every man from private to general officer the cause for which they fought—the vision of the South as a nation unto itself. What he did say was that that nation cannot win a long war because it cannot compete with the Union's might in economics, military personnel, matériel, men, or food.

Sooner rather than later, I fear, Mr. Lincoln will find a general or two who are tactically intelligent and emotionally callous about killing Southerners whether in uniform or not. When that happens, God save us. We shall be generations upon generations mending our Southern heritage, if such mending shall ever happen at all.

If we lose this fight, as I fear we may, I can foresee that we may never recover our honor among the states. If this happens, the United States may be united, but in name only.

JEM

Hope, Not Fate

May 30, 1863
Horlbeck Creek Farm

My Very Dearest JEM,

The news of the triumph at Chancellorsville and the unfortunate death of General Jackson has finally reached us here on Horlbeck Creek. Again, I am compelled to seek pleasure in that I have not also received news of your demise. I do believe that should you fall to the stray cannons' fury, Father Michael or John would somehow get word to me, bypassing the military's typically less than disciplined handling of such matters.

So Pandora and I hope.

I miss you desperately, but especially when I retire and when I rise. As I will myself asleep and I turn toward "your side," I feel your presence with me. Then in the morning, my brain fogged with sleep and dreams, I physically reach for you.

It is wonderful to enter the world of Morpheus in the evening with you as the last thought of my day. And though my false awakening seems a less than optimal way to start the day, the feeling of physically reaching for you stays with me.

On May 30, in average years, we would expect corn to be almost knee high and beans and peas to be flowering. This spring has been very different. Perhaps it was the unusually cold winter. The ground was particularly challenging to till, and we never really got the soil to the soft consistency of past years. I think the beans and peas will do just fine. Once they break the ground, there is no stopping them. But the corn emerged in erratic bunches of plants. One row will show seedlings ideally six inches apart, and another row right beside it will have several corn slips six inches apart and then nothing for another four feet. It is baffling as all the seed came from last year's harvest, which was very typical if not abundant.

Nate is really worried about the soil conditions in the potato fields. Potatoes need loamy soil with generous amounts of sand to encourage the tubers to grow unimpeded, but again, that is not what we got when we tilled those fields. If we can keep the rabbits from eating the potato seedlings when they begin to break the ground, we may be okay anyway as both Irish and sweet potatoes are hardy plants practically immune to insects. Nate read that if you spread human hair or dog hair around the potato rows, the rabbits will stay away. So Boomer and Colin are just about bald, and let's just say my tresses are now easily combed and cannot be braided. Nate, of course, is as bald as a watermelon, but Audrey Lee contributed her share of her beautiful white locks. Audrey Lee says I now look like I am a teenager again. I wish I felt that way too. It is too early to tell if this will deter the cottontails, but it sure gave us something to talk about.

We are beginning to see the end of our last year's canning and milling of our corn. I think we will be fine, but just in case this year's garden does not come around, we are eating a bit less each day.

Colin sends his love. He and Nate have been about setting gopher traps. At least that is what Nate calls them. You know the holes that tortoises make that go deep in the ground? Well, Nate and Colin look for one that has a root across the top of the opening, and they tie a sturdy piece of cord around the root and leave a loop on the ground in the hopes that the gopher will snag its foot on it. I must say I was less than enthusiastic about cooking their first catch, but there is a substantial amount of meat around the legs, and they cook up rather tastily with dumplings.

I was thinking just yesterday about the first day when you came into John's medical office looking to introduce yourself to your new tutor. Bartholomew Jennings thought you might be a proper suitor for me, and he began to commence with trying to get us together right there in the waiting room. I remember that I was a bit perturbed at Bartholomew, but only slightly. I thought you were the most handsome man I had ever seen. You looked like you were dressed to meet President Millard Fillmore instead of my older brother. That August morning, sparks flew between us, and we knew, though we would not admit it for a good long while, that we were attracted like Bartholomew to a bottle of bourbon!

I do believe that if you will get your handsome self back to South Carolina, I might just make those sparks fly again!

Darling, please do everything in your power to stay out of harm's way, although that is more than a bit silly to say when you are the spearpoint in this conflict. I do pray that Chancellorsville will soon lead to another Southern victory and the politicians on both sides will seek to find a peace acceptable to all. Until then, read the rabbi's advice every day and find time to talk to Father Michael.

It is time for me to put down this pen, blow out this lamp, settle into bed, and turn over and reach for you again as the god of sleep and dreams takes me away.

Always yours as I always have been,

Red

CHAPTER 22

For Want of a Horseman

It is Sunday, June 28, 1863, and General Lee and his armies, except for Jeb Stuart, are encamped at Shetter's Woods, or nearby, just on the outskirts of Chambersburg, Pennsylvania. The march from Chancellorsville to Fredericksburg, across the Rappahannock and the Potomac into Maryland, and on to Pennsylvania had been without incident. The marching had been so easy over good dry roads that Lee's soldiers joked that they had eaten breakfast in Virginia, drunk whiskey in Maryland, and had supper in Pennsylvania. Not quite the truth, but they had marched hard and had marched fast.

To Lee it was an affirmation of himself and the South—a procession as much as a march. He was served fresh raspberries by a friendly Marylander, and he gave his autograph to "a true Union woman" who came out to see him at Shetter's Woods. But the impeccably groomed, gray-bearded commander who rode sartorially dressed upon the steel-gray Traveller was worried, and it showed, if not in his countenance than in his brow, which was wrinkled more than usual since leaving Virginia.

Lee's grand strategy, which had been approved by President Davis's cabinet, was to strike deep in Union territory—a heart-beat away from Washington and Lincoln. Lee was confident—he was always confident—that the strategy that had worked before back in September would work again. Lee knew that his armies were rested, decently fed, and in good spirits and could be brought to battle in less than a day's time. It had been quite awhile since such a favorable combination of elements had been at Lee's disposal.

But he was worried. Lee had not heard from the flamboyantly plumed Jeb Stuart for days, and that meant he did not know that Union general Hooker was on the same side of the Potomac and moving north toward him but staying between the Confederates and the Union capital.

In fact, on this Sunday, Stuart and five thousand of his cavalrymen were on the outskirts of Washington. They were too few to be able to take Washington and were seventy miles away from being able to guard Lee's flank.

As he met with his commanders, Lee placed his right finger on a map that had been drawn by his departed friend Stonewall Jackson. He traced a line from the northernmost range of the Blue Ridge Mountains to the west and came to rest, though not purposefully, on the small college town of Gettysburg, Pennsylvania. He was heard to say, "Hereabouts we shall probably meet the enemy and fight a great battle, and if God gives us the victory, the war will be over, and we shall achieve the recognition of our independence."

The Giant Gopher Rodent

June 7, 1863
Horlbeck Creek Farm

Precious JEM,

It is a beautiful Sunday afternoon here in South Carolina as I write this. I am sitting under a willow tree at the Horlbeck Creek dock on the Wando. Colin and I walked here after lunch at Nate and

Audrey Lee's. Colin is fishing for bream with gopher-hole crickets. I bet you don't know what those are. I sure didn't. Nate has been doing more educating Colin in the ways of the South Carolina Low Country. As Colin tells it, first you find a gopher hole—yep, the same hole where they snagged that creature we called a tortoise, but Nate insists on calling it a gopher.

He just laughs at my "citified" ways as he calls them, amazed that I would think a gopher is a rodent instead of a tortoise! "Girl," he says, "there ain't no giant gopher rodents in South Carolina."

The way Nate relates it, some Yankee must have married a Low Country Southern belle, and this man must have gone hunting for rabbits one winter Saturday, stepped into a tortoise hole, and sprained his ankle. The next day when he limped into church, folks asked what happened to him, and he replied, "I was rabbit hunting, and I stepped into a gopher hole." According to Nate, "The rest is history."

Anyway, back to my story about those crickets. According to Nate (of course), the biggest bull bream (I think that is a male bluegill) really like those gopher-hole crickets because they have never seen anything like them. So you find a gopher hole. An abandoned one is best according to Colin. How you know it is abandoned is beyond me. Anyway, you cut down a young pine sapling about ten feet tall, then you ram it down in that hole and turn it around and around, and when you pull it back out, those gopher-hole crickets are all in the branches just waiting on you to grab them and put them in a bag. Only when we got to the dock did Colin tell me that when you start picking out those crickets from the limbs, you have to really look out for rattlesnakes because they like gopher holes too.

You may have to get me out of jail when you get home because I might just kill Nate Billington the next time I see him. I guess I have to measure the chance of finding a rattler against the value of those crickets because Colin is hauling in one fish after another. He even caught a nice flounder on one.

JEM, I am glad that you were able to care for General Jackson in his last days. It sounds like he was truly a God-fearing Southern gentleman. Please let me know of your continued friendship (and hopefully your work on triage) with Dr. Paisley. He sounds like a man much like you and John. I don't think it wise that you go too fast with plans. Let that wonderful idea speak for itself to Dr. Paisley. If he is the physician scientist that you believe him to be, he will see its merits and approach you because he is interested. Then you can see that he has seen the value for himself, not just you selling him on the idea.

Whatever is to come next, whether skirmish or battle, I want you to know that I am there with you, if not in body, then totally in spirit. Nurse and physician. How I long to return to those days.

Now there is a thought I have not uttered until this very moment. Yes, I would very much like to return to Charleston and open a medical practice with you. And just think of the opportunities for learning there for Colin. Keep that idea in the back of your beautiful brain and reflect on it until I see you again.

I could not live in Charleston right now with the almost certainty of the capture of our lovely city by the Yankees. Knowing that the first cannonball of this conflict flew from the Charleston Battery, I can only imagine what destruction they might render in revenge. I have tried to convince Father to take Mother from the asylum and join me here on the farm, but he will not hear of it as Mother is in steady decline. As travel by boat from here to Charleston is treacherous these days, I am not sure that I shall ever see Mother alive again.

That is enough of my maudlin dawdling. If I don't bring a halt to Colin's fishing and head for home, we will be cleaning fish until midnight!

As the sun is just starting to grow orange as it makes its transit to set behind the reeds across the Wando River, and as Colin gathers up his fish and fishing pole and frees any leftover crickets, I will leave you with this story that is often on my mind these days:

Do you remember the morning in early June when Colin was about four and we took him to spend the day and night with Nate and Audrey Lee? We picnicked down on the creek with fried chicken, biscuits, and peach cobbler. And then you decided (for it certainly was not my idea) that we should go skinny-dipping in the creek. Do you remember how cold that water was even in June? I don't think we stayed in the water but a few minutes, but when I got out I had goose bumps in the strangest places! And since we did not bring a towel with us, we dried off with the picnic blanket, little knowing that an army of ants had invaded the blanket. So we dried off, they attacked us, and we had to get in that cold creek again! The next time we got out, we shook that blanket really well, dried off, put our clothes on, and ran back home, only to take off our clothes again as soon as we got in the door. Love was made all over our farmhouse that afternoon and late into that good night!

I love you, my dearest physician. Come back to me. I shall be waiting for the adventure of the rest of our lives.

Come home and give me goose bumps again,
Red

Warrior and Gentleman

June 26, 1863
Shetter's Woods
Chambersburg, Pennsylvania

My Dearest Red,

My sincerest apologies for being inconsistent in my correspondence to you, but since we crossed the Rappahannock on June 17, my days are consumed with marching. And I mean marching for me too. With horses so important and so scarce these days, I had to give up Coal to the cavalry before we began this march. I have opportunities to ride in the ambulance wagon from time to time, but I think the walking does me good. Time to think. Time to get to know the boys while they are still whole and wholly optimistic about their futures. I am convinced that it will aid me when the battle comes should I recognize a face on my table.

We march from morning to day's end, and although I am not treating the mortally wounded, the marching brings on its own set of ills. Many of our boys are clad in little more than makeshift uniforms hardly recognizable as uniforms at all. Few still have their regimental dress from their home units and are, instead, covered from head to foot in ill-fitting accouterments surrendered by those no longer in need of them in the afterlife they have already entered. In other times and places, such actions would be shameful, but shame is an emotion long and readily abandoned when one's own body is cold and the feet are bare. Even so, General Lee issued stringent orders that the army is to march in exact and precise columns.

We are in the most beautiful land I have seen since leaving Horlbeck Creek. Even the barns show unique designs, and everything is just so green and lush. I know that our boys have been tempted to break rank and go onto the farms ripe with fruit and rich with vegetables and confiscate a few for "the good of the cause." General Lee's orders strictly forbid such behavior. I know that I shall not quote the order precisely, but here is what I remember that he said to us all before we crossed the Rappahannock:

> "I cannot hope that heaven will prosper our cause when we are violating its laws. I shall, therefore, carry on the war in Pennsylvania without offending the civilians and the tenets of Christianity." Further, he told us, "To totally restrain from the wanton destruction of private property of Maryland's and Pennsylvania's citizenry, commissary officers are to formally requisition food and other supplies from local authorities or directly purchase such from farmers, paying them with Confederate currency."

Our boys have carried out his orders to the letter. As we were settling into our camp today in the roadside grove known as Shetter's Woods, which we came to understand was a favorite picnicking spot for locals, one local matron came forward and asked for Lee's autograph. He complied and wished her well. She was heard to remark as she walked away, "Oh, I wish he was ours," even as she returned to her home displaying a Union banner.

Our own men are little different. General Lee passed our unit yesterday astride his horse Traveller as he moved from the front to the back of the column of marchers and back again to the front. He has a nobility and graciousness of bearing that I have not seen in another general officer. His fleeting presence transports the men, no matter how tired and ragged, as if it were the first day of their imagined glory as soldiers of their beloved South. But I can see the toll this war has taken on him. He has aged in the short year that I have been in his presence.

As officers we see that his vision is more expansive than any of us are afforded, yet he seems to understand that even superior strategy and tactics will inevitably fall to the greater numbers of soldiers with better equipment unless we strike decisively and make morale an issue in the North. Nonetheless, no Yankee general has proven General Lee's match, so we all continue to believe that one more victory may actually be at hand.

The scuttlebutt is that our objective is a small Pennsylvania town known as Gettysburg, some twenty-five miles to the east, two days' march if we march as hard as we have thus far. I do not grasp the significance of the town, if any, other than it is the most distant we will have thrust into the North and that we are not far from Washington should we prevail again.

I want to believe as others, but I fear that a crippling victory is just illusory. It is impossible for me to imagine that triumph is even a word to be considered when it must come at such a cost of lives and limbs as I have not yet observed. Yet we continue our march toward our destiny. That much is clear.

As physicians, we are told, not to be repeated among the men, that Gettysburg may be the largest gathering of soldiers at any one place since this war began, and thus, regardless of the outcome of the battle, I shall be consumed for days to come with blood and death. Pray for me that I may keep Benjamin's advice ever in front of me.

My darling, I could not sleep this night, and these words have taken me unsteadily to the first faint rays of false dawn, so I must again say a reluctant goodbye. I do not know when I shall write again.

But rest assured that my love for you grows stronger each day, and if God is willing, I shall return to you. Until then, pray for me as I shall pray for you. Pray that we shall be sustained by each other's love until we shall return to each other's arms.

Lovingly and longingly,
JEM

CHAPTER 23

Murder in the Shadow of the Battlefield

From the *Chambersburg Public Opinion*
July 8, 1863

Last Sunday, Brother Leon Clodfelter found a gruesome scene of Confederate slaughter at the home of Sister Petronella Neuenschwander when he stopped to pick the family up for church. The details reported by Brother Clodfelter and others are simply too ghastly to report in this family newspaper.

Sister Neuenschwander and her children, Brecht and Addy, were buried in the community cemetery on Monday last. To add mystery to the horror, the Neuenschwander home burned to the ground sometime after dark on Wednesday evening. Brother Clodfelter had no information about the fire.

Evil beyond Understanding
July 2, 1863
Shetter's Woods
Outside Chambersburg, Pennsylvania

Widow Petronella Neuenschwander and her two children lived three miles outside Chambersburg, Pennsylvania, in a well-kept Pennsylvania Dutch farmhouse. The clapboard siding was a weathered gray. Mr. Neuenschwander had only painted the trim to suit the missus. The grass in the yard was neatly cut, the work of her teenage son. Apple trees were showing the first evidence of treasures to come, and peaches would be ready for picking before long—maybe a few early ones to tempt the palate by the middle of July. The kitchen garden was well laid out in neat rows with a white picket fence surrounding it. Just beyond were three acres of corn and beans. Neighbors helped neighbors in Pennsylvania Dutch country, and clearly, Petronella's neighbors, the closest a mile away, had done the planting for her again this year—the second since her husband went to war and the first since General Pope's letter notifying her of her husband's death at Second Bull Run.

Three hounds of mixed heritage barked tentatively as a wagon pulled up on the north side of the house just at dusk dark. As she had most summer evenings about this time, Petronella Neuenschwander was putting up the dishes from dinner and calling to her children to get in their beds on the north side of the house—the side with no windows and an unseen covered wagon parked near the wall. Petronella poked her head out the back door, yelled at the dogs, and returned to her bedroom on the south side of the house. Two nice windows gave her a bit of extra summer sun—just enough to step out of her house-dress and put on her nightgown. Most nights she would light the kerosene lamp and read the Bible in German. But tonight she was tired. The sound of cannon thunder, she figured from Gettysburg, had agitated her all day. She missed her sweet Ambroos more today than any time in many months, so she swept and swept again. She had mopped. She had checked on the corn and picked and shelled some early peas. She had sweated over the woodstove and the special meal she fixed for Brect and ten-year-old Addy. Now she slept the sleep of impending death.

Boston Williams drove the covered wagon. Davey Little and Tommy Nagley were secreted inside, and Abraham Whetstone was mounted and following close behind. Boston parked the wagon, nearly silently, about thirty yards from the side of the house with no windows.

That Whetstone and his three compatriots had arrived at Chambersburg at almost the same time as the Confederate army was no coincidence. He had planned to forage for valuables and take a little blood in southern Pennsylvania but was thwarted by the Union forces, who were pushing quickly northward from Washington. He assumed that a fight was coming. No better diversion for Satan's spawn than a good battle.

Waiting for the dogs to settle, Whetstone eased off his mare and tied her next to the gelding at the rear of the wagon. Boston broke off half of the bale of hay in the wagon and dropped thirds of it at the horses' feet. They would be quiet long enough.

Whetstone reached in his left saddlebag and took out a squirt can of oil that he used to whet his knives and to oil the hinges on the doors of his victims. He put three drops, always three drops, on each of the three hinges on the back door. Silently Whetstone entered with Davey, Boston, and Tommy trailing behind. He got the prime meat. Davey, Boston, and

Tommy would get what was left—alive if they were lucky, but probably not. Whetstone was in a lusty mood tonight.

As the terrors eased themselves into the darkness of the house that only a moonless country night could provide, Whetstone smiled and thought, *My pupils have done well. My performance? I had never any doubt. Not a lot of money—some silver—but oh my, the blood.*

The two bits a day that Abraham Whetstone paid Mary Skirett for his room and board and for boarding for his gray mare were easily won at the beer-stained and cigar-burned poker table once covered in green felt in the back room of the Wounded Duck Tavern. Whetstone did not mind the few miles' ride to the Duck. He could gamble in his own neighborhood, but best to have his face seen by as few people as possible who might remember him should he feel the need to satisfy his blood urge again.

The incident with David Little at Mary Skirett's stable (he refused to call it a fight as it was one-sided) had drawn enough of the little turd's blood to satisfy Whetstone for the time being. After all, he had not come to DC to kill. He could cut off enough ears and beat up enough whores to keep his more base desires at bay. He had come to DC to recruit. He was expanding. There was money to be made in murder of the unsuspecting, but doing it alone presented him with more risk than he was willing to assume. He knew that his name had likely made its way from Grant's army in Mississippi to DC for sure, and probably to the Confederates as well, after those two kills outside Lee's encampment in Fredericksburg. That had given him such pleasure coming so close to the military that he despised so intensely. He could care less about North or South.

Whetstone had joined up with the Fifty-Eighth Indiana Infantry at Princeton and fought reasonably well before he was arrested for raping and killing a Confederate civilian, her two teenage daughters, and a female house slave during the Fort Donelson campaign. "Hell, I thought I was hired to kill Rebels; that nigger just got in my way" was his only defense during his impromptu court-martial in front of General Grant's tent.

After Fredericksburg, his kill total was seven. *Seven is such a nice number,* he often thought as he made his way to DC. *Ten is a good number too.*

All in good time. Killing gave Whetstone a kind of pleasure he had never before experienced—sexual, primal, wolfish, evil. But murder did not always pay the rent, so he began the idea of a gang. His gang. Davey Little was Abraham Whetstone's first acolyte. Davey was faithful, more like a cur dog than Whetstone's equal, but he had his place in the gang as Whetstone imagined it. No more than four people. Only three horses—his mare, one to pull the wagon, and one more tied off at the tail of the wagon. A covered wagon pulling up to a solitary homestead was like hiding in plain sight.

By mid-April Whetstone had recruited two more people. Boston Williams from the seldom spoken of Negro underbelly of Washington was the first. Williams had escaped from a plantation down near the mouth of the Rappahannock where slaves died in equal numbers from malaria, heat stroke, and beatings regularly delivered. Water was Boston's delivery from the misery of the plantation life. A natural swimmer, at five he was swimming in the creek on the plantation. At ten he swam across Robinson Creek. At fifteen, he swam across the Rappahannock and the Potomac. He went on to an existence in the Negro ghetto of Washington, DC. He never wished to return to the plantation—never that—but he yearned every day for a way to leave Mr. Lincoln's city.

Boston found his way most unexpectedly when Abraham Whetstone, after a rare supper out on a cold early March night, found him rummaging through Whetstone's saddlebags for food. As the edge of the cold steel of the bowie knife pressed against his neck, Boston Williams thought he was getting his wish to leave DC, but he was wrong, at least about his mode of delivery. Whetstone gave him a piece of hardtack and a half bottle of gut-reaming whiskey. By the time Boston had finished his bread and drink, he was a member of the Whetstone gang.

The final member of the gang was an amoral western Virginia hillbilly, Tommy Nagley, raised by his daddy on cow's milk and moonshine after his mother died giving him birth. And usually shine was in better supply than milk from the decrepit milk cow kept out back of the shack perched precariously on the side of Friars Hill. Friars Hill stood six miles as the crow flies west-northwest of the small town of Falling Spring. Six miles took all day to walk, so Tommy and his father made do with what little they could eke out of the rocky soil, or kill, or gather from the woods around them, or steal if they did make the trip to Falling Spring. With the pittance they got in Falling Spring for cloudy moonshine and ratty vegetables, stealing was the only thing that made the trip worthwhile.

Clarence Nagley was a first-generation hillbilly married to a second-generation hillbilly, mean as a diamondback, and just as quick to strike the son that he called "Uppity Nagley," a joke that only Clarence found funny. At fifteen, Tommy Nagley took his last beating with the belt his father called "the viper" because the buckle left two fang-like tears in his skin. He had the fang marks all over his back, but no more. This time when he saw the signs of rage building from the lead-laced moonshine eating at his father's brain, Tommy was prepared. As Clarence reached to loosen his belt, Tommy reached for the eight-pound wood maul that he had put in the corner when he came in to cook supper.

"Come on over here, Uppity. Yeah, you been actin' jest like them uppity niggers you wuz named for. What the shit you thank you doin' with that maul? I seen you put it in the corner. You come here rat now and get yer ass tore up."

Those were the last words Clarence Nagley would ever utter, and he never heard his son's reply: "I'ma killin' you, you gawd-damned sumbitch," Tommy roared as he brought the maul down on his father's head, splitting his head and torso like a white oak log. He dragged the body deep into the woods, where the foxes, wolves, eagles, and buzzards could make some use of an otherwise useless creature who had tormented him his entire life.

The next day, Tommy Nagley gathered up his few personal belongings. Then he located all the flint, matches, and kindling in the house, and tied them up with a small cast-iron frying pan, the last bit of chicory-laced coffee, and a bit of sowbelly in a bedroll of sorts made from a tattered thin plaid wool blanket. He tied the knapsack around the end of a sassafras walking stick with a hard knot on the end of it rubbed smooth from going up and down the steep terrain around Friars Hill. To an Irishman, it would look a lot like a shillelagh. And it was not unlike a shillelagh in purpose as a tool or a weapon, if the need arose. He had killed more than a few rabbits with it in the winter—tracking them to their dens in the snow and dispatching them with a quick blow with the knob of his walking stick.

Finally, Tommy Nagley put on every piece of clothing he owned. He found his father's flintlock pistol, his store of black powder, and ten lead balls. He thought about burning down the shack, but people would see the smoke, and it was waste of a good match, so he walked away and never looked back.

He had not much in the way of supplies when traveling from home in western Virginia in the middle of winter, but he would make do. Without question, he would make Falling Spring on his first day. From there he just did not know. Maybe toward Washington. Possibly toward Pennsylvania. As fate would have it, it was on the outskirts of Washington, DC, that Tommy Nagley finally stopped. It was within a half day's travel to the city if he needed, but it was countryside, which made him comfortable.

On his eighteenth birthday, he was drinking real whiskey in the Wounded Duck and unquestionably had the constitution for drinking enormous amounts of Virginian bug juice, having been suckled on the nectar of the corn plant since birth.

A lot of drinking brings on lots of pissing. One night as Nagley relieved himself on the outside back wall, he felt cold steel against his face. He did not move even though he was now pissing on his own pants leg. He did admit to pulling a card from the bottom of the deck as the huge gun barrel of Abraham Whetstone's .45-caliber Colt revolver pushed into his ear canal, drawing blood. Soon after, he was issued an invitation he was not to forget. In fact, years later, in the last conscious moment of a violent death, he would remember that fateful birthday.

It was of no consequence to Abraham Whetstone that Little, Williams, and Nagley "accepted" the invitation to join him under the menace of bodily harm, if not imminent death. They were not natural-born killers like their mentor, but they learned quickly Whetstone's methods, which were neither unknown nor abhorrent to them.

Petronella Neuenschwander and her children were finally discovered when Leon Clodfelter stopped by in his buggy to pick them up for worship at the First Lutheran Church of Chambersburg.

Leon knocked on the front door but heard no sound. When he walked to the back and found the three dogs' heads sitting atop the pointed slats of gate of the kitchen garden like medieval pikes, he ran to the back door and pounded on it until it opened a crack. Something was holding it closed, something that slowly gave way to his increased pressure on the door. He pushed until he could just squeeze between the door and the frame.

Leon believed philosophically in the presence of evil in the world, but he had never really experienced it. An occasional theft of a watermelon was the extent of his familiarity. Today would change that forever.

As he stepped inside, the smell was hellish, but so had been the Confederate wagon train that had passed just the day before, heading back, he guessed, to Virginia. The coppery smell of blood. Blood everywhere that he could see. On turning around toward the back door, he found that he had been pushing the headless corpse of Petronella Neuenschwander. On that recognition, he added his vomit to the unholy smells.

Moving farther down the hall of the Neuenschwander home, Leon found human entrails draped across the doorframes like Christmas garland and every square inch of floor covered with more blood than he thought possible from three scarcely recognizable human bodies. He vomited until he had nothing left in his stomach, and then he was taken with the dry heaves. Leon held on to the edges of the kitchen sink as his body was racked with cramps. Finally, when the waves subsided, he looked in the tub to find the head of Petronella. The heaves began again, until he eventually made his way to the front porch, where he lay in exhausted agony until he regained his breath. When he regained his mind, Leon found in his hand an ace of hearts he must have picked up from the sink. It had these words penned in black ink within the heart: *Greetings from Abe.*

Today, Leon Clodfelter had no doubt that the Evil One not only existed but also lived on earth and had personally paid a visit to Shetter's Woods, Pennsylvania, on July 5, 1863.

CHAPTER 24

Aftermath of Armageddon

The sights and smells of three days at Gettysburg were like nothing Dr. James Edward Merriweather's subconscious could conjure up in his worst nightmares that had been with him since the battlefield casualties had entered his field hospital on the first days of this war. At Gettysburg, July 1 was unremarkable, if such a term can be applied to the six thousand wounded and dead from that first day of fighting.

But nothing had prepared the doctor for the sheer number of boys and men who poured like flash flood waters into his field hospital. He literally stood in pools of blood up to his ankles. More than one-third of all Confederate troops who marched into Gettysburg were killed or wounded—twenty-two thousand on days two and three combined. Many of the dead and wounded from the fighting on July 2 were merely left on the battlefield. When they could be reached in safety, the dead were gathered together and buried on the battlefield near the places they had fallen. The wounded who could be reached were carried back to field hospitals, and so many limbs were amputated so quickly that they were thrown into a pile as high as a man was tall and later buried all together.

Rain showers peppered the defeated Confederates as they prepared to retreat in defeat on July 4. The seventeen-mile train of wagons filled with wounded and the beyond-exhausted foot soldiers began the slog toward Virginia over rain-soaked Pennsylvania bogs that once had been roads. Six thousand Confederate casualties were just left on the battlefield to be treated in Union hospitals. Many were handled by Confederate doctors who chose to be captured with the wounded.

The retreat was hard on everyone—mentally and physically. Merriweather had not bathed since arriving at Gettysburg. Blood was caked on his clothes, and his shoes and socks were stiff with dried blood. The smell of death was woven among every thread of his uniform and clogged every pore of his skin, and every fold of his brain was saturated with it. Merriweather withdrew at night into his nightmares, unable to banish from his eyes the faces of men who had survived the battle only to die in the retreat.

The Confederate army fortuitously managed to escape an attack by General George Meade, who had planned to trap them against the rising Potomac. But Meade was indecisive, and Lee, impatient with Meade's reticence to attack, declared on the morning of July 13 that he would wait no more and ordered the Army of Northern Virginia to ford the Potomac, now returned to its banks, and move to the relative safety of Williamsport.

After making rounds of the wounded on July 15, Dr. Merriweather, fresh from a bath and with a clean uniform, finally recorded an entry into his diary.

Surgeon's Diary

July 15, 1863
Williamsport, Virginia

Nothing prepared me for the sheer awfulness I was to face at Gettysburg. I thought that this would be much like previous battles, where our work was intense for hours, but at the end of the day, we found a time to reflect on the good done that day in our field hospitals. At Gettysburg, there was no time for anything except for cutting and sawing and tossing away limbs from young bodies.

There were so many wounded that there was utterly no time to probe a wound, remove the lead projectile embedded in the muscle, and suture the wound. There were so many boys waiting for our attention that a rifle wound where the lead remained in the limb often meant the leg would be amputated in the hopes that the time we saved would save others who waited for our ministrations.

Limbs were amputated, cauterized, and sutured up with no anesthesia unless the patient lapsed into blessed unconsciousness. So much blood. So much pain. Such a hellish din. Long after we'd left the field of battle, I continue to feel the grind of the saw's teeth on bone, the feel of the blade cutting through sinew and muscle. I taste the coppery essence of blood. I smell the reek of abdominal wounds and cauterized flesh. The sounds and feel and taste and smells reside with me constantly.

I am a beast of burden for the screams of the boys whose limbs I have removed—so mangled were they as to be unrecognizable as human appendages. I think that I shall never be rid of these sensations the rest of my days.

My mind is unable to grasp with any logic known to me the sheer magnitude of the dead and dying left on the battlefield each day. Indeed the manhood of entire towns was lost on those days—and with it, weddings, and births, and families—to be replaced only with an unending grieving for what was, for what is, and for what shall never be. How shall they sensibly ever deal with such loss? I do not know. And for us, Gettysburg's survivors, we have abandoned any hope of returning to the innocence of normality. We only seek to endure to the end of this national disaster.

JEM

Michael O'Malley

Father Michael O'Malley had grown to manhood in the slums of Galway, Ireland. At an early age he saw sex in the side street, blood in the gutter, and diseased citizens put aside by families who could not cope medically, financially, or emotionally with the gravities of a disease-ridden relative. He gave dinner scraps when he could to urchins his own age who roamed in packs and lived in dirty unheated squats.

As a priest he never outgrew those memories of his early

life, and they had, in an entirely unanticipated way, prepared him for service in the church. However, the chaplaincy was an altogether different kind of service. Yes, there were poor in corps the equal of Galway or the slums of Richmond, and his ANV "parishioners" were fighting to stay alive by killing their counterparts across the field of battle.

Battle produced a different kind of spiritual need. The hereafter was often hours away. Heaven and hell were places as real as the thickets of Chancellorsville, or the open fields of Antietam, or the bounty of Manassas. Death was a one-ounce Minié ball away.

Father Michael O'Malley was initially unequipped theologically, spiritually, or emotionally to minister in this environment. Although he had never experienced the level of depression of his friend Dr. James Merriweather, he had come close at Antietam, so massive was the number of casualties.

He had grown in his listening and counseling skills, and in his techniques, and in his letter writing to relatives back home of boys on the brink of death, but the three days of Gettysburg shook him to his Roman Catholic core.

Following St. Paul's admonition, Father O'Malley was a doer. He had found that a gentle touch and time given to listening without impatience was almost always a better healer than any words he could say to the wounded. But to whom does a Chaplain go for solace? Finally, Michael O'Malley gave in to his friend's suggestion that, if he were not willing to talk, perhaps writing words to himself would be a start of the conversation that he needed to have.

Chaplain's Diary

July 16, 1863
Northern Virginia

I am not a diary writer, and this may be the last entry I write in this war. I am writing because I am not ready to accept James's invitation to talk about my obvious distress that he has clearly observed. I am writing because my surrogate correspondence for boys at the brink seems to bring them the grace of God so that they can die relieved of some kind of burden I do not comprehend.

I pray that I, too, shall feel the full and certain knowledge of God's peace in my soul.

What compels otherwise sensible men to risk life and limb for the amorphous concept of *country*? I understand James's desire to serve his profession in time of war. Even so, as much as I love him as a brother, I do not understand his love for the land he calls the South.

That is a question of little consequence in my struggles with God and is one that can wait until I am old and gray—assuming I do not encounter a stray grapeshot—and can sit with my dear friend James in debate on the subject of the rationality or irrationality of such decisions.

I do my best to apply the rabbi's advice, and generally I am successful at that as a process of staying personally sane and doing the most for the most in the shortest time available to minister during and after the battle. However, when the day is done—whenever that may be—and I am alone, I cannot find God. When I pray the rosary, it is reduced to a tool much like Benjamin's advice. How can that be? For as long as I can remember, the repetition took me to a place of tranquility. Since Gettysburg, the disturbance in my spirit is the terminus to which I return each time I pray.

My agitated spirit, or perhaps it is the Evil One's influence, causes me to question if my God is just my own creation—a convenient three-letter word for a tin into which I can drop every unexplained phenomenon that I encounter. Damn. I thought I had put such considerations behind me as a seminarian. Why again now?

Whatever and whoever the Almighty is, I cannot find the means in my understanding of him to grasp that such slaughter as Gettysburg falls is anywhere in the realm of godliness.

I gave up on the idea of predestination the first time I returned to Galway after seminary. God, whoever that being is, surely does not guide the affairs of mankind. If anything was proven at Gettysburg, that is it. But what of omnipotence? Why would an omnipotent God allow such butchery even if free will is the plan for mankind? Of course, this same God allowed Africans to capture and sell their own kind to be sold again and again into the system of economic slavery that now unquestionably drives significant numbers of the politicians who are responsible for this conflict.

Hell's bells! This diary writing is only getting

me back to my original questions. I will talk with James to see if hearing these concerns in my own voice helps. Regardless, I shall keep writing the letters requested by the boys. At least there I can see a tangible result.

Michael O' Malley

PART VII
CIVIL DISOBEDIENCE

CHAPTER 25

A Child Is Born

As slaves, Moses and Sarah Billington prayed to the Almighty that their loving, as they called it, would never result in children. Such was their abhorrence for life on the Van Landingham plantation. Even with a much better existence as slaves for Jacob Billington, they still prayed to remain childless. The Lord had answered their prayers. Then in May of 1780, when Tyler Billington's ultimatum bought their freedom, they prayed a different prayer. But still Jehovah honored the prayer they had prayed for so many years. *Perhaps we are to be like Abraham and Sarah. Maybe our faith is not enough,* thought Sarah Billington with tears in her eyes. Her desire to give her husband a son permeated every fiber of her as a believer.

Sarah and Moses would pray another thirteen years, and on a beautiful Easter morning of 1805, Sarah at forty-five and Moses at fifty-eight became parents of a seven-pound, seven-ounce son (as weighed on the pecan scale). Two weeks later on Sunday, April 20, Jacob, ever the Presbyterian, at Moses and Sarah's request, baptized the child in the parlor of the now well-appointed home of Sarah and Moses. When he asked, "What name is given this child?" Moses answered, "Simon Abraham Tyler Jacob Billington."

Taking the pitcher of water from the basin that Jacob's wife, Martha, had brought for the occasion, and with Martha holding the enameled bowl beneath the child's head, Jacob declared as he poured the warm water over the baby's head, "In the name of the Father, the Son, and the Holy Spirit, I baptize you Simon Abraham Tyler Jacob Billington."

As Jacob handed the squirming Simon back to his father, who placed on the baby's head a God-white napkin with needle lace edges sewn by Sarah, Moses interjected, "We are not yet done."

Sarah, speaking in almost a whisper and with the intonation of a prayer, asked, "Mr. Jacob and precious midwife, Martha, would y'all be willin' to be Simon's godparents? We would be mighty proud to know that he is loved, looked after, and prayed for by two sets of parents."

As Martha Billington wailed with joy, Jacob fairly bellowed out, "Holy God in heaven, yes!" To which Simon added his voice to the holy chorus in the parlor of his home on Horlbeck Creek.

Bringing the Word to the Creek

In 1823, as pastor in secret to slaves along Horlbeck Creek, eighteen-year-old Simon Billington heard the Lord calling him to bigger pastures. Simon had worked full time for his father, Jacob, since his thirteenth birthday, when his father declared he was a man and should work full time. Before his father declared him a man in the eyes of God and according to the Old Testament, Simon had worked part time, mixed with learning to read and doing his figures. He read mostly the Bible as his mother had taught him. He learned from his father, whose first financial commandment was to trust in God. The second was to trust yourself, and the third was to trust nobody else, especially the white man, unless such person was a member of the Jacob Billington family. Clearly his skills in all forms of practical figuring—measuring, calculating rows per acre and yield versus expectations, budgeting for the family business minus expenses; making payment to the family, tithe to the Lord, and payment to Jacob Billington on the land; and saving—came directly from his father. And if truth were told, it often came from Tyler Billington, who advised him in the vagaries of commerce at the Charleston markets.

In May of 1777, Tyler Billington returned to Horlbeck Creek from a Revolutionary War skirmish without his right arm and unaware of his father's slave purchase a year earlier. He gave his father an ultimatum—"Free your slaves or lose me."

Jacob would not lose his son, and though he still believed the Holy Book condoned, if not outright approved of, masters and slaves, he hired the "other" Billington family on Horlbeck Creek and paid them a salary that would allow them to buy ten acres of land surrounding the small cabin they had built themselves and that was included at no cost. With a tributary of Horlbeck Creek on its northernmost boundary and two pecan trees shading the cabin, the land was as fertile as any owned by Jacob.

Moses's ten acres included in the bill of sale a right-of-way from his home through the land owned by Jacob Billington to the road leading to the dock on the Wando River. Once Jacob made the decision that he would never own slaves, he also made the decision that he would never have them reduced to the plight of being pseudosharecroppers—in economic slavery beholden to him. The deeded right-of-way across his property meant fiscal freedom. More importantly, it meant physical freedom beyond the ten acres. The boundaries of the lives of Moses, Sarah, and Simon were now mostly, if not totally, of their own choosing.

On Sunday, June 15, 1823, Simon Billington opened the front screen door of his home to find his mother and father waiting for him at the dining room table. At the heart of his home in 1823 was still the cabin with homemade plaster floors his mother and father had constructed as slave quarters forty-seven years before.

"You a bit later than usual, Son. Everythang all right?" his father perceptively asked.

My father has always had "the gift," he thought.

"No, sir, not really. I jest been thinkin' some on my future."

"Yo' future's here with us," his mother said with a stridence she did not intend but which came through nonetheless in her surprise at her son's response.

"I been truly blessed to have such wonderful parents, even if y'all do work me as unpaid labor from Monday 'til Saturday. And we are sho' blessed among our fella Negroes to have had the fellowship and advice of Mr. Jacob Billington and his family. And God has allowed me to preach his Word to slaves here about the creek."

"Son." Moses spoke quietly as he perceived his son was having a crisis of self. "Your mother and I had no choice about our future for most our lives, so it is hard for us to understand how you would want ever to give up what we done built here. He'p us understand."

For the next half hour, without interruption, Simon Abraham Tyler Jacob Billington told his parents that God had called him to do bigger things. Not more important or more fulfilling than he found on the farm with his parents, but bigger. He envisioned a congregation that could meet without fear, a wife and family of his own, a legacy built on the foundation of Moses and Sarah Billington.

Another foundation was laid that day, the makings of a powerful preacher, full of God's power and full of understanding of the plight of thousands of slaves in South Carolina and across the nation. He wanted to serve God and his fellow Negroes—free and in bondage—and build bridges of understanding even if only a few Charlestonians were willing to help. He knew they were there. Jacob Billington and his family were examples.

With the family holding hands and with their heads on each other's shoulders, Moses prayed for a blessing for his son and let him go.

CHAPTER 26

The Inevitability of Age

No one in the parlor that evening when Simon Billington told his parents about his plans thought about the future soon to be unswervingly in front of them all. They had different reasons. Simon was full of piss and vinegar befitting any eighteen-year-old about to embark on a sacred calling. His parents, although dreadfully fearful for their son, ignored all their reservations, so desirous were they that their only son, a free Negro—and there were simply not many of those in South Carolina—make his mark upon Negro society beyond Horlbeck Creek and maybe, just maybe, heal the need of a nation for a collective Sunday "Come to Jesus" reckoning regarding slavery. The result was that Simon did not think to ask, "What of Mother and Father?"

When Simon met *his* burning bush, his father was seventy-six; his mother, sixty-three. Without question, there is *old-old* and there is *young-old*. Moses and Sarah fell into the latter category. Even so, young-old farmers are hard-pressed to make a living from farming much beyond the age of sixty-five.

Simon sat on his bed that evening with his head in his hands, readying himself for prayer. The warm, moonless summer night was punctuated with stars, with the calls of crickets and cicadas, and with the whoosh of an owl's great wings as it passed his open window on the way to the barn. At that moment, Simon felt himself remarkably close to his Creator, more so even than amid his "experience" walking home on the Wando Road earlier in the afternoon. *How could I have been so ignorant, so selfish?* he thought. *I never considered my parents when I made my announcement.*

"They still often outdo me physically with their endurance and persistence," he said out loud to himself and perhaps to the Almighty, "but that is no reason to ignore their age as if it is insignificant."

Even a young seventy-six or sixty-three was still not very far away from the ills that were inevitable with aging. Simon realized that once he moved on, his parents could not continue the farm as a business venture as they had for the past almost forty years, no matter how much they wished it so.

Simon learned a great lesson that night about the missives of God as he sat on his bed. Jehovah's messages are seldom without a very healthy dose of common sense and logic. And he could not escape the naked truth that he was needed awhile longer here on the farm. Maybe God also needed him to preach awhile yet along the creek—a proposition to which he was not opposed at all. He loved the people along the creek.

He prayed a single sentence before drifting into a dreamless but restless sleep: "Thank you, Lord, for leading me through my selfish desires."

Charleston would have to wait.

The next morning, the Billingtons in their former slave cabin, now a fine home, rose before daylight and ate a breakfast of bacon, eggs, and biscuits with dewberry jelly. At the first hint of false dawn, Sarah began harvesting tomatoes, Moses was in the pea patch, and Simon was starting on his acre of butter beans.

"Lord," Simon said out loud, "if hell is not a burning fire, surely it is an endless butter bean row in June in South Carolina that must be picked. And, Lord, why can't the best butter beans be at the top of the bush instead of at the bottom, where the dewy grit makes them so nasty to pick?"

The Almighty chose not to elucidate his young servant on those questions. When Simon glanced over at the pea patch, he saw that his father had finished one row and was making his way back down toward the house on the next one.

His father, seeing Simon standing and stretching his back and looking over at him, laughingly called out, "Preacher man, you havin' some troubles? You wanna switch rows?"

"You jest keep to yore patch, ol' man, and I'll keep to mine," Simon retorted with a peal of laughter.

"Hey, Son, look yonder. Mama's comin' to help you out. Lord A'mighty, I do believe we raised one of them sissified preachers that likes to tell people what to do but who can't do it theirselves!"

"Moses, that is enough," shouted Sarah, sure enough making her way to the butter bean patch with a basket in one hand and a pail of cool well water in the other. "You leave the boy alone if you want what I got in store for you come bedtime tonight!"

In another family, such implied intimacy might have been less than apropos. Not with Moses and Sarah Billington. There were no secrets in the family, and Moses had explained to his young son early on that physical love between his father and mother was God's blessing in a world where blessings were often hard to come by.

The Blessing

On a hell-hot June morning in South Carolina with 95 percent humidity, working until about 11:00 a.m. was about all anyone could reasonably expect to labor without a long break to recover mind and body.

A majority of the population of the state of South Carolina in 1818 were slaves, and slave owners seldom took consideration of heat or humidity, or the day of the week, and expected their slaves to work in the cotton and rice fields from dawn until dusk six days a week.

As free Negroes, Sarah and Moses occasionally worked the same hours, but it was their choice. And while the heat and humidity gave no quarter to their freedom, it sure felt like God was in his kingdom at the end of a hard day.

This day the family came in from the fields about 11:30 and headed directly to the well at the back of the house. Drawing a bucket of icy spring water, they all doused their heads. Once cooled down, they made their way to a dinner of leftovers from breakfast at the table on the porch in the shade of the massive pecan trees. The shade knocked a good five degrees from the midday temperature and provided a small breeze that helped keep the bugs at bay.

"Daddy, will you bless our food?" Sarah asked Moses with no request really implied, as Moses always blessed the food unless he passed that honor to Simon for special occasions.

"God our Almighty Father, Maker of everything in heav'n and here on this creek bank, we thank you for our food that you, in your infinite mercy, have provided to us who are undeserving. Today, Lord, we thank you 'specially that you have called our son child Simon to preach the Word and to serve the peoples beyond these few acres on the Creek.

"Now we humbly ask that you bless this food for our bodies

and bless our bodies as we work these fields this day. And, Lord, if you could, would you bring us a cloud or two? Amen."

"Daddy," Simon said with a mischievous grin on his face, "that's maybe the finest blessin' I ever heard you deliver. Maybe the good Lord will forgive you for all that trash-mouthin' you gave me out in the pea patch this morning." With this, Simon and his mother roared in laughter at Moses's expense, although he soon followed too. "Hard work makes for a happy family" was one of Moses's favorite aphorisms, as Simon's jostling of his father plainly denoted.

Simon split a biscuit from breakfast and slathered it with a mixture of soft butter and jelly blended together, with two slices of bacon on top of the jelly–butter mixture. He closed the biscuit and barely got his mouth around it for a bite. After he finally finished his creation, he broached the subject that had been on his mind all day.

The Call

"Mama. Daddy. I need to tell you about a conclusion that God laid on my heart last night as I prayed. I have realized that I heard only half of what God was tellin' me about movin' on from the farm to Charleston to spread his Word. God needs me to stay here on the farm awhile longer."

"Well, I'll be," Sarah almost shouted in response. "What brought this on?"

Simon thought a moment. He wanted to make sure that he got his next few words as perfect as he could construct them. He said, "We all have to face the facts that y'all are not goin' to be able to keep runnin' this farm as a business for that much longer at your ages."

"Hold on there a minute, Son." Moses was clearly perturbed. "We worked this land for years 'fore you came along, and I 'spect we'll just keep on keepin' on after you leave."

"Wait up now, Moses. Let's hear out Simon's ideas." Sarah spoke quietly so as to calm the conversation before it erupted into an argument. "We have put off talkin' about what's gonna happ'n when we cain't work the land like we been used to workin' it. We need to listen to what Simon's 'bout to say. He's likely to be right. It's just mighty hard for us to admit what he's thinkin' might just be true."

"As usual, Mama, you right," Moses admitted with a smile creeping on his face, starting with the laugh lines around his eyes.

"Okay, Son, let's hear what you got on your mind. I can see them gears a-turnin'."

Over the next hour Simon explained to his parents that he believed God was calling him to stay here awhile longer; he did not know for sure how long. He told his parents that he believed that when they had completed the preparation for life on the farm when it became their source of food instead of their business, he would move on, but only when everyone was satisfied that it was time.

He was rather sure that his parents had squirreled away substantial savings, but his father seldom talked about the family's finances. Simon knew that they had paid off the gentleman's agreement mortgage to Jacob Billington at year eight. After that, they put half of what they had been paying him into savings and put the other half of the mortgage payment toward improving the slave cabin until it was the fine farmhouse in which Simon had come of age.

Simon was young, but he knew that farming was a calling much like preaching, and as a business it always faced the vagaries of weather and the economics of supply and demand.

Moses and his family were not wealthy by South Carolina plantation standards, but they were certainly among the most prosperous of the freed Negroes in Charleston County, in large part because Jacob Billington shared his expertise about the Charleston produce markets. He also shared his very substantial home safe with Moses.

Neither Moses nor Jacob believed in banks. First, to bank in Charleston meant placing their wealth, such as it was, in the hands of capitalists they did not completely trust. Second, money in Charleston was simply not money close at hand. So Jacob Billington had bought his safe years ago when he was beginning to see his farm prosper. The safe, behind a false wall in the pantry, weighed nearly three hundred pounds. For additional protection he bolted it through the floorboards and then bradded the bolts into the nuts with a sledgehammer. "Not impossible to haul off, but damn near it," he often told his wife and children. He'd said the same to Moses when he offered to keep his money for him.

To Moses, the knowledge that what he put in the safe was physically secure and near at hand was worth many times more than the pittance of interest he might earn in Charleston.

Preaching the Word in Charleston

Simon Abraham Tyler Jacob Billington worked another four years on his parents' farm. When he stepped on the small sailboat from the dock on the Wando River headed to Charleston to preach the Word, he felt uneasy assurance. He reasoned that he was as assured as one could be, given the devolving politics of Washington and Columbia, that his parents would be able to live reasonably comfortable while farming for a hobby and not a livelihood—the inevitable destination of any man who chose farming as his life's calling.

Jacob, Martha, Tyler, and Mason Billington stood on the dock with their dearest friends, Moses and Sarah, to watch their godson sail off to Charleston, confident in the knowledge that he had met God's first condition of his charge.

CHAPTER 27

Clifford's Alley

In the summer of 1863, Simon Billington celebrated his twentieth anniversary as pastor of Emanuel African Methodist Episcopal Church. He had his own family: two grown but unmarried daughters whom he adored but who were also total mysteries to him. Ruth Evangeline was thirty-one, and Mary Hannah was twenty-eight, and they both still lived at home. His wife of thirty-four years, Miriam Lightfoot Billington, was, on the other hand, a miracle.

Simon introduced himself to Miriam Deborah Lightfoot the first Sunday he attended the Emanuel African Methodist Episcopal Church on Calhoun Street in Charleston. She was the daughter of Pastor Charles Lightfoot and the first soprano in a choir that only had exceptional voices. Miriam was tall—actually statuesque. She had skin the color of creamed coffee and just as smooth and brown eyes that were as dark, deep, and mysterious as the eddies in the deep tannin-stained pools created by flowing water in the outside bends of Horlbeck Creek. Miriam Lightfoot was hard to miss, and Simon was smitten.

Simon was not just a Sunday Christian. He quickly became known in the area of Clifford's Alley, where he rented a room from Geneviève Ardoin, a Louisiana Creole Frenchwoman who typically passed for white and who had immigrated from New Orleans with her sister, Amélie Ardoin, owner of a successful French bakery and coffee purveyor near Meeting Street. Simon worked the docks during the day and preached on and around Clifford's Alley until dark most days of the week except for Sunday, when he was always in church admiring Miriam Lightfoot in the choir while, at the same time, trying to listen to her father's sermon. It was not easy to look beyond Reverend Lightfoot into the choir, for he was an imposing man in speech and stature.

The Courtship of Miriam Lightfoot

With Pastor Lightfoot's permission (he was of the old school when it came to his daughter's suitors), Simon courted Miriam for a year before he roused the courage to ask her father for her hand. On a mild November Sunday in 1828, before Sunday dinner, with Miriam's assent, Simon had worked up the courage to ask her father for her hand. In the Lightfoot household, Sunday dinner was eaten about 3:00 p.m. as Pastor Lightfoot was a tad longwinded preacher and as his congregation were enthusiastic recipients and often participants of his Sunday sermons.

Finally, Simon eased into the parlor from the kitchen where he had left Miriam and her mother, Adele, whispering and giggling while gathering the essentials of Sunday dinner. He found his hoped-for father-in-law reading the Sunday edition of the *Charleston Courier.*

"Pastor Lightfoot," Simon stammered, "uh, suh ... I need ... I mean, I want to ... I mean, I would like to ... ask you a question before dinner today."

"Spit it out, son. Is this somethin' to do with my *only* daughter?" Charles Lightfoot emoted theatrically for the benefit of the women, who were listening behind the parlor door.

"I am so sorry to upset you, sir," Simon said apologetically.

"Simon, how many times you eaten Sunday dinner at my house? And how often you been holdin' hands with Miriam under my table?" Charles Lightfoot asked the questions with a smile beginning to crease his face. "You think I don't know what you are goin' to ask?"

"No, sir. I s'pect you do," Simon agreed.

"So," Charles Lightfoot said while rising from the settee to his full six feet four inches, "the only question is whether I am goin' to say yes or no. Would you agree?"

"Yes, suh; I think that 'bout sums it up, sir."

"Simon, I don't think I can give you a yes with you still workin' at the docks and preachin' on the street corners."

"But, Pastor Lightfoot, I *will* have a better job by the time we get married. I promise."

"You promise? I just don't think I can say yes on a mere promise to provide for my daughter. So here is what I *am* prepared to do."

"Yes, suh. I'll do whatever you wants," Simon said a bit too quickly and overenthusiastically.

"Let me finish, son. How would you like the full-time position as associate pastor in charge of evangelism and membership at Emanuel Church startin' next Sunday? Thataway you can give some proper notice to your employer at the docks and quit preachin' for nothin' on Clifford's Alley.

"You willing to make that commitment to the Lord before you marry my daughter? And you gonna have to get you a better suit. We'll talk 'bout that later when we talk a little church business."

"Yes, suh," Simon fairly whispered, he was so excited. His response was almost drowned out by the giggles of the women who were obviously in on Charles Lightfoot's charade and who had now rushed through the parlor door to give hugs and kisses to the two Charleston preachers in the parlor—one the senior pastor of all the city's Negro congregations and the other the newest.

Simon and Miriam were married a year later to the day they'd gotten engaged in an overflowing church. Simon's parents, Moses and Sarah, and godparents, Jacob and Martha, all now very elderly, and Tyler Billington, now a successful Charleston attorney, sat on the first row on the groom's side. Pastor Lightfoot officiated with his usual flair and élan, but he kept it short as instructed by his wife, who watched him carefully, ready to give him the signs if necessary.

Two years later, in 1831, Miriam gave birth to their first child, Ruth Evangeline. A year later, Moses Jacob was born healthy but died of the ague in his third month. It was three years before Miriam gave birth to a healthy daughter, Mary Hannah. However, a long labor and complications at birth meant that Miriam and Simon would have no more children.

When Simon was appointed as senior pastor in 1843, stepping into his father-in-law's shoes but never replacing him, Ruth Evangeline was eleven and Mary Hannah was eight. Ever perplexing to their father but raised by every matron member of his congregation at Emanuel African Methodist Episcopal Church, they were loved beyond all reason and so were shielded from the ugliness that Charlestonians frequently exhibited to freed Negroes even though they lived and conducted commerce in each other's midst.

Simon never believed the old saw that death occurred in threes, yet in his second year as pastor, death took Simon back to Horlbeck Creek three times.

In the midwinter, he preached the funeral of Jacob Billington. Martha, now feeble in body and mind, barely comprehended what took place. Tyler, his wife, Margaret, and their son Nathaniel, whom Simon had played with on the creek bank in earlier days, attended. Mason, a sea captain, was in the mid-Atlantic. Moses and Sarah stood with the family for the blessed short sermon.

In midsummer, Martha, who had lived with Tyler in Charleston since Jacob's death, passed away with her children, her grandchildren, and her godson at her bedside. Three days later Simon preached her funeral, as she was laid to rest in the family plot next to Jacob on Horlbeck Creek.

On a frosty late autumn afternoon, Simon returned to Horlbeck Creek for what he hoped was his last time. Not that he deplored it, just that his life was no longer here. His father and mother had died within three days of each other, Moses of old age, primarily, and Sarah of a broken heart.

CHAPTER 28

The Sweet Potato Vine

The impact of the Emancipation Proclamation on slaves in the South was, for some time, minimal. But in whispers in plantation slave quarters late at night, the *idea* of the proclamation gestated slowly at first until after the Union victory at Gettysburg, when it burst into flame, as right and proper ideas tend to do in societies where they are profoundly needed.

However, even before Gettysburg, Geneviève Ardoin's boardinghouse and brothel had seen a steady increase in the number of runaway slaves showing up at her doorstep asking for a safe place to sleep for the night. The message that Geneviève Ardoin was friendly to runaways had steadily made its way to the plantations in and around Columbia and the South Carolina Low Country by what became known as "the Sweet Potato Vine."

The first slaves to take advantage of the Sweet Potato Vine were at Chestnut Hill Plantation north of Columbia. But the idea of the surreptitious communication system was devised after Dr. Cyrus Knotts, a sympathizer with the cause and a professor of religion from the University of South Carolina, spent a very pleasant evening in Geneviève Ardoin's brothel, where he had made known his opposition to the practice of slavery to his sweet companion for the evening, Cocoa, a nineteen-year-old runaway slave from Charlotte who possessed the skin tones and voice to match her name.

Always a bit mysterious in his dealings when he visited Charleston, he was never acknowledged or referred to in conversation, even by those who had known his given name and family history for years, as anything other than Professor. The professor's cousin in the bright yellow house at 107 East Bay Street knew she should never expect her favorite northern relative to be home at whatever time he had promised, so she worried neither a jot nor a tittle when she found that his bed was still made up from the morning when she retired at 1:00 a.m. to read her Bible. She thought to herself, *He will be back when he is back, as he is fond of saying.*

At 2:00 a.m. as the professor was about to enter his carriage to return to his cousin's home where he slept on visits to the Holy City, the still fetching Miss Geneviève, as she was known to most of Charleston, in a green satin dress barely containing her more than ample bosoms and accentuating her slightly yellow-tinted French Creole complexion, called to him. "Professor, may I engage you in conversation for a moment before you leave? I believe I have a proposition for you that you will want to hear."

"Anything for you, my dear," the professor responded as he paid the carriage driver to wait while he returned to the establishment worthy of comparison to any whorehouse in New Orleans and wholly belied by the rundown exterior that hid the delights tempting all the senses inside its rather substantial front door.

Geneviève Ardoin's proposal was simple. "Devise a safe and straightforward way to let my brothers and sisters across

South Carolina know that should they find the courage and the means to walk or run away from their masters, they will find a powerful and silent friend here on Clifford's Alley who will help them take the next step toward their freedom.

"Do that," she said with a lascivious smile on her still unlined face, "and my ladies and I will be ever so grateful anytime you grace our lovely city."

Recruiting

Two weeks after his return to the university, during supper with the head of the agriculture department, Knotts peppered him with inquiries about the proclivities of the South Carolina variety of the South American sweet potato. Over an aged rib eye, and bolstered by some fine Kentucky bourbon, the Sweet Potato Vine was born unbeknownst to the head of the department of agriculture who sat across the table.

At fifty-five, the professor remained unmarried and had no desire to engage in the legally required condition for sexual relations in South Carolina. When one of his plantation belles could not be enticed to bed in his spacious home under the live oaks on the Broad River running directly through the city of Columbia, there was always the brothel upstairs at the Gamecock Inn. The Gamecock Inn was a legitimate business on the first floor, and its name honored the Revolutionary War hero General Thomas Sumter, known as the Carolina Gamecock. Fittingly, the brothel was merely known as Cocks, and should one mention the name to anyone within fifty miles of Columbia, they knew precisely the establishment and could likely talk about its reputation for the exceptional women of both races it employed.

He had been so involved with creating the Sweet Potato Vine that it had been almost a month since Knotts had engaged in a romantic evening with any of his several young belles, and he yearned for their company. Yet the need for a return visit to Charleston would not subside so that he could concentrate on the women. Seldom did affairs of academia or business take precedent over his affairs of the heart; however, this niggling of his synapses was different.

On the other hand, his was a life composed of patterns, and this was no time to break his arrangements with the female sex just because a war was on. The professor argued with himself, *Maybe I could entice Miss Regina Wellington to dinner and dessert tomorrow evening, then be off to Charleston the next day. After all, she is the daughter of the president of the University of South Carolina.*

His better angel prevailed, and he settled the war of desires being fought in his head. *Hell,* he thought to himself, *the ladies of Columbia will just have to bide their time for a while longer. I have a date with Miss Geneviève.*

The next morning the professor left early for Charleston on his roan filly Clementine.

Geneviève Ardoin's Blessing

Three days later during an evening of numerous goings-on at Ardoin's, Knotts explained his idea for the surreptitious communication system to Geneviève, whose ladies would help to get the message out to the plantations in the Low Country. The process the professor devised over dinner with his colleague from the agriculture department was simple in design and execution.

Starting backward, the professor explained to the buxom madam lounging on the other side of the bed eating éclairs from her sister's bakery.

"First," he said, wiping custard from his blond mustache,

"we recruit ladies from your establishment and from Cocks in Columbia to explain the process to their enslaved sisters and brothers.

"We—you here and me in Columbia—must purchase a goodly number of sweet potatoes. I would start with the purchase from Bailey's Remedies & Sundries. Bailey is not a proponent of slavery, and he may just be the ally we need down the way. For sure, he will not divulge our plan should the authorities question him.

"Into each potato your ladies will carve 'CAA'—for 'Clifford's Alley Ardoin.' And whenever any of your ladies visit the market—and I suggest you alternate who that might be often so as to deflect any suspicion from you—they take with them two or three of the sweet potatoes carved with the CAA. If they come in contact with brothers and sisters still in slavery, they should strike up a casual conversation and tell them about the process.

"If the person they talk to is interested, they give them a carved potato and ask them to explain the significance to their fellow slaves when they return to the plantation. If their fellow slaves are not ready the first time they are approached, they will be soon enough, so ask the next time again. We must remember that being comfortable, even in dreadful situations, is a compelling emotion, and leaving the only thing they may have known may be painfully slow to begin.

"However, I expect they already have a good idea of who is willing to risk everything they know for the one thing they don't know—freedom. Keep the faith. The message will get out, and the humble sweet potato will keep the authorities away from your environs here on Clifford's Alley.

"What are your thoughts about what I have said thus far?"

"Professor, when slaves decide to take the plunge into the great unknown of freedom, they must be zealous in their desire. They must see no other path and must not be able to stand to be a slave another day. The moment they make that decision, they must become Negroes, instead of niggers, in their own hearts." As she said these words, tears streaked down Geneviève Ardoin's face and tumbled like a river over her naked breasts and onto the silk duvet that was pulled up to her waist.

"I will take that beautiful thought back to Columbia with me when I begin my work there. If I may, I would like to start the process first. It may take more time because they do not know you in Columbia."

"Of course they know me in Columbia. Where do you think Cocks ladies are trained and got their start? Right here on Clifford's Alley. Besides, I own 30 percent of all the payin' business that goes on above that tavern. There are some things even the mysterious professor doesn't know about me. But you can still start first."

"Well, I'll be damned!" The professor laughed as he wiped the tears from her breasts with the immaculately white silk handkerchief that he always seemed to have nearby for just such an occasion. No ordinary handkerchief, this. The touch of the silk was like a butterfly alighting on her skin. It felt incredibly sensuous.

However, even the naked woman in whose bed he currently lounged could not sidetrack the professor. "They must act the part of free Negro. If the people they meet on the street believe they are free, they will treat them differently. I know that their treatment is not perfect, not even acceptable in most cases, but it's a whole lot better than they'll be treated if they act like they are still slaves and are jerked off the street by slave hunters so near to their final destination."

He was on a roll now and continued: "To take their first step toward freedom, they must have the intellectual wherewithal and the resources to quickly leave the plantation, and they must be meticulously exact in their actions if they are to reach your door. As they make their way here to you, in their actions and their mannerisms they must be as unremarkable as the sweet potato they carry with them.

"The wherewithal must come from within them. The symbol of the sweet potato represents the risks taken on their behalf. If they are to bring anything else but the clothes on their back, it must be that carved sweet potato."

"How will they know my house is the right house?" Geneviève asked.

"When they reach your door, they will see the red ribbon on the doorknob and see a small basket of sweet potatoes on the stoop. That basket of tubers is the signal that all is well inside—no authorities are engaging your ladies for the evening. To enter beyond your threshold, they must give you a single sweet potato with 'CAA' carved into its skin. That way you will know that they are who they say they are.

"And should you ever be questioned about the basket on the porch, you tell the authorities that the basket of sweet potatoes is there for the hungry to take one or two away for dinner."

"I like it. And what is more, I am known to love roasted sweet potatoes, and my ladies routinely buy them from Bailey's or the market, s it will not be unusual for them to be out and moving about and starting conversations with other Negroes."

Call in the Dogs

With his last bite of éclair washed down with a steaming cup of very strong coffee with chicory, the more severe Cyrus Knott came to the forefront—a side of him Geneviève had not seen.

"Geneviève, from the moment they enter your home, they are your responsibility. Have you thought about the next steps?"

With that question, the professor had shifted the conversation from the vision of freedom to the mechanics of how it would happen.

"I have an idea. I am not without friends and more than a few strings I can pull, but I would leave using influence and threat until all else has failed. Too much to risk. I think we should maybe keep that part of this story separate from the other part. Reasonable deniability will protect us both at the most critical points in the process.

"What about you, Professor? You have to get your folks from Columbia down to Charleston, and that is a good hundred miles as the crow flies."

"You are, of course, right about having some secrets between us. As for my folks from Columbia, they will travel down the Congree all the way to Charleston. As you suggested, let's leave it at that."

The professor spent the night with Geneviève—asleep—in her big feather bed on the third floor. He awoke at first light, as was his habit, to find Geneviève dressed and ready to go down to the first level for breakfast. "Will you come down after your bath and have breakfast with us ladies? I believe your bathwater is drawn just as you like it."

"Of course, darlin'. And then I must get to my cousin's. She will not know how to act if I actually show up for dinner and spend the rest of the day in conversation with her about the Bible as she is always wont to do."

Once he had returned from Charleston with the Sweet Potato Vine process agreed upon, it was to Josephine, one of his lovely dark-skinned companions at Cocks, that Knotts turned. Josephine often encountered the house slaves from Chestnut Hill Plantation at the market in Columbia as she purchased foodstuffs for the inn, and on occasion, they might even have coffee together at one of the tables outside the vegetable market. Josephine was as smart outside the bedroom as she was creative inside it, and over dinner with the professor, she eagerly agreed to take the first steps to get the Sweet Potato Vine started at Chestnut Hill Plantation. The professor felt no obligation to ask about what the steps might be, as he had other needs that required Josephine's attention.

The next day he penned a one-sentence letter on university stationery letting Geneviève know of his success in Columbia:

June 1, 1863

University of South Carolina
Columbia, South Carolina

My Dearest Geneviève,

Call in the dogs and piss on the fire. The revolution has begun!

Yours,
The professor

CHAPTER 29

An Unexpected Visitor's Proposition

By the time the professor returned to Columbia and wrote his letter announcing the revolution, Geneviève Ardoin had already begun to set up her required contacts, deciding to talk only with people whom she knew she did not have to convince to join in the venture. That simple idea reduced the amount of secrecy and surreptitiousness to a livable level not so different from the conditions required for her business on the second floor of her Clifford's Alley home.

On Monday, May 25, 1863, Geneviève Ardoin paid a visit to Bailey's Remedies & Sundries and spoke with the owner, Matthew Bailey. She was dressed in a blue and brown striped silk taffeta dress that accented her French blue eyes and played down, if possible, her more famously prominent attributes.

"Mr. Bailey, I hope I am not disturbing you so early this Monday morning." Her Cajun French accent was a bit more prominent than usual. "My sister, Amélie, speaks highly of you and your business in helping her acquire the necessities for her bakery and coffee shop. I am Geneviève."

"Miss Amélie is one of my most regular customers, especially as the war has drawn nearer. It seems everyone needs their pastries now and again, even if they have to cut back on other things.

"Ma'am," he said, "what can I do for you this fine spring

morning? And take whatever time you need. Monday mornings I usually spend with the inventory, and anything that will take me away from that onerous task is a blessing indeed."

"Mr. Bailey, I know that you and your family are not slave owners or supporters of those who are. I know that your business at one time before the war was to frequent Clifford's Alley, bringing vegetables and fruits and sundries to its people. That was a big risk on your part, and the people along Clifford's Alley hate that the war has caused your cart to remain parked, but we understand."

"That was the idea of my son Andrew Ryan. He was the one who drove the cart. But since he is now a Confederate naval officer, it is no longer possible. That cart was another of the good things that this war has taken from us. Won't you sit so we can talk awhile more comfortably?"

"Mr. Bailey, your son sure had some good friends on the alley who miss him, sir. And your business's relationship with the folks on Clifford's Alley is why I am here this morning," Geneviève said as she sat down in the oak rocking chair, her dress flowing outward in voluminous pleats and stripes.

"Sir, you no doubt know the nature of my business."

"I do, and it is none of my business to pass judgment," Matthew said. "So what can I do for you this morning, Miss Ardoin?"

"Mr. Bailey, as you may or may not know, some of my ladies have visited your store before for various reasons. I trust they are always polite and courteous to you and other customers."

"They are fine examples of comportment, and they are welcome here."

A Well-Conceived Plan

"Thank you, sir. That is what I wanted to hear you say. Over the next few days and perhaps longer, some of my ladies are going to be coming here to purchase sweet potatoes, in quantities a bit larger than in the past. I do love a good baked sweet potato, but that is not why they are coming." Geneviève's voice grew quiet, almost to a whisper. "My establishment is soon to become a safe house for runaway slaves from South Carolina. Does that bother you?"

"Miss Geneviève," Matthew said with a title usually reserved for Charleston's ladies, "it is about damn time. Please pardon my vulgarity. I am afraid that my language in front of ladies is another casualty of this conflict. I apologize. How can I help? And please call me Matthew."

"If you will call me Geneviève. I mostly need you to protect my ladies should anyone inquire why they are making larger purchases of sweet potatoes, and perhaps sundries that will aid our travelers on their journeys."

"Consider it done. It is an honor," Mathew said, thinking back to the reason his family came to the United States to begin with. "From our days in Ireland, opposing oppression is in my family's blood. If you need more from me, perhaps in the way of remedies, I will be personally offended if you do not ask."

"That is wonderful news indeed, Matthew." She felt a bit strange calling him by his Christian name as she usually only called white men by their first names when they were undressed and in her bed.

"You will know *my* ladies when they come to you because they will pose a question: 'Sir, do you have any nice sweet potatoes today?'

"Should you have any worries about their presence, merely say, 'No, but I believe the market has some nice ones.' And they will leave and actually go to the market."

"Geneviève," Matthew asked, "can you tell me more about what happens once they arrive at your establishment?"

"I believe it is best for all concerned that beyond me, each person involved only know about their little piece of the puzzle. That way should the authorities inquire, you can honestly plead ignorance."

"What a well-conceived plan. Now, can I interest you in a few sweet potatoes?" It was a question too good to resist, and they both laughed, if nervously.

CHAPTER 30

Mother Emanuel

Simon was sitting in his office at Mother Emanuel on an early May Monday in 1863 reflecting on yesterday's sermon and praying for guidance in the week ahead. The weeks had become more treacherous for Negro Christians in Charleston as the war progressed. Almost weekly now, his church had been receiving in membership a fellow Christian who had been worshipping for years at a local congregation with both white and black members. But things were changing in the Holy City.

Simon was not sure when he first used the moniker "Mother Emanuel." He remembered using it as the associate pastor even before he and Miriam were married, albeit believing it did not originate with him. Regardless, the name fit the role he now considered a church should play in any community and especially the community surrounding Calhoun Street in Charleston. Besides, it just rolled off the lips, and that made it practically unforgettable. *I wish the same for my sermon this week,* he thought to himself and laughed, just as a familiar face stepped into his office and sat in the chair across from his desk.

"Pastor, I need your help," she said, her voice highly accented from her early years in New Orleans.

"Geneviève Ardoin!" Simon fairly yelled out her name, such was his love for the woman who sat across from him.

No Judgment Zone

Simon knew that had Geneviève Ardoin not taken him in and placed him under her wing during his early days in Charleston, he would not be sitting across the sizable oaken desk from her right now as pastor of the largest Negro congregation in Charleston. She fed him literally and spiritually. He knew the business that was just in its infancy in the floors above him, but she never tempted him with pleasures of the flesh—either her own or that of her women. Their understanding of each transcended their circumstances.

At the time, Geneviève lived in a two-story shotgun house, run down with the door hanging akimbo on its rusty hinges. There was a swept dirt yard that was muddy up to one's ankles when it rained should a customer step off the flagstone pathway. Inside, there was a woodstove for heating and cooking and a threadbare settee in a tiny parlor on which Simon slept each night. Physically, Geneviève Ardoin's was as far removed from Simon's home on Horlbeck Creek as one could imagine. Blessedly, Simon was a spiritual person who took little note of outer trappings. Geneviève Ardoin was the archetype of the persons on Clifford's Alley to whom he preached every afternoon until he was hoarse. Criticism of her never entered his mind. Besides, he saw Miriam every Sunday, hoping that she saw beyond the fact that he slept each night in the settee downstairs in the whorehouse on Clifford's Alley. She did.

Simon knew what had transpired on Clifford's Alley in the years since he had left. Geneviève had purchased the two shotgun houses on either side of her. Collectively they became known as the Three Sisters. The one to the far left served moonshine disguised as whiskey to seamen. The one to the far right was a New Orleans–style boardinghouse—the only place in Charleston one could find authentic etouffee. Geneviève lived on the added third floor of the one in the middle. The whorehouse was on the second floor with a vast Charleston-worthy parlor on the first floor that was known to have welcomed many of Charleston's finest citizens at one time or another. All the business in each house transpired behind the weatherworn clapboard siding and dirt yards.

Judgment was left to the Almighty. Simon had enough on his hands.

Covert Missionaries

"Geneviève, how have you not aged a day? And look at me."

"Good clean living, Brother Simon. Good clean living."

The laughter was so loud that Head Deacon Alonzo Gibbs opened the door to make sure everything was all right. It had been a long time since Alonzo had heard his pastor laugh, and he was glad—whatever the source.

"Simon Abraham Tyler Jacob Billington," Geneviève said, trying to sound motherly by using his full name and hoping to quell the laughter, "I am here on serious business."

"I thought clean living was your business." Simon could not resist.

And it was another five minutes before either could speak, tears rolling down their faces.

"All good and needed laughter aside, I do have important business, and I need *your* help."

Over the next hour, Geneviève told Simon every detail about the Sweet Potato Vine Revolution as she was now calling it, knowing that unlike others who got the runaways to her door, Simon's job, should he agree, was to get them out of Charleston. And for this, partial knowledge, meant as protection, would be inadequate.

Simon was the smartest person Geneviève had ever

encountered. He could take care of himself and the runaways. At least that was what she told herself.

At the end of the hour, Simon agreed that Mother Emanuel was entirely a good and right vessel in which the escaped slaves of South Carolina could place their total trust to take them to the next leg toward freedom.

The last order of the day was to agree on a signal that would tell Simon a group of four runaways was about to show up at Mother Emanuel.

"Simon, do your parishioners ever bring you vegetables from their gardens?"

"Of course. Do I see sweet potatoes in my future?" Simon grinned.

"You do. In fact, one of my ladies will deposit a small sweet potato in the offering plate on Sunday, a week and a day before a group of four runaways will show up on Monday morning at the parsonage's back door asking if you have any sweet potatoes they might have. Will a week give you enough time to arrange whatever it is you are going to do next?"

"The Lord and I will make it enough. I will stop by and order some etouffee when I am ready to begin. I know it will be at least two weeks before I can partake of that most Cajun of dishes. I need to see a wayward seaman on this side of the harbor, and then he and I need to make a trip to Horlbeck Creek and extend an offer to an old friend who I believe will not refuse.

CHAPTER 31

The Reprobate

Simon laid out his plan almost as soon as Geneviève Ardoin left his office. He had a two-week window in which to make arrangements to move four runaway slaves out of his church, out of Charleston, and on to the next leg of their dangerous journey northward. He hoped to accomplish it more quickly, but quick, or at all, depended on the answers of a reprobate seaman he had befriended through the years and his godbrother across the Charleston Harbor up Horlbeck Creek.

The Reverend Simon Billington and the Mother Emanuel Church were fixtures within Charleston as the church's unofficial parish lines were bounded by the harbor to the east, the battery to the south, the Ashley River to the west, and roughly Grove Street to the north, although at times Simon was known to visit the Charleston Neck farther north where the lowest rent and the fewest jobs were found for free Negroes and poor whites.

Simon was a pastor for whom compassion for others was the key element of his usual calm and almost always comfortable approach to theology. He was oblivious to how others might perceive him or talk about him or even treat him; therefore, as he made the rounds of his parish—he took his carriage on every street at least once every week—it really was of no consequence to him whether people he encountered were free, slave, white, or slave owner. If help was needed, he gave it. This was the "unto the least of these" commandment, he called it in his sermons. Simon was practicing what he preached when he first met Bartholomew Jennings, to whom he now intended to turn for help in getting runaway slaves across the harbor, up the Cooper and Wando Rivers, and to the mouth of Horlbeck Creek.

Jennings had been a former seaman on the coastal schooner the *DeMille* before the war and was a full-time reprobate since. Since the war began, Bartholomew had lost all contact with the civilizing relationships of the Bailey family. And the discipline that life on the *DeMille* brought him was nonexistent since Charleston Harbor was, for the most part, closed and the *DeMille* had been sold for its timber and brass. The maritime traffic that one time made Charleston a premier port on the East Coast had now moved to Wilmington, where it could be more easily defended by the Confederate guns at Fort Fisher.

Bartholomew Jennings was reduced to begging when he could not catch his supper handlining around the docks where, at one time, he had been warmly welcomed.

It was early evening, just dark, on a hot July day when Reverend Simon Billington smelled Bartholomew Jennings before he met him for the first time. He recognized the signs. The man was near death from dehydration, malnutrition, and likely any number of parasites.

He stank of vomit, piss, and shit in equal measure as he lay under the stoop of an abandoned squat just beyond the western edge of Clifford's Alley. People walked so far around him that Simon could not even get their attention to ask for help. Finally he returned to his carriage and drove away, looking for a horse trough into which he could dump the pitiful Bartholomew

Jennings. Simon considered just riding on. *The man will not be the only person to die in his condition this night in Charleston, and probably not in Clifford's Alley,* the preacher thought to himself. But the Almighty's commandments did not exclude those who smelled rank and putrid, so Simon drove on until he found a half-empty horse trough two blocks away. After knocking on several nearby doors, Simon was finally greeted through a barely opened door by the familiar face of a member at Mother Emanuel. She gave him a bar of lye soap and quickly closed the door.

Simon returned to the unconscious man in the doorway, rolled him onto a blanket kept in the carriage for cool mornings, looped a rope around both his feet and the blanket, tied it to the underpinning of the carriage, and dragged him the two blocks to the trough. Holding his breath, he grabbed him by the seat of his soiled pants and the neck of his ragged shirt and dumped him unceremoniously into the tepid dirty water of the trough.

After Bartholomew Jennings spit and spewed water and shook his tangled mess of hair until he regained a measure of consciousness, the Negro in reverend's attire standing in front of him told him in no uncertain terms to keep his ass in the water until he had removed all his clothes and scrubbed every inch of his body and every piece of his clothing. This was no time for modesty. After almost twenty minutes, the smell became at least bearable, and after Jennings put his dripping clothes back on, Simon turned the trough over to empty its fetid contents into the dirt street. He would return tomorrow to see about getting it filled again. Now he had to get the man dried off and find him something to eat.

Simon would not allow Bartholomew, whose name he finally got from the man, to ride inside the carriage, but he did let him stand on the side step of the carriage and drip-dry as they made their way back to the parsonage.

When Simon opened the back door and asked Miriam for some old rags so Bartholomew could dry off, she refused. Instead, she brought out two nice towels, a pair of dry pants, underwear, socks, and a shirt—all Simon's. "I believe the golden rule is 'Do unto others as you would have them do unto you.'"

All Simon could say was, "Yes, ma'am." She was, of course, correct in her theology and in reminding him of his.

A few minutes later Miriam brought out a strong cup of coffee and a plate with two biscuits and a slice of country ham. Miriam never did anything halfway. "There is more when you are ready. But go slow to begin with," she advised.

As Bartholomew Jennings ate, Simon asked about his past and was interested to discover the former seaman was as at home with boats and waterways around Charleston as he was with drink and hangovers and whorehouses.

Bartholomew Jennings had come close to death on that stoop in Clifford's Alley, and he intended never to let it happen again. He was not sure of his path to sobriety and a meaningful existence, but he was sure he had found the man who could help. So on Sunday next, and most Sundays after that, Bartholomew Jennings was the only white face in worship at Mother Emanuel. He was a regular worshipper from that point on and a part-time custodian—enough to keep himself fed and housed on Clifford's Alley.

On This Rock I Build the Plan

Five years later, it was to Bartholomew Jennings that Simon turned to plan out the next step of the Sweet Potato Vine Revolution.

After asking Bartholomew about boats and the best departure points and times, Simon determined that perhaps it was best not to know precisely how Bartholomew was to acquire the necessary craft.

Bartholomew was ever the bearer of unexpected information as he cleaned in and about the grounds of the church. Simon was still surprised when Bartholomew told him he had made the trip from the Charleston docks and up the Wando River to the small and now decaying jetty at the mouth of Horlbeck Creek a number of times since the war began, ferrying Mr. Matthew Bailey to meet his daughter Mary Assumpta Merriweather and her son, Colin.

"Well, let me ask you, Seaman Jennings," Simon said, being overly formal. "Did you also happen to meet a farmer and his wife, Nate and Audrey Lee Billington?"

"Well, hell yeah! Pardon my French, Parson. About my second trip, I found Mr. Nate fishing off the dock with Colin, who called him Uncle Nate. On the trip back to Charleston, Mr. Bailey told me that Mr. Nate and Miss Audrey Lee were the first people on Horlbeck Creek to help out Dr. James Merriweather and his wife, Miss Mary Assumpta, when they moved to the creek from Charleston after a shotgun wedding at the Stump."

Bartholomew was not done. "I have known Mary Assumpta since she was fourteen and helped her brother Dr. John Bailey lance a carbuncle on my ass. She is a pistol, Preacher."

Bartholomew continued, "Nate and Audrey Lee helped them fix up the farmhouse that her father gave them when Miss Mary Assumpta's mama threw her out of the house for marrying a Protestant, an older man who got her daughter in a family way before they got married.

"Mr. Nate showed them how to make a profit from farming, and Audrey Lee even delivered their son Colin. As far as I can tell, they are as close to a natural family as you are ever likely to encounter. Anything else I can tell you, sir?"

Reverend Simon Billington, godbrother to Nathaniel Billington, could see the pieces coming together as clear as day, but first he had to make a trip to Horlbeck Creek to make a proposition, explain the risks, and do some planning about the future steps of the journey once the first of his four "sweet potatoes" were ready to move on from Horlbeck Creek. From that thought forward, Simon always referred to the runaway slaves as "sweet potatoes." *I'll have to let Geneviève know so that she can use the same language.* A load of "sweet potatoes" was unlikely to draw the attention from even the most curious official.

"Thank you, Lord, for putting that thought into my head," Simon said out loud with his face to the heavens.

Three days later, Simon Billington and Bartholomew Jennings docked a "borrowed" oyster boat at the jetty on Horlbeck Creek.

CHAPTER 32

Reunion

The boat bearing Simon and Bartholomew that tied up just after false dawn at the jetty extending out into the Wando River was so nondescript that a nonsailor might have assumed that it had been long abandoned and had floated unaided against the wharf and now bounced with the waves of the incoming tide. The boat was built of cypress with a single mast and a brown sail extending upward through a small forward cabin, and while it looked abandoned and about to sink beneath the swells, the water-soaked cypress boards were tight and heavy and seaworthy in the sometimes choppy waters of Charleston Harbor. Yes, the boat would do just fine. Bartholomew would have to devise a lie about the bags of sweet potatoes in the cabin and the fact that they were sailing away from Charleston, not toward it. But if anything at all, Bartholomew Jennings was a consummate liar.

Simon Billington had walked the road from the Wando River dock to his family's farm hundreds of times over the years. It was just a couple of miles from the river. If he was just fishing or exploring with his godbrother, Nathaniel, it was usually less trouble to walk the two miles than to harness up the mule to the wagon then find a place to park the wagon and stake out the mule. But Simon was much younger in those days without cares except to find a way to escape his chores. Today it was hot, and he was sixty-three years old—almost a decade younger than Nathaniel.

Simon brought Bartholomew with him today. If plans worked out as he foresaw them, Bartholomew would be at least as frequent a face in this venture as Simon himself. Besides, it might even be best that Simon did not make too many trips. Bartholomew was much less noticeable in an oyster boat with his cargo covered in burlap sacks in the small cabin.

After their casual walk up the Old Shell Road, Simon stopped short when he beheld the Jacob Billington farmhouse for the first time in almost twenty years.

Nate and Audrey Lee Billington's farmhouse was no longer whitewashed but was weather-beaten to a gray patina on the heart-of-pine clapboards. Had he not known what it looked like the last time he was on the creek, he would have walked on by. Time and age and the war had plainly beaten down the once fine and comfortable, but never extravagant, farm home. He expected that his own family home had suffered a similar fate. That was of no consequence whatsoever. Nate had leased the land, not the house.

The money for the ten acres nearby that Simon had leased to Nathaniel at the death of Simon's parents had continued to come to him yearly, always soon after the beginning of the fiscal year, until the war beginning in 1862 had prevented even reasonably safe travel across the Wando River and Charleston Harbor. If Simon knew Nathaniel, the trifle that was the lease money for the last two years was in a rusted tobacco tin behind a loose brick on the fireplace behind the firewood. Simon might forgive the debt. Nathaniel would not forget it.

Simon decided, after all, that before he met with Nate and Audrey Lee, he would visit the old homeplace. As he approached, thirty yards away he could tell that, although the siding had the same weathered gray skin, there was not a spiderweb to be seen on the porch or under the eaves. The porch was swept, and wild azaleas had been planted around the foundation. When he opened the door, he saw that every stick of furniture was covered with a piece of rough muslin, and aside from dust in the corners, the floor was clean.

"Can I help you, sir?" a familiar voice called to him a ways away.

"Do I know you, sir?" the elderly man continued as he walked forward until both the man and Simon knew exactly whose face each saw for the first time in two decades.

Simon Abraham Tyler Jacob

Nate is old. He must be nearing, what, seventy-five? Simon asked himself. But Nate's walk was steady; no cane was necessary. He had a slight limp in the left leg, probably the same rheumatism that Simon felt when the weather changed or when he had climbed the choir loft stairs too many times.

"Oh, my dear God in heaven. I was so afraid that with this war that I might never see my brother again." Tears were forming in Nate's eyes.

"Nate, I have felt the same, especially as the fighting has consumed the South. But that is no excuse for not seeing you before now. Just my pride. And maybe a little fear at coming back to the homeplace."

"Brother, this farm, mine *and* yours, will always be your homeplace, and you will never find me encouraging you to come back to farming. The Lord knew what he was doing when he took you away from the creek."

"Nate, do you by any chance know this fellow I have with me? I think you might. He is Bartholomew Jennings. Bartholomew, this is Nate Billington, and yes, he and I have the same last names, but I will save that story for the trip home."

"I believe I have seen him a few times transporting Mr. Matthew Bailey here to visit with his daughter and grandson. Is that right, Bartholomew?"

"Indeed it is, sir. Mr. Matthew, Dr. John, and Dr. James and Miss Mary Assumpta have treated my seafaring and other ills more times than I can remember. Is Miss Mary Assumpta near?"

"She is. You passed the road to her house about a mile back. I know she would be glad to see you if you have time."

"We'll see," Simon said, and then he changed the subject a bit. "Nate, what possessed you to keep up Mama and Daddy's old place like this?"

"Simon Abraham Tyler Jacob Billington." Nate's voice faltered a bit and then took on an emotional edge, something between pride and righteous indignation. "Do your Christian names not tell you what your family means to mine?"

"It does, indeed, but Brother, clearly I have missed something as it relates to you."

"No. It has just been unspoken. My grandfather's evil deed. Your parents' Christian benevolence even when they were still slaves. My father's ultimatum that assuaged his sin. My father's recognition that being freed was not enough unless economic freedom came with it.

"Your parents' magnanimous act of forgiveness when they chose to live on and make a living from the same land on which months before my family had enslaved them. Then they freed my family for all time of the ignominy of that unprecedented sin that occurred on July 4, 1776. My small act of keeping up your home is my worship, my penance, and my pride, my brother."

Bartholomew knew best to merely stand quietly aside in the holiest moment he was ever likely to experience in his life.

Simon lifted his face to the heavens and prayed out to the forests and fields, "My dear sweet Lord. My heavenly Father. My Rock and my Forgiver. I know right now at this place, for the first time, what it means to truly be in your presence and not to be worthy of that gift."

CHAPTER 33

Sweet Potatoes to Horlbeck Creek

Simon, Nate, and Bartholomew spent most of the rest of the day around the dining room table, with Audrey Lee keeping them supplied with coffee and sweets and with the kind of criticism all good plans need. She listened. She digested. She spoke. The plans changed and improved.

There would be no prearranged signal. It would be just too hard, if not impossible, to arrange such between Charleston and the creek. Instead, the oyster boat with Bartholomew at the tiller, and sometimes with Simon aboard, would dock at the old pier, be dragged up into the reeds that had grown up on either side of the jetty, and bring the cargo of "sweet potatoes" to Nate and Audrey Lee's door. Nate and Audrey Lee would assess their needs, provide them clothes and nourishment, and take them to Simon's homeplace, where they could adequately rest.

Bartholomew would return to Charleston in the late afternoon the same day unless conditions were unfavorable. If it seemed unwise to set out late in the day, or if the weather had worsened, or worst of all if he saw suspicious boats on the Wando, he would ask Mary Assumpta if he could bunk on the floor until the next day.

Simon's homeplace had not been lived in for decades, so there was some risk should other residents along the creek observe regular activity there for too long—particularly if they saw stove or fireplace smoke.

Nate and Audrey Lee's farm, as did Simon's homeplace, sat just off the road and so was not ideal for clandestine activities. However, Mary Assumpta's Horlbeck Creek farm was perfect—if she agreed to take the risk.

Nate knew Mary Assumpta's inclinations and that she had as strong a set of morals as anyone he had ever encountered. He also knew that she had been visited not long ago by the black dog of melancholia and was still recovering, whether or not she would admit it. Would their proposition be good medicine or too much sugar for a half dime as Nate's granddaddy used to say when a good thing on the tongue turned sour later in the stomach?

Nothing to do but for Nate, Simon, and Bartholomew to head out to Horlbeck Creek Farm and lay out the plans and the options of the Sweet Potato Vine Revolution to Mary Assumpta.

The Proposal

At midafternoon on a South Carolina summer day, anyone with a lick of sense had found some shade and the small breezes always found there. Mary Assumpta and Colin were sitting on the front porch when the delegation approached. Colin was studying his algebra, and Mary Assumpta was writing her daily letter to James. Her letters after Gettysburg were the hardest for her to write since the war had begun, so it was a relief when she looked up and saw two familiar faces, one she had not seen in far too long.

To Colin's surprise, his mother literally jumped up, leaped off the porch, and ran to the open arms of Bartholomew Jennings, who whirled her until he and she were both dizzy with delight.

"Bartholomew Jennings, you look better than I have ever

seen you, and I have seen some parts of you that looked pretty bad."

"Miss Mary Assumpta," Bartholomew said, fairly laughing as he called her name, "let me introduce you to Reverend Simon Billington, the man who pulled me from the brink of death and is the cause of why I am here before you today." This last addition was said with evident pride.

"Mrs. Merriweather, it is my pleasure to finally meet the person whom Bartholomew worships almost as much as he does the Almighty."

"Reverend, I would put my life in this man's hands without a thought. So I think pretty highly of him too. Having seen him at his worst, I say that it is such a pleasure to see the result of your work."

"Well, a few years ago I just happened by the right place at the right time, and Bartholomew and the Almighty, and my lovely wife, Miriam, did the rest."

"Reverend, may I introduce you to my son Colin. His father, James, is a physician with the Army of Northern Virginia, and Colin is ten but has had to grow up faster than he should."

"Proud to meet you, Reverend Simon and Mr. Jennings. My mama has mentioned you a time or two when talking about her nursing days in my uncle John's office."

"I see the apple did not fall far from the Baileys' tree with that one, Miss Mary Assumpta," Bartholomew said, eliciting a big smile from his friend.

"Gentlemen, is this a social call? Or are you here with Nate to help me in the okra patch once the sun starts setting a bit? Or is there some other business on your minds?" Mary Assumpta knew there had to be an agenda of some kind when an elderly gentleman farmer, a reprobate seaman, and a free Negro minister were standing just beyond her porch.

"Actually, Mrs. Merriweather," Simon spoke up, "we have a unique proposal that Nate believes you might very well be interested in."

"Okay then, let's ease up on the porch. Colin will get us something to drink. Then we can talk a bit about your idea. Who is going to start with this proposal? And, Reverend, please call me Mary Assumpta."

Simon began with a very condensed version of the beginning of the Sweet Potato Vine Revolution and the visit he'd received from Geneviève Ardoin. He talked about the roles of Mother Emanuel Church and himself in getting the runaways safely out of Charleston and across the harbor.

Sensing a reticence in Mary Assumpta, Simon tried to salve any misconceptions. "Mrs. Merriweather, I fear I have frightened you with the boldness of our scheme."

"Reverend, I expect Nate has already told you that I am not easily put off by challenges. In fact, Colin's and my life on this entire Horlbeck Creek Farm started as a great experiment as neither his father nor I had the faintest idea of how to make a living from farming. My husband was a physician, and I was his nurse. But with the goodwill of Nate and Audrey Lee, we are making as much of a go of it as we can given the circumstances of this godawful war. Does that answer your question?"

"Indeed it does, ma'am. May I ask Nate, with whom I share a surname, to tell you a bit more?"

Nate began. "Colin, do you remember the story I told you about my father when he came home from a Revolutionary War battle with just one arm and found that while he was away fighting the British, his father had bought two human beings?"

"Yes, sir," Colin responded.

"The Reverend Simon Billington is the son of the two slaves whom my grandfather freed the very day my father returned from the war. The reverend's full name is Simon Abraham Tyler Jacob Billington. The name Tyler is for my father, and the name Jacob is for my grandfather. Reverend Simon and I are godbrothers, much like Miss Audrey Lee and I are your godparents."

With the lesson in lineage complete, Nate described what would happen from time to time with Bartholomew's trip across the harbor and up the Old Shell Road with his cargo of "sweet potatoes."

"Mary Assumpta," Nate continued, "I think after a day or two of rest in Simon's homeplace, which will give me and Audrey Lee a chance to assess their condition and their plans for the next leg of their journey, that the best place for the four 'sweet potatoes' is here at Horlbeck Creek Farm until they depart. You are much farther off Old Shell Road and away from prying eyes.

"So, my darlin' Irish daughter"—a pet name Nate used to describe his deep love for Mary Assumpta—"tell us honestly what you think about housing four runaway slaves until they can start the next leg of their journey north."

Priorities

Had this been a year ago, Mary Assumpta would not have hesitated. But a year ago she had not lost a child, and her husband had not been broken down mentally and spiritually. Acting impulsively was Mary Assumpta's most fundamental nature, but today, sensing the risks that her agreement would place on Colin and potentially on James, she hesitated.

"Gentlemen, well ... except for Bartholomew," she said, which brought a needed lightness to the discussion, "I really need to think this through. I am 100 percent in agreement with what you are doing. Although I love my South, I abhor slavery.

But this has the potential to have very negative effects, especially on James should word of my actions reach his commanding officer. And to think of the effect that slave hunters might have on Colin should they get wind of the scheme and come looking. I just don't know if I am able to take those risks when my actions could have such repercussions on those I love."

Simon spoke up. "I purposefully told Geneviève Ardoin that I could not begin immediately, knowing that securing a craft to traverse the harbor and securing Nate's agreement would need at least two weeks. How about Bartholomew and I return five days from today? Will that give you enough time to reach a decision? And please, make this your personal decision. Do not let my views cause you to act in a way that is not in your family's best interests. Will you promise me that?"

"Reverend Simon, that is so very gracious. I promise. I see why the special bond between you and Nate has spanned the years. I am sure Nate will tell me more. But before he does, I will ask Audrey Lee to come over and bring Nate with her, and we will decide by your deadline."

"I can ask no more of you except to take care of my godbrother and his precious Audrey Lee. And I know you will. He has already told me that much."

Nate walked with Simon and Bartholomew back up the lane to where it intersected with the oystershell road. They stopped for a few words before going in opposite directions.

"Simon, as much as anyone, Mary Assumpta is a casualty of this conflict. I watch over her with that in mind. God chose not to give Audrey Lee and me a child, but since she arrived on the creek, Mary Assumpta has been our child in every sense that is important. I will not let her make a decision that will harm her and her family. You and I can work this out. Go back to Mother Emanuel assured that God will still continue the work you began here on the creek."

CHAPTER 34

Middle Ground

Mary Assumpta lay awake long past the time she would usually be asleep. She was staring at the knots in the pine ceiling and finding faces of Jesus in them. But mostly she talked to herself and then to the Almighty.

From my earliest memories, I went full bore in everything I did. Top of my class at Saint Mary's School, I loved homework. Who does that? Thought I'd be the first female admitted to the Medical College of Charleston. Nurse with John as if I were his medical apprentice, not his baby sister. I leapt into the waiting arms of James Merriweather, and if the truth be told, I set a trap for him like a tigress on the prowl. Gave up everything I had ever known in Charleston, including the love and affection of my mother, to marry him and move across Charleston Harbor, which might as well have been across the Atlantic.

"So, God, why is this decision so perplexing?" she asked out loud.

"Mama, is everything all right?" Colin called.

"Yes, baby boy. Mama is just praying a little louder than usual."

Soon after breakfast, Colin hitched ol' Jake to the carriage, and he and his mother rode to Nate and Audrey Lee's, talking at length during the ride.

"Colin, you heard what that was about yesterday, didn't you?"

"Yes, ma'am."

"Well, today I want you to go in a back room or to the barn or wherever you can find a cool spot, and I want you to work on your reading and then some more on your algebra. You are going to be tempted to come and listen to what your aunt Audrey, Uncle Nate, and I are talking about from yesterday. But I want you to stay completely out of it today."

"But, Mama, I was in it yesterday."

"I know you were, but it happened so quickly that I could not shield you from that grown-up discussion, although I really think that I should have. Whether or not I, not you and me, participate in this very important but dangerous venture has to be my decision with Aunt Audrey Lee and Uncle Nate's help. Just like you are not old enough to go to war, even though you want to join your daddy, you are not old enough to join in this undertaking in any way.

"I know that's really hard because I depend on you every day to do things that most ten-year-olds never do, or else we would never be able to live here on the farm until Daddy gets home.

"I will tell you everything I decide on our trip home. We will stay up tonight past your bedtime, and I will answer every question you have, but baby, this is a decision that only Mama can make. Promise me you will attend to your studies?"

"I promise, Mama, as long as you tell me stuff on the way home."

As gut-wrenching a deal as she was likely ever to make with her precious son was settled with a loving head bump—their special sign of agreement—just as ol' Jake pulled up to the hitching rail. Colin unhooked ol' Jake from the carriage and led him to the pasture behind his uncle Nate's house and let him loose. Colin headed down toward the creek, where the shade would linger the longest. Mary Assumpta knocked on the front screen door, knowing that Audrey Lee already had a pot of coffee ready to pour up.

Seeking Out Advice

"Did you sleep last night, darlin'?" Nate asked. "By the way, what did you do with Colin?"

"Colin is probably down by the creek catching up on his reading and algebra. I explained to him on the way over that this has to be my decision. I think he understands even though I know he doesn't like being left out."

Audrey Lee spoke up. "I think that's smart, Mary Assumpta. It is so easy for all of us to forget that the boy is only ten. All right, you are here, and we are here. Where do you want to start?"

"I want to start with you, Audrey Lee. Let me tell you my dilemma, and then I want to hear what you think. Nate, you just have to be quiet for a while. Besides, you heard what I said.

"As I lay awake last night, I realized that this is the first major decision of my life that I must make entirely by myself, and it scares the shit out of me that I might make the wrong decision."

Mary Assumpta, on the verge of tears, nearly pleading, asked, "Audrey Lee, what *do* I do?"

Audrey Lee got up and poured herself the dregs from the coffeepot that had been sitting on the edge of the hot stove long before Mary Assumpta began talking. Audrey Lee really did not want the coffee, but she needed to let the emotions in the room settle a bit before she spoke. Nate recognized her technique. It had been used on him a few times through the years to significant effect.

"Mary Assumpta, I am going to tell you exactly what I think about the two choices that you have as I see it. I will even tell you what I think you should consider about each of the choices. You did not come here to have me pose more questions to you. You have enough questions of your own. Is that okay?"

"Audrey Lee, I need to hear your wisdom. And maybe in a minute Nate's too." Nate smiled an impatient smile. He cared remarkably for this young woman sitting at his kitchen table.

"The first choice as I see it," Audrey Lee began, "is to throw yourself entirely into this venture and not look back. The moral imperative in front of you is as compelling as any you are likely to encounter in your life, but it will not be the only one. There will be others. There are others right here. Right now.

"If you choose to become wholly involved, you must go into it knowing that you risk your reputation and that of your family at the least, and perhaps even your life in a worst-case scenario.

"To consider this truthfully, I believe it is fair that you assess this decision in front of you in light of the decision James made a year ago when he enlisted and left you on the farm with Colin, hoping that Nate and I would help you keep things together until he returned. And we are doing pretty well at that.

"While there is some potential for negative effects on James, the primary negative effect is going to be on Colin. Only you can determine if he can handle the intermittent extreme levels of stress. Once this gamble begins, the stress will only be reduced from time to time but never totally alleviated until this war ends. Have I hit any nerves?"

"You did hit a few, and that was what I needed to hear."

"Nate, anything to offer?" Audrey Lee tossed him a bone.

"Just this one thing," Nate offered. "A lot of our boys rode off to war with visions of glory in their eyes, and there is that element in this endeavor. You must do your best to completely put that idea aside. This will be dirty, tiresome, dangerously repetitious, and without an end that we can see right now."

"Okay, ready for what I see as your other choice?" Audrey Lee asked. And then she moved on, not waiting for Mary Assumpta to answer.

"Mary Assumpta, the desire and the need to resist oppression as you have told us was in the blood of your not so distant relatives. I know you have a desire in you as mighty as a hurricane to help other people, and should you choose to forgo this enterprise, your life will continue down the path that the Almighty put you on when you were born. Just think what will need to be done when this war finally ends. We know now that there is not going to be fighting in the north. The Union victory at Gettysburg eliminated that possibility once and for all. All the fighting and all the destruction and death is going to be here in our land—the land we love and cherish in spite of all its faults. The opportunities to fulfill your destiny, whatever that is, will not end should you tell Nate and Simon a polite no.

"This second alternative is where you choose *your* family as the primary way of fulfilling God's promise on this earth. Colin needs you. James needs you right now, and who knows how much he will need you when the war is over. And what's more, *you* need Colin and James. They, and hopefully future children, are your destiny, but this course could change all of that if things go awry.

"That is how I see your second choice. You wanted my opinion, so here it is. I honestly believe you really have only one choice. You knew yesterday, and you know this morning, that the only reasonable thing for you to do is tell Simon and Nate no.

"Any misgivings you are experiencing now are just like hen chatter at a quilting bee—nothing to do with the real job at hand. I know you, my lovely and precious daughter. I know you know what is right, but only you can do what is right."

Telling her lovely adopted daughter what she thought was best for her had left Audrey Lee mentally and physically drained. She did something Mary Assumpta had never seen her do before: she poured herself half a glass of homemade peach brandy before 3:00 p.m.

Hard to Tell

Mary Assumpta had, as Audrey Lee surmised, reached the same conclusion—and generally for the same reasons. But she had thought early this morning before daylight of a way to be involved with almost zero risks for her or her family.

"Nate, Audrey Lee, I really cannot disagree with anything you have said, and as much as it is opposite my nature, and maybe it means I am finally an adult, I must decline the level of participation you outlined yesterday."

"Oh, dear Lord, thank you. Thank you. Thank you," Audrey Lee prayed out loud. She had been so fearful that the red-headed, hardheaded, spitfire Mary Assumpta would show up this morning full of piss and vinegar, ready to take up arms.

Mary Assumpta was not done. "I do have one consideration that I think will improve your operation and allow me to at least stay in touch with events. Why not plan for Bartholomew to stay with Colin and me on each trip he makes? I will provide him shelter and food, and he can return to Charleston early the next morning or stay as long as he needs until conditions are favorable for a crossing.

"No one will ever be able to question my relationship with Bartholomew, and maybe on some trip he can haul my father over for a visit too. What do you think?"

Nate spoke up. "This may be hard to believe, but Bartholomew suggested that very thing yesterday afternoon should he be caught late or in bad weather."

As Colin and his mother rode home, Mary Assumpta told him of her decision. It was clear to Mary Assumpta that Colin was mightily disappointed. Colin had hoped he could "go to war," as he put it, to help the runaway slaves, but he also remembered vividly the weeks when melancholia visited his mother after the stillbirth of his brother, and he did not want her to risk that again. He told his mother so.

Bartholomew was right, Mary Assumpta thought to herself, *the apple really did not fall far from the tree.*

CHAPTER 35

Sweet Potato Vine Coda

Judging from the backgrounds of the majority of its citizens whose families had immigrated to the South to escape oppression in other locales, the Sweet Potato Vine Revolution was as Southern an idea as it was the antithesis of the institution of slavery to which the economy of the South was temporarily bound.

As the vision of emancipation as a legal construct spread to the plantations of the South like boll weevils on cotton, pathways to freedom, quietly referred to as the Underground Railroad, were secretly communicated to people who wanted to know about them for the right reasons. They were as secret from the slave hunters as morality was absent from the reasoning that drove such men to hunt other human beings for profit.

The Sweet Potato Vine was as surreptitious to the powers that be as the Underground Railroad, and its efficiency would have surprised those same people had they known anything about it.

June moved on to July and August, when the dog days slowed most everything down in the South to a steady crawl. The Sweet Potato Vine Revolution, like its namesake, proliferated, so much so that Geneviève Ardoin's Three Sisters brothel, boarding-house, and barroom could not handle the flow of runaways that caused, equally, a problem for Reverend Simon Billington, his oyster boatman, and his compatriots across the Charleston Harbor.

Numbers meant conspicuous notoriety. And notoriety was the enemy of the Sweet Potato Vine. Therefore, Geneviève Ardoin decided something had to be done, and as usual she would do it herself, even if it meant abandoning the safety of the Three Sisters temporarily and traveling overland to Columbia. She figured that given the atrocious reputation of the Confederate mail service, she would arrive in Columbia by carriage several days and maybe weeks before a letter. And she was correct.

Geneviève arrived in Columbia in her rather fine carriage driven by a free Negro decked out in a livery uniform that would have made a Londoner proud. She went directly to her only destination, the Gamecock Inn. As she expected on this Friday evening, the professor was engaged with the woman on the second floor. Upon finding his room for the evening, she opened the door unceremoniously; grabbed the woman's garments, which could only loosely be called clothes; threw them to Evangeline Robicheaux, the Cajun beauty she had enticed out of New Orleans; and told her to take a quick bath and make herself useful with another customer. The professor had more pressing matters to which to attend.

Butt naked, or was it buck naked? Geneviève used the two terms interchangeably. Regardless, the professor was unquestionably provoked by her interruption.

"Madam, do you have no manners?" the professor laughingly

asked, making absolutely no effort to cover up the provocation still on full display.

"Sir, and I use that salutation generously, I am here on sweet potato business, so clean up, put on some clothes, and meet me downstairs at my table."

"Professor, we have a good problem on our hands," Geneviève began. "We have an oversupply of sweet potatoes in Charleston, and we need to slow down the supply process, or else we are going to have far more sweet potatoes than we anticipated. Some are going to end up in the root cellar of the sheriff, if you get my meaning."

The professor had regained a measure of ivory-tower-developed and, some would say elitist, composure. "I was expecting this might happen at some point. I just didn't think it would be this quickly."

"Is there any reason that we cannot divert some of those sweet potatoes from my neck of the woods to the Gamecock Inn? After all, it would just be a branch venture for you, and I can offer any assistance necessary to help keep the supply lines flowing but not jamming up to the point that we begin losing too many potatoes."

Cocks easily added safe-housing runaways from in and around Columbia to its other illegal and secretive enterprise, although it was hoped that the safe house was a much less open secret than the brothel. This allowed the Three Sisters to resume an efficient operation in the Low Country. The Underground Railroad had "stations" to both the east and west of Columbia, not so bad a ride in the false bottom of a horse-drawn wagon. The runaways were moved out of South Carolina mostly to Quakers who had settled in and around Greensboro, North Carolina, and who welcomed them in the meetinghouses or in their homes until they could board the next relatively safe "train" to Indiana or Ohio, or the more accident-prone "train" through Virginia and on to Washington and beyond.

Once the supply and demand forces for sweet potatoes were in the balance, Horlbeck Creek worked without a major flaw. If runaways fell to the authorities or slave hunters, it usually took place on their journey to the Three Sisters.

Reverend Simon did more than a little counseling before he approved the runaways' next step in the journey to Nate and Audrey Lee Billington. Simon had to use all his skills as a pastor and persuader, and as a fellow person of color, to justify why the next three white people they were to be delivered to could be totally trusted and why the worst thing that could happen to the runaways was if they chose to separate from the group and had to fend for themselves and find their own way overland or by sea to freedom.

The runaways who came to Horlbeck Creek reached their northern destination by one of three means. First, they could be moved overland almost due north until they entered the Piedmont area of North Carolina, and then Greensboro and Winston-Salem, where they were received by the large Quaker congregations who would see to their immediate safety and then to their transportation on to Indiana and Ohio, where there were substantial Quaker populations. Some might even reach freedom as far away as Canada.

Depending on the size of the supply on hand, potatoes could be ferried out beyond the harbor to meet a coastal trader who would then take them by an Atlantic route to markets in New York or Boston.

Finally, if the weather was unfavorable or the agent transporting them really favored it, they would keep as a group close to the shoreline, usually in pirogues, and hide in the almost infinite number of small creeks and the dense reeds in midday and move at night and early morning when conditions were more favorable. Eventually, this coastal route arrived at the semifriendly confines of the Chesapeake Bay estuary, and from there on to the Potomac and freedom in Washington, DC, and beyond.

Beyond the late summer of 1863, it was not known the exact number of runaways who were conveyed to the North and Midwest during the remainder of the war, but in the three-month period of that summer when numbers were kept, thirty-three groups of four moved through Horlbeck Creek, and another twenty-eight groups moved through the Gamecock Inn from the area surrounding Columbia. Once a substantial and steady number were being moved through the Columbia and Horlbeck Creek terminuses, the proprietors of the Sweet Potato Vine agreed that it was not in the best interests of the business to keep precise figures, as such figures only gave the authorities and slave hunters reason to shut down the Vine and destroy both runaways and their guides.

The story of a whorehouse madam from Clifford's Alley, a professor of religion from the University of South Carolina, a free Negro pastor from Charleston's Calhoun Street, an Irish businessman from Meeting Street, a former seaman of dubious credentials, and a farmer and his wife from across the Charleston Harbor suggests a tall tale more than a sophisticated network of covert operatives making life-altering, under-the-table decisions. Yet just such a system, right in the middle of the War between the States, started at the whorehouse on Clifford's Alley and moved around 250 plantation runaways from South Carolina to freedom and a future.

PART VIII
THE BEGINNING OF THE END

CHAPTER 36

The South's Lament

In the ancient past, as the Spinners beneath the roots of the great ash tree at the center of the earth looked at the fabric that was to be the fate of the United States of America, they wove the land into existence on one July 4. And one sister turning to the others must have said, "Has a nice ring to it, don't you think? Perhaps we shall find another use for it." And they did.

Eighty-seven years later in human years, a hiccup in time within the roots of the ash, July 4 was woven again into the tapestry of the United States of America with great men, cannons, rivercraft, mules and horses, cordite smoke, uncalled for needless death, and mistakes aplenty.

On July 4, 1863, Hiram Ulysses Grant celebrated victory on the bluffs over the Mississippi River at Vicksburg, whereas the day before Robert Edward Lee was retreating toward Virginia after he'd personally accepted defeat between the hills of Gettysburg, Pennsylvania.

Grant's victory at Vicksburg, more than any other, would propel him to commander in chief of all Union forces a few months later when he would meet Lee in the Virginia wilderness.

So unconditional a defeat was Gettysburg that Lee, on August 8, offered his resignation to President Jefferson Davis. Davis rejected it, but Lee was never again bulletproof.

The war of total destruction prosecuted following Gettysburg and Vicksburg was unlike the war that had been fought to this point in almost all regards. The strategy approved by President Lincoln was to bring the South not to peace but to total and humiliating surrender. It was a stratagem with a single tactic—destroy the South's civilian population's capacity and backbone to sustain the fight by showing them in their fields and front yards the horrors of war that had heretofore been confined to the fields of battle. For decades upon decades upon decades, the decision would blemish the South's ability to return wholly to the Union. Such was the hatred of Southerners for the deeds of the Union army, equaled only by the loathing of the Union army for the Southern populace.

Dear Lord,

With Gettysburg and Vicksburg as sure signs, I pray that you will compel President Davis to see this conflict for himself as we see here away from the smell of the cannon smoke. And, Lord, show him the virtue of making peace.

But, dear Lord, I fear that the South is a bobcat caught in a varmint trap—no amount of reasoning will calm that bobcat short of a shotgun. Please show us the way out of that trap, for what have we gained if our ground be ruined, our bellies be empty, and our menfolk be moldering in the earth?

Finally, heavenly Father, I pray for your

strength to sustain my family here and in battles
to come until we are whole again.

Amen.
A soldier's wife

Normalcy

Human beings have a remarkable capacity to find normal in the most abnormal of circumstances if the abnormal is tolerable to some degree when compared to the unbearable recent past and lasts long enough for the sedating properties of repetition to take effect.

For three weeks after Gettysburg the Confederates retreated to find shelter. Finally secure from the mostly rear skirmishes of General Meade that had characterized this prolonged retreat, General Lee settled his army in the Luray Valley of Virginia's Blue Ridge Mountains.

During the three weeks of the retreat, the physicians did what they could for the wounded. A few got better. Many deteriorated. Death was everywhere. When wagons filled with wounded broke down, they were left to the Yankees.

However, once settled in the Luray Valley, the medical staff of the Army of Northern Virginia spent five days *and* nights treating men whose injuries had become septic from the environment in which they were stowed on the trek or whose wounds had opened from the constant jolting during the wagon ride from Gettysburg.

After the seventeen-mile caravan of wagons gathered in and around the Luray Valley, and the pressing day-and-night doctoring that strained physicians' Hippocratic oaths and their personal well-being, was done, a kind of strange normality returned to the soldiers' days.

Soon the unbidden smells, sounds, and tastes returned as if the battle still raged and would not be put aside. Piles of arms and legs regularly appeared in dreams and daydreams. Then came the recriminations of lives not saved. Then the guilt.

James Merriweather knew that he was among the fortunate because he could go to Father Michael O'Malley and, without shame, yell because it felt good, weep at his own inadequacies, curse the idiocy of politicians and generals alike, or stridently question the existence of a merciful God and know that he would be heard but not judged.

Following just such an eruption of emotions after supper, James and Michael O'Malley returned some two hundred yards from the dense woods to Michael's tent. There was some danger from Union snipers, James supposed, and the worry of what the memory of Abraham Whetstone might do to his always fragile psyche. However, it would not do for the men, healthy or wounded, to hear the moans of their healer, so they took the risk.

On returning to Michael's tent, the priest brought out his bottle of medicinal corn whiskey. He would have much preferred good Irish rye, but he accepted what he could get. Only in Michael's tent did James take a drink. Depending on the session in the woods, it might extend to two shots in one day. Never more. Never more often. Michael accepted the role of James's bartender seriously, and therefore so did James. Since his return to duty in late spring, he was faithful to his friend's dosing regimen.

After a toast to friends and family, and sipping the whiskey that barely covered the bottom of his dented tin cup, James thought a moment and then probed the priest sitting before him. "Michael, I am doing everything I know how to do and doing some things that come only from resourcefulness borne more from failures than successes. The dying that surrounds me three weeks after the battle hounds my every step. It seems my shortcomings outweigh my abilities. A few questions for your insights, Father?"

"The Almighty and I will do our best," Michael replied with a laugh.

"An easy one to begin. Can you conceive of a hell worse than what our wounded experienced in the last three weeks?"

"You planning on another trip to the underworld?" Making light of the black dog that walked beside James since he'd enlisted was one of Father O'Malley's methods for not letting a conversation digress too deeply into his friend's depressive psyche.

"No, nothing like that. But then I did not plan to make those first two trips either. It is just that in my mind and based on conversations in the minds of my colleagues, there is the involuntary ability of our senses—smell, taste, and hearing especially, and sometimes even sight—to reconstruct the worst of what we have experienced at the most unexpected times."

"In your dreams, do you mean?" Michael probed a little for himself.

"Sometimes. But my dreams are mostly fantastical images, and I have come to accept them to some extent as a method of my mind emptying itself. No. I am talking about out of the ether when least expected, I smell gutshots. I taste the coppery essence of newly spilled blood, or I hear soldiers crying, 'Oh

God, please. Stop the wagon from bouncing. Doctor, where are my legs? Oh Jesus, not my legs.'"

"James, I have prayed with boys days after a battle who have told me of similar things, thinking that they are possessed by the Evil One. Although I cannot explain it or define it, I think that it must be connected to your dreams and is likely God's or the mind's way of sorting out the torrent of impressions that flooded your senses almost all at once. From what I have observed, the mind needs time to sort out what the senses have recorded, and if we do not allow that time, it or the Almighty will find the time on its or his own.

"It seems to me that the workings of this phenomenon must be akin to the private silent meditation that monks have practiced for centuries. They are purposefully trying to rid their minds of anything that would prevent them from experiencing the voice of God."

James was intrigued that his friend had apparently intuitively reasoned out a practice that might just improve medicine. It was not the first time.

"Michael, you and I must talk about this some more. Perhaps in years to come we can prescribe or even require that people who experience intense distress go through a period where they do something like those monks."

With another dram of corn liquor in the bottoms of their tin cups, the conversation turned to politics and peace. After a few minutes with even fewer conclusions than the discussion of dreams and hallucinations, they said their temporary farewells, and James left to check on his wounded soldiers before he returned to his tent to write until, he hoped, the glorious power of deep sleep transported him far beyond the Luray Valley.

Red-Haired Colleen

July 20, 1863
Horlbeck Creek

My Beloved Physician,

Word of the defeat of the Army of Northern Virginia at Gettysburg reached us soon after you all had successfully evaded the trap of General Meade at the Potomac. My heart bleeds mercy drops for each of the brave men who gave his all for our blessed South. None more than for you, my dear husband.

I have waited until now to write, hoping every day to receive correspondence from you and believing that not hearing anything from the War Department was a positive sign.

When I read the page from your diary from July 15 that you included with your letter, I cried for two days without consolation. I fear that Colin thought his mother was bordering on madness again. I have stayed strong since your enlistment, crying only at night when our son could not hear me. But your account of the horror of Gettysburg left me unable to function beyond my body's inevitabilities. I neither ate nor drank and seldom moved from my bed. Colin took care of himself and the animals until I finally emerged, but no more than a shadow version of myself.

Darling, you and I have shared operating rooms and surgeries on farms and in dirty back rooms of public houses, but I know that our experiences and those you had in previous battles could not prepare you for the hellishness of the decisions you had to make in the field hospital at Gettysburg.

I know how much you value your skills as a surgeon, learned at the side of John. I know that you took pride in using those skills to cure and rehabilitate, and that time will come again. This war will end, and you will be the physician you have been and still are.

I pray for you every day at morning and evening, for that is when I feel closest to the Almighty here on the banks of the creek. I pray for courage for you that you will, even in the midst of battle, see every boy as a mother's precious son, indeed when the battle forces you to make choices that attack your conscience and leave you with great remorse, knowing that had circumstances been different, you could have easily saved a limb, sent a son or husband home whole again, and kept a family whole.

I pray that your nights will be peaceful. But if nightmares return, I pray that you will allow your intellect to process those night terrors and the day terrors that caused them, and lock them both in a lead-lined box in the recesses of your remarkable mind. Remember, I have seen you work, and I know that you are best in the worst of conditions. If Colin had gone to war and was wounded in this hideous conflict, there is no one—including your mentor, John Bailey—that I would want caring for him but you, my darling. That is the attention I know that you bring to every soldier under your care. And remember, talk about them and your experiences with Michael. I expect that he could benefit from a little talking of his own.

I am doing well. Tired, but that is good for my sleep. I have much to keep me busy and my mind off the war, which so far has not affected us here on the creek. We occasionally hear cannon fire, which causes us to worry, but it comes from the south and is restricted thus far to Charleston Harbor.

Do not worry about us. Ol Jake remains reliable, and we're thankful that Nate and Audrey Lee adopted us long ago. Although I despair for you, I am most thankful that you are on the healing end of the conflict and not the killing. I do love my South, but I confess that my support for the war, though still strong, wavers each time I hear of a neighbor who lost a son or a husband.

Let me, for a few lines, turn to a brighter subject that I trust will brighten your day as just writing about it has mine. My love for you grows each day. It seems that as I miss you more, my love becomes more too. We will have a lot of catching up to do when you return to us.

I often think fondly of our first time in that cramped spare bedroom above John's office. We had finally cleared the patients out about five o'clock that day, and John had walked on ahead to Mother's for supper. I told him that I was making a side trip to the dressmakers to be fitted for my Easter dress and would be late for supper. You said to him you would lock up and were then having supper at the pub.

Do you remember how we thought we were caught when Bartholomew started banging on the front door after another of his drunken visits to the Three Sisters brothel? We panicked and threw our clothes back on, sure it was John returning, having left without his key. I still get a chuckle when I think of how we giggled that Bartholomew would be shocked to know that this was not the only banging going on in the office that afternoon!

You seduced me, James Edward Merriweather! You wormed your way into my good graces after I had so valiantly and virtuously resisted your charms for so many months. Or perhaps, having just turned eighteen, I was tired of stolen kisses and secretive caresses, and I seduced you. Please hurry home so I can do it again!

I do love you so. Hurry home to us. Nothing you have experienced is beyond my love to heal you.

Your loving redheaded, blue-eyed colleen,
Red

Unexpected Visitors to the Creek

August 15, 1863
Horlbeck Creek

My Darlin' JEM,

We finally received the complete news about the crushing defeat at Gettysburg and the surrender of Vicksburg. At first, the newspapers reported Gettysburg as a victory of sorts, but now we finally know the entire truth, and I pray for you even harder, hoping that the Almighty will bring something good from such defeat.

I have desired since the war began that the Army of Northern Virginia would deliver a monumental Southern victory early in the conflict and that it would move the Union toward our position as a separate nation. My feelings were that the South could then move toward a legitimate and lasting Confederate States of America whose culture and climate and peoples could come together and rise above the past's dependency on slavery.

Nate, Audrey Lee, and I, and also Father when he has made the crossing, have talked about the economic and political future of the South. We agree that slavery cannot be long for this land, nor should it be. With the Emancipation Proclamation, it seems to me that the war has turned from the politics of keeping the Union together to the immorality of slavery. Whether the war rages for a few more months or many, the continuation of slavery is not a position on which the Confederacy can stand. Nor should it. Now with the defeats at Gettysburg and Vicksburg, I pray daily that President Davis will again rise to the statesman he was before the war and sue for peace, although I do not anticipate it. Of course I am looking with eyes that see inevitable hardships coming our way if the Union demands our surrender or we theirs. I do not believe that we shall see that day.

We have just begun to see tangible effects of the triumvirate of Union successes. As slaves in the Low Country encounter the powerful idea of the Emancipation Proclamation and take faith from Gettysburg and Vicksburg, here on the creek we have on occasion encountered runaway slaves from the west who made their way out of Charleston and across the harbor.

Perhaps you know the story of our neighbor's grandfather and his conversion from slave owner to freedom giver when his father (I do not know his name) returned from fighting the Redcoats with only one arm to find that his father had purchased two Negroes. I did not hear the story until our neighbor told it to Colin while they were fishing down on the Wando. The son presented an incontestable ultimatum to his father: free these two people or lose me forever. It was a natural choice for the father, and he lived the remainder of his life exhibiting fairness toward all people.

When we arrived here on the creek, the elders—our neighbor's grandparents and the two slaves his grandfather had freed—were dead and buried on the farm near each other. The slaves' son, who was born late in life, and our neighbor here on the creek grew up with each other. Thus, the idea of free Negroes is as natural to him as rain and sunshine.

Accordingly, as runaways have made their way across the harbor, hoping, I figure, to travel on toward Greensboro, where there are Quakers to take them on to the North, our neighbors have provided them with temporary shelter, clothing, and some advice as to the best way to move on from here. I have seen some of them from a distance when Colin and I have been working the okra. They walk down Old Shell Road toward the Wando. I do not know where they go from there.

I expect that knowing me, you are now wondering how I fit into all of this. Well, I do not. Having an opportunity to help people oppressed by the wealthy and not fully participating causes me pause. But I had to consider what my participation might mean to you and to Colin should things go awry here on the creek. So after talking with our neighbor's very wise wife, I decided that my highest moral obligation was to Colin here and my husband at war. So you need not worry about us.

Knowing that our neighbors are doing some extra cooking, I have taken over some of our dried peas and beans to make sure they are not sacrificing their own well-being. It is not much, but I think they appreciate it. It is a small thing and something we often do for each other.

We continue to farm with Nate and Audrey Lee's help as we agreed in the spring when we planted our joint plots here on our farm. Our yields have been better for both our families than in the past when we planted separate plots on each farm. Thank the Almighty, we have stored enough to make it until next spring. Our smoked pork will probably take us through Christmas. I expect Colin and Nate will be looking to kill a deer or two come cooler weather. Tending and harvesting the fields, and canning, and helping Colin with his studies makes up a full-time job.

Father has made his way to this side of the harbor a couple of times since June, I assume by cajoling or shaming Bartholomew to transport him to us. What a treat it has been to see both of them. Father does not talk about Mother unless I ask, and he says that she no longer recognizes him at all. He says that she remembers things sometimes from years and years ago and acts as if she is still living at that time. She even asks about Joseph as if he had not died but was a grown man. But yet she does not recognize Father.

You will be pleased that Bartholomew seems to be (I use that qualification because you never know about Bartholomew) sober and, believe it or not, attending church services regularly, where he also works as a custodian to make enough to put a roof over his head and beans in his belly. The Almighty is assuredly surprising!

I trust that when this reaches you, you will be far beyond the distresses of Gettysburg. Colin and I pray for you daily and tell each other stories over supper. Recently we laughed when I told him how I designed John's extra bedroom upstairs at his office just for you and how you and I would sneak upstairs and eat pastries from Amélie's. Yes, silly boy, I keep it clean! But I am sure you remember that those éclairs were not nearly as sweet as our lovemaking on the sly!

Yours and yours and yours, forever and ever and ever,

Red

Lifted Spirits

September 10, 1863
Northern Virginia

Dearest Mary Assumpta,

Thank you, my dearest darling, for your letter of August 5. Your bit of good news about the crops lifted my spirits as I have been in dire need of finding something positive on which to reflect. To know that you are doing well with the help of Nate and Audrey Lee and that you are watching after your own affairs is all for which I could hope, and finding out that Colin is thriving learning in this mess of a war is such an uplifting thing among the overwhelming tragedy I see every day.

I am relieved to know that you are currently meeting your food needs. Here we are so often reduced to restricting our already paltry rations as delivery to us is frequently interrupted by the Yankees destroying our rail lines. It is only on the most special occasion that we have anything even resembling fresh.

The boys are good at finding ripe persimmons and chinquapins as we march, but they are no substitute for a good meal.

Your recollection of our first intimacy makes me glad that as an officer my mail is not read before Private Semmes delivers it to me. I have read that section so many times that I have permanently embedded my fingerprints in the paper. And each time I read it, I must stifle my chortles. Darling, any laughter is a reprieve from the dreariness that surrounds us always. Thank you for that.

I have spent considerable time talking to Michael as we have finally settled in since our serendipitous pullback from Gettysburg. However, even the retreat cost us many lives of so many young men. Michael is, of course, the blessing he has been since he first thankfully revived me, at least most of me. As you so perceptively wrote in your letter, I have listened recently to Michael's story of his fight with his own demons. He has yet to tell me in detail of their nature, only that Gettysburg was the place of their creation, or perhaps their emergence or reemergence. I trust that in his time, he will tell me. I will watch him as he watched over me, and if need be I will intrude.

Thanks to my dear friend's ear, my nightmares have subsided as we have become more distanced from the horror fields of Gettysburg. And as you and the rabbi so wisely suggested, I have tried to place those experiences as far back in my conscious mind as I am able and do my best to focus only on the needs directly in front of me. Michael has had a recent idea that on some level, at least, the nightmares and daytime emanations are the mind's way of finding time to sort through so much intense information received in such a short time for such a prolonged time as was the case for our three-week retreat.

At Gettysburg we were overwhelmed with so many boys who were going to die regardless of our skills, and so much of our time was taken with them, that others died needlessly and still others faced amputation because they were thrown into the milieu. We are confident that had we been able to attend to the severely wounded whom we could have saved, we could have then had time to remove shrapnel or bullets from limbs without having to remove them.

Perhaps I am now ready to again pursue training colleagues in the process of triage.

I must stop, my dearest. Every day is long and exhausting as we continue to care for the wounded long after the cannons' fire of the battle has ceased. I lament each day that I am not able to use even the simplest of the sanitation skills I learned from John. Water and whiskey are our antiseptics, and carbolic acid, if we are lucky enough to procure it, which is almost never.

Pray for us. Pray for me. Hold my Colin to your breast and tell him about his father. The picture of his face has become so intermingled with the faces of boys from the battles that I am losing the ability to recall it.

Your darling physician (and lover!),
JEM

CHAPTER 37

The Luray Valley

Had it not been for the sounds of pain and the smell of latrines and of festering dying flesh, the Luray Valley would have been otherwise a place of uncommon beauty. The August temperatures were so moderate as to necessitate a coat in the late evening and early morning. Campfires were kept smoldering all day long, anticipating the early sunset behind the Massanutten Mountains. And even at midday, it was not unusual to find a campfire still going as the sun rose late above the Blue Ridge Mountains. Chicory-laced coffee was usually found brewing in an enamel pot dented and scratched from its many campaigns.

Some claimed the dents improved the taste, but when pressed most would admit that they were just dreaming about the taste of real coffee. The camp coffee was at least mostly roasted chicory root. Only the occasional New Orleans recruit actually liked the taste. Sometimes when broken rails had delayed delivery of rations, roasted acorns replaced the chicory. However, the supply of ground coffee never ran out. Not that it mysteriously regenerated itself, but rather that no one would ever want to be accused of using the last precious grounds.

Notwithstanding its taste, it cut the chill and reminded all of better days back home.

It was mid-August. In the early morning sunlight shining on the highest western ridges of the Massanutten Mountains, James Merriweather saw that even now some leaves on the sugar maples were getting a first start, turning a bright yellow. For a moment he was completely removed from his immediate surroundings. *The fall in Richmond is filled with colors too, but not until October,* he thought, surprised at how easily his mind wandered away. "Was I just back home again?" he said out loud to no one.

"Did you speak to me, Doctor?" Father Michael asked as he walked up and poured himself the last strong cup from the communal pot.

"Let me introduce myself. I am Dr. James Merriweather of Richmond, Virginia."

"The hell you say! You are just some soldier wannabe hanging around for the coffee," the priest parried. "James," he said with a handshake and hug attached, "I have not seen you to even say hello since we departed those killing fields of Gettysburg."

"Have you been in monastic contemplation?" James asked, knowing better.

"I wish. You know what I have been doing."

"I was trying to get a smile from you," James said. "Seems I failed."

"You did, but it was not your fault."

James turned counselor. "Want to walk and talk a bit about it?"

They placed their tin cups, still three-quarters filled, on the table outside James Merriweather's tent and walked toward the creek some fifty yards away that ran parallel to the camp until it emptied into the Shenandoah River to the north. It had no name as far as Merriweather could discover, but it did have some boulders scattered on its shore and sounds that smoothed rough edges about as well as whiskey.

"James, I find that writing these damnable letters to so many Virginia families is the most onerous task of this war for me. There are times, knowing that my words smother last faint hopes and verify their worst fears, that I think it better to let hope wither of its own accord. For whether cut down by a Minié ball or shrapnel, dysentery, or pneumonia, it will always be *my letter* that did the killing. And that weighs heavily upon me."

CHAPTER 38

The Army of Northern Virginia stayed encamped in the Luray Valley from late July through the winter of 1864 with General Lee maintaining his headquarters at the Orange County Courthouse a few miles away. In the early days, the army left briefly to skirmish with the Yankees in what was called the Bristoe and Mine Run Campaigns. But neither rose to the description of a campaign by either army. However, both armies had specific goals. The Rebels hoped to cause the Union to divert some of its divisions and so relieve the Confederates fighting in the west. The Yankees hoped to do what they had not done following Gettysburg—trap and defeat General Lee. Neither army succeeded. So both set up in familiar positions opposite the Rappahannock and Rapidan Rivers and prepared for winter.

For James Merriweather, it was a time to reflect on the idea of triage—an idea he had abandoned with the murder of his colleagues Willie and Bobbie Jean McCarty following the Battle of Fredericksburg. As awful as Gettysburg was on the senses, both physical and moral, there were some tragedies he firmly knew were preventable.

He believed the impending winter lull presented the time to think about it again and present it to new colleagues: Dr. Claude Paisley and Dr. Hunter McGuire. And this time Father Michael O'Malley would be part of the discussion.

Five months earlier at the beginning of May, at the Battle of Chancellorsville, James Merriweather was asked by the senior surgeon to assist in the treatment of General Stonewall Jackson. At the end of ten days, Jackson succumbed to pneumonia that had attacked him as a result of his weakened condition. But Merriweather knew he had found two like-minded colleagues in Claude Paisley and Hunter McGuire. Paisley was a bit older than Merriweather, maybe by five years, and McGuire was much younger by at least ten.

On the first night after treating General Jackson, as Merriweather rode back to his quarters from the makeshift surgery at Wilderness Tavern, he was despondent because he had not done enough to save the life of the godliest man he had ever met. Nevertheless, Merriweather always found that being on horseback freed his mind to think beyond the blood, smells, and distress of his daily existence, and this evening he found an ember of hope that he might just be able to rekindle the interest in triage if he could persuade Drs. McGuire and Paisley to assist him. He planned to talk to his new colleagues soon after camp life had settled back to normal after the elation of the Chancellorsville victory and the despair that was felt throughout the Army of Northern Virginia at General Jackson's death. Sadly, Gettysburg entirely extinguished that small hopeful fire. There would be no talk of triage. There was nothing but to cut, cauterize, and discard during three unending days of battlefield surgery.

Claude Paisley

Malcolm Paisley settled in the Shenandoah Valley of Virginia, finding the area reminiscent of the Scottish Lowlands from which his parents had fled for Ulster. Soon after settling, Malcolm met his future wife, Kaithren, while attending services with the local Presbyterian congregation. Love at first sight and marriage shortly thereafter was common among early settlers, as was the birth of children. Sixteen months after that first Sunday, Kaithren Paisley gave birth to a son, McLeod Montgomery Paisley.

It seemed to his parents that McLeod had sprouted from toddler to soldier in one giant gasp. At eighteen he fought the Redcoats with General Washington, and fought them well, rising to the rank of captain at age twenty. At the end of the war, as a reward for his exemplary service, he was awarded a grant of land in the colony of his choosing. He chose an area just west of Kings Mountain, North Carolina—an area already populated by numbers of Scottish Irish immigrants. McLeod, still a young man and unmarried, soon remedied that state of affairs, marrying Glynnis McGregor, the only daughter of the mostly self-taught and slightly apprenticed physician Dr. Michael McGregor. Son Claude was born just over eight months later, the strapping image of his grandfather Malcolm.

When Alabama gained statehood in 1819, it granted plots of land to encourage development and immigration, especially of professionals. Twenty-year-old Dr. Claude Paisley, the third-generation physician in his family, had learned and apprenticed at the side of his father and grandfather. He asked his parents about taking up the newly formed state of Alabama on its offer, which was a twenty-acre plot of land on the outskirts of the capital city of Cahaba.

Soon after arriving in Alabama, Claude Paisley discovered that Cahaba was more hospitable to mosquitoes and politicians than physicians, and he quickly purchased a five-acre piece of land in the small town of Selma, where he would move and build his medical practice and establish his family.

However, when the shots were fired in Charleston Harbor and war declared, Claude Paisley could not resist the call of Virginia, the land that had given his American family its roots. Therefore, he rode north with his wife and two girls, all on horseback, to enlist in the Army of Northern Virginia. It was an arduous trip made less so for him by his vision of serving his country as his father had served his. Paisley's wife, Priscilla, and daughters, Claudia and Margaret, did not travel with the same enthusiasm, yet they exhibited no less horsemanship. Priscilla was a country girl, the only kind that Alabama produced—other than those from Mobile. Daughter Claudia was fifteen, and sister Margaret was twelve. Folks in Dallas County, Alabama, said the girls must have been on a horse as soon as they could walk, so accomplished was their horsemanship—and this was not far from the truth.

Taking after her father, Claudia was an accomplished athlete. Strong and lithe, she found that the outdoors was her kingdom. At twelve, miles from her home, she was camping by herself with only her mount for protection on the banks of the Alabama River, where she caught her supper of bluegills and shellcrackers, and scaled, gutted, and washed them out in the swiftly flowing dark waters of the river. She cooked them in the cast-iron skillet with bacon grease, both brought for that purpose in the saddlebags strapped to the back of her dappled mare Abby. Heaven for Claudia Paisley was found on the banks of her very own river.

Margaret, on the other hand, was Daddy's little girl, and Mommy's, and that attention inevitably produced a prototypical Southern belle-in-waiting with all the charms and none of the bitchiness so familiar in many of the female variety of Southern gentry. Margaret was sweet and as smart as her sister, but she was a homemaker, and she loved every stitch of every dress she sewed and the kneading of lard into the flour of every biscuit she baked. She would be fine wife material in a few years for some lucky landowning Southern gentleman.

The Paisleys themselves were far from landed gentry, although Claude had continued to farm the original plot granted to him. Actually, he had his land cultivated for him so as to meet the conditions of the land grant. Claude Paisley liked to say that he "loaned his land" to Elijah Burns and his common-law Cherokee wife, Juda, whom Claude had discovered living in a lean-to just beyond his property line soon after he started to build his cabin. He befriended them and gave them work and food in exchange for their help in building the cabin and clearing and planting the land in his first and only spring in Cahaba.

Once he decided Cahaba, free land or no free land, was not where he wanted to put down roots, Paisley made an offer to Elijah and Juda, who were now living in a tent between the cabin and the creek at the bottom of the hill. Ever aware of the history of treatment of the poor Lowland Scots by the landgrabbing English who had driven the Paisleys to Ulster, he offered to loan them the twenty acres on nine nonnegotiable conditions, as follows:

1. They were to keep the cabin in presentable condition but could add to it as needed.
2. Juda would teach Elijah to read, and they would read the Bible and pray daily.
3. Any children would be taught to read and write by age seven.
4. They were to farm at least five acres in vegetables and sell them reasonably or give them to other pariahs like themselves.

5. Claude would purchase the seeds necessary to begin planting the first year with no expectation of repayment.
6. After the first year, Elijah was to hold back seeds enough to plant the next year.
7. Any profit made from cotton or corn on the remaining fifteen acres was to be split according to the following system:
   a. Years one and two—20 percent to CP, 60 percent to EB, 20 percent to be placed in the Bank of Selma
   b. Years three and four—30 percent to CP, 50 percent to EB, 20 percent to be placed in the bank
   c. Years five and six, 40 percent to CP, 40 percent to EB, 20 percent to be placed in the bank
8. After year six, if conditions 1–7 were met, Claude Paisley would sell the land to Elijah and Juda for one-fourth of their savings in the Bank of Selma, or
9. If they so choose, they could continue the plan in perpetuity but could withdraw no more than 20 percent of the savings held in their name at the Bank of Selma in any calendar year.

In year eight, at the end of a better-than-normal year for cotton and corn, Elijah and Juda Burns became landowners in Dallas County, Alabama.

It was early autumn when Claude Paisley and his family arrived in North Carolina, and not long after, Margaret would become the talk of Kings Mountain, the women's final destination.

As they rode up to the stately but less than elegant country doctor's home, their grandparents McLeod and Glynnis rushed out to embrace their daughter-in-law and the grandchildren they had never seen. They knew their granddaughters well as the girls had written them weekly letters since their mother had taught them to write—and in the style and with the decorum necessary for proper Southern women. After all, Southern propriety bordered on the religious, and manners and morality were often spoken of in the same breath.

They would reside on Kings Mountain while awaiting their father's return.

Hunter McGuire

Young Dr. Hunter McGuire was Virginia-born and Virginia-loyal, and medicine was as much a part of him as was his devotion to the South. McGuire grew up in the small town of Winchester as one of seven children. At an age that he frankly could not remember, he began to follow dutifully behind his father, an accomplished eye surgeon. At twenty, he graduated Winchester Medical College. Always the scholar like his soon-to-be mentor James Merriweather, he studied in Philadelphia and briefly taught anatomy at Tulane before he enlisted in 1861 as an infantry private with the Winchester Rifles, a unit from his hometown. Hunter McGuire was not shortsighted with his choice of the Rifles; he was merely filled with conviction and desire to defend the homeland where he was raised. Being a physician was secondary to protecting his home.

After the first battle, his instincts to heal overcame his desire to fight, and he spent hours upon hours tending to his wounded Winchester neighbors. His superiors, who could easily see that his skills at medicine far exceeded his ability to shoot a long rifle, made him a regimental surgeon. His orders were to report to General Stonewall Jackson, who took a look at the youthful unbearded face of his new surgeon and rubbished his apparent lack of experience. McGuire, who treated Jackson's wounds after the First Battle of Manassas, soon became the general's confidant in matters of medicine and served as his personal physician. McGuire took General Jackson's death as a personal defeat. It was McGuire who heard and recorded his mentor's poetic final words: "Let us cross over the river and rest beneath the shade of the trees."

McGuire was a quiet and contemplative physician. Even in the insanity of Gettysburg, he was never heard to shout. Instead, if he could not be heard calling for an instrument over the din of battle or the mewling of the injured on the tables in the surgical tent, he would walk to the case where the instruments lay and, without saying a word to fellow physicians or nurses, return his full attention to the soldier on his table.

Dr. Hunter McGuire was a doer—had been his entire life. His father told a story about his son enough times that Hunter was embarrassed to hear it. At age ten, on daily visits to his father's medical practice, and without being asked, Hunter routinely cleaned up after his father's surgery, never repulsed by the blood or diseased eyes that sometimes had to be removed and lay upon the table.

Triage Resuscitated

If patience was a virtue, then James Merriweather, since Chancellorsville, had been meritorious indeed. But now with the cessation of fighting in the fall of 1864, he was provided with a reasonable outlook of finally nurturing that ember he'd found months before and reestablishing his triage procedures. By November, James had moved to his postbattle doctoring in the town of Orange, Virginia, where the more severely injured were being housed and treated at Saint Thomas Episcopal Church.

Once the cold air of November settled on the Massanutten and the Blue Ridge Mountains, and once camp life slowed down for the physicians who remained in the Luray Valley, except for regular rounds of the diseased or recovering, James Merriweather invited three people to spend a day in Orange learning about the revolutionary procedure triage.

In Drs. Paisley and McGuire, James had obviously chosen well, but he showed his growth in understanding of the gravely wounded by also inviting Father Michael O'Malley. Michael surprised James by bringing enough of his whiskey substitute for communion wine for a small serving for each person to be added in, or after, the just made coffee they found on arriving.

Once settled with coffee and a dram, James explained his ideas about triage and the modest research that he and Dr. William McCarty had conducted after Antietam by together selecting at random twenty-five wounded men and, without consulting each other, grouping the recovering injured men into three triage-like groups.

"Gentlemen," James said, trying to remain objective (and modest), "after three days of repeating the process with a new random group each day, we found that we agreed on men in the three groups 75 percent of the time, far surpassing our expectations."

"Any thoughts before I continue?" James added, now rolling along like a preacher in midsermon.

"I want to hear more of the research," Hunter McGuire spoke up, "but I am also interested in Father O'Malley's ideas about the ethics of this process. Is this playing God, Father?"

Michael began, "Gentlemen and James, I am honored to be with you."

On seeing that the newcomers did not understand his humor—although James distinctly did—he backtracked.

"Dr. Merriweather and I go back a ways to Fredericksburg. I expect you heard about the brutal murders of two of James's colleagues soon after the fighting had ended. Willie Joe McCarty, to whom James referred earlier, his wife, Nurse Bobbie Jean, and a second nurse made up the team who were permitted the task of implementing a test of the procedures we will be discussing today.

"We all deal with death as our constant companion, but murder just seems inherently more evil, and James and I spent many hours supporting each other in dealing with that evil—truthfully, we never have recovered from it. So your colleague and I often use humor to deflect from the misery around us and sometimes just to be a redbug under each other's skin."

Claude Paisley, moving to pour another cup of coffee minus the fortification, added, "I knew I was going to enjoy this association. We already knew about Dr. Merriweather's skills as a surgeon. James, my good man, it's good to know you can take a barbed torpedo from the clergy as well."

"I don't expect it to be the last you will hear," James said. "You will know that he has accepted you into his realm of the spiritual and mystic when he tosses those barbs at you too. And he can take as well as he gives."

"Let them fly," Hunter McGuire added. "Now back to my question, which I believe was more in the spiritual realm. Father?"

"I hope you will dispense with the title. It just gets in the way most of the time unless I am dealing with the brass," Father O'Malley replied, drawing hearty laughs from everyone.

"Hunter, your question is certainly a perceptive one and one that has not really been addressed to this point. Is that right, James?"

"No. It has not, but it should be addressed going forward if we choose to redeploy the process on a larger scale."

Michael showed a contemplative brow full of too many wrinkles on his young face as he considered his response. "Let me see if I have your question formed in my head: 'Is it ethical to choose to treat an injured soldier who will likely recover if treated and to allow a moribund soldier's life to end untreated?' Did I get that right, Hunter?"

"That is better than I stated it. Thank you. Does Michael always do that, James?"

"Always. Michael," James added, "I would add only one thing to your description. A third group consists of those who would likely recover regardless of treatment. Not sure it adds anything to the ethics discussion, but it is how we divided them. So move us forward, Father, with your revelations."

Michael began, ignoring James's return torpedo. "There are three ethical questions, it seems to me, and Hunter's is definitely one of them. The first is very general: Is it moral—and I will use *moral* and *ethical* interchangeably—to be engaged in any process of choosing one life over another?

"I would just answer that that decision has been made for all of us. We are here, engaged in doing what we are doing, because others instigated this war. Are Confederate lives more valuable than Union lives? We might here in this room say, 'No, a life is a life.' However, the politicians have, by their actions, placed some lives above others. Otherwise, there would be no war.

"Although there are many ethical dimensions in that line of inquiry, they are not apropos to our discussion, and we should move on. Otherwise, to discuss them will engage us in the politics of war, and we could go no farther in our understanding of Hunter's question of the ethics of this process of triage."

Claude spoke up. "In fact, to take that a step further, the three of us all chose to take part in this war; however, had we not, we would have been conscripted. Michael, I agree, let's move on and not waste our breath on things that have been decided."

"So then," Michael continued, "the second question—Hunter's question—gets us closer to the heart of the matter: Are there any moral conflicts if, when faced with a choice of two people who are dying, a physician chooses to treat one person rather than the other?

"That is really but half the question, for as James described the procedure, the critical matter is this: Are you acting morally if you choose to treat the person who, with your efforts, is likely to survive and you leave the other person to expire from obvious catastrophic injuries?

"Gentlemen, I am sorry this is such a contorted analysis, but it seems that every question begets other questions just as complicated as its parent."

"Not a problem for me, Padre," Hunter spoke. "Claude? James? Y'all want to let Michael continue?"

"Absolutely. Let's get to the end before we add our interjections," James responded with Claude's nodding agreement.

"Well, I shall trudge ahead," Michael agreed. "That last question—the key one for the triage procedure—begs this one: Isn't the current process of taking whoever is brought to your tables by the orderlies, without regard for the severity of the injury, more morally questionable than the triage procedure under consideration? The immorality occurs, it seems to me, because soldier A, who would otherwise live, dies from waiting because soldier B, who is beyond hope, is being treated before him and receives no benefit from the attention."

Michael had been sitting as he talked, but now he stood. "All of that said, here is the position I have argued myself into. Feel free to poke holes in it.

"As much as we would like them to be, and as often as religious leaders proclaim them to be, moral ethical positions are seldom black or white. I have found them to frequently be dependent on circumstance. And as we all grow older and have more experiences from which to draw, a range of grays become the dominant colors, and stances taken from afar look very different on closer examination.

"Had I not experienced war, I might view the decisions of triage very differently, but today I am very clear that I can defend with total honesty and conviction the decisions at the heart of this procedure. Perhaps the presence of a chaplain at the triage stage of treatment would be an appropriate addition—not to add to the decision-making, but to comfort and pray for the doctors and the injured.

"One final thought to add perhaps another moral dimension for your consideration. I am torn more by the proposition that you all are making these triage decisions in order to return the injured back to the fighting, only to face once again the horrors they escaped, than I am by the triage decisions themselves. I am interested in how you all as physicians deal with this question."

James, the convener of the group, rose to speak. "Before we begin to interrogate the priest, perhaps this is a good place to break for the morning. I have arranged for Bell's Tavern, just a short walk, to provide dinner for us. I have but one condition for our dinner—we may talk only about family and home and our lives before the war began. Shall we adjourn?"

"Hear, hear!" was the reply in unison.

The Triage Team, as the four began referring to themselves in ongoing communication, recruited and trained two nurses per physician, and Michael recruited two other chaplains.

Even with the prospect of another winter like that of 1863, the Triage Team looked to each person expanding training to other physicians and chaplains within the command to which they were assigned and to the working dinners at Bell's Tavern. Equally received as the medical and moral discussions during training was the lack of such a discussion during dinner at Bell's Tavern. When James Merriweather suggested having regular dinner meetings during the winter, the senior physician of the group, Claude Paisley, suggested that dinner discussions continue to focus on home and family and that medical issues be held in abeyance until the tables were cleared and after-dinner wine was served.

The Triage Team offered family-like support to each other that had heretofore been entirely absent in their lives. It was a small thing in the scheme of the war and soon forgotten to history.

CHAPTER 39

Winter Lull Redux

In early December 1863, the Army of Northern Virginia moved from the Luray Valley and settled in for the winter south of the Rapidan River in Orange County, Virginia, with the Army of the Potomac twenty-five miles away in Culpeper County near Brandy Station.

Had the commanders of the warring armies listened to the stirrings at the center of the universe in the roots of the great ash tree, they could have saved themselves, and principally the soldiers under their commands, another winter of misery and agony. The Fates, or Spinners if you like, were clearly pissed when the politicians refused to listen to the voices of the 23,055 Yankee and 23,231 Rebel casualties who shouted above the blood and cannons: "*Enough. Enough. Enough.*"

Hence, the Sisters twisted among the roots in their anger, and in their despair wove yet another tapestry and called up another winter more severe than the last. Perhaps, even more starvation and deprivation, disease, and dysentery would do what the Minié ball and shrapnel had not.

Yet still no one paid attention, so the Spinners gave up hope, deciding that this unholy conflict could only be resolved when at least one of the armies had slaughtered or suffered the killing of enough of their own young men to sour the politicians and commanders until they declared, "*No more.*" Unfortunately, as the Spinners had observed from afar since the beginning of time, politicians at war are usually reduced to cretins, and commanders look for immortality just beyond the next battle.

When the winter of 1863–64 came, it came like the thunder of a twenty-four-pounder Howitzer, proving to be even more severe than the previous year for the Army of Northern Virginia.

Rations were halved and halved again until the men were half themselves. General Lee was overheard at one point saying to a subordinate, “The question of food for this army gives me more trouble and uneasiness than everything else combined.”

Amazing Grace

November 10, 1863
Horlbeck Creek Farm

My Beloved James,

Do you remember the hymn "Amazing Grace"? I find myself singing it and thinking of the lyrics of my favorite verse every few minutes, although I have changed them slightly:

Through many dangers, toils, and snares
My James has yet already come.
God's grace has brought him safe thus far,
And grace will bring him home.

Through my heartaches, fears, and pain,
My hopes unknown abide.

That grace has kept you safe thus far
And grace will bring you home.

(Adapted from "Amazing Grace" by John Newton, 1779)

It has been more than three months since I have heard from you, my darling, and only God's grace has sustained me, but even that has ebbed and flowed as I am frightfully sustained only by the familiarity that not knowing is the only hope I see. I wish that God's grace would bring me faith that all is well with you, but faith, I have concluded, must have some foundation beyond empty hopes.

What a god-awful state of affairs this is that I daily find myself in, but after kissing Colin good night and assuring him of your well-being, I kneel on your side of the bed, thinking that I can still smell the scent of your essence lingering in the corn shucks of the mattress. And then I realize I have made it through another day of hope borne by the unknown, and I thank the Almighty for that nourishment of my soul.

My final conscious thoughts as I move over to my side of the bed are, And grace will bring you home. I awake with anticipation that today is the day I will see "my fears relieved" because Nate will bring me your letter as he comes to tend the winter collards, although I know he is just coming to check on Colin and me. I kiss him on the cheek even when he opens the door, and he shakes his head in regret of another day without a letter.

Who knows when you will receive this, if at all, but do not despair. I have not retreated into my melancholia. I am just lonely beyond my ability to even comprehend it. I take great joy in my lovely Colin and dears Nate and Audrey Lee, who are my almost constant helpmates. But I need you. Hurry home, my dearest.

I close by just saying that we are well, and I will write again tomorrow with better news. For now, I go to your side of the bed and pray.

Yours in grace, blessings, and love,

Red

Tensions Simmer in Charleston

November 11, 1863
Horlbeck Creek

My Most-Loved James,

After yesterday's letter, I slept fitfully and arose before dawn. Colin is still asleep. I am not sure of the time. We have no working watches or clocks, but the sun suffices. I just know it is still very dark, and I don't even detect the first stirring of the morning birds and insects. I do hear a cricket somewhere here in the house chirping to my candlelight. I am thankful for his song.

I really do have much for which to be thankful, although yesterday's letter was not overflowing with apparent expressions of it. I do hope that you found my messages of hope there in the words of loneliness. My anticipation that you will return is powerful. There is no tangible reason, and I do not attribute it to faith. I find faith a very scarce commodity these days. Yesterday I could not feel your presence near to me no matter how hard I yearned for it, but here in the predawn darkness, in the flickering light of my one small candle, you are close—almost as if, in this place and time, you feel the stirrings of my heart. Bless you, my darling.

You would not believe Colin—skinny as a bean sprout and tall as an okra plant, and sometimes his attitude is just as prickly. I pay him no mind. Of course, I never gave my parents a minute's grief!

He is all boy. The woods are his schoolhouse just as much as the books his grandfather brings him when he visits. I fear that he has taken more after me than you, and of course Nate encourages these weekly forages into the woods and the creeks and rivulets at the mouth of the Horlbeck that rises and fall with the tide. Recently, crabs and mussels and occasionally oysters have been added to our diet of catfish, flounder, rabbit, and squirrel. We are still waiting on the first deer of the season, but Colin (I can hear Nate's words) tells me that we need to wait until the first hard freeze when the deer will, being in rut—he really likes that word—begin to move around and are easier to harvest.

Colin has turned into a regular little engineer. Nate has continued to teach him necessary carpentry skills, and Colin seems to have a talent for using those skills to repair dozens of things around the house. Just last week the pump up and died. At least that was my explanation. Next thing I knew, your son had it torn apart and was doing something with the leathers. Who knew a pump needed leather anything? I didn't, but Colin, by way of Nate, thankfully did.

We had a passable harvest, and our trial run with our two families combining our efforts on one farm seems to have been a good idea. Nate and Audrey Lee took vegetables to the Charleston Market three times during the summer, but we only have Confederate dollars to show for it, and some salt pork that he got in barter, but it was good for him and Audrey Lee to get away just for the day. On his return, he told us that after the shelling from the Federal gunboats in August and the CSA submersible David that did damage to USS New Ironsides in Charleston Harbor, tensions are running high in Charleston, and the journey from here to there, although not really dangerous, is far from a casual sail across the river. I don't see Colin accompanying him from this point on, but Father and Bartholomew seem determined to continue to make the trip. Just having Bartholomew's mouth around brightens up the house.

Father says that Mother is now confined and strapped to her bed. Only Father's connections with the doctors have prevented her from being moved to the ward for the criminally insane. Father has accepted that she is beyond recovery. Father confided that he prays for her timely and peaceful demise, and I totally understand, but I would find it very hard to attend services for her. Not from the spite I once held—that is entirely past—but because I would not risk the danger that would be involved for Colin and me.

I surely hope that your winter this year is milder than last. From what you wrote of last year's struggle, it is hard for me to see how General Lee can keep an army together under such conditions. Please watch yourself. Hungry men who are desperate to return home have little to lose in injuring whoever may get in the way.

I see the first glimmer of false dawn in the east. Time for me to stoke up the stove and get your son some breakfast of eggs (3), biscuits and jelly (4), two slices of bacon only because I will not cook more, and a cup of black coffee. Yep, he now drinks coffee.

That is <u>your</u> son. Hurry home to see him. He needs his father, and I need my lover.

Yours in every way you can imagine,

Red

Good News for a Change

November 9, 1863
General Lee's Headquarters
Orange County, Virginia

Blessed Red,

I have not heard from you for so very long, since before Gettysburg. I expect that our twenty-three-day retreat until we finally settled in safely here in the Luray Valley made it nearly impossible for mail to get to us. Richmond, through which all mail flows, had other matters pressing down. Had the Yankees captured our wagon train, the Army of Northern Virginia would have been destroyed, and this experiment in independence would have been demolished with it.

If your letters are lost in a back room somewhere in Richmond never to be placed on a railcar, or if they eventually make their way to me, I understand. I trust you have been keeping your head down on Horlbeck Creek. I am thankful that it is remote enough to stay away from the politics and hotheads on either side of this fight.

I have good news for a change. Except for two small encounters with each other in early fall at Bristoe and Mine Run that amounted to naught for either side, we began our winter lull of 1863–64 almost two months earlier than last year. Perhaps our foraging armies will be more successful starting before the snows come. Lord, our boys need it. Nourishment right now is the primary need of this army. Malnourished boys are dying needlessly from dysentery every day. most physicians think the miasma lurks in the air of the tents, so even on the coldest days there is a mandatory fifteen-minute airing out. I am not convinced at all of the airborne theory. But should I want to disinfect a tent as John taught me about the operating table, I could not. No one knows anything about disinfectant, and if they did, it could not be procured.

Sorry. I got entirely away from my good news. Imagine that. Actually, the fact that most of our doctoring of the wounded has been reduced to those who can be housed in the Saint Thomas Episcopal Church in Orange is part of the good news. This development has allowed me to approach my two colleagues with whom I served General Jackson to tell them about my ideas for triage. This time, I also included Michael's insight into ethical questions that might arise. We met here at Saint Thomas Episcopal Church, and I am so very excited to write that we are making plans to implement triage across the entire army with Drs. Claude Paisley and Hunter McGuire. Claude is my senior physician commander, and Hunter was General Jackson's personal doctor. Their experiences in battle and their mind-sets have uniquely prepared them for the idea of triage. With an excellent discussion led by Father Michael on more than a few ethical questions, we agreed to move forward in training a triage team for each of the three armies under General Lee's command: Longstreet's First Corps, Ewell's Second Corps, and the Third Corps of A. P. Hill. Michael will be training a chaplain for each team.

I do not look forward to what fate may send our way this winter here so near the Blue Ridge and

Massanutten Mountains, but it will be more bearable because my colleagues and I are working again on triage. I hope our discussions can explore two more topics, the use of antiseptics in the operating theater and in recuperation tents and postbattle depression in soldiers. Since Michael was so well received and has some training and experience through me with depression, he may be the one to introduce first when we are ready. Also, the treatment does not require the acquisition of chemicals, only education of physicians and chaplains. There will be no new treatments anytime soon. We have enough on our hands finishing up the triage training in each corps.

Michael would not mind me telling you this, so I want you to know that he is struggling with the writing of letters to the next of kin about the death of their loved one. He knows better, but still he tells me that he thinks the family back home, when they receive his letter, somehow holds him responsible for the death. Keep him in your prayers. It is easy to forget that men of God are first men of this earth with much the same measure of fears and foibles as any of us. As I have seen Michael's humanity, it has only amplified his spiritual gifts in my eyes.

Pray for the boys of the Army of Northern Virginia as they battle infections, dysentery, and ague, the last of which I prefer to call respiratory distress. I have taken to wearing a cotton cloth across my nose and mouth, placing a few drops of whiskey on my hands between patients, and washing my hands as soon as I come out from attending the men. I have been keeping meticulous notes about my own health since I began these procedures. It feels good to be back doing some uncomplicated research. John taught me well to question, probe, investigate, and document. And that is what I am doing this winter.

Night has long ago closed in behind the mountains, and these days I seem to feel an ache in my bones as it does so. Guess I ought to record that too.

My darling Red, it must appear that I seldom think of you and Colin, but nothing about that would be truthful. There are a thousand things a day that remind me of each of you: a boy's face that looks like an older version of Colin, a mop of flaming red hair on an orderly, the song of a bird bathed in sunlight.

If my damned honor permitted me, I would strike out to you tomorrow. Of course it would kill Father, although I think Mother would understand. Regardless, I am sure I cannot, and you know I cannot, so we must just wait and pray and let our longing sustain us.

Yours in all things, past and future,
JEM

Boomer Rousing

December 1, 1863
Horlbeck Creek

O How I Love You, My Darling,

I received your wondrous letter filled with hope and faith for at least the near future. I forgive you for not writing sooner. You have been most busy saving future lives of boys who will return to their families and run down tree-canopied lanes instead of moldering away in the soil of northern Virginia.

I am so pleased to read that the adventurous and inquisitive spirit that took you from Richmond to Charleston, through John's office door, and into my life has returned after so long an absence. I know you did good work—better than most, even at your worst—but I know the remarkable James Merriweather is fully present when he is questioning accepted canons and researching and trying new methods. I shall pray my very hardest that from this moment, your work is your laboratory as often as is possible and feasible.

War must be a lonely hell above all else. I know what it would be here on the creek if not for Colin and the ever-present Nate and Audrey Lee. I pray that the camaraderie that you have forged will sustain you when my letters are lost, or when I am lost in myself and fail to write. Undoubtedly the Almighty placed the members of the triage team in your path. We know that he indeed placed Michael there.

Oh, my darling. Your presence consumes me as if you are sitting right here next to me in the darkness of this early morning. Your presence whiffs the candle as you stand looking in on Colin. The smile on your face lights up his doorway.

Father says that Charleston is awash in a hurricane of restlessness these days. He tells us, with evident pride, that some dry goods and sundries, and the vegetable markets, and even a few restaurants and bakeries remain Charlestonian as ever, yet they struggle. What a crime against our culture it would be should the Yankees occupy our Charleston and, in their contempt for it, destroy it. Father says he will not be surprised should he awake one morning to find Federals patrolling the streets in their immaculate blue and gold. Bartholomew, of course, regales Colin with his opinion that any two Southerners are worth any ten Yankees, and therefore the Yankees, knowing that fact better than anyone, shall not attempt such a tactic.

I often think the world of Bartholomew's mind is far better

than what likely lies ahead for our beloved South Carolina. Damned politicians. Polecats, all. I firmly believe that we shall prosper again in time, whatever the near future holds because of men just like you, James Merriweather, and Father, Nate, Audrey Lee, Bartholomew, John, and Andrew Ryan from whom we have heard almost nothing since he enlisted in the navy. And yes, Lauraleigh Bailey, whom I have forgiven, and Colin and his brothers and sisters to come.

The South is and shall be in times to come filled with such people as these. So, my darling, do your beautiful work—heal, repair, and resurrect, even. Teach and inspire, and on mornings like this, with your letter in my hand, I will sit and luxuriate in your presence and take your presence into my soul, ready to start the next day and the next and the next.

I hear Boomer rousing Colin with his licks and yelps, so it is time to attack this day with you next to me.

Surrounded by your love, I go forward in faith and grace,
Red

Surgeon's Diary

December 7, 1863
General Lee's Winter Encampment
Orange, Virginia

I am struck by just how easy it was to reinstitute the procedure of triage and to see it planned out for all three corps of the ANV. I am convinced that bringing Michael into the process at the beginning answered many questions that I could not have successfully argued to their needed conclusions. It was most helpful that Claude and Hunter knew his reputation before we began the conversation. I could kick myself for not involving a chaplain when Willie and I applied triage at Fredericksburg. Had we had a chaplain's perspective, I think it may have continued on in my absence. What a difference that would have made at Gettysburg.

We have taken to calling ourselves the Triage Team in our intrateam communications. We are just as careful not to use that term with brass around. The progress we have made could be undone on a general's whim.

Once we broke up our first meeting at Saint Thomas Episcopal Church, the Triage Team agreed that we should recruit and train two nurses per physician and that Michael would recruit two other chaplains. By December 1, the teams were in place, and I reported to Dr. John Bailey at HQ in Richmond (now risen to the rank of colonel) that the First Corps of Lieutenant General James Longstreet, Second Corps of Lieutenant General R. S. Ewell, and Third Corps of Lieutenant General A. P. Hill each had ready a trained triage team awaiting his approval and his recommendation to General Lee. I heard back almost immediately of his support and the fact that he would draw up the recommendation for General Lee's review.

I kind of expect that we may hear from General Lee's adjutant before we hear from John. At least I hope that is the case as then we would have more time for ongoing training.

Even with the prospect of another winter

like that of 1863, I find myself almost unaware of the winter's cold with the preliminary success thus far and the hoped-for next steps with depression and antiseptics.

JEM

Poking the Bear

December 25, 1863
General Lee's Headquarters
Orange, Virginia

My Precious Colleen,

In whatever twist of fate that causes such things, this morning's mail delivered to me the most excellent Christmas gift I shall ever receive: three of your letters at one time, two from November and one from early December.

It is now early afternoon, but I am not sure, as I have been mesmerized by the longing and loneliness of your words. I first read the letters in order. Then in reverse order. Then in order again and again. I think it would make no difference at all if I turned the pages over on my bed and picked each up at random. Your letters are harp strings to my tired brain. Bless you, my darling, for your trust, your patience, and your hope when that is all you have to sustain you. I will do my best to do better with my letter writing.

Red, I think there will be many days ahead in which to write. I have seen signs and portents all about. As I pass near to General Lee's offices I sense that we are not yet spent with death. We shall continue to fight even though _our_ war for independence is lost. It seems that we are fighting for better peace terms, but I do not see peace conferences. I fear that if we merely poke the bear, he shall turn and devour us in all his ferocity and anger. But poking is all we are able to do with the numbers of men we have lost and the conditions the remainder must endure. Peace is not on any horizon that I can see. We must pray for our land and for our people—that the politicians in Richmond will look at the tracks of the bear in the snow outside their windows each morning, see it getting closer and closer, and decide that saving our precious Southland is more important than saving face.

Enough of my navel-gazing. I am just so pleased to see you returned to the redheaded feisty Irish lass who captured my heart with her laugh. How is it possible that the prettiest girl in Charleston would be blessed with the most raucous laughter as well? I can see you now at Murphy's Irish Pub on Meeting Street hushing the entire supper crowd with your laughter at another of Bartholomew's outrageous tales of shipboard life. I _will_ come back for that laugh and the rest of you too!

It is good that Boomer and Colin are so close. A boy in the country needs a dog, and from how you describe him, Boomer is the perfect companion. Spirited boy and strong-willed pup. I trust Boomer hits the proper combination of keeping Colin out of your hair but not away from his chores.

Darling, as your father speaks of your mother, I understand entirely. I care for so many men, older _and_ younger, who beg me for their death. Like your mother, who has already passed beyond this world and is waiting for blessed release, they are oblivious to everything except the constant pain. You must remember the Lauraleigh who dressed you in a handmade lace white frock for mass every Sunday, and that birthdays and holidays were the canvas that she painted for her family. I pray for her daily, but mostly for your father. His quiet strength in the face of such dementia is beyond the pale of our abilities to understand. If there are heroes in this conflict, your father is indeed one of mine.

Our Triage Team continues to meet as we can, and we correspond back and forth regularly about ideas on our minds since our own orderlies and not the mail service can deliver our letters. I asked Michael to introduce the topic of postbattle depression in soldiers at our last meeting, and as you would expect he was a perfect combination of science, ethics, compassion, and godliness. We all agree that we have seen this condition in many men but, lacking a cause for its symptoms, could not formulate a plan for its treatment. After Michael's synopsis of Robert Burton's work on the topic, his book The Anatomy of Melancholy has been passed from person to person. I believe that we shall soon be developing a medical course of treatment, but not to be implemented until we have successfully brought triage to the level of standard practice.

Forgive me, but I must speak of one more medical remedy I spend much time reflecting upon. My dearest Mary Assumpta Bailey Merriweather, your words are the best personal restorative that I have in my kit, and I administer it daily.

I am beyond blessed to be yours,
JEM

Gray Days

February 3, 1864
General Lee's Headquarters
Orange, Virginia

Dear Mary Assumpta,

I know that this letter will echo my mood. I am so sorry, but I have no other. Michael is no better. The Triage Team cannot meet, not with the conditions here so dire, and when we correspond our words seem to match the gray skies that never let up. Perhaps a week of blue skies and cold, clear mornings will also clear our attitudes.

These days I am a reflection of thousands of bored and lonely soldiers freezing from lack of clothes and starving from lack of nutrition. Promise of food and new shoes and uniforms and underwear on the next train that never arrives is a formula for desertion at the least and insurrection at the worst. Boredom, not Yankee artillery, is the enemy in the winter, and drilling in the mud and ice is not a cure. It only makes these men hungrier for home.

I have looked at so many sunken faces from malnutrition and eyes that look a thousand yards distant yet see nothing that I have lapsed into a kind of somnolent grayness myself. I walked by a storefront here in Orange yesterday, and in the window I saw a stoop-shouldered old man. I actually turned to see who was so close to me and was shocked that it was I. That image shook me out of my state of mind for the instant, but I have no idea how I shall fight it off the next time and the next when it comes slinking like the black dog of depression.

I trust that ol' Jake will continue to bend his will to the harness and the plow in near spring and that his stubbornness is of no consequence. When I look around at the dearth of food for our men, I worry that you all will have enough seed to plant decent crops of corn and potatoes to sustain you in the coming months. But knowing Nate, I expect my worries are more borne of the weather than anything else.

When you married this citified doctor raised on the streets of Richmond, I know you had no thoughts that you would find yourself with calloused hands and a body bone-tired at the end of the day. But God willing, I will return to you entirely, and we shall again retreat to Charleston and make our home as we imagined it to be. Remember? We were under covers on a crisp October evening, having made more than a little love and noise! We laughed when we said we hoped John's neighbors did not call the constabulary about burglars next door. I wonder, do you think that was the tryst when Colin was conceived? The timing seems about right.

I could write more, but how could I improve on that thought? It will remain with me, as has your love. I shall come home to you.

Your lover and your husband,
JEM

Cocoon

February 27, 1864
Horlbeck Creek

My Dearest Companion,

I sit with your letter of February 2 open on the table in front of me as I write. For the last few minutes, I have been reliving the beautiful and boisterous evening of lovemaking you wrote about. Good thing Colin was outside for a while and my shaking had calmed when he finally burst through the door with the rabbit he had just killed.

Darling, I grasp your feelings of the grayness of melancholy creeping toward you. I don't know if you received any of my December letters. I find it most discouraging that, in addition to the Yankees, we must fight a second war with our own Post Office Department. The "commodity" most likely to bolster people at home and at the front is the mail, it seems to me. And the mail is the least costly and most straightforward to administer. But the reality of that truth has escaped the politicians in Richmond.

I know for sure that you did not get a letter from me after December 15 and not until the message I am writing at this moment. There is a reason. I vowed not to allow the pain of last year to return to me again, but I could not stop it. From Colin to Audrey Lee and Nate to Father, they all expressed their regrets with hugs and not a few tears. And I accepted them with smiles and proper Southern graces. But for days extending into fortnights, I liken my outlook, as it says in Corinthians, to "seeing through a glass darkly." I must have functioned, or Colin would have complained, but I remember little. Thank goodness there is not much to be done on the farm this time of year and that what needs doing, your darling son can do and does do on his own.

This day, your vivid recall of our lovemaking pushed me from my cocoon and back into reality. Soon after, I must have fussed at Colin to take that damn rabbit outside to clean it because the next I saw of him was with a pot of cut-up rabbit pieces, pink and ready for the salt and flour and the frying pan for supper. Seems he prefers my fussing to my acquiescence.

Darling, I read once that surviving produces its own set of values and morality. James Edward Merriweather, we shall survive. You will return to me, and I will be whole when I see your face again. We will do whatever it takes. Promise me that.

And you damn well better not forget it. You get your ass home, so I do not have to come looking for you!

Your loving (and gracious) Red

Easter Evil
March 5, 1864
Washington, DC

Abraham Whetstone, Davey Little, and Tommy Nagley, still covered in the dried bloody enamel of their work in Shetter's Woods, arrived back in DC's Hell's Bottom and the boardinghouse of Mary Skirett at dusk dark. Boston Williams's decapitated body lay somewhere south of Gettysburg. He had not been a favorite of Whetstone from the beginning, with him being a former slave and all, but Whetstone thought that Williams's penchant for violence might overcome his skin color. When, at Whetstone's suggestion, Williams failed to urinate into the mouth of the decapitated head of Petronella Neuenschwander, he thought no one saw. He was mistaken.

If Mary Skirett took any notice of the bloody clothes, she said not a word, only putting out her hand for past rent unpaid during their excursion to Gettysburg. Paid up, the three walked out of the lobby to the water trough, where they stripped naked and washed bodies and clothes. Walking naked up the outside stairs to their room was enough to dry them off in the hot July Washington night. They did not care that the trough was now bloodred, nor whose job it would be to empty it and fill it again in the morning. Such mundane doings did not concern master artists of the human condition whose canvases were walls and whose media were blood, organs, and offal.

Whetstone had no illusions about what he was. He was not insane. He knew he was pure evil. He craved to be the most evil man as likely had ever walked upon the earth. And he was just getting started. By his count, he and his surrogates had dispatched somewhere south of sixty people over the last six months. His carnival of killing outside of Gettysburg was his finest piece of art, he knew. There had been a bloodlust that night. But he was pissed his work was forgotten in the streams of dark red gold that had flowed from Little Round Top.

It was March 18, 1864, and Whetstone was bored. Except for a killing here and there to replenish his funds, he had no art of any substance to exhibit since Gettysburg. And when Abraham Whetstone was bored, his darker demons suggested fun things that made him smile. He had smiled a lot in the last three days.

In preparation for his next exhibition, Abraham Whetstone cleaned himself up, sized up a gentleman about his size who was visiting one of Mary's whores, and using a garrote formed from a three-foot piece of piano wire with sticks about four inches long and an inch thick attached to each end, quietly dispatched the whore's visitor to his Maker with the joy of sin still percolating around in the gentleman john's amygdala.

In the gentleman's clothes, Whetstone looked rather

presentable, according to Davey and Tommy at least. Not that they ever had seen a gentleman's trappings that were not covered in blood.

The next morning Whetstone left Hell's Bottom, and over breakfast at Ebbitt's Boardinghouse on Fifteenth Street, he casually inquired about where he might spend a quiet Easter Sunday outside the environs of the politics of Washington and the war. He listened and nodded at several suggestions, but he deemed them too near to his current abode. As he was about to look for suggestions elsewhere, a gentleman evidently in Washington on business suggested Saint Mary's Catholic Church in Annapolis. If Mr. Whetstone were willing to make a not unpleasant ride, he would be pleased by the welcoming Christian congregation he would find at 109 Duke of Gloucester Street, and if he arrived on Saturday afternoon, he could participate in the annual Easter egg hunt on the lawn facing the river.

As Whetstone considered his plans for the next display of his work, he knew that three men together, and of the age to be at war, would look too conspicuous to accomplish what he intended, so he killed Tommy Nagley with the rope garrote, demonstrating to Davey Little the technique so that he could dispatch his own gentleman and acquire his own set of clothes presentable at an Easter egg hunt in Annapolis. At midnight, they tossed Tommy Nagley's body into Mary Skirett's pigpen. His remains were gone by morning.

Whetstone and his remaining devil's miscreant set off from Hell's Bottom on Wednesday, March 22, expecting to make the just over thirty-mile ride in two days without pushing hard. They would arrive in plenty enough time to scout out Saint

Mary's and the surrounding neighborhoods, find a boarding-house and stable, and make their final plans for Easter Sunday.

Whetstone had considered with some pleasure the stealing of a couple of boats, rowing them across the river, and anchoring them at the river's edge among the reeds. They would then mingle with the Easter egg hunters and snatch a couple of young Annapolis Catholics for their pleasure. *No,* he thought to himself, *the risks just outweigh the rewards. But we could,* he thought, arguing with himself, his eyes glistening as he considered the plan again, *plant our own eggs ever closer and closer to the edge of the river and maybe even entice the baby papists into the boats without even a yelp.*

Finally, he convinced himself that he was not really interested in children so young. Maybe one day. Besides, he had a better plan.

Father Robert Constantine Fucillo was newly arrived at Saint Mary's, and tomorrow's Easter Mass would be his first Mass with the congregation. He had been sent down (to his mind) after six years at Saint Michael's Church in Baltimore, and he had every intention of teaching the Annapolitans how real Roman Catholics celebrated the resurrection of their Lord and Savior Jesus Christ of Nazareth. To begin the transition, he dressed in his finest vestments for the Easter egg hunt. To the onlooking parents, a few faithful parishioners, and Whetstone and Little, the new priest was clearly overdressed for an Easter egg hunt.

All the better, thought Whetstone.

The egg gatherers and the parents returned to their carriages and to home as the sun began to dim and the cool breezes gathered around the river. The Reverend Fucillo walked to his single-story vicarage to disrobe, but then he waited. *I shall enjoy the beauty of God's vestments a bit longer,* he thought to himself as he poured a substantial draught of brandy in the gold and silver communion cup. *God will understand,* he rationalized as he brought the gold chalice with silver crosses on each side to his lips again and again. So much the easier for Whetstone and Little, who watched him through the window he'd left open to catch the March river breezes.

Soon the priest could be heard snoring loudly, at which time Whetstone and Little entered and did their worst.

Easter morning in Annapolis was as glorious as Easters are supposed to be but very seldom are given the vagaries of spring weather. Congregants gathered outside the heavy wooden doors to the cathedral that had been finished and dedicated in 1862, it was so declared, to the glory of God and Rome. The Annapolitans had worshipped since before the revolution in a chapel rather than a cathedral, and the new Saint Mary's, as most parishioners still thought of it, instilled reverence in all who entered, but not to Abraham Whetstone.

And not on Easter Sunday, 1864.

At 10:45, as the worshippers in their Easter wartime best began to enter the narthex and opened the doors to the nave, they were first assaulted by the smell of intestines ripped open and spread in the center aisle all the way from the narthex to the transept. As they tried to divine this unfathomable blasphemous act on Easter Sunday, their eyes were drawn upward from the floor of the nave and to the altar, where the priest's staff stood in its stand with a human heart pierced by the crucifix.

The worshippers turned to their left, away from the intestines in the aisle, to scuttle their children from the carnage, and their eyes naturally fell on the pièce de résistance of Abraham Whetstone's Easter evil. Father Fucillo, in his golden vestments, was splayed from his chin to pubis and was nailed by his hands and feet to the prized gold-leaf wooden statuary of the crucified Christ—the centerpiece of the north transept and the only part of the old chapel to be included in the new cathedral.

By the time the authorities arrived at Saint Mary's, the artists were halfway back to Hell's Bottom. Not a single parishioner recalled any peculiar faces in the days leading up to the tragedy or the day before at the egg hunt. However, John McMasters, who had returned from business in Washington especially for the Easter egg hunt, had a faint twitch of recollection at the back of his hippocampus.

The War Comes Home

On the chilly, crisp Wednesday night of February 17, 1864, the CSS *Hunley*, under the command of Lieutenant George Dixon, silently made its way just beneath the calm star-sparkled waters of Charleston Harbor, moving slowly ever closer under hand-cranked power toward the USS *Housatonic* sitting at anchor. Only at the last moment, a seaman in the crow's nest roused the *Housatonic* of the *Hunley*'s approach. The *Hunley* rammed the *Housatonic*, embedding the 135-pound explosive charge on the end of the *Hunley*'s long spar into the *Housatonic*'s starboard quarter near its munitions stores. As the *Hunley* reversed, the munitions officer exploded the torpedo, sinking the *Housatonic* in minutes.

Unfortunately, the Confederate victory was short-lived as the *Hunley* failed to return to port and all eight crew members were lost. It would be a month before names of the crew were released to families. Among the dead was Munitions Officer First Lieutenant Andrew Ryan Bailey.

Andrew Ryan had thought about joining up as soon as South Carolina seceded, but he couldn't put his heart into leaving his family for a cause that was in such contrast to his upbringing. Over the years the family business had received criticism for its willingness to openly sell to white, black, Jew, and, on occasion, Natives in the area. Andrew's brother Dr. John Bailey treated all who came through his door. However, once cannon shots were exchanged, philosophies were put aside. Andrew Ryan enlisted in the Confederate navy three days later.

Having grown up on the Ashley River, he was a river rat. Swimming was as natural to Andrew Ryan as walking. He had built so many bateaus and sailing skiffs that he had lost count. If he was going to fight, Andrew Ryan was going to do it on the water.

After managing his family business, Andrew Ryan entered service as a steward first class responsible for ensuring that the naval expeditionary force based in Charleston had sufficient and appropriate stores and equipment. He was initially satisfied with his job because it was so familiar, but he had enlisted to fight.

After months of living at home and walking to the navy yard each morning, his enlistment seemed to him to have no purpose, although he had risen to the rank of chief steward and then to chief petty officer. On April 12, 1862, he approached his commanding officer. "Captain Fuller? May I enter and speak, sir?"

"Come in, Chief. What's on your mind this morning?"

Andrew Ryan spoke confidently but calmly and respectfully. "Sir, when I enlisted it was to fight. I recognize that men must be fed and that we must have the stores and equipment required should the fight come to us, and I have fulfilled those expectations."

Captain Earl Fuller had served with some officers who rode roughshod over their enlisted men, but he was not one of them. "Go on, son. Speak your piece."

"Well, sir, I grew up on the water of the Ashley River. I could swim before I could walk, and I have been designing and building boats since I could hold a saw and hammer. Captain, I have more to offer this navy than what I have given thus far. I am not sure exactly what path that might be, but I am a fast learner and a willing worker whatever the job. I just want it to be with boats and ships."

Fuller rose from the desk he had rescued from the schooner *Daufuskie* that he had captained before the war but that was now dry-rotting not far from the naval yard.

"Bailey, I have a hundred men who can bake and manage our stores. But we are in very short supply of experienced sailors at any level." Fuller paused, and Bailey held his breath in anticipation of what he hoped would come next.

"Son, down in Mobile they are building something called a submarine. You have any idea what that is?"

"Well, sir, I know *marine* is related to water and *sub* is a prefix meaning below." He would have made his eighth grade teacher mighty proud at that moment. As it was, he just surprised his commanding officer.

"Well, I'll be damned! A sailor who knows his boats and his

grammar. I am not sure we can rightly call a submarine a boat or a ship. For the time being, let's just call it a craft that attacks enemy ships from under the water."

Captain Fuller smiled as he asked his next, obvious question: "Bailey, is that more what you are thinking about this morning?"

"Yes, sir, it is. I will do whatever you need me to do, sir," Chief Bailey responded, trying to hide his obvious pleasure.

Captain Fuller's face became a bit somber and severe. "It will require that we send you by rail to Mobile to work under the tutelage of Mr. H. L. Hunley, who is financing the building of this craft.

"I want you to learn where every bolt is attached, how the propulsion system works, how the heck people breathe under water, and the job of every crew member that will be aboard.

"Then I want you to personally escort the craft back here to Charleston and train us in how to operate it."

Fuller paused again thoughtfully, and then he spoke, "There is one last thing. We cannot trust an enlisted man with such an important task, so as of this moment, you are now Midshipman Andrew Ryan Bailey.

"Bailey, the trip to Mobile likely will be hazardous. Several seamen have already died testing the prototypes, and the return will be even more dangerous than the trip down. All of this must be carried out in total secrecy. You should tell your family that you have been deployed indefinitely to Wilmington to procure supplies and equipment necessary to defend the port from the inevitable attack by the Yankees, but speak nothing of Mobile or of the submarine now or in the future. Your assignment here will remain secret."

When the Confederate navy finally notified Matthew Bailey of his son lost at sea, the short paragraph was the first he had heard of his middle son in more than a year:

> Dear Mr. Bailey:
>
> The navy of the Confederate States of America regrets to inform you that your son Midshipman Andrew Ryan Bailey, munitions officer on CSS *Hunley*, died on February 17, 1864, after piloting the first submarine to successfully sink another warship, the USS *Housatonic*. The *Hunley* ran aground as it withdrew and sank with all eight souls aboard.
>
> Sincerest condolences,
> Stephen Mallory
> Secretary of the Department of the Navy

Reluctant Warrior

> March 20, 1864
> Charleston, South Carolina
>
> Dearest Mary Assumpta,
>
> Just yesterday, I received a letter from Stephen Mallory, secretary of the CSA Navy, informing me that Andrew Ryan was among eight sailors who were lost when their submarine sank in Charleston Harbor after successfully sinking the USS *Housatonic*. I knew that Andrew Ryan was working on something very secretive as I had not

seen or heard from him in weeks, though he was stationed at the Charleston Naval Station.

Andrew Ryan was a reluctant warrior, more at home in the shop and the streets of Charleston, but when his country called, he answered. I do not know if we shall receive his body, as the exact location of the craft the CSS *Hunley* is unknown. At an appropriate time when this war is over, we will have a memorial service in his honor.

Do not worry about me. With Bartholomew's help, I will weather this just as I accept the care of your mother. I will be over to see you soon with another load of sweet potatoes, and we will discuss this more fully.

Lovingly,
Father

Mary Assumpta read her father's letter as if in a dream. As much as she comprehended the realities of the war, like most members of most families south and north, she never conceived that those realities would include the name Bailey or Merriweather. And now they had.

After two days she took Colin aside and told him how his uncle Andrew Ryan had died a hero fighting for his country and that when the war ended, they would travel to Charleston to remember him suitably. And then they both knelt and prayed long and hard for the return of the father and husband they so desperately missed.

Figuring that James did not need to worry more about home than he already did, Mary Assumpta chose not to write to him of Andrew Ryan's death. Life at Horlbeck Creek went on, but the war had come to the creek.

Tragedy Strikes Again

April 12, 1864
Horlbeck Creek

Dearest, Dearest James,

Father is dead. I am an orphan, and I need you so. I am not sure that I can go on, and yet the best I can do is write this damn letter knowing that you may not even receive it and that by the time you read it and send me your words of healing, I will be in a completely different place. And I will be at that place without you. And I do so desperately need your arms around me.

I will not retreat into depression as I did when the baby died. Nothing will ever again be so hellish as that experience. But I have no confidence in my ability or even desire to rationally make the decisions that must be made within the next few days.

As always, I will lean on Nate and Audrey Lee. Dear Lord, I do not think that they ever contemplated what they were taking on when they agreed to watch over Colin and me as you went to war. We are awash in grief and unable even to decide on the simplest things that we should do next. We are all forlorn as our lives have been defiled by his death.

I have never seen a more distressed human being than Bartholomew Jennings when three days ago I opened the door to his barely audible knocks and yells. He could scarcely speak, and I dissuaded him from talking as my only thought was to get him inside and get him warm and changed into a pair of your pants and a heavy woolen shirt. Luckily we had a fire going against the damp and chill, and I poured a large draught of brandy for him—brandy Father had brought us on his last visit.

Pitifully, Bartholomew finally told us that Father had perished. They were crossing the harbor with a cargo of sweet potatoes when a late winter storm roared through and capsized the oyster boat that Bartholomew was captaining. A swirling and unpredictable wind had churned the Wando into four-foot whitecapping waves that simultaneously swept over the vessel as the wind flipped it on its side. The sail had become waterlogged, and the wind drove the mast and sail over and into the gray-brown rollers. There was nothing that Bartholomew could do except to abandon the craft.

Dear God, James, they were twenty-five yards from the dock. All perished except for Bartholomew. Their bodies have not been seen. Bartholomew, ever the seaman, dog-paddled, looking for Father. The last he saw of him, Father was holding on to the mast as he and the boat slid beneath the surface with Bartholomew frantically trying to reach out to him. Bartholomew continued to tread water until he could triangulate his position using trees on the shore so that he might be able to return and recover Father's body once the storm had passed. Then, his clothes and shoes waterlogged, he somehow made his way to the dock and eventually to our door.

There was enough light, and I sent Colin with Boomer to fetch Nate and Audrey Lee as I knew I was in no state of mind or body to fathom what would need to be done in the coming days and weeks.

Nate, Audrey Lee, and Colin with Boomer following faithfully behind the wagon were back here within half an hour of my sending Colin. Bless his heart, Colin must have run all the way. Nate and Audrey Lee salved our pain-mine, Colin's, and Bartholomew's-with no attention to their own distress, for they have really come to know Father in the last few months. I almost had supper fixed when Bartholomew arrived, and Audrey Lee finished it up by adding a few touches as only she is able. Once I had settled into the reality that I could handle Father's death, I begged them to return home, but they would hear nothing of it.

We spent much of the night remembering Father, but before we all crumpled and slept where we sat, we had evolved the conversation to smiles and fond stories of the man who had "tamed" Lauraleigh O'Brien. But with morning my misery returned even stronger as the sure knowledge that Father was lost became clear in the full light of day.

As I write this, we have not recovered the boat or Father's remains. Pray for us, my darling. We are struggling to keep our senses about us, and prayers are all we have. We hold no hope for his survival and only little more for the recovery of his remains.

I love you, my darling, more today than I have ever loved you. Please return to me, my dearest.

I need you in more ways than I can name,

Mary Assumpta

Love's Caresses

April 12, 1864

General Lee's Headquarters
Orange, Virginia

My Precious and Irreplaceable Red,

It is just after sunset as I write this, and for some reason that I cannot comprehend logically, you have been on my mind today in a fashion that is utterly unlike how I experience you always being by my side.

Early this morning long before dawn, I heard a lilting voice humming "Galway City," and I pulled back my tent flap expecting to see a nurse who loved the old Irish ballad as much as you, but there was no one I could see, so I returned to my bed and turned to the wall, hoping to sleep until dawn. However, almost as soon as I closed my eyes, I felt a soft touch on my shoulder. I thought it must be the same Irish nurse needing my attention for the feverish patient I attended before I retired last evening, but when I turned, I was again alone.

Throughout the day, I heard your name for me, JEM, spoken near me. Not a single soul other than Mary Assumpta Bailey Merriweather calls me that name. Red, I felt your presence surrounding me throughout the day, and I rejoiced in every touch and whisper and soulful note. I thought as I experienced each new glimmer of you that if I were descending into madness, what a lovely way to make a visit.

For whatever prompted this, bless you, my darling, for I have needed you this week. As the officers hurry the men in preparation for the next saga in this monstrous conflagration, the sense of dread all about us is palpable in the boys' sweat, peppered with fear's unpleasant scent.

If you are calling out to me, I am here, thinking of you every second of every minute. I only pray that this letter reaches you and strengthens your resolve if you are in a time of need, and most of all that it embraces you tightly with my love.

One of the great tragedies of the conflict in which we are engaged so long is that war does not often inspire love letters as much as dirges to events long past by the time you receive the missive, if at all. So, my blessed sweetheart, because of you I write this letter not with a hint of pessimism, but only with *love. With the binding faith that you and I shall soon be together again, I write love's letter.*

This moment my mind's eye feels the excited anticipation of touching all the extraordinary places of your body. Soldier's mouth to maiden's lips. Tongue touches tongue, and you whisper in supplication. Not yet my Irish lass.

I know every crease and valley and knoll, and I travel to them again and again. You are quivering. You are keening in anticipation.

Now we are ready.

See what you do me?

Bless you, my love,
JEM

Recovering Matthew Bailey's Remains

On the afternoon two days removed from the storm, the winds had subsided enough that Bartholomew and Nate took Nate's pirogue out to see if they could see a sign of the oyster boat. The water where Bartholomew had triangulated that the craft went down was not particularly deep—maybe fifteen feet or so—according to Nate, who had fished the area many times. However, it did not take long for them to call off the search as the water was still so murky and muddy from silt pouring from recently tilled land along Horlbeck Creek. Their visibility was limited to a foot or two beneath the surface. Indeed they were wasting their time trying to sight the boat, but before they returned to the dock they would try one more thing. Nate brought out the long pole that he had brought with him—the pole that he used to shake the mature pecans off the highest branches of his trees—and he probed the bottom with it, hoping to hit the boat's hull. His efforts were fruitless, probably, Bartholomew surmised, because the currents had moved the boat down the shore toward the harbor.

After two more days of calm winds, the silt settled and the waters were about as clear as they ever got. Nate and Bartholomew made another attempt to find Matthew Bailey. Soon after daylight they again paddled out to the spot Bartholomew had triangulated, but this time they rowed slowly parallel to the shore, keeping the same distance from shore. After an hour filled with false sightings of the craft, driftwood floating on the surface, they finally spotted the top of the mast just inches below the surface. The oyster boat had drifted about 150 yards down the bank after it sank.

Bartholomew eased over the side of the pirogue into the cold water and tied a sturdy rope as securely as he could to the mast. Clamoring back aboard and nearly tipping the low-sided pirogue, Bartholomew bitched and moaned about how cold the water was as Nate paddled to shore. Each had a change of dry clothes back at the dock, but it would be awhile yet before they returned to the wharf.

They paddled into shallow water where several cypress trees were growing. After winding the rope one revolution around a tree for leverage, they put their backs into pulling on the rope—not with really any hope of moving the waterlogged and water-filled boat to the shore, but to tell Mary Assumpta they had tried. Finally the line was wound several times around the sturdy cypress that sat a foot or so off the bank. The boat should be secured from drifting any more until they could return with a plan for getting it to the shore.

After a dogged trip back to the dock paddling against the outgoing tide, they changed into dry clothes, secured the pirogue to the pier, and thankfully rode in the Bessie-pulled wagon the two miles back to Billington Farm. As they rode slowly—Bessie only had one speed—Nate suggested that they would likely have to use a pulley system if they hoped to make any progress in winching the oyster boat to shore. Accordingly, Nate dug into the rusty tools in his barn until he found two pulleys that he had last used to haul hogs (and deer) off the ground for gutting, skinning, butchering, and aging. In fact, the dirt floor of the barn was stained a dark rusty red below the cross-beam where the animals were hung and bled out.

After a dinner of Audrey Lee's breakfast leftovers of bacon, biscuits, and honey, they hitched Bessie up again and returned to the unwelcomed task that awaited them even if they were successful.

Using the two pulleys, one attached to the mast where it was fixed to the boat and the other tied around the cypress tree, little by little they hauled the boat to the shore. For the most part, the boat was not much damaged as it was made of cypress itself, but Matthew Bailey's body was not in the craft.

With the sun beginning to set and nothing good to report, they returned to give Mary Assumpta the news.

Matthew Conroy Bailey's body was never found.

Dead in Absentia

It took a month for the oyster boat to dry out, for Mary Assumpta to patch the sail, and for Bartholomew to recaulk the open strakes with tar-laced rope. Two days after the work was done, anxious to return to his Sweet Potato Vine responsibilities, Bartholomew set sail back across the Wando River for Charleston.

He carried with him a letter signed by Mary Assumpta and witnessed by Nate and Audrey Lee Billington identifying

Bartholomew Jennings as her agent to petition the South Carolina Court of Common Pleas in Charleston requesting that the court declare Matthew Conroy Bailey as *dead in absentia* since Bartholomew had personally observed Bailey drown as the oyster boat with him aboard slipped beneath waves in the storm of April 9, 1864.

In a sign of pressures of many such pleas since the war began, the court issued a judgment to that effect immediately so that the disposition of Matthew's last will and testament could move forward.

After a week of reestablishing the Sweet Potato Vine process, Bartholomew, pleased to be able to continue his work with Simon Billington, delivered four runaway slaves to the Billington farm on Horlbeck Creek. At least as important to Bartholomew, he also delivered to Mary Assumpta the court's disposition of "dead in absentia" and Matthew Bailey's last will and testament, which the court order had procured for Bartholomew from the Bank of Charleston.

Before Bartholomew had departed Charleston, Mary Assumpta already had begun the next steps that would be required of her. Once she recognized that it would be up to her to decide on how to develop a plan to handle her father's assets in the environment of the war, she wrote to her brother John suggesting that their father's last will and testament not be opened until the war was done and John had returned to Charleston. She also wrote that she would ask Bartholomew Jennings to securely close up the house and live in the apartment above the surgery until the end of the war at no cost to him other than maintaining it as necessary.

She would also direct Bartholomew to sell any perishable goods in Bailey's Remedies & Sundries, keeping the proceeds for himself, and then boarding up the doors and windows until the family, including James, could decide on the business's future after the war.

Memorials

The last duty Mary Assumpta assumed was to plan a memorial for her father and brother Andrew Ryan. After talking to Bartholomew, her confidant, and Nate, her advisor, she asked Bartholomew to ask Reverend Simon Billington if he would officiate at a small service in his church. Mary Assumpta knew that Simon and her father had grown close through the secrets they shared through the Sweet Potato Vine.

Bartholomew and Reverend Simon planned a short service and were very cautious about who was invited so that sensitive identities were kept protected. For anyone who might ask, her father and brother Andrew Ryan had developed a special relationship with Reverend Simon after Andrew Ryan convinced his father to sell vegetables, fruits, meats, fish, and other sundries along Clifford's Alley, the traditional Negro section of Charleston. This was the truth, just not the complete truth.

Reverend Simon took it upon himself to visit the Baileys' longtime parish priest Father Quigley to ask if he would say a few words. Now retired, Father Quigley enthusiastically agreed to share in the service. Perhaps the most diverse assemblage ever to assemble in Charleston gathered at Emanuel African Methodist Episcopal Church for a midmorning celebration of the lives of two Southerners who not only loved the South but also whose humanity had extended to all of Charleston's citizens, and many citizens-to-be once the war was done.

Mary Assumpta thought to herself as she shook many hands on this warm May morning, *Andrew Ryan and Father would really appreciate the show of brotherhood this day. Maybe, just maybe, this will be an omen for Charleston's future.*

Mary Assumpta returned to a reasonable semblance of rational thought and actions necessary to plant the spring's common gardens with Nate and Audrey Lee. She knew that she was at a crossroads. The war was inching closer, and she was more alone than she had ever been in her entire life. Decisions affecting the Bailey clan were in her hands. She needed James's advice. She had decided to stay here on the farm although she and Colin could have moved back to Charleston. She knew this farm was the place where James would return. Mary Assumpta kenned that he would find his peace here, not in Charleston, at least not immediately on his return. She would stay. She would be his rock, his sure port in the storm of his recovery.

To survive and keep moving forward with maybe a little success here and there was her vision for Horlbeck Creek Farm.

But down deep in her soul Mary Assumpta knew her life must be more than soldiering on in the face of adversity until James returned–if not for herself for Colin. Remarkably, Colin recognized the need first and decided that a practical joke was just what his mother needed on April Fools Day.

Divine Laughter

There is a word in the Southern vernacular whose origin scholars attribute to the fourteenth-century word *pismire*—a word for an ant that predictably became *piss ant*. In the South, *pissant*—always one word—is indeed literally used to describe small biting ants that in the scheme of things are of no consequence, unlike their more vicious cousins the fire ants. Metaphorically, *pissant* can be used affectionately to describe a cute or precocious child, or derisively to define a person who, as Nate would say, "doesn't use the sense God gave a pissant."

April 2, 1864
Horlbeck Creek

My Dearest Lover,

I don't think I ever told you this about myself, but when I was a child, April Fools' Day was my favorite day of the year. I expect you can imagine why. With older brothers, it was my chance to get back at them for the pranks they had pulled on their curly redheaded little sister. Well, little did I know that Colin had inherited my Irish precociousness and fondness for a good practical joke.

The little pissant must have been planning for a while his antics to take my mind off the war. Below is what your son did to his mother yesterday—if I can keep from laughing long enough to write it.

This happened yesterday in the late morning, just before dinnertime. I had missed Colin during the morning but was not worried. I was in the barn busy sorting through the dried butter beans we'd saved from last year's crop, removing the smallest beans and those the weevils had gotten to. I had been diligently about my chore for more than an hour, letting my mind wander to bedroom thoughts of you, when Colin came running up to the barn where I had spread the beans on an old door set on sawhorses.

"Mama! Mama! Mama!" he yelled as he ran toward me. "Boomer's tangled with a bobcat, and he is hurt bad, Mama."

I jumped up and spilled the lapful of beans I had just sorted onto the dirt floor. "Where is he, Colin? We have to get his cuts cleaned out and put some turpentine on them right away."

"He's down by the creek, but he won't come to me. He's hurt real bad. Come on, Mama." As he said this, he grabbed my hand, emphasizing his apparent distress. Did I see crocodile tears on his face? Maybe.

As we ran toward the creek, Colin would stop every fifty yards or so and ask me, "Listen, Mama. Do you hear Boomer crying?" His question was asked with all the conviction of a Methodist preacher welcoming new converts to the kingdom on Baptism Sunday. Little pissant.

"Mama, he might have tried to crawl toward home, so we have to listen real careful."

Colin, leading me by the proverbial nose, would change direction again, go a few yards, listen again, and then change directions again and again. We did this enough times that, truth be told, we were nowhere near the creek.

Finally I intervened, thinking Colin was so upset that he was just irrational. After all, I thought, he is just an innocent ten-year-old little boy. And something like this could scar him for the rest of his life.

Was I ever wrong about the innocence of your son! Anyway, I took his hand and told him, "Colin, let's just head in the direction of the creek, and you can show me where you last saw Boomer. Then we can go from there. Okay?"

"Okay, Mama. But let's hurry. Boomer's hurt real bad." Crocodile tears again. Did I detect the beginnings of a grin too? Little conniver.

With me leading the way and holding Colin's hand, it took us ten minutes longer than usual to get to the creek as Colin had led us out of the way so far with his "stop and listen" tactics. Finally, I could see Boomer's small outline at the base of a big sweet gum tree we often picnicked under. He was lying very still, and blood covered most of his side and belly. Except, as I got a little closer, I began to think that maybe it was not blood at all, and this was some kind of trick—never even thinking that this was April Fools' Day.

Just as I was about to cuff Colin about the ear for taking me away from my bean-sorting chore, I smelled something that smelled a lot like fried chicken, accompanied by the definite sound of giggling. Colin now had a full-blown grin on his face, and before I could say anything, Nate and Audrey Lee jumped out from behind the tree, and they and Colin in unison shouted, "April Fool!" At which point Boomer popped up and leaped up into my arms, coating me with his "blood," which I quickly deduced was a jar of my canned tomato sauce.

Damned pissants, all of them! But oh how we needed the laughter that engulfed us all for the next five minutes.

As it turned out, Colin had planned most every part of his little joke on his mama and had had little trouble convincing Nate and Audrey Lee to be part of his gang. Boomer, of course, was an enthusiastic member and played his role to perfection thanks to Colin's working with him every night last week. I had wondered why Colin, right before he went to sleep, would tell Boomer to "Lay down and stay" while he would get up and tell me, "I'm going to the outhouse one last time." Almost every time, Boomer would be right where Colin had left him, and Colin would give him a bite of corn bread. At least that is what I now surmise from finding corn bread crumbles on Colin's bed every morning. But I was beginning to worry that Colin might have a urinary infection.

He did—of the pissant variety!

Oh, JEM, I have not had so much fun since you left. I hope I have told this story well enough that it will bring laughter to you and maybe to Father Michael too.

I have thought a lot since April Fools' Day just how divine is love and laughter in making our lives complete as the Almighty intended. I will silently pray that you may find a little laughter from time to time to go with all my love that is yours

Now and forevermore,

Red

CHAPTER 40

Thunderheads on the Horizon

In war, soldiers live on omens. Victory is found in the hawk's dazzling plunge to sink its death talons into the unsuspecting squirrel's spine. Death to the enemy surely follows a murder of crows alighting at dusk. And most feared is the death sound of the call of the owl at false dawn. As the victors write history, so too do they give meaning to omens.

The war that had been fought before July 3–4, 1863, was as different from what was to come as the steady morning rain is from the thunderheads and their frequent violent parturition of tornadoes on hot southern afternoons. If there were omens assigned to the almost simultaneous Union victories at Gettysburg and Vicksburg, and surely there were, the politicians and generals on both sides of the Mason–Dixon Line saw them the same.

The South was defeated on those two days. Thunderheads were on the horizon; that much was clear.

The only question was how soon and by what means the end would come.

Surgeon's Diary

April 15, 1864
General Lee's Encampment
Orange, Virginia

This evening, General Lee's adjutant, Lieutenant Colonel Walter H. Taylor, informed the medical officers (we are the last to find out such things) of an address that General Ulysses Grant made to the Army of the Potomac two days ago. I will try to record it as accurately as I can remember.

According to Taylor, an ANV infiltrator heard Grant's address. Dressed as a Yankee, the private had lived among the Yankees for more than a week, never staying with any unit long enough to arouse too much suspicion. When asked about his accent, he always playfully overemphasized his drawl, saying that he lived just across the border in Maryland. According to the intelligence he brought to General Lee, Grant shouted at his men at one point that the war that Lincoln had demanded that he pursue against the South would be total war. They were to kill the soldiers, burn the cities, houses, farms, and barns, and rape the land. According to the infiltrator, roars of approval ripped through the Yankee ranks.

"Gentlemen," Colonel Taylor finished, "in short, your jobs are likely to get a lot uglier over the next year. Be prepared for the worst."

As Taylor reached for the tent flap, Claude

said, "Colonel, before you go, can you tell us anything about medical supplies? We are desperately low, and there has been miserably little resupply over the winter. Is there no ether to be had?"

"Doctor, these men are as tough as any soldiers ever to go to war. They will bear the pain of the medical tent just as they have dealt with it on the battlefield. I will wire Richmond again to request ether and bandages, but as our ether gave out before Gettysburg, I expect no more of that. We can hope for bandages."

We talked a bit about coming battles after Taylor left. The tactics of total war scared us more for our families than for ourselves. We agreed that if there had been a surprising aspect of the war so far, it was that our families had not been much affected by it. Apparently that was about to change. Each person left the tent not with worries of war occupying their thoughts but with worries of whether or not the Union onslaught would bring Grant's armies near our homes and families.

I expect I am worried more than most of my colleagues as Charleston, having initiated this fight, is squarely in the sights of Union cannonry.

JEM

Trepidation and Home

April 15, 1864
Horlbeck Creek Farm

My Dearest Husband,

It has been so long since I used that precious word husband that it sounds like music to my ears just to write it. It has been a long winter (aren't they all?) here on the creek. Our correspondence since you all finally set Orange as your winter headquarters has been so ordinary that one might think we are merely lovers temporarily separated by family business concerns instead of war. I have thought on this and find it interesting how the mind can put away the most horrific past events when even a semblance of peacefulness finds its way to us.

As the days warmed up in mid-March, our minds here on the farm turned inevitably toward the commonplace tasks of readying the fields and garden for planting. And those thoughts, I guess aided by the rare regularity of our correspondence, brought a sense of normality. An example:

One afternoon Colin had taken Boomer out, hoping to kill a rabbit for tomorrow's supper. I expected them back toward dusk dark, and I was sitting in the rocking chair in the front room (perhaps even napping a bit in the rocking chair) when he returned much earlier than I expected. He slammed open the back door, and before he could ask when supper would be ready, I, without thinking, called out, "JEM, is that you?" I was quickly brought back to reality when Boomer jumped into my lap and lay down for his stroking. Even so, that comforting fantasy has remained with me since that day, though Colin continues to joke about it, accusing me of taking a few nips of the medicinal whiskey I keep in the cupboard. JEM, he is growing up so fast.

The winter for Colin, with little to do except mending harnesses, feeding ol Jake, and occasionally taking him for a walk over to Nate and Audrey Lee's or down to the pier, has been the perfect time for his studies, which must give way almost totally to fieldwork from late March until the heat of July kills everything except the okra. I think you will be surprised at his skills in mathematics. I sure don't remember attempting geometry when I was ten years old. Math and science come easily for him, in no small part due to Nate's practical knowledge of both areas. We saw Nate and Audrey Lee usually twice a week during winter—once for Sunday dinner at their house and once for a midweek early supper here at our house. There were plenty of opportunities to teach with Nate posing questions and observations to Colin about the natural world or about the processes of how things, mechanical and natural, work.

As you might expect with Father gone, our news from Charleston is limited to Bartholomew's trips, which have dwindled to maybe once monthly as the authorities have become wise to the workings of the Sweet Potato Vine. In Bartholomew's words, "The fear in Charleston is worse than the trepidation a Baptist preacher feels coming out of Miss Geneviève's 'boardinghouse'!"

According to Bartholomew, Charleston lives with a fear that the Union navy will sail en masse up the harbor to bombard the city into ruins. They have not been successful yet, but the threat is so great that Charlestonians constantly live in anticipation that it could happen any day. Nate says he would expect any attack on the city to come by land as the mouth of the harbor is so small, and the Union is satisfied for now with the effect of its barricade, which has taken Charleston out of the war for all practical purposes. I will be interested in what your thoughts are.

Of course we are not directly affected yet, but should travel across the harbor be shut down, we would face disaster with our crops, so I guess we shall just see. We cannot wait for planting, which will commence next week according to Nate, to Colin's great disappointment.

Darling, my candle is burning low, and my eyes are heavy. It is time for me to tuck your mathematician son and his dog in for the night and then make my way to bed as well.

I do genuinely pray that this prolonged absence of major battles in the east is perhaps a sign that peace is near, but I fear my prayers have no more substance than inclinations. Darling, I tell myself that regardless of how long the fighting continues, I cannot miss you more than I do at this moment, but I know that I am being delusional. Just the same, please live in the confidence that no woman has ever loved her husband more than I love you.

Now as before and always, all my love,
Red

All Necessary Viciousness

April 15, 1864
General Lee's Encampment
Orange, Virginia

My Dearest Red,

I know it has been awhile since my last letter. I hope that my procrastination has not burdened you unnecessarily, and I do hope that this missive has arrived in short order.

Red, we are busily readying for the next campaign, although most probably the attackers will be dressed in blue and marching to the cadence of the "Battle Hymn of the Republic." From what little I have been able to glean from campfire gossip, General Lee's strategy will be to defend Richmond until peace can be sought with the Yankees. The boys in butternut and gray are likely to be formed into defensive positions, still as the rabbit that hears the hawk's wings in the pines. They will spring their trap on those Yankees. As the saying goes, "I have told you more than I know," as neither tactics nor strategy often make their way to the surgeons' tent.

Regardless of the plans of either side, I pray that the end of this conflict will come mercifully and quickly.

I expect that by now you have read the news that Lincoln has appointed General Ulysses S. Grant as the commander of all Union forces. This week, we were briefed by officers of General Lee's immediate staff about what to expect from Grant. A Confederate plant in the Army of the Potomac returned recently to relay the news to General Lee that Grant has been directed by Lincoln to employ "total war" upon the Southland on all fronts and with all necessary viciousness to bring our nation to its knees in total surrender, begging for mercy.

As for my surgical colleagues and me, we expect that little will change in the surgery tent or in post-op in this next campaign, whatever its tactics. Pain is pain and death is death. There is no nobility found in the blood at the surgeon's feet. Death and pain are equally contemptible whether obtained in the glory of Chancellorsville or the ignominy of Gettysburg.

However, we are prepared to employ the triage process. If anything, our team is overtrained. The spiritual member of the group sends his kind regards too, emphatically demanding that I let "his fellow redhead born in the land of God and worshipping the only 'true' faith" know that her priest is saying the rosary for her daily! Actually, I have suggested to Michael that I think it would be good if he wrote to you himself. He keeps so much in, and he might even give you a bit of insight into my own well-being. Michael has practiced with us so much that I do believe he has picked up enough skills to relieve us in the surgery should it ever be necessary. He is a constant questioner about any procedure or anatomical feature he does not completely understand. I think his "queries" have actually sharpened our own skills.

As the weather has improved in northern Virginia, many of the men on French leave have returned to us. If they brought with them even the smallest contributions of food or libation from home, they are spared any discipline other than a tongue-in-cheek lashing. Our officers are too glad to have more bodies in uniform to inflict any significant punishment, and really their compatriots understand their motives because, officer or not, we are all besieged with the same feelings of longing for our homes and loved ones.

I shall leave it right there. I could write all night about the camp goings-on and only cover a smidgen of how the men overcome their boredom and prepare to fight all at the same time.

Once I know a definite location for our next fight, I will write again. In the meantime, I trust you will forgive me when I must put my thoughts of you aside to take up the scalpel or the saw. I pray that I shall be

In your arms again soon,
JEM

Prophylactics
April 27, 1864
Orange, Virginia

Captain James Merriweather and Chaplain Michael O'Malley met around the freshly stoked cook fire faithfully every Wednesday morning at gray dawn just to talk. No one was around but the cooks, and they were too busy trying to figure how they would perform another culinary miracle with the derisory small rations they were provided.

The first thing to go on the fire was the coffeepot, and soon the hot steaming chicory-laced, dark-caramel-colored potion was being poured into battered enamel cups extended at the ends of arms. The coffee was always poured by Corporal Robbie Robinson from Cold Harbor, Virginia, who weekly had to endure the "question of the day" before he could resume his duties after the coffee was poured.

"Robinson, where in Virginia do you call your home?"

To which Robinson faithfully answered, "Sirs, it is the same place as it was last week at this time—Cold Harbor, Virginia."

"And on what body of water can we find Cold Harbor should we desire to visit when this war ends?"

"Sirs, it does not reside on or near a body of water."

"Chaplain O'Malley, I think we may have discovered a spy in our midst," Merriweather would offer.

"Do you think he may be poisoning our fine army?" O'Malley would respond.

"No. Can't be that, because poison would surely make his beans taste better!"

"Robinson, see if you cannot find a more suitable answer by next week, or we may have to report you to our intelligence officer."

"That's a good one, sirs—intelligence officer!" Robinson

laughed to himself as he refreshed their cups and made his way to his duties to await the same routine, only slightly altered, at the next predawn Wednesday morning meeting.

These meetings about nothing and everything and anything were the best prophylactic they had found for keeping the black dog of worry and depression away from their psyches. The sessions began soon after Merriweather's return to his unit more than a year ago, following his reassignment of duties to Richmond during the winter lull of 1863, when he was obliged to "get his head on straight," as O'Malley referred to Merriweather's orders.

Their conversations began with a question, an overheard comment, an observation, a reflection, or a position on an issue past, present, or future. It really did not matter the form, for it would consistently prompt an hour-long rambling discourse. On this Wednesday, April 27, 1864, Merriweather began with a question not typical of most Wednesdays, but really not atypical either, asking O'Malley if he had had a chance to read Mary Assumpta's "April Fools' letter" that Merriweather had passed along at his wife's suggestion.

"James, that colleen of yours seems back to normal based on that letter. That is a relief. And Colin ... the lad seems to possess a rare gift of unique intellect and a sense of humor. I just pray that this struggle to which we give our energies will not one day sap his extraordinary abilities. He sure seems to have lifted his mother's spirits with his little caper."

"Michael, I know Mary Assumpta well enough to know that things are not as normal as she described in the letter, and I expect Nate and Audrey Lee killed a precious chicken for lunch that day. Nonetheless, I really enjoyed her telling of the story.

"It worries me about what effect this total war we hear about might have on the farms of Horlbeck Creek. With its being so close to the most desirous Union prize of Charleston, I fear a stray group of Union sailors might decide to explore up the creek. What disaster they would wreak on the utterly helpless farms they would find.

"And even if no such events were to happen, is it inevitable that they will experience severe shortages? I just don't know how to keep my mind from going there."

"James, you are forgetting Benjamin's advice to worry about what is directly in front of you. I know about your worries. I feel them too, about my parishioners in Richmond, knowing that the city very well may be leveled when the Union army enters it.

"Enough of such talk this morning. Let's talk a bit about a more straightforward subject—whether this war is a fulfillment of the book of Revelation."

And so they went on through two more cups of coffee until Mother Nature called, and then they rose to return to their tents for morning ablutions.

"Michael," Merriweather called to his friend, "thanks for another good session. May God bless you until this time next week."

"And you, my brother. I wonder if Robinson will come up with a better name for his hometown?"

"And spoil our repartee? Never!"

And so another Wednesday began. The war dragged on to the consternation of politicians and the public above the Mason–Dixon Line and to the fading hope of a return to better days to the people below it.

Better days would be a long time coming.

Familiar Fears

May 1, 1864
General Lee's Encampment
Near Chancellorsville

Dearest Red,

Since my last letter we have moved the twenty miles or so east, and we are now camped in the familiar environs of Chancellorsville. From the first step my mount took, I was accompanied by the familiar sound of the swoosh of bats' wings as they leapt at me from overhanging tree limbs and flew before my eyes to reside in my gut, flapping their unholy wings. I smelled whiskey on their rodent breaths as they escaped my insides and returned to their darkened haunts.

Darling, I know these hallucinations are conjured by my own unconsciousness. However, if it makes any sense at all, that I know their source makes them even more fearsome. On any day, the command of my mind is often all the influence I am able to muster amid the hellishness of time that is measured by one more soldier's life dripping off my surgeon's table.

The retreat into my unconscious self just at the thought of battle days before it commences has me wondering how I will perform when I am needed most.

Pray hard for me, my darling. Until we left Orange, I was sure the black dog was at bay for good. But now, instead, I have learned that he is but a single event—a miniscule sensation away. During my visit last year with Mother and Father, Father told me about my grandmother's long and laborious trek from her darkness into the light as my grandfather patiently guided her back to sanity. Now I understand.

Pray patiently for me, darling. I am on a journey. I see that now, and I also see that I likely always shall be. Yet I have several tonics on which to depend should I falter: (1) our every Wednesday morning talks, (2) seeking out Michael, as I shall tonight, for his counsel and instruction, and (3) more importantly, I think, the fact that I have found a healing as personal with me as the malaise, and it resides in my mind—my written words to you, my beloved.

Pray gently for me, my love. Do not let your prayers be burdened, but let them be light in the knowledge that the hand of the Almighty has been at work in me this day.

Yours in more ways than I understand,
JEM

CHAPTER 41

Grant Enters the Field

May 4, 1864

Rapidan River, Virginia

It is not unfair to say that few other Southerners outside the army had heard of Ulysses S. Grant. For that matter, the Northerners who knew of him were found mainly within the confines of Washington, DC.

Such lack of renown bothered Grant not a whit. He was a military man. Five feet eight inches tall, one hundred and thirty-five pounds, single-minded, Grant did not have *retreat* in his vocabulary. His tenacity and victory at Vicksburg on July 4, 1863, would, a few months later, see him appointed by President Lincoln as commander of all Union forces.

Grant's unwillingness to retreat even in the face of unwinnable odds would cost his army thousands of unnecessary deaths, but it also forced the Army of Northern Virginia to adopt a single-minded defensive strategy for the remainder of the war, unlike the creative forays that had characterized Robert E. Lee's approach to war. Even the horrific defeat at Gettysburg was strategically remarkable, even in the face of the tactical failures that turned the battle and ultimately the war in favor of the Union.

On May 4, 1864, General Grant sent his forces across the

Rapidan River into the heart of Virginia, and though his ultimate victory over the Army of Northern Virginia would be very long in coming, on this day he seized the strategic initiative. He drove his men incessantly. He pounded the enemy even to the loss of thousands of his own men. But unlike his counterparts before him, he did not know the word *withdraw.*

On May 5, 1864, Grant commenced what would come to be known as the Overland Campaign in the woods known as the Wilderness near the small town of Locust Grove, Virginia. On the first day he lost 17,500 men to Lee's forces.

The story is told that Grant, after that tragic first day's battle, retired to his tent, threw himself down on his cot, and wept over the loss of Union lives with absolutely nothing to show for it. A number of officers new to Grant's command and standing near his tent had expected their leader to drink and rage himself into a stupor, so they were stunned at the sounds of sobbing instead.

As the group of officers moved away, either from embarrassment or to give their commander privacy, they whispered conspiratorially among themselves, wondering if the new commander of the Army of the Potomac would follow past unsuccessful Virginia forays by retreating back across the Rapidan River and regrouping.

The next morning, the story continues that Grant emerged from his tent not forlorn and disheveled but well-groomed and resolute as he gathered his officers around him. While his conversation that follows is inexact, it is accurate in the tone of his dialogue, if it could be called that. It was more a sermon than a discussion.

"I expect that some of you expect me to—maybe even would be happy to speculate that we will now—retreat and regroup. Shall we retreat to consider our losses, tend our wounded, and develop a new strategy to fight that gray-bearded wraith riding tall on that gray ghost horse?

"Retreat? Never. We shall advance and advance and advance if it takes all summer to defeat those detestable Rebels. I assure you that General Lee is not a supernatural being. He puts on his pants just like the rest of you, eats beans like the rest of you, and yes, shits like the rest of you. And a Minié ball will take him out of his saddle just like it will any other man."

It is unclear whether that story is true or merely apocryphal. In the end, it would not matter, for Grant would prove its truth again and again until surrender came at Appomattox Court House eleven months later.

Hell and Death

May 5–6, 1864

The Battle of the Wilderness

Chancellorsville, Virginia

Like Major General Joseph Hooker's strategy a year before, Grant's Army of the Potomac's attack through the wilderness of Chancellorsville meant that the Union army's advantages of numbers and weapons were negated almost entirely by the brambles, briars, and brush that became the stretch of land outside Chancellorsville, Virginia, once the trees had been cleared for timber. A forest would have been relatively straightforward; the Wilderness was hell.

On May 6, the battle was step-by-step blind fighting and often at close quarters, although few casualties ever saw the enemy, the thickets were so dense.

Implausibly, the fighting on this day gave birth to another antagonist as a brushfire from a sparking flint broke out in the dry-as-kindling leaves and twigs on the forest blanket. As the day ended in the Wilderness, the beast spread with an enthusiasm for the destruction that lay before it. Deadly, all-consuming, ruthless, and wanton, it fed upon the bodies of the wounded and dying, caring not a whit for birthrights or families, or politics or rank, leaving in its wake little except an asphyxiating stink of brimstone and charred, unrecognizable flesh.

The two armies that fought that day, in what was a draw at best, would remember it for the rest of their lives. They would try unsuccessfully to forget the voices of wounded comrades and enemies lying on the wilderness floor. They would be unable to remove from the mind's eye pictures of men in blue and gray wounded and unable to crawl to safety, calling to their friends for rescue and to their mothers for absolution as the raging hellfire raced toward them. But no help came, only death riding on a pale and fiery horse.

Cold Death
May 31–June 12, 1864
In and Around Richmond, Virginia

In the six weeks following the beginning of the Overland Campaign's Battle of the Wilderness, Grant and Lee faced off at Spotsylvania, North Anna, and Cold Harbor.

In the Overland Campaign, there were few definitive victories by either army. Casualties were devastating with a total of almost eighty thousand dead or wounded across both armies, with Grant's army bearing the brunt with nearly forty-nine thousand men removed from action by death or injury. Lee suffered much smaller numbers, losing twenty-nine thousand killed or wounded. The South and North's casualties were both at almost 50 percent of their armies. And although Grant lost nearly twice as many fighters, his personnel resources were abundant, so he could throw men into the battle until Lee ran out of men and, therefore, the will to fight.

The Overland Campaign officially ended after nine days at Cold Harbor, giving Lee his last major victory of the war and leaving Grant questioning his strategy of sending men to sure death against the defenses of the South. Cold Harbor was afforded the distinction of the bloodiest standoff of the war, especially for the Union army. At Cold Harbor, Virginia, at dawn on June 3, 1864, Grant threw 108,000 Union soldiers against Lee's 59,000 Rebels manning the impregnable seven miles of Southern defensive fortifications. Grant's frontal assault resulted in almost 7,000 casualties in the first hour, and some said most of those were lost in the first ten minutes of the battle.

The Overland Campaign was over. Though sustaining heavy losses, the Army of the Potomac had pushed Lee to within sight of Richmond. Grant's relentlessness meant that Lee was now forced to fight a defensive war. And as Cold Harbor demonstrated, Lee was certainly a military strategist capable of executing a defensive strategy and causing heavy losses for his foe. Yet Lee and Grant knew that it was not Lee's strong suit, and as the only tactic left for Lee to employ, it would spell the end of the Confederacy sooner or later. If the nine days of fruitless Union assault on the seven miles of Confederate defenses were any indicator, it would be much later.

After Grant had had enough of the slaughter of his army and withdrew from Cold Harbor, Lee moved to Petersburg, twenty miles south of Richmond, to protect the precious railroad center.

Capturing Richmond would have been significant, but many governments have moved operations from a capital in time of war. Capturing the railroad center was far more strategically critical to Grant, and its defenses to Lee, than was Richmond. If Grant were to destroy the railroad center with its five rail lines and well-built roads, the war would be over, as supplies to Richmond and the Army of Northern Virginia would be cut to practically naught.

On June 18, 1864, after several unsuccessful Union attempts at capturing Petersburg, Grant began prosecuting what would ultimately be a nine-month siege of Lee's army at the town. Grant's strategy was to encircle Petersburg, cutting off supplies to the Army of Northern Virginia from the south. For the Confederates it was nine months of hanging in and hanging on, hoping the citizens of the North would tire of a seemingly never-ending war.

The siege was tedious and tiring. For both armies, only drilling, salt pork, bad beans, and terrible coffee broke the boredom at the rear. At Petersburg, ennui was the commanders' worst enemy, and its grip on the psyche of officers and enlisted men alike would only grow in the next nine months of Grant's siege.

Quiet Your Mind

May 15, 1864
Cold Harbor, Virginia

Dear Mary Assumpta,

I am writing this letter at James's request. A little more than ten days ago, following the Battle of the Wilderness, James experienced a kind of amnesia, which he and I believe is closely associated with his depression.

On May 5–6, the Army of the Potomac attacked General Lee's forces through the area near

Chancellorsville known as "the Wilderness"—called that because, unlike the farm fields around it, it is overgrown with briars and brambles, and bushes and small trees that have grown up over the last few years after the area was cut for timber and just left alone. It is the kind of woods where you cannot see more than ten yards ahead of you and is in essence a killing field.

We were prepared for a large number of casualties and successfully implemented our triage process based on experiences at the same spot a year earlier. However, what we could not anticipate was the uncharacteristic lack of rainfall during the last two weeks of April and the first week of May. The undergrowth was a tinderbox waiting for the right situation to ignite it. During the fighting, a bit of unseen sparking flint from a soldier's rifle dropped to the ground and began to smolder in the dry leaves and small branches.

As evening approached, the battle dwindled down to only an occasional shot as the armies retreated. But soon we saw a column of smoke rising from the middle of the undergrowth, and then as the night encroached we could see orange flames rising toward the sky, racing across the ground, and consuming everything in their path, including the wounded from both armies. This awfulness went on until a God-sent thunderstorm doused the flames.

Mary Assumpta, the only thing that survived that hellfire was the stink of burned human flesh, which lingered all night on the damp air of the rainstorm. The next morning when fighting resumed and I resumed my triage duties, James was noticeably absent from his surgical table. During a short break in the multitude of wounded descending on us, I walked to look for James, fearing that perhaps a sniper had taken his life at first dawn. Shooting our surgeons is a prized sniper tactic as it creates such a conflagration among the men that morale suffers for days.

Thankfully, I found him about thirty yards from his tent, walking an almost perfect circle around it, talking to himself as he walked, and asking anyone he encountered, "Who am I? Won't someone please tell me how I got here?"

I walked carefully and slowly toward him, holding a cup of water in my left hand, with my right hand extended to encourage a shake. "James," I said to him, "come with me back to your tent and let's lay you down. You have been up all night long caring for the wounded, and I know you need to sleep just a little."

"Padre, did I do good? I heard so many boys crying for their mothers, and I could not get to them because of the fire," James pled for assurance.

"You did really good, my son. But now, you have to rest so that you can help some more of our boys so they can get home to their mothers."

"Is my mother okay? Did this fire spread all the way to Richmond? Oh God, I am so worried about Mama." Tears now streamed down his sooty face.

"Your mama is just fine, James. The fire was just right here in Chancellorsville, and God sent a rainstorm during the night to put it out. See yonder? All you can see is a little smoke."

With that assurance, I was able to lead him to his tent, where I found his precious stash of laudanum that he kept for the wounded who could get no relief any other way. He drank the two drops I dissolved in a bit of water and slept the rest of the day on May 6 and through the night.

I stayed with him as much as I could that day—in between ministering to the dying and performing my triage duties during the day's battle. Just at dark, James roused and said he was hungry and thirsty. I took care of those needs, and he dropped quickly back into his opioid stupor.

At morning, he woke me with, "Michael, what the hell are you doing in my tent? Are you okay?"

I told him about the last two nights and a day, but he remembered nothing: not surgery on the fifth, or wandering around his tent, or my ministrations. However, he knew perfectly well where he was, who he was, and what his job was.

I have read that this is called a fugue state where one loses all touch with reality—usually as a result of some trauma—only to regain one's touch with reality a few hours or days later, remembering nothing that occurred during the amnesia.

Mary Assumpta, after I talked with James about what had happened, everything I observed about him convinced me that he was unharmed and able to perform all his regular duties. Of course, I will keep as close a watch on him as I can, and I have asked Drs. Paisley and McGuire to seek James out from time to time to check on him, so I believe he is in good hands.

One of the best things that could happen to him now is for you to write him a long letter about the day-to-day goings-on on the farm. He needs to see that there is another reality awaiting him when this all-consuming fighting is over. There will be nothing better to quiet his mind. Pray, too, that the end is soon—for all our sakes.

Yours in Jesus Christ, our Lord and Savior,
Father Michael O'Malley

Move or Die

It was June 30, 1864, and Abraham Whetstone had had enough of Washington, DC. The boardinghouse of Mary Skirett was good enough, and Mary was a no-nonsense landlord who saw no reason to ask questions as long as the rent was paid on time.

But it was the politicians who just chafed his ass, acting so much like Union army commanders to suit his taste that he knew he would end up killing one of them if he did not get himself away from the temptation. He had no moral compunction against killing self-important well-off politicians. In fact, he would rather enjoy pissing on the corpse of a congressman in his fine house in the Georgetown area, but there were too many soldiers in DC. Too many watchful eyes, too much risk.

As the two criminals packed their meager belongings on their horses, Whetstone thought back to the tales he had heard in the Wayward Sailors Pub during their art adventure of

Annapolis. The pub was a simple affair—a nautical theme. What else would you expect in Annapolis? Whetstone and Little had been frequent figures around suppertime at the pub since they'd arrived on the Wednesday before Easter. Most nights they had fried fish and beer.

As they had waited for the Easter Spectacular, as he still thought of it, a story was told by an old and grizzled fisherman who ought to have known that of which he spoke. He said that a shark has to always keep moving or it will die. *I am like that,* Whetstone thought. *Move or die. And it is time to move on from DC.*

So on no particular morning, and for no specific reason other than his nervous system was on high alert, he and Davey Little rode south and west toward Kentucky.

"Abe? Why the hell are we going to Kaintucky? Ain't even no war goin' on there."

"That's the point, you little shit. Kentucky'll give us a little time to hide from pryin' eyes. We git ourselves into one of them hollers, ain't nobody will even know we are alive.

"Besides, they got the best whiskey in the world, and I aim to take us some."

Whetstone and Little spent two weeks holed up back in a holler that was only about twenty-five feet wide at the bottom with steep, woody, rocky bluffs to either side. They did not know how far deep in the mountain the holler extended. They had stopped after about two miles. It had been a long time since either of the outlaws had experienced the deafening silence they found in the holler.

In recognition of their contribution to the world of artistic expression, they named it—what else?—Butcher Holler. Davey carved the name in the massive white oak at the base of the hill extending its branches to the top of the bluff to find the sunlight. They found that it was always cool in the daytime under the shade of the oak and frequently downright cold on the late July nights. It was not hard to imagine how cold it would be in winter. Too cold.

They would not stay long enough to find out.

Their plans made, at least in Whetstone's mind, they rode out toward civilization on the first day of August. Their destination was the small bourbon-producing town of Bardstown.

With his plan beginning to take shape, Whetstone looked for the first tavern in town. He was interested in a glass of that famous bourbon, but he was more interested in listening. The town only had a population of about sixteen hundred, which was both good and bad for his plans. With a city this small he would easily be remembered, as he intended to be recalled as an alcohol speculator trying to make up his mind about where to invest his sizable fortune (according to his persona) and in what. He spread the word that he would be returning to Washington in a few days to relate to his investors what he had seen and experienced, and he would be back again tomorrow to sample their wares.

He reasoned that if you are likely to be remembered as a stranger in a small town anyway, then you'd best control what people will remember. The citizens of Bardstown would never see Davey Little, only the well-dressed gentleman with the midwestern accent, that is, if he was lucky. Right now he was thirsty. Whetstone noted that the Talbott Tavern had hung its shingle prominently where visitors would easily see it, just as he had. An hour after he entered the tavern, he left, sure of the impression he had created. He'd also left with a good idea of just who and what would be the focal point of his next art exhibition.

After two days of frequent visits, tavern regulars had not seen the "liquor broker" in three days. He left late on the seventh, saying he would return with the contracts that he intended to fill out that evening and that would make the next day, in his words, "seem like Christmas in August in Bardstown."

Not a soul thought to ask where he was staying while he was in town. Maybe it was his bluster, but just as likely it was that it was the beginning of dog days in Kentucky, and the patrons were dead tired of chopping tobacco and hoeing weeds around the corn that would be turned into sweet bourbon with a bit saved for milling. The Ohio Valley in summer was hot and humid, and people's thoughts were on beer and whiskey, not on where the stranger was staying.

Whetstone and Little had camped five miles outside Bardstown and a good two miles off the road that led from Louisville straight to Talbott's Tavern. They were low on cash. Mr. Jackson Talbott and his customers would remedy that situation tomorrow. But before Whetstone visited Talbott's for the last time, tonight they would pay a visit to the Elijah Craig Distillery on the outskirts of Bardstown and help themselves to as much sweet Kentucky bourbon as they could carry in five of the six army canteens they carried, keeping one back for water.

The barrel-aging warehouse was not hard to find, just two miles back toward Talbott's Tavern. Framed against the August sky, lit by the almost full moon, the black warehouse storing the precious nectar stood almost proudly in profile on a slight hill away from the distillery itself.

Whetstone was prepared should they encounter anyone on guard duty. He carried his bowie knife, and Davey Little carried a piano wire garrote. All the guns would stay on the horses, pegged one hundred yards off in the woods on the opposite side of the road from the distillery. Theirs was a small recreational mission tonight of nonartistic value. If they did their jobs well, no one would even know they had visited the warehouse.

As was suspected, no guard was anywhere near. The place was too open with wide spaces easily observed between the house, the distillery, and the warehouse. Besides, the good people of Kentucky did not steal bourbon from their neighbors; they just asked for it.

Having slipped in a side door, Whetstone's eyes adjusted to the darker inside of the warehouse. He found a stack of barrels labeled 1859—five-year-old bourbon, here for the taking. On a table next to the racks holding the barrels of liquid delight was a wooden mallet used to pound the plug into the bunghole on the side of the barrel. Whetstone whacked gently at the side of a plug on a barrel just enough to loosen it but not enough to knock it out and spill the angel's breath. The bunghole was in the center stave on the side of the barrel and had been rotated up just above horizontal so that when it was tested monthly, it was easy enough to get at the bourbon, dip in a small ladle that held maybe a quarter cup, and bring the prized liquid out to meet the lips of the master distiller.

Tonight, that ladle would make many trips into the white oak barrel with its insides charred to an ebony blackness. The barrels were always white oak, and the insides were charred awaiting the clear distillate, which had its secret proportions of corn, rye, and malt and sometimes wheat to add a milder, smoother taste.

Whetstone was practically salivating as the last canteen was filled to the brim and capped off. If they adopted the Kentucky technique of sippin' instead of throwing the shot back, the night's take might last them to celebrate whoever won this inglorious war.

Job done, they decided to celebrate when they arrived back at their camp. Davey Little had no more than been given a shot of bourbon in his tin cup when he threw his head back and with it the bourbon, barely tasting the good whiskey, the first good whiskey he'd had in his life. He was enjoying his defiance of Whetstone's admonition to sip, and he never saw Whetstone's lightning-quick backhand that knocked him off the saddle he was using as a seat.

"Damn, Abraham. Whatja go and do that fer?"

"'Cause I told your sorry ass that if you ever cross me, there will be consequences. Just count your blessings that it was the back of my hand and not the blade of my knife. Maybe next time." Whetstone howled with laughter as Little spit blood for five minutes.

Whetstone had no qualms about killing Davey Little. He was a simpleminded little convenience, and when Abraham tired of him, Davey's life would end. Davey knew he was Whetstone's serf—little more than a slave—but certainly better than he had gotten from his father. He was proud of his status. It was the only status he had ever had in his entire life. Little knew and accepted the conditions where he was allowed to continue to apprentice under a true evil genius.

Tomorrow that genius would once again exhibit his work at Talbott's Tavern and be gone from town and well back toward Butcher Holler before the first body was found.

Honey in Winter

For those who waited and wondered on Horlbeck Creek, the war weeks of the summer of 1864 dragged on like honey in winter. Any news of the war in the east was always about Grant's constant siege of Petersburg. When Mary Assumpta finally got news from the front, it was a letter about James—but from Father Michael, not James. When she looked at the handwriting on the envelope, her spirit sagged.

In fact, she did not remember coming inside off the porch and sitting at the kitchen table to read it. She thought to herself that she did not need to read it to know that it would likely be less than joyful news. It was, indeed, disquieting. Father Michael's words were hard to read.

The rest of that day she moved in and out of a fog that was not quite despair, and as she readied herself to retire, she thought about the letter again. Colin had been a godsend to her that day as each of his requests brought her back to the reality of the now, even if for only long enough to tell him exactly where he had left his whittling knife or to answer his requests for supper. And each time, he returned to wherever an eleven-year-old country boy goes when his freedom of movement is almost unlimited within the safety and comfort still found at Horlbeck Creek Farm. Gratefully, his mother whispered a thanksgiving to herself that she had no need to worry about him as she worked through her own anxieties.

Her last thought of that day was a prayer, and she prayed that James's episode was just an anomaly and not a harbinger, but in her heart she knew, and she searched for words that weren't there. Tomorrow perhaps she would find them, and then she would write.

Country Boys Will Survive

July 8, 1864
Horlbeck Creek, South Carolina

Dearest Lover,

I received Father Michael's letter yesterday, and I want you to hear my words from your staunchest supporter and your most stubborn Irish lass: I understand and accept totally your body's and mind's reaction to what you experienced on that day in June.

James, the horrors you witnessed were surely hell's designs for its vilest sinners. And to know that mothers' boys in both armies suffered such a wicked and malevolent death—well, that is beyond what a sane and sensitive mind should endure, much less accept. I surely hope that their mothers never know how they died.

That your mind would not let you consciously and customarily continue as if such aberrations of God's world were normal—even for war—is a measure of the strength of your body to keep your mind safe for the future, not any weakness on your part. As Benjamin might say, "My son, you can now return to taking care of the boy on the table before you."

James, Michael suggested that I write you a long, long letter about the pleasant goings-on on the farm as a measure of helping you see that here we live in a different world beyond your experiences, one to which you can aspire to return. But the world where you are right now is the one where your special gifts are most needed.

So I thought about his advice long and hard and even prayed my rosary, so you know I was serious about getting the Lord's help. I understand his suggestion. It is reasonable—perhaps for other war marriages. Just not the right thing for us. From the beginning, nothing about our love has been easy or ordinary. Perhaps that was

God's way of preparing us for where he needed us. Although he sure has not revealed that to me. I just know that the last thing you need for me to do right now is to be "blowing smoke up your arse" as my grandmother used to say. Yes, she actually said that. Seems doctors used to actually do this for a variety of ailments. Of course it never worked, which accounts for my granny Bailey's frequent use of it when my grandfather was trying to flatter her!

I know that you realize that not everything is lovely here on the creek. We are at war too. Yet we are not in penury, and we do more than just survive. We worry about you and about our future. It would be unnatural if we did not. But most days our worst worries are nothing that a little pot liquor and corn bread cannot make better.

We don't eat as much meat as we did a year ago, which would just be foolish, not knowing what lies ahead but fearing hard times are likely. Nate, Audrey Lee, and I have butchered as many hogs as we ever have. However, we have smoked and salted and stored almost three-quarters of the meat in a cave near the creek in the deepest woods on Nate's farm. He designed and built a door that fits perfectly into the hole—invisible unless you know it is there. Even then, it is hard to find it. Nate created ceiling hooks that we screwed into the soft limestone of the cave, and we have hung the meat from them. So we will be okay. We season our vegetables with just a little salt pork, fat mostly, and seldom have meat at a meal unless it is game that Colin has killed, which is about once a week. He is a good shot.

I do have one interesting story that might brighten your day a bit but probably not really surprise you at all.

The last time Colin and I walked down to check on the food in the cave, we went with Nate and Audrey Lee, to make a picnic out of it. As we followed Nate and Colin (there was no path I could see) through the thick woods, I said to Audrey Lee, "Is there nothing Nate cannot do?"

She laughed at me and asked, "Don't you know what his favorite saying is?"

"I cannot even imagine, but I bet Colin knows," I said to her. Colin, come here a minute." I yelled to him to get him away from Nate, who was walking a dozen yards ahead.

"Colin," Audrey Lee whispered to him, "what is your uncle Nate's favorite saying?"

"That's an easy one. It is the last thing he says to me every time we are together." Colin giggled at that thought.

"He tells me, 'Boy, you just remember that no matter how bad things get, you are a country boy, and a country boy will always survive if he can hunt, fish, and plant and if he knows the woods better'n anybody else.'

"Then he makes me repeat it back to him." Colin said this laughing. Then he ran up to Nate and jumped on his back. "Hey, Uncle Nate, you know what Aunt Audrey Lee just asked me to tell Mama?"

"Let's see. I would have to guess it had something to with your uncle Nate not doing his chores, maybe?"

"Nope. She asked me what your favorite saying was. I guess she didn't know you tell it to me every time I see you."

"Well, I'll be damned. My last secret, and now your mama knows that too."

At that point, Nate, with Colin on his back, turned to face his wife and adopted daughter and just raised his arms and shrugged. He said to Colin just loud enough that everyone could hear, "Colin, get used to it, son. The world is really ruled by the womenfolk."

"And don't you forget that, Nathaniel Billington!" Audrey Lee returned his joust, laughing, running up to him, and hugging her husband and adopted grandson.

James, we are not living in high cotton, nor do we need to. Most of our clothes are filled with patches where they have been *mended over and over. I expect they will last until you get home. If not, I guess I will just have to stitch together some of this Confederate money I have been saving from the sale of vegetables by Nate in Charleston and make me a paper dress. Might be all it's worth before long.*

Don't you worry about us, James Edward Merriweather. Don't concern yourself about what happened recently. Do your job. Return boys to their mothers and sweethearts, and you get yourself home to your sweetheart just as soon as you can. You hear me?

With all my most profound and dearest love,

Red

Atlanta Burns

August to September, 1864

Chattanooga to Atlanta

The Siege of Petersburg was only one tactic in Grant's overall strategy of total war. Back on March 20, 1864, during the winter lull, Ulysses S. Grant and William Tecumseh Sherman, both Ohioans, holed up in a parlor of the Burnet House, a Cincinnati hotel, to devise a strategy to crush the Confederacy's will and ability to carry on.

Grant and Sherman had a symbiotic relationship. Sherman trusted Grant and quickly told people they were wrong for labeling him as a drunk mostly because of his lack of social graces. Grant refused to believe Sherman was insane just because Sherman approached every goal with a remarkable intensity not seen in many other commanders. Grant rescued his old friend Sherman, elevating him to second in command.

In the Cincinnati hotel room, Sherman presented his plan for quickly marching across Georgia to the sea, marching across the Carolinas, and then joining with Grant in Virginia. The key to Sherman's strategy was not to depend on Union supply lines to keep his army moving. Instead, the bold plan was to feed off of and destroy the land as they went.

Grant approved the audacious plan, as did Lincoln when it was presented to him. In almost all regards, the strategy of total war prosecuted by the Union army against the South was unlike any before it on US soil. The reasons were strategic, tactical, and most of all political. Lincoln was fighting for his political life in the summer of 1864. He needed battlefield victories in the fall if he was to win his political victory in November and, therefore, if his plan for the reuniting of the country was to come to fruition.

In the fatigue-inducing southern midsummer heat, Sherman slogged his way from Chattanooga across northern Georgia to Atlanta. And on September 2, 1864, while Lee and Grant were still exchanging blows in Petersburg, Sherman captured Atlanta, burning much of it to the ground despite the orders to his men to burn militarily significant targets only. A Southern telling of the battle of Atlanta still has the entire city burned to ashes by the Yankees, but according to Northern reporters, much of the city remained—just not its rail lines and its ability to supply General Lee. There was general looting, but the citizens of Atlanta were personally harmed only in a few instances, and the soldiers committing the acts were prosecuted.

Asuncion of Mary

August 3, 1864
Petersburg, Virginia

Darling Mary Assumpta,

When I write your name, it causes me to pause and think about how much is in that name. Soon after we first met, being the Protestant that I am, I commented on the uniqueness of your name—seems like maybe the second day working for John. Rather brusquely, you told me that Assumpta was Irish for Asunción—the assumption of Mary into heaven. So, Mary Assumpta—the Asuncion of Mary.

I recall thinking, An Irish virgin Mary. I wonder, is she? A virgin, I meant—not the Irish part. Your Irishness was apparent with your surname and your feisty attitude. Knowing that the feisty and virginal parts of you would never be mutually compatible, I am forever grateful that we remedied that in short order. I trust you have asked for absolution for that mortal sin we committed above John's office. Me, I thanked the angels for that afternoon, right after I asked the Almighty for forgiveness for deflowering the most beautiful woman I had ever seen.

These days as I write, often I see angels hovering near to you and Colin. Today was like that when I started this letter. Of course, you always have a couple of earthly angels just a mile or so up the road. I fear there will never be a way to repay Nate and Audrey Lee for all they have done. But we shall try when I return. Your letter about the food stored in the cave and Nate's advice to Colin shows just perfect examples of what angels they are.

Thank you, darlin', for admonishing me to quit feeling so sorry that I would ask Michael to write to you instead of doing it myself. You are totally right, of course. And thank you for understanding the visits of the black dog and giving me an entirely different perspective on them.

I am so very thankful that the fighting itself has not reached Horlbeck Creek, and as you have written and Nate has said so eloquently, the practically worthless Confederate dollars will require that you all live off the land. The officers colloquially call the CSA dollars "graybacks," but the enlisted men call and then use them as "cigar lighters" since, had they ever been paid in them, they would have had no store in which to spend them, and if they had a store, no one would accept them. So they might as well be used as tender of a different sort.

You all are blessed to be in a wonderful location to more than survive. You are away from Charleston proper and the problems that will eventually reside in every city. Most of all, you are surrounded by fertile farmland, Horlbeck Creek, and the Wando River for fish and crabs and such, and the woods for game. And you have two strong "men" who can harvest the woods and water.

My only worry is that if the Union army takes Charleston, as surely it must be on Grant's agenda, there may be some adventurous men who will want to cross the harbor. However, that is a worry grounded in no facts whatsoever, but perhaps it is worth your time and that of the Billington to develop a plan for going to ground should it become necessary.

Speaking of Grant, since he began the siege of our fortifications here at Petersburg away from the front lines, the daily life of our soldiers is filled with the boredom of drilling, eating, drinking bad coffee, and playing poker, just to start over again the next day. Several men have been disciplined for fighting over poker games when the stakes they were fighting over were sticks or acorns or whatever they were using for money that day. No one was ever hurt—oh, I patched up a couple of cuts and bruises, but nothing more serious—and most fights ended in laughter. But rules are rules—military discipline at all times and all that.

We had an interesting event on July 30 that broke the monotony. At about 5:00 in the morning, we heard the most god-awful explosion you have ever heard. The Yankees had tunneled under our defenses and planted four tons of gunpowder in the hopes that when it was ignited, their troops could just flood through the opening and seize the day and, with it, General Lee. The Yankees being Yankees, they had really not thought of what was to happen after the blast, and in their inevitable attacks following the explosion, they were easily defeated by our Confederate boys.

There were several hundred of our boys killed that morning, but there was little to be done as a surgeon because most of those killed were gathered up in baskets, the force of the blast had been so great.

Soon after the explosion of the mine, the siege resumed, and along with it the monotony. Even when the Union army is firing mortars on us, monotony is created. It is the same scheme at nearly the same time every day—whistle of the mortar round, explosion, silence, wait for the next time. The worst part is that they send the mortars over our lines at either 4:00 a.m. or 11:00 p.m. Most of the men sleep through it. I, on the other hand, keep an ear out for the "whistling Willies" as we call them and crawl under my bed. Though I must confess I have no idea what protection a canvas cot will do should a lucky round hit nearby. No worries, my love. "Them Yankee mortarmen cain't hit a bull in the butt with a bass fiddle," as my first sergeant says. He is not far from right. Still, we change the location of our tents once a week, just to make it more difficult for them.

I break my personal monotony by studying Robert Burton's work on depression so as to better understand my own psyche. As best I can understand it from the text and my personal experience, it is not a condition that one chooses, but instead, like other diseases, it finds us, or better said, we have built in us a propensity toward depression, and the tendency may be lessened by certain habits of body and mind, but it will always be present.

I trust that Michael's description of the Wilderness battle was not too graphic and not too disturbing for you. I will not dwell on the trigger that caused the arrival of the black dog except to say that the sounds and smells of that night sparked in me such a connection to those boys. And because we could do nothing for them, which was the antithesis of my entire reason for being here, it tipped me over that edge and into darkness. On the positive side, I guess, my amnesia was short-lived compared to other instances, and I can feel no lasting effects except to spur me to study more about it.

I do so miss you and home. It seems sometimes that I have been absent at the time Colin is growing and changing so rapidly. I pray to be home soon. Perhaps this siege will convince our pols of the total fruitlessness of continuing.

Keep me and all of us here in your prayers,
JEM

Rumors

September 30, 1864
Horlbeck Creek Farm, South Carolina

My Dearest Captain Doctor James Edward Merriweather,

I don't know why I wrote that salutation so formally. I just like the sound of it. Probably because I just want you to know that I want every bit of you back in my arms as damn quickly as you can manage.

Crops are in except for okra, which we will continue to get until frost, but that is just in the kitchen garden. Colin will eat every bit that we can pick. That boy loves okra any way that I can cook it. I even roasted some this week with a bit of salt and pepper, and I must agree, it was delicious.

Audrey Lee and I put up a great deal less of the corn and the peas and beans and tomatoes than we usually have. In fact, most of what we did put up was quart jars of vegetable soup that included okra ... again! We just figured that dried beans and peas and corn will be much easier to move than jars should we have to go to ground, and I think Nate intends to store our dried crops in the cave with cured meat. I know for sure that he is especially keen on storing our crop seeds in containers that he will make airtight. Don't ask how. The canned vegetables and an amount of cornmeal we will keep in our kitchens, and I think some dried peas and butter beans. Plus we can stretch our kitchen gardens awhile longer, surely enough until good winter sets it.

I dread to bring this up to you, darling, as you have enough to worry about on your own, so just consider this a request for information–nothing more–on something we might need to make plans here on the creek. Bartholomew visited with us a couple of days last week and brought some fresh shrimp and smoked catfish with him. As you can imagine, we had a good ol' Low Country shrimp boil with Irish potatoes (what other kind?) and some late corn Nate had planted in mid-June hoping for a few ears in September, seasoned with some of Nate's precious sausage.

What an enjoyable afternoon and evening on the porch in the shade of our water oak that Colin has named the General Lee because he says it is so inspiring. After Colin had wandered away to do his last chores, Bartholomew told us the news that the Union army had captured Atlanta on September 2, practically burned it to the ground, and killed every living Southern thing they came across. And they occupy it still. Bartholomew said the high-society womenfolk in Charleston are suffering from the vapors at the mention of the name of the Union commander General William Tecumseh Sherman. Bartholomew says rumors are that he is headed through Georgia straight for Charleston and will rape every Southern belle in the Holy City. Bartholomew swears it is the talk in every bar, whorehouse, and church Sunday school class.

I invited him to come and live with us for the duration, but he declined. I think he rather likes all the gossip. Of course, you know me well enough to know that I do not deal in rumors and that I know Bartholomew Jennings well enough to know that he *does. However, they are enough for me to ask you if anything at all about Sherman's plan has been discussed by General Lee and his commanders.*

Even if Charleston were sacked, there is really not much reason to think that the Union would expend resources exploring a few farms across the harbor. And looking at the atlas you bought for Colin before you left, the best I can figure, their next target would much more likely be Columbia, which is still aiding the war effort, and then on through North Carolina to Virginia. Besides, with the Union blockade, Charleston has been effectively shut down for the last year. Nothing in or out. Boats like Bartholomew's that ply the harbor and rivers are generally ignored.

It is interesting to me that even though I can see Union warships blocking Charleston Harbor if I walk down to the river, this is the first time I have actually looked at that atlas with the purpose of making some wild-ass conjectures about the war. Maybe the rumors have affected me just a tat. I promise you, it is nothing serious.

So, darling, if you do hear any news about Sherman moving from Atlanta, it would help us here in really putting substance to our plans about going to ground.

Yours,

Red (Mrs. Mary Assumpta Bailey Merriweather, and don't you forget it!)

Surgeon's Diary

October 10, 1864
Petersburg, Virginia

I find it interesting that when I have had almost endless time to diary my thoughts, the less likely I am to do it. Perhaps there is not the need for a cathartic release that comes when words to paper release emotions. But here I am, so let's see what happens this October morning in Petersburg, Virginia.

This is the first fall-feeling morning we have had here in mid-Virginia, and perhaps that is the impetus for my writing. If spring mornings are an indicator of God's forgiving and resurrective nature, then fall's first explosion of crystal clear wind is a cleansing from the sweaty and dirty hot summer days. On the other hand, it is not easy to create a metaphor for that which connects winter and the Almighty. Perhaps the innocence of the first snow inevitably followed by its decline into dirtiness describes the human condition and maybe teaches us that God's spring is always around the corner for man's repeated and repeated transgressions. Hmm. Sober thoughts on an October Saturday morning. Wonder what Michael and Benjamin would think of my metaphors?

While new injuries from war wounds have become less than routine, there remains doctoring to be done. Dysentery remains almost as big a killer of our young men as the war itself. With so many men in such confined areas, it can disable an entire company in two days and last for two weeks, even with treatment. To see a man go from energetic to febrile and coffin pale in three days of contracting the disease is disheartening to all. Out of a company of a hundred men, twenty-five will die even with our best efforts.

I have concluded, by the way, that if a company were to employ a regimen of antiseptics to their sleeping and eating quarters, they would likely remedy the problem.

After recovering from the amnesia, I met with Claude Paisley and Hunter McGuire individually to ask pointedly if they had lost confidence in my abilities as a physician. Graciously, they told me that each of them had considered just walking away, going back to their families, and traveling to the western territories, such was the effect of the overwhelming horrors they faced routinely.

Bless them both. They are true friends, and I am in a much better place because of their honest conclusions as physicians.

We continue to hear reports of Sherman's intent to march from Atlanta to Savannah, but it is nothing more than scuttlebutt. At this point, he still occupies Atlanta. Regardless of his actions, they are not likely to affect us directly unless he should turn north toward Virginia, which I expect is his intent.

JEM

A Reason to Believe

Before November 8, 1864, perhaps the Confederacy's best hope for peace rather than surrender lay in the election of 1864 and Lincoln's longtime war critic and opponent George B. McClellan, the Democrat from New Jersey. Lincoln was very unsure of his reelection late into the summer of 1864. Former commander of the Army of the Potomac McClellan and the

Democrats favored a negotiated peace in one form or another, and the Union populace was tired of war with what seemed to be so few victories and so many young men and husbands dead. Peace sounded very reasonable. Total victory seemed a faraway dream that might never come given the stubbornness of the South to continue fighting, often successfully, despite odds that should have brought out the white flags of surrender.

Grant's slow gains and his mostly unsuccessful Siege of Petersburg did not bring confidence to the people and politicians of the Union or to Lincoln. Lincoln needed an overwhelming victory by his Union army that pointed confidently to a sure end of the war, or he expected he would lose the election in November. Then all the social gains he had made would likely be removed or so diminished in negotiation as to be unrecognizable.

Brash and bold General William T. Sherman was Lincoln's best bet to regain the confidence of the people, and Sherman delivered Atlanta in no uncertain terms.

The overwhelming Union victory and occupation of Atlanta provided the Union with the reason they'd been looking for to give Lincoln a second term.

CHAPTER 42

The Devil Goes Down to Savannah

After occupying Atlanta for two months, on November 5, with Grant's and Lincoln's blessings, Sherman ordered Generals Slocum and Howard to ready their armies to move out of Atlanta and move southeast.

A week after the order to ready the troops, Sherman punctuated Lincoln's presidential win as sixty-two thousand troops marched out of Atlanta, burning anything of potential military value and a notable number of other buildings out of sheer enthusiasm. His final destination was the sea and Savannah.

On the first evening after leaving Atlanta, Sherman met with his officers and summed up their purpose. Captain Randall Peterson, Methodist chaplain from Mystic, Connecticut, recorded Sherman's words as best he could remember them when he returned to his tent:

"Gentlemen, congratulations on the total destruction of Atlanta. We have placed doubt and fear into the very heart of every Georgian. Now we must remove any doubt that lies deep in every Georgian's soul so that they no longer fear and doubt. They must believe. Believe they can do nothing to aid their army. Believe their Southland, as they have known it, is no more. Believe that their God wears the robes of the Union army of the United States of America. Believe that any future they may have will come from the benevolence of the US government, and not from their own initiative.

"Gentlemen, we will empty their fields and gardens, their barns, pastures, and feedlots, their cupboards and storehouses. We have a righteous army to feed. And when we have completed the harvest, we will burn what remains to the ground. Burn the barns and storehouses, but not the homes. Do not harm civilians or burn their homes unless they threaten your life. Any man who wantonly injures a civilian or their home will be court-martialed and punished."

Sherman cut telegraph wires as he went. He did not want anyone, including his superiors, and especially the press, which he despised, to know where he was or his tactics. Casualties were light on both sides, which was the primary goal of his strategy. Destroy property. Instill fear and loathing. Remove the desire to make war. Remove a hope for the future, but do not kill the people.

On December 21, a little more than a month after Sherman's army left Atlanta, Savannah mayor Richard Arnold surrendered the city to the Union army, eliciting a promise from Sherman not to burn Savannah as he had Atlanta. Sherman agreed ... almost: "As long as my army is not attacked, your city will be safe."

The next day, Sherman telegraphed President Lincoln: "I beg to present you as a Christmas gift the city of Savannah, with one hundred and fifty heavy guns and plenty of ammunition, also about twenty-five thousand bales of cotton."

With Sherman occupying Savannah, the citizens of Charleston were apoplectic with fear. After all, the war began in Charleston, and with the loathing Sherman had demonstrated for Georgians, the Charlestonians held no doubt—none—that Sherman would soon march the hundred miles and burn their city to the ground.

Little did the citizens know that Sherman held an affinity of sorts for Charleston as he had spent four years there at Fort Moultrie in the 1840s. Sympathy or not, had Charleston been militarily significant, Sherman would have destroyed it, but Sherman's eyes were north on Columbia and on to North Carolina and to Grant's army in Virginia.

Charleston was insignificant—blockaded and impotent.

But the Merriweathers and the Billingtons and Bartholomew Jennings were ignorant of any of these plans, as was Captain James Merriweather as he continued to endure Grant's Siege of Petersburg.

There was no bliss in their states of ignorance, only worry and anxiety.

Requests to Petersburg were caught in the time warp that plagues all wartime correspondence and exacerbated exponentially by the incompetence of the Confederate mail service.

Plans were made in the absence of knowledge. Information from Charleston was so distorted that it was useless.

Letters and Diaries

October 15–November 15, 1864

Horlbeck Creek, South Carolina, and Petersburg, Virginia

To the families along Horlbeck Creek, the anticipation of what the redheaded devil who now occupied Atlanta would do next was well-nigh debilitating.

Two topics seemed to occupy every discussion, especially if Bartholomew Jennings was part of the group: Has Sherman left Atlanta, marching south? And is he headed to Charleston? The unflappable Mary Assumpta and the experienced Nate both knew worrying right now was useless, but it was hard not to get caught up in it.

Finally, Mary Assumpta reasoned that they needed to do some planning, but until they heard something reasonably reliable indicating that Sherman had left Atlanta and was headed south, to prepare any plans would be a waste of energy. So the Merriweathers and Billingtons returned to farming.

They dug sweet potatoes and harvested the late season acorn, butternut squash, and pumpkins. After keeping back enough for themselves for October of these winter vegetables (so named because they would keep throughout the winter), they banked the rest in the cave with pine straw where they could breathe, heal any tears in the skin, and grow sweeter.

They sowed seeds of collards and turnips next to each other in the kitchen garden. The seeds were broadcast down two wide rows next to each other but three feet apart. No need to be particular with the greens; they would pick and eat them long before they started to crowd out their neighbors. Often turnips and collards were cooked together in the same pot with a piece of fatback. Greens, pot liquor, and corn bread were banquet cuisine for even the most highbred Southerner. No high society on Horlbeck Creek, although Mary Assumpta's mother had aspired to enter Charleston society and open the debutante door for Mary Assumpta. However, Mary Assumpta, even had she not married a Protestant and been pregnant at the time, would have dashed her mother's dream in some other way.

Mary Assumpta knew that she had not pushed Colin to be attentive to his studies this last month, rationalizing that he was getting the best kind of practical education from his uncle Nate. She was not far from wrong. Nate was masterful at whatever the task he and Colin were working on to connect it to Colin's studies in a half dozen ways. But Colin, like most eleven-year-old boys, was masterful in getting his uncle Nate off the topic he was teaching and on to fishing or hunting and required some pushing by his mother. Usually this was taken care of at the supper table with generally the same question to her son every time he was with Nate: "So, Colin, what did you learn from your uncle Nate today?" If Colin had been studying at home, she asked the same question—just an adjustment in form from Uncle Nate to his textbooks. Colin normally could not escape his mother's scrutiny of his learning, but far too much of October's worrying took her away from her motherly duties. As his mother and "uncle" went back to their farming, Colin went back to the books.

Amid the fruitless worrying, Mary Assumpta had put off writing to James. No good reason, just lethargy. Inexcusable. She chastised herself as she now finally sat down to write. In her defense, it had been at least as long since she had received a letter from her husband. Finally, almost as if coordinated to her decision to quit worrying about Sherman's departure from Atlanta, the letters started arriving and leaving Horlbeck Creek Farm.

October 15
Petersburg, Virginia

Dearest Mary Assumpta,

The cooler temperatures here have significantly improved morale and remarkably lessened the number of men we have been treating for dysentery and lung infections. Pray that the trend continues. This siege has to end soon, and General Lee will need every man ready to fight General Grant, whose army is likened to some huge steam engine, slowly but surely moving our Rebel forces out of the way as he makes his way toward Richmond.

JEM

October 20
Petersburg, Virginia

My Dearest Colleen,

Word here is to expect Sherman to move out of Atlanta as soon as he has news that Lincoln has been reelected, but no talk of his intended direction. The indication here is that Sherman's victory at Atlanta will push Lincoln past George B. McClellan.

We remain so bogged down here that neither Sherman leaving Atlanta nor Lincoln being reelected would have much impact on our lives.

Michael sends his best. He has started an early

morning Bible study group on nondrill days and has seen it grow each week. He needed a sign from the Almighty, and it seems this might just be it.

JEM

November 1
Horlbeck Creek

Colin says the deer are finally in rutting season and expects to put venison on the table in short order. I expect that he will do precisely that. He is quite the hunter. I keep thinking that surely his shells are running short, but Nate keeps reloading them for him. Another remarkable Nate Billington skill. As repayment, Colin always saves the tender backstraps from the deer for Nate and Audrey Lee. And I did not even have to tell him to do it. You are going to find a young man when you get home.

First frost of the year last night. About three weeks early, but thankfully we had already dug and banked up the sweet potatoes, and of course the greens do fine, frost or no frost.

Bartholomew visited last week and says Charlestonians are moving around like chickens on worms after a hard rain. They have blinders to everything except Sherman. They see him around every corner according to Bartholomew, who brought us some fresh coffee beans. I did not ask how he procured them given the blockade. But you know Bartholomew, always the trader.

Red

Surgeon's Diary

November 15, 1864
Petersburg, Virginia

It appears that Lincoln has won a second term, so any reasonable expectation of peace talks is as unlikely as this army is of breaking this god-awful siege anytime soon.

Sherman has left Atlanta and is moving southeast, burning everything in his path. Headed to Charleston? That is the assumption, but that is not good enough information to send to Mary Assumpta. She will likely know as much as we do about Sherman departing Atlanta.

It pains me not to be able to tell her if she's in harm's way.

JEM

November 20, 1864
Horlbeck Creek

Precious James,

With Sherman not even three hundred miles to the north, we are anxiously wondering about his next moves. The Courier recently ran a story reprinted from the Baltimore American, and they are entirely sure he will march directly to Charleston and burn it to the ground. We have only very generally started discussing our plans should he become a threat to our farms here on the creek.

Red

December 12, 1864
Horlbeck Creek

Dearest Husband,

Why the hell have I not heard from you about Sherman's intent? We are nearly paralyzed with fear. I can only imagine what the people of Charleston are feeling. From the last report we got, he is more than halfway to Charleston. I expect he is really much nearer.

We must have some reliable information. We live in fear and foreboding.

Red

Christmas Eve, 1864
Horlbeck Creek

My Dear James,

Christmas is tomorrow, and we shall be saying a prayer for the Almighty's protection and a prayer of thanksgiving that Sherman has chosen Savannah and not Charleston.

Just writing that makes me feel spiritually and morally dirty inside, but I cannot help myself.

Red

Preparing for the Worst

January 1865

Horlbeck Creek, South Carolina

It did not take but hours for the news of the surrender of Savannah to reach the westward-leaning ears of Charlestonians. A significant number of Charlestonians with means had left the city long ago to escape the unrelenting naval bombardment. For those who remained, panic was the order of the day.

In Charleston, the *Courier* ran a story on January 5 reprinted from the *Baltimore American* that pronounced, "General Sherman's future movements may be easily divined. Charleston is too near and too coveted a prize to long escape his grasp." Those levelheaded Charlestonians who had remained calm—mostly the business community—also now believed the end was near.

However, for the entire month of January, Sherman peacefully occupied Savannah while finalizing plans for the next part of his campaign, which was to destroy Columbia for the same reason he destroyed Atlanta and then move upward through North Carolina and into Virginia to join up with General Grant.

Across the bay and up Horlbeck Creek, Mary Assumpta had not received the hoped-for letter from James with the reliable information about Sherman's plans she had looked for, so the Merriweathers and Billingtons had to move forward on the information Bartholomew brought with him in the *Courier*. Bartholomew was convinced enough by what he had read and seen that he finally accepted Mary Assumpta's invitation to join them on Horlbeck Creek. Nate and Audrey Lee offered him the Simon Billington house, which he gratefully accepted. Over the months of working with Nate and Audrey Lee with the Sweet Potato Vine, they had become fast and trusted friends, so it was not an imposition or looked at as one by either party.

Wasting no time, for they had no idea if Sherman's assault on Charleston was imminent or if he would be enjoying the spoils of his victory at Savannah awhile longer, they met in the living room of Simon Billington's parents' home the next day—a bright and clear Sunday morning. Audrey Lee supplied biscuits; Mary Assumpta, the dewberry jam.

Bartholomew brewed coffee he had brought with him from Charleston. After all, he still had contacts who slipped beyond the Union navy's grip on the harbor and ferried goods from small ships—boats, almost—to meet certain risk-taking Charleston "businessmen" on Kiawah Island on the fourth Wednesday at midnight. From Kiawah, Bartholomew sailed up the Stono River to Wappo Creek, to the Ashley River, to Charleston, and around the battery in the dead of night to dock in his usual spot with other oyster boats. He only "traded" in coffee, from which he could make as much as the rum traders at much less risk. His trade kept him in whiskey and women at Miss Geneviève Ardoin's "restaurant" (two vices for which he weekly prayed for forgiveness from the Almighty and his dear friend Pastor Simon Billington).

Bartholomew had never returned to the drunk he had been

when Simon Billington pulled him from the gutter one night when he was so drunk that he was in danger of imminent death from alcohol poisoning.

After the day of discussing and discarding places where they could avoid Sherman's troops for a few days or live for a time if necessary, they finally agreed that an abandoned oysterman's shanty known to Nate, half a mile north from the mouth of Horlbeck Creek, was viable in most ways. It was set back from the bank of the Wando River about fifty yards and was surrounded by thick river reeds that had grown up around it. So thick were the reeds that surrounded it that anyone unfamiliar with the location could literally stand three feet from one of its plank walls without ever seeing the hut.

Several hundred yards from the dock up Old Shell Road, a path led down to the shanty, but like the hut itself, one had to know where to look. Two hundred yards down the bank from the dock lay a small tidal stream, dry at low tide. At high tide on Wednesday Bartholomew and Colin would pull his boat far out of the water and well into the reeds then hide it with a thick cover of reeds to boot. The next tide would cover up any indication that it had been dragged through the mud.

Monday morning after good sunup, everyone met on Old Shell Road at the farm lane that led to Horlbeck Creek Farm and walked to the hut. At best, Mary Assumpta agreed, it was workable as long as the men cleared it of swamp rats as big as small cats and covered up all the holes where they could get back in, as they certainly would try once they discovered the warm bolt-hole right in the middle of their territory. Boomer would keep the rats at bay once they moved in.

Mary Assumpta could just imagine the old oysterman whose

shanty they would make use of—grizzled face, wrinkled skin the color of milled cypress wood and just about as tough, and arms the size of cypress knees from working the oyster tongs from dawn to dusk. She was thankful the oysterman had left a small stove/heater when he abandoned the shanty. The stove would do fine for them, but they would have to make a trip to bring some well-dried hardwood from home that would burn clean with little smoke. The smell of woodsmoke carried a long way on cool, windless days in January.

They would bring blankets for sleep, make mattresses from piles of reeds, and use only the barest utensils for cooking and eating. They would get water from the river for cooking. They would have to decide on baths, probably necessary, as they were in really close quarters in the hut. They would initially bring enough food for a week, figuring that if Sherman's soldiers did visit, they were not going to stay on this remote piece of land when Charleston and Miss Geneviève Ardoin's were so close. If troops were quartered on the creek for longer, every three days Nate and Bartholomew, traveling a different and circuitous route each time, would check on the farms, gather any foodstuffs they could find, and then make their way to Nate's hidey-hole where the larder for the remainder of the fall and winter was stored.

The first time Nate took Bartholomew to the cave, Nate stopped several yards from the entrance and asked Bartholomew if he could find it. After fifteen minutes, Nate walked directly to the entrance and, to Bartholomew's amazement, opened the door and invited him in. Once inside, Bartholomew asked an obvious question, to him at least: "Nate, why don't we just hole up here? Looks like the obvious place to me."

Nate responded that he and the women had considered just such a plan. "As far as I know, we are the only people who know about this cave, and that seems ideal. But when we thought it through, we agreed that we had to have a place where we could store our preserved food through the rest of this winter and beyond and where we could know that our seeds for next spring would be entirely protected.

"Bartholomew, if this war ended next week, it will not be the Yankees who will descend on our farms."

"I think you got that right based on what I seen in Charleston already," Bartholomew added.

Nate continued, "Based on what we have heard about Sherman and what he is likely to keep doing in the Carolinas, there will be starving Southerners looking for a meal wherever they can find it. We must take into account this probability when we plant this spring. Therefore, anything that would endanger our crop seeds must be prevented.

"So although coming here at all is not the best strategy, if we vary our route every time, we should be fine. After all, probably no one but Colin knows these woods as well as I do. Be sure you don't wander off, because you might not find your way back. Not as easy as navigating on the water."

They both laughed—Bartholomew a little nervously—before gathering dried beans and peas, a small slab of bacon, and enough sweet potatoes to last them a week if Sherman routed Charleston. They headed back to the Simon Billington home to store the food in the root cellar behind the house.

For the Billingtons and Merriweathers, January passed as had every other January on the creek—colder than the thermometer indicated and generally dreary most days.

But there was no news about Sherman's plans to burn Charleston.

After his second week, Bartholomew, suffering from lack of gossip, cabin fever, or lack of whiskey, returned to Charleston to take his chances—promising to sail over with all due speed should he hear the "Battle Hymn of the Republic" being sung anywhere except in Mother Emanuel Church.

CHAPTER 43

Hopes for an end of the war were present at the beginning of 1865 in both the North and the South, but prospects were not improved, merely different. And only slightly that. Lincoln's reelection in the fall bolstered hopes for the reunification he spoke about, often to the consternation of many in the North who, because the war was into its fourth year, feared the South would never return to the Union. Confederates, whose land had borne the totality of the physical destruction, certainly understood that the end was close and that in whatever form it was manifested, it would not be good for them.

In the North and South, the battle-weary were ready to go home, and the war-weary at home were ready for them. Yet the Siege of Petersburg continued into its eighth month, and the prisoner of war camps at Andersonville, Georgia, and Camp Douglas in Chicago continued to grow, as did the horrors they fostered.

Still, letters from and to home rekindled the human spirit again and again, especially on the worst days.

Anniversary Remembered

January 9, 1865
Petersburg, Virginia

My Darling and Precious Bride,

Where have twelve years gone since we said our vows in the Seaman's Chapel? I awoke this morning with the heaviest of hearts knowing that the best I can do today to tell you how much I love you and to celebrate our wedding day is to write this letter. They say that if two hearts are in tune, they can commune over time and distance. I believe that as you worry about what fate holds in store in the form of William Tecumseh Sherman, you will spend at least equal time today thinking about the man a few hundred miles away who is doing precisely the same thing.

I have already asked the Almighty this morning as I sat down to write to intervene and speed this letter to you so that you may feel every fiber of my love in the ink on this page.

Yours this day and for eternity,
JEM

January 9, 1865
Horlbeck Creek

Dearest Love of My Life,

An eternity ago we vowed to love one another until we die. Even with all that has transpired with my family and with the war, I would do it again a hundred times over. I grew up surrounded by family—brothers who, when they were not teasing me to tears, were spoiling me, and Father and Mother, who doted on their only daughter and youngest child. I never knew loneliness—not even for a moment. But over these last two years, loneliness has been my most constant companion. There were times at night—the loneliest time—when I missed you so much that I thought I could not run this farm and take care of Colin another day. In the morning, I would awake and find you were always the first thought on my mind, and that thought sustained me for another day, and another, and another.

I could never let you down. I never will. I thank the Almighty for creating such love as I have for you. Since the first moment I realized I loved you—weeks before we consummated our love in your bed above the surgery—that love has been all-consuming. Today, miles and worlds apart, we celebrate our wedding day—the day we made it public. We must renew our vows when you return to tell the public again. Think we might entice Michael and Benjamin to come from Richmond?

Oh, how I pray that you will be home in my arms and my bed long before this time next year. Sometimes I wonder how you could love such a flighty, headstrong, freckle-faced Irish lass as me, but God in heaven, I am blessed that you do, James Edward Merriweather.

Yours this day and for eternity,
Red

Scuttlebutt

January 10, 1865
Petersburg, virginia

mary Assumpta,

I finally heard some scuttlebutt that I consider decently reliable. Sherman will stay in Savannah until the end of the month and then move north to Columbia. The less reliable gossip says that he plans to unleash the might of the union army in a fashion on Columbia that will make its citizens wish they were Atlantans.

JEM

February 9, 1865
Horlbeck Creek

James,

Bartholomew arrived yesterday with news from Charleston that on February 2, Sherman's army was making apparent preparations to leave Savannah. This is all we know.

Assuming it would take Sherman five days to reach Charleston and assuming that he left Savannah on February 4, he may be on our doorstep.

We will move to our bolt-hole in the morning and be there for at least a week. James, pray for us. We are in fear for our lives.

Red

Relief and Decisions

February 17, 1865
Horlbeck Creek

Dearest, Dearest James,

We are safe from the Yankee devil!

Yesterday before dawn, Bartholomew sailed to Charleston to seek out news of Sherman's movements. He returned and rapped on the shanty door just at dark to tell us that reliable information in Charleston, by way of Savannah, was that Sherman turned north with his sights on Columbia. We left everything in the shanty to be retrieved another day and walked back home by the light of a waning moon that seemed to make the pieces of mother-of-pearl on Old Shell Road glisten like opals in a Charleston jeweler's case. Once home, Nate and Audrey Lee left us assured that all was okay, and I held Colin longer than your eleven-year-old son normally allows me.

James, we awoke this morning grateful for the beauty of Horlbeck Creek Farm even with its grasses turned brown and most trees now bare. The shanty provided shelter and concealment but, unfortunately, little in the way of privacy. As farmers, we generally gave up privacy long ago, and Colin knows more about conception, birth, death, and shite than I ever did at his age, but it is a bit different when one is glimpsing human nakedness and smelling the inevitable odors of five people who have not bathed in a week. We took our sanitary "jobs" outside, but it only took a couple of days for the smell of the temporary latrine to filter its way to us on winds that seemed always to blow from south to north. And poor Boomer. With so many smells to choose from, he did not know whom to sniff next!

The week spent at the shanty humbled us and showed us the immensity of our blessings when compared to so many who were left with nothing but smoldering embers after the unholy Sherman burned them out. With every day spent sitting outside the shanty anticipating every moment that Bartholomew, who was lying in the reeds just off the riverbank where he could see the dock, would make before returning with word that the Union army had just landed on Horlbeck Creek, we had nothing else to do but plan. We talked of plans for this spring's planting and about a postsurrender South where a lifelong pride in self-sufficiency will have been replaced with the urgency of hunger and the need to regain a measure of Southern respect in replanting burned fields without mules since they were slaughtered by the Union army. And here we are with fields with soil needing only to be turned over, and ol Jake for that task. We talked about our seeds in the cave, and we still worry. We may not possess a more precious commodity after the war than the crop seeds or a more daunting task than deciding what and how much to plant and how to protect our food source for the next year.

We talked about ways to plant that could most help those in greatest need while protecting our own interests, which, I think, is the only sane way to approach things. The last two years we have divided tasks and harvests equally with Nate and Audrey Lee here on our farm, and it has worked beautifully to have two more people available to work the land. We see no reason to vary from that this year. However, Nate and Audrey Lee will offer portions of their farm's arable land for anyone in need on the creek who wants to work it on their own. Unfortunately, it must be with human power alone. Ol' Jake is just too old to do more than he is doing. But that is not an impossible task. This loamy, sandy soil, as you know, is not hard to work, and Nate said he had experimented in the past with just planting seeds without tilling at all, and it worked reasonably well. Providing the land is easy. Deciding how to, or if we should, "loan" some of our seeds to others is another and infinitely more complicated choice, and we don't have much time before we must come to a resolution that we can live with. Fairness takes on a different meaning when talking about the potential of losing some of our families' critical sources of food. We know we must depend on our crops. Perhaps we can add some wild game to our larder, but Nate said that he expects there will be so many people out hunting game that we really should not even consider the idea.

We made some decisions that were easier. With first planting just weeks away, we decided to get sweet potatoes in the ground much earlier than usual. We will plant more of them and eat a few less. If there are people who need food, supplying them with a few sweet potatoes will be a start at least. They can eat some and hopefully keep some back for planting next spring.

Nate also suggested we plant one smaller plot each of corn, peas, and butter beans earlier than usual. It is a gamble with late frosts infrequently coming after Easter, but if we have to replant, we will. These early starts like the sweet potatoes might give us a small early harvest to help out the hungry without significantly affecting our traditional plans.

Not knowing what the landscape of the South physically and politically is going to look like once this war is over, all we can do is plan in a way that gives us options to help those in dire need even though with some risks, but not so much as to endanger our own families.

Between now and harvests, we will conserve as much as we are able. There is not much room to help anyone in need right now out of last year's harvest, but we are praying that will change with this year's planting.

Darling, I can think of nothing better for your return to us than coming home to a working farm that is just waiting for your hand. I know you will add these considerations to your prayers too, and ask Father Michael to do the same.

Making these plans has put me into a state of contemplation about our family's future in months and years to come, and I realized again just how much I have depended on you, even when you are not here. Many days I turn at the slightest sound, expecting you to ask, "What's for supper?" only to turn back disappointed and elated at the same time to have heard your voice, if only in my heart.

Hurry home, my love. Your redheaded, feisty colleen is going to keep you busy for a long time. We may not go outside for a week. And we will have to make up an excuse to send Colin to stay with Audrey Lee and Nate so that our lovemaking all over this house will not be restrained by worrying about what an eleven-year-old is thinking or seeing or hearing.

Yours in breathless anticipation,

Red

A Siege of Dysentery

February 22, 1865
Petersburg, Virginia

Dearest Mary Assumpta,

I began this day—another cold, damp, and fuscous Petersburg Wednesday—with my daily visit to the infirmary tents that are set off some three hundred yards from our main camp: canvas monastic hospices of dread and death. There is little hope found there. When a soldier comes down with the runs—usually dysentery or cholera—confinement to the infirmary tent, known by the inhabitants aptly as the Death House, is mandatory.

The officers are so fearful that the entire army will become infected that even suggesting the use of triage to separate those with less severe symptoms from the more severe symptoms is not an option to be considered. Immediate confinement is decreed at the first indication, which is often well into the fever stage of the infection, as the men will ignore treatment of even minor ailments for fear of being "sentenced" to the Death House.

Tragically, we had two doctors come down with dysentery a few days after a visit. They were allowed to remain in their own tents, but the tents had to be moved to the area of the infirmary tents. Both died within two weeks of becoming symptomatic.

Our surgical team has accepted my experience that handwashing with lye soap immediately after a visit will keep them safe, although they still wear a cotton mask out of fear that the diseases are carried in the air. I do as well to keep them happy, but I am of the opinion that these diseases are waterborne or contracted through direct contact.

Enough of this. Today when I returned from my rounds, and as I was washing my hands with lye soap and rinsing them with a bit of precious whiskey in place of medical alcohol, I noticed your letter from January 9 on my bed—delivered while I was out.

My darling, darling Red, nothing could have

lifted my spirits like your memories of our wedding (and those special occasions leading up to it). Darling, you are never far from my thoughts, but as you can surely tell by the paragraph with which I led this missive, there are dark forces that push the brilliance of your love—the red of your hair, the cream of your skin, the fire of your touch—to the recesses of my consciousness. This moment, the glory of your love assaults me—body, mind, and soul. God bless you, my angel.

I pray that my letter to you written on our anniversary has made it to you. It surprises me not at all that in the midst of this craziness, we wrote our love letters to each other on the same day. That yours arrived when I needed it most is just another example, I believe, that though evil events separate us this day, the day will come when the Almighty brings us back to each other and to another life beyond this war that surely awaits us.

Finally, let me close with a piece of information that I hope has already reached you. Sherman is not aiming for Charleston. He is en route to Columbia as I write this.

Pray for Columbia. Pray for the men of the Army of Northern Virginia. Pray that this god-awful siege will cease so that the beginning of the end of this useless war may commence.

Pray for me as I pray for you,
JEM

Surgeon's Diary

March 4, 1865
Petersburg, Virginia

Scuttlebutt between officers is that a few days ago General Lee sent a message to General Grant requesting a conference to work out the differences between the Union and the Confederacy.

As I have reflected much over these last long months here at Petersburg, I am struck with the logic that the climax—the beginning of the ending of this war—actually occurred with the Confederacy's almost simultaneous losses at Gettysburg and Vicksburg. And since those four days in July 1863, all of America—North and South—has been caught in a kind of metaphysical, political opera whose authors have long known the outcome but who are unwilling to step away from the precipices of power to bring it to closure.

As much as I am optimistic that the scuttlebutt is real and not merely my hopes, I hold few expectations for the prospect of a resolution of reason rather than of rifles. Even so, since the fall of Fort Fisher, I have felt an unmistakable sense that this conflict is nearing an end. I pray it is so. If tomorrow comes with news of peace, I shall yet remain as perplexed about the Almighty's intentions in this conflict as when I first encountered a cavalryman who had met his end at the intersection of his head and a chain shot from a Yankee cannon—his head severed as cleanly as if by a surgeon's saw.

I have long prayed that slavery's taint upon our Southland will end with this war.

Even so, I struggle this day, and shall do so beyond it, with an Almighty who allows (I cannot conceive that it is by his design) so much death to achieve this noble end. Surely there was another way.

Looks like I need another conversation with Father Michael and Rabbi Benjamin.

JEM

PART IX

THE END OF THE END

CHAPTER 44

War in Four Movements

The beginning of the end, or perhaps more appropriately the beginning of the ending of the Civil War, as Captain Merriweather had noted in his diary, began in the stifling heat of early July 1863. But as the Fates had decided and as the calendar pronounced for all to behold the signs, this was to be a sonata in four movements. The events of July 1863 were but the final somber notes of the second movement. The third movement had begun with renewed energy as General Grant arrived in the east. But Petersburg dashed those hopes, and darkness once again emerged as the dominant theme of this national sonata.

Assurance of peace had long ago been dashed on the cold shores of reality, but a spark of hope was reignited on February 15, 1865. The Confederate guns of Fort Fisher, which had for the entire war defended the port and city of Wilmington, were finally silenced by the coordinated bombardment of Union ships and an assault by a landing force of two thousand sailors and marines—the first in the nation's history—on the fort's sea face, as infantry attacked its land side.

A fortnight later the mayor of Wilmington surrendered his city to Major General Alfred Terry on the steps of city hall. They exchanged handshakes and went inside to work out the terms of the city's surrender and occupation.

Wilmington was the last major East Coast Confederate port

taken by the Union, and its taking shut down the South's last major supply line from Europe. The sonata's third movement ended with restoration of hope bordering on assurance, at least for the North.

For the citizens of Wilmington, the fourth movement was another story as tens of thousands of Union troops transformed it. Its citizens fled the city for the countryside in fear that it would become another Atlanta or Columbia. There was little hope in Wilmington or across the South.

A Chance Encounter

Mrs. Corinne Brooks managed a small boardinghouse on Harrison Street in Wilmington as her husband and son were off to war with the North Carolina Fifth Cavalry. Early in the false dawn of the morning on February 25, Corinne Brooks alerted her tenants that she would be leaving presently—her single bag already packed. She advised them to do the same. The Yankees would be in Wilmington directly, and without a Confederate army to protect them, she knew the best she could hope for was to be taken in as a refugee by a farm family outside the city.

As Corinne Brooks made her way from the city, she encountered a section of the Confederates who, after staying to ensure the complete burning of the Confederate warehouses on the Wilmington waterfront, were marching to join the Army of Northern Virginia. As the last of fifteen soldiers walked toward her, she greeted the last man, extended a hand to him, and handed him a letter addressed to Robert E. Lee. She asked Sergeant James Calvin Armstrong if he would see that her message was delivered to General Lee.

First Sergeant Armstrong was too weary and too kind to tell the obviously equally spent Southern matron carrying her single heavy, timeworn, and clearly prized leather suitcase that there was almost no chance whatsoever of her letter reaching

General Lee. Instead, he just said, "It would be my pleasure, ma'am. I will deliver it personally.

"You take care of yourself now, and find a place to hide. Them Yankees are goin' to be mighty full of theirselves after taking Fort Fisher and Wilmington."

Duty Fulfilled
April 2, 1865
Petersburg, Virginia

First Sergeant Armstrong was responsible for himself and the ten men who marched ahead of him to make sure everyone stayed the course until they joined the Army of Northern Virginia at Petersburg or wherever that army might now be located. The section did, in fact, meet up with General Lee's army the first week in April as the army was preparing to abandon the defensive earthworks that had served them so well for so long.

As fate would have it, First Sergeant Armstrong, looking to inquire about how his section should join the larger force, approached a thin, well-groomed, and dignified lieutenant colonel who was watching the ranks as they dispersed and making notes about the movements. The nearer Sergeant Armstrong got, the more he believed he knew the officer. However, as a rule, top sergeants did not start conversations with lieutenant colonels. Nevertheless, First Sergeant James Calvin Armstrong decided to breach protocol.

"Colonel, pardon me, sir, for my lapse in proper military manners, but did we not attend the same Presbyterian church some years ago in Norfolk? My father was the minister of the First Presbyterian Church on 820 Colonial Avenue where your family attended, and you and I were in the same Sunday school class.

"My father was Reverend George D. Armstrong, and I am

his eldest, James Calvin. I must have been about twelve when my father assumed the leadership of the church. Does that sound familiar?"

"Well, I'll be damned! Of course I remember you. I am Walter Taylor." That Lieutenant Colonel Walter Taylor did not use his official title was not lost on James Calvin Armstrong.

"I also remember the one time we sneaked out of Sunday school and preaching to go fishing. As I recall, we did not catch any fish, but we both sure caught whippings when our fathers found out!"

Taylor laughed out loud at the memory, turning the heads of several noncommissioned officers who had never heard him laugh. After all, he was Robert E. Lee's adjutant, and whatever burdened his boss showed heavily in Taylor's countenance as well.

"I might still have a scar or two on the back of my thighs from that peach tree switch my father used. Good training for VMI, where my parents sent me a year later."

"After that whipping," James Calvin remembered with a smile, "every Saturday night my father made me pray for a half hour before supper, kneeling on grains of rice the first few minutes to focus my attention on the voice of the Almighty. I am afraid my focus never got nearer to the Almighty than those grains of rice."

"So, First Sergeant Armstrong," Lieutenant Colonel Walter Taylor asked, "what brings you to Petersburg and the Army of Northern Virginia?"

Armstrong's attention was finally drawn to the braided aiguillette on Taylor's right shoulder indicating his position as an adjutant and the golden color indicating that he was closer than anyone else in the Army of Northern Virginia to its commanding officer, General Robert E. Lee. Even so, Walter Taylor had not yet made any reference to indicate his position.

"Sir, we are the final Confederate section from Wilmington,

and General Bragg ordered us to remain, set fire to the stores in the CSA warehouses and the dock, and guarantee they were burned to the waterline before we departed.

"I can assure you, sir, that we completed our assignment. Nothing remains that could be used by the Yankees, although there sure was a lot of material that our boys could have put to good use.

"General Bragg, with verbal orders only, directed that we should move as quickly as we could to join the Army of Northern Virginia. I am not sure of General Bragg's personal intentions, but I believe he planned to return to the Army of Tennessee."

"You are well-informed, Sergeant. He is, as of this date, serving as an advisor to that army. What can I do for you today, James Calvin?"

First Sergeant James Calvin Armstrong, his fists closed so tightly that his fingernails drew blood, fought hard to keep back tears at the use of his Christian name by this influential officer standing before him. Having known him in childhood or not, Taylor's personal greeting that breached army protocol was an honor beyond any expectation.

"Sir," First Sergeant Armstrong finally replied, "my men and I are here to lend any assistance to the Army of Northern Virginia that may be required of us. Just direct us to the person who would need us most, and you will not be disappointed in this group of soldiers. I promise you that."

Lieutenant Colonel Taylor gave his childhood friend directions to report to Dr. James Merriweather, figuring this would provide him and his men the best chance of surviving the final days of this conflict. As Armstrong began leading his men away to join up with Dr. Merriweather, Lieutenant Colonel Taylor noticed the unopened letter Armstrong was clutching tightly in his left hand, having just taken it from his tattered gray blouse's front pocket.

"Sergeant, is that a letter to be delivered to someone here at this command post? If so, I will be glad to have it delivered as you report to Dr. Merriweather."

Sergeant Armstrong told Lieutenant Colonel Taylor about the matron who had given it to him and of the sentimental, if not realistic, promise he'd made to her to deliver it to General Lee.

"Well, well," Taylor said, smiling. "As I am General Lee's adjutant and about to return to his tent to report on the progress of our withdrawal, you delivered it to the only man who can assure you with 100 percent certainty that it will be placed in General Lee's hands."

First Sergeant James Calvin Armstrong executed the crispest salute of his military career and responded with a simple "Thank you, sir."

CHAPTER 45

Prayer for Peacemakers
April 2, 1865
Commanding General's Tent
Petersburg, Virginia

"Walter, do you have that report for me on the progress of our withdrawal from this godforsaken mudhole?" General Lee asked, clearly perturbed.

"I do, sir, but before I deliver it, perhaps you might want to read this letter that was hand-delivered just now all the way from Wilmington."

"Indeed. Let me have it." Lee spoke considerably more sternly than he had intended to his adjutant. *If any single member of this army has seen the power of this conflict to bring out the worst and best in me, it is Walter Taylor. He deserves better even if these days are grim,* Lee thought to himself.

"Walter, I had no reason to bark at you. I hope that you will accept my apologies."

"No need to apologize, sir. Every man among us knows the heavy burdens you carry on our behalf."

Lee sat on the edge of his cot, his portable desk pulled near, and read the boardinghouse matron's letter—its words demanding of him to do his duty as commanding general in the final days before him and his army.

March 8, 1865
Wilmington, North Carolina

Dear General Lee,

I wrote this prayer when it was clear that my home was to be overrun and taken over by Yankees. Please excuse my penmanship and the emotions of my words. I am but a merchant's wife who has not heard from her husband and son in four weeks.

Dear Lord,

I am but a soldier's wife and mother, and I am done, Lord. Won't you open the eyes of our leaders so that they may see this conflict as we common folk see it? Turn them, Lord, into blessed peacemakers.

Lord, we Southerners are a stubborn and proud people, and what will we have gained by our angered pride if our ground is ruined, our bellies empty, and our menfolk moldering in the earth?

Rescue us, Lord.

Corinne Brooks
Wilmington, North Carolina

Simple Prayer Long Remembered

Although no one could logically attribute the end of the conflict to the effects of the letter, General Lee carried it with him in his vest pocket—the envelope and single page stained with dirt and fingerprints and, perhaps, with tears.

When Walter Taylor was asked about what it was that General Lee had been observed reading from time to time—always appearing to be the same single page—Lieutenant Colonel Taylor replied the same way each time: "He is reading his favorite prayer to the Almighty."

Robert E. Lee vowed to himself that he would not forget the letter from Corinne Brooks of Wilmington, North Carolina, when the conflict was ended. To that end, on his last night in Petersburg, he wrote to Corinne Brooks and put the letter into the hands of his adjutant, Lieutenant Colonel Taylor, with orders that it be mailed or hand-delivered to her if necessary.

> April 2, 1865
> Petersburg, Virginia
>
> Dear Mrs. Brooks,
>
> When you receive this letter, I will be either a casualty of this conflict or a prisoner of war, or I will have returned again as a private citizen to my beloved Virginia. Regardless of my outcome, I want to thank you for your letter and your prayer. It reached me as you intended. You chose a fine man in First Sergeant Armstrong to ensure it was delivered. Through the Almighty's divine providence, I received it when I needed it most, and it gave me such direction and strength as I need in these final days.

Your words and your concern for husband and son most eloquently spoke to me that I must not be the cause of more casualties. Enough boys have died.

Be assured that I will be an instrument of your prayers and find your son and husband and return them to you safely.

Your obedient servant,
Robert E. Lee

CHAPTER 46

Exchange of Letters between Generals

On April 7 and 8, and early on April 9, Generals Grant and Lee exchanged battlefield correspondence whose manners belied the horrendousness of the conflict that had brought them to these momentous seventy-two hours.

Friday, April 7
Afternoon and Evening

On the afternoon of April 7, General Grant wrote to General Lee suggesting that the events of the week before should convince General Lee of the hopelessness of continuing and that Lee could prevent further bloodshed by surrendering.

The same evening, General Lee responded to General Grant's proposition in the very same way that had endeared Lee to his troops—saying that no situation was hopeless. Even so, he agreed with Grant on the desire to spill no more blood on the field of battle. Still, offering no suggestion of surrender, Lee asked Grant for the terms he would offer should the situation present itself.

Saturday, April 8
Morning

General Lee's courier with his commander's response arrived late at General Grant's encampment, and so it was the next morning, April 8, that Grant responded to Lee's question. He wrote: "In reply, I would say that, peace being my great desire, there is but one condition I would insist upon,—namely, that the men and officers surrendered shall be disqualified for taking up arms again against the government of the United States until properly exchanged."

General Grant, in the first of several gracious propositions he was to extend to his enemy over the next two days, offered to meet at the location of General Lee's choosing as they definitively agreed on the terms of surrender.

On receipt of General Grant's morning letter, General Lee responded that he had not intended to suggest that surrender was among the immediate options he was considering. He was only asking as to the surrender conditions should the situation change regarding the Army of Northern Virginia.

Instead, Lee moved his Army of Northern Virginia toward the village of Appomattox Court House. However, intelligence reached him that the stores to feed his army that had been placed at Appomattox Railway Station had been seized by the Union forces.

Sunday April 9
Early Morning
The situation was clearly changing. Even so, General Lee, as only he was prone to do, prepared to make one more push through Union lines on the morning of April 9 with plans to join the Army of North Carolina. He assumed that the Union forces at the front were lightly armed Union cavalry. He would be wrong. As the morning skirmishes progressed, scouts returned with intelligence that two corps of Union infantry supported the Union cavalry. To continue would be slaughter.

Sunday, April 9
Midmorning
Calling a halt to fighting, General Lee retired to his tent an old man—warworn, a warrior no more, and worse, defeated. At his field desk, he wrote to General Grant accepting the proposed terms of surrender in Grant's letter of the previous day. As the commander of the Army of Northern Virginia exited his tent to give the message to a courier, Lee was heard to say to no one in particular, "There is nothing left for me to do but to go and see General Grant, and I would rather die a thousand deaths." Ever the leader, General Lee knew that unless he acted quickly, his men would soon begin rampant foraging of the farms in the area.

Lee dispatched the letter immediately by courier, who met up with General Grant as Grant and his army moved steadily toward the village of Appomattox Court House. Upon reading Lee's letter, Grant stopped and wrote a letter to General Lee saying that he would move forward to meet General Lee in the village—leaving the site of the meeting to General Lee's discretion.

Sunday, April 9
Late Morning
Grant's couriers to General Lee, Lieutenant Colonel Orville Babcock and his orderly Captain John Luther Dunn, found General Lee resting against an apple tree on the bank of the Appomattox River. On reading General Grant's reply, General Lee, accompanied only by his aide-de-camp, Lieutenant Colonel Charles Marshall, and Private Joshua O. Johns, immediately rode toward Appomattox Court House accompanied by Federal couriers Lieutenant Colonel Babcock and Captain Dunn.

As the delegation rode away from the Confederate encampment, Lieutenant Colonel Marshall and Private Johns rode hurriedly ahead to find a suitable location for the meeting as Lieutenant Colonel Babcock and Captain Dunn escorted General Lee to meet with General Grant.

The McLean House
Appomattox Court House, Virginia
Sunday, April 9
Noon

Wilmer McLean, too old to enlist, and after sustaining damage to his home in the First Battle of Bull Run, moved to the crossroads village of Clover Hill. Renamed for the fact that it was the location of the courthouse for Appomattox County, it became Appomattox Court House, Virginia. McLean hoped to escape the war altogether in his new abode, but the war found him again.

When Lieutenant Colonel Charles Marshall and Private Joshua Johns rode into the hamlet looking for a place to meet up with General Grant, it was near noon and eerily quiet—unusual for the county seat and especially for Clover Hill Tavern at this time of day. One man sat on the courthouse steps, his head in his hands—Wilmer McLean. With sounds of the early morning fighting on the ridge above his home still echoing in his ears, he was contemplating how the war had found him yet again. To the north were Lee's forces around the Appomattox River. To the southeast were the Union forces strategically occupying the ridgeline above the village and behind his home.

Lieutenant Colonel Marshall dismounted and walked up to the man on the steps. "Sir, if you have a few moments, I would like to ask you about the best place to hold a meeting this afternoon between Generals Lee and Grant. Would you have a suitable location in mind at this spur of the moment?"

"Gentlemen, I will not ask the nature of the meeting,

although I do have the appropriate place for the kind of gathering I perceive this to be.

"I would be honored if you would use my home. It is there," he said, pointing due south about seventy-five yards to the two-story red brick house facing the Richmond–Lynchburg Stage Road. White porches spanned both floors at the front. A well sat in the middle of the front yard with a gravel pathway circling it. An underground icehouse was to the front left, and the kitchen and slave quarters were in the back.

"I believe it to be far enough from the tavern or the courthouse not to draw attention, and the parlor is large enough to hold several people. I have a marble-topped table and a smaller writing desk, both with comfortable chairs. Does that sound as if it would fit your needs?"

"Would it be possible for us to take a quick look at your home?" Lieutenant Colonel Marshall asked.

After a quick review of the home, Colonel Marshall sent Private Johns scurrying to meet General Lee with the location.

Upon hearing the report from Private Johns to General Lee, Captain Dunn addressed the general: "General, with your permission, I will ride to meet General Grant and give him this information."

"Captain Dunn, you need not ask my leave to ride to your commander, but I will long remember the honor you give me this day by asking. Thank you, sir."

Dunn would also remember that day and that General Robert E. Lee remained a gentleman of Virginia and West Point at the worst point of his life and military career.

After the war, and with the Virginia economy in shambles, Wilmer McLean could no longer make a living from farming.

Unable to keep up the mortgage payments, he sold the house in 1867 and returned home to Manassas.

For the rest of his life, in thousands of odd moments, Wilmer McLean would find himself contemplating the ideas of fate and predestination. A troubled man, he did not understand at all that the Fates were about to make him the most famous citizen of Appomattox County next to Patrick Henry.

CHAPTER 47

Surrender
Sunday, April 9
Early Afternoon
The McLean House
Appomattox Court House, Virginia

At 1:00 p.m. General Lee arrived at the McLean home. Slowly, almost apologetically, Lee dismounted his faithful Traveller, handed the bridle to Private Johns, brushed the dust from his best uniform, walked up the nine steps to the porch, entered the parlor, sat down, and began talking quietly with Lieutenant Colonel Marshall about Marshall's plans for the future.

A half hour later, the sound of horses signaled the approach of the man to whom Lee would surrender his army. General Lee rose uneasily from his chair as General Grant entered the parlor and greeted Lee cordially in the center of the room. The two commanders offered a very dissimilar appearance with Lee in his best dress uniform and polished boots and Grant in his road-spattered field uniform, the top two buttons askew.

General Grant asked General Lee if he remembered the two meeting once during the Mexican War, and General Lee said that he did. With geniality, the conversation continued for almost a half hour until General Lee, the misery of defeat weighing heavily on his shoulders, brought their conversation back around to why they were there.

Moving from the center of the room, they sat on either side of the small marble-topped writing desk. General Grant appeared to be discomfited as he had to ask his counterpart if he was indeed ready to accept the terms of surrender. General Lee quickly said that he agreed to the terms as General Grant had outlined them in his letter the previous day.

The discussions around the acceptance of the terms continued across the small walnut writing desk until General Lee asked General Grant to put the terms in writing so that he could sign his agreement should anyone question the gentleman's agreement between commanders.

General Grant agreed, and as he wrote out the terms, Lee returned to the square marble-topped table across the room. To the observations of Lieutenant Colonel Marshall and Private Johns, their commander, a profoundly religious man, closed his eyes and prayed for several moments as General Grant completed his writing.

After General Grant delivered the written terms, and once General Lee had reviewed them more hastily than judiciously, Lee asked if the terms allowed his men to keep their horses. General Lee explained that many of his men owned their mounts and that the horses and mules would be desperately needed for farming back home. Grant, firmly but not unkindly, said he would not change the terms as they had been spelled out and agreed upon. However, perhaps remembering President Lincoln's wish to return Confederate combatants quickly to their homes and businesses, in an act of remarkable generosity, Grant told Lee that he would order his officers to allow any Confederate who claimed an animal to keep it. And when General Lee mentioned that his men had had no rations for many days, General Grant ordered that twenty-five thousand rations be sent to the hungry Army of Northern Virginia. Then he asked General Lee if that would be enough.

With this gentleman's addendum to conditions of surrender, General Lee added his signature to the document, telling General Grant, "This will have a very happy effect on my army."

The Confederates were allowed to return immediately to their homes, unhindered by Union forces so long as they observed the terms of the surrender and the laws where they resided.

The meeting ended around 4:00 p.m., and as Lee left the house and rode away, the men who had accompanied General Grant to the meeting cheered in celebration, until General Grant ordered an immediate stop. "The Confederates are now our countrymen, and we do not want to exult over their downfall," he told his adjutant.

Lee delivered the final address to those who remained of the Army of Northern Virginia on April 10, and afterward the army immediately dispersed and commenced their journeys homeward.

The healing had begun.

Return to Richmond

Like his men, General Lee was anxious to return home to his family, so he rode out on Traveller early on Tuesday, April 11, bound for Richmond, to the salutes of both the Confederate and Union soldiers whom he encountered.

Lee arrived at Richmond on April 15. The night before,

he had slept for the last time under the stars to the sounds of Traveller grazing nearby, occasionally raising his head to whinny at forest sounds throughout the night.

Robert E. Lee was almost uncomfortable with the reception he received as he entered the front door of his home, having stabled Traveller, making sure he had hay and water. And then as he had with General Grant, he again passed cordialities with the gathered guests in *his* parlor, there to welcome him back home and to civilian life. But to the old and weary warhorse, it was torturous. Finally, the guests dispersed, and he was able to embrace his family and all who wanted to hear every detail of the meeting with General Grant.

"Father, was he evil?"

"No, Son. He was a gentleman. An officer," Lee replied quietly.

"Robert, did he make demands just to humiliate our boys?" Mary Custis asked.

"No, dear. He did everything in his power to ensure our boys were not humiliated by Union troops. No one could have done more."

After pouring himself a brandy, Lee, now father and husband, patiently answered every inquiry until the brandy ceased to calm his nerves and just made him sleepy. Caring not for supper, telling Mary that his stomach had to adapt to such rich food a little at a time, he retired to read his Bible and offer his evening prayers in his bedroom.

Back in His Element

However, after only two weeks, Lee became increasingly restless. And with profound apologies to Mary Custis and the promise to quickly return, he rode Traveller to Appomattox Court House. Lee's primary reason, as he explained it to his wife, was to visit the wounded who were now housed with the Union casualties. Lee knew he would also likely read over a bit of paperwork regarding the surrender and respond with explanations here and there to questions from Union officers about the location of specific documents or matériel—things that would soothe his restless mind. And he would think on his future.

Lee was back in his element, and he found it much more natural than his brief time at home. He no more remained a military leader than the new class of plebes who would soon be entering his beloved West Point. Lee was contemplating his future, and as was his custom in planning the strategy and tactics of a battle, he made notes to himself, notes with stray ideas about the next stage of his life. As he was writing his last note—"to lead an institution of higher learning"—he was surprised when a Union officer delivered to him a handwritten letter from General Grant. The courier who delivered the message, to Lee's pleasant surprise, was Captain John Luther Dunn, the courier who had graciously escorted General Lee on his way to the home of Wilmer McLean.

The letter from General Grant read as follows:

> April 18, 1865
> Headquarters of the Army of the Potomac
> Near Appomattox Court House, Virginia
>
> Dear General Lee,
>
> I have just returned from Washington after relating the terms you and I agreed on, and I find that I much prefer running an army than dealing

with the endless and inane questions from politicians. But that is not the reason for this correspondence. There is a field surgeon of yours who has come to my attention. As I expect that you have seen on your visits to the wounded, we will be here in Appomattox tending to those who gave their all for the cause for some time to come.

Would you be so kind as to ask Dr. James Merriweather of your medical corps if he is still tending the wounded, as I have been advised that he is to visit me at his earliest convenience? I have received many recommendations from my medical staff that he has frequently been in the medical tents doing remarkable surgical work with our doctors and on the soldiers of both armies.

My army and my surgeons clearly need his expertise for a few days longer if he would be so inclined. I will, with deep gratitude, help speed his journey home in any way he sees possible following his time with us.

Very respectfully, your obedient servant,

U. S. Grant
Commanding

PART X
THE AFTERMATH

CHAPTER 48

Homecoming Delayed
April 19, 1865
Union Headquarters
Near Appomattox Court House, Virginia

It was ten days after the surrender, and medical care for the wounded after the week of fighting around Appomattox Court House remained as problematic as it had been during the entire war. Men died by the scores each day, some from poor surgical techniques, many from gangrene or other postsurgery infections, and even more from dysentery.

At the direction of General Grant (with a recommendation from former CSA general Robert E. Lee), the chief medical purveyor for the Army of the Potomac, Dr. Charles Sutherland, directed Union surgeons from the Appomattox Campaign and invited the few former Confederate surgeons who remained to meet in the front of the medical tents now housing all wounded, both Union and Confederate. Two Confederates, Dr. James E. Merriweather and Dr. John Bailey (formerly Sutherland's counterpart with the Army of Northern Virginia), were the Union army's special guests for the occasion and joined Sutherland on the quickly erected one-step-high platform.

Dr. Sutherland introduced the two speakers for the day and gave a brief outline of the day's topics: the importance of field hospital cleanliness, the use of disinfectants, and the process of triage. Sutherland's remarks were necessarily short because he knew little about the topics himself.

Dr. John Bailey spoke first.

"Gentlemen and ladies—good to see we have some nurses with us this morning—I am pleased to officially introduce to you Dr. James E. Merriweather, although he needs no formal introduction, because you have already met him in the hospital tents as he was making rounds. I want to tell you a bit more about him this morning.

"In 1852 when James, a year removed from his studies at the University of Virginia, apprenticed with me, I had already begun to do research into the importance of operating room cleanliness and the use of disinfectants during surgery and in my own practice. James Merriweather was an eager apprentice and became an exceptional research-based physician in his own right. James was always the questioner of his own methods *and* mine. His mind-set was not to accept a less than a favorable outcome but to ask why. Those whys brought him to you today, and I can proudly say to you this morning that he far surpassed my knowledge through his work with battlefield surgery. But Dr. Merriweather went a step beyond anything that we had discussed in my practice. You will hear him talk about the practice of triage. This process emerged from his questioning the practice of taking every wounded soldier on his surgery table just as the soldier was presented to him. He determined that this 'first come' practice actually was costing the lives of many who died waiting because the surgeon who could successfully treat them was treating wounded who could have waited, being in no danger of succumbing to their injuries, or who would not survive even with surgery.

"Dr. Merriweather proposed to do research into the triage system—a system he had devised and used to some degree in every battle since Antietam, where his scientific observational mind first observed how the sheer mass of wounded prevented appropriate care for each soldier.

"Fellow surgeons and devoted nurses, I am proud to introduce a genuine medical pioneer—my partner, my friend, the husband of a nurse, and also my brother-in-law—Dr. James E. Merriweather."

Teaching Again

In the days that followed the gathering of physicians, Dr. James Merriweather's task was to teach the other surgeons the three-step triage system and, using it, to scientifically assess the state of the wounded of Appomattox and apply treatment based on the assessments of the surgeons. As operating theater cleanliness and use of disinfectants during surgery were the other two legs of his three-legged stool, they necessarily accompanied his teaching of triage.

Merriweather found a physician of like mind in the person of Union physician Jonathan Letterman, who had worked out a system of medical management to organize treatment of Union wounded as they were removed from the battlefield and to the medical tents.

The two physicians were seldom seen separately as they made it their practice to routinely seek out and often question the opinion of each other. There were neither arguments nor heated discussions between the two. Their pursuit of the truth allowed for no such wasted time as hurt feelings caused.

During the day they were to be seen relentlessly prowling the hospital tents answering questions of the physicians and patients alike and attending to the wounded in equal measure.

Together they established a level of care and built a system of wartime medical knowledge and practices that would live far beyond them in the medical corps of the US Armed Forces.

The first week after the gathering, physicians assessed the wounds of the injured assigning each patient a number. The triage system had begun.

Those assigned to category three were provided every form of succor available to the physicians to keep them comfortable. They were beyond mortal help.

The injured in category two had significant, but neither life-threatening nor amputation-requiring, injuries. Their wounds were cleaned and dressed, and they were moved away from the dying and were provided either writing supplies or, if they could not write, a volunteer who could write a letter for them to let their loved ones know that they were not mortally wounded but would be delayed in getting started back home.

The casualties assigned to category one were given the highest priority. These were the soldiers who faced amputation of a leg or foot or hand. The skills that the field surgeons had gained in the bloody hospitals on both sides of the conflict were employed in every effort to save damaged appendages.

However, to Dr. Merriweather's dismay, the surgery was often still crude, but at least a limited understanding of the role of sanitation had been employed since the gathering.

Doctors Merriweather and Letterman were a formidable team as they worked to repair the physical ravages of the infernal conflict, as James Merriweather referred to the war. When they were not cutting, they were instructing other physicians. The colors of the uniforms were no longer important to the doctors or their patients. Their only goal, as emphatically urged by General Grant, was to return the soldier on their operating table home with as intact a body as surgical skills would permit.

Merriweather was saddened that he could not teach his

colleagues the surgical means to save infected limbs, and amputations continued to be a primary method for too many young men. But the wounds created by grapeshot or pieces of shrapnel from a cannon's exploding shell were, for the most part, beyond the skills of the doctors. However, where the injury was from a single bullet or piece of shrapnel, the muscle was incised and the offending object and its remnants were carefully removed. Then came the setting the bone if broken and rinsing the incision with a disinfectant of carbolic acid if available, or turpentine as a last resort. The divided muscle was sutured back together, and if the patient survived the surgery without going into shock, the chances were at least even that some function would return to the limb.

Even limited function in a limb meant walking behind a plow in the spring, stepping out in the cool of the summer shadows at dusk hand in hand with a spouse, or returning to church without need of a crutch on a crisp fall Sunday morning to the thanks of the congregants for their sacrifices.

These were the thoughts that drove Dr. James Merriweather and his fellow physicians after Appomattox, until finally their work reached an end.

Unexpected Kindness

In an act of uncommon kindness, General Grant provided each former Confederate field surgeon with a mount from the Union stable, and one by one the doctors in gray made their way back to their families, each with a hope to return to a life that bore at least some resemblance to the life they had left behind when they enlisted.

James Merriweather stayed another few days, watching with intense personal pleasure as colleagues employed "his" techniques and soldiers recovered. The quick improvement of the status of the wounded did not go unnoticed by General

Grant, who, at Dr. Letterman's suggestion, rode from his headquarters to meet with Dr. Merriweather before he departed for home.

"Captain Merriweather," General Grant spoke as he entered the spare office of James Merriweather, surprising James as he was finishing organizing his files for the office's next inhabitant and getting together a few belongings to carry with him on his way home.

"Sir, I am sorry I didn't respond immediately. It has been awhile since I have been addressed by my Army of Northern Virginia military rank."

"I was thinking on my way here," General Grant said, "how I might address you, and I decided that as I was a military man, using your rank would be the most appropriate way to show my great respect for you. I trust I have not offended you."

"General, I still carry my military service proudly, and I thank you for recognizing my rank. Can I help you, sir?" James responded, hoping his response carried the respect he had for the man who stood before him.

"Captain Merriweather, you helped me when you helped my surgeons and when your efforts saw young men of North and South returned to their families. I am here today to hopefully help you on your way home. I have ordered my quartermaster to select a fine mount to carry you on your journey. If your mount tends to want to turn north occasionally, I hope you will be patient with him!" Both laughed at the unexpected humor as the atmosphere of the meeting changed from the customs associated with rank to that observed in the presence of fellow officers who had survived the worst humankind could offer.

"Captain, your newfound colleague Major Letterman wrote me to ask, almost at the point of insisting," he said with a smile, "that I meet with you before you left us so that I could express the thanks of all your colleagues and that of the Army of the

United States and most of all, my personal thanks for your unselfish service these past weeks here at Appomattox Court House."

"General," Merriweather said with more than a hint of personal inflection clearly added to the military address, "I could do no less."

"Captain, as you make your way home, I want you to carry with you two letters of recommendation—one from me and the second from General Lee, which I personally asked him to pen on your behalf. I hope that you will not need to use either, but you will have them.

"And I want you to carry with you these fifty gold dollars. It is a miniscule recompense for the service you have delivered to your country during the last few weeks. I doubt the emblems on the coin will make you popular should you need to use it, but the gold will overcome those feelings right quickly, I expect."

"General, I don't know what to say. This is totally unexpected."

"Say nothing, Captain. Just get your Southern ass back home! And, Captain ..."

"Yes, sir, General?"

"That's an order."

The surgeons near Merriweather's quarters likely had never heard their commander laugh with such unhindered enjoyment.

Merriweather would carry these few moments with him the rest of his life.

Doctor James Merriweather's final act before departing for Horlbeck Creek was to write what he intended to be his last letter home, anticipating a two-week journey by horseback. He would be wrong.

CHAPTER 49

Last Letter Home

April 22, 1865
Appomattox Court House, Virginia
Quarters of Doctor James E. Merriweather

Darling Red,

I have given this letter to the postmaster of the Army of the Potomac in hopes that it will arrive before I do. However, with the war only being over for the Army of Northern Virginia and not the Confederacy as a whole, and now with Lincoln's death at the hands of the idiot Booth, I am unsure my plan will succeed.

Since I last heard from you, I have seen and experienced things I could not have imagined even a month ago, much less when I departed Horlbeck Creek.

I witnessed the most humble, most gentlemanly, most honorable—the greatest man I have ever known—brought low. As I observed General Lee resting his eyes under the apple tree on the bank of the Appomattox River, sure of what he must do, it was as if the death of every soldier weighed down on him. Resting yet restless, he laid his head back against the trunk and closed his eyes only to slam them open again and to stare the thousand-yard stare of the infantryman in battle, looking into the future and the past simultaneously, I guess. Just as he had set his head against the cool of the tree trunk, in moments he would lower his head in his hands. I saw his lips move, I expect in prayers of supplication for strength for the next few hours. His prayers of intercession for the South had clearly not succeeded. The Almighty chose to answer the prayers of the man who was riding toward Appomattox Court House even as General Lee was gathering up his last full measure of courage to disobey Jefferson Davis and surrender for the sake of his men, the South and the Union united again.

I have had a chance to observe the "drunken devil" as we called General Grant. I now know him personally as a man equally worthy of the honor we have given to General Lee. It took two gentlemanly warriors—each giving full respect to the other—to reach the accord that freed our Southern soldiers to return home honorably so that one day they, like their commander, may see the value in again being citizens of the United States.

Red, General Grant asked me to stay awhile after the surrender to work in hospitals in and around Appomattox Court House and work with Union surgeons on the techniques started in John's surgery in Charleston with a few new ones added myself over these years of "the Struggles" as I have come to think of them.

That is why the letter, if it is delivered before me, has a date so long after the surrender. I know you have worried about my personal struggles as you have not heard from me in far too long. I can tell you that I am better than I have been in some time—the horrors visit me less frequently, but they do visit from time to time. However, thanks to Benjamin and Michael, the effects of their visits are usually short-lived.

I promise you that I will depart tomorrow morning on my way back to you, the only person I know (including a priest and a rabbi whom I love dearly) who can free me from my struggles.

So that is the thought I will have on my mind as I ride south to Horlbeck Creek tomorrow morning.

Until I hold you again,
JEM

Last Letter to the Front

April 11, 1865
Horlbeck Creek
South Carolina

My Beloved Physician,

The word of the surrender of General Lee into the hands of Ulysses Grant at Appomattox Court House reached us this morning. I cannot tell you that it was greeted with wails of remorse and of sackcloth and ashes—although the South has each in abundance. There was only relief here on the banks of Horlbeck Creek and also, I hear, in Charleston. I impatiently await your homecoming.

My darling, we are completely spent beyond any reasonable measure. Here on the creek, we are the fortunate ones, if such a sentiment can be said of any persons in South Carolina.

Darling, come home to me quickly, but please be safe.

Bartholomew brings us news (okay, probably rumors) of roving gangs taking advantage of the lack of law enforcement. I am desperate to have you in my arms, and I pray for you without ceasing. Colin pesters me hourly about when you will be home. He spends every afternoon at the head of the lane looking for you and returns for supper disappointed but always with an "I bet he'll be here tomorrow!"

Come home, my beloved, so that Colin and I can salve your wounds and heal your soul.

Darling, you will not find most of South Carolina as you left it. After four years of war, much of it is again a wilderness. According to Bartholomew, many of our fellow citizens are literally scraping the forests for roots and mushrooms and scouring the underbrush for wild berries. I would like to think that God has blessed us here on Horlbeck Creek, but I do not believe that the Almighty sees our work here on the creek as fruitful and allows other souls—people more deserving than we—to suffer the evils of this conflict only because of where they live.

I did not want to write about this when it happened, for fear I would disturb you in your work, but now that I know for sure that you are coming home, I can tell you about the destruction here at home.

After the word of General Lee's defeat at Gettysburg, it was clear to everyone that this was not to be a quick and glorious little war, and what little remained of the state's treasures was gathered in Columbia and hidden away beneath the floors of warehouses on the banks of the Congaree River. William Tecumseh Sherman—not content with his jubilant destruction of man, beast, and property on his vainglorious march to Savannah—turned his sights toward Columbia to punish South Carolinians for the cannons fired on Fort Sumter. And, like Atlanta, little remains in Columbia untouched by Sherman's fiery sword and uncontrollable rage to destroy all evidence of the loveliness that once was the South.

I am tired, my darling James Edward. Tired of being worried. Tired of nightmares. Tired of seeing Colin growing up too fast without a father. He is growing toward manhood too quickly—experiencing a childhood filled only with war and worry. Tired of questioning my faith in the providence of the Almighty. Tired from lack of sleep. Tired of fear for your safety. Tired of the inner disquiet that I would have to raise our son without you. I need you here as you need to be here. And so I await word of your return.

Oh, I almost forgot. Ol Jake finally left us since last I wrote. Bless him, he provided for us in his death as he had in life. We have learned to waste nothing. We have struggled in the garden without him, but I expect that the lessons ol Jake taught us will be with us for some time to come.

Darling, give my concerns no thought. They are just the ramblings of a tired spirit but also of a faithful one who relishes nursing you back to your former self. I have not lost my ability to nurse the body and soul.

Darling, the light of another day that brings you closer to us is almost gone, and I must stop to cook supper. Colin caught us a nice mess of bluegills, and they await the frying pan.

I rest uneasily, tired each night. And I shall continue until I will see you coming toward us down the lane, the azaleas on either side welcoming you back. Then I will know that our endless night is finally over.

In breathless anticipation,

Red

CHAPTER 50

Trying to Leave Appomattox

After spending two unplanned weeks, James Merriweather left Appomattox, Virginia, early on the Sunday morning of April 23, expecting that his four-hundred-mile ride home through southern Virginia and North and South Carolina would take him three weeks. It took him five.

Although General Grant had been generous in providing mounts to the physicians who stayed on after the surrender to treat the wounded men encamped around Appomattox, the horses were not of his best stock, understandably. But Merriweather's dappled gray mare was different. She was sure of foot and swift of step and seemed to have an innate sense to protect Merriweather when he was in the saddle. Sixteen hands high, she was still in her prime. A cavalry mount, she had been trained to ignore the sounds of fighting, but lately she had become skittish. Assuming he would not encounter any more fighting, she became the perfect mount for James Merriweather. Even so, Merriweather spent most of the first three days assuring her that forest noises were not to be feared.

When Merriweather set out from Appomattox, he had a plan. First, he wanted to journey alone so that he might purge his subconscious of the horrors that had been inflicted upon it. He trusted that he would return to Horlbeck Creek Farm at least resembling the father and husband who had left it in June of 1862 to join the Army of Northern Virginia.

The second part of his plan was to follow a rough railway map that he had sketched with the help of General Grant's cartographer, Captain Jedediah Hotchkiss, who, as he was riding to the surrender ceremony, had been shot in his left leg by a Confederate sniper, Corporal John Anderson.

Corporal Anderson was one of many riflemen on each side of the conflict who were provided with two weeks' rations and ordered to work on their own to try to demoralize the opposition by targeting officers where possible. Anderson had been in the woods area around Appomattox for fourteen days, rations running low and entirely cut off from any information. When he spotted the line of Union soldiers moving along the road to Appomattox, he honed in on an officer near the rear of the column. Anderson was shooting his Whitworth rifle downward from his roost in a tree on a rather steep hill. Whether he was tired or just confused about how to adjust his aim for shooting downhill, Anderson failed to compensate. And instead of hitting Captain Hotchkiss in his chest on the left side at the level of his heart, his bullet fell low and struck Hotchkiss in the left thigh, lodging in the femur and breaking it six inches above his knee.

The Union column unleashed a barrage of return fire at Anderson, and when no more shots came from the hillside, Sergeant Sean McGinnis was directed to yell in his most forceful sergeant's voice toward the direction of the shot.

"Hey, Johnny Reb, ain't you heard? This damn war is over. Now if you will get your sorry ass off your perch and surrender, I promise you that you will not be hurt."

"How am I s'posed to know you won't just shoot me? I did just shoot that cap'n yonder in the leg," Anderson yelled back.

"'Cause," yelled a frustrated McGinnis, "General Grant will shoot us if we shoot you, and I do not want to be shot after this damn war is already over. So one more time, get your Rebel ass down out of that tree so we can see you."

Tired and hungry, cold from a late April frost, and bedraggled so as to hardly resemble a soldier at all, Anderson stumbled his way down the hill toward the Union column, tossing his rifle ahead of himself to indicate his intentions to follow the directions of Sergeant McGinnis.

Anderson was tied with his hands behind his back but suffered no other indignities. He was marched to the Union encampment on the outskirts of Appomattox, where he was released five days later.

Jedediah Hotchkiss

Fate created many peculiarities over the days spent at Appomattox after the surrender. That Union army captain Jedediah Hotchkiss became a patient of Dr. James Merriweather was surely one of the strangest. As soon as Hotchkiss was presented to him as a patient, Merriweather promptly incised the leg, excised the bullet, and set the femur, saving Hotchkiss the trauma of amputation.

Captain Hotchkiss, having known immediately upon being shot earlier that morning that his leg was broken, had become resigned to losing his left leg above the knee. Awaking late the same night from his body's unconsciousness brought on by the pain of surgery, he reached down immediately to feel for his left leg. He had heard the stories of soldiers who declared that their foot itched or felt pain long after it was amputated, so Hotchkiss was not sure if he was dreaming when he felt pain when he touched his leg.

As Merriweather made his postsurgery rounds the next day, Hotchkiss was recovering remarkably and was sitting up and sketching what appeared to Merriweather to be maps and topography in a notebook that he'd had with him when he was brought to the medical tent.

"Captain, you need to lie back and allow your body to recover," remarked Dr. Merriweather. "You had two traumas yesterday. You were shot, and then you were operated on to save your leg."

"So, Doc, it is true. I do still have a leg. I am not dreaming?" asked Hotchkiss.

"It is absolutely true. And if you rest and let it heal, change the dressing every day, and continue to keep it clean with the carbolic acid solution in this bottle before applying the new dressing, you have an excellent chance of saving the leg."

"Doc, are you a Johnny Reb?" Hotchkiss inquired.

Thinking for a few seconds about how to best reply, Dr. James Edward Merriweather responded, "Geographically and philosophically only, Captain. I was officially mustered out of the Army of Northern Virginia yesterday with the signing of the surrender, and as of today, I am a simple country doctor who must soon be making his way back to Charleston, South Carolina."

Merriweather, noting the maps on a notepad, continued, "I see you were drawing roads and rail lines with topographical details in your notebook. Is that your line of work?"

Stopping to consider if he would be violating the secrecy of any orders, Hotchkiss answered, "I am the official mapmaker for General Grant. Not sure what I will be doing now that the war is over. Hopefully not getting shot at again."

After hearing that, Merriweather decided he had nothing to lose by asking, "I have been thinking about my trip back home and thought I would try to use the rail lines as a sort of compass to get me from Virginia to Charleston. What do you think about my plan?"

Most grateful for the unexpected positive outcome from surgery, Hotchkiss sketched an outline of the railroads that would lead Merriweather south to Horlbeck Creek Farm.

Four days later, Dr. Merriweather looked in on Captain Hotchkiss for one last time. Hotchkiss was moving about gingerly with the aid of a crutch, gathering up his belongings in anticipation of a long train ride back to Boston.

"Captain, it looks like we both have the same idea," said Merriweather. "I am heading out myself this morning, but I wanted to stop in one last time to wish you well."

"Dr. Merriweather, be careful heading home. Stay off the railway right-of-way, and travel in the forests to either side. There are still some very angry people out there who may try to take their anger out on you regardless of the uniform. You ride safe. Better to be slow and arrive late than in a pine box.

"By the way," said Hotchkiss, handing Merriweather a slip of paper, "this is my address in Boston. If you ever find yourself in my city, I would like to have you stay with my family and me so that all of us can adequately express our gratitude to you."

"I will do that, Captain." And with that promise, Dr. James E. Merriweather executed a crisp salute.

Captain Jedediah Hotchkiss of the Union army reciprocated in kind and extended his hand. "God bless you, Johnny Reb."

Best-Laid Plans

According to Hotchkiss's directions, Merriweather would follow the Southside Railroad east until he reached the railhead at Petersburg. There he would pick up the Wilmington and Weldon Southern intersecting line and follow it south until he reached the port of Wilmington, North Carolina. There he would find the Wilmington and Manchester Railroad and follow it southwest to Florence, South Carolina, where he would begin the final leg of his journey to Horlbeck Creek Farm fifteen miles east of Charleston.

For the third part of his plan, Merriweather figured he could reasonably travel no more than twenty-five to thirty miles a day. Though he would be using the rail lines for navigation, he planned to stay away from the cleared spaces provided by the railbed. Merriweather did not intend for a similar fate to befall him as had befallen Captain Hotchkiss, so his travel was often through a rather dense forest and underbrush, always keeping the railway in sight. Therefore, his trip was much slower than he'd anticipated.

The final part of his plan was the most tenuous. He hoped that the rail line would provide opportunities to procure or forage for food and water. However, he was totally unprepared for the miles of utter destruction that he was to encounter over and over again. At practically every crossroads he found death, starvation, and hopelessness.

CHAPTER 51

Jemima and Job

Dr. James Merriweather figured he would talk to his mount as he rode, so he named his dappled gray mare Jemima. Jemima was a name often given to slaves, but its heritage was one Merriweather knew. Jemima was the strong and beautiful daughter of Job from the Old Testament. Feeling a bit like Job as he left Appomattox, he thought it altogether fitting as he was departing on Sunday, April 23, 1865.

Regardless, the first two days' journey was uneventful as he made his way toward Petersburg following the Southside Railroad that connected Lynchburg in the west with Petersburg in the east. Jemima was a solid mount and steady once she overcame her initial skittishness. They stayed some fifty yards off the railroad right-of-way, keeping trees and brush between them and the cleared right-of-way. They saw but did not make any contact with numbers of former Confederates who were walking on the railroad.

The largely pine forest in which they traveled and the fallen pine needles on which Jemima walked muffled almost completely the sounds of their journey. Besides, they provided a reasonably soft layer for Merriweather's bedroll at night. At twilight Merriweather led Jemima to the edge of the right-of-way, where she could graze on hard-to-find patches of grass. There was no grain to be had for her, and Merriweather knew that grass alone would not provide the nutrients she needed for the long journey, but he had no choice right now. He could only hope that he might find a better option along the way.

The two-day ride from Appomattox, which at times was almost pleasant, changed dramatically when he reached Farmville, where he found widespread destruction in and around the small community. Three battles had been fought within a half day of Farmville. The battles at Cumberland Church, High Bridge, and Sayler's Creek had all been fought in early April and all within a two-day span.

He had hoped that he might add to his supplies in Farmville, but Grant's Union forces had passed directly through Farmville and had raided the town and surrounding farms of anything that could feed his army and its animals. Unlike Sherman, Grant saw the end of the conflict perhaps only days in the future and did not raze homes or needlessly slaughter the livestock, but he did not stop his army from resupplying itself where it could.

Farmville, being roughly equidistant from each of the battles, had served as a gathering point for the Union wounded and dying. Merriweather had intended to spend the night in Farmville and take whatever time he needed the next day to find supplies, but as he encountered combatants in need of medical attention, he could not just pass them by. He mainly treated infections that had taken hold after quick amputations. For these unfortunates, cleaning, disinfecting, and redressing wounds was seldom sufficient, as they often required additional surgery to excise infected tissue before any disinfectant could prevent further damage. The cries of the men reminded Merriweather of the squeal of a wild pig caught in the steel teeth of the jaws of a bear trap. And in ways and for reasons not clear to him, these cries affected him beyond even the horrors of Gettysburg. Perhaps it was the mere fact that they came after the war's end, and he could more easily foresee the fate that awaited the men even if they survived this second surgery.

With permission of the Union commanding officer, Merriweather was able to add four bottles of carbolic acid, as the commander saw it as a pittance of what he deserved for stopping his journey home to tend to men who, just weeks before, had been his enemy. Merriweather and Jemima had eaten relatively well while in the Union camp, and they had full bellies as they left Farmville on April 26, 1865, headed toward Burke's Station, the midway point between Appomattox and Petersburg and the junction of the Danville and Southside Railroads.

Stench of War Endures

As Merriweather made his way to Petersburg by staying off the railroad right-of-way, he nonetheless was traveling parallel to the route that Grant's Union army had marched only days before on its way to Appomattox and the surrender of the Confederate forces. Therefore, there was little in the way of sustenance for him or Jemima. By the time they reached Petersburg on day six, they were only images of their former selves when they had departed from Appomattox full of food and anticipation. On day seven, April 28, they made a turn south, and that alone was enough to sustain Merriweather for one more day.

Just south of Petersburg, Merriweather again encountered a gathering of wounded Union soldiers brought to the encampment from the battles of Sutherland Station, Five Forks, White Oaks, and Dinwiddie Courthouse. These battles had taken place only a few miles from each other during the last days of March and early April. General Grant and a similar contingent of men with General Meade were pushing steadily and swiftly toward Appomattox and had left the wounded to be tended by nurses and a single field surgeon, First Lieutenant Silas

Shrewsberry, a young physician with minimal experience and even less knowledge of how to care for the severely wounded.

As Merriweather eased Jemima into the encampment, a morning fog was settled around the men. The smell of infected and decaying flesh had bonded with each molecule of water vapor. The smell told Merriweather that he would not be leaving this day.

He tied up Jemima to a hitching post and unsurely but resolutely made his way to the medical tent, where he found Dr. Shrewsberry and five nurses tending to a hundred or so severely wounded Union and maybe twenty-five captured but technically, if not practically, free wounded Confederate troops. Merriweather introduced himself.

"I am James Merriweather, formerly a physician in the medical corps of the Army of Northern Virginia. I believe I can be of assistance."

Silas Shrewsberry patted a soldier he was tending on the shoulder and stepped over to meet James Merriweather. "I am Silas Shrewsberry. I was only recently conscripted into General Grant's medical corps. Two days after graduating from the Harvard Medical School, I was commissioned a first lieutenant and transported to meet up with General Grant for this Appomattox Campaign."

Shrewsberry continued, eyes lowered, seeming to stare at the blood on his boots as he spoke. "These nurses and I are doing all that we know to do, but we are losing boys every day to infections that set in after surgery."

Merriweather led Lieutenant Shrewsberry away from earshot of the wounded. "Lieutenant, would you be so kind as to call your head nurse over so that I might have a few words with you together? I think I can help you all change the direction I see here."

Lieutenant Shrewsberry walked over to a handsome nurse comfortably in her fifties, and they returned to where

Merriweather was busily observing the lack of sanitary conditions that assailed his senses. "Dr. James Merriweather, this is Nurse Amelia Brown. Nurse Brown followed her husband down from Philadelphia. Unfortunately, Colonel Brown was killed at the Second Battle of Manassas. With two sons fighting in the Western Theater, she decided there was no good reason to return to an empty house in Philadelphia."

Nurse Brown spoke in a soft but convincing voice: "Dr. Merriweather, we are glad to have any help we can get. I have written far too many final letters home for fine young men. And I am not sure I can bear to write another, especially now that the war is over."

Glad to find willing souls, if such a sentiment as "glad" could be used in the circumstances that faced him, Merriweather gave instructions as if he were still in command of *his* field hospital.

"Nurse Brown, do you have a quartermaster assigned to this camp?" asked Merriweather. She answered in the affirmative.

"I need you to speak to him personally and have him erect additional tents at least fifty yards away from us so that these soldiers can be moved while we clean up this field hospital. And have him requisition at least five healthy soldiers to help in moving men and equipment."

Nurse Brown responded in her most authoritative motherly voice, "Don't you worry, Dr. Merriweather. Sergeant Brookside owes me more than one favor for the extra biscuits I have slipped to him when I have had time to cook. We have been together for two years now, so I don't think we will have a problem."

By midafternoon, tents were erected with clean cots that came from nobody knew exactly where—and they would not ask. Sergeants in any army are miracle workers, and such was the case in the Petersburg field hospital encampment.

As soldiers were moved and placed on clean beds, the soiled cots were washed in a strong solution of carbolic acid and water and placed in the direct sun to dry. Just outside the field hospital tent, the orderlies built three fires with cast-iron washpots hung above the flames and filled with water. Once the water was boiling, every instrument was placed in the first pot for twenty minutes, after which they were removed and placed in the second pot containing carbolic acid and water for ten minutes, and then they were placed in the third pot of boiling water for another ten minutes. When the instruments were removed from the third pot, they were rinsed in the carbolic acid and water solution, dried, and wrapped with a clean cloth.

By the end of the second day, April 29, the medical tent had been thoroughly disinfected and readied for the return of the men from the auxiliary hospital tents. There they had been kept as comfortable as possible, their wounds treated twice daily with the standard carbolic acid and water solution and dressed with clean bandages.

At least a quarter of the infections cleared up to the point that the men needed no return to the field hospital and remained in the temporary tents away from the more critical infections.

James Merriweather celebrated April 30, the birthday of his wife, Mary Assumpta, by teaching surgical techniques learned from his mentor, Dr. John Bailey, to Silas Shrewsberry, Amelia Brown, and Jubilee Martin.

Jubilee Martin, whom Nurse Brown had invited to attend, was a slave in 1861 when Dr. Alden Dennell, an aging physician in nearby Petersburg, bought her and immediately freed her. Alden Dennell needed help, and though he tolerated the institution of slavery, he would not abide the evil personally, so it was an easy choice to pay for Jubilee's freedom and offer her legitimate work in his office. Dennell knew that a newly freed young black woman was free as to her legal status but pragmatically remained a slave to the system of the economics of the South.

Jubilee Martin served as a nurse in Dr. Dennell's office

throughout the war, and after word of surrender in Appomattox, she moved to the Petersburg field hospital encampment, where she would remain until it was dismantled permanently. Only then would she return to her position in the office of Dr. Dennell in Petersburg.

Merriweather showed how to incise and remove infected flesh around the wounds that had not begun to heal properly. Once the dead tissue was removed and what remained was healthy, the area was resutured. Then application bandages soaked in the carbolic acid solution were applied. For the next twenty-four hours, nonsurgical nurses wet the bandages with the solution every four hours. If the wound showed no signs of the return of infection after the first day, the external sutures were covered with an ointment made of turpentine and beeswax and the wound covered with clean bandages, and the soldier was moved to the auxiliary tents for recovery away from the cries of the less blessed wounded.

The two surgical teams of Merriweather and Martin and Shrewsberry and Brown worked throughout the day and into the early night by kerosene lanterns. By 11:00 p.m. fatigue had replaced aspiration, and the teams simply had to stop to eat and rest. They had operated on more than seventy-five men that day.

Weary but Resolute

The morning of May 1, 1865, broke clean and clear. The stench that had assaulted Merriweather on his arrival had all but disappeared. There were injured remaining to be treated, but Dr. Shrewsberry and his team were now equipped with the knowledge to attack the problem and not let it again gain a foothold in the camp. Merriweather knew to a certainty that they had lost far too many young men to the trauma of a second surgery or to an infection that had spread too far beyond the site of the amputation to be treated.

As he put his left foot into the stirrup and settled into the familiar sway of Jemima's back, he said a prayer for the soldiers who would not be going home and another, more fervent prayer for those who would return forever wounded by this terrible conflict.

Weary of mind and body, James Edward Merriweather and Jemima headed doggedly southward.

CHAPTER 52

The Long Night of Not Knowing

Merriweather and Jemima departed the Petersburg field hospital encampment on May 1, 1865. By the calendar, he was ten days removed from Appomattox Court House. Geographically, Merriweather had traveled only about a hundred miles and remained in Virginia. Mentally, he was still fully engaged in the war.

Merriweather left the Petersburg field hospital with his two saddlebags filled with jerky, a dozen of Nurse Brown's biscuits, a pound of ground coffee, two more bottles of carbolic acid, a small bottle of morphine, a bundle of clean bandages, a box of Lucifer matches, and five sticks of tinder. When he mounted Jemima, he found a scabbard attached to his saddle and, in it, a US Army–issued .56-56 Spencer carbine loaded with seven cartridges. In his saddlebag he found a box of twenty-five more cartridges. Looped around the saddle horn was a ten-pound bag of oats, his canteen filled with water, and a velvet bag with a drawstring of gold cord in which he found a pint of good Irish whiskey. The creative Sergeant Benjamin Brookside, quartermaster for the Petersburg field hospital encampment, had been busy again.

The hallucinations started with a simple, albeit one-sided, conversation with his dappled gray mare three days south of the Petersburg field hospital encampment. Merriweather rode unaware of his surroundings. Occasionally, Jemima would stop to urinate, and he took the opportunity to do the same—totally unaware of his surroundings or his bearings. If he slept, it was upright as Jemima steadily moved in the direction of her choosing. When James was awake, he was oblivious to the fact that he had been asleep or awake. Occasionally, he heard himself yell something unintelligible and profane into the air and felt Jemima jolt at the sound, but never enough to throw her rider from the saddle. Where she could find it, Jemima would stop and graze on grass and drink water from puddles from the rains that had soaked and chilled her rider to his marrow. Merriweather never felt hunger himself in the midst of his hallucinations. Sporadically, he would take a drink from his canteen.

On the third day, the path out of his hallucinations and back to reality started when Merriweather, entirely outside his rational self, was unceremoniously separated from his saddle by a low-hanging two-inch oak branch sometime during the night and somewhere just north of the ruins of the Goldsboro Bridge in North Carolina.

In the Pitch-Black and Alone

As he gradually regained consciousness after the blow to his head by the tree limb, Merriweather's first sensation was that he was cold and very wet. A cold rain had been falling on him for more than an hour. The second sensation was that his face was covered with a viscous and sticky substance with hard bits of something embedded in it. It was blood, he realized when he touched his fingers to the area and felt a lightning stab of pain. Third, there was an intense and relentless almost-nausea roiling both his head and his stomach as he had not eaten since midday the day he had left the Petersburg hospital headed south. However, the last sensation as he regained consciousness was by far the worst—the palpable sensation that he was utterly and completely alone.

It was the all-encompassing aloneness that brought him finally and totally back into the material world as he realized that he could not determine if Jemima was dead, alive, proximate, or gone. He could see nothing. The woods were the color and consistency of pitch. It occurred to him almost incidentally that he could hear nothing, and he wondered if the blow had rendered him deaf. He had landed and remained, until consciousness returned, in muddy clay that had effectively sealed his left ear canal, and the blood from the gash on his head had flowed down and congealed in the canal of his right ear. He realized finally that he had some hearing when he scratched at the wound on his right temple and heard a faint noise seemingly inside his head and much like the sound of kernels of corn flowing into a hopper before being ground into meal. At that sensation, he clapped his hands. When he heard the clap as if from a great distance, it occurred to him to check his ears. Once his ear canals were reasonably free of foreign matter, he called rather unsurely the name of his equine companion.

"Jemima. Are you here?" He listened for any sound that might represent a response from the night forest.

He thought that perhaps he heard the corn-kernel-like noise again. This time, he called loudly (and painfully), "Jemima! Where are you?" Again he heard corn-kernel-like noise, but this time he could determine the direction. From behind him, he felt Jemima emerge from the darkness. As he turned to find the source of the sound, the altogether lovely spectral gray presence eased over to him, placed her forehead directly on his chest, and gave him a nudge. Merriweather wrapped his arms around her neck and caressed her as if she were a wayward child returned to the fold of home.

"Oh, Jemima, girl, am I glad to see you. You must be as frightened as I am." He noticed bloody scratches on her withers and more on her hindquarters. Her tail was thick with beggar's-lice and cockleburs. "Girl, what have I put you through?" he wondered. It mattered not to Jemima as she nuzzled his whiskery face with her soft nose, and he thought it the loveliest caress of his life.

He felt with his feet the ground around him until he found a relatively mud-free patch. He tied Jemima off to a nearby small oak tree, hoping that he could soon get his bearings and determine just how desperate were their current circumstances. His first order of business after tying off Jemima was to check his saddlebags to see if his precious box of Lucifers was dry enough to use one to start a fire. Somewhat to his surprise, they were dry. The box had been coated and sealed with wax before it was placed in his saddlebag.

He took a single piece of kindling, and using the Iver Johnson pocketknife given to him by his father on his tenth birthday that he'd carried in his pocket every day since, he by feel rather than sight stripped the stick of kindling into thin strands that would catch fire quickly. As he worked blindly in the night, he recalled a wisecrack his father made anytime James would ask, "Father, do you have your pocketknife?"

"Son," his father would always wryly reply, "do I have my pants on?" That simple memory and the chuckle that came with it convinced Merriweather that he would survive at least this night mentally intact.

Once he had a decent fire going, he pulled his saddle from Jemima so that it and she could dry. Merriweather removed the saddlebags so that he could do a more thorough inventory by the fire, and he found that he had barely touched his rations beyond a piece or two of jerky and a half-eaten biscuit. He could not rationally, here in the dark of night, reach a reasonable conclusion. Was this the night of the day he departed Petersburg field hospital? Merriweather simply could not answer with any assuredness. His stomach told him that it had been more than just a few hours since he had last eaten, but how many? With his own hunger, worries for Jemima assailed him. He looked at the bag of oats Sergeant Brookside had procured for him, and he was alarmed that it seemed to be unopened. A feel of Jemima's side told him she had not eaten recently.

He fed Jemima first, a handful at a time, knowing that she would gorge on the entire ten-pound bag if given a chance. He gave her water from his canteen in his tin coffee mug. He followed the same regimen for himself with a single piece of jerky and the rest of the half-eaten biscuit. It was only enough to ease his nausea, but it was sufficient for now, until he could get his bearings. He was tempted to add a good slug of Brookside's Irish whiskey to his water, but he would wait until he was sure, in the light of day, that his senses had returned.

Using a clean piece of cloth and carbolic acid diluted with water from his canteen, he cleaned the gash on his head as best he could, being careful not to start it bleeding again. As he palpated the area around the wound, he found a lump the size of a hen egg but no other obvious problems.

He took the bedroll from his saddle, placed the waxed cloth groundcover next to the fire, and covered himself with his gray CSA wool blanket. For the past several minutes he had been busy and unaware that he was cold. Now that he had gotten still, and even next to the fire, he was very cold and very troubled, each perhaps caused by the other.

He needed to plan. Although it made him uneasy, he knew he must wait until good light as the night distorts reality and confuses the mind. Few good decisions are made in the deep of night. So he would wait.

CHAPTER 53

Where the Hell Am I?

The sun rose at 6:30 a.m. although Dr. James Merriweather did not know that fact, as his watch had not been wound in three days. It was May 4, 1865—a Thursday—but he did not know that for a fact either. These details are incidental when compared to the fact that he did not know where he was.

Merriweather had wandered in a mostly subconscious mental state interrupted by periods of semiconsciousness when he was aware enough to relieve himself when Jemima stopped for the same reason. But when he was back on Jemima, her gentle rocking and swaying produced in him a hypnotic-like state filled with hallucinations. It was a miracle that he had remained upright on Jemima.

Today was the fourth day since leaving the Petersburg field hospital. However, he had no idea at all the direction he had traveled in this time or how far.

Once the sun finally rose today, Merriweather could use it and his field compass to move south from his current location, the only direction he cared to know. But he could not tell if his southerly travels were in Virginia or North Carolina. He could not say whether traveling south would take him toward

Wilmington, his final North Carolina destination before entering South Carolina, or to the Atlantic Ocean somewhere north of Wilmington. He could not tell if he was near or far from a rail line—the feature that he had used thus far to guide his progress.

Merriweather's principal task this morning, after rebuilding the fire from the smoldering embers, was to try to figure out where the hell he had landed when that oak tree limb knocked him from Jemima's back and into a state of total unconsciousness.

At 6:30 a.m., good light—enough that Merriweather could make out landforms—was gradually mutating. Dawn was never a sudden thing, he thought, but rather it always seemed to metamorphose slowly from the depth of night like an embryonic moth emerging daily from its dark cocoon. This day's journey from darkness to light must wait a bit longer as the sun must still rise high enough to burn away the morning fog that lingered around him.

Merriweather drank a single cup of russet-brown coffee, heating up a dab of his precious coffee in a cup of his precious water. He needed his head to clear this morning. And thus it was worth it. He fed Jemima four handfuls of her oats, leaving about a third of the bag. It was not nearly enough, but it would have to do for a while.

As he chewed on a piece of jerky and ate a biscuit with it, waiting for the fog to lift, it occurred to him that the presence of the fog indicated that perhaps he was in a depression near water. Flowing water could lead him inevitably to its mouth in a larger creek or river, and people settled near water. He moved far enough so that its crackling would not camouflage the sound.

Sure enough, he thought that he heard running water, but in an unknown wood encased in fog, he could not be sure of its direction. So he must wait. As he waited, he wound his pocket watch and set it at 6:30. He knew the general time of sunrise and figured he would only be off by half an hour at the worst, and at least he could now mark time from this moment forward, knowing that at some point in the future he would make corrections that would set him surely southward to Mary Assumpta.

Fog

The fog was a stubborn creature this morning (his and the earth's), so he moved back to the warmth of the fire, took out his notebook, and wrote a diary entry:

Personal Diary
Early May 1865

I know not the day or my location, but that will change once this smothering fog, my own and the earth's, dissipates, and it will. Once the sun is high enough that I can see it, I can at least use it as a starting point to move southward toward home.

No use to fret about where I am. I am blessed to be alive and warm with a bit of food in my belly and to have the company of Jemima. I expect that since it has been awhile—I honestly don't know how long—since she has drunk her fill, she will lead us to water. Therefore, I will give her the lead and expect she will not disappoint me.

The last memory that I am sure was real and not hallucinatory was when I was about two hours south of the Petersburg field hospital. I was telling Jemima about the farm on Horlbeck Creek and saying that she would have pastures to roam without worrying about her next meal. I talked to her about missing Mary Assumpta's birthday and wondering if Colin had remembered. And that was it—the last memory of which I am sure.

I seem to recall the screams of the cannon rounds as they flew overhead, the fire when they exploded, the smell of cordite, and the plaintive last calls for mama that inevitably followed.

I had flashes of blood rising up to Jemima's forearms that flowed endlessly from the cuts of my scalpel and the rasp of my saw on virgin bone. I recall yelling at the demons that rose up from the morass of the blood and tissue at Jemima's feet.

At some point, we entered the pitch-dark pits of hell, and I clung to Jemima's neck, calling out to Mary Assumpta to save me. But only the demons answered with their otherworldly laughs and shrieks.

It seemed, though I know it cannot be so, that we entered a craft of some form that swayed to and fro on the bloody waves that broke upon its bow. No sails. They were in tatters. No rudder. It had long been broken off, and so we drifted upon the sea of blood. But we were not alone. The broken bodies of young men bumped the side of our craft, and they cried out each time, "Help me, Mama. Help me." And each would then slowly sink in the bloody sea, to be replaced by another and another and another. Our craft was moving swiftly as I could feel a sour wind upon my unshaven face. We gathered speed as if propelled before a cyclone. Yet the force pushing us was not the wind, but the fetid and odorous vapors of a decaying battlefield.

As our barque gathered speed, I felt the bottom of the craft scrape on perdition's reef and knew that I was lost and beyond hopefulness. With a mighty crash *and a blow to my head, I was flung upon the rocks. My last thought before I lapsed into total blackness was what would happen to Jemima, or was it Mary Assumpta?*

I thank my Lord and Savior Jesus Christ for reaching his strong arms down—wherever down was, as I still do not know—to return me to this world. For as evil as it can be, hell is worse. I know. I have been there.

JEM

CHAPTER 54

Nothing Like a Bear

By 8:00 a.m. on May 4, his twelfth day since departing Appomattox, the sun had burned the last remnants of the wet and dense fog that had surrounded Merriweather since before dawn. A quick mental self-assessment—his full name and age, the names of his wife and child, the name of the creek on which his farm was located in South Carolina, and the name of his dappled gray mare—convinced Merriweather that his intellectual faculties were reasonably intact.

Though he had completed his morning constitutional in the woods, Merriweather felt nothing like a bear. His belly had a piece of jerky, part of a biscuit, and a cup of coffee in it, but he was not nourished. His skin had a gray pallor to it, like the color of a seagull's back.

Jemima's ribs were showing, and when he cinched the saddle this morning, he noted the billet strap around her abdomen was two holes tighter from the discolored crease in the strap that showed where it generally fell. She needed nourishment as much as he. Merriweather also knew she needed water, but he would let her thirst help her find more water than he could provide her from his canteen. He was aware that Jemima, the mare he had grown so fond of, was hurting, and he swore it would be the last time she would long for food or water. But he was wrong.

"All right, Jemima," he said to her, "it's time to head toward home." And he gave Jemima slack reins and gently urged her forward with a nudge of his knees to her shoulders. She responded, and they moved eastward. It wasn't toward home, but Jemima was in charge this morning, and Merriweather hoped it was toward the water.

After generally moving eastward for twenty minutes, Merriweather noted that the elevation of their travel was downward. A good first sign. In another five hundred yards, Merriweather saw tall swamp chestnut oaks, sweetbay magnolias, and occasional palmettos, all of which grew in areas near water.

He stopped Jemima to listen. He heard moving water straight ahead to the east and dismounted. Jemima had done her job. No reason to burden her with his weight at this point.

They fought through the thick underbrush of briars, small trees, and honeysuckle vines until, finally, they broke into an opening and saw the Little River. They were, remarkably, only about ten miles north of where the Little River emptied into the Neuse River near the once-bustling town of Waynesboro, North Carolina, and within a short trek to the Wilmington and Weldon Railroad in Goldsboro and a turn southward toward home.

Merriweather dropped the reins, and Jemima walked with her head down to the water's edge on the inside of a bend where the river had deposited a crystalline white sandbar that sloped off gently into deeper water. Jemima stood up to her forearms in the water and drank for what to Merriweather seemed an eternity. He was worried that she might drink too much, but she stopped presently and ambled back to the shore, where she began grazing on the bright green grasses that grew in the fertile loamy soil. Merriweather walked over to her, opened the bag of oats, and fed her handful by handful until they were all eaten. *The oats should give her a boost of nutrition,* he thought to himself, *until we can find additional food, now that we are at least on a tributary of civilization, if a civilized South still exists.*

Three times Merriweather dipped his tin cup into the sweet water of Little River until his thirst, real and imagined, was slaked. He filled his canteen, more for convenience than for need as he would now follow the river southward to its mouth, which he anticipated would be the Neuse.

Baptism

Merriweather removed his clothes and walked slowly until he was waist deep in the moving current. He scrubbed himself with a bar of lye soap that he had acquired before leaving Appomattox. The soap was harsh on his skin, but harsh was what he wanted to remove the odors that he smelled sporadically emanating from his pores. His hair was long and oily. He would remedy the oil here, and he would use his straight razor to trim his hair when his bath was completed.

He eased back to the sandbar, feeling the warmth of the sun through the sand on his wet feet. He returned the bar of soap to its small canvas bag in the saddlebag, dried off with his blanket, and returned to the water's edge with his shaving kit. He had not followed his own teaching about hygiene. At the field hospitals, his bathing had been cursory with a ewer and basin. He simply did not take the time for himself. Other concerns were more pressing. He had let his beard grow while at Petersburg, so he knew that today's shave was likely to be a battle of the straight razor and a five-day growth of his beard. Nonetheless, he stropped his razor, honing its blade, and lathered his face with his badger-bristle hairbrush with the cursive *M* on its top. He picked up the matching straight blade and began the onerous task at hand. Mary Assumpta had given him the shaving kit as a wedding gift, and its use brought him pleasure.

After shaving, he took his hair about an inch from his skull and cut it off with the razor, not a style that Mary Assumpta would have preferred, but one less thing to worry about for a while.

His ablutions completed, he returned to the water, rinsed his hair, lay down in the river, and let the force of the moving water baptize away the sins of war.

CHAPTER 55

Discovery

Thursday, May 4—the warm, white sandbar on the Little River was inviting, and Merriweather considered staying here for the remainder of the day and setting out fresh on the next morning. But it was not yet midday, and he and Jemima were reasonably nourished, at least for a while, so he set out, following the course of the river. Had he been able to travel as the crow flies, his trip would have been less than five miles long. However, rivers never trek as the crow flies, and Little River was no exception.

His journey was to be twice as far and more than twice as long time-wise as he and Jemima would often have to make their way through thick underbrush. To compound matters, the river had at least two oxbow lakes, and Merriweather simply had to follow the course of the river as it frequently bent back around on itself.

Merriweather's best prospect for a shorter journey was to encounter a farm whose boundaries included the banks of the river. This was a rather good bet as the bottomland next to rivers was prime farming land because the silt deposited by frequent spring floods refreshed the nutrients taken out by overfarming.

There were times when the underbrush was unusually thick, and Merriweather was tempted to cross the river in hopes that the other bank would be easier. But he knew that there were as many sandbars on the inside bends on his side as on the other, so he and Jemima continued staying as close to the river's edge as the undergrowth would allow so that he would not miss any signs of farmed land on the far bank.

Toward 3:00 p.m., he still had not spotted any obvious signs of homesteaded land, and both he and Jemima were tiring. He staked Jemima on a grassy bank by another large sandbar, took his carbine, and walked about one hundred yards away from her in the hopes that he could take a squirrel or two for supper. His taste for jerky had worn thin, as had his supply.

He sat down on a dry spot at the base of a large tulip poplar facing toward a group of oak trees up a slight rise. In a half hour, the woods absorbed his presence and returned to its primal nature. There was no wind this afternoon, and that always made seeing squirrels much easier. Sure enough, he soon heard a sound like a shallow cough that an infant might make—the bark of a gray squirrel or maybe a fat fox squirrel. He spotted two fox squirrels playfully chasing each other around the trunk of a sweet gum tree. He knew he would never score a hit with the squirrels running and jumping, so he waited patiently. In a few minutes, they settled down and started eating the acorns they had in the pouches of their mouths. He took aim just below the squirrel at the limb the fattest one was sitting on, steadied the gun against the trunk of the tulip tree, and fired. One of the squirrels fell to the ground in front of him at the base of the sweet gum, and he watched the other run to a nest two trees over. Knowing that he might have only dazed the fallen squirrel, he eased over and, seeing that it was only unconscious, dispatched it. Next, he moved toward the nest. As it was already starting to get dusk dark in the woods, he did not have time for the swamp forest to grow silent again after the sound of his rifle, so he decided he would shoot into the nest in hopes of harvesting the other squirrel. It was not sporting he knew, but damn, he was starved and night was coming on quickly.

He made his way back to the sandbar with two fat young gray squirrels after skinning and cleaning them at the water's edge. He staked the two pink-meat carcasses in the sandy river bottom so that the cool moving water would keep them fresh as he foraged for the implements to build a fire.

He found two oak saplings about a half inch in diameter, cut them off at their bases, and stripped them of their leaves and branches, leaving a *Y* of branches at the top. The bottoms he had sharpened into points that he would drive in the sand on either side of the fire. He repeated the procedure with two more saplings.

Next, he cut two small sweetbay magnolia trees about the same size as the oaks and stripped them, leaving a *Y* branch at the large end of each. These last two saplings would make the spit on which he would affix the squirrels. Once the two squirrels were secured to the spits, he gathered up the bay leaves he had stripped off, filled the chest cavities of the squirrels with them, and fastened each squirrel's stuffing with two small twigs that he had sharpened and inserted between the ribs. Sweetbay leaves were a staple of Southern cooking. He had no salt, so the pungent leaves would suffice nicely.

Once the fire had a nice bed of coals, he drove the two oak saplings with the *Y* branches at their tops on each side of the fire so that the spit with the body of the squirrel would be about six inches over the edge of the coals. After laying the spits holding one squirrel each in the *Y* of the oak saplings, he dragged up a driftwood log and took a seat before the fire. He planned on rotating the squirrels about every five minutes, figuring that thirty minutes would be more than enough time to cook them done without toughening them.

Shadows

As he moved from the log he was sitting on to turn his supper on the spit for the first time, Merriweather caught a movement in the peripheral vision of his left eye. He did not turn to look straight in the direction of the movement, for he knew the human eye, as a vestige of its past as predator and prey, could detect much more with peripheral vision than by turning the head. When forest was virgin and the water as pure as the air, a turn of the head might just be enough for a (now extinct) large eastern panther that had hunted this North Carolina coastal plain to decide that this particular member of the (also now extinct) Tuscarora tribe on the sandbar was lunch and not just another tree near the water.

Merriweather did not have to turn his head, as the moving shadow called out to him. "You a Johnny Reb? Or did you murder a Confederate cap'n and steal his horse and them clothes?"

Merriweather was so surprised at the voice that he stammered, "Yes, sir. I mean, no, sir. I mean, yes, sir. I am a Johnny Reb."

The intruder, still only a shadow, was unconvinced. "Hell, I don't believe you. I might as well shoot you rat'chere. I sure could use a good horse to git me back goin' on my farm. Sherman's damn Yankees kilt ever last animal I owned and just left 'em rottin' in the fields 'cept for the milk cow and one ol' mule I managed to hide down in that thicket yonder."

Regaining a bit of his battlefield-physician-acquired composure, Merriweather answered the shadow, who had now moved slightly to Merriweather's right and behind a solid swamp oak trunk. "I am Captain James Merriweather, and I served as a field surgeon to General Lee and the Army of Northern Virginia."

"No provin' it by me. Sheeit. Look at that saddle. Got 'US Army' wrote on them saddlebags."

Merriweather was beginning to panic a bit as he began to see himself from the shadow's perspective. "If you will just come out, I can explain everything. I am from Charleston, South Carolina, and I am just trying to get back to my family and my farm, which I fear may have suffered the same fate as yours."

The shadow, aiming a single-barrel twelve-gauge shotgun at Merriweather, moved to the other side of the oak tree and then toward Merriweather, keeping a black gum tree between the two of them. "Nope. I thank I shall jest shoot your sorry ass right now. Look yonder at that rifle scabbard. Damn US Cavalry carbine. That proves it sure 'nough."

Merriweather decided he would go redneck on the shadow. "Now, just hold the hell on for a minute. When have you seen a damn Yankee kill two squirrels with a carbine and not leave a mark on them, and then cook them up stuffed with sweetbay leaves over a campfire? You got the drop on me. Why don't you bring your sorry ass over here, and I'll share a squirrel with you. Did any of Sherman's Yankees share anything with you when they were passing through?

"On your way over, stop and look in the saddlebag on the right side of Jemima, and you will find my diary. Take a look at it and see if you still think I am a Yankee."

The shadow decided the stranger did sound rather Southern and figured it wouldn't hurt to look in the saddlebag. The shadow did not read fluently, but he could make out the pain in words written after the retreat from Gettysburg, and he knew no Yankee could write such words about the boys who fought and died in the Pennsylvania mud—his own boys. The shadow had given his two sons to the fight. Jeremiah, eighteen, and Emanuel, twenty, had died fighting side by side during Pickett's charge on Cemetery Ridge the last day of Gettysburg.

CHAPTER 56

Shared Despair

With tears streaming from his eyes into his scraggly beard, the shadow moved toward James Merriweather. "Sorry to put the fright into ya, but we have had some Yankee strays, and some Rebs too, who seem to think the war ain't over yet. I ain't got much left, but what I got, I'm gonna keep. But hell," the shadow said to Merriweather as he moved toward him while opening the breech of the shotgun, "my shotgun weren't even loaded anyway."

Merriweather waved for the farmer to come over to the fire and have a seat on the log. "I got two big fox squirrels here, and I can't eat them both. You are sure welcome to one of them. I also got a little whiskey that might go good with a little branch water from this river."

"That is most Southern of you, Cap'n. I had a little shine I made with some weevil-eaten corn. It was hardly fit to drink and didn't last long, but I sure ain't had no good sippin' whiskey in more'n three years now."

"I haven't got much in the way of provisions, but what I have, you are welcome to," Merriweather told him as he extended his hand to shake with the shadow.

"You know my name, and it's time I quit thinking of you as 'the shadow.' May I ask your name, sir?"

"Damn, sorry about that, Cap'n. Damn war has 'bout

robbed me of all the manners my mama taught me. I am David Johnson, and me and my wife, Tillie Jean, live on what's left of our farm two bends up and jest 'cross the river."

"Pleased to meet you. And no need to call me Captain. I was never fond of the title, but my bosses said if I was to be an army surgeon, the rank came with the job. And I must admit there were times that a soldier's respect for the position made it just a little bit easier to do what had to be done to remove an arm or a leg.

"I am just James. May I call you Thomas? If this war has taught us anything, it ought to be that social order has nothing to do with a man's value."

"Cap'n ... sorry ... James. If you don't mind, just call me Tom. That's a sight better'n what my Tillie calls me when I come home from the woods with nothin' fer supper."

Merriweather, realizing that Tom had been out foraging for anything he could find that could be safely eaten, made a suggestion. "Tom, why don't we take both these squirrels—and I still have some jerky and hard biscuits, and a little coffee and of course that whiskey—and bring them to Tillie Jean so that we might have a proper supper together?"

Thomas was totally dumbfounded and could hardly talk. Finally, with tears welling and his voice breaking, he managed to speak: "James, that'll be the kindest thing anyone has done fer us in ages, but I won't take your food. Looks like both you and the mare ain't ate decent in many a day."

"Well, I guess Jemima and I will just have to head up this river until we locate that fording spot and make our way up and introduce ourselves to Tillie Jean without your help."

"Hell, no you ain't. Tillie'll cuss me good if you do that, and I already had my one cussin' fer today. I don't need another."

Johnson and Merriweather put the saddle, the saddlebags, and scabbard on Jemima, and Thomas took Jemima's reins and started walking southeast along a game trail through the brush—clearly not the first time he had been this way.

Two bends up, the river shallowed up to a natural ford. The water was rushing, but it did not get above their boots. As they reached the east bank, Merriweather admitted, "Tom, I have been lost for four days now, and I was just hoping to find a farm so that someone could get me back on my way home. Does this river have a name?"

Tom laughed a deep and hearty laugh all the way from his belly, a laugh long suppressed by war. "Hell, James, I thought you looked a *little* bothered—more'n just hungry—when I come up on you. This here is the Little River, and 'bout ten miles down it runs into the Neuse. Does that help you get your bearings?"

"The Neuse runs into the Pamlico Sound, right?" asked James.

A bit puzzled, Tom responded, "It does, but it is a three-day ride from here to New Bern. Is that where you're headin'?"

"No, I just need to find the Wilmington and Weldon Railroad. I have been using the railroads as my map home. I can follow the Wilmington and Weldon to Wilmington and then pick up the Northeast Railroad that'll take me to Charleston. I expect there are more direct routes, but as I am unfamiliar with North Carolina roads, following the railroad seemed the best choice for me. What are you thinking?"

Tom smiled again as they walked toward a weathered gray clapboard farmhouse. "Shit, James. The Wilmington and Weldon ain't more'n five miles directly east from our farm. I'll walk you there myself. Might just pick up a rabbit or two on the way. I ain't been huntin' in that direction in a while."

"I can't ask you to do that, Tom. I can find my way to the rail line."

Tom threw his head back and roared with laughter at that. He was so loud that an attractive woman, even in her tattered dress, came out on the falling-down porch to see if her husband had finally gone over the edge of reality for good.

"I ain't had two laughs in the same day, much less the same afternoon, in I don't know when. I find you as confused as a Yankee in a New Orleans whorehouse, and *you* tell me you can find your way to a rail line you ain't never seen? Bullsheeit is what that is." And he roared again as they neared the farmhouse.

"It'll be good dark in another hour, and you ain't goin' nowhere today, or tomorrow, without me. We'll sit down and have supper of them squirrels, such as it is, and then you'll stay the night under our roof."

"I can't impose on you folks like that. I have a bedroll, and Jemima and I will sleep just fine under the stars," stated James Merriweather.

"The hell you will," a very Southern and very feminine voice drawled to Merriweather. "We may not have much left after this damn war, but we sure as hell have some southern hospitality left. Now, no more questions. What is this I hear about squirrels?"

Gettysburg Diary

Tillie Johnson placed three cracked unmatched china plates and pewter utensils on the table. She placed the two roasted squirrels, which Tom had cut into pieces, on a battered old tin serving tray that might have been used to feed the dog back when they had a dog. But it was clean, and it was full of fire-roasted squirrels. Tillie even produced salt that came from a vein that ran near the top of the ground where the farm dropped off sharply toward the river.

Tillie asked Tom to bless their food. "Dear heavenly Father, the source of all that is good and kind, please forgive our frustrations and teach us humility. Please look after our boys. For that peace of mind, these squirrels, and this new friend that you brought to us this day, we are thankful. In Jesus's name I ask these things. Amen."

The house was battered, looking like Sherman's troops had slept here and tried, it appeared, to break every keepsake they could find. But it was clean, and the damaged furniture had been repaired as best as was possible with the hand-carved dowels or metal wrapping made from fence wire. There were places in the floorboards where one could see the earth beneath the floor. There were no curtains or even glass in the windows, and no rugs to cover the bare places in the floor. Yet it seemed not to affect at all the feel of warmth that pervaded the home.

After supper, Tillie made a small pot of coffee from Merriweather's precious stash. She poured it in an intact china cup for her guest and in tin cups for herself and Tom. James offered them a dash of his Irish whiskey, and they accepted it gratefully. The coffee had cooled enough to drink, and Tom spoke. "James, me and Tillie have suffered more in this war than just our farm. We lost both our boys on Cemetery Ridge. Until I read your diary, our only comfort was that they died together. But when I read your diary on that riverbank a few hours ago, I knew for the first time that there was good men at Gettysburg who cared for our boys. That brought me such peace that I'd like you to read a bit more of it to me and Tillie."

Merriweather took the tattered notebook from his saddlebag that had been brought into the house with his bedroll and began to read: "Nothing prepared me for the sheer awfulness I was to face at Gettysburg. I thought that this would be much like previous battles. There our work was intense for hours, but at the end of the day, we found a time to reflect on the good done that day in our field hospitals."

He stopped before the next entry as Tom and Tillie were softly crying. "Are you sure you want me to continue?" They both nodded, and James finished reading the entire diary entry of July 15, 1863, to the war-broken husband and wife.

As his emotions threatened to overwhelm him again as they had on the trail, Merriweather was not sure he could go forward to Mary Assumpta. How could he rightly bring such pain to his beloved wife? Merriweather placed the carbine next to his bedroll with a cartridge in the chamber and the hammer cocked. Such was the depth of the despair that he experienced as he tried to sleep that coolish May night in front of the dying fire in the fireplace with drafty breezes coming through the floor and windows.

Sometime during the early hours, long before dawn, Merriweather released the hammer and ejected the cartridge. His time might come, but it would not be tonight.

CHAPTER 57

Former Glory

Guided by Tom Johnson, Merriweather and Jemima walked eastward and directly to the Wilmington and Weldon Railroad just north of Goldsboro. This was his path south to Wilmington. After a long embrace with Tom, Merriweather mounted Jemima and rode south toward the town of Goldsboro, North Carolina.

He entered Goldsboro hoping to find supplies for the next legs of his journey. Instead he encountered hurricane-like devastation at every turn. In late March the hurricane, in the form of General William Tecumseh Sherman's more than hundred thousand Union troops, had occupied the town of fifteen hundred for more than three weeks.

Before the war, Goldsboro had been a growing community, so much so that the county seat had been moved from Waynesborough to Goldsboro in 1847, after the Wilmington and Weldon Railroad was completed. At the start of the war, Goldsboro was a flourishing community thanks to the lumber and grain mills that had brought a significant level of prosperity to the town. As a measure of the success, there was recently built a number of stores, two hotels, two churches, and numerous fine homes.

But the Goldsboro that James Merriweather found resembled its former glory not at all. As Merriweather entered the town where the railroad intersected with the main street, he had simply continued to give Jemima her lead. They passed through as pale ghosts in the bright sunshine. Each side of track was lined with vestiges of fine houses that now lay plundered by the Union soldiers who had encamped there.

Merriweather passed the infrequent resident, but no eye contact was ever made between them. Now and then a Union deserter, seeing Merriweather's gray uniform, tattered as it was, would step out under the porte cochere of an occupied house and yell insults. The insults never even registered on Merriweather's consciousness. Such was his dogged determination to move through Goldsboro leaving no hint that he had ever passed that way.

Surprise at the Wilmington Star Hotel

Merriweather plodded on and reached Wilmington before noon on May 9, 1865, emaciated of spirit and body, hoping beyond hope that he could purchase enough supplies to last him and Jemima for the seven days he anticipated the trip would take to reach home.

He followed the Wilmington and Weldon Railroad into Wilmington and to where it terminated at the depot on Water Street—at least what had been the depot. Merriweather found little that remained of the glory that had been Wilmington before and during much of the war. The citizens of Wilmington were accustomed to imported foods and colorful cloth goods from Europe, even during the Civil War. After the fall of Norfolk, Virginia, in spring of 1862, Wilmington became the last remaining Confederate East Coast port where goods could be sold and where supplies from European allies could enter and be transported north to supply Confederate forces using the Wilmington and Weldon Railroad.

Wilmington remained critical to the Army of Northern Virginia until the winter of 1865, when the Union army successfully captured Fort Fisher, which protected the Cape Fear River and Wilmington on the river some thirty miles north. With the capture of Fort Fisher, the Union blockade of Wilmington was complete. The Union army had placed a choke hold on the city of Wilmington and the Confederate Army of Northern Virginia. The citizens of Wilmington fled in advance of the Union army, which was moving swiftly toward the city. Making things worse for the citizens of Wilmington, Confederate general Braxton Bragg left the city and took his six thousand troops, but not before burning the riverfront warehouses containing anything of use to the Union army.

From the burned-out warehouses and depot, Merriweather rode at a slow pace south on Water Street until he reached Byrne's Star Hotel at the corner of Market and Princess Streets. He was not sure what he expected, but what he found was an all but abandoned hotel. The Union blockade at the mouth of the Cape Fear River had not only strangled the supply line for Lee's Army of Northern Virginia but also had starved out, except for the most stalwart among them, the citizens of Wilmington.

Merriweather tied off Jemima to the hitching post in front of the Star Hotel where she could get water from the trough that sat under the hitching post. The accumulated water in the trough had to be from a recent rain, but Merriweather checked it and it was free of algae and safe for Jemima.

As he stepped on the wooden sidewalk, his boots made a hollow ringing sound that seemed to echo down Market Street. He really thought that he would find the hotel locked up or else demolished on the inside. Actually he found neither. The Yankees' main objective for Wilmington was the blockade that rendered the Wilmington and Weldon Railroad useless. The Union forces around Wilmington, except for a small force to occupy the captured Fort Fisher, had quickly moved through Wilmington with minimal damage to property.

Merriweather tried the front door and found it open. As he entered, off to his left was the hotel's restaurant, where he found a single civilian drinking a cup of coffee and writing in what appeared to be a journal.

"Hello, sir," Merriweather ventured. "Could you tell me if this hotel is open for business and, if so, where I mind find the proprietor?"

"Phillipa!" the man called out in the direction of the kitchen at the far end of the room. "Get your cute little ass out here, and bring another cup of coffee. I think you might have a paying customer.

"Pardon me for being so rude. Let me introduce myself," the man said in a clearly educated voice. "Captain, I am Cicero Harris, the former publisher of the *Wilmington Daily Journal*."

"Glad to make your acquaintance, Mr. Harris. I am Dr. James Merriweather, formerly of the Army of Northern Virginia medical corps. Please dispense with that 'Captain' business. I only wear this uniform because it is all the clothes that I have, and the bars on my shoulder might be useful to get me out of trouble at some point on my way home."

"Well, I will get rid of the 'Captain' if you dispense with the 'Mr. Harris.' Deal?"

As Merriweather was about to ask again about the hotel's manager, a very attractive woman, whom he assumed was Phillipa, elegantly carrying a cup of coffee in a china cup sitting on a matching saucer, strolled to the table where he was now sitting with Cicero Harris. It was impossible to easily determine her age. The war aged everyone beyond their actual years. She was dressed in the style that Merriweather would describe as English country estate hunting attire. She wore polished boots that came to her calf, dark olive-green corduroy slacks, a dark tan shirt with the collar open just enough to show a trace of the cleavage that peeked out from beneath, and a brown Harris

Tweed jacket with faint blue and green stitching that made a plaid, but only if you looked very closely.

A few gray strands that created a notable, rather than aging, appearance highlighted her ebony tresses. She could be, Merriweather surmised, anywhere from thirty to fifty. Her demeanor said that she was definitely the kind of woman of whom you never inquired about age.

As she approached the table, Merriweather stood, although Cicero Harris remained seated, and introduced himself. "Miss Phillipa, I believe. I am Dr. James Merriweather. Please pardon my rather dusty and dirty attire. I have been on the road to Charleston since the surrender at Appomattox Court House."

Phillipa Byrne extended her right hand and ever so slightly curtsied as Merriweather took her hand in his. "Dr. Merriweather, Mr. Harris and I are ever so glad to make your acquaintance. Three is so much better company than two, don't you agree? Cicero and I have said the same things to each other so many times that we complete each other's sentences.

"If I understood Mr. Harris's shouting at me, I believe you are looking for accommodations." As she spoke, she looked directly at Cicero Harris with a devilish look that told him in no uncertain terms that Southern gentlemen do not yell at Southern ladies, war or no war.

"Yes, ma'am," Merriweather responded, "that is the case. I assume from the looks of things that you do have a room available. Do you also provide food to go with this excellent cup of coffee?"

Phillipa Byrne said, "We actually are still supplying both, although the former is in much greater supply than the latter. But we do still have some cured meats, some sweet potatoes, Irish potatoes, and acorn and butternut squash, and a few apples that were hidden away from the Yankees in our root cellar, along with a small supply of tea and coffee, sugar and rum from the Caribbean, and a rather excellent supply of European wines from Germany and France.

"Mr. Harris here is an accomplished cook when you can break him away from making up stories of death and destruction at the hands of the malevolent Yankees for his recently defunct, but soon to be operational again, newspaper once our citizens begin to return."

Cicero Harris took insincere offense at the implication. "Whoa there, Miss Phillipa. I only write the stories as I see them. Besides, once I get the paper back on its feet, then we can get back to the truth."

"I'd be careful, Dr. Merriweather," Phillipa spoke in a raspy sotto voce alto. "By the time this yellow journalist records your visit, you will be Stonewall Jackson come back to life." At that, they all laughed at Cicero's expense, including Cicero.

"Before I sign your register for posterity's sake and get a key to my room, can you tell me where I might be able to find a livery stable for my mount Jemima?"

Cicero Harris spoke up. "I have done business personally with Mr. Samuel Currie, owner of livery stables on the corner of Princess and Second Street just a block from here toward the river. I don't know if you will find him on the premises, as horses are scarcer in Wilmington these days than people. But if he is not around, you are likely to find food and water about the place for your mare, and you should help yourself. If you do run into him, he will be a bit gruff, but pay that no mind as he prefers horses and mules to people. He will take care of the mare at a reasonable rate."

"Thank you, sir. Miss Phillipa, I will tend to Jemima and be back presently. May I leave my saddle and belongings here until I return?"

"Of course. They will be okay right where you dropped them."

Merriweather took the bit from Jemima's mouth and walked her with just a halter the one block to the Currie Livery Stables. "Mr. Currie, are you here around the stable? I wish to board my horse," Merriweather shouted, but no answer returned.

Merriweather looked about the place that had been swept and mucked out before it was abandoned. Temporarily, he surmised. In a far dark corner away from casual eyes, Merriweather found a hundred-pound croker sack of oats with a crudely written note attached to it. He struck a match so that he could read it. "As there are no horses left in Wilmington, I have gone to ground in the country. If you find this note and there are any oats left, help yourself, but leave some for the next person." It was signed, "C. A. Currie, Owner."

Merriweather led Jemima to the rear of the stable and into a stall with a water trough half filled and a wooden feed bucket nailed to the back wall of the stall, into which he poured five pounds of oats. He would go slowly over the next few days until Jemima had regained some weight and stamina.

Using all of his former military folderol and just a bit of fudging about how he had obtained Jemima, he pinned a note to her halter: "I am Captain James E. Merriweather of the Army of Northern Virginia, and I am the owner of this mare given to me personally by General Robert E. Lee at Appomattox for medical service to the Confederacy. I am currently residing in Byrne's Star Hotel should you require my services."

He was a bit leery of leaving Jemima, but he had no other choice. He shut the stable door and latched it so that it might appear to someone wandering by that it was locked up tight.

Upon returning to the Star Hotel, he found that his belongings were no longer in the dining room where he had dropped them, but Cicero was still in his same seat, writing in the same notebook. "I hauled your things up to your room, which I believe is room 202. You will find a room key on your bed, but I doubt that you should need it with Phillipa and me as the only potential thieves about. And Phillipa does lock the front door at dark, which is about 7:00 p.m., give or take a few minutes this time of year."

Merriweather bid Harris good day and started toward his room when Harris called out to him. "Once we lock the door, we make our way back here and serve ourselves supper. Tonight we are having cured ham, red-eye gravy, baked sweet potatoes, and sweet tea. Unfortunately, we have no ice."

Merriweather expressed his thanks for the information and headed toward room 202. There he found his saddle, saddle blanket, saddlebags, carbine, and bedroll stacked neatly on the floor at the foot of the four-poster bed.

The bed, and in fact the entire room, reminded him of the bedroom above his mentor's medical office in Charleston. The furniture was not the same quality, but the same pieces were in the room: a bureau to hang his outer garments, a side table for personal items, and a washstand with ewer and basin and soap dish. In a remarkable coincidence that brought a smile and then tears to his eyes, the soap in the soap dish was the same milled French soap that Mary Assumpta had attentively picked out and left for him. He remembered that moment as giving him the first insight into the workings of the mind of his future bride.

Unlike his bedroom in Charleston, room 202 had a separate bath with a plumbed tub, basin, and toilet. Apparently Wilmington had benefited in some unique ways as a significant European trading destination in the South. After taking a few minutes to figure out how everything worked, he ran a tub of water and washed his uniform and shirt as best he could with the hand soap. So dirty were his clothes that the soap hardly made a lather at all. When he had wrung them out by hand and let the water out of the tub, there was a substantial coating of dirt and grime on the bottom of the bath. So he repeated the process until no residue remained after rinsing his clothes. The Star Hotel, expecting guests to wash some of their clothes, provided a clothesline that ran the length of the room on which Merriweather hung his well-worn uniform, gray underwear, and socks with holes in the toes and heels.

Next, he ran a tub of water for the first all-over bath he had had since his "baptism" in the Little River several days before. The water was cold, but it was still well and truly delightful to be in a porcelain bathtub again. After thirty minutes of soaking off the trail dust, he dried himself with very white towels with "The Star Hotel" embroidered on them, hoping that he did not leave them dirty as well as wet. Covering himself with the bathrobe, he opened the bathroom window and then the window in his room, hoping that his clothes would be reasonably dry before supper.

Beyond tired of body and soul despite the pleasing bath, Merriweather climbed naked beneath sheets and went immediately into a two-hour profoundly dreamless sleep. He awoke to a knocking on his door. "James, this is Phillipa. I just wanted to let you know that I am locking the front door presently, and we will have supper in the dining room in about twenty minutes."

Used to going from sleep to complete alertness in seconds during his war campaigns, Merriweather replied, "I will be down shortly, but don't wait on me for supper."

He heard an alto voice in return: "Of course we will hold supper. We shall not miss the conversation that you will surely provide. See you in a few minutes."

Merriweather's underwear, socks, and uniform shirt were damp but would soon dry on him as he wore them. His pants were still rather wet, but he had no other choice, so he put them on. His captain's blouse would have to wait until tomorrow.

When Merriweather entered the dining room at 7:30, he found Cicero and Phillipa sharing a glass of white wine. Cicero waved him over. "We decided we could wait on your for dinner, but the wine could not be delayed. Come, let me pour you a glass of this sweet German Riesling before we have our evening meal together."

Merriweather was not sure food had ever tasted as good as the elegant meal they shared, made of the most ordinary of Southern fare. "Cicero, supper was remarkable, as was the company. Phillipa, the modern conveniences provided to your guests shall surely bring my wife and me back once I am home and I have settled my affairs."

Phillipa looked at bit pensive at the mention of a wife, for she had had her eye on the handsome physician from the South Carolina Low Country, but she recovered quickly. "Why, thank you sincerely, James. That means a lot to me coming from a cultured gentleman such as yourself," she said with a wry smile on her face.

Neither the face nor the smile was lost on Merriweather. He thought it was a face that was unadorned by makeup and didn't require any. Her beauty, he thought, was entirely natural with none of the affectations so prevalent in Southern society before the war. He noticed that she spoke with a Carolina accent, but it was pure with no artificiality to it. She walked with the grace of a Carolina catamount, totally aware of the effect the rhythm of her backside had on him and Cicero. He speculated that antebellum plantation-bred young women were likely reduced to spiteful Southern bitches in her presence because there was nothing they could do, and nothing that their fathers could buy for them, that would produce the natural sexual magnetism that Phillipa Byrne exuded from every cell of her body.

After dinner over a coffee, Cicero inquired about Merriweather's experiences in the war and especially how he had come to be in Wilmington. Merriweather spoke in general terms of his medical service in the Army of Northern Virginia.

But he did not talk at all about any of his personal turmoil. Merriweather spoke of Appomattox and General Grant's generosity in providing him Jemima, and he said that General Grant had paid him in US dollars for the medical services Merriweather provided to the Union army following the surrender at Appomattox. He told of how his journey home was planned out but how it had become sidetracked at Farmville and Petersburg. He recounted the Johnsons' hospitality extended to him in spite of the losses they sustained to farm and family.

The publisher in Cicero Harris was particularly interested in Merriweather's account of Goldsboro, and he posed a question: "Are you able to talk about your impressions as you rode through Goldsboro? I think it would be a story my future readers would be most interested in."

"It was a like a ghost town," explained Merriweather, "except it was not abandoned. As I came down the railroad tracks in the middle of the village, the people I saw walked about, it seemed, with no purpose to their movements. Their eyes were downcast, and not a single citizen made eye contact with me. The Union army of General Sherman must have occupied every building in town, and although they did not destroy it physically, they appear to have broken the Southern spirit of this entire community. At least that is what I surmised."

Cicero reacted, "We have gotten word that one hundred thousand Union troops occupied the town that had held about fifteen hundred residents. So I expect your account is accurate. It makes me wonder how the citizens of Wilmington will respond when they return. They will come back to a city almost exactly as they left it, except for the warehouses on the docks, but any Confederate currency they have will be worthless, and who knows how long it will be before the banks will have any substantial reserves of dollars."

Phillipa agreed. "I have no idea how this hotel will function if the money is no good. We can barter, but only up to a point, and we cannot survive on bartering. Who will be our guests? In the past the hotel has been a center for tradesmen, but how long will it take for trade to resume? I worry that the next few years may be worse for us here in Wilmington than what we experienced in the war."

Merriweather added his concerns to those of Cicero and Phillipa. "I have no idea what I will find once I get home. I had one letter from my wife, Mary Assumpta, that reached me at Appomattox, and things had gotten rough on our farm near Charleston."

The conversation had evolved into a discussion of economics, and Merriweather took the opportunity to discuss paying the bill for his stay with Phillipa. "I will settle up with you in dollars when I depart the day after tomorrow. And I will need to purchase some supplies needed over the next several days, so I hope you all can point me toward anyone who is willing to sell me a few dried goods for the trip.

"Even better, if you could procure the supplies for me, I will then pay you. The fewer who know I have dollars, the better.

"But let's talk about that tomorrow. Right now, I am going to bid you both a fond good night. And again, thanks for an excellent meal and even better company. I will see you in the morning."

CHAPTER 58

Southern Hospitality Brings Moral Uncertainty

Merriweather walked to his room with a somewhat renewed sense of himself. He had had a civilized conversation with two Wilmingtonians who saw the future for what it was likely to be but who faced it nonetheless with a resolve to succeed. If Cicero and Phillipa could see triumph in the face of oncoming adversity heaped upon them by the conclusion of this war, then he saw no reason why he could not do the same.

Merriweather entered his room and shut the door with no need to lock it. After placing his clothes in the armoire, he slipped between the crisp North Carolina cotton sheets. He had cracked the windows on either side of his room, and a cool sea breeze was rustling the curtains—a sound that was just at the level of Merriweather's awareness—before he slipped into the arms of Morpheus. But the rustling he heard now was to the left of the bed, nearest the door, where there were no windows.

Presently, he felt a sensation of coolness as the coverlet was pulled back from the bed. The May night was moonless, and his room was swathed only in black shadows. A shadow was now lying next to him. Merriweather could count in years the last time he had felt the suppleness of an attractive woman's skin touching his own, and his senses were immediately awakened. "Phillipa, is that you?"

Phillipa replied in a hushed whisper, "Shh. Just enjoy the

moment. Cicero is passed out with his head on the dining room table. It is just you and me, and we are all the world that we need be concerned about tonight."

Merriweather whispered his doubts to Phillipa: "I am just not sure about this. You are a very attractive woman, but I am married, and my wife is waiting for my return." However, doubts or not, it was evident to Phillipa that his animated state of affairs that she now felt against her body belied any moral uncertainty on his part.

"Look, James," Phillipa whispered with a hint of insistence, "I am not here in your bed presuming anything but a night or two of unexpected enjoyment in a city that has been devoid of all pleasure for a very long time and that will continue to be devoid of it for the foreseeable future."

Hearing no rejection of her rationale, Phillipa took the next step in her logic and went to remove James's cotton drawers. As she grasped the band and lingered there a moment, she heard an audible gasp. James placed his hand on hers, but he did not stop her from continuing. She slid his drawers to his knees, and he kicked them to the bottom of the bed.

Beyond the point of no return, he drew Phillipa to himself, and she rested her mature woman's body on his.

He reveled in the softness of her breasts on his chest and the counterpoint of the hardness of her nipples against his skin. Phillipa could feel the boniness of his chest and his legs as she eased him into her body. After the excited newness of the moment, the tempo of their breathing produced its own pleasures and they delighted in each other.

This was no rip-your-clothes-off-in-the-passion-of-the-moment affair. There was only tenderness as Phillipa moved her body in rhythm to his. They experienced sexuality in its primal simplicity, but it was more than that. It was not love, but neither was it just selfish ecstasy. There was an unspoken thankfulness that they had, in the most unlikely of times and places, found themselves together here on this May evening in room 202 of the Star Hotel.

The two now sweltering bodies moved synchronously as a boat moves to the rhythm of the rolling waves of the ocean. The tempo of their crashing waves was mutual, beautiful, and fulfilling.

James and Phillipa shared themselves with each other in a postcoupling state of harmony devoid of time, place, and worries. At some point in the night, Phillipa lifted James's arm from around her shoulders and picked up her gown from where she had stepped out of it. As she eased into her bed dress, it seemed that every nerve ending of her body was aroused again by the feel of the silk as it slid down her body.

Phillipa kissed a sleeping James tenderly on his forehead and whispered, mostly to herself, "Again tomorrow, my captain?"

She quietly opened the door and made her way to her own suite on the third floor. Easing into her feather bed, she quickly lapsed into a contented sleep, the kind that only follows a mutually pleasing sensual encounter.

The next morning as dawn's first soft rays were entering room 202, James awoke in stages, wondering if last night had been another hallucination, but he knew differently because he felt differently physically. He was rested but in a pleasantly tired kind of way. However, making its way surely to his conscious mind was a conundrum he could not escape. How could he reason away the immorality of the unexpected sensual encounter?

Generosity without Expectations

Merriweather bathed away, for the moment, the lingering traces of last night's dalliance with Phillipa Byrne, and when he had finished, he dressed, including his captain's blouse, and walked down to the dining room.

Cicero and Phillipa were already in an animated conversation. Merriweather hoped it was not about last night. He was relieved when he neared and learned that they were talking about procuring supplies for him so that they could keep secret the US dollars he carried with him.

"Cicero," Phillipa said with a hint of frustration in her voice, "you are still drunk from last night if you think finding any supplies will be easy. Even harder will be convincing any seller to give them to us on credit. You need to go to your room and take a bath. You reek of last night's drinking, and your breath smells like two-day-old shrimp hulls."

Merriweather observed that Phillipa could intimidate a man as easily with the honed blade of her language as with her coquettish personality and animal sexuality. She was definitely a woman of many interesting dimensions.

As Cicero passed Merriweather on his way to his bath, he whispered, "Watch it, she is fuller of herself this morning than usual."

"Oh, I shall," said Merriweather.

"I heard all of that." Phillipa laughed. Phillipa's laugh was as authentic as the rest of her. There were no hidden sides of Phillipa Byrne. Merriweather noted that he had not heard her laugh until this very moment. He also realized that laughter was a commodity in short supply on his trip from Appomattox.

"James, come over here and let us talk about how to provide for the remainder of your trip," said Phillipa without a hint of last night's clandestine coupling in her voice and her eyes.

"Let me pour myself a cup of your coffee first, and I will be yours for as long as you want me." Just as he said it, he realized the unintended double entendre, and he smiled to himself.

Phillipa began with a proposition. "I suggest that we outfit you from the hotel's supplies."

"No, Phillipa," James said, more forcefully than he intended. "I cannot let you do that. You and Cicero are almost as desperate as I."

Phillipa rejoined Merriweather with her businesswoman's logic. "Well, we may certainly be close to that state once we outfit you, but Cicero and I have enough to keep us going for several days. We will have adequate time to resupply the hotel, time that you do not have."

"Yes, ma'am. If you insist, I will take you up on your generous offer."

With a lilt of dissembling sarcasm, Phillipa responded, "You may not think me so liberal when you find out how many of those Yankee dollars you are going to fork over."

They ironed out the arrangements over another cup of coffee, and Cicero returned just in time to help with bringing up supplies from the root cellar. Once the supplies were laid out on a dining room table and ready for his departure the next morning, Merriweather asked Cicero if he would give him a walking tour of the Wilmington riverfront.

CHAPTER 59

The Reporter

As they walked among the abandoned classic antebellum homes that lined the streets just off the Cape Fear River, Harris queried Merriweather about his service at the Gettysburg and Appomattox campaigns. Merriweather thought to himself that perhaps this was an opportunity to unburden himself of some of his demons to a person he clearly liked and whom he was very unlikely ever to see again.

For Harris, Merriweather's would be a critical first-person account of the sacrifices made at Gettysburg and of the utterly untenable position of General Lee at Appomattox as the Union army surrounded and strangled the Army of Northern Virginia and beat it into submission. Harris also saw Merriweather's story as an antiseptic for the people of Wilmington, thinking that it might start the healing of the great open wound of slavery the war had laid bare for all to see.

"James," Harris spoke as they ambled, "I have a proposition for you as you settle in somewhere down the road—whenever that may be."

"All right, let's hear it. After what I have witnessed on my way to your fine city, I am certainly open to hearing options for the future."

"As we have talked these past days and this morning, it is clear that you have a keen eye for detail—especially from a personal perspective. I am pretty good at the objective view and the occasional sharp editorial. But I could use an occasional story from someone who has experienced this war and its aftermath firsthand and can tell our readers about it with all the emotion you can muster.

"Could that be you, my friend?"

James, flattered at Cicero's offer, responded with one reservation: "I will do it as long as I am not held to a schedule. I don't know what will be required of me once I make it home."

"Done," Cicero said, and they walked on.

Options

As they turned back toward the hotel, Merriweather asked Harris's opinion about his plan to follow the North East Railroad to Charleston. Harris responded after a thoughtful pause.

"James, as I see it you have three options. The first is as you have laid it out, of continuing to follow the railroad right-of-way, staying away from obvious settlements until you have determined them to be friendly. By friendly, I do not mean free of Yankees. Right now, there are many Rebel ne'er-do-wells who, finding out that the Confederate dollar is good only for wiping their sorry assess, will as soon slit your throat as take an offer of help from you."

Merriweather was a bit taken aback by Cicero's blunt assessment. "Do you really believe that my life will be in danger from other Southerners?"

"James," Cicero said emphatically. "Did you think all those boys you operated on were their mothers' angels sent on God's mission?"

Merriweather had to admit to himself that he had not considered such a question.

"Good God! James." Cicero was clearly on his editorial soapbox. "How many scoundrels do you think enlisted as a lark that lasted right up until the Minié balls started flying and their mates' heads were taken off with grapeshot? Those white trash subhumans are on their way back home just as you are. So at least hear these next two options."

As they talked, they had meandered down to the riverfront, where they let the river breezes flowing off the Cape Fear cool them as they sat on a bench in the shade of a massive water oak that must have been six feet in diameter with branches as big as a man and almost touching the ground.

"Well, you certainly have my attention. Please continue," Merriweather told his companion.

Harris apparently had considered this discussion and would have brought it up even if Merriweather had not first broached the subject. He continued, "The second option as I see it is to continue to reside at the Star Hotel until the rail lines have been repaired and you can safely travel to Charleston by train car. I would expect that this would be midsummer at the latest. The South's postbellum conditions will be a drain on the North's resources, and the powers in Washington will be as anxious as we to have a working rail system, especially one connecting Charleston and Wilmington with points north."

Merriweather, in spite of his indiscretion last evening, had not wavered in his yearning to get back to Horlbeck Creek with all due haste. Cicero had made a valid point, but what would he do in Wilmington?

"Cicero, you seem to extend to me some hospitality that is not yours to offer. Surely Phillipa would not agree."

"When you came down this morning," Harris said, "that was the very conversation Phillipa and I were having, right up until she said I smelled like two-day-old shrimp.

"The reality of Appomattox will soon fully take hold of people, and we both agreed that your medical and surgical skills could be put to great use as our Wilmington people begin to return to their homes. Phillipa would set you up with a surgery just off the hotel lobby.

"We would not want you to touch the dollars you will need to get yourself back on your feet, so in whatever way your patients might pay you, you would, in turn, contribute a reasonable share of that back to the running of the Star."

A fresh start certainly intrigued James Merriweather almost as much as the knowledge that he would be providing an essential service needed for Wilmington to get its collective feet back under itself. "It is a proposition I certainly will give due consideration this evening."

Harris continued. "I have one other thing for you to consider, and it may be the most onerous of these two new ideas. Are you ready to hear it?"

"I am. Let me hear it," said Merriweather, leaning forward with his elbows now rested on his knees.

"I have the means—let us just leave it at that for now—of engaging a captain of a very successful Confederate blockade-runner who is now out of a job given the surrender at Appomattox. I have little doubt that he could easily be persuaded to transport you to Charleston. It would mean that you would have to give up your mare Jemima. But I will pay you a fair price for her that would equal whatever fare the charter would entail. And I will treat her as you would treat her.

"There is some risk. Our man has been dubbed as the 'Havana Banana' by Rear Admiral Francis DuPont, the commander of the Union blockade, because he liked nothing more than a not so subtle message to DuPont in the form of a cluster of ripe bananas delivered to him personally each time he successfully docked his blockade-runner in Wilmington."

Harris finished, "James, this would be the quickest and easiest way to return home. What are your thoughts about it?"

"It would also be the most gut-wrenching of the choices. I

just don't know how I could give up Jemima," Merriweather replied with evident consternation.

"Cicero, I would not be here today talking to you without her. She carried me to safety when I did not know who or where I was for three days after I left Petersburg."

It was evident to Harris that Merriweather was reluctant even to think about this option. "Well, why don't give yourself at least one more day to consider your options? No need to make a decision today."

An additional night in Phillipa Byrne's Star Hotel was a pleasant, if unsettling, thought. "Okay, Cicero. I will accept your offer of another night."

CHAPTER 60

Logic

As Cicero Harris made his way back to the Star Hotel, James Merriweather detoured and strolled along the riverfront, thinking about the three choices that confronted him. He might face a dangerous weeklong journey by horseback, not knowing from hour to hour what he was to find or who was to find him. If Merriweather stayed in Wilmington until the government repaired the rail lines, he would face a different a kind of dangerous liaison—Phillipa Byrne. Or he could be back at Horlbeck Creek Farm in a matter of two days, but at the sacrifice of his beloved Jemima.

The spring afternoon was waning as Merriweather made his way back to the Star Hotel and a bath before supper. After his bath, he lay on the bed staring at the intricate designs of the plaster ornamentation of the ceiling but not actually seeing them. Upon reflection, he decided that he could eliminate one of his options.

Having put aside traveling by horseback, he decided not to decide yet on either of the other two options in front of him. He would make his decision after supper, when the night would help still his mind.

Temptation

He rose from his bed, dressed, and made his way to the dining room, which smelled of fried fish.

Phillipa had taken some catfish from a trotline that she regularly maintained in a section of the Cape Fear River undisclosed even to Cicero. She brought back a half dozen "squealers" as the smaller catfish were called in Wilmington.

With supper concluded and cups of coffee all around, Merriweather leaned back on the legs of his dining room chair, his belly full of fresh catfish and baked sweet potato. "Phillipa is there no limit to your resourcefulness?"

"Stop it, or you will make me blush," Phillipa retorted. "I didn't grow up in a hotel. I grew up on a farm east of Kinston, and my daddy taught me to set and run a trotline on the Neuse before I was ten.

"Just because there may not be food in the city doesn't mean there is no food to be had. You just have to know how to find it," she proudly declared.

Merriweather congratulated Phillipa on her fishing and culinary skills and thanked them both for a conversation that deepened his understating of the plight of Wilmington after the fall of Fort Fisher and Confederate general Bragg's burning of the warehouses full of supplies before the Union army swept through. With next to nothing in Wilmington to eat and the way to procure food eliminated, it was no wonder the city was practically abandoned.

Merriweather stood and pushed his chair back to the table. "I have some decisions to consider before I retire for the night. I will see you both in the morning with a decision so that I can move forward tomorrow with final preparations for my departure."

With that, he made his way to his room to ponder his two remaining options. He was intrigued by the potential to help a city like Wilmington recover its former glory, but there was so much that he did not know, and there was only one person who could tell him what he needed to know—Phillipa. He was not sure of the room number of Phillipa's suite, but he would just look for a light under the door.

He was right, of course. He lightly knocked on the highly polished walnut door and frame of room 323 and called to Phillipa, "I need to talk to you about your offer of a medical office. Are you decent?"

"I am," Phillipa said as she opened the door. Clearly, Phillipa's notion of decent was not the same as Merriweather's, but he stepped into the room nonetheless.

Phillipa's suite was decorated in English country estate. A painting of a foxhunt with horses and dogs hot on the trail of a red fox hung on the wall behind the head of her bed. The bed was built and stained to match the beautiful walnut entry and door to her suite. A second picture, this one of a young woman fly-fishing for salmon, decorated the opposite wall. If he was not mistaken, the woman in the painting was a younger version of the vision who stood before him now in a translucent gown of beautiful white French lace accented at her neck and waist with satin ribbons of emerald green—a deeper version of the green of her Irish eyes.

It occurred to Merriweather that Phillipa had anticipated that he would come to her tonight. He was here, and she was radiant with her dark curls falling on her rounded feminine shoulders. Without any hesitating, Merriweather closed the door and reached for the ribbon at her neck.

The evening's encounter was a bit more athletic than the previous night, but no buttons were torn off or garments ripped. However, bedcovers lay tangled at the foot of the bed as a result of their athletic pursuits. Each more comfortable with the needs of the other, they found that exploration was the theme of the evening's lovemaking. After an altogether pleasing journey, they now sat propped up by the head of the walnut bed imbibing glasses of fine sherry, and they had the conversation that Merriweather intended when he'd first knocked on Phillipa's door.

"James," Phillipa responded after hearing that he had eliminated travel by horseback, "I cannot disagree with Cicero's assessment. Although he has not been publishing the *Daily Journal*, he has kept up rather well with the postsurrender news. He regularly walks in the afternoon to the small Union garrison now occupying Cassidey's Shipyard to spend an hour or two talking with Captain Sean Crowley, the garrison commander, about the coming months.

"Cicero said he found that Crowley, the only officer in the small group, was as hungry for conversation as he was, and was rather forthcoming with news that made its way to Wilmington by way of a Union army communication system.

"Crowley reports that there are roaming bands of displaced Confederates making sporadic attacks on travelers."

Merriweather was pleased with the confirmation that his conclusion not to travel by horseback was the logical decision. He also knew that he could not logically accept Phillipa's offer to set up a medical office for him.

Logic be damned. Emotionally, the last two nights tore away at the fabric of Merriweather's judgment. One moment his decision-making was reduced to that of a hormone-riddled teenaged plantation scion. The next minute he knew he could not abandon Mary Assumpta to the farm. Alternatively, after his trial by cannon fire, he had earned the right to be happy with this beautiful woman whose breasts peeked seductively above the sheet that had slipped from her shoulders as she animated her thoughts with her arms and hands.

Ultimately, he knew what he needed to do, and he told Phillipa.

"These last two nights have replenished a side of me that every soldier must put aside or else go mad. Letters from lovers only make it harder to do the work of war. Romance has no place in war, no matter the tales told by old men and unsuccessful general officers.

"I thank you for recognizing that perhaps there was a bit of romance left in this body of mine. I will take that gift to Mary Assumpta, although she will never know its source. So I really must, with much regret, turn down your attractive offer of a medical practice here by the Cape Fear River. Although I would reserve the right to take you up on it at some point in the future should life's peculiar hands of fate bring me back to Wilmington. Deal?"

"Deal," Phillipa said with a tear in her eye and a smile forming on her love-blushed face.

A kiss on her cheek and he was gone to find Cicero Harris to ask if he would make arrangements for his transport by sea to Charleston.

Intuition and Something More

Cicero had secured the agreements and negotiated the fare by midday. Merriweather spent the late afternoon riding Jemima. Afterward, he brushed her down after their ride, and he fed and watered her generously. A long hug to her neck and a gentle hand from her mane to her flanks, Merriweather walked away with tears streaming down his face for the gentle dappled gray mare.

Phillipa had said her farewell at the hotel. No kisses. Just the hug of a friend and a promise by both to stay in touch.

Cicero and James left the hotel at eleven and walked to the docks beyond the destroyed depot, and there they waited. James carried his saddlebags and his carbine, his gold in a hidden compartment in his saddlebag.

On May 9, 1865, although the moon was full, the sky was also full of clouds—a night of little moonlight but gentle breezes. It was the kind of night favorable to slipping by the Union army occupying Fort Fisher, but it was also a night where sound carried remarkably far over the water. Although Confederate forces had surrendered at Appomattox almost a month earlier, there were isolated skirmishes regularly occurring, mostly in the western front, but also by Rebel guerrillas who refused to believe that General Lee would ever surrender the fight.

Captain Jean-Joël Leclair skillfully eased his steam and sail blockade-runner almost silently next to the dock at the foot of Red Cross Street. He threw lines to Merriweather and Cicero, who tied it up to the dock.

Merriweather handed his saddlebags to Leclair and said his farewells and thanks to Cicero Harris.

"James," Cicero began, "I will take care of Jemima. She is now my horse. I promise I will not sell her. Should you find your way back to Wilmington, she is still yours."

"I know you will. Thanks for every kindness that you have extended to me over these last few days. I shall not forget it," James responded.

"Don't forget, you owe me a column on the recovery in Charleston by the end of June," Cicero reminded James. "Now get on this piece of illegal flotsam and get yourself home to Mary Assumpta and your boy."

With that, James Merriweather stepped one foot on the deck of Leclair's boat. Just then he was overcome with a foreboding of evil like the fog that was silently and swiftly moving up the Cape Fear River and surrounding the *Pride of Paris* and the dock where he tentatively stood with Cicero Harris.

The captain had treated him fairly, and he trusted Cicero

Harris's work on his behalf to secure his passage, but he felt deep in his gut—rationally unexplainable—that he was making a mistake. He would explain later to Cicero Harris that he was convinced the feeling was the Almighty, God, Jehovah, and Yahweh—all rolled into one Deity—powerfully speaking to him in the most intimate depths of his soul.

Merriweather paid Captain Leclair his full fare, and by the time he told Cicero Harris why he had changed his mind, the night and the fog had already absorbed the *Pride of Paris*.

CHAPTER 61

Homecoming
May 27, 1865

Mary Assumpta Bailey Merriweather still looked like a Southern belle even though she had never sought that sobriquet. Mary Assumpta's physicality was beyond her control. She need not put on a ball gown to stroll down the archetypal staircase to look the part of a Southern belle. It came to Mary Assumpta naturally. She possessed a beauty that wealth could never provide or that a war could alter. After three painful years of worrying about James's role in the fighting and the seemingly ceaseless farmwork, her complexion was still as fair and smooth as her hair was red and curly after a rare warm evening bath.

Mary Assumpta was overcome with a feeling of well-being. It had been more than a week since she had felt the feeling this intensely. She thought of it as a movement in her spirit, and she knew it came from James. She hoped, oh how she hoped, it was because he was getting closer to home.

Beneath the surface of this calm was a sensation she could not put into words. It was a sense of a presence just behind the lovely awareness of well-being. It lurked and glanced and slithered and consumed the oxygen in her kitchen as she worked on supper while standing at the window facing the lane.

She could not ignore a feeling that all was not well. A cold shiver ran up her spine as if she were being watched. It erased the warm glow she had felt moments before.

Evil Comes to Horlbeck Creek

Abraham Whetstone and Davey Little had come across a creek swiftly flowing southward—a tributary that they figured would take them within sight of the Holy City. It was getting late but was not quite dusk, the time when the woods became still and quiet. As their mounts moved slowly, the smell of a campfire permeated the copse of swamp oaks that surrounded and hid them. As they edged toward the source of the smoke, they saw a man in a Confederate captain's uniform as he sat warming himself by a late afternoon campfire. He was at the head of Horlbeck Creek.

They stopped, tied off their horses, and waited until they could see that the man was by himself. Whetstone motioned Little to stay with the horses. This kill was to be Whetstone's singular pleasure. As silent as a copperhead moving through a patch of wet leaves, Whetstone walked silently by the gray mare staked out near the water grazing on new spring grass. She did not make a sound. Neither did her owner, who died as he sat by the campfire humming "Onward Christian Soldiers."

The death of the Confederate captain, undoubtedly on his way home from the war, was not satisfying for Whetstone. There was no sexual arousal, just a momentary pleasure of knife slicing through jugular. And the only thing of value that he found in the saddlebags was a brass telescope with "CSA" engraved on one side and the initials JM etched on the other.

Whetstone called for Little to bring the horses, and they

camped where the officer had fallen. No reason to waste a good campfire.

Traveling Mercies

Following James's letter of April 22, Mary Assumpta had done some rough calculations with Bartholomew's help and figured that if James rode steadily on horseback, it would take him three weeks to travel from Appomattox to Horlbeck Creek. She knew James well enough to allow him at least a week or more after the surrender to conclude the doctoring he would never leave unfinished. Therefore, Mary Assumpta had been looking for James in earnest every day since May 10, and she was worried.

Nate and Audrey Lee tried to assuage her worries by telling her that with railroads destroyed and renegade gangs on the prowl, James would know to be extra careful and stay away from well-traveled roads, which would add a few days to his journey. She appreciated Nate and Audrey Lee's advice but was getting more worried every day. Working in the garden and sweeping and mopping the house was a poor way to avoid the increasing anxiety she felt.

As she worried about James's return, Mary Assumpta prayed for simple things now that the war was formally over in the Confederacy's eastern states. Her prayers were to be a member of a family again and to feel her husband's arms surrounding and enveloping her late into the night and early in the morning. She prayed for the return of the father that Colin hardly remembered; to know the conviction of the presence of a loving God; and the sanguinity that single-mindedness brings.

And most of all she prayed never again to dangle on Pandora's hope as her best promise.

Death Stands Near

Although Whetstone and Little did not know the name of the tributary whose path they were tracing as they followed it south, they could see that it was broad enough to lead to somewhere interesting—and their only aim in life at this point was to keep things interesting from one kill to the next.

Their ultimate goal was to enjoy the *pleasures* of Charleston then to die in a gun battle on its streets. Although they had no specific knowledge that they were traveling directly toward Charleston, it did not really matter.

They had spent yesterday taking care of business, as Whetstone put it, at the Boone plantation. They were excited when they came upon fields that they recognized as the layout of a plantation. If the Union had not destroyed it, there would be rape and plunder aplenty for them both.

As they watched during the day from the dense woods on the banks of Horlbeck Creek, they observed some slaves still attached to their former master. Ridding the renewed Union of a few traitorous slaves was downright patriotic in Whetstone's mind. After all, he had fought with Grant in Mississippi. He laughed to himself anytime he thought of that bit of irony.

A little reconnoitering before nightfall and they knew precisely which quarters held their prey for the evening's pleasure. The murderous pair waited until ebony dark and walked right up to the slave quarters that lay less than seventy-five yards south of the plantation house. Unseen, they slipped soundlessly into the cabin that held two slaves asleep on the corn-shuck mattresses on the dirt floor. With practiced stealth, they simultaneously drove foul, sweat-soaked, balled-up bandannas into the mouths of the two sleeping slaves, Abba Boone and her thirteen-year-old daughter, Juba.

When Abba and Juba Boone failed to show up for breakfast at the main house the next morning, Cuffee Boone, the oldest former slave still on the plantation, was dispatched to their cabin. He found their violated bodies left on the dirt floor where they used to sleep with intestines pulled out from chest cavities and breasts sliced off. The cabin stank of the blood, urine, and feces the bodies had naturally expelled at their deaths. And there was also the unmistakable smell of semen.

Cuffee added the odor of his own bile to the scene. He walked as fast as his old legs would take him, shouting as he went, "Masser Nathan, Masser Nathan." As he arrived back at the main house, out of breath and terrified by what he had seen, all he could say was, "Masser Nathan, the devil done been here last night."

He was, of course, unfortunately correct.

Bloodlust in the Afternoon

Satisfied for having done his "patriotic duty" the night before, Whetstone and his barely controllable associate slept past daylight and then rode slowly south, keeping Horlbeck Creek on their right. By late afternoon they reached the outskirts of the Nate Billington farm and saw an old man and his wife sitting down for supper. While age did not matter to Whetstone if his bloodlust needed satiating, on a day like today, with the taste of new blood still fresh in his primeval memory, he decided to spare the Billingtons. Instead, the pair rode a bit farther, and at last light they stopped as Whetstone saw a scene lit by a hurricane lamp almost identical to the one he had just passed up. At two hundred yards, using his new brass telescope, he could see the curls of red hair on the head of a shapely young woman preparing supper.

He saw nailed to a post on the front porch of the house a large hand-painted sign on two weather-beaten boards nailed to two smaller vertical boards behind: "Welcome Home, Dr. Merriweather." Whetstone might just need to work a little more carefully, but an unexpected person was a problem he had encountered before. *Only requires a little more planning on my part,* Whetstone thought to himself. *Damn Davey Little is useless except for the cutting.*

The two dismounted. Whetstone and Little would stay the night here in the neck of woods that extended out from the banks of the creek and then see what developed in the morning.

The redhead and the old couple Whetstone and Little had observed yesterday began working in the garden plots a half hour before daylight. Whetstone took his brass telescope from his saddlebag and watched the redhead—and only the redhead. Red hair. Red blood. Meant to be.

Abraham Whetstone touched himself as he became aroused at the redheaded beauty's obvious femininity and her conspicuous lack of pretense as she worked in the farm's garden plots. If the view from the brass telescope could arouse him, he knew how he would feel with her blood on his hands and face.

Whetstone sent Davey Little around behind the house toward the barn, and he returned after a half hour with the news that the son was scything the grass along the lane from the road to the house. The boy was young, but muscles formed from farmwork defined his arms and legs. Little figured him for a fighter. Just more fun. More blood made for more pleasure. But first, Whetstone said they needed another day to plan; they would leave the boy alone for now. They would strike in the morning. Mornings were prime hunting times as prey were often oblivious to early day dangers lurking right beneath their windows.

Wilmington, Jemima, and Horlbeck Creek

As he stood, one foot on board the blockade-runner that would take him to Charleston, he was overcome with a premonition. *The voice of God?* James wondered. Regardless, he decided he had come too far with his faithful Jemima for her to be butchered and eaten by starving Wilmingtonians. No, he would take a few days more and travel as he had done since he'd left Appomattox.

On his last morning in Wilmington, the fog was gone even before the sun could burn it off. *Strange,* James thought to himself as he walked to the stable. *Last night the fog seemed to move with the* Pride of Paris. Even now, the portent of evil remained after the fog's leaving, and James shuddered as he had the night before. But this morning he was resolved, and he paid no attention to any feeling except that engendered by the thought of going home.

As he walked to the stable, he heard Jemima nicker as she smelled his approach, leading him to the back where she was hitched. After soothing her with familiar whispers, he quietly placed the saddle, the saddlebags, and all his accouterments, especially his carbine, on Jemima's back. Then he left Cicero a short final note and rode toward the Wilmington and Manchester Railroad. He would return to his previous ways and ride far enough away from the railroad's right-of-way to allow him to see any dangers it might pose from renegades who were riding its more open pathway. Merriweather would follow the Wilmington and Manchester to Florence, South Carolina. From Florence, James followed the North East Railroad to Moncks Corner, where he turned and rode east until he found a spot where he forded the headwaters of the Cooper River.

Merriweather had studied his military map and was looking for a horseshoe lake where the Cooper wound back on itself. From this geographic marker, he would travel east until he intersected the Wando River.

When he found the Wando, James knew home was no more than a three days' ride. The Wando was wide and deep at the point where he intersected it, but unless he wanted to travel days out of his way northward to find a fording place, he would have to put his trust in his faithful Jemima to swim them both across.

Jemima swam strong and steady as James held on to the saddle horn, freeing her of his weight on her back. Back on land, Merriweather made his way southeast until he found the headwaters of Horlbeck Creek, where he was on familiar ground. He and Colin had explored the length of the Horlbeck Creek, almost up to its headwaters, camping and shooting game. He was not home yet. But in another two days, he should be.

The Malodor of Murder

The next day James let Jemima set her own pace after her swim across the river. As he moved slowly along the banks of Horlbeck Creek in the shroud of piney woods, he smelled the unmistakable odor of rotting human flesh mingled with the smoke of an almost dead campfire. There was no stench so foul as decomposing human beings. Not animals. Not swamp gas produced from decaying plant matter. He dismounted and walked on until he found the murdered Confederate captain. The hair on the back of his neck stood upright when he saw the knife wound from one ear to the other and the almost decapitated head. *Whetstone?* he thought to himself. When he found the card, reading "Compliments of Abe," stuck in the officer's mouth, he knew, and he cried out to the evening stars, "Dear God, no! Not on Horlbeck Creek."

James spent a few minutes gathering his thoughts. He would like to give the officer a proper burial, but the best he could do was find out his name. The officer was Captain John Morse from Charleston. James would let authorities know where to find the body when he could. Right now, night or not, he had to get to Horlbeck Creek Farm. As he turned to mount Jemima, he noted something strange, three distinctly different sets of boot prints. The one near the campfire was apparently the officer's, but had Whetstone added an accomplice? James had to assume so. It did not change anything except to make his journey more urgent.

Seeing the gray mare staked out near the creek bank, he could not in good conscience leave her, so he tied her lead to the back of Jemima's saddle, and they headed south as fast as the encroaching darkness would allow. By dawn, he had reached the very familiar sight of the Boone plantation. Hearing screaming and otherworldly wails, he rode to the plantation house, where he found the former slaves in a state of hysteria with the owner, Nathan Boone, trying to calm them with no success as he, himself, was on the verge of panic as well.

James Merriweather had not intended to stop at the Boone plantation, but the scene he found before him gave him no choice. "Nathan," he asked, "what has happened here?"

"James, it is good to see you back home. Last night two of my Negro workers were silently slaughtered as they slept. No one heard a thing in the other cabins where they slept, only feet away from the cabin of Abba and Juba."

"Can I go see the scene?" James asked.

"Of course. But first, do you have anything in your saddlebag that might calm my people down?"

When James had departed the Petersburg field hospital encampment, Nurse Brown gave him a small bottle of laudanum in anticipation of other wounded he might encounter on his way home. He surmised now would be as good a time as any to use it.

After he had instructed Nathan Boone on how to deliver just two drops in a quarter cup of water to each person, James walked with his horses to the cabin that held the bodies of Abba and Juba Boone.

Whetstone, he thought to himself, *is making his way from farm to farm down Horlbeck Creek. And there are only two more farms between here and the Wando—Nate's and my own.*

Stone-Cold Killers

James knew Nate Billington's place was only five miles farther down the creek and on a good road. Pushing his Jemima to a steady canter, he arrived at Nate's in a half hour.

A hundred yards from Nate's house, James saw the imprints of two horses and two men in the sand beside the road. He urged Jemima into a full sprint to Nate's front door.

He dropped Jemima's reins and ran to have Audrey Lee greet him with a kiss. He brusquely asked her where Nate was. He was looking for another rifle. "Hunting in the swamp before we head to work with Mary Assumpta in the pea patch," was her answer.

"When he returns, you stay here, but you tell him to run to my house and bring his rifle and his pistol. I think there are killers about and they are stalking Mary Assumpta and Colin."

The Warrior

James reached Horlbeck Creek Farm, staked out Jemima and the gray mare a half mile up Old Shell Road and far enough off the road to be unseen by passers-by, and then fast-walked, staying on the soft and silent grass to the side of the road until he reached the lane that led to his farm.

On reaching the lane, James soldier-crawled on his belly with his pistol snapped tight in its holster on his left leg, his ever-sharp combat knife strapped to his right. He held in front of him his US Army–issued .56-56 Spencer carbine given to him by Sergeant Benjamin Brookside, quartermaster for the Petersburg field hospital, when he left that facility. The carbine was loaded with seven cartridges with seven more in his pocket. He had crawled almost fifty yards down the lane in the wet morning grass when his peripheral vision caught a movement in the barn, and it wasn't a mule. Someone had arrived in the barn before daylight with evil intentions.

James crawled another fifty yards closer to the barn. At this position, if he had to, he could make it to the side of the barn in a ten-second sprint. In an uncanny coincidence, as soon as the thought had cleared, he saw Colin open the back door of the house and walk toward the barn.

Jesus, no, James thought to himself.

Colin would be in the barn before James could get there. Adding cruelty onto cruelty, James saw a shadow enter the back door that Colin had left ajar. James sprinted to the barn. He chose Colin. He had to trust that Mary Assumpta could defend herself until he could get to her.

James sprinted to the side of the barn unseen and unheard as its occupant had been focusing only on the boy. As Colin reached to open the barn door, the dirty hand of Davey Little grabbed his hand, and he clasped his other hand over Colin's mouth. James could hear a faint squeal escaping between the man's closed fingers. He tried to stay composed. A surgeon's calm could save his son; a father's impetuousness—likely not.

But what James saw next would have caused a man on a lesser mission to betray his calm just enough to allow evil to prosper. Abraham Whetstone entered his home's back door. He let it register a millisecond only on his cerebral cortex. Instead, James focused wholly on the wretched piece of human malevolence holding his son. Colin saw his father, although Davey Little did not. His eyes grew wide at the sight of his father, and he tried to yell even more. Davey Little spit out the words, "Shut your feckin' mouth, or I'll gut you from chin to pecker and show it to you while I watch you die."

James held his finger to his lips, and Colin quieted. Colin saw his father silently remove his combat knife, and he remained utterly still as his father leaped the three feet to Davey Little's back and plunged the knife with surgical precision deeply into the back of Little's neck, severing his brain stem. For all intents, Davey Little's bodily functions ceased the moment the knife's tip entered his spinal cord. Colin was safe.

Medically, Little was not dead. The point of the knife James inserted into his chest, severing his aorta, removed that technicality.

James did not have time to hug his son, only to whisper to him to leave the barn and hide in the cornfield. Colin was a faithful son. He would be scared but grateful later. He ran for the field and lay flat between two rows of shoulder-high stalks of sweet corn.

As James left the barn, he saw through the kitchen window the red hair of Mary Assumpta pulled tight by a large and hairy hand. The other forepaw held a bowie knife to her throat. As James raised the carbine to take aim, he paused. He had no clear shot. As much as it disturbed him to leave his view of Mary Assumpta and her attacker, he crept around toward the back door, where he would have a direct line of sight. He would delete Abraham Whetstone once and for good.

Never Felt a Thing

Whetstone paused his licking of Mary Assumpta's face before moving to her neck. "I seen the Welcome Home sign on the porch. You a doctor's wife? Your boy make that sign? Looks like the work of a retard."

"You piece of gobshite. You leave my son out of this!" Mary Assumpta shrieked out the words, spitting on his hand as she yelled. Her voice bordered on hysteria, but her mind was calm as she inched her left arm toward the open drawer of the counter she was pushed up against. She had freed her arm unnoticed when Whetstone released it to wipe her spit from his hand.

"I like 'em feisty. Makes the blood explode when I gash that throat. Gotta clean up your neck a bit, though, before I slice it open. Bein' a doctor's bitch, you can appreciate bein' clean an' all," Whetstone told her, his brimstone breath burning her nose as he began to slither his tongue down her face to her neck.

However, his tongue never reached her neck. So intense was his drive to satiate his unholy desires, his member thrusting against her pelvis, that he never felt the revolver Mary Assumpta held against his chest or the .36-caliber round as it entered his heart, the polished revolver covered with a dishcloth that she had silently pulled from the drawer with her free arm.

Redheaded Colleen

From his angle, James could not see beyond Mary Assumpta's arm reaching behind her, but he heard a shot and another and another: six in total made by the Colt 1851 Navy revolver he had purchased for Mary Assumpta before he left for the war, the one he had taught her to shoot out behind the barn.

Before Mary Assumpta blew out Abraham Whetstone's candle that late spring day, as he slid down the counter smearing bright red blood as he went, he learned the last lesson of his pathetic subhuman existence as Mary Assumpta whispered in his ear, “You never stood a chance against a tomboy Irish lass with a revolver and a temper.”

Forgetting but Not Forgiving

On May 22, 1865, the day after Mary Assumpta and James killed Abraham Whetstone and Davey Little, respectively, a burning pit was dug in the middle of the cornfield nearest Horlbeck Creek. The pine kindling placed under a thick layer of dry oak limbs burst into life when Colin touched it with a piece of burning tinder tied to a long green oak sapling. As the fire exploded to life, Nate added another layer of tar-filled pine knots and to that another layer of dry oak fireplace logs. In fifteen minutes, it was impossible to stand near the pit. *Just right,* Nate thought to himself as he loaded Davey Little over his shoulder, using Little’s corpse to protect himself from the searing heat.

“James, you want to do the honors for Whetstone?” Nate asked.

Not hesitating, James picked up Whetstone and tossed him in beside Little.

James, with the disposers of evil along with the survivors, sent the two perpetrators of inhuman wickedness to hell with a cold and calculated vengeance. Audrey Lee Billington had decided that she would stay at Horlbeck Creek Farm should someone come to inquire about the smoke and smell. “Just the remains of ol’ Jake the mule,” she would say. “Burned right where he died.” It was only a small lie. Jake *had died* in that same field.

It took three days for the fire to cool enough that the ashes could be shoveled out and placed on a screen for the larger portions to be sifted. It was impossible except for a few bones and a couple of buckles and buttons to tell what was oak and what was evil. It really did not matter. The remains left on the screen were put in a croker sack weighed down with fieldstones. The finer ashes would be used to add needed potash to the cornfield. *Good from bad,* James thought.

At almost dusk the same afternoon, Colin and James paddled Nate's small pirogue to the middle of the Wando River. Nate, with his arms encircling Mary Assumpta on his left and Audrey Lee on his right, watched silently as the croker sack was lowered into the murky depths of the dirty river.

As they walked home down Old Shell Road in the cool of the early evening, no words passed between them about the killing or the burning or the disposal. Nor would they ever.

In early June, a Federal officer stopped at Horlbeck Creek to ask about a Union army deserter and his partner who had brutally killed some slaves up at the Boone plantation a few weeks earlier. He wanted to warn everyone nearby to be on the lookout. "These two are stone-cold killers," he said to James.

"Yes, sir, Major," James responded. "We will be on the lookout. We don't want their kind here on the creek. "

The officer rode north back to his unit.

EPILOGUE

January 2, 1868. Mary Assumpta had chosen this day in mid-February five years earlier when she finally emerged like the early crocuses and redbuds from her dark, depressive winter. It was the first time since the stillbirth of her son that Colin had led her to the flower garden where a tiny grave was marked by the small wooden cross he had engraved with "Baby M. 1-2-1863." That February day in 1863, she promised Colin and vowed to the Almighty that once the war was good and over, January 2 would be a day not to be forgotten but to celebrate. She had done enough mourning for a lifetime.

Those who had arrived on New Year's Day and gathered at noon on Thursday, January 2, 1868, had little idea that this date would hold special significance in their lives going forward. Mary Assumpta, James, and Colin had invited each to a gathering at Horlbeck Creek Farm to celebrate a reunion of family and friends, and except for Rabbi Benjamin Cowan, Reverend Simon Billington, and Father Michael O'Malley, this was all that those who gathered knew. Still, it was enough. Recriminations and Reconstruction had occupied far too much of all their lives since Appomattox. To come to a place physically untouched by weapons of war was a balm for the soul of each. Yes, there had been less apparent wounds found here at the farm, but they had been put to rest and would not be resurrected.

The invitation read as follows:

> November 1, 1867
> Horlbeck Creek Farm
>
> Dear Precious Family and Friends,
>
> We invite you to gather with us at Horlbeck Creek Farm on January 2 to celebrate the joys of life. We will celebrate the special place in our hearts and lives that each of you holds.
>
> Talk of the war or Reconstruction will not be tolerated. We will talk and laugh about the special relationships we have in the lives of each other. Discussions of plans for the future are encouraged.
>
> We invite you to come and enjoy a Low Country dinner as we gather at our home on January 2, 1868. Bartholomew Jennings will provide transportation from Charleston, and lodging will be provided at our home and in the homes of Nate and Audrey Lee Billington and Reverend Simon Billington.
>
> No excuses will be accepted.
>
> Lovingly yours,
> Mary Assumpta, James, and Colin

Going forward from the get-together, the day would become known among the Merriweathers, the Baileys, and their friends as "Naming Day," and it would be celebrated each year with a gathering of family and friends to eat and commune and to celebrate the naming of the smallest casualty of the war, Timothy Ryan Merriweather.

The original Timothy Merriweather had been a graduate of Oxford and a towering intellect at the College of William and Mary. As the spiritual leader of the Merriweathers of Virginia, his wisdom and wit were legendary.

Ryan Bailey was the middle Bailey child between John and Mary Assumpta. He had been Mary Assumpta's confidant. He was good in every way a Charleston gentleman should be. Few would remember the day he died on the submarine CSS *Hunley*'s successful but ill-fated mission, yet every January 2 among the Baileys and Merriweathers his story would be told.

At dawn on January 2, 1868, Horlbeck Creek Farm was covered with a shroud of cold, foggy vapor, but by midmorning when the guests started arriving, the sun had burned the mists away to reveal a glorious, almost warm Low Country winter day.

The Baileys, the Merriweathers, and guests who gathered on that first Naming Day were familial, spiritual, or existential—although it would be impossible for a stranger to tell who fit into which category.

Dr. Winston and Beatrice Merriweather, James's mother and father, and his siblings Rachel Lee and Patrice represented Richmond. James's brother Timothy, who had served in the Union army on the western front during the war, was somewhere in the Indian Territories and sent his regrets.

Traveling with the Merriweathers from Richmond were Rabbi Benjamin and Abigayil Cowan and Father Michael O'Malley. Benjamin and Michael, with the Reverend Simon Billington, would preside at the graveside naming ceremony to be held that afternoon after dinner.

Traveling the short trip from Charleston were John Bailey, now the patriarch of the Bailey family, and the Reverend Simon Billington, the son of former slaves and longtime pastor of Charleston's Mother Emanuel Church, transported by the very close family friend Bartholomew Jennings.

Nate and Audrey Lee Billington opened their home, and Reverend Billington his guesthouse on his family's farm, to the Richmond pastors who arrived on New Year's Day thanks to Bartholomew Jennings, who transported them all in two trips from Charleston in the same oyster boat that had saved so many runaway slaves.

For sleeping, James's mother and father would take Colin's bed, and Colin would sleep on a pallet next to Bartholomew, who resumed his customary place on Mary Assumpta's sofa for the night. Bartholomew was now a married man, and his nights on the sofa were few these days.

Three months earlier he made an honest woman of Ophelia Boudreaux, one of Geneviève Ardoin's women, and even with a personal invitation from Mary Assumpta, Ophelia could only envision how sick she would become on Bartholomew's small boat, being pregnant just a few weeks and suffering from morning sickness most days of the week. So she respectfully declined but sent with Bartholomew a beautiful watercolor of a baby sweet potato wrapped in swaddling clothes. The caption below the drawing, in Ophelia's beautiful calligraphy, read as follows:

God's Little Sweet Potato
Timothy Ryan Merriweather

Mary Assumpta had sworn no mourning, but the tears she profusely shed at the opening of Ophelia's gift were tears of joy. She would proudly show the painting to all who gathered, but very few knew its real significance.

The last time James had seen his counselor Benjamin Cowan, it was the winter of James's recuperation in Richmond during the Army of Northern Virginia's winter lull of 1863. When Benjamin stepped on the dock at Horlbeck Creek, James noted that he had aged since he had seen him last, but still there was a strength and joy in his step that belied his eighty-four years.

Not mistaking Benjamin's bedraggled white bush, James rushed to his friends with Mary Assumpta a step behind. During the war, Benjamin and Abigayil had become his and Mary Assumpta's counselors and friends, but also much more. A ménage, perhaps. A unique family at a distance. Being neither Merriweather nor Bailey, Abigayil and Benjamin loved and advised as James and Mary Assumpta's genetic families could not.

As James and Benjamin walked toward the wagon, Abigayil walked directly to Mary Assumpta, the former's magnetism drawing the latter into a strong sisterly hug. As they slowly walked arm in arm, Abigayil spoke softly to Mary Assumpta, a bit more than a whisper but not vocalization that Benjamin could hear.

"Mary Assumpta, the last two years I have seen Benjamin become increasingly feeble. His mind is as strong as ever, but his movements have become that of a rabbi emeritus who sees his influence in his congregation diminishing. But when your invitation arrived, I thanked Yahweh that Benjamin stood straight and spoke in his old voice again—the voice that had enthralled so many congregants through the years. And I knew there was no doubt we would travel to Horlbeck Creek."

The bond that Mary Assumpta had felt in Abigayil's writing was even stronger at their first face-to-face meeting. This was going to be a different connection than her relationship with Audrey Lee, who had become Mary Assumpta's adoptive mother figure. This was a feeling of sisterhood.

Mary Assumpta whispered to Abigayil when she stepped up in the wagon, "We must find some time just for *us*. No men."

Abigayil whispered back, "Amen to that." And the bond was formed between these two Southern women—a bond built upon different generations, ethnicities, and religions.

Family and friends talked long into New Year's night, all heeding Mary Assumpta's *suggested* guidelines. There was excited chatter of rebuilding and building late into New Year's night at each of the three homes.

Talk of what had been, what might have been, and the current Reconstruction mess was left on the porch of each home.

At Nate's home, James's sisters inquired and then listened as Nate told the story of his family home and his family's decades-old connections to the Reverend Simon Billington. In fact, Simon was telling much the same story to Father O'Malley and Benjamin and Abigayil Cowan. Mary Assumpta had asked that Benjamin Cowan lead the design of the celebration with Simon Billington and Michael O'Malley, knowing that Michael and Benjamin had restored James's spiritual and mental health more than a few times in the war years and that Simon had held a special relationship with her father and with Ryan and presided at their memorial service in Charleston—neither body ever recovered.

Had either group stepped out on the porch, they likely would have heard the laughter that echoed up and down the hill between the two houses.

At Horlbeck Creek Farm, the talk was a bit more personal as James broached the subject of whether or not the family would continue to live the farm life. Nothing definite was said, but James's father, Winston, thought to himself as he looked at Mary Assumpta while James talked, *They are all ready to go back to Charleston.*

It was clear to Winston, and no doubt to Beatrice, that the desire to practice medicine again was active in their son, and no doubt Charleston offered many opportunities for Colin's education and future.

However, as Winston and Beatrice talked after the bedside oil lamp had been doused, it was also clear to both that there was something else—dark and foreboding almost—that underpinned their desire to leave the farm.

Two days earlier, Nate and James, with help from Colin, had brought tables from the Billington farms. With Mary Assumpta's inside and outside tables, all were placed under the century-old live oak, its leaves still in winter a dark, almost black green, its branches sweeping low to give plenty of shade, its gray-brown corrugated bark scratched where Boomer and squirrels had played their daily games.

At 12:00 sharp the celebration began with a prayer by Rabbi Benjamin. In his best Hebrew, Benjamin repeated the traditional Jewish prayer before meals: "Barukh ata Adonai Eloheinu, melekh ha'olam, hamotzi lehem min ha'aretz." And just as eloquently, he translated: "Blessed are you, Lord our God, King of the universe, who brings forth bread from the earth."

By two o'clock dinner had been consumed, and talk and laughter had quelled in anticipation of the occasion that would shortly follow. Mary Assumpta stood to give directions, but Father O'Malley interrupted, saying, "Mary Assumpta, if I may, I would like to offer another blessing." And as had been agreed upon the evening before among the clergy, he offered a post-meal prayer of thanks: "Bless us, O Lord, through these thy gifts, which we have received from thy bounty. Amen."

After Mary Assumpta explained what would follow, the group stood quietly as Reverend Simon Billington, having promised Bartholomew to keep his remarks short, stepped behind the small cross and began.

"My friends, I believe there is no verse of the Old or New Testament more relevant for this celebration than Matthew 19, verse 14: 'But Jesus said, Suffer little children, and forbid them not, to come unto me: for of such is the kingdom of heaven'" (KJV).

"We are here today to affirm that the soul of the earthly remains at our feet is already with God in heaven. Therefore, it is right and appropriate that we should, as Mary Assumpta has *gently* directed us, celebrate this child and not mourn his passing. Any sadness we reserve for the fact that *we* must wait a bit longer to visit this beloved child.

"Mary Assumpta, James, and Colin, what name is given this child?"

Colin spoke up. "Reverend Simon, this child is to be known as Timothy Ryan Merriweather."

Simon turned and spoke to Father O'Malley, "Michael, may I have the chalice containing the holy water?"

As agreed, Michael had brought the communion chalice from his church and a flask of holy water for the occasion, and as he held it, Simon dipped his fingers in the cup three times, allowing the water each time to drain on the small river rocks that covered the resting place of Timothy Ryan Merriweather. Reverend Simon Billington gently intoned the words of infant baptism he had said hundreds of times before during his ministry: "Timothy Ryan Merriweather, I baptize you in the name of the Father, the Son, and the Holy Spirit."

A quiet reverence for the moment was punctuated only with smiles. Simon paused to let the holiness grow. Then he turned and spoke to Benjamin Cowan, bedecked with his yarmulke and his tallit—his prayer shawl embroidered in gold—topping his flowing black robes indicating his status in his synagogue.

"Rabbi," Simon said, indicating it was now time for Benjamin's benediction.

Benjamin took the hand of Simon on the one side and Michael on the other and said to the assembled, "In a moment I want you to cross your arms and take the hands of the persons next to you. But before I lead us in prayer, Nate Billington has a special presentation to make."

"Colin, this could never replace the love you put in the original, but Aunt Audrey Lee and I want to present this cypress cross with your brother's name on it to you to present to your parents. Would you do that for me?"

Colin took the new permanent grave marker from his uncle Nate. Still, the gatherers held back tears as Colin's presence in this holy moment held total sway over them.

The cypress tree was likely more than two hundred years old when Nate's father had pulled it from one of the swamps off the Wando River. Nate had been barely old enough to go with him without getting in the way. Boards cut from the tree had cured in the rafters of the Billington barn, waiting for the right occasion to use the wood that had been growing long before America was a nation. This was the time. The nature of the cypress would make the cross impenetrable to weather, and the presentation from Nate to Colin to Mary Assumpta made sure the day would not be forgotten by anyone.

Still, no tears were shed, though more than a few lips trembled to keep their promise. Before Benjamin continued, Mary Assumpta held the beautifully crafted cross as she had held Timothy Ryan for the few brief moments before he was taken from her on January 2, 1863. She spoke up.

"I trust that you will remember this day each year on January 2 and also remember the names of family and friends who have gone before you. And do more than that—remember why they were special. Our Timothy Ryan was named for two important people in the Merriweather–Bailey family.

"Timothy Merriweather was a giant in his spiritual influence on this family. He was questioning the Bible's endorsing slavery as an acceptable practice and was labeled a heretic before time regarded him as a hero.

"And ... he was a Protestant!"

At first, only silence followed Mary Assumpta's playful poke at her *mixed marriage*, as Catholics and Protestants alike did not know how to respond or if they should at all. But finally, Father O'Malley could restrain himself no longer and cackled. It was the first time since the war that he had really howled in laughter, and he broke the spell for everyone. The forced smiles turned into the joy of spontaneous and effortless laughter.

"And," Mary Assumpta continued finally, "Ryan was the best of us Baileys. He was the quiet pioneer who made sure people in *his* city of Charleston were fed regardless of their station, and yet he gave his life for the land he loved. He teaches us that we Southerners, if anything, are very complicated.

"I hope that you will share stories like these each year and celebrate as we have here today. Benjamin, I believe I interrupted you."

"Indeed you did, but I will forgive you, my daughter." And

with that Benjamin roared with laughter as he brought Mary Assumpta to himself for a mighty hug.

"Now, as I was saying, join arms and let us pray the Lord's Prayer as our benediction." He paused before continuing. "What? You think a rabbi does not recite the Lord's Prayer? Have you forgotten that Jesus was a Jew before he was a Christian?"

Laughter again echoed off the limbs of the giant oak that held them in its embrace.

Benjamin led the gathered friends and family in a Lord's Prayer that would have made a Methodist preacher proud.

"Now," Benjamin spoke again, "grab someone, hug them, and tell them 'shalom.'"

As hugs were exchanged, the secret that Mary Assumpta had whispered to Abigayil that she could share at the naming celebration began to circulate.

Mary Assumpta and James were expecting again. New life for a new South.

CPSIA information can be obtained
at www.ICGtesting.com
Printed in the USA
BVHW071533120819
555662BV00001B/10/P